PENGUIN BOOKS

WOMEN OF THE TAGORE HOUSEHOLD

Chitra Deb was born in Purnea on 24 November 1943. She took her MA and PhD in Bengali Literature from Calcutta University. She has edited and translated a number of volumes, and also has a few children's books to her credit. She has researched and written extensively on the contribution of women in the social and cultural history of Bengal.

~

Sona Roy stood first class first in MA in English. She took her PhD Arts degree from Jadavpur University, taught at Rabindra Bharati University and Burdwan University, and retired as professor of English, Calcutta University. She is currently guest faculty at Presidency College, Kolkata.

Smita Chowdhry took her MSc in Chemistry from Lucknow University and her PhD from Allahabad University. A member of the Royal Society of Chemistry, UK, she taught in a college in Kolkata till she retired.

Women of the Tagore Household

Chitra Deb

Translated from the Bengali

by
Smita Chowdhry
and
Sona Roy

PENGUIN BOOKS

PENGUIN BOOKS
Published by the Penguin Group
Penguin Books India Pvt. Ltd, 7th Floor, Infinity Tower C, DLF Cyber City, Gurgaon 122 002, Haryana, India
Penguin Group (USA) Inc., 375 Hudson Street, New York, New York 10014, USA
Penguin Group (Canada), 90 Eglinton Avenue East, Suite 700, Toronto, Ontario, M4P 2Y3, Canada
Penguin Books Ltd, 80 Strand, London WC2R 0RL, England
Penguin Ireland, 25 St Stephen's Green, Dublin 2, Ireland (a division of Penguin Books Ltd)
Penguin Group (Australia), 707 Collins Street, Melbourne, Victoria 3008, Australia
Penguin Group (NZ), 67 Apollo Drive, Rosedale, Auckland 0632, New Zealand
Penguin Books (South Africa) (Pty) Ltd, Block D, Rosebank Office Park, 181 Jan Smuts Avenue, Parktown North, Johannesburg 2193, South Africa

Penguin Books Ltd, Registered Offices: 80 Strand, London WC2R 0RL, England

First published by Penguin Books India 2010

10 9 8 7 6 5 4 3 2

Reprinted in 2014

To Baba and Ma

ISBN 9780143066057

Typeset in Sabon by InoSoft Systems, Noida
Printed at Repro India Ltd., Navi Mumbai

A PENGUIN RANDOM HOUSE COMPANY

Acknowledgements

Most photographs have been lent from personal collections of members of the Tagore family. We would like to thank *Ananda Bazar Patrika*, Indira Sangeet Sikshayatan, Rabindra Bharati and Vishwa Bharati Museum for some of the photographs in this book.

We would also like to acknowledge all those who gave interviews and valuable material. We thank Samareshwar and Sanat Bagchi; Dr Asit Kumar, Bandana, Chittaranjan and Kalyanakshya Bandopadhyay; Atasi Barua and Ratna Barua; Dr Arun, Arun, Dwijendranath and Partha Basu; Sujata Bhattacharya; Samar Bhaumik; Sunil Gangopadhyay; Bani, Dwarkanath, Gauranga, Gautam, Jayantamohan, Partha, Sudipta and Sumohan Chattopadhyay; Bela, Dipti, Gauri, Meera and Subhas Chaudhuri; Sunil and Tapan Das; Namita Dasgupta; Sanjay De; Bhabatosh Dutt; Shovanlal Gangopadhyay; Prakriti and Pranati Ghoshal; Bipul and Buddhadev Guha; Susheema Guha Thakurta; Champa Haldar; Akshay Kumar Kayal; Manimala Devi; Manjushri Devi; Dr Kalyani Mallik; Dr Amritamoy; Bhaskar, Jagmohan, Jayanta, Jimutendranath, Kamala, Nripendra, Prasen, Prasun, Pravatkumar, Sanjay and Sudhamoyee Mukhopadhyay; Ajit Poddar; Purnima Devi; Ena, Kshitish, Mukula and Suvra Roy; Savita Devi; Saha Gaur; Sunanda Sen; Ira Sengupta; Sripantha; Surupa Devi; Amita, Amiya, Chitra, Menoka, Mihirendra, Parul, Purnima, Srimati, Supriyo and Surama Tagore and Uma Devi.

We would like to thank for help in preparing the third edition Rina, Rita, Sandip, Sauri and Snigdha Bandopadhyay; Sudeshna Basu; Dr Amrita, Shankarlal, Shubho and Swapna Bhattacharya; Srilekha and Surhita Chakraborti; Aloma, Hena, Indrajit, Smita,

Sudebi and Supurna Chaudhuri; Geeta, Kishore, Maitreyi, Manjari, Prabuddhanath, Ratna, Rekha, Sanmohan, Sheila, Sibdas and Sucharita Chattopadhyay; Ashok and Surasri Das; Bakul Das Gupta; Milan Dutt; Ashok, Kamala, Maya, Mitendralal, Niradhiprakash, Rajashri and Shyamal Gangopadhyay; Abhaypada, Ira and Mira Ghosh; Ruby Goswami; Suchitra Goswami; Jayani Gupta; Debal, Madhumita and Neelangshu Haldar; Rama Kar; Anil and Sunanda Maitra; Amit, Gopallal and Padma Majumdar; Ratna Mitra; Arya, Gopa, Krishna, Nandita, Parthanath and Pranati Mukhopadhyaya; Tapati Mustaphi; Bimal Kumar Pal; Priyaranjan Rakshit; Rita Devi; Arun Kumar Roy; Chitralekha, Shaktidas and Supurna Roy; Kamalendu Sarkar, Vishwaranjan Sarkar; Debabrata Sau; Krishna Sengupta; Smita Sinha; Shyamasri Sinha Roy; Sunetra Devi; Amritendranath, Arundhati, Bani, Debaprasad, Gauri, Indrani, Jayashri, Ira, Manujendranath, Mitindranath, Neelakshi, Ranjan, Sandip, Satirani, Saumya, Srilekha, Shubhashri, Shyamashri, Subhra, Sudip, Suhita, Amitendranath and Sumitendranath Tagore; Asmita Trivedi and Ashok Upadhyay.

Preface

Even today there is a good deal of curiosity about the women of the Tagore family in people's minds. While studying the history of women's emancipation or liberation in Bengal it became obvious that in most fields the women of the Jorasanko Tagore family played the lead role. They appeared, either individually or jointly, as torchbearers to dispel the darkness. A perusal of available material shows that a great deal is still unknown about these women though there is no dearth of material. This is just an initial effort to elucidate their role in the cultural life of Bengal.

The topic is certainly important and serious. Every endeavour has been made to present it in an interesting and humorous vein so that every reader may enjoy it. The first publication was an article in the annual issue of the *Ananda Bazar Patrika*. The appreciation shown by numerous readers made me want to make it a more detailed study. The present book is the fruition of my efforts.

I first spoke to Shri Ramapada Chaudhuri about my plans regarding the topic. He not only encouraged but also advised me to delve deeply into the records. But for his encouragement, help and advice this book would never have been written.

While penning the book I received the maximum help from the various characters portrayed herein as well as their relatives. My gratitude to them knows no bounds. But for their unstinting help and cooperation this saga of the women's emancipation in Bengal could never been written. The vice chancellor of Vishwa Bharati, Shri Surajit Sinha, very kindly allowed me to go through the necessary records in Rabindra Sadan.

A genealogical table of the Jorasanko Tagore family has been appended to the end of the narrative. All members of the Tagore family have helped in this arduous task. Shri Kalyanakshya Bandopadhyay deserves special mention. Shri Sanjay De has shown commendable patience in arranging the genealogical table. I convey my thanks to all of them.

CHITRA DEB

Preface to the Third Edition

I had the desire to furnish some more information about the ladies of the Tagore family and hence this enlarged edition. Though the genealogical tables of the various branches of this family were mentioned earlier, each branch had not been properly tabulated. In these vast tables the names of the daughters and their families had been ignored. The prevailing idea regarding the maintenance of a family tree was to guard against legal battles regarding inheritance. Hence a daughter, her husband and child progeny had no place in a man's family tree. However both a son and a daughter represent a family equally. Research led me to the fact that this was a favourite topic with the ladies, especially the elderly. They not only remembered the names of the men and women belonging to the various offshoots of the family but often helped clarify the various relationships. Sujata Bhattacharya was such a rare personality. Acting on her suggestion I found and met a number of people who helped me discover many forgotten offshoots and establish their relationship with the Tagore family anew.

Mr Debabrata Sen has taken great care in preparing the genealogical table while Mr Subimal Lahiri is responsible for correcting the errors. My thanks to both of them.

CHITRA DEB

Dawn was breaking over Calcutta. The first rays of the sun had just crossed the boundary of the sky and fallen on the roof of the mansion. The indistinct veil of darkness had not moved away totally. Two Arab steeds, treading the dew-laden grass, emerged onto the hard surface of the road. Leaving the main entrance behind, they trotted towards the Maidan. The durwan at the gate forgot his duties. The neighbours are nonplussed, the pedestrians stunned. Everyone gaped in silence and disbelief. The two men seemed oblivious to all these people. No, an error. Lo! One of the riders was a lady! People wondered if their eyes were deceiving them. A horsewoman on the streets of Calcutta! That too a Bengali, not an Englishwoman. But there was no room for doubt. The erect horsewoman in full riding habit was Kadambari, wife of Jyotirindranath Tagore. She was out for a ride on the Maidan with her husband.

Even today, it reads like a fairy tale. But this was very much fact, not fiction. It is the story of a family that transcended the barriers of the four walls of their mansion and grew in all directions. The old-fashioned palatial mansion standing at the end of a narrow lane, almost lost in the hustle and bustle of Jorasanko, appeared no different externally from other such mansions of the time. However, this home of the Tagore family was the cradle of the Bengal Renaissance. Many of the rebels who repeatedly sought to jar a somnolent society into alertness were permanent residents of this mansion. This was the age when Bengali art and literature had become confined, practically, to some old manuscripts, songs by village bards and the so-called babu culture of the decadent rich. It was then that a small ray of light from the western horizon seemed to touch the eastern sky. The Renaissance! This faint blush slowly turned into a raging fire. While many were bewildered, some went astray and others turned into rebels, the members of the Tagore family took up the task of rousing the nation. The above anecdote is but one illustration of this endeavour.

A cursory glance over the contemporary events of the Renaissance period shows that no collective effort had been made at the time to dispel the dark gloom enveloping contemporary society. There were a few scattered sparks more akin to the light of small earthen diyas, but they were all disjointed. If the efforts of the Tagore family were removed from the backdrop, this would be the true picture of Bengal at that time. One wonders whether light from these lamps would have been able to herald the Renaissance as we see it reflected in our lives today. More likely it would have remained just a memory like the Chaitanya Movement in sixteenth-century Bengal. However, there is no point in pondering over disasters that may have happened. We only wish to emphasize that during the confrontation of oriental and occidental ideas, it was in the Tagore family that a tolerant attitude of synthesis developed. Thus its members were as easily inspired by the oceans of the west as by the mighty Himalayan peaks.

Almost the entire gamut of artistic values and aesthetic norms of modern Bengali culture is a contribution of the Tagore family. Naturally, the name of the poet Rabindranath Tagore comes to mind as the catalyst that initiated this flame. He alone is enough to immortalize not only the Tagore family but the whole of Bengal. But it is also true that the Tagores were not like the other contemporary wealthy families.

It was probably from the time of Dwarkanath Tagore that this family began to develop a distinctive lifestyle of its own. All ideas—whether oriental or occidental—had been assimilated unhindered. That is what brought about the co-existence of the Brahmo Maharshi Debendranath and his son civilian Satyendra Nath. A gathering of poets, musicians, dramatists, art critics and philosophers under the same roof was also made possible thus.

In this golden era, the women of the Tagore family did not remain as obscure shadows behind the confines of the four walls. They participated wholeheartedly in laying the foundations of the new era, some of them directly while others as able helpmates of their husbands. It is easy to write about this today but the actual task was an arduous one. Old Brahminic constraints, especially those of Manu, and the need to protect women during the long Muslim rule had more or less made them akin to mere home adornments. In the beginning, these strict rules had been followed in the Tagore family also. The residence was divided into the 'sadar' and 'andar' mahals, the latter was where the womenfolk spent their lives. No man, unless he was a close relative, was permitted to enter this domain. A trip outside was always undertaken in a well-covered palki. The palki-bearers were usually dressed in dhotis and red, sleeveless shirts and wore gold wristlets and earrings. They were accompanied by durwans or security guards carrying heavy sticks. Every aristocratic family used a distinctively coloured coverlet for the palki. That of the Jorasanko Tagore family was bright red with a deep yellow border while the palki-covers of the Pathuriaghata branch of the Tagore family were deep blue with sparkling white borders.

Even in a palki, where could the women folk go? If it was for a bath in the holy water of the Ganges, the bearers would literally dip the palki—with the ladies inside—in the river! This was the accepted custom. Whenever they went to visit relations on social occasions like weddings, the palki would be carried right into the inner courtyard of the andar mahal. Houses number five and six in Jorasanko were within a stone's throw from each other; and yet the ladies had to use the palki to visit each other. Thus women, even of the Tagore family, had to overcome many hurdles and cross innumerable boundaries drawn by society, for simple acts of self-emancipation. The task was far from easy. Some of them have left behind memorable contributions in the field of art and literature, but the role of others, many of them unknown, was not negligible. To the beginner, treading even an easy path seems fraught with risks. These women not only had to make their own pathways but also had to protect these against weeds and other impediments. It is a matter of great credit and pride that the women of the Tagore family were able to ignore the constraints imposed by society. They showed the courage to stand alongside their men in almost every field of life with honour and dignity. This book is a chronicle of those women, now lost in the lanes and bylanes of memory.

The favourable winds of the Renaissance were welcomed by many others. Ishwarchandra Vidyasagar, Mrityunjay Tarkalankar and a number of others were the harbingers of female education. So were Maharshi Debendranath and his sons. While in England, Satyendranath would dream of smashing all the wooden shutters of their house and liberating the women. Hemendranath regularly taught them, while Jyotirindranath took it upon himself to widen their horizons by narrating well-known tales from both Indian and English literatures. The women were not only eager to learn but also had the courage and strength to tread new paths.

How is it that only the women of this particular family had so much freedom? Considering the prevailing situation, it appears that the strictures of Hindu society were not able to tie down the women of the Tagore family. The main reason was that the Tagores were Pirali Brahmins, considered more or less 'untouchable' by the orthodox Hindu Brahmins. Moreover, Debendranath's initiation into the Brahmo sect had automatically loosened the strict bonds of conservatism. An observation in support of this theory is that no young man was able to return home after marrying a Pirali girl. Satyendranath's wife Jnanodanandini's father Abhoycharan Mukhopadhyay left home in a huff as a young man. Later, due to unavoidable circumstances, he had to marry a girl belonging to the Pirali Roy family of Jessore. Meanwhile, Abhoycharan's father had been searching for his son. As soon as he heard that his son had married a Pirali girl, he was overcome with rage and grief. He tore his sacred thread and cursed his son, saying that no child of Abhoycharan's would survive! A Brahmin cursing someone by tearing his sacred thread was considered a calamity in those days. There are many other examples of the conservatism of the Tagore. Among the five sons-in-law of Maharshi Debendranath, four had to sever relations with their families just for having married into Pirali families. They all lived with the Maharshi as ghar jamai. In a patriarchal society, it was considered demeaning for a son-in-law to take up residence in his father-in-law's house. Jnanodanandini heard that one man's father had stood near the gate and cursed his son. Maharshi's fifth son-in-law, Janakinath Ghoshal, lost the right to his paternal property, albeit temporarily, for marrying Swarnakumari, the daughter of Pirali Debendranath. At the time of Jyotirindra's marriage, Debendranath wrote to a friend, 'We are lucky to have found a bride for Jyoti.' Why such a statement? At that time, hardly any family equalled the Tagores in wealth, education and social status. Debendranath explained, 'Brahmins other than Piralis do not give their daughters in marriage to us and the Piralis too are scared because of our faith in the Brahmo religion.'

The restrictions of society had not hardened into chains to shackle the inhabitants of this house. Rather, they had left gaps which enabled the Tagore family to evolve a culture of its own. It was no imitation of others but something totally new.

The most important gifts that Bengali women received from the ladies of the Tagore family were self-confidence and a wide road on which to march ahead. This preceded contributions to music, art and literature. This is why the various activities of these ladies, like cantering on horseback along the Maidan, and travelling to England, crossing the kalapani (as the Bay of Bengal was called then), attending parties at the Viceregal Palace, lecture-tours in the USA, school education, lessons in painting, music, play-acting, writing books, participation in the national movement and establishment of various women's organizations, became important. These acts were necessary to sow the seeds of courage in the faint hearts of Bengali women and to give a jolt to the static society. The role of Rabindranath's sisters and sisters-in-law was no less important than that of his brothers in creating a literary atmosphere for budding poets. Even in his later years, Rabindranath always turned to the women in his family while trying to give shape to his ideas on music, dance and drama. The women of the Tagore family deserve to be remembered for this alone, even if their own contributions to artistic fields were not as spectacular as those of the men.

It has been mentioned above that social constraints and taboos were never too rigorous for the women of the Tagore family. What exactly were these constraints that were unable to impede the women of this family? What was the life of a woman in those days? Needless to say, it was not a happy one. Even without going into the so-called 'records' of a few hundred years, it is obvious that there had been a tremendous devaluation of women in Indian society. In those days, men considered women chattels who had to be provided with only the bare minimum of subsistence. A woman could be sacrificed any number of times according to the wishes of her lord and master, her husband. In a patriarchal society, where only the men earned, money power enabled society to shackle women easily with numerous bands. A woman had no right to the property of her husband or father. Their helplessness enabled the men to perpetuate unbridled acts of self-indulgence. This is why the first and foremost agenda of social reformers in the nineteenth century was the liberation of women—not in its present context—but more along the lines of drawing attention to women's education, women's rights and emancipation.

Apart from grave social injustices like child marriage, polygamy and the practice of *satidaha,* numerous petty restrictions had fettered the women. These included denial of many things like literacy and education, wearing shoes and blouses, going outdoors, singing, riding in a coach or talking to men outside the family. One cannot but wonder how the women spent their time. Looking after the home and family? But women do that even now. Did life revolve around cooking, eating, and again cooking after eating? Numerous examples in the pages of contemporary literature negate this view. Saralata, a character in Dinabandhu Mitra's play *Neeldarpan* said, 'There are no means for a dejected woman to alleviate her misery.' This was so because it was impossible for a woman to go out even into the garden with a few companions, let alone into the city. Women had no colleges, organizations, Brahmo Samaj—in effect, nothing. How did the inhabitants of such a world put up with it? Probably they were so used to this state of affairs that they had no sense of loss. After all, Chinese women considered small feet a sign of beauty, ignoring the pain and discomfort that binding the feet caused. Just as bandages bound and narrowed the feet, so had centuries of repression narrowed the vision of most women. Things would perhaps have continued thus for many more years with only an occasional feeling of loss, had not a gust of fresh wind shaken them to the core.

Moreover, though one cannot be too sure, all women were not absolutely unresponsive and vegetating. This does not seem possible. Some had already begun to feel restive when the ladies of the Tagore family lit the lamp of women's emancipation. Though many of the social restrictions mentioned above were also in force in the Tagore family, women here were never deprived of education. Not only were they encouraged but suitable arrangements were made to make them literate. Vaishnavis (women devotees of Sri Chaitanya) were employed from the time of Dwarkanath's father to teach the womenfolk. While Dwarkanath was learning to read, write and spell at the local pathshala, his elder sister, ten-year-old Rasbilasi, could already read *Hari Kusum Stabha* by Rup Goswami. The benefits of this education were immediately apparent. Like their menfolk, the women of this family became models for Bengali women for all ages to come.

The antecedents of the Jorasanko Tagore family are well-known today. The mansion, mysterious as a fairy palace, has long been the focus of Bengali curiosity. Many will be able to affirm when Panchanan, the descendant of Purushottam, came to Calcutta to improve his fortunes or the auspicious moment when Panchanan's paternal grandson Neelmoni took up residence in a suburb of Calcutta. Our interest lies in the Jorasanko *thakurbari*. However, we have also discussed the ladies of other families who excelled in many fields. Their achievements have necessarily been mentioned briefly in appropriate contexts since it is not possible to single out each one. For quite some time, the main Kushari or Tagore family had been rent with internal strife and squabbles. The first court-case relating to the property disputes of the Tagore family was that between Gobindaram's wife Rampriya on one side and Neelmoni and Darpanarayan on the other. Rampriya was an extremely intelligent woman with a forceful personality. After her husband's death, she lodged a case at the Supreme Court, claiming her right to his share of the property. This was the first case of the Tagore family in the courts of the British. It was also the first time that a case relating to the rights of a Hindu widow regarding inheritance reached the Supreme Court. It was probably around this time that Neelmoni and Darpanarayan decided to divide their property mutually. In June 1784, Neelmoni left his ancestral home and moved for good to Jorasanko, which was a part of Mechhua Bazar. He was accompanied by his wife Lolita Devi, three sons and a daughter Kamalmani, while his brother Darpanarayan stayed on in Pathuriaghata. The Jorasanko *thakurbari*, as well as the family, became the cynosure of all eyes a few years later, from the time of Prince Dwarkanath. He was the man behind the wealth, ostentation and impeccable aesthetic taste of the Tagore family. Not only had he acquired unlimited wealth but he also wanted that the 'twain should meet'—the East and the West. He certainly succeeded, otherwise he would not have stood out among the other wealthy persons of his time. However, leaving him for the time being, we had better return to the andar mahal.

In those days, there was no dearth of families as wealthy and aristocratic as the Tagores. It is possible to mention at least thirty such families who not only equalled but in some cases surpassed the Tagores in wealth and fame. The members of such families also left their mark in various fields of art and culture later on. The reason for choosing the womenfolk of the Tagore family lies in the fact that this family were pioneers at that time.

Among the ladies of the Tagore family, Swarnakumari and Jnanadanandini are well-known. But every history is preceded by a previous one and we should not forget their grandmother Digambari and great-grandmother Alakasundari.

When Dwarkanath lost his father at the early age of thirteen, it was his mother Alakasundari who took up the reins of the household in her capable hands. In his will, Ramlochan instructed his minor son Dwarkanath, 'Until you attain maturity, all signatures, orders and necessary decisions will be taken by your mother . . . when you reach the age of maturity, you will keep all income from the parganas (landed property) with your mother—as I did—as long as she lives.' These instructions give an insight into the administrative capabilities of Alakasundari. She was deeply religious and a bath in the Ganga was a part of her daily routine. Ramlochan was a disciple of Harimohan Goswami, whose wife Katyayani Devi was the deeksha guru of Alakasundari. That she was not blind in her religious faith is clear from the Maharshi's writings, 'She did not like the frequent visits of Ma Gossain (Katyayani Devi).' In those days, it was customary to place a dying person on the banks of the Ganga, with the feet immersed in the water. This was known as antarjali yatra. During her last illness, Alakasundari did not agree to perform this ritual but, unfortunately, no one paid any heed to her protests. Even her eighteen-year-old grandson Debendranath did not try to prevent it. Alakasundari had said in deep distress, 'Had Dwarkanath been here, none of you would have been able to take me forcibly.' She had wanted to live a little longer, this craving for life was very natural.

Desire for 'Ganga-yatra' or 'antarjali' has been found in some other women of the Tagore family also. Dwarkanath's elder sister Rasbilasi too was a very devout lady. Her husband Bholanath Chattopadhyay was a class-fellow of her elder brother Radhanath Tagore. Though he hailed from a well-known family of Chandernagore (Chandannagar), Bholanath was forced to leave his home, family and society for marrying into the Tagore family. A decade later, after the birth of two sons, Bholanath became an ascetic and left home. He died about fourteen years after renouncing the world. Sometime before his death, he came to Calcutta and sent for his sons. He met them at the Kali Temple in Thanthania (Bidhan Sarani). Both Madanmohan and Chandramohan were adults by then. Bholanath advised his sons to try and build a house of their own rather than continue to live forever in someone else's home.

Madanmohan purchased a house on the eastern side of Dwarkanath's mansion and moved there with his family. Rasbilasi had always wanted to bring an idol of the goddess Durga and worship her at home. But she was unable to do so because her [Brahmo] brothers objected. Such anecdotes here and there help us realize the problems faced by Rasbilasi and Bholanath. If the son-in-law lives with and is dependent on his wife's family, both he and his wife are looked down upon even now and this seems to have been equally true then. Bholanath's family were Shaktas (devotees of the Goddess Kali) while the Tagores were devout Vaishnavas. When Madanmohan decided to hold *Shyama*-puja (worship of Goddess Kali) in the new mansion, Rasbilasi objected, saying, 'I shall not stay in a house where blood will flow.' It was customary to sacrifice goats during such worship. Since Rasbilasi was now established in her own house, her feet were on firm ground. Her wishes prevailed. During such puja, only fruits were to be sacrificed in future. When her end drew near, Rasbilasi expressed a desire for a 'Ganga-yatra'. This desire was not unusual. After lingering on the bank of the Ganga for four or five days, she passed away.

Like the pale light of dawn foreshadows the sunrise, Digambari's religious nature and spirited behaviour embodied the dedication and strength of character of the Tagore family. In those days, when a husband was considered the lord and master, not only in this life but also in future ones, Digambari had the strength of will to seek the opinion of renowned religious scholars. Her query: whether it would be righteous to sever all relations with a husband who had deviated from the religion of his forefathers? She was alone in her protest, in a patriarchal society, yet no one criticized her. Hindu society looked upon her with great respect and admiration.

What put Digambari on the horns of such a dilemma? Had Dwarkanath's negligence hurt her sensitive nature irretrievably or did she want to be relieved from the bonds of unbearable wedlock? For an answer, we have to turn to Digambari's life, which today is part fact and part fiction.

Digambari was born in Narendrapur, in the Jessore district of Bengal. She was only six when she came to Jorasanko as the wife of Dwarkanath. It was after her marriage that the fortunes of the Tagores began to improve. She was thus considered the Laxmi (goddess of wealth) of the family. Tales about her looks are legendary. Her pink and white complexion coupled with curly jet-black hair, delicate hands and feet, made people compare her to the goddess Jagaddhatri (a form of goddess Durga). It is said that during Jagaddhatri puja, the idol was sculpted with her features. It was probably from her time that the proverbial good looks of the Tagore family originated. When Digambari's dead body was being taken for cremation, many swore that they saw an ethereal halo round her feet! Along with her incomparable beauty, Digambari had a forceful personality. Even her mother-in-law Alakasundari held this daughter-in-law of hers in awe. What about Dwarkanath? He certainly loved his wife deeply. But this is not a tale where people live happily ever after. It is a tale of life, the ups and downs of which have woven not only the intricate designs of the andar mahal but also the glorious history of the awakening and emancipation of women.

During this time, the Tagores were devout Vaishnavas. They were often referred to as the 'orthodox of Mechhua Bazar' by the Tagores of Pathuriaghata. Let alone meat or fish, even onions were taboo in the household. With regard to cooking vegetables, even use of the verb 'cut' was eschewed in favour of the verb 'prepare', to avoid feelings of violence! Dwarkanath himself worshipped the family deities Laxmi and Janardan daily. It is reasonable to presume that Digambari assisted him in such duties. Her beautiful countenance, full of piety and devotion, clad in a neelambari sari (traditionally the garb of Radha) must have evoked respect in all. There was no inkling of any dark cloud of disaster in their conjugal life then.

A sudden storm shook their lives, rocking the very foundations of orthodox Hindu norms. Dwarkanath's business prospered. It was as if the goddess Laxmi had showered her blessings on him. But success brought with it other problems in the garb of luxury and modern ideology. According to Hindu religious texts, association with persons of other religions defiles the body. Thus, when Dwarkanath began associating with the British, he could no longer perform the daily worship himself. He appointed eighteen Brahmin priests to carry out not only this task but other religious functions also. Then he started eating meat and drinking sherry, mainly when entertaining his business associates. From now on, his life and Digambari's began to traverse different paths.

Though Dwarkanath's tastes were similar to other wealthy gentry of his time, he did not give way to unbounded dissipation in the beginning. He built for his pleasures a garden house at number 5, Belgatchia. This house bore ample testimony to the excellent aesthetic taste of Dwarkanath. He decorated according to his own taste the garden with fountains and paths of coloured tiles, the house with chandeliers and modern English furniture. The details of his griha sanchar (moving to the new house)—a lavish feast accompanied with music and dancing, an English band and local jesters, with nothing spared—were published in the local papers. One jester apparently came dressed as a cow and pretended to graze in the garden!

The house had ample arrangements for enjoyment and no one knows how much wealth was squandered there for a night's pleasure. All this bears complete testimony to Dwarkanath's love of ostentation, like other wealthy gentry of his time.

This house was built in 1823. At that time, Dwarkanath was the dewan of the government and later rose to even higher posts. In the beginning, Digambari failed to notice the change that was coming over her husband. Her days were taken up in looking after the family, daily worship and meditation. Her elder son Debendra had just got married. His bride Sarada too was from Jessore. Jessore was the abode of a large number of Pirali Brahmins. Sarada was also six years old at the time of her wedding. She belonged to Dakshindihi in Jessore. Her original name was Shakambhari, which was changed to Sarada. In those days, it was a common practice to rename a new bride. Digambari's day began before four in the morning. At 4 a.m. she would begin her daily worship. Besides chanting the Hari naam (The names of Vishnu/Janardan) one lakh times, she regularly read the *Bhagwat* and *Raas-panchadhyaya*. A Vaishnavi named Daya read aloud various religious texts daily while a Brahmin called Paran helped arrange the various accessories for her daily worship. He also assisted with the preparations for cooking, though she always cooked her own meals. On specific days of the calendar, like Ekadashi, she usually had only some fruits but on four Ekadeshi days she observed a complete fast. According to prevalent belief, no Hindu wife whose husband was living should fast on Ekadashi. When Alakasundari hinted at this, Digambari was able to convince her that such fasting would never harm Dwarkanath.

Occasional rumours began to reach Digambari. Neighbours and friends began to pass comments. Digambari chose to ignore such rumours and comments as malicious gossip. After all, scandal-mongers were always ready to cast aspersions on a successful and wealthy man. She immersed herself in prayers, to forget such news. But it was not possible for her to remain indifferent for very long. Banquets, drinking bouts and other revelry continued unabated at the garden-house. The rooms were aglow with flowers, chandeliers, mirrors and other accessories of a lavish lifestyle. Ultimately, Digambari heard that wine flowed like water at Dwarkanath's parties. She also heard that limericks were being composed:

Belgachhiar bagane hoy chhurikantar jhanjhani,
Khana khaoyar koto maja amra tar ki jani?
Janen Thakur Company.

In the garden at Belgatchia, knives and forks rattle,
What do we know of the joys of *khana* ?
It is known only to Tagore and Company !

Another one was by Rupchand Pakshi, a noted satirist of Bagbazar:

Ki maja ache re lal jale
Janen Thakur Company.
Mader gunagun amra ki jani
Janen Thakur Company.

O! The pleasures contained in red water,
Are known only to Tagore and Company.
How are we to judge the merits of wine?
It is known only to Tagore and Company.

And yet Digambari refused to believe what she heard. She decided to visit the *mlechha* (forbidden) banquet and judge the truth for herself. This sudden decision by a devoted wife was extraordinary. She sought to reform her wayward husband and went to Belgatchia accompanied by her terrified young daughter-in-law Sarada and a few female relatives of her household. She still believed that the loving husband she knew could not alter so drastically; whatever she had heard was false.

One wonders whether Digambari's steps faltered as she crossed the threshold of the andar mahal and entered the baithak-khana (the outer portion of the mansion, meant for the menfolk). No one recorded this historic moment. Doubts may arise as to whether she actually went to Belgatchia, though circumstantial evidence points to it. Digambari witnessed her husband feasting at the same table with Englishmen and -women. A meal cooked by Muslim bawarchis was being served. She thought she was in a nightmare. But she realized the truth of all the rumours. Though her heart seemed to break, she still remembered her duty. She entreated Dwarkanath to forsake such company and abandon such a way of life but all in vain. This happened after Alakasundari's death. While his mother was alive, Dwarkanath had never touched food proscribed by his religion.

What would another woman have done? Drowned in a sea of tears or remained indifferent, as did most wives of wealthy men in those days. Digambari did not choose either path. For a spirited lady like her, religion and duty stood above all else. She suppressed her grief and asked the opinion of Brahmin pundits (scholars). Her query: should she leave her husband for the sake of religion or abandon religion to follow in his footsteps? In Sanskrit, a wife is termed saha-dharmini, i.e. one who shares the same religious practices as her husband. Dwarkanath had not formally renounced his religion but one who did not baulk at sharing the table with *mlechhas* had certainly given up the tenets of his faith. After a great deal of discussion, the pundits gave their decision: 'It is certainly the duty of a wife to revere her husband and look after him but conjugal life with such a man was not permissible.'

Digambari did not falter in the path of duty. Except for looking after his material comforts (seva) she severed all relations with him. Her devotion to her husband was so great that no outsider ever learnt anything about this step. Every morning she would go near Dwarkanath's bed, sink into a pranam and move away. All this did not have the desired effect on Dwarkanath. He severed all relations with the main house and shifted permanently to the adjacent baithak-khana bari. A bawarchi-khana (where Muslim cooks prepared non-vegetarian dishes) was also constructed on the south side. Whenever Digambari had to speak to her husband on family or other related matters, she would bathe immediately after in seven drums of Ganga water to atone for such an act. This she did, irrespective of the hour, whether night or day. Her body was unable to stand such hardship. She developed a high temperature and passed away. Her image always remained untarnished in the memory of her son Maharshi Debendranath. What about Dwarkanath? Did the memory of Digambari not haunt him? That he felt her loss at every step is evident from his remark when the Carr Tagore Company lost a valuable ship. With a heartbroken sigh, he said, 'Laxmi [a devoted wife is termed Grihalaxmi, an embodiment of the goddess of prosperity] has left, who can bar the entry of Alaxmi?' (the opposite, i.e. adversity).

The spirit and courage of conviction shown by Digambari, considering her circumstances, were not evident in her daughters-in-law. The life of Sarada, Debendranath's wife, revolved round her husband. Jogmaya, Girindranath's wife, on the other hand, showed much devotion to the ancestral religion, like her mother-in-law. Tripurasundari, the wife of the youngest son Nagendranath, came into the family much later.

Both Sarada and Jogmaya were literate. A paid Vaishnavi

used to come and teach them to recite texts like *Shishu-bodhak, Chanakya sloka, Ramayana* and *Mahabharata*. She also taught them to write on banana leaves. This practice was prevalent not only in the Tagore family but in many other families also. Besides Sarada and Jogmaya, other women of the family could also read and write. They were not scared of the popular belief that literacy would lead to widowhood! Such prejudice was more prevalent in the villages.

Sarada was very fond of reading. Whenever she had some leisure time, she would sit down with a book. She often called her sons to read the Sanskrit *Ramayana* or *Mahabharata* to her. It has been said that if she did not find any other book, she would read the dictionary! *Chanakya sloka* was a great favourite with her.

Jogmaya was also a voracious reader. In those days, women who sold flowers also supplied books. They were mainly printed in the Bat-tala area of Calcuta. The ladies were thus able to buy books of their own choice. *Nabanari, Laila Majnu, Hatim Tai, Arabian Nights, Lamb's Tales, Paul and Virginia*—all these had been collected by Jogmaya. Her husband's lyrical novel *Kamini Kumar* was also stocked by the saleswoman. Swarnakumari said about this book that though it may not be a memorable creation in terms of its poems or plot, it should be preserved in the literary circle. This was the first book in contemporary Bengali society to feature a man and a woman as the hero and heroine. Other commonly read books were *Maan-bhanjan, Provash Milan, Kokil Dyut, Annada-mangal, Rati-bilap, Vastraharan, Geet Gobinda, Gulebakawali* and *Basabadatta*. Jogmaya knew Bengali well and, according to Satyendranath, often acted as their tutor.

Nothing much is known about either Sarada or Jogmaya. Both were deeply religious but their lives followed different paths. Though she had no inclination or love for the Brahmo faith, the gentle-natured Sarada tried her best to be a worthy partner of her husband, Maharshi Debendranath. The picture we get of her is of a typical Hindu wife, dedicated body and soul to her husband. She often worried about her husband's well-being. Once when Debendranath decided to take a boat-trip on the Ganga at the height of the monsoon, Sarada was in tears and insisted on accompanying him with her infant children. Her plea: 'Where do you wish to go without me? If you have to go, take me along.' The story of her getting Rabindranath to write to his father when the latter was in the Himalayas is well-known. Where the welfare of her husband was concerned, both upasana according to the dictates of the Brahmo faith and worship according to the Hindu scriptures were equally acceptable. Her daughter Saudamini has written, 'There was no end to the number of pundits who fleeced her, promising to perform various rites to ward off all Father's evils.' A devout wife, she wanted to follow the custom of touching the husband's feet before departing for the last journey.

A perusal of Jnanadanandini's *Puratani* also tells us that Sarada was not a very active person. Her household did not need much supervision either. She would usually recline on a divan while the maids applied beauty preparations known as rooptan to her daughters-in-law. While thus seated, Sarada would also mediate over the quarrels and complaints of the women of the andar mahal. This was the usual practice in most aristocratic families. Like the menfolk, the ladies also reclined on cushions. But whenever Debendranath ate at home, Sarada always went to the kitchen to supervise the cooking. Jnanadanandini further mentions that Debendranath would send for Sarada fairly late at night—after everyone was in bed. She would change into a freshly laundered cotton saree and spray herself with a little attar. According to Abanindranath, in those days, married ladies, irrespective of age, dressed up like new brides before entering their bedrooms, complete with sindoor, alta, attar and a floral garland! Compared to this, Sarada's toilette seems to have been very simple.

Sarada's picture, as drawn by the various Tagores, is always gentle though not too clear at times. It is a delight to imagine her seated on a small carpet, spread on the tiled floor of her room on the second floor, clad in a Baluchari saree. The room was lit by a small oil lamp, which would illuminate the bright vermillion mark in the parting of her white hair. Though she passed away before her hair could turn completely white, the description is heartwarming. There was always a stream of visitors, praising her brilliant sons. On her face was a glow of happiness mixed with a blush of modesty. Lest one consider her proud, she would lower her head diffidently when she heard her children praised.

The portrait of Jogmaya that we have from various reminiscences is no less beautiful. Her complexion was like molten gold and when she walked past, she exuded the fragrance of a lotus. She was very fond of children. Satyendranath writes: 'Mejo-kakima's room was our real meeting place—it was where we studied, rested and chatted with each other. In those days, formal education was not the norm for ladies of our family but Mejo-kakima and some others knew Bengali well. As a matter of fact, they were our first tutors.' After converting to the Brahmo faith, Debendranath decided to do away with the daily worship of the ancestral deities Laxmi and Janardan. Jogmaya then made a request that this charge be given to her. Her request was granted and she, with her two daughters and two sons, shifted to Dwarkanath's baithak-khana house while the Maharshi's family resided at number 6, Jorasanko. Since that time, the Tagore family of Jorasanko was split in two. Though the relations between the menfolk were always cordial, the movement of the ladies was restricted and they only met during festivals.

The severance of communication with Jogmaya hurt the Maharshi's children deeply. Even among them Saudamini's grief seems to have been the most. She had lived all her life in Jorasanko with her husband and children and Jogmaya had been her companion through thick and thin. Now Saudamini had to bear the entire responsibility of the Maharshi's family alone. Saudamini played an important role during the early days of women's education in Bengal. However, it was more due to circumstances than to her own efforts.

As mentioned earlier, the Tagore family as well as other aristocratic families made arrangements to educate their womenfolk. Such opportunities were non-existent in the villages. It is doubtful if any village woman—barring one or two intrepid ones—had the courage to openly sit down with books. Rassundari—a housewife living in a remote village—had become literate. She was neither a member of the Tagore family, nor had she ever come in contact with them; yet she was the first Bengali woman to have written her autobiography. One would have expected this pioneering step, in writing about oneself, to be taken by a lady of the Tagore family. It had not been easy for Rassundari to learn to read and write. She had to do so in the privacy of her room, behind locked doors. Otherwise she would be bombarded with derisive comments from the elderly, 'Kalikal has come. It seems now women will do men's jobs.' Incessantly hearing such bitter comments made Rassundari feel, 'Education seems to be only the means to earn money and not endow one with any other virtues.' Satyendranath Tagore's mother-in-law—Jnanadanandini's mother—also had to read and write in secret. She used to close the door at night and write 'letters and accounts'. Shibnath Shastri's mother, Golokmani Devi, also had to employ many a subterfuge to become literate. Prannath Chaudhuri's sister, Prasannamoyee Devi of Pabna, used to dress up as a boy before going to the 'Kachari Bari' for her studies. Three of Prasannamoyee's aunts—her father's sisters Bhagabati, Krishnasundari and Mrinmoyee—could read and write well but the youngest—Kashishwari, a child widow—was really well-educated. She used to teach small children. Prasannamoyee writes, 'Kashishwari returned from pilgrimage with her head shaven and pretending to be Hothi

Tarkalankar, opened a "Pathshala" in the village.' In this context the name of Drobomoyee, the daughter of Hothu Vidyalankar, alias Chandicharan Tarkalankar is also worth remembering. But all these were exceptions. Most women never had an opportunity to study.

The situation was much better in Calcutta. Vaishnavis used to come by turns to educate women. At the Jorasanko residence of the Tagores, every girl had to devote time for reading or being read to. Thus the reading habit was inculcated early. Even if initially one did not want to read, an interest in stories and tales helped develop the urge to read. After some time, English governesses replaced the Vaishnavis. Aristocrats like Raja Nabakrishna, Radhakanta Deb Bahadur, Brahmananda Keshab Chandra Sen, Prasanna Kumar Tagore and Raja Baidyanath Roy had arranged for the education of their womenfolk. However all this was confined to within the privacy of the home. Prasanna Kumar's daughter Harasundari and daughter-in-law Balasundari became adept in many arts. But for her untimely death, Jnanendramohan Tagore's wife Balasundari may have pioneered the movement for women's liberation in Bengal. She was tutored by a governess from 9 am to 3 pm daily. She could also speak and write English, though she never went out of the andar mahal. Perhaps she had just begun to prepare mentally to step out of doors when she passed away. Mrs Wilson of the Central Female School used to teach the wife of Baidyanath Ray. So even though the Tagore family had a foreign teacher—Mrs Gomes—the appointment of such ladies within the home did not call for much courage.

Though the Zenana Mission had established a number of schools, these were out of bounds for the women of aristocratic families. Yet a number of people had begun to realize the importance and necessity of female education. So efforts were made to open a good school for girls. Apart from Ishwarchandra Vidyasagar, Raja Dakshinaranjan Mukhopadhyay, Ramgopal Ghosh, Madan Mohan Tarkalankar and many others were enthusiastic supporters of this ideal project. Despite tremendous opposition the Bethune School was established in 1849. It was originally called Hindu Female School. John Drinkwater Bethune, one of India's greatest well-wishers, founded this school with help from eminent Indian scholars. The school was originally housed in the baithak-khana of Raja Dakshinaranjan's mansion at Sukia Street. It is to this school that five-year-old Saudamini came in 1851. One would naturally expect a girl from the Tagore family to be the first student. But this was not so. The first two students were Kundamala and Bhubanmala, the daughters of Madanmohan Tarkalankar, who was ostracized and made an outcaste by the village society for sending his daughters to school. Another nineteen girls were also admitted shortly after.

There was a social outcry fanned by the newspapers. *Samachar Chandrika* raised numerous objections. According to this paper, innocent girls should not be sent to school as it entailed a grave risk of molestation. Men smitten with lust would rape them whenever they got an opportunity. They would not be spared because of their tender years. After all, it was a relationship similar to that of a hunter and his prey! Strange attitude, since other girls' schools had been set up earlier. The Juvenile School had been opened in May-June 1819. It started with eight students but the number later rose to thirty two. Later, the 'Ladies' Society' also did a lot of work in this field. In 1821 Mary Anne Cook founded a number of free schools in Calcutta. Within a year, three hundred girls began to study and in 1872 this number rose to six hundred. Girls' schools were also opened in Serampore, Dacca, Birbhum and Chittagong while the first school for Hindu girls was opened in 1847 at Barasat near Calcutta. Yet there was such opposition to the 'Hindu Female School'. It was even suggested in the papers that parents who were sending girls to study in this school 'may not be respectable and of questionable lineage'. The student strength of Bethune School fell sharply to seven girls. The opposition, including *Sambad Prabhakar*, protested against such base allegations. Debate raged on views for and against. But debate in newspapers is quite separate from real life. The aristocratic families went on hesitating about sending their daughters to Bethune School. At this juncture Saudamini was chosen to set an example. The pretty child of five, dressed up in a 'peshoaj', was ready to go to school along with her cousin Kumudini. Debendranath sent Saudamini to school as he felt that others would follow suit. His presumption proved correct. Thus in 1851 Saudamini was admitted to school to pave the way for other Bengali girls. Were there no problems? Of course there were. The police mistook her for a stolen English girl—her complexion was marble white—and came to rescue her!

It is not known how far Saudamini's formal education advanced. She was the Griha Rakshita, the one who had sole charge of the home. Supervising the manifold duties of the household left her with little time on her hands. Not only supervision, she was the one who had to dress her sisters' hair in the latest mode when they went out. The house had to be decorated with alpana whenever there were any festivities and there were myriad other jobs. The Maharshi kept a careful eye on such activities. Saudamini's days were taken up in being the ideal mistress of a large household. She had also dedicated herself to looking after her father. She always cooked special dishes for the Maharshi. She was an expert at serving and entertaining people. Debendranath had once asked her to teach the other girls of the family to cook. Saudamini carried out her father's wishes with deep devotion. Not much is known about her literary activities. Her reminiscences of her father—*Pitrismriti*—and a few Brahmo sangeet composed by her are all that we have been able to trace. The song 'Though poor, I shall worship you' may have been heard by many. A perusal of *Pitrismriti* leaves one with the feeling that Saudamini could have contributed much more had she so wished. She appears to have chosen to give only stray glimpses of a few pictures. About her days in Bethune School, Saudamini writes: 'When the Bethune

School for Girls was first established in Calcutta it was difficult to get students. So my father sent me and my cousin sister there. Shri Haradev Chatterjee, who was devoted to my father, also admitted his two daughters. Shri Madan Mohan Tarkalankar also sent some of his daughters to study in Bethune School. Thus Bethune School was started with a few students.'

This reads like a news column. This is not a report by a third person but the comments of a student of the very early days of Bethune School. Saudamini could have given us much more information. Innumerable limericks and satires had been composed about the students of Bethune School. Needless to say Saudamini also had to move amid considerable adverse conditions. Ishwar Gupta, popularly known as 'Gupta Kabi', lamented:

Joto chhundigulo tudi merey ketab hatey nichchhe jobe,
Takhan AB shikhe Bibi sheje bilati boley kabeyi kobe.

Now that all the young lasses are taking up books, they will learn A-B and certainly prattle away in the foreign tongue.

Yet, far from being an opponent of female education, Ishwar Gupta encouraged it. Numerous satires were penned about women educated in Bethune College and consequently gone astray. '*Swadhin Zenana*', '*Boubabu*', '*Pas Kara Maag*', '*Sikshita Bou*', '*Maag Mukho Chelay*', '*Sreejukta Boubibi*', '*Pas Kara Adurey Bou*', '*Kalir Meyey O Nababbabu*', '*Barbadal*,' '*Pundit Meyey*', '*Phachke Chhundir Kirti Kando*', '*Hurko Bouer Bisam Jwala*', '*Kalir Bou Haar Jalani*', '*Maag Sarvyasya*', '*Behadda Behaya*', '*Meyey Chheler Lekha Para Apna Hotey Dubey Mora*'.

[Translation of the titles: 'Independent Woman', 'Wife As Man', 'Educated Woman', 'Educated Wife', 'Henpecked Man', 'Madame Wife', 'Educated Pampered Wife,' 'Daughter of Decadent Age and Nababbabu', 'Change of Husband', 'Scholarly Woman', 'The Doings of a Fast Girl', 'The Perils of a Wayward Wife', 'The Headaches of a Wife Belonging to the Decadent Age',

'Wife: Be-All and End-All', 'Wanton Woman', 'Education of Woman Akin to Suicide by Drowning'.]

There was no end to such names. The context and lament of all these was the same. Doom was at hand with women treading on male preserves! Such literary creations went on for fifty years, right up to the early days of the twentieth century.

Saudamini was fully apprised of such social controversies. It is from her writings that we have the following anecdote. Debendranath's cousin Chandrababu's house was just beyond the boundary of Maharshi Bhawan at Jorasanko. He was scandalized to see the ladies of the Tagore family strolling on the terrace. He came over and said, 'We are ashamed to see the women of your household walking about on the open roof. Why don't you stop them?.' Saudamini goes on to say, 'When Durga Puja was observed in our house, on Vijayadashami day, the boys and men-folk dressed in new clothes and accompanied the idol. We women would watch the immersion from the-second floor roof. This was the only day in the whole year when we were permitted to go up.' Not only was Debendranath broad-minded enough to see no wrong in such behaviour but he had also realized that change was imminent. Thus he had replied with a smile, 'Why should *I* stop them? The Almighty will surely set things right.'

It would be erroneous to label Debendranath a reformer on the basis of Saudamini's *Pitrismriti*. He was tolerant so long as his children did not stray into the wrong path. He sincerely observed many dictates of the Hindu society inspite of being a humanist. Widow remarriage, inter-caste marriage, unlimited freedom of women were never condoned by him. Similarly, he never tried to do away with age-old family customs and norms of behaviour observed by women. He knew that such customs nurtured the essence of Bengali life. Any effort to remove these would uproot and destroy that very essence. He always opposed customs that were anti-tradition. Saudamini writes, 'Once Mother pierced the noses of my two younger sisters and sent them to our father to ask for nolaks (rings worn through a hole made in the partition between the two nostrils). As soon as he saw their noses pierced, he commented, "You look like clowns. Take it off at once, only wild savages pierce their ears and noses to wear ornaments, this is not worthy of civilized society."' It was a matter of great credit to steer successfully the raft of one's family amidst such opposing thought processes and it required a cool head and great perspicacity, considering the prevailing conditions at that time. Fortunately we are provided with numerous intimate glimpses of Debendranath's life from Saudamini's writings. For instance, after he had to repay the debts incurred by Dwarkanath, Debendranath abhorred even minor debts. Saudamini writes in *Pitrismriti*:

> He was scared of even the smallest debt; when any of his sons borrowed money and requested him to repay the loan, he would refuse: 'Am I to repay loans all my life?'

She also writes about his thrifty habits:

> He would never spend more than four annas (25 paise) on a meal. A man whose father's dinner cost a minimum of Rs 3000 was quite satisfied with spending only four annas. He sold off all the coaches and horses, keeping only a palanquin for the ladies.

Had Saudamini not penned her reminiscences, such anecdotes would have remained unknown. Debendranath had another characteristic trait inherited from his ancestors. He had great respect for women. Saudamini writes, 'Whenever a lady came to visit him, he addressed her as 'mother' and showered her with affectionate care. He gave everyone of them a patient hearing, trying his level best to allay their fears and worries. Thus they always departed with their hearts full of ease and peace. Once I visited a relative. On my return, Father asked me what the gentleman was doing when I called. When I said that he was lying down, Father queried, "Did he not sit up on seeing you?"

My reply in the negative saddened him. He was upset that this gentleman did not show due respect to a lady.' Saudamini's pen gives us a vivid picture of this aspect of Maharshi's character.

Among Saudamini's younger sisters, Sukumari died young. Like her sister, Sukumari was also involved in a historic event—though without an active role. Debendranath got Sukumari married according to Brahmo rules. The shalgram shila, kusha grass, tulsi and bel leaves, Ganges water and the sacred fire—a must for every Hindu marriage—were not there at the wedding ceremony. This marriage took place on 26 July 1861 and was the first Brahmo wedding. Till then, no separate rites were followed in the various facets of the domestic lives of Brahmos. Naturally this caused tremendous commotion. Though, apart from idolatrous rituals, all norms of a Hindu marriage had been observed, many did not consider the marriage to be consecrated and legal. The bridegroom, Hemanta Mukhopadhyaya, was the grandson of Shyamlal Tagore, a descendant of Darpanarayan Tagore. Rakhaldas Halder published the details of the wedding in London's *All The Year Round* magazine on 5 April 1862.

Giving his daughter in marriage like this and refusing to perform his father's shradh according to Hindu rites further alienated Debendranath from his relations. However, his brother Girindranath's family and Dwarkanath's three daughters, Janhabi, Rasbilasi and Drobomoyee, remained by his side. For women of that era, the three sisters showed tremendous courage. Debendranath's uncle Ramanath Tagore and his two cousins also did not sever relations. Thus the family of Nilmani Tagore remained tied by an invisible bond.

Saudamini and Sukumari's sister Swarnakumari was the first successful woman writer of Bengali literature. Her other elder sister Saratkumari confined herself to the kitchen and beauty aids while her younger sibling Barnakumari did not do much except taking part in a few dramatic ventures of the family. But Swarnakumari was a rare exception whose achievements lit up the andar mahal of the Tagore family. Another lady, inextricably connected with Swarnakumari's achievements and success, was Jnanadanandini, the second daughter-in-law of Debendranath. Though she was not born into the family and became a member by marriage, it is impossible to visualize her apart from the traditions and achievements of the Tagores. She was a part and parcel of their culture, education and ideas. As a matter of fact, Jnanadanandini was the first to step into the wider world, overcoming all opposition and restrictions, and paved the way for women's emancipation. It did not take women long thereafter to shake off the bonds of purdah and other strict norms of society. Thus it may be better to talk about Jnanadanandini before Swarnakumari. It is not possible to view them separately since they belonged to the same era and were members of the same family.

Jnanadanandini was the second daughter-in-law of the Maharsi. Naturally one would think of the eldest before her. The role of Sarbasundari—wife of the philosopher Dwijendranath—in the Tagore family is obscure. We get glimpses of her in some writings, traditionally dressed in a broad, red-bordered saree. She always had her head and face covered down to the chin, as was the prevailing custom. Her small figure seems to have been hidden perpetually behind the pillars of the mansion. Making herself one with the family and caring for her children, she seems to have been lost among the numerous members of a large family. Her short life appears to have been devoted to the service of others. She had nine children, of whom two died shortly after birth. Her last son was stillborn and she passed away at the early age of thirty-one, due to a complicated labour. According to Prafullamoyee, 'I was near her when she died. Shortly before the end, she was unable to talk and gestured that she wished to see her husband and children. I immediately sent word to my eldest brother-in-law. But she breathed her last before he arrived.' Well, this was the life of most women in those days. Jnanadanandini was not a woman who should have been lost thus; with tremendous strength of purpose, determination and grit, she contributed greatly to forge the path for women's advancement. She was fully supported in this task by her husband Satyendranath Tagore—the first Indian to join the Civil Service.

Jnanadanandini was only seven at the time of her marriage. This type of wedding was known as gauridaan, popular in those days. She had just begun to learn the alphabet in the village pathshala. She, whose days were mainly spent playing with her dolls, herself entered the Tagore mansion dressed like a wax-doll with traditional ornaments, the border of her saree covering her head and face, right down to her neck. Perhaps the little girl carefully raised the saree-border (ghomta), while her scared doe-eyes tried to look around for some vestige of her known family life. Needless to say she did not find any. Which bride of the Tagore family was able to retain the traditions of her maiden days? But Jnanadanandini found a new path to move ahead. That in itself is history.

Satyendranath was not only the first Indian Civil Service officer but also a pioneer of women's liberation in Bengal. He was keen that his shy girl-bride should become the ideal of Indian women in every way. In England he saw the freedom enjoyed by women. They were at liberty to move both in and out of the house at will. There was no discordant note anywhere. There was no furore in the English Society over it. Then? His thoughts were: 'Women are the flowers of the garden of life, what good will come of it if they are allowed to wither away within four walls due to lack of light and air?'

Satyendranath began to dream: He would demolish the doors of the andar mahal. His wife had crossed the 'kalapani' and arrived in England. His beloved 'Jnenumani', who had accepted him as her very own before she had a chance to know her own mind, was again acclaiming him as her chosen one before the eyes of the world. He was being welcomed with a garland woven out of her love, akin to the celestial flower parijat. Thus began his struggle to inculcate his ideas in his wife. Letters followed in quick succession.

> Does it not upset you that our women are married so young that they have no idea of marriage and are unable to choose independently? Your marriage was not yours, it was *kanyadaan*. Your father just gave you away.

Such letters from across the ocean brought new messages to Jnanadanandini.

> We were not free to marry according to our choice. Our parents got us married. Until you reach adulthood, are educated and mature in every way we will not enter conjugal life.

Such letters worried Jnanadanandini as the message was often not clear to her. One wonders what her replies were. It has not been possible to trace even a single letter of hers. Satyendranath's letters, though intimate, were formal in language, almost bookish, because at that time this was the style of correspondence even between a man and his wife. Hemendranath also used the same formal style but Rabindranath always wrote letters in the colloquial mode. However, the letters are replete with Satyendranath's dreams and heartfelt desires:

> Women's liberation and well-being are at the root of all commendable and beautiful achievements of this society. I wish you to be the ideal example for our women but a great deal of this depends upon you.

Jnanadanandini was only thirteen at that time. Perhaps she pondered on these thoughts while pacing on the terrace alone, on a full moon night. Satyendra's letters tell us:

> You were the embodiment of all the shyness and timidity of norms of behaviour prevalent among our women. Are you still the same?

Slowly, Jnanadanandini began to change herself.

Satyendra's dreams of Jnanadanandini joining him abroad remained unfulfilled this time. The Maharshi flatly refused to accede to his proposal. Well, every wish is never granted. The young daughter-in-law remained within the four walls of the mansion. Her education began afresh under the tutelage of the Maharshi's third son Hemendranath. The shy Jnanadanandini, veiled right down to her neck, would sit with the other young womenfolk of the family. Hemendranath's reprimands would often startle her but her education continued upto *Meghnad Badh Kavya* by Michael Madusudhan Dutt.

Meanwhile, Debendranath took a memorable step. Realizing that the progress of the young women was not satisfactory, he engaged the young acharya of the Brahmo Samaj—Ayodhyanath Pakrasi—as a private tutor for them. This was the first time that a man who was not related to the family entered the andar mahal. He took great care in teaching the young women the school text-books. During this time, Keshab Chandra Sen lived with the Tagore family for some time. This diligence towards education greatly impressed him.

The history of Jnanadanandini's endeavours is not clear. It is well-known that she was able to turn her husband's dreams into reality. What was the dream? It was just that women should be educated and become capable of standing next to men as equals. It is well nigh impossible to comprehend the importance of this today. Perhaps, what Jnanadanandini achieved was not a very difficult task but as the pioneering step it was a tremendous one. When told today that she was the first Bengali lady to step out of doors, a derisive smile may touch our lips. What was so great or daring about that? Where was the need for such a commotion? Yet commotion there was and plenty. In later years, Jyotirendranath wrote—'Women going out of doors, riding coaches and mixing freely with men may appear commonplace, natural and normal to you but all this was not achieved easily. Criticism there was in plenty, as were differences of opinion and alienation in the family and a lot of heartache. We have only arrived at this juncture slowly, advancing step by step.'

Satyendranath was posted to Maharashtra on his return from England. The prevalent custom in those days was that when a man had to go out of town on service, his wife remained with the family. Satyendranath requested permission to take his wife with him to his place of work. The thought of Jnanadanandini imprisoned behind the four walls of the home—akin to a black hole—while he was away, was unbearable for him. She had already suffered a great deal. Her husband's liberal views had created unpleasant and unwelcome circumstances, which she had had to face on her own. From some of Satyendranath's letters, we get a hint that Jnanadanandini's relations with her mother-in-law were often bitter. The Maharshi's wife often refused to speak to her second daughter-in-law. From *Atmakatha*, the autobiography of Satyendranath's daughter Indira, we learn that the Maharshi's wife took away Jnanadanandini's jewellery on the pretext that a lot of expense had been incurred to send Satyendra abroad. This jewellery was used by the Maharshi's wife at the time of the marriages of her two daughters. Whatever the real reason for her doing so, it was certainly not paucity of funds. The Maharshi was so annoyed when he heard about it that he gifted Jnanadanandini a diamond necklace. Apart from coral ornaments, Jnanadanandini had no fascination for jewellery. The Maharshi did not object, Satyendranath's request was granted.

Protests and objections galore were raised. No daughter-in-law had ever gone out of the ancestral home and this was preposterous. After all, even men were not allowed to enter the andar mahal at will. As long as they were bachelors, the andar mahal was out of bounds for them. It was only after marriage, when a separate bedroom was allotted to him, that a man came in at night to sleep. Any leniency would tarnish the sanctity of the andar mahal which was kept safe from any contact with the outside world. This norm was observed strictly in every household. The Maharshi's wife reprimanded Satyendranath, 'Are you planning to take the womenfolk of the household to the Maidan for a stroll?' There was a storm of protests from other members, too. Satyendranath felt that there would be no harm if he did so. After all, this custom of purdah was not our own but an imitation of Muslim ways. Moreover, where was the need to have norms similar to those followed by Muslim nawabs?

Satyendranath never liked such conventions. This was perhaps the reason for a humorous but daring act of his some years ago, though later he found the memory amusing. This was shortly after his marriage. Young Satyendra was an avid radical. His best friend Manmohan Ghosh once wanted to meet Jnanadanandini. Neither of the two friends saw anything objectionable in this wish, but how was Satyendra to *show* Jnanadanandini to Manmohan? She was not allowed out of the andar mahal while no unrelated males, not even men-servants, were allowed within it.

After a lot of planning and cogitation a plot was hatched. It was both adventurous and romantic. We have the account from Jnanadanandini herself:

> Both of them entered the andar mahal late at night matching each other's steps so only one footfall was heard. My husband made Manmohan sit on the bed and himself lay down. Both of us sat inside the mosquito-curtain. Both of us were tongue-tied with shyness. After a while, my husband got up and escorted his friend outside, stepping together as before.

It was not done as easily as it reads. To bring his friend in, Satyendra had to cross the main entrance and the outer courtyard. Every step was dogged with the risk of being noticed. That he attempted such a deed was only because of his progressive outlook.

This time, with the Maharshi's permission, Satyendra was in seventh heaven. He would be able to take his wife to Bombay and there was a glorious chance to open the gates of women's liberation. Preparations for the journey began, but a problem arose over Jnanadanandini's dress. No one had bothered about such matters since aristocratic women were never seen in public and a saree was adequate. Jnanadanandini, in her reminiscences *Puratani*, tells us that in winter they wore a shawl over the saree. *Puratani* provides us with many such domestic details. Satyendranath wrote, 'If you have to change your mode of dress, please do not hesitate. The way our women wear the saree is practically the same as not dressing at all. It is impossible to go out into civilized society thus attired.' The question that arises is: why didn't Bengali women take to any other apparel all these years? Did they really not wear anything except sarees? Bengal had been under Muslim rule for many years. The few paintings of nawabi harems show women wearing aesthetic and decent dresses. Why was this not adopted by Bengali women when the Muslim influence could be noted not only in the dress but in the general behaviour of men? The peshoaj was in vogue and even the Maharshi had thought of appropriate dresses for young girls. Well, an order was placed with a French shop and an 'oriental' dress was tailored for Jnanadanandini. Not only was it cumbersome but getting into it was a Herculean task. Jnanadanandini failed to wear it by herself and Satyendra had to help her get ready. It was this initial problem with dressing that made Jnanadanandini ponder over women's apparel. The tasteful and modern way of wearing the saree by Bengali women is the fruit of Jnanadanandini's efforts.

Satyendranath suggested that both of them enter the coach from the main gate. There was again a wail of protest and even Debendranath disagreed. In those days women riding in open coaches was considered deplorable. Debendranath insisted that the convention of women going by palki had to be maintained. Perhaps, the thought of his daughter-in-law—who was asuryamsparsha (untouched by the sun)—crossing the main gate on foot, before the eyes of his employees, was repugnant to him.

The family palki put Jnanadanandini onto the ship for Bombay. This was the last time that Jnanadanandini rode a palki.

After spending two years in Bombay, Jnanadanandini, dressed tastefully, set foot in Calcutta. That day heralded the victorious advancement of Bengali women. This was during the sixth decade of the nineteenth century. Winds of change were blowing all over but it took quite a while before the rigorous rules of purdah were relaxed in Bengal. This time, Jnanadanandini did not have to face reprisals alone: other women of the Tagore family as well as some other Brahmo women stood by her side. But the day she returned from Bombay, she was alone. Swarnakumari has immortalized that moment by a stroke of her pen. 'The wails of disaster that lashed the household, as they saw the daughter-in-law of the house alighting from the coach like an English-woman, are indescribable.' Tears streamed down the cheeks of even the old servants. Jyotirindranath has endeavoured to preserve these times beautifully:

> I remember the time when our womenfolk first began to go out in coaches. In the beginning I never allowed the door of the coach to be opened. Slowly I began to open the door—first a quarter, then half and then the full door. I used to be acutely embarrassed if any outsider saw the women of our family. First we used a covered tightly shuttered coach, then a covered coach with the door open, followed by a top-open phaeton and lastly an open phaeton.

Jnanadanandini herself was very diffident to begin with. She herself narrates:

> When my husband threw his first dinner party in Bombay, I was determined not to sit down at the table though I had laid the table myself. When dinner was served and one of the guests—an Englishman—took my hand and led me to the table, I drew away my hand, ran off to my bedroom and shut the door.

Another incident:

> I was introduced to the Lieutenant General of Bombay, Sir Bartley Frere, as the wife of the first Indian Civilian. He was very courteous and began to converse. Unfortunately my knowledge of English was negligible and I was unable to follow a word of what he said.

Refusing to admit defeat Jnanadanandini was bent on adapting herself to her new role. Thus when she came back to her old rooms at Jorasanko she was more of an outcaste. Swarnakumari was very sympathetic and she observed: 'The other womenfolk of the household were diffident about associating or sharing meals with Jnanadanandini.' Several of Satyendranath's letters also allude to this:

> Do you take your meals alone or are others keeping you company? What makes you feel that Baba Mohasay (Maharshi) will not come to Calcutta while you are in the house? There is no need for people to denigrate you. Do you enjoy the food as it is cooked?

It is clear that Jnanadanandini had few friends at Jorasanko to share in her joys or woes even during her days of pregnancy. In this context her behaviour was even more daring.

She accepted an invitation to the Government House and accompanied Satyendranath there. At that time, the begum or wife of the nawab of Bhopal was the only one to have come out of purdah. Initially the other invitees mistook Jnanadanandini for her. Prasanna Kumar Tagore of Pathuriaghata was one of the invitees to the dinner. He was so embarrassed to see a woman of the family attending an open party that he left in a towering rage. Since no Hindu woman had ever come to the Government House, it was incomprehensible to the orthodox why one should do so now. Satyendranath was delighted and wrote, 'What an astonishing scene. My wife was the only Bengali lady amidst hundreds of English women.' Slowly other doors also began to open as this step, ridiculed as a 'disease', proved contagious.

Jnanadanandini not only removed obstacles from the path of

other women, she also managed to broaden the men's outlook to a great extent. The best example is Jyotirindranath. Though they were about the same age and Jnanadanandini was very fond of her brother-in-law, Jyotirindranath, far from being progressive, was rather conservative in his views, like his eldest brother Dwijendranath. His feelings became clear when he wrote a satire mocking Keshav Chandra Sen. However, the company of Mejodada (Satyendra) and Mejo Bouthan (Jnanadanandini) soon changed his views.

Our debt to Jnanadanandini may appear obscure to the women of the twentieth and twenty-first centuries. She trod many unfamiliar paths to engineer the advancement of Bengali women. She travelled all the way to England alone with her infant children. Crossing the kalapani at the time was a venture that even men baulked at. Two of Bengal's noted sons—Rammohan and Dwarkanath—did make the trip, never to return. When Satyendra went, it caused a great deal of anxiety. Considering all this, one wonders what gave Jnanadanandini—a housewife, with only a cursory knowledge of English—the courage to undertake the trip. Prasanna Kumar's son Jnanendramohan Tagore, the first Bengali barrister, was shocked to see her disembark alone. His comment: 'What was Satyendra about? Why didn't he come along?'

One wonders why Jnanadanandini went to England. Was it to fulfill young Satyendra's dream or to become an ideal for Indian women in every aspect? We are surprised to learn that she undertook the voyage only to acquaint herself with women's liberation. On her return home, she was able to use her experience to usher in a golden dawn with numerous possibilities for women.

This does not mean that no one else had achieved anything or adopted English ways of life. Taru and Aru Dutt of the Rambagan Dutt family were educated abroad. Rajkumari Bandopadhyaya was persuaded by Mary Carpenter to go abroad. There were a few others but none of them blended with the Bengali culture. The totally Westernized Bengali families had been alienated from society. Rajkumari was the first Bengali Kulin Brahmin lady who went to England of her own volition. But for an untimely death she may have been able to undertake various projects for women's education. Jnanadanandini was the first to spearhead the winds of change.

The first to join the women of the Tagore family were other ladies of the Brahmo Samaj. For sometime past women had been permitted to attend the prayer meetings of the Brahmo Temples. Their seats were separated from the rest by a bamboo curtain or chik. In about 1872, suddenly some Brahmo men informed the 'Acharya' that they wanted to sit along with their womenfolk, outside the chik. No time was wasted, Annadacharan Khastagir and Durgamohan Das sat with their wives and daughters on the seats allocated for all and sundry along with other men. Since no objection was raised by the other Brahmos, Keshab Sen was forced to permit women to attend prayer meetings openly. Thus began the public opposition to the custom of purdah. In 1879, when the Prince of Wales visited Calcutta, the ladies of the family of Jagadananda Das were allowed by the latter to meet the royal visitor. This caused a wave of protests.

Jnanadanandini gifted Bengali women a graceful mode of dress for moving out of doors. Not that much was wrong with the earlier way of wearing a saree but it did not please the eye. On her arrival in Bombay she discarded the cumbersome oriental dress for the neat way Parsi women had of wearing the saree. Though she made minor alterations but she basically adhered to this mode of dressing. Swarnakumari's young daughter Sarala remembered that when her mother and Mejomami (Jnanadanandini) returned wearing the saree in a new way, all the womenfolk of the family adopted it. This attracted other Brahmikas too.

This mode of wearing the saree was called the 'Bombay style' in the Tagore family as it had been imported from Bombay. For the common Bengali it became 'sarees of the Tagore family'. On her return from Bombay, Jnanadanandini advertised in the papers offering to teach others to wear the saree the way she did. A number of aristocratic Brahmikas came to her to learn to wear the saree, the first one being Saudamini who was later married to Bihari Gupta. Jnanadanandini also began the practice of wearing petticoats, chemises, blouses and jackets with sarees. We have to remember that other Brahmikas had been pondering on an appropriate dress for going out-of-doors. Manmohan Ghosh's wife used to wear a gown as did Indumati, a granddaughter of Debendranath. However not every Bengali lady was willing to step into a gown. Durgamohan Das's wife Brahmomoyee used to wear a dress which was a quaint mixture. To create a typical Indian dress, Jyotirindranath had pleats put in pajamas and tried to blend a sola topee with a pugri. Similarly Brahmikas joined a long veil to the top of a gown and created a dress that was half English and half Indian. The novelty of the 'Bombay Style' attracted every lady. There was no provision for covering one's head in this dress so ladies wore small hats. The front resembled a crown while a small piece of cloth hung at the back. It has not been possible to see a portrait of Jnanadanandini with such a hat on. Her daughter Indira brought into vogue the custom of partly covering one's head with one end of the saree. By her time, the fashion of wearing the saree in the traditional way had been revived.

The modern style of wearing the saree was not an invention of Jnanadanandini. Keshab Sen's daughter Suniti Devi—the Maharani of Coochbehar—had attempted to simplify the awkwardness inherent in the 'Bombay Style'. She used a brooch to keep the saree in position and used to wear a small triangular piece of cloth similar to a Spanish mantilla on her head. Her sister Sucharu Devi, the Maharani of Mayurbhanj, sported a style at the Delhi Durbar which had much in common with the present mode. According to her, this was the original way of wearing a saree in the family of her in-laws. Women of northern India still wear the saree gracefully with the pallav over the right shoulder in front—this seems to be an old style. Bengali women also adopted this but, remembering Jnanadanandini's style of having the pallav on the left shoulder, they followed the same tradition. Hobble sarees, in imitation of Hobble skirts, were also in vogue for sometime but were never popular. They were too tight for the tastes of many people. Along with sarees came the fashion of various types of lace-adorned blouses and jackets. According to Rabindranath, 'cut pieces of silk from English tailoring shops along with bits of net and cheap lace were used to stitch blouses for women.'

Jogen Basu had penned a satirical character 'Model Sister' and the Hindu Society considered ladies dressed in the latest mode akin to her. Jnanadanandini is silent on this topic but we learn from the writings of her two sisters-in-law Saudamini and Swarnakumari about their trials and tribulations. When these ladies—dressed in chemise, blouse, shoes and socks—went out in coaches, they were assailed with derision.

Among Hindus there is a convention that no holy rites may be performed wearing stitched clothes. This led to controversies for quite a while. With changing times, though Muslim dresses were not allowed for women, the 'Brahmika dress' could not be debarred. The new style of wearing the saree earned the synonym 'Brahmika Sharee'. For weddings however the old conventions were strictly followed. During the wedding of Gaganendranath's nine-year-old daughter Sunandini in 1901 some members of the groom's party objected saying that the bride could not be given away wearing stitched clothes. Gaganendranath knew this fully well. Though a Tagore, the old convention was in vogue in his family. He smiled and said, 'You can see for yourself, the bride has no blouse on.' The saree had been draped in such a way that it was impossible to realize that she had no blouse on. The groom's party was amazed. Gaganendranath had dressed his daughter following his own artistic taste. This was much appreciated.

Apart from modernizing women's dress, Jnanadanandini introduced two other hitherto unknown habits. They were: evening outings and celebrating birthdays. She brought both the ideas from England. Sumitendranath mentions how birthdays were celebrated in the Tagore family according to the lunar calendar, so it was not really the birth *day*. The family accepted from the family priest the holy water obtained after bathing the shalgram shila, touched a live fish (usually kept in the family well) and had 'payas' (a form of rice pudding) at lunch.

Since the Maharshi's family adopted the Brahmo doctrine, such customs were not followed in his family. So it is safe to assume that Jnanadanandini was the pioneer in celebrating birthdays. All the youngsters of the family were invited on her son and daughter's birthdays. The employees were also remembered during these festivities. Surendra's birthday came during the rainy season, so all the servants were presented with an umbrella each. Indira was born in winter so her birthday meant a blanket for each servant. It was with Jnanadanandini's encouragement that Sarala and Hironmoyee too celebrated Rabindranath's birthday for the first time at Satyendra's residence at 49, Park Street. On that day it transpired that Jyotirindra's birthday was on a date close by. From the next year, arrangements were made to celebrate his birthday as well, mainly due to Jnanadanandini's efforts. However, the custom of lighting candles according to the number of birthdays was started by Hironmoyee.

There are other instances of Jnanadanandini's independent nature. After Satyendra's return from Bombay, she did not wish to remain as a mere member of the joint family at Jorasanko. She was the first to leave the ancestral home, to move to a separate residence with her husband, son and daughter. This was unheard-of in Bengali families at that time. Even in affluent families, after a daughter's marriage, the son-in-law was kept as a 'ghar jamai' and a separate wing was prepared for them. Thus Jnanadanandini was the precursor of the modern nuclear family. Without going into the merits or demerits of this system, it is obvious that this is the favoured norm today. However, though Jnanadanandini moved away from Jorasanko, her ties with the family remained intact. She always took great interest in all family matters and was the one to whom everyone unhesitatingly turned in times of need. With whom would young Rabindranath stay in England? Jnanadanandini of course. When Sushila was on her deathbed, we find Jnanadanandini by her side. She was also by the side of Mrinalini when each of the latter's five children was born. When Prafullamoyee's husband was slowly going insane, it was to Jnanadanandini that she turned for solace. She says, 'Plagued by worries, I used to sit alone in my room and weep. At that time my second sister-in-law Jnanadanandini used to live on the second floor. She would always take me to her room and console me just like a mother. Had she not been there, I shudder to think what I would have done.' Renuka was ill and who would take care of Rabindranath's two motherless young children? Why, Jnanadanandini was always there to help. Who encouraged Abanindranath to take up painting and also arranged for an art teacher for Pratima? Naturally, Jnanadanandini. She was there to shoulder all responsibility and provide succour.

Not only the grown ups, Jnanadanandini also remembered the trials and tribulations of the young members in a large household. She made every effort to detect and encourage the talent latent in each one of them. She collected all the young children and brought out a magazine called *Balak*. Sudhindra, Balendra, Sarala, Pratima, Indira—all of them owe their first literary efforts to *Balak*. Though she was the editor, Jnanadanandini wrote only one article. She translated the daring escape of Debagorio Mogrievitch from Siberia as published in the *Contemporary Review* and named it 'Ascharya Palayan or the Amazing Escape'. Not only did she bring out a magazine but Jnanadanandini established a litho press to encourage the youngsters to draw and paint. Most of the expenses were borne by her.

Another contribution of hers was the dramatization of two fairy tales for her grandson Subir. These were '*Saat Bhai Champa*' and '*Tak Doomadoom*'. It is a Herculean task to dramatize such tales or fables, especially the second one, but their appeal to the young is immeasurable. Jnanadanandini described so well the episode where the jackal's nose is cut off that one yearns to hear this well-known tale again and again. One also regrets that she did not do the same with other fables and tales. When the jackal says, 'Oh no, no! Do not be worried—a few cuts will not blemish my looks. After all I am not bare bodied like humans, the scar will be well concealed by my fur,' a child's imagination rapidly transports it to the land of fables and family tales. The rhyme, '*Naker badaley narun peloom, Takdoomadoom doom*,' becomes epic poetry for them.

Very few mothers have thought thus for their children. Jnanadanandini's other writings also show the preponderance of concern for children. Three articles by her were published in *Bharati* magazine, one of them was 'Kinder garden' and another 'Women's Education'. The first deals with children's education and the other with that of women. According to Jnanadanandini, the main purpose of women's education was to be an ideal mother. This was the predominant view at that time. Apart from compositions for children we also have two other works by her—one is the Bengali translation of a Marathi story '*Bhau Saheb Bakhar*'. It is a story written with the third Battle of Panipat as its backdrop. The other is an article entitled 'Patriotism and the criticism of the English'.

As the wife of the first Indian Civilian, Jnanadanandini was on intimate terms with the current anglicized Bengali Society. She had also been abroad and so it was natural that her tastes would be similar to those prevalent among the English. However she had adopted just enough Western ways as was necessary for the full flowering of a woman's self, and no more. Just as she had no inhibitions about wearing jackets and shoes or going out for a drive to the Maidan, so had she no difficulty in concerning herself about the well being of her motherland. She rebuked in no uncertain terms people who, behind a mask of false criticism, spent their time begging the English for favours and exhorted her countrymen to stand on their own feet. She knew that our permanent development and improvement could only be achieved by us and no one else.

We find Jnanadanandini in the forefront in practically every walk of life. Due to her natural ability she was even requested for help when plays were staged at home. Whether it was at the time of rehearsals or tying the pugree for her young brothers-in-law Jnanadanandini was the one everyone turned to. There was no dearth of theatre-fiends among the members of the Tagore family. They would stage a play at the drop of a hat. Even when the Jorasanko Theatre wound up, the private performances in the 'Jorasanko courtyard' ended, still the dramatists refused to call it a day. For the staging of *Raja o Rani*, Jnanadanandini's house became the venue for the rehearsals.

The roles were also allotted as follows:

Raja Vikram	—	Rabindranath Tagore
Rani Sumitra	—	Jnanadanandini Devi
Devdutta	—	Satyendranath Tagore
Narayani	—	Mrinalini Devi
Kumar	—	Pramatha Chaudhuri
Ila	—	Priyamvada Devi

Other roles were also performed by the members of the Tagore family. The play was a huge success and all the players performed superbly. It was difficult to choose the best. Among the audience were some actors and actresses of the public stage in disguise. The consequences were astounding. Abanindranath was one of the witnesses and writes that they were invited by the owners of the Emerald Theatre to a public show of *Raja o Rani*. While watching the play they were stunned! 'When Rani Sumitra appeared on the stage, she was exactly like Mejo-jethima (second aunt). She had copied Mejo-jethima in toto in dress, hairstyle, mannerisms, voice and acting!' This drama staged by Emerald theatre was a tremendous success. The actress who played the part of Rani Sumitra and copied Jnanadanandini so well was Gulfam Hari. Motilal Sur as Raja, Mahendranath Basu as Kumar and Kusum Kumari as Ila also acted well.

The staging of this play by the members of the Tagore family gave rise to a controversy. *Bangabasi* magazine was the perpetrator. It brought out an article 'New fashions of the Tagore family'. A detailed text of the actors and actresses and their personal relationships was given. It was pointed out that the parts of husband and wife were enacted by men and women who were forbidden to do so by the dictates of Hindu society due to their relationship. Rabindranath/Raja—was the younger brother-in-law of Jnanadanandini/Rani, Satyendranath/Debdutt was elder brother of the husband of Mrinalini/Narayani while Pramathanath/Kumar was the uncle of Priyamvada Devi/Ila. Had such minor details bothered Jnanadanandini, she would have halted in her tracks much earlier.

Apart from her own literary pursuits, Jnanadanandini always encouraged others to write. Her help to the younger family members in this respect has already been mentioned. She was the inspiration behind Jyotirindranath's translations of Sanskrit plays. Earlier Jyotirindranath had never read any Sanskrit plays. Jnanadanandini requested him to read *Shakuntala* to her; Jyotirindranath was bewitched by the beauty of the play and began to try his hand at translating Sanskrit plays. Rabindranath was also encouraged to write for children by Jnanadanandini. It was through her publication *Balak* that Rabindranath was urged to write for young people.

Jnanadanandini showed an insatiable interest in practically every field of life but we would like to mention one more incident before passing on. Once, on her return from Bombay, she invited a photographer to take pictures not only of her mother-in-law but almost all the women members of the family. But for her energy and endeavour many members would perhaps have been lost to us since there would not have been even a photograph for us to draw some conclusions about them. Probably Rabindranath Tagore's well-known poem 'Chhabi' would never have been penned. Thus Jnanadanandini alone helped Bengali women to move forward in their quest for fulfillment.

Swarnakumari—the brightest star of the andar mahal—was inextricably entwined in every endeavour of Jnanadanandini. She stormed the firmament when some women were just contemplating on certain actions. Before she had finished her education Swarnakumari wrote an entire novel. Society was aghast. Well, the nineteenth century was the time for such feelings. Who would not be surprised to see one trying to erect a mansion over weak foundations? It was barely ten years ago that Bankim Chandra had begun his career as a novelist, with his successful Bengali novel. The memory of *Durgeshnandini* was still fresh in every mind amid the plethora of dramas, satires and caricatures all round. When and how did this eighteen-year-old woman start writing novels? It was not just a first attempt but more like an appearance—a startling appearance indeed. In the year 1876, a dull December evening was brightened by the appearance of a novel *Deep Nirban* by an unnamed author. The novel caught the imagination of all and sundry. While various conjectures were rife about the possible author it was rumored that it had been penned by a young woman. It was as if a hornet's nest had been stirred. No one believed that such a novel could have been written by a woman. The erudite language, the command over the plot sans any feminine inhibitions, how could it be by a woman? The review in the paper *Sadharani* ran as follows:

'We have heard that this has been written by an aristocratic lady. Such power of composition, sympathetic attitude, erudite writing and mastery of the subject by a lady is rare not only in Bengal but even in more advanced countries.'

Praise it certainly was but a tinge of suspicion was also there. Was it really by 'A lady!' Who was the lady? Might it not be written by a man using a woman's nom de plume?

Swarnakumari's Mejodada, Satyendranath, was out of Calcutta at the time. He was convinced that his brother Jyotirindranath was the author. He wrote in his congratulatory letter 'Jyoti's jyoti can never be hidden.' This certainly proved true. As Swarnakumari's glow spread wide like the lustre of a newly mined gem, there was no longer any room for suspicion.

Why was there such a commotion regarding Swarnakumari? Was she the first Bengali authoress or novelist? History disproves this though it would have been natural and perhaps expected that the first woman writer would emerge from an educated, cultured and aristocratic family like the Tagores. But before *Deep Nirban*, Martha Saudamini Sinha's *Nari Charit* (Women's Character) and Nabinkali Devi's *Kanuni Kalanka* had been written. Hemangini Devi's *Manorama* and Surangini Devi's *Taracharit* had also been published. Krishnakamini Das was the first Bengali poetess. Her *Chittabilasini* was published in 1856. Apart from *Phoolmani o Karunar Bibaran* (Description of Phoolmani and Karuna), this is the first book written by a Bengali woman. Later, a book of non-fictional articles was first written in 1861 by Bama Sundari Devi of Pabna. It was called 'The list of superstitions that have to be removed for the progress of this country.' The first woman playwright was Kamini Sundari Devi who wrote *Urbashi* in 1856. According to many, the first Bengali woman novelist was Shiva Sundari Devi. Her novel *Tarabati* was published in 1863 (another source places it in 1873). Shiva Sundari was the wife of Harakumar Tagore of Pathurighata. Her youngest son Shaurindramohan not only translated *Tarabati* into English but in 1881 sent the same, along with his book of lyrics, to friends in various places. It is worth mentioning that the ladies of the Pathuriaghata Tagore family also had literary tastes. At least six or seven such ladies—daughters and daughters-in-law—were known to pen plays and poems. Manorama, Jatindramohan's daughter, wrote *Pitridev-charit* in verse. Her real name was Chaturbarga-pradayini, though she was known as Manorama. In between working on her father's biography, she also penned the story of her birth. It is very similar to what prevails in most Indian families even today.

Krame krame teen kanya prasab korile,
Chaturtha barete Karta anandete bole.
Teen kanya pore bujhi hoibe ek chhele,
Anuman kori ami rakhi tai bole.
Bedona jakhan punoh tahar hoilo,
Karta tobe shawl, taka loiya boshilo.
Gopaler ebar chhele hoile por,
Sakolere ebe ami dibo purashkar.
Putra na hoiya holo e hotobhagini
Harishe bishad tahar hoilo thakani.
'Jaha hoiyachhe taha thakuk banchiye'
Eyi katha boli bahire gelen choliye.

Three daughters arrived one after the other.
The fourth time, the master conjectured hopefully,
'After three daughters, there is sure to be a son.
I feel it would be so and hence say it.'
When my mother went into labour,
The master sat down with a bag full of coins,
'If Gopal has a son this time,
I shall reward everyone.'
This unfortunate girl arrived instead of a son.
The master's happy anticipation turned to grief.
Still he said, 'Whoever has been born, may she enjoy a long life.'
And saying thus, he went outside.

The 'master' mentioned above is Manorama's paternal grandfather Harakumar Tagore. Jatindramohan's daughters never went to live with their in-laws. Brahmin youths were found to marry the daughters of the family and they came to live as ghar jamais. This was because the doors of their own homes were barred against them once they married into the Pirali family. Manorama's husband Pundarikakshya Mukhopadhyay was the stepson of her father's sister. After the death of his sister, Jatindramohan got his brother-in-law remarried and treated the new bride as a member of the family. He later gave his daughter in marriage to this lady's son. The literary value of the above poem may not amount to much but it mirrors the social reality of the day. This is also reflected in the following lines about her grandmother:

Kahar emon buker chhati achhey bolo
Nija kanya haraiya puno biye dilo

Who can show such grit and large-heartedness
To get her son-in-law remarried after losing her daughter?

She was also in charge of managing her father's household. Apart from *Pitridev-charit*, her other creations were the plays *Biraja, Mohini* and *Aniruddha Milan* as well as the books of verse *Gourgeetika* and *Mankunja*. She had also learnt to play the instrument sur-kannan at home from her father's younger brother. Some writings of Shaurindramohan's two daughters Shreejayanti and Jayjayanti were also published. Jayjayanti wrote *Manas Kusum*. She turned to poetry to overcome her heartache. She says, 'I had no desire to bring this, the outpouring of my pain, in to the public eye. This belongs to the innermost recess of my heart and is my private prayers. It is neither a beautiful rose nor has it the fragrance of a lotus, mallika or juhi in bloom—it is just a posy of wild flowers.'

Her poems reiterate the same feelings:

Janina likhite ami moorkho ashikshita
Bhashaheen chhandaheen bhaabheen gatha
E shudhu maram byatha
Jhara phuler mala gantha
Bhab-boney bhabpushpa koriya chayan
Brahmomoyi paadpadme kori nibedan.

I am illiterate and know not how to write,
My poems express neither rhyme nor reason,
This is just an outflow of my heartache,
A garland made of flowers that have dropped from the tree.
I have endeavoured to collect blossoms of feeling
And lay them at the feet of the almighty Goddess.

In the poem *Amaar Sansar* she writes:

E mayar songshare keno ghar bendhechhile?
Ashay nirash kore sheshete bhangiya dile.

Why did you build my home in this transient world
Only to break it up, dealing a blow to all my dreams?

The poem *Utsarga* also draws our attention :

Asru diye gantha mor e malyakhani
Keho na loyuk tobu tumi lobey jani
Hridayer jata katha bhasaheen byakulata
Murta hoye uthibe go parashe tomar
Manas Kusum tai dibo upahaar.

Others may reject this garland, strung with my tears,
But I know you will accept it.
All the unspoken words of my heart
As well as unexpressed longings will find form by your touch.
It is thus that I gift *Manas Kusum* to you.

Jayjayanti's two novels were *Mahamilan* and *Jeevanmukti*. Kalikrishna Tagore's wife Saudamini wrote *Bhaktiras-tarangini*. The first woman to write her autobiography was Rassundari Devi (1876). In the early period of writings by women (1872) we come across the names of quite a few. These were mostly non-fictional articles. Articles dealing with serious topics like prevalent society and its modernization, women's education and morality were written by Kamini Dutt, Swarnalata Ghosh, Madhumati Gangopadhyaya, Bibi Taheran Leccha, Golapmohini Devi, Ramasundari Ghosh, Khiroda Mitra, Madame Saudamini and many others. None of these women were connected to the

Tagore family. Apart from Shivasundari and a few others, they did not even belong to the aristocracy. Yet their love of literature and pursuit of education commands our admiration. The year 1876 is especially memorable. It was in this year that Chandramukhi Basu requested permission to appear in the entrance examination at Dehradun, Rassundari wrote her autobiography, Faizunnessa Chaudhurani, the nawab of Kumilla, composed *Rupjalal*, an epic of love written with an admixture of prose and poetry, and finally Swarnakumari's *Deep Nirban* was published. Women from all walks of life struggling for self-expression seemed to have come together in this one field. The efforts of a member of the Tagore family, a domiciled Christian girl, a housewife in a remote village, and a Muslim landlady blended into one. However, apart from these factual recordings, it is difficult to accept any of the precursors of Swarnakumari as a literateur or novelist. The way they carried out their responsibility was praiseworthy but at that time the literary efforts by women only invited ridicule and pity. Yet the first novelist in world literature was not a man but a woman. Her name was Morasakisi Kibu (978–1031 AD). This Japanese lady wrote the first novel *Genji Manogatari*.

Slowly Swarnakumari gained due recognition in the world of Bengali literature. Ridicule and pity gave way to astonishment tinged with respect. The path of self-expression for women seemed to have broadened further.

Apart from novels, Swarnakumari wrote satires, poetry, songs, humorous skits, non-fictional articles, travelogues, musical plays, reminiscences and school texts. The list seems impossible and unbelievable especially for a lady. It is surprising that she was not influenced by any of the women writers before her. Her ideal was Bankim Chandra though her penchant for history reminds one of Ramesh Chandra Dutt. Her aspiration to emulate Bankim as an ideal author has shorn Swarnakumari's creations, albeit partially, of grace. This loss however is negligible. Whatever may have been the case elsewhere, in literature feminine styles were not popular. Yet Swarnakumari began writing short stories and novels while quite young. Of course there are other examples of writers beginning this early. Taru Dutt, who passed away due to an incurable illness at twenty-one, had composed a number of memorable poems and two novels in English and French. Many authors wrote in English at the time. Learning the language had been facilitated by English teachers. Swarnakumari also translated her stories and novels but that was much later.

Swarnakumari seems to have been favoured by exceptional good fortune. Impediments seem to have blossomed into fragrant flowers in her case. She was never touched by the storm Jnanadanandini faced whenever she tried to foray into new paths. Swarnakumari on the other hand was showered with admiration, respect and glory. This is what one would call good luck. One wonders whether she really never faced any opposition. It appears that she never considered them as such and trod firmly along her chosen path. Due to a detached nature Swarnakumari was always able to hold herself aloof from mundane family affairs. This was coupled with her complete dedication to literature. As a child she had been blessed by the Maharshi. On reading one of her compositions he had said, 'Swarna, may flowers bloom forth from your pen!' This was coupled with the affection of her brothers and overriding everything was her husband Janakinath Ghosal's love. He shielded her from all the trials and travails of life and eased the path for her success in the literary field. Swarnakumari's fame as an author never caused the slightest dent in their marital life.

What were other women doing while Swarnakumari was preparing for a literary career? It is not very easy to get an insight into the andar mahal of other families, but we may consider the Tagore family: to begin with, Swarnakumari's elder sisters and sisters-in-law were immersed in household chores. From early morning they would settle down to paring and preparing vegetables coupled with feminine gossip. Saudamini, Sarat Kumari, Barnakumari, Prafullamoyee, Sarbasundari, Kadambari and many others were regular participants. When the Maharshi returned home, Sarada Devi would come along to supervise. Other dependent ladies also joined in. Various tidbits of gossip livened up these routine chores. Sometimes the young girls were also lured by the attraction of various anecdotes and news. Sarala used to go often but she never saw her mother attend any of these sessions.

Saratkumari loved to spend her time in beauty care. She took the maximum time to smear herself with various beauty aids called rooptan and swim about in the tank inside the house. Her husband Jadunath (Jadu Kamal) Mukhopadhyaya had an excellent sense of humour. Many people were curious about the fair complexion and exceptional good looks of the Tagores. On being asked the secret Jadunath solemnly replied, 'Milk and wine!' This led to the idea that in the Tagore family children were bathed in milk and wine directly after birth! This intimate anecdote about Jadunath's love of humour has been mentioned by Indira in her memoirs.

In the Tagore family along with beauty care the women had to be proficient in culinary arts. Saratkumari was a superb cook. Jnanadanandini writes, 'Once when the income from the zamindari had declined, my father-in-law instructed that all the daughters-in-law must be taught to cook.' Saudamini writes the same thing. She says, 'To make us proficient, my father had directed that each one of us would have to cook a dish everyday. Each one got a rupee daily; we had to purchase fish and vegetables with that money and cook it.' This is the reason why all women of this family were good cooks. This was also the norm in other families too. According to *Kahini*, the reminiscences of Binayini Devi, the women of Aban and Gagan Tagore's family spent a lot of time in the thakur ghar preparing for the daily worship of the household deity. Most women in other families also spent their days similarly. Some indulged in dolls' weddings, some played cards and *pasha* or a particular game known as 'Dus Panchish'. In most wealthy families women did not do much manual work. As there was no scope for education, a great deal of time was spent in gossiping and scandal-mongering. Thus in educated families the need for women's education was being gradually felt and encouraged. This included embroidery and tailoring, literacy—especially reading good books—cooking, nursing and even childcare. Such education also included household jobs. Thus the notion that all uneducated women of the time were adept at housekeeping is false. Many frittered away their lives in idle pursuits. Swarnakumari never spent her time thus. Remaining aloof to such pursuits she shielded herself from many unsavoury situations.

The novel *Deep Nirban* was followed by *Basanta Utsav* and almost simultaneously came *Chhinna Mukul*. Her admiring readers crowned her with fame. Nowadays most people have forgotten that Swarnakumari can claim to be the pathbreaker in the composition of musical plays akin to opera in Bengali. She composed *Basanta Utsav* before Rabindranath's *Balmiki Protiva* and even Jyotirindranath's *Maanmoyee*. This was staged almost as soon as it was written. This was the golden era of the Tagore family. Swarnakumari's elder brother Jyotirindranath was a great appreciator of drama and his wife Kadambari a lover of literature. Satyendra and Jnanadanandini's frequent visits were like a sudden gusty wind which blew away all that was old and mouldy. The 'Hindu Mela' was organized with tremendous enthusiasm. Now the young men and women of the Tagore family became keen to bring out a new magazine. Bankim's *Bangadarshan* had come out five years earlier and was widely read. Would it not be possible to bring out an equally good magazine? The Maharshi's eldest son was rather conservative and would have preferred to improve *Tattwabodhini*, but the more modern Jyotirindranath did not see eye to eye with him. He felt that it would not be possible to modernize an old magazine. Ultimately Jyotirindranath's view prevailed. The brothers and sisters spent days and nights planning and drafting. What would the name of the magazine be? Someone suggested *Suprobhat*. This did not find favour and ultimately the matter was put to vote! The name accepted by the majority—*Bharati*—was both beautiful and symbolic. In its early days *Bharati* was the brainchild of Jyotirindranath and Kadambari. Much later, in 1884, Swarnakumari took the helm. About seven years before 1884, Dwijendranath was the first editor of *Bharati*. From the very first copy, young Rabindranath began his harsh criticism of *Meghnad Badh*.

Let us return to the former context. Recitals of vulgar music and dance were never allowed in the Tagore mansion, but members of the family were never denied enjoyment of quality music. This was because they themselves were adept and well versed in the arts. Any family celebration was accompanied by various performances. About ten years previously Ganendra, Gunendra, Saradaprasad and Jyotirindra were the ones behind the 'Jorasanko Theatre'. Though that had eroded with time, the love of drama was still there. So Jyotirindranath began afresh. Though the old theatre audience was not allowed in, the various plays became a great success. Jyotirindranath, who had enthralled audiences playing the part of a courtesan, began with renewed enthusiasm. Most of the old timers were not there, some having passed on. This time the womenfolk of the family came forward to participate. Though it was a performance staged within the four walls of the home and the audience comprised only relations, the event raised the hackles of many. Staging a dramatic performance within the precincts of the home as well as the appearance of aristocratic ladies on the stage—both incidents were unheard of, even considered impossible.

Swarnakumari's *Basanta Utsab* was enacted at a private party of the Tagores. One day as the family had gathered in the verandah and were chatting away, suddenly the talk veered towards how Basanta Utsav (Holi or spring festival) was observed in the olden days. Amidst arguments and counter arguments, Jyotirindra—as usual in the forefront—suggested that they should also celebrate Basanta Utsav according to old traditions. The proposal was met with great enthusiasm and all the necessary ingredients like aabir (dry colours), kumkum (red powder), water spouts, etc., were collected. It was decided that the festival would be observed on the terrace garden under coloured lights. To add to the gaiety, Swarnakumari wrote *Basanta Utsav*. Thus Swarnakumari penned the first musical drama. Rabindranath was unable to participate in this family celebration as he was away in England.

Kadambari played the role of Leela—the heroine of *Basanta Utsav.* Swarnakumari enacted the part of the nun whose blessings enabled Leela to get back her lover. Her saffron dress enhanced her detached nature well. Jyotirindranath was the hero. In a later presentation of *Basanta Utsav*, Rabindranath not only acted opposite the hero but also engaged in battle, wielding a tin sword! For quite sometime, the three of them were engrossed with writing musical plays and enacting them. Later on, Swarnakumari wrote *Bibaha Utsav.*

Swarnakumari's writing flowed like a perennial spring. Apart from Rabindranath, no other member of the Tagore family was such a prolific writer. Though this is not the place to discuss her literary ability, it is true that Swarnakumari has not received her deserved place in Bengali literature. We could easily consider her a bridge between Bankimchandra and Rabindranath—two writers at opposite poles. Though she mainly followed Todd in her historical novels and short stories, her mastery even in that field is unmatched.

Swarnakumari wrote quite a few historical novels. *Deepnirban*, *Mibar Raj*, *Bidroho*, *Phooler Mala*, *Hooghly Imambara*—all were popular. The ingenuity she showed in bridging the gaps in history is commendable. Considering the novel *Kumar Bhim Singh*, Todd mentions Raj Singha's first wife Kamal Kumari but does not give the name of his second wife, though he writes about their two sons Bhim Singh and Jay Singh. Bankim Chandra in his novel *Rajsingha* transformed princess Charumati of Kishangarh as the valiant Chanchal Kumari of Roopnagar. Five years later when Swarnakumari began to write *Kumar Bhim Singh* she unhesitatingly named Kumar Jaisingh's mother Chanchal Kumari. This may have been a little off the track as far as Todd's history was concerned but the readers accepted it without a murmur. Thus a half-mythical, nameless character attained shape and form in the hands of Swarnakumari.

Swarnakumari won more acclaim for her social novels and short stories than for her historical creations. Many of us still hold the view that the Tagore family, especially their womenfolk, had hardly any close contacts with the ordinary Bengali society. Hence their writings seldom portray the realities of social life. Even Rabindranath felt that 'lack of real acquaintance with the rest of the world had crippled them.' This was perhaps the reason behind his strong objection to translations of Swarnakumari's works. Though detached from mundane affairs of daily existence, Swarnakumari was not oblivious to the real problems in life. She certainly was able to feel the human soul that is above society and family. Thus both her best novels are social ones.

Let us consider her first novel *Snehalata*. According to the critics of the twentieth century: 'This is the first time in Bengal that a novel has been written about the problems raised by modern views.' As we said earlier, Swarnakumari was exceptionally fortunate. There had been considerable discussion and writings on the problem of widows but it was she who won the accolade. The Maharshi himself was against widow remarriage; so it surprises us to see Swarnakumari concerning herself about them. The widow Snehalata only followed the path trod by Kundanandini of *Bisabrikshya*, but Binodini of *Chokher*

Bali could not forge a new path either. Swarnakumari judged the problems of widows not as a social reformer but from a woman's view point. She viewed a woman's problem keeping in mind the entire gamut of her emotions like love, fear, debts, age-old convictions, diffidence and so on. This unusual outlook certainly brought a new dimension to Bengali literature.

In the nineteenth century many eminent reformers had not only begun to ponder upon the problems faced by widows but had also begun to take practical steps. On 7 December 1856, Ishwarchandra Vidyasagar persuaded his favourite disciple Sureshchandra Vidyaratna to marry Kalimati, a child widow. This created tremendous enthusiasm especially in the Brahmo Samaj. Though widow remarriage was accepted by the Adi Brahmo Samaj much later, young Brahmos like Durgamohan Das, Shibnath Shastri and others set glaring examples. We know about the liberal views of Satyendranath Tagore as regards women's emancipation. Durgamohan Das's outlook was much bolder. He married his young stepmother to one of his friends amid tremendous opposition from society. His wife Brahmamoyee was also an exceptional character. Equally bold and broad-minded was Shibnath Shastri. He had been forced by his father to marry Birajmohini though his first wife Prasannamoyee was there. After embracing Brahmoism, Shibnath decided not to establish conjugal relations with his second wife but get her married afresh. This idea was nipped in the bud as Birajmohini violently opposed the scheme. Such views were never encouraged in the Tagore family. In 1872 Keshab Sen propagated a special marriage act (Teen Ain) legalizing inter-caste marriages. Ishwarchandra then sent a few hapless widows to Rajnarain Basu's daughter Leelavati, requesting her to arrange for their remarriage. Leelavati showed tremendous guts and had eight widows remarried between 1884 and 1890.

Swarnakumari was also concerned about the fate of widows. She, along with a few of her friends, founded an organization for women's welfare called Sakhi Samiti. The name was suggested by the poet Rabindranath. The main purpose of this organization was to educate widows and young unmarried girls as teachers for women. At the time women, especially married ones, seldom went to school; yet the quest for education and knowledge was increasing. Thus governesses were in great demand—usually foreign missionaries or men had to be employed. Swarnakumari realized that educated Bengali women could easily get these jobs. Economic independence would doubtless make the plight of widows easier. Though Sakhi Samiti's achievements in this field were not much, such an organization was necessary to spread education among women and help them become independent. Such a need exists even today.

Let us return to *Snehalata*. Swarnakumari tried to make widows financially independent by educating them but she never tried to have them remarry. She had also wondered if this was the real solution to the problems faced by widows. *Snehalata* was the result of such deliberations. After Snehalata's death when we read the views of Jagatbabu—one of the main characters of the novel—we are stunned since they must have been the opinion of Swarnakumari herself. After Snehalata's death, Jagatbabu felt, 'Had Snehalata not been educated she would have borne her lot with equanimity. Perhaps she would not have caused her own death.' The strong conviction, which enables one to accept all deprivations and misfortunes as dictates of fate, are certainly weakened when logical arguments begin to rent the mind. As a woman Swarnakumari was unable to ignore this truth. She realized that making women self-reliant and economically independent alone would not solve their problem. In her play *Nivedita*, written for the Hiranmoyee Widows Home (Shilpashram), she portrays another ugly facet of this problem. She neither tried, nor was able to show the path that would lead to a solution. She wanted to rehabilitate widows in society with full honour. She felt that education, economic independence or even remarriage sans reverence would not lead to a woman's fulfillment.

A few of Swarnakumari's contemporaries also distinguished themselves by writing social novels. One of them was Kusumkumari Devi and the other Saratkumari Chaudhurani. Kusumkumari's novels *Snehalata, Premlata* and *Shantilata* were praised by both Ishwarchandra Vidyasagar and Bankimchandra, Saratkumari's works were appreciated by Rabindranath himself. While writing the history of Bengali literature Sukumar Sen unequivocally regards *Snehalata* as the first novel dealing with the problems of modernization in Bengali society.

Swarnakumari's other popular novel is *Kaahake* (To Whom). In this novel she deals just with the love of a young woman. This novel pleased critics who had earlier thought Swarnakumari's writings lacked feminine grace and charm. This novel does not deal with social problems but is just the autobiography of a modern woman. The educated heroine tries to analyse her feelings regarding her conception of love. Swarnakumari's masterly analysis of a woman's heart and mind, ignoring the usual feminine restrictions and diffidence, have few parallels even today. Her acquaintance with the daily life of common people was certainly slight, but she tried to make up for this lack by psychoanalysis. Many critics have found the environment of *Kaahake* resembling that of Swarnakumari's own, i.e. one present in educated aristocratic families of the time. It is perhaps also the reason why *Kaahake* is so true to life. Though Swarnakumari's life had no resemblance to that of the heroine, there is no gainsaying that she was completely at ease in her surroundings. Not only was she able to portray contemporary educated society but two of her main characters were moulded on Debendranath and Satyendranath. *Kaahake* was not only popular with the Bengali public but was appreciated by foreigners too.

In the nineteenth century, writing novels in English was in vogue. Some wrote in English while others translated their Bengali creations. In every aristocratic family, children were taught English from childhood. Not only were the textbooks in English but the governesses and teachers were also Englishwomen. For such people, proficiency in the language was natural. Thus even ladies wrote novels in English. It has been possible to record the names of 194 such ladies between 1850 and 1910. There may have been about fifty others who used pseudonyms rather than publish their names.

Swarnakumari was quite enthusiastic about translating her literary works. Two of her novels, fourteen short stories and a play were translated. *Phooler Mala* was the first to be translated by Christina Albert. This was published in the *Modern Review* as *The Fatal Garland*. The original novel had not been very successful. Probably this led to Rabindranath's poor opinion about the translation. When the poet was in England in 1913, Swarnakumari sent him the translated book. She hoped this would widen her literary circle in English society. Rabindranath opined, 'I know that publication of this work here would not be fruitful. The translation is not upto the mark and has not reached the high standards of English compositions.' (28 January 1913)

He expressed the same opinion to Indira Devi in his letter: 'Nadidi sent me the translation of her *Phooler Mala*. Had she been acquainted with the literary circle here she would have realized why such stuff will never be acceptable here. The work must have what these people term *reality*.' (6 May 1913). It was a very difficult task for Rabindranath because his poems had won acclaim abroad. If he mentioned the superiority of his works he was sure to be misunderstood. Since the award of the Nobel Prize, many authors felt that translations of their creations might win similar laurels. While discussing such people Rabindranath did not spare Swarnakumari too. He wrote to Rothenstein, 'She is one of those unfortunate beings who has more ambition than ability, but just enough talent to keep her mediocrity alive for a short period. Her weakness has been taken advantage of by some unscrupulous literary agents in London and she has had stories translated and published. I have given her no encouragement but

I have not been successful in making her see things in their proper light. It is likely that she may go to England and use my name and you may meet her but be mercyful [sic] to her and never let her harbour in her mind any illusion about her worth and her scope. I am afraid she will be a source of trouble to my friends who I hope will be candid to her for my sake and will not allow her to mistake ordinary politeness for encouragement.'

It has not been possible to ascertain the date of this letter. This was probably the time when *An Unfinished Song*, a translation of Swarnakumari's novel *Kaahake*, had been published in London. Undeterred by all odds, Swarnakumari translated this novel herself and it was published in London in December 1913. From the December of 1876 to that of 1913, Swarnakumari appeared before the London reading public on a snowy and foggy winter evening, traversing a long path. To them it was a book written by a foreigner and one which amply justified its name. Critics were lavish in their praise. *The Clarion* said, 'Remarkable for the picture of Hindu life; the story is overshadowed by the personality of the authoress, one of foremost Bengali writer [sic] today.' The editor of the *Westminster Gazette* was even more vocal in her praise. 'Mrs. Ghosal, as one of the pioneers of the women's movement in Bengal, and fortunate in her own upbring [sic], is well qualified to give this picture of a Hindu maiden ['s] development.'

One wonders why Rabindranath was so apprehensive. Proving all his qualms baseless, the second edition of *An Unfinished Song* was published by the same company in 1914. Thus it appears that Swarnakumari was able to attract the attention of foreign readers, albeit temporarily. *To Whom*, another translation of *Kaahake*, had been published from Calcutta in 1910. The translator was Swarnakumari's niece Sovana. Between the two translations, the one by Swarnakumari appears more spontaneous. Her other niece Indira helped her partly in this task. *Divya Kamal*, a play by Swarnakumari, was translated into German under the name

Princess Kalyani. Some short stories by her were also translated into English. Swarnakumari thus earned acclaim as an authoress both at home and abroad.

In our country an author is acknowledged only when he writes novels. Swarnakumari, though a successful novelist, also tried her hand at other literary ventures. Her short stories were popular. The first successful Bengali short story was written by Rabindranath. His predecessors who wrote short stories were not even sure what their creation should be called. Thus the story 'Kumar Bhim Singh' by Swarnakumari was named a historic novel at times and a historic play at others. During the infancy of Bengali short stories, Swarnakumari wrote quite a few about Bengali women. Malati and Lajjabati, Hem and Bhabini of 'Gahona' and Jamuna are women who are hidden behind a multitude of mundane incidents and ultimately lost. Swarnakumari portrayed their diffidence and shyness. In a patriarchal society girls have always been neglected. Parents worry themselves sick about allowances for a son studying abroad, yet consider medical attendance a wastage for a dying daughter. Swarnakumari came across innumerable such cases during her social service. These hapless and helpless girls have come alive in her short stories.

Apart from her activities in Sakhi Samiti, Swarnakumari always encouraged other authoresses. In those days women writers were usually good friends and called each other sakhi or *soi*. Competition there was among men but the educated women were above petty jealousies. No harsh criticism of another authoress' work has ever been observed. Swarnakumari had a number of *sakhis*—Saratkumari and Swarnakumari called each other '*Bihangini Soi*' (two ladies sworn to eternal friendship and calling each other by a special name), the poetess Girindramohini was Swarnakumari's '*Milan Biraha Soi*' and there were many others. The first art and craft exhibition was held under the auspices of the Sakhi Samiti. Swarnakumari was keen to bring forth the artistic excellence of the various handicrafts by women. So far such creations were only used to beautify the home. Society was condescending and the artists never got due acknowledgement. The art and crafts exhibition held in the premises of Bethune College provided them the first opportunity. Rabindranath composed a play *Mayar Khela*. The actresses and the audience were all women. Their excitement and joy knew no bounds. The actresses were mainly from the Tagore family with one or two outsiders. However, in the craft competition, the first five prizes were bagged by women from other families. It has been possible to obtain a list of names of those who participated the first year (1888), including the first five competitors and their works:

First Prize	Miss Manuk	a picture of Ranjit's cane bridge
Second Prize	Srimati Bhubanmohini Dasi	a scene depicting a wedding night, made of kheer (milk concentrated to a solid state and cooled) and engraved stone moulds for makingsweets.
Third Prize	Srimati Girindramohini Dasi	a village scene in clay and a picture of Devi Chaudhurani worked in tapestry.
Fourth Prize	Miss Sarkar	fine embroidery.
Fifth Prize	Srimati Basantakumari Das and	embroidery with gold silver thread (zari) or zardosi work.

The winner of the third prize, Girindramohini, was a poetess. The fifth prize went to Basantakumari who was a member of the working committee of the Sakhi Samiti. Her husband Jnanendranath, the second son of Srinath Das, was the editor of a magazine called *Samaj* and an advocate of women's liberation. Basantakumari was the first woman member of the

Indian National Congress and attended the Bombay session along with Swarnakumari and Dr Kadambini Gangopadhyaya. The other members of Sakhi Samiti were Swarnalata Ghosh, Baradasundari Ghosh, Lalita Ray, Sarala Ray, Manmohini Dutt, Thakamani Mullick, Saudamini Gupta, Prasannatara Gupta, Hiranmoyee Devi, Saudamini Devi, Chandramukhi Basu, Mrinalini Devi, Bidhumukhi Ray, Prasannamoyee Devi, Surabala Devi, Girindramohini Devi and Swarnakumari herself. Just like her friend Girindramohini, Swarnakumari also composed poems, songs and gathas. Gathas have gone into oblivion now but in the nineteenth century poems depicting a tale were known as gathas. Saratkumari's husband Akshay Chaudhury started this mode of writing which enthused Swarnakumari, Rabindranath and many others. The gathas composed by Swarnakumari were hailed by some magazines rapturously. Unfortunately these do not evoke any enthusiasm today, not even the excellent songs therein. Swarnakumari stands apart for two more achievements. These were: editing a magazine and her articles on scientific topics. Her pen matched those of her contemporary male writers.

There were several Bengali magazines edited by women. Between 1875 and 1900 at least twenty-six women editors appeared on the scene. However, the most eminent among them was Swarnakumari. Later a number of other ladies of the Tagore family came forward in this field. Apart from Jnanadanandini, others like Indira, Hiranmoyee, Sarala, Protiva, Progya, Hemlata and many others left their mark as editors.

The first women's magazine with Thakamoni Dasi as the editor came out in 1875. The magazine was published by her father and she was only a figurehead. About two years later *Bharati* was brought out by the Tagore family; seven years later, after the sudden death of Kadambari, Swarnakumari took up the reins of this magazine. But for Kadambari's untimely death, Swarnakumari's capabilities as an editor would perhaps never have come to light. According to Saratkumari, 'Swarnakumari amply showed the latent power of a woman in coping with a disaster.' It was for *Bharati* that Swarnakumari had to compose articles, plays, satires, and farces.

No one ever dreamt of women playwrights turning their abilities to satires. Apart from a number of plays, Swarnakumari wrote two satires. She proved that she was equally adept in comedy also. *Paak Chakra* and *Kone Badal* portray in minute detail the life within the four walls of the andar mahal. The amusing songs of these two compositions are also insights into contemporary life. Swarnakumari composed quite a few charades too. Indians are not very familiar with charades. These deal mainly with unravelling a particular word, with the help of a couple of scenes. For example, in Bengali the synonym for mountain is 'pahar'. To explain this word, one actor pretends to have fractured his leg (*pa*) and is examined by a doctor. The diagnosis is a broken bone (*haar* in Bengali) and this provides the clue to the entire word. The charades 'Scientist Husband' and 'Lajjasheela' by Swarnakumari are incomparable. Rabindranath named such compositions 'Fun and laughter'. Swarnakumari's credentials as the first writer for children are unimpeachable. Her *Galpey Swalpey* (1889) has been able to portray the feelings of children admirably.

Swarnakumari left the rosier path of a novelist for the more difficult one of writing serious articles. This was because, like Bankimchandra, she was keen that her writings simultaneously help in social reform. Her sincerity shines out even in a difficult article like 'Prithibi'. Even today, when men and women in rockets are being sent to outer space, we have few women writing serious articles on scientific themes. Yet Swarnakumari began writing scientific articles barely seven years after the publication of Bankimchandra's *Bigyan Rahasya*. This was much before Ramendrasundar had entered the literary field. Swarnakumari collected the opinions of the most eminent geologists of the world and wrote seven articles. These were the precursors of scientific discourse among women. At that time, the School Society had encouraged the publication of books on Geography and Science for school students. Swarnakumari wrote her articles to cater to the newly created curiosity regarding the earth in Bengali minds.

The main hurdle faced by Swarnakumari while writing scientific articles in Bengali was the lack of suitable synonyms. She encountered this while trying to express the views of eminent geologists like Laplas, Harcell, Thompson, Norman, Lakiere, Godfrey, Balfour and Figuey in Bengali. She writes that the main obstacle while writing scientific books in Bengali is the lack of suitable synonyms. She gave this matter considerable thought and even created some terms herself. In the Introduction to her book on the collection of the opinions of eminent geologists she says:

> 'The terms used by previous authors have been generally accepted but in some cases the commonly accepted words have been substituted by others, e.g. a volcano is usually termed "Agneyagiri" in Bengali but the word *Jwalamukhi* used in Sanskrit literature is more apt. I see no reason why it should not be used in Bengali and have ventured to do so in this book.'

The number of appropriate synonyms coined by Swarnakumari is considerable. Her preference was always for simple terms. For example:

Fern	—	*Parnitoru*
Penumbra	—	*Upacchyaya*
Sensitive	—	*Mohishnu*
Solar spot	—	*Surya bimba*
Pygmy	—	*Balkhilya*
Triassic	—	*Tristar*
Universe	—	*Biswa-akash*
Hypnotism	—	*Swapni kata*
Deduction	—	*Abaroha*

The apt choice of synonyms do her credit. We have unknowingly accepted another one of her suggestions:

> As in the animal world, so in the sphere of words, only the fittest will survive. There is no harm in using the same scientific terms in every language. It will enrich the language.

She established the reasonableness of this dictum by using English words in her Bengali compositions.

Along with social work and creative writing, Swarnakumari also attended the Congress sessions. Her husband Janakinath Ghosal was one of the main leaders of the Congress. He was intimately involved with the Indian National Congress for a number of years, right from its inception. Janakinath also adorned the post of the General Secretary of the Congress and it was his favourite sphere of work. Swarnakumari was, along with her husband, also imbued with ideals of nationalism. She attended the fifth and sixth sessions. These sessions were also attended by two other ladies. Swarnakumari's concern for the motherland was not only reflected in her novels written in later years but also in the life of her younger daughter Sarala. She had contemplated dedicating Sarala to serve the country rather than to get her married. According to many, Swarnakumari's personal experiences bore the greatest influence in *Troee*—a novel written towards the end of her life. The character of Jyotirmoyee particularly was modelled on her daughter Sarala. We find many other characters and incidents of the Tagore family here. This novel also gives us an inkling of Swarnakumari's thoughts on the freedom struggle. She did not believe in the terrorist movement. Her heroine believes, 'India will achieve Swaraj without any bloodshed when the rulers and the subjects will unite under the same flag of equality and friendship.' Swarnakumari's preference for the Civil Disobedience movement is also evident in her support for processions protesting police excesses. She never approved of aping the West but the independence, self-sufficiency and particularly the political involvement of Western, especially English, women drew her admiration. She realized that though men ridiculed such actions, in their heart of hearts they respected such women and were often like string puppets in their hands. She often wondered when Indian women would also move forward. Swarnakumari's literary achievements did not depend on any formal acclaim. However the Calcutta University honoured her by conferring on her the highest award: the Jagattarini Gold Medal. The first person to have been awarded this medal was Swarnakumari's younger brother Rabindranath. Swarnakumari was the first woman to win it. She certainly appears to have been the brightest star in '*Thakurbarir* andar mahal'.

Returning to the family school of the Tagores, where Swarnakumari as well as Jnanadanandini took their first lessons, another very competent pupil was Neepamoyee. Hemendranath, with his deep love of learning, wanted his wife to be accomplished in all walks of life. His daughters certainly fulfilled his wishes but what about Neepomoyee? Certainly she never created any commotion like Jnanadanandini did but a look into her life gives us an insight into the preparations for women's liberation in the precincts of this mansion as well as in the attitude of their menfolk.

Neepomoyee's father Haradev Chattopadhyaya was a close friend of Debendranath. Her younger sister Prafullamoyee also later entered the Tagore family as a bride. Acceding to Debendra's request, Haradev had sent his two daughters to school along with Saudamini. Haradev's two daughter were Annada and Saudamini—the elder sisters of Neepomoyee and Prafullamoyee. Inspite of their close friendship, the social disparities between Debendra and Haradev were great. This led to great furore at the wedding of Hemendra and Neepomoyee.

The furore was only to be expected. Haradev was a Kulin Brahmin. When he decided to marry his daughter to a Pirali Brahmin, and that too according to Brahmo rites, all his relatives were distraught by the bogey of social ostracism. To avert contact with such a calamity, Haradev's eldest son left home with his wife and son. Though Haradev was heartbroken, especially for his grandson, he remained firm in his resolve. Debendra was his dearest friend and who was 'society' to object to a marriage between the two families? Moreover the social dictates and norms had begun to slacken. Around then, in 1856, the wife of a Kulin Brahmin had successfully sued her husband for maintenance. Vidyasagar had already initiated the remarrying of widows. Society had not been able to forbid these. So Haradev took heart and went ahead.

His relations and the so-called 'protectors' of society were not to be deterred. They arranged for a hundred *lathials* to kill the groom and to abduct the bride. Probably they also had in mind an old and doddering Kulin bridegroom for the twelve-year-old Neepomoyee. Fortunately, matters did not come to a head. News of the plan leaked out and Haradev arranged for police protection during the wedding. As Hemendranath, the bridegroom, arrived just before sundown, people were charmed by his good looks and dress. Clad in a Benarasi *jor* (dhoti), bedecked with pearl and diamond chains, bracelets and rings, it appeared to young Prafullamoyee that the Lord Shiva himself had come to wed her sister.

Neepamoyee, exquisite in her bridal finery, walked round Hemendra seven times and garlanded him. After the prayers, according to Brahmo rites, the bride and groom entered the *basor ghar*. This is the room where the bride and groom spend the night with friends and family members, mainly from the bride's side. Hemendra has given details in his book *Amar Bibaho* (My Wedding). Since the wedding was according to Brahmo rites, ladies of non-Brahmo families did not attend. Thus Hemendra did not have to face any crude pranks that were common to such occasions. Moreover, to deter the ladies present from such revelry, Hemendranath had brought up the topic of women's education. His information that most women of the Tagore family were adept in Sanskrit and English left the ladies spellbound and speechless. This observation by Hemendra indicated that all Brahmo ladies were not educated at that time. Though the term Brahmika implied an educated Brahmo woman, obviously there were others beyond this sphere. Sukumari and Hemendra's marriage according to Brahmo rites further narrowed the social circle of the Maharshi's family.

In the Tagore family, life was flowing unfettered along novel lines. The educated society outside was also full of new ideas. The greatest changes were brought about by the Brahmo Samaj. Keshab Sen attended a tea party at the residence of a preacher, Mr Borson, along with several Brahmo ladies. A storm in the teacup indeed. At this juncture Hemendra took another bold step. He arranged for his wife to have music lessons.

Such a daring action was unheard of. Ladies of quality certainly never learnt to sing. It is difficult to ascertain when exactly this social taboo was first enforced. It was probably during the time of Aurangzeb. Singing was confined to Bengali men and courtesans. Though the gentry often sold their souls and submitted them at the feet of such women, with their tinkling ankle bells and sweet voices, teaching a genteel woman to sing and dance was absolutely taboo. It was considered almost a heinous crime! Women were dependent on Vaishnavis, Jhumur and Khemta-walis for music. Usually, women from the lower rungs of society embraced such professions. They had open entry into the homes of aristocratic families and brought along tales of their own experiences. Slowly, association of such women with the good families declined, due to the strong objections raised by educated men. It is possible that most women hummed on their own since both Kadambari and Swarnakumari could sing. Of course, they had had no training in classical music from any one.

Hemendranath asked for the Maharshi's permission. The latter, with his conservative attitude, at first baulked at the thought of his daughter-in-law taking lessons in music. Yet he had never been one to forbid something that was truly harmless. With his permission, Hemendra arranged for Neepamoyee to take lessons in music from the reputed singer and family-friend Vishnu Chakravarty.

It is surprising that such an act, which should have sent the pillars of society into a flurry of apprehension, or provided food for slanderous gossip to the neighbourhood, especially the women, did not even cause a murmur. Was it because, unlike Jnanadanandini, Neepomoyee remained confined within her home? Certainly, human nature is strange. One brother sent his wife to England so that she could become the ideal of modern Indian women. The other quietly helped his wife acquire every accomplishment within the four walls of the home. If Jnanadanandini was considered to be an ideal for the modern Indian women, in her own way so was Neepamoyee. Yet their ways were totally different.

Our curiosity about Neepamoyee remains. The mother of eleven well-accomplished children, she could sing, paint, had literary interests and cooked superb oriental and Western dishes. Whenever a new bride came into the family, Neepomoyee was entrusted with her training. It was she who transformed Bhabatarini of Phooltali village into Mrinalini, the poet's wife. She never mentioned anything about herself and there are no means of knowing her views on life in general. She spent her life within the pattern followed by ladies of other aristocratic families and exerted no influence on the world outside her home.

Neepamoyee's paintings certainly make us curious. There is a painting of *Hara Parvati* by Neepamoyee, published in the *Punya* magazine of 1900 (Bengali 1307). The painting is of mediocre quality and Neepamoyee's talent as an artist perhaps did not amount to much. Still, this pastime of hers leaves us curious. At that time painting was not in vogue in Bengal. The old art of making 'patas' was nearly lost as a result of negligence. The overall scenario of Indian art was not promising either. Yet Neepamoyee had taken lessons in painting. Thanks to Dr Amritamoy Mukhopadhyaya, it has been possible for us to see an unpublished diary, 'Maharshi Parivar' by Kshitindranath,

Amritamoy's maternal grandfather. Here, Kshitindranath has written about his mother and also mentions her artistic works:

> We three brothers still have a few paintings by our mother. Under the tutelage of Kalidas Pal she painted a portrait of Irudidi. She also drew one of Cleopatra. Under the guidance of Mr White, she painted a picture of Didi.

Unfortunately, every painting of Neepamoyee has been lost. It seems she never developed a style of her own, despite lessons from Indian and foreign teachers. Her children could all draw and paint. Kshitindranath also mentions that Mr Kalidas Pal was paid Rs 30 and Mr White Rs 100 per month. There is hardly any art that Hemendranath did not encourage Neepamoyee to learn. Apart from painting, she also learnt to play the tabla and karatal from the well-known maesteo Benimadhab. According to Khagendranath Chattopadhyay, Neepamoyee first acted in *Manmoyee*. Kshitindranath remembers seeing her read Milton's *Paradise Lost* and the Sanskrit play *Avijnanam Shakuntalam*. Unfortunately, all her achievements remained behind the scenes. After Hemendranath's untimely death, she moved into almost complete seclusion. The multifaceted and exceptional talents of her daughters are the only testimony we have of Neepamoyee's abilities.

Neepamoyee's younger sister Prafullamoyee would also have remained unnoticed had her memoirs not been brought to light by Sudhindranath's eldest daughter Rama. Even though Prafullamoyee, unlike Swarnakumari and Jnanadanandini, did not play an active role in the emancipation of Bengali women, Sarbasundari, Neepamoyee and Prafullamoyee were also part and parcel of life in the Tagore family.

There are not many women like Prafullamoyee. Her name seems to have been a mockery of fate. It means 'one who is always cheerful', yet practically her whole life was spent in tears. Very few knew that a room in this fairy-tale Tagore mansion hid a mountain of tears turned to stone. Had Prafullamoyee not bared her heart towards the end of her life, no one would have had an inkling of a beautiful face harbouring a heart rent with sorrow, amid the laughter of the Tagore family. After all, the life of a woman is woven round pleasure, pain, laughter and tears.

Prafullamoyee's grief was never clearly expressed. A sudden catastrophe finds vent in lamentations and tears but the heart-rending sorrow that piles up slowly finds no such relief. Prafullamoyee had been blessed with everything that a girl could desire. Her elder sister Neepamoyee had been married into a rich family. The brother-in-law reminded her of Lord Mahadev. Occasionally, Prafullamoyee accompanied her mother to visit her sister. She observed wide-eyed the large mansion, well-furnished rooms, showcases filled with curios and a host of servants. Saratkumari and Swarnakumari were also charmed by Prafullamoyee's looks. Her fair complexion, like the golden petals of the champa flower, her doe eyes, beautiful figure and sweet singing voice captivated everyone. Saratkumari and Swarnakumari chose her as the bride for their younger brother Birendra, the fourth son of the Maharshi. Apart from his good looks, Birendra was deeply interested in the study of mathematics. The two sisters Saratkumari and Swarnakumari thought it would be an excellent match and arranged for Birendra to see Prafullamoyee. Previously, such norms were unknown in the Tagore family. An old and trustworthy maid was sent to the prospective bride's place with some toys! If the maid approved of the girl, the wedding was fixed. But with changing times, it was considered appropriate that the groom see his would-be bride. One day, when Prafullamoyee had come to visit, Saratkumari and Swarnakumari dressed her up. They tried to persuade her to come before Birendra. Prafullamoyee, the village belle, was overcome with shyness; she refused and ran inside. This did not stop the wedding from taking place. While reminiscing in her old age, Prafullamoyee herself recounted these happy memories.

One spring afternoon, Prafullamoyee, her head and face covered, arrived in a palanquin to her husband's home, just as her sister had done a few years ago. The new bride was decked with ornaments by her-in-laws. Necklaces, collars and *jheeldana* for the throat, bangles, bracelets and armlets, pearl and gold earrings, tops for her ears, a tiara for her hair, anklets of various designs, toe-rings, a heavy gold waist band and many other items. Her life amid loving in-laws seemed like a dream, she felt that her cup of happiness was brimming over.

While reminiscing, Prafullamoyee has drawn intimate pictures of the family life of the Tagores. These are informal and homely and do not give any indication either of the winds of change blowing across the family or the steps that were being taken by the men and women to modernize their lives. She mentions that all the womenfolk, her husband's sisters and sisters-in-law, would have their meals together. Having first arrived from the village, Prafullamoyee always had her head and face covered with the end of her saree. This covering extended well below her chin. Her husband's younger brother Jyotirindranath would try to peep in to see how she managed to eat!

'My way of eating prompted him to tease me.'

Prafullamoyee began taking lessons in music and would sometimes sing along with the adolescent Rabindranath. However, all her dreams of happiness burst like a bubble within four years. Birendra gradually began to show signs of mental instability and finally went insane. It has been said that his obsessive passion for mathematics was the cause. He would, using a piece of charcoal as chalk, work out complicated problems on the four walls of his room. An English mathematician was wonderstruck when he saw this. Unfortunately, Birendra's lunacy manifest itself as suspicion towards everyone. It was a Herculean task to make him swallow a spoonful of rice or vegetable. As is usual in such cases, many people blamed Prafullamoyee for Birendra's condition. Three interminable years passed but Prafullamoyee's fortunes did not reverse. Slowly the smiling face withered away with grief.

While Prafullamoyee's tears were flowing like the incessant sravan rain, the rest of the household was busy rehearsing *Basanta Utsav* and *Punar-basantay*. It surprises us that it was so. Why and how was it possible? But then, immersed in plenty, who remembers the slow withering of a young woman behind closed doors? People commiserate for a few days and then they forget. This is the norm in every family. Still it is strange that it should have been so even in an enlightened family like the Tagores. Couldn't the Maharshi have shown this heartbroken woman some way to fulfillment? It was only after Prafullamoyee's son Balendranath's death that the Maharshi employed Hemchandra Vidyaratna to read and expound the Gita and Upanishads to her. This went on for a year. Rabindranath had endorsed this act and Prafullamoyee was able to transcend her sorrow through spiritual teachings. This however was much later.

Prafullamoyee's ill luck seemed to have abated for a while. Balendranath, though a sickly child from birth, won acclaim for his talents at an early age. When Sushitala alias Sahana entered the family as his bride, Prafullamoyee again began to see a ray of hope. She went on with her devoted care of her husband. Her dreams of a happy future were once again rudely shattered by a cruel fate. Balendra came down with typhoid. At that time, there was hardly any treatment known. As the fever gripped Balendra, and there was a tussle between life and death, the world seemed to be crashing around Prafullamoyee. On the fateful night, it became impossible for her to watch Balendra in the throes of death. She went out, only to be requested by Rabindranath a little later, to come to her son as the end was near. Though Prafullamoyee had been steeling herself for the call, she had not expected it so soon. She came and stood by her son's bedside. To quote her:

> Everything came to an end. Dawn was just breaking. Just as the sun was awakening the world with its gentle rays, the lamp of my son's life was extinguished.

Prafullamoyee bore this crushing blow with fortitude, mainly out of concern for her sixteen-year-old daughter-in-law. Ironically, her quiet acceptance of this catastrophe amazed her family. Some were even peeved. Rabindranath wrote to his wife:

> Nabauthan (fourth sister-in-law) lost her only child yet her interest in property matters has surprised and even annoyed the family.

The letter was written the day before Balendra's sraadh. Prafullamoyee's reminiscences reveal that she tried to bury her grief under a welter of activities. She writes:

> My loss can only be appreciated by those who have lost a son. His memory seems to engulf and reduce me to ashes. I had bought so many knick-knacks to decorate his room. I felt like throwing all these into the fire. Consideration for my daughter-in-law stopped me from doing so.

Further disasters—death of daughter-in-law, husband and brother, as well as financial difficulties on being denied her share in the property—rent Prafullamoyee's life. She seems to have risen above such vicissitudes of fate. When she began *Amader Katha* after her grief had been assuaged by time, she had neither any complaints nor any feeling of betrayal. The calmness of spirit she attained in the deepest sorrow may never have been hers had she wallowed in pleasure. The nectar that came to Prafullamoyee after she had churned the ocean of pain and grief—one that the world craves—allowed her to feel Balendra's presence in everyone and in everything around her. Her spiritual master Paramhansa Shivnarain Swami guided her with wise injunctions and ideals of sacrifice. She mentions:

> Bala also said that renunciation would give me peace.

This was her greatest reward. About the feeling she says:

> I feel as if he is still playing about in the courtyard. The first rays of dawn appear to portray his smiling face, when the sun sets I feel he has gone to sleep on my lap. I have not lost my son. I feel I have him all the more. Today I see him in a myriad forms before me. He has come to rest in my heart forever.

Such spiritual experiences also contributed to the enrichment of the Tagore family. Otherwise one might have felt that their women frittered away their time in pursuits like cooking, riding, dressing and other trivial social activities, contributing to making Bengali women more materialistic. This was not so. This family was a confluence of the East and the West. The quest for material objectives combined with spiritual aspirations. Prafullamoyee, delving deep into the ocean of grief, was the first to come up with this immortality. To quote her:

> Had my life been one of unalloyed pleasure without a trace of sorrow, perhaps I would have never sought the spiritual peace which is like nectar. When a man seeks this touchstone he is blind to the outer world and he considers himself blessed when such peace comes to him. It is the Almighty who helped me strive for this spirit and in its light I am able to perceive my son amid all beings.

Life flowed on despite personal sorrow and misfortune. While dark clouds of disaster were engulfing Prafullamoyee's life, in another corner of the large Tagore mansion preparations were afoot for another wedding. One day, riding the traditional palanquin, clad in a typical red Benarasi sari, another young girl entered the mansion at dusk.

> Her dusky wrists were covered with gold bangles, she wore a pearl necklace and her feet were adorned by golden *charan chakras*.

The youngest son Rabindranath felt that this must be a fairy princess. She seemed to bring him tidings of the princely mansion he had been seeking. The sphere of his imagination increased manifold.

Kadambari did not hail from the famous Roy family of Jessore. Her father, Shyamlal Gangopadhyay, was a resident of Calcutta. His family had had links with the Tagores for many years. Kadambari's paternal grandfather Jaganmohon had married Dwarkanath's first cousin Shiromani. Again, Dwarkanath's nephew Nabinchandra Mukhopadhyay had married Annadasundari whose father Ramlal was Shyamlal's elder brother. The family was also connected to the Pathuriaghata Tagores by marriage. Shyamlal himself had married Troilakya Sundari whose maternal grandfather Mathuranath was Radhanath Tagore's son. Hence the Maharshi had no objection but Satyendra was against the match. He had just returned from England, fired with modern ideas. He had thought of Dr Surya Kumar Goodive Chakravarti's well-educated daughter as his brother Jyotirindra's bride. How could one think of an eight-year-old child as a suitable girl? Moreover Shyamlal's father had been an employee of Dwarkanath, who had sheltered him along with his two sons. Jaganmohan was employed as a taster. It was his job to taste the freshness of the *sandesh* supplied everyday. How could one consider his granddaughter for Jyoti? Moreover Jyoti was likely to go abroad. Would he accept such a wife on his return? Maybe both lives would be ruined. None of Satyendra's arguments held water. The Tagores, being Piralis, and Brahmos to boot, were practically outcastes in society and Jyotirindranath was married to Kadambari as the only available choice. Her name was possibly Matangini. In the Tagore family a girl's name was often changed after marriage. So 'Matangini' merged into Kadambari. Proving all Satyendra's apprehensions wrong, Kadambari became a fitting daughter-in-law of the Tagore family.

She created a terrace garden on the second floor and named it 'Nandan Kanan' (Garden of Eden). To quote Rabindranath: Rows of palms were arranged. Numerous flowering shrubs like chameli, gandharaj, tube-rose, oleander and champak were also placed alongside. She also set up an aviary. Slowly, the entire house seemed transformed. Kadambari always had a fair eye for interior decoration. It was she who raised young Rabindranath's aesthetic sense to a high plane. These values were never lowered by the poet.

Kadambari appears to be associated with practically every creative activity of the andar mahal. Yet, according to Prasanta Kumar Pal, when Kadambari entered the Tagore family as a child bride, books on elementary arithmetic (*Dharapat*) and Bengali (*Barna Parichay* Parts I, II) had to be purchased for her. This was mentioned in the annual accounts of the family. This practically illiterate girl was within a few years able to establish herself as the centre of literary activities in the famous Tagore family. She seldom participated in any event herself. To light up the life of others with encouragement seems to have been her forte. She had the sense of romantic beauty in full measure. Probably it blossomed in the congenial atmosphere of the Tagore family, but the seeds must have been latent in her subconscious mind. This is perhaps the reason why her influence on the most important member of the family—Rabindranath—was unmatched.

So much has been written about Kadambari that it is futile trying to say more about her. The reason for such discussions and even occasional criticism is Rabindranath himself. Kadambari's influence on the young man and her contribution in moulding his mind is immeasurable. Her untimely death left a deep imprint on him. He had himself expressed this in innumerable poems and lyrics. Thus it would be fair to surmise that Rabindranath himself provided the means to many who imagined various nuances in their relationship. Rabindranath was fully aware of this situation. In his later years, he would jokingly say, 'It is just as well that Natun Bauthan is no more, otherwise we may have been fighting over property rather than my still composing poems about her.'

To begin with, Jyotirindranath was fairly conservative, but under the influence of Satyendranath and Jnanadanandini his views relaxed. Casting aside orthodox ideas, he taught Kadambari to ride. The lessons were given on the lonely banks of the Ganga but once she became proficient, Kadambari would ride out to the Maidan daily with her husband. We have already mentioned the reactions of neighbours and passers by who were aghast at such scenes. Needless to say Kadambari's daily excursions caused a great deal of commotion in society. But it would be wrong to describe Kadambari as the only Bengali woman to ride a horse in public. Some other Bengali women who were either her contemporaries or came slightly after her also did. Modern Bengali women had begun to learn horse-riding as a part of English education. The British were emulated by the 'Desi Sahibs', most of whom were the Indian Civil Service officers. Satyendranath had been asked by many people whether his wife could ride. The three Bengali Civil Service officers after him, Ramesh Chandra Dutt, Biharilal Gupta and Surendranath Bandopadhyay, became completely anglicized in their mode of life. Surendranath's wife would out for a ride every evening in Sylhet. Lord Satyendra Prasanna Sinha's daughter Romola, as well as daughters of Maharani Suniti Devi of Coochbehar, were proficient horsewomen. Some of Hemendranath Tagore's daughters were also adept at riding, through they came much later. The modern women those days showed a broad outlook in many spheres, but perhaps the most remarkable was in the choice of their own life partners. The women of the Tagore family were never able to adopt such views. They just tried to modernize the existing age-old traditions.

Being carried away by unbridled waves of liberty, which often turns to license, may be intoxicating, but no woman of the Tagore family ever indulged in such heady, albeit shallow, conduct. Thus their influence on the modern Bengali women has been the greatest and most enduring.

Kadambari not only rode out in public but she presented to the eyes of ordinary women an enchanted vision of courage and a sense of daring. They saw someone who was an ordinary housewife, like themselves, and not a woman brought up in the anglicized society. She was adept at slicing betel nuts finely, an art in itself. Not only was she regularly present when vegetables were pared but she also looked after the younger family members. If a child came down with fever it was Kadambari who stayed at his beside. Although she was only a year older to him she had drawn the young Rabindranath—who had just lost his mother—into her affectionate fold.

What singled Kadambari out from others was her great love of literature. She read Bengali literature not as a pastime but really as a passion. She read Dwijendranath's *Swapna Prayan* as well as Bankimchandra's *Bishabrikshya.* Often Rabindranath would read to her in the afternoons while she fanned him. She preferred being read to than reading on her own. She also gave a lot of thought to *Bharati* magazine. Though her name never appeared anywhere in the magazine, she was the inspiration behind it. This became clear after her death.

After Jyotirindra's marriage, quite a few changes took place in the Tagore mansion. The Maharshi had begun to live elsewhere and Jyotirindranath was given half of the second floor. The strict division between the andar mahal and the outer mansion was also relaxed. Not only was a terrace garden created on the second-floor roof, but this became the venue for regular sessions in literary reading. Apart from many family members, a number of friends also became regular visitors. These included Akshay Chaudhuri and his wife Sarat Kumari, called 'Lahorini', and Janakinath. The poet Biharilal Chakravorti would also drop in occasionally. Jyoritindranath, Rabindranath and Swarnakumari were permanent members of these meetings. Kadambari enjoyed Biharilal's poems. She invited him often to partake of meals she had cooked and also presented him with an *asan*, or a small mat, that she had made. On this she had embroidered a few lines from 'Saradamangal', as a query. By the time Biharilal could pen a poem in answer, Kadambari had passed away. Biharilal named his work 'Saadher Asan' in memory of the gift. Eulogizing the lady who had gifted the *asan* he wrote:

Tomar shey asan khan
Adore adore ani,
Rekhechhi jatan kore chirodin rakhibo;
E jibane ami ar
Tomar shey sadachar,
Shei snehamakha mukh pasoritey naribo.

I have preserved your *asan*
With great devotion and shall do so all my life,
Alas, I shall never perceive your affectionate
Countenance ever again.

Every evening a music session was held in the terrace garden. Cushions would be strewn on woven cane-spreads, a silver dish would hold garlands of sweet-smelling bel flowers covered by a wet handkerchief and there would be a glass of iced water as well as a dish of paan (betel leaves with condiments). Kadambari—fresh from a bath, her hair done up—would sit there while Jyotirindranath played the violin and Rabindranath sang. The music would appear to permeate the atmosphere at sunset, as the sea breeze blew in and the sky slowly filled with stars. Such romantic imagination was essential to awaken the latent feelings of beauty and romance in the adolescent Rabindranath.

Later, there has been a great deal of gossip about Rabindranath and Kadambari. Some certainly hinted at unfair suspicions. This was prompted partly by Kadambari's death within a few months of Rabindranath's marriage.

Kadambari's contribution in moulding Rabindranath's mind was incalculable. Going through the history of his becoming a poet, it appears that Kadambari was the inspiration behind all his literary efforts. The more he tried to prove his worth to impress her, the more she seemed to ignore him with an indulgent smile and teasing comments like:

Rabi is the darkest among the brothers and neither is he good looking. He has a peculiar voice and will never be a good singer. Satya sings much better. He will never be able to write like Bihari Chakraborty.

Rabindranath's impulse was to become perfect, to achieve so much that she would never be able to find any fault with him. He never realized that it was exactly what Kadambari wanted—to spur him on so that no one would ever be able to find any fault with her Rabi. By the time he realized this Kadambari was lost forever. She not only nurtured the lamp of his genius but lit up the wick and disappeared into the darkness. She has been remembered innumerable times by the poet. 'I was very fond of her. She also loved me a lot. It is this love that has attuned my heart to the Bengali woman.' That is why he wrote:

Nayano samukhe tumi nai
Nayanero majhkhane niyechho je thnai.

You are no longer before my eyes
You have taken up abode in the midst of my eyes.

This embodies his lifelong quest for her.

We do not intend to discuss Tagore's poems but Kadambari cast her shadow upon innumerable lyrics and poems composed by him. He portrayed her eyes in his paintings. All in all, Kadambari is to us today a representation of an inimitable personality. Rabindranath described a woman as half human, half imagination—the exact definition of Kadambari. Thus the real Kadambari has blended with the romantic dreamgirl *Natun Bauthan.*

Kadambari's role in the Tagore family is memorable for her aptitude in acting and singing. Jyotirindranath, already an appreciator of drama, had been further enthused by his talented wife. When the Jorasanko Theatre became defunct, he began composing plays, satires and musical dramas. These were enacted in the spacious courtyard of the andar mahal. Since no outsiders were involved, no eyes were raised when Kadambari began to take part. Her first appearance was either in Swarnakumari's *Basanta Utsab* or Jyotirindra's *Aleek Babu.* The latter was originally named *Emon Karma aar Korbo Na* and was written before *Basanta Utsab*, so probably it has a better claim. If it is assumed that this satire was staged directly after its composition, since Rabindranath played the hero, then this must have been before his first trip abroad. This would also have been Kadambari's first stage appearance.

However, whether it was the first or second, *Emon Karma aar Korbo Na* was an eminently successful play. Many members of the Tagore family had enacted the different roles with pleasure. They were:

Rabindranath	—	Aleek babu
Dwijendranath	—	Satyasandha
Jyotirindranath	—	Chinaman
Abonindranath	—	Aleek's friend
Jadunath Mukhopadhyaya (Saratkumari's husband)	—	Gadadhar
Barna Kumari	—	Pisni alias Prasannadasi

Very little is known about Barnakumari, the Maharshi's youngest daughter. Older than Rabindranath, she survived him by quite a few years. Though she never tried her hand at art or literature, Barnakumari left an imprint by her superb characterization of Prasanna. Her acting left its mark on young Indira. As Prasanna, she brought to life the daily mannerisms of the maidservants. Though she never took part in any other play, she had a natural aptitude and often advised others during rehearsals. Barnakumari was married to Satishchandra, the younger brother of the poet-cum-litterateur Rajkrishna Mukhopadhyaya. Satishchandra was a doctor of international repute and one of the founders of Carmichael Medical College (known at present as R.G. Kar). He was a German scholar as well. He succumbed to cancer at a comparatively early age.

Like Saratkumari, Barnakumari considered the home as her main source of occupation. She was an expert cook, a superb needlewoman and a good singer. Her favourite pastime was singing Brahma Sangeet, written by the Maharshi, after prayers. An avid fan of Bankimchandra, she also wrote. Diffidence prevented her from publishing her creations under her own name. Today it is virtually impossible to identify her writings from the host of publications under pseudonyms in old copies of *Bharati*. The bond between her and Rabindranath remained intact until his death. Even in her old age she made it a point to come to Jorasanko on *Bhai Dwitiya* to put the traditional 'phonta' on Rabindranath's forehead.

Coming back to play-acting, the most difficult character in *Emon Karma aar Korbo Na* is that of Hemangini, who was a romantic girl of the nineteenth century steeped in Bankimchandra's novels. She immortalized herself by successfully transforming passionate sentiments into dialogues filled with fun and laughter. Many people believe that the part was played by Kadambari. However, Akshay Chaudhuri's wife Saratkumari enacted the role in the performance that Indira remembered. Rabindranath's biographer Pravatkumar Mukhopadhyaya followed Indira in naming Saratkumari Hemangini. On the other hand, poet Sajanikanta had asked Tagore directly about the identity of 'Hey'. This was because when Tagore's *Bhagna Hriday* (Broken Heart) was published he dedicated it to 'Srimati Hey'. Tagore queried 'What do you think?' Sajanikanta replied, 'Hemangini. In *Aleek Babu* you played the part of Aleek and Kadambari Devi that of Hemangini. You have taken advantage of those names.' The poet agreed, saying that this was the truth and all other conjectures false.

This pseudonym 'Srimati Hey' has also been subjected to numerous interpretations. Indira thought that 'Hey' was the short form of 'Hecate', the three-headed goddess of Greek mythology and the nickname of Kadambari. It would be unfair to surmise that Kadambari never enacted the role of Hemangini just because Indira never saw it. If the first performance was in 1877, Indira was not in Calcutta and even later on she did not always live in Jorasanko. Jnanadanandini also never acted in these performances. *Aleek Babu* was staged a number of times later. When Rabindranath produced the play he altered it to keep Hemangini behind the scenes right through. Abanindranath's explanation was that there was a dearth of women to play the role. This may have been true but one cannot help thinking that lack of a suitable actress may not have been the sole reason. Perhaps Kadambari was considered irreplaceable. Idle conjectures do not lead one anywhere.

Despite doubts about her portrayal of Hemangini, Kadambari's participation in *Basanta Utsab* and *Maanmoyee* are well recorded. She not only acted well but also sang beautifully. The granddaughter of the well-known musician Jaganmohan Gangopadhyay, music was in Kadambari's blood. Not only did a piano arrive when she took up abode on the second floor of the mansion, but also both Jyotirindra and Rabindranath began practising in earnest. Musical soirees were a regular feature of the evening sessions in her roof garden Nandan Kanan. We are forced to believe that Kadambari had enthralled her family with music, literature and play-acting. Consider *Bharati* magazine—Dwjendranath was the editor, Jyotirindranath the overall-in-charge and Rabindranath the main writer. What then was Kadambari's role? To Saratkumari, she was the ribbon that held the bouquet of flowers together. It was she who bound the others from behind the scene. Her contribution became apparent only when this thread was lost forever.

Had Kadambari not extinguished her life and gone into oblivion, she might have been able to keep alive the cultural fountainhead of the andar mahal a little longer. With her death the halcyon days of the Tagore mansion began to disappear like migratory birds. Thereafter, the individual, and not the collective efforts, of the women members began to gain ascendance. What prompted Kadambari's suicide? No definite answer to this riddle has been found till date.

Kadambari died a few months after Rabindranath's marriage. It was sudden but perhaps not unexpected considering that she had made an attempt earlier. The life of this talented, beautiful and cultured woman certainly lacked peace and harmony. According to a biographer of Rabindranath, Kadambari was extremely sensitive, sentimental and an introvert. She was also schizophrenic. Many others, though not in full agreement with the above analysis, have also described Kadambari as high-strung. The agony of a childless life had greatly aggravated her sensitiveness. Perhaps some sudden hurt unleashed these feelings—held long in check—flooding away all logic and reason.

Conjecture has been rife about this incident and many theories were put forward. The most popular one is concerning her feelings for Rabindranath. This was lent credence by her death only a few months after Rabindranath's marriage. Her feelings for Rabindranath's wife are not known since it has not been possible to obtain any record of Kadambari and Mrinalini's relationship. It is also unknown why Kadambari was not entrusted with the task of transforming Bhabatirini to Mrinalini. According to some, this was done by Neepamoyee while others hold that Jnanadanandini was the one. Even in the article by Hemlata which describes in detail Rabindranath's marriage, Kadambari is conspicuous by her absence. It is strange that she who had been so enthusiastic in choosing a bride for Rabindranath should suddenly withdraw herself quietly from the scene. Possibly she had a difference of opinion with someone else over the choice of a suitable girl. Probably this led Pravatkumar Mukhopadhyaya to comment, 'Kadambari's sudden death was the result of internecine quarrels among women.' However this 'woman' could not have been Rabindranath's wife since she was a young girl. Probably Kadambari's difference of opinion had been with Jnanadanandini. There may have been deeper reasons which overwhelmed Kadambari over a trifling incident. Some people at the time blamed Jyotirindranath for the event.

Nothing definite can be surmised from the details available regarding Kadambari's death. According to Indira, 'Uncle Jyotirindranath often did not return home. He spent a lot of time at our Birjitalao residence and was very friendly with my mother Jnanadanandini.' One day Kadambari had specifically requested Jyotirindranath to return home early. Unfortunately there was a musical soiree at Satyendranath's place and Jyotirindranath was unable to return at all. This proved to be the last straw. The hurt seems to have provoked Kadambari to destroy herself forever. A woman called Bishweshwari or Bishu used to supply sarees regularly to the household. Kadambari procured some opium through her secretly and swallowed this to depart from the world.

But, on the contrary, Amal Home had been told by Barnakumari that Kadambari came across some letters in Jyotirindranath's pocket. These were, according to some, from a well-known actress, Binodini. The letters were a clear indication of the intimacy between the actress and Jyotirindranath. This upset Kadambari greatly and she finally chose to end her life. In a dying declaration she said that these letters were the cause of her taking this step! Apparently the letters and Kadambari's declaration were destroyed by the orders of the Maharshi. Kazi Abdul Odud mentions that a well-known member of the Tagore family told him that the lady with whom Jyotirindranath had become intimate was not an actress, and also that this had led Kadambari to attempt suicide once before.

Some writings of contemporary poets also show that they held Jyotirindranath responsible. He certainly failed in his duty as a husband to alleviate the loneliness of his wife. He certainly did not pay her the attention she needed and seems to have become indifferent towards her. His absorption in new creative ventures, pandering to sudden whims, the company of Satyendranath, Jnanadanandini and their children had certainly drawn him away from Kadambari. In the prevalent norms of the day, it would have been quite natural for him to come in contact with actresses too. At that time a barren woman was a focus of disdain and, in the joint family of the Tagores, Kadambari thus never attained the position befitting her. She loved children and brought up Swarnakumari's and Janakinath's youngest daughter Urmila as her own. Unfortunately, just two months after she began school, Urmila tripped down the stairs and died. This was a tremendous blow to Kadambari. She immersed herself in housework, the care of her husband and literary pursuits but it all proved to be of no avail. Kadambari's loneliness reached the breaking point with Satyendra–Jnanandini's return to Calcutta. Jyotirindra and Rabindranath expressed a deep attraction for them and their modern lifestyle; added to that was Rabindranath's marriage. Kadambari lost her mental balance and chose the easy way out. Against this backdrop, the reasons described by Indira and Barnakumari—both or any one of them—may be true. There does not seem to be any scope for a third conjecture.

This was also the reason why some poems composed just before and shortly after Kadambari's death draw the attention of critics. The first one was by the poet Akshay Chaudhuri. According to Jagadish Bhattacharya, '*Abhimanir Nirjharini*' portrays a woman's agony and hurt towards an indifferent husband. He also holds the view that 'Nirjharini' was none other than Jyotirindra's wife Kadambari.

Rakhite tahar mon, pratikhone sajatan
Hashe hashi kande kandi—mon rekhe jai,
Marame marame dhaki tahari sanman rakhi,
Nijer nijashya bhule tarei dheyai,
Kintu shey to ama paney phireyo na chay.

I always endeavour to please him,
Smiling when he does and weeping with him,
To keep up appearances and his image
I hide all my hurt in my heart,

Forgetting myself I only dream of him,
But alas he has no time for me.

These lines remind us of the gifted and gentle Kadambari. On the other hand Tagore's biographer has perceived the shadow of Kadambari's first attempt at suicide in Rabindranath's 'Tarakar Atmohatya'. The young Rabindranath knew about his *Natun Bouthan*'s heartache.

Jodi keho shudhayito
Ami jani ki je shey kohito
Jatodin benchechhilo
Ami jani ki tarey dohito.

Had any one queried, I know what she would have said,
As long as she lived, I knew what fire devoured her.

Hence the self-imposed exile of the star from the world of brightness (jyoti) to that of darkness. After Kadambari's death Rabindranath wrote in '*Puspanjali*': 'What joy is there on earth for those who are noble, with a heart capable of great affection? None at all. They are like the veena whose every string vibrates when smitten by the cruelties of the world. The music thus produced captivates everyone—but no one sighs at the thought of this pain appearing in the garb of music.'

It is obvious that this 'veena' was none other than Kadambari. Immediately thereafter he says: 'The veena is smitten by all and sundry—most of them cruel and heartless who do not care to remember her. They do not consider this veena as God's blessing. Considering themselves to be the masters, they often tread upon this manifestation of all that is gentle, sweet and pure in a fit of disdain or indifference!'

Another poet reprimanded Jyotirindranath in more stringent terms. Biharilal in his '*Saadher Asan*' tells the virtuous woman not to come to earth again since a queer man does not appreciate her:

Purush kimbhutmati cheney na tomay.
Mon pran jouban—

Ki diya payibe mon.
Poshur matan era nitui natun chay.

How can you hope to win him with your heart, life and youth,
Like a beast he is always seeking novelty.

Considering the evidence of contemporary people as well as thoughts recorded by poets in their poetry, it is clear that the malicious gossip linking Kadambari's death to Rabindranath's marriage was baseless.

A moot point is Jyotirindranath's reaction to this death. Within a month of Kadambari's death he embarked on a boat trip in the steamer *Sarojini* with Jnanadanandini, Surendranath, Indira and Rabindranath. To a casual observer this may prove that the young poet of 'Tarakar Atmohatya' was correct when he said: 'Jyotirindranath has remained the same before and after.' However we can disregard all accusations, saying that no proof has ever been found of Jyotirindranath's licentiousness. The Maharshi always endeavoured that his children follow a high moral code and his children did not fail him. At that time licentiousness was the norm in aristocratic society, but the Tagores of Jorasanko had always been different. But Kadambari's death left Jyotirindranath shattered. He not only lost in his business ventures but was battered by life itself. How can we explain otherwise a gifted playwright abandoning everything and limiting himself only to translations? His desertion of a full social life seems an effort to forget himself. Jyotirindranath was only thirty-five when Kadambari died yet he never remarried. On being asked his answer was, 'I still love her'.

Critics may call this repentance. Perhaps that is the truth. Exiling himself from society and family he punished himself—the indifferent husband who failed in his duty to his wife. Unfortunately nothing is known about Jyotirindranath's feelings during this period. It was rumoured that he even lost his mental balance at some time. Neither his *Aamar Jeebansmriti*, nor the diary he maintained in his old age gives any inkling of his feelings. Apart from a few cursory remarks Kadambari is absent in these. Yet the bare room he occupied in Shantidham—his Ranchi house—was adorned by just one picture. It was a pencil sketch of Kadambari by Jyotirindranath. Recently some doubts have been raised about this sketch. Indira's description of this sketch *Nijehate Anka* does not clarify who the artist was. Quite a few Tagore women could draw well and so the sketch might have been by Kadambari herself. She perhaps took lessons in drawing from her artistic husband. Thus Jyotirindranath's exile certainly was not an effort to forget Kadambari. In the quiet loneliness of Shantidham Jyotirindranath probably tried to reminisce over his incomparable wife who was able to inspire the latent talent of Rabindranath himself.

Some critics are also of the opinion that the relations between Jyotirindranath and Rabindranath were severed for unknown reasons. They have tried to put forward Rabindranath's rising fame as a poet and the suicide of his *Natun Bouthan* as plausible reasons. Both appear fallacies since Jyotirindranath was never jealous of Rabindranath even after he went into self-imposed exile. Relations between the two were not broken at any time even after Kadambari's death. Apart from the boat trip on board the *Sarojini* the two brothers lived in adjacent rooms at Satyendranath's house for a number of years. In his diary, written during his last few years, Rabindranath was mentioned a couple of times. Jyotirindranath made observations about Rabindranath's activities, like singing and lecturing and even his sporting a beard. He not only sketched Rabindranath but on his sixty-third birthday he sang the songs of *Balmiki Protiva* before a dozen guests. He had visited Shantiniketan and had even thought of buying a house there. But slowly he began distancing himself from society and family.

Rabindranath's letters also bear proof of their initimacy. He was the main enthusiast about publishing an album of his Jyotidada's paintings. He not only read Jyotirindranath's translations of Sanskrit plays but also wrote to him, 'You have completed the translations of almost all Sanskrit plays.' Later on he became a world-renowned poet but his own life was beset by catastrophes. Devastated by the death of his wife and children and plagued with the many problems of Shantiniketan Rabindranath found it difficult to keep in touch with his closest relations, let alone the recluse Jyotirindranath. Thus we can conclude that Kadambari's death did not create any rift between the two brothers. Jyotirindranath sought her immortal soul while Rabindranath was able to rediscover himself. Thus Kadambari's spirit remains mingled in his music, songs, poems and paintings.

At the time of Kadambari's death Bhabatarini (Rabindranath's wife, who hailed from Phultali) was a mere girl. Dwijendranath had blessed her saying that she would one day become 'Swarna Mrinalini' (a golden lotus). Bhabatarini slowly lost her identity in Mrinalini. This transformation created no ripples in the minds of the modernists or the outside world. Still Mrinalini was no ordinary person. When she entered the Tagore family, veiled down to her throat, the ten-year-old had no conception of the qualities of her husband or of the grandeur of his family.

Rabindranath always said that there were no incidents behind his wedding, it just happened. The beginning had been out of the ordinary. The old custom of sending a maid to select the bride was rejected. Instead a committee comprising of Jnanadanandini, Kadambari, Jyotirindranath and Rabindranath was set up. They set out for Jessore from where most brides of the family had come. They stayed at Jnanadanandini's paternal home in Narendrapur. Eligible girls from the neighbouring villages like Dakshindihi and Chengutia were interviewed. Not a single girl was found who could match his sisters-in-law in looks. Ultimately Bhabatarini, the eldest daughter of Benimadhab Ray, an employee of the Tagore estate, was chosen.

Rabindranath unquestioningly accepted the bride chosen for him by his elders. Though he personally sent out invitation cards to his friends, there was no ostentation. Unlike that of his brothers, his marriage was held in a portion of the Jorasanko mansion itself. Decked in an heirloom Benarasi *Daurdar* shawl, the groom skirted the west verandah of the mansion and arrived at the marriage venue. Thus was solemnized his wedding with the young, inexperienced Bhabatarini. We have an eyewitness account of the wedding from Hemlata Devi. She writes: 'After the wedding when the bride and groom were taken to the "Basor" Rabindranath began to play pranks. Instead of filling up the small clay pots—a traditional ritual—he started turning them upside down. On being chided by his aunt Tripurasundari he replied that since everything had turned topsy-turvy, he was doing the same with the clay pots. On being requested by Tripurasundari to sing, he looked at his veiled wife teasingly and began "Oh my beautiful one!" The song had been composed by the fourth of his elder sisters, Swarnakumari.'

It has been said that because Bhabatarini had an accent peculiar to Jessore, she hardly spoke during the early days of her marriage. One wonders if Rabindranath was happy with such an unequal marriage. Small incidents, perhaps insignificant in themselves yet indicating a deeper happiness, force us to believe that he was. After her marriage Bhabatarini's transformation into Mrinalini began. To begin with, the Maharshi asked Neepamoyee to instruct her in the deportment, speech and mannerisms of the Tagore family. Later Mrinalini went to Loreto School along with Neepamoyee's daughters. However, according to another view, Mrinalini's instructress was Jnanadanandini and she was tutored individually at Loreto School rather than attending regular classes. Through Bhabatanini merged into Mrinalini, she never became ultramodern. Her lessons in English, piano and music in Loreto School, as well as lessons in Sanskrit at home from Hemchandra Vidyaratna, did not find expression in any creative venture. Yet she knew Bengali, English and Sanskrit well. While in Selaidaha, Balendranath often read to her. Mrinalini would translate English tales and her way of storytelling left an indelible imprint on her daughter Mira. Her life seems to have centered round the wellbeing of others. She appears to have been a silent figure, slightly hazy, among the more vociferous characters around her. Yet she also acted in family plays like the other women members, translated the *Ramayana*, collected folk and fairy tales under Rabindranath's direction and stood by the side of everyone both in happiness and sorrow.

In the first staging of Rabindranath's *Raja O Rani*, Mrinalini enacted the role of Narayani while her elder brother-in-law Satyendranath played Debdutta. It was quite a grandiose performance and not just a family affair. Though it was her maiden effort Mrinalini's acting was natural and flawless. Akshay Chaudhuri was so overcome by shyness that he was unable to come to the stage after accepting a female role in *Naba Natak*. The same could have happened to Mrinalini, especially as she was acting opposite her elder brother-in-law, but it did not. According to Ajit Kumar Ghosh: 'The way Mrinalini acted, wielding a broom and shaking her nose ring—it was absolutely true to life.' Still it has to be admitted that Mrinalini showed no desire to participate in her husband's plays. Apart from bit roles in *Mayar Khela* or some plays put up by the Sakhi Samiti there is no record of her acting. Thus there is no point in looking for Mrinalini's real talents in the field of music and literature. It was much later that Mrinalini shone forth in all the glory of a traditional Indian woman. This was when she stood by her husband to help him achieve his great ideal. From the cocoon of the ordinary emerged the extraordinary.

Mrinalini's role in the Tagore family was that of a superb housewife. Her personality was dignified. Though the youngest, she managed to influence everyone around her. Adept at dressing others, she seldom spent much time on her own toilette. Her stock answer was: I feel shy to dress up in the presence of grown-up nephews and nieces.' Once she was persuaded to wear a pair of rather showy earrings. Rabindranath happened to appear suddenly and she immediately covered her ears out of shyness. Her great joy lay in cooking and entertaining people. In the Tagore family every woman was given expert training in housework. New brides first learned to make 'paan', i.e. betel leaves rolled with a number of condiments. Later on they graduated to pickle and preserve-making as well as preparing *bori* (small balls made of ground pulses and dried). Such training was considered mandatory though the family was wealthy. Mrinalini showed a great aptitude for such things. This was a time when changes were taking place both outside and inside the house, otherwise how could Jyotirindranath and Kadambari have created a Nandan Kanan on the second floor roof? Men were also allowed entry here; and yet we know the trouble Satyendra had to endure in order to take his friend Manmohan into the andar mahal. No snide comments were heard when Mrinalini joined Loreto School. Chandramukhi and Kadambari had already achieved what was then deemed impossible. Still, women tend to cling to traditional customs just as the last rays of the sun are loath to leave the earth. So even though some women had brought about memorable changes in the world outside the home, the Tagore women still had to learn the art of making mango cakes, various coconut-based sweets and preserves like *kasundi* using mustard and chillis—so dear to the Bengali palate. Mrinalini was an expert at cooking sweets. Her *maankachur jeelapi*, *malpoya* from curd, sweets from ripe mangoes and *chirer pooli* were sweets par excellence. The poet also would come up with unusual requests. Rathindranath writes, 'On the day the session of the *Khaamkheyali Sabha* would be held at Jorasanko, Father told Ma that nothing ordinary would suffice. Every dish had to be unique.' Mrinalini never let her husband down. Her mastery often inspired the poet to experiment with out of the way dishes. Mrinalini usually had to help him out. He would then tease her saying, 'See how I am training you in your own job!' Mrinalini's retort was, 'Who has ever been able to match you? You always come out on top.' In later life the poet would often tell his daughter-in-law Pratima, 'Bauma, you will never believe that I taught your mother-in-law various dishes and supplied her with innumerable menus.' If the others present protested saying, 'But she was a very good cook herself,' the poet's smiling rejoinder was, 'Of course, otherwise how would my menus be so successful.'

After her education was complete, Mrinalini took up the translation of *Ramayana* into a simple and abridged version. This she started under her husband's direction while they were living in Selaidaha. Death intervened before she could complete the work. The poet handed the manuscript to his eldest daughter Madhurilata, hoping that she would complete it. Madhurilata's untimely death put a stop to this project and no trace of the manuscript could be found. Rabindranath had another notebook wherein Mrinalini had translated some slokas from the *Mahabharata*, *Manusamhita* and the Upanishads. She had also begun to collect fairy tales as Rabindranath had specifically requested her to do so. Abanindranath got the story of 'Khirer Putul' from her and wrote it according to her narration. A grateful Abanindranath acknowledged her narration to be the origin of his fairy tale. How about other writings by Mrinalini? On being questioned Swarnakumari's spirited rejoinder was, 'She never felt like writing since her husband was the most renowned writer of Bengal.'

Very true, but this does not dispel our doubts. Did Mrinalini dedicate all her heart into quiet service? Has nothing remained behind for us to ponder upon? Is our only glimpse of Mrinalini to be restricted to Dwijendranath's wife Hemlata's memoirs? Fortunately a few of Mrinalini's letters were preserved. These clearly show her sense of humour even among the mundane affairs of daily life. In her letter to Sudhindranath's wife Charulata, we find Mrinalini accusing her of long silence. This simple yet humourous letter stands at par with the best literary creations. She says: 'You never informed me about your lovely newborn daughter. Were you afraid that I would be jealous? Even since I heard she has a lot of hair I have started using 'Kuntaleen'. Even the thought of your daughter with lovely hair laughing at my bald pate is intolerable. I am really upset that the arrival of our pretty grandchild has completely banished us from your heart.'

Even after she moved to Shantiniketan, Mrinalini's concern for the family members at Jorasanko was undiminished. All her nephews and nieces enjoyed visiting her at Selaidaha. She was a particular favourite of both Balendranath and Nitindranath. Mrinalini's sympathy and kindness were not limited to her near and dear ones. She had the rare quality of sharing the joys and travails of outsiders too. While in Selaidaha, one day Mula Singh, a Punjabi, approached her in tears. He narrated his destitute condition and requested her to save the entire family from starvation by providing him with a job. Though Rabindranath was away, Mrinalini immediately had him appointed as a watchman. A few days later she found Mula Singh still looking upset. When she asked why he said that all his salary was spent in procuring four *seers* of atta (about four kilograms of wheat flour) which was their daily consumption. The kind-hearted Mrinalini arranged to provide him with four *seers* of atta from her own household budget. She continued this even when Mula Singh's salary was increased. The picture of Mrinalini that emerges before our eyes is that of a universal mother. This came to the fore after the establishment of Shantiniketan. Rabindranath had once called her '*Seema Swarger Indrani*' (queen of heaven) but in Shantiniketan she became the benevolent Annapurna. According to eyewitnesses, 'Mrinalini was not a beauty, but her whole face glowed with an inner light of motherliness. One look at her urged the viewer to glance at her again!' This was evident in the way Mrinalini—herself the mother of five—drew the young inhabitants of Shantiniketan into her fold.

One wonders about Rabindranath's expectations from his wife. His letters to her indicate his ideas on their life together. In one of them he writes, 'Do not over-exert yourself to make me happy. Your true love is enough. It certainly would have been excellent if our views were the same in every field, but this is not always possible. I shall be delighted if you can join me in all my endeavours, I can always tell you all that I want to know, and if you can learn what I want too, it will be a happy state of affairs. If both partners try to keep pace with each other going ahead becomes much easier. I do not wish to overtake you in any way, but I am also scared of forcing you. All of us have our own tastes, likes and dislikes. It is not right that you mould all your views completely with mine. Do not worry, but if you endeavour to protect me from unwanted strife and fulfill my life with your love and care—it will be invaluable for me.'

Mrinalini certainly matched all of Rabindranath's expectations. She stood by his side through thick and thin. When he went to Shantiniketan to establish a school according to his own ideals, friends and relations opposed and heaped derision and ridicule on him. They cannot be blamed either. They were only trying to warn him against total ruin by his impractical action. He had five minor children, three of them daughters—yet the poet was pouring his assets into the Ashram School! Mrinalini was also worried but she helped her husband willingly in his endeavour. It is doubtful if the poet would have been able to immerse himself in this work had Mrinalini objected. She handed over her jewellery whenever there was financial hardship. According to the poet: 'Women, though dependent, have a strange ability to control the menfolk.' Mrinalini wholeheartedly shared her husband's dream and hence never baulked at parting with her large store of jewellery. Apart from wedding gifts she had received plenty of heavy jewellery belonging to her mother-in-law. Rathindranath writes: 'Towards the end Ma only had a few bangles and a gold chain left.'

Mrinalini not only gave her jewellery but she also helped her husband in the daily life of the Ashram. She may not have been termed modern, as many other women had begun to surpass the Tagore women in the field of education and culture; ultra-modernism never entered the blood of the Tagore women. For years, only Jnanadanandini was the one to exhibit this trend. Mrinalini had the traits of a great woman. In his book *Charitrapuja* Rabindranath wrote: 'The life history of a great and saintly man is immortalized in his work and life mostly outside the home while that of a woman is woven in her husband's work though her name is never mentioned therein.'

This is very aptly applicable to Mrinalini. Had we not decided to narrate in minute detail about the women of the Tagore family, there would have been hardly any scope for discussing Mrinalini on her own. Her presence in Rabindranath's life, the Tagore family and Shantiniketan Ashram school is akin to that of a flower's fragrance. It cannot be seen but it fills the heart nevertheless.

Had Mrinalini lived longer, Rabindranath's plans for the Ashram School would have been even more successful. She looked after the Brahmacharya Ashram. She drew into her fold the little students to help them forget the loneliness of being away from home. Even though away from home, the boys never lacked a mother's love and care. Unfortunately she could not stand the hard work and passed away eleven months after the establishment of the Ashram School. There was a lot of resentment about her treatment during her last days. Despite all Rabindranath's care and love, the winter-lotus withered away and his beloved *Bhai Chhuti*, as he addressed her in his letters, was lost forever. Who knew that she would take chhuti (leave) so early from her family and life? At every step thereafter Rabindranath felt her loss:

'There is no one to whom one can confide everything.' In his poem '*Smaraney*' he has poured out his anguish for Mrinalini. When daily life became a babel of words, he remembered his departed wife again and again.

Tomar sangsar majhe hoye tomaheen
Ekhono ashibe kato sudin-durdin—
Takhan e shunya ghare chirabhyas-torey
Tomare khunjite eshe chabo kar paney?

In your home bereft of you,
Times both foul and fair will come,
Then, in keeping with a lifelong habit of seeking you,
Whom shall I turn to in this empty room?

He felt that his Ashram School was incomplete without Mrinalini: 'I can give them everything but not a mother's love and care.' Mrinalini certainly can be placed alongside many other ideal mothers of our country.

While talking about the daughters-in-law of the Tagore family, it may be best to discuss another one of them at this juncture. We have already mentioned Jogmaya. She was Girindranath's wife and a lover of literature and deeply religious. It was she who shifted to the baithak-khana baari with the family deity Lakshmi Janardan. Though officially the Tagore family was split into two, yet there were no rifts in their feelings for each other. On the contrary, Nagendranath's wife Tripurasundari maintained hardly any contact with the Maharshi's family. She was of a suspicious turn of mind. Due to certain property disputes, she suspected that the Maharshi's family wanted to poison her. She lived in Sudder Street and on her rare visits to Jorasanko refused all refreshments unless tasted by some member of the Maharshi's family. The Maharshi's sons and those of Jogmaya were always on affectionate terms, especially close being the family of Gunendranath. These two families always thought of themselves as one. Moreover, since Gunendra's family did not embrace the Brahmo faith, their relationship with Pathuriaghata or the

Koilahata Tagores was not severed either. Thus this family served as a bridge between all the other branches. Socially they were in touch with the other Tagores while their emotional involvement was with the Maharshi's family. So it would be better to think of houses number 5 and 6 in Dwarkanath Lane as one. Originally, both houses stood within the same compound, but later it was not so. Number 5, the tastefully decorated baithak-khana house of Dwarkanath, has been completely demolished except for the *bene bari* adjacent to the andar mahal. Jogmaya was the virtual mistress of this baithak-khana bari.

Jogmaya chose eight-year-old Saudamini of Phultali, Jessore, as her daughter-in-law. In the beginning Saudamini yearned for her village, where she, along with other girls, had learnt to swim by floating pitchers in the ponds. 'In that tiny village mundane affairs kept us happy.' She often thought of the walls of her mansion as cages. Slowly Saudamini integrated into the family. Her days were passing happily. Sometimes she would go on boat-trips with her husband and children. In due course of time, she took over the task of managing the household from her mother-in-law. The affairs of the family thus continued to be run on traditional lines. Saudamini's granddaughter Pratima has written: 'Often she would sigh for the bygone days.'

The capabilities of Saudamini were not originally discernible in her large family. They came to the fore only when she, with her minor children, had to face numerous problems. The expertise with which Saudamini took up the reins of her family at its most precarious juncture is incomparable. Seeing the sudden premature end of Gunendranath due to licentiousness and ostentatious habits, she swore to protect her sons from the clutches of a lavish lifestyle and never allowed them to go astray along the path of unbridled pleasures. It is well-nigh impossible for us to visualize the difficulties of such a resolve. Within the renaissance in education and other cultural aspects of the nineteenth century raged the filthy streams of the babu culture. Along with establishment of schools and magazines as well as social service, there was the lure of drink and dancing girls. Scions of aristocratic families were growing attached to both Indian luxuries and occidental lasciviousness.

It was inconceivable for the son of wealthy parents not to be steeped in luxury. It was the norm to train them from adolescence to become *alaler gharer dulal*. The Tagores lacked neither fortune nor aristocracy. Though at that time aristocracy was linked with ostentation and licentiousness, Saudamini held the reins of her family in her capable hands. She ignored all comparisons with other wealthy families, choosing to emulate the members of Maharshi Bhawan. No such undercurrents were flowing there beneath the pleasures of life. Ultimately she won the battle. Disregarding the beckoning pleasures of the so-called babus, her sons Gaganendra, Samarendra and Abanindra became accomplished like the sons of the Maharshi. Saudamini never declared her wishes or forced any decision on any of her sons. Yet she kept a close watch and her influence on them was supreme. None of them ever raised any objections to her dictates. This amazing woman—outwardly like steel yet gentle within—commanded the respect of even Rabindranath. Many years later he once said to Rani Chanda: 'Our Gagan's mother was not educated in the usual sense of the word. Yet her courage and common sense in running her home and bringing up her three sons is astounding. The respect they have for their mother is rare.'

Saudamini not only brought up her sons well, she also transformed the debt-ridden zamindari her husband left behind. There was no dearth of advisors. Many showed sympathy for the twenty-four-year-old widow, with five minor children. But her innate common sense was such that she could distance herself from such undesirable well-wishers and stood firmly at the helm of her family's affairs. She reminds one of Bara Bou, i.e. Kumudini's mother in the novel *Jogajog*.

Her preoccupation with the family led Saudamini to neglect herself. She sang well. As Benayini remembered, 'Ma would play the harmonium and sing devotional songs after lunch.' She was fond of reading the *Ramayana* and *Mahabharata*. Abanindranath's reminiscences were full of his mother's evening toilette. Gunendranath, who had excellent taste, often procured rare and beautiful objects. Once he gifted Saudamini a tulip-shaped flower vase. According to Abanindranath: 'When Ma sat down before the mirror to comb her hair, the mirror reflected her face and also a tulip.' Though nothing is known about her artistic or literary tastes, she certainly possessed many sterling qualities. One can't help but feel that the various talents exhibited by her granddaughters must have been latent in Saudamini. This helps explain her uncanny knack of detecting even a spark of genius in the younger generation. Hearing Gaganendranath's daughter Hanshi sing, she arranged for her to have music lessons. She would request Harish Chandra Halder to draw designs on pieces of cloth and urge her granddaughters to embroider these into nakshi kanthas. She knew how to spin. Sarees woven from the thread spun by her were fine enough to match those from Shantipur. She had presented each of her granddaughters with a spinning wheel. They had to spin a certain amount of thread daily and show it to her. She also patronized cottage industries. When village women came to peddle hand-made toys or dolls, she would buy the entire stock to encourage them.

She always sympathized with the freedom movement. Apart from regular financial help she secretly allowed the Anusilan Samity the use of her house. Such incidents lead us to conclude that Saudamini may not have been 'modern' but she certainly possessed exceptional and rare qualities. Observing her and a few other women who entered the family by marriage, it is clear that these women, though not involved with the Brahmo Samaj, and unaware of women's education and other modern ideas like women's liberation, were unique in many ways. In this context Girindranath's two daughters Kadambini and Kumudini deserve to be mentioned. They both lived in the house number 5 for a number of years. Kadambini's husband was Jogyesh Prakash Gangopadhyay. Girindranath had had his eye on this exceptionally handsome young man. The details of the wedding are unknown. According to Ardhendrakumar Gangopadhyay, 'Our home was very close to the river Ganga. In those days it was customary for the young and the old to take a bath daily in the river. One day, young Jogyesh Prakash went for his accustomed dip and never returned. The whole day there was no sign of him and late at night the news came from the Tagore mansion that he had been married to Girindranath's daughter.' Abanindranath in his *Apan Katha* mentions Kumudini's room. The description closely resembles Suryamukhi's room in Bankimchandra's *Bishabrikshya*. The walls were decorated with pictures by artists of the Jaipur School, oil paintings and *patas* of Kalighat. Books also found a pride of place. Kumudini was an expert in needlecraft. A pair of bangles crafted by her with gold beads and turquoise flowers surpassed even those made of gold. This also showed her artistic bent of mind. She had a number of pet pigeons. Her days were spent in worship, reciting devotional texts, needlework and care of her pigeons. The artistic imagination of the child Abanindranath was always fired whenever he spent some time with this aunt.

The number of Maharshi Debendranath's brilliant granddaughters is far from negligible. The influence of talented parents combined with an encouraging atmosphere helped them acquire many accomplishments. A number of his granddaughters-in-law showed equal talent. This was a time of unprecedented women's emancipation in Bengal. Many women themselves took the first step in moving out of the confining walls of the home. In the first phase, the achievements of the Tagore women had astonished everyone. The situation had changed in the time of the Maharshi's granddaughters. A number of contemporary women with outstanding achievements appeared on the scene, apart from the Tagores. This is not to say that the Tagore women were sidelined. Far from it. They were no longer the pariahs, but the symbol of aristocracy and worthy of emulation. Social outcry against their actions had given way to approval and praise. The culture of the Tagore family also began to leave its imprint on literature and art. Actually the fifty years from 1875 to 1925 give us a glimpse of the golden era of the Tagore family. This period also heralded a revolution amongst the women of Bengal. In the Tagore household, Jnanadanandini, Swarnakumari, Mrinalini, Saudamini were now joined by Protiva, Indira, Sushama, Sovona and others. Though they were contemporaries, a chronological sequence is being adopted to discuss them. Other women also came forward to match the Tagores and women's emancipation was enriched by their collective efforts.

Among the Maharshi's granddaughters, two of the eldest were Saudamini's daughter Irabati and Hemendranath's daughter Protiva. We will consider the progeny of the Maharshi's daughters also as members of the Tagore family. Irabati was about the same age as Rabindranath. Her husband Nityaranjan was the grandson of Suryakumar Tagore of Pathuriaghata and the nephew of Raja Dakshinaranjan Mukhopadhyay. Nityaranjan lived in Benaras and being an orthodox Hindu he had severed relations with the Tagores of Jorasanko. Irabati came to her parental home after eighteen long years of marriage! We have anecdotes of her fertile imagination, when she would mention a 'king's palace' to fool Rabindranath. She often told him about her visits to this palace. This fired the young boy's imagination. He felt that the 'king's palace' must be nearby but did not know where it was. His eager question: 'Is the king's palace outside our home?' further amused Irabati, who would reply, 'No, it is within this house.' She never realized how her words fuelled young Rabindranath's imagination. He would ponder, 'I have seen all the rooms of this house, where is that palace?' He never knew about the 'king' or the whereabouts of his kingdom but always felt their house was the 'king's palace'. Thus Irabati's role in igniting the imagination of child Rabindranath is not negligible.

Irabati's younger sister Indumati had even less contact with the Tagores. Her husband Nityananda (Nityaranjan) Chattopadhyaya was a doctor in Madras. The two sons-in-law were known as 'Elder Nitya' and 'Younger Nitya' among the Tagores. In Madras, Indumati and her husband moved about a great deal in Anglo-Indian society. Thus Indumati became accustomed to foreign ways of living. All her existing photographs show her wearing a gown.

Protiva or Protivasundari was just five years younger to Rabindranath. She was the eldest child of the Maharshi's third son Hemendranath. Protiva means 'genius' and she really exemplified her name. Hemendra spared no pains to have her accomplished in numerous fields. Thus Protiva had very little time for recreation in her early life. She and her sisters had no contact with the other young members of the family. The door leading to their apartments was always bolted. On the other side of this locked door, Protiva and her sisters carried on their lessons with single-minded devotion. Protiva was believed to have been the first Hindu (Brahmo) student of Loreto. According to another view, she studied in Bethune School. At that time there were no arrangements for holding public examinations for girls. Thus Protiva never appeared in any, though she went up to the highest class.

It is strange that neither Hemendranath nor Protiva thought of appearing for a public examination. This was the time when Chandramukhi Basu was labouring to open the doors of Calcutta University. She was a contemporary of Protiva. Chandramukhi's contribution to spreading women's education is exceptional. She first appealed to Reverend Heron, the principal of the Native Christian Girls' Missionary school of Dehra Dun, for permission to appear for the entrance examination. Heron tried to dissuade her but, moved by Chandramukhi's heart-rending plea, he asked the University for permission. After all, if boys could appear, why not this girl? Wherein lay her fault?

The Calcutta University was extremely reluctant to grant Chandramukhi the requisite permission. After a great deal of pleading, a meeting of the Syndicate was held on 26 November, 1876. Chandramukhi was granted permission on condition that she would not be considered a regular candidate and, even if the examiners awarded her pass marks, her name would not appear in the list of successful candidates—who were all male! What a praiseworthy decision by Calcutta University! No girl from the Tagore family came forward to sit for the examination, though Protiva had been educated upto the same level as Chandramukhi. Thus the girls of the Tagore family—though they were among the first batch of schoolgirls—were denied the pride of place among the first batch of college-going women. But then the successful members of the Tagore family had never shown any interest in going to school or college. Perhaps the same attitude was the reason for Protiva's disinclination.

Chandramukhi can be named as the first woman graduate along with Kadambini Basu. Kadambini later became a doctor. All was not achieved by the efforts of these two women alone. Their plight had attracted the attention of quite a few. Dwarkanath Gangopadhyay of Dacca known as *Abala Bandhab* (Friend of the Weak) strove tirelessly to persuade Calcutta University to grant permission to women to appear for an additional test examination. He was helped by the Vice-Chancellor Sir Arthur Hobhouse—a great emancipator of women. Kadambini passed and was granted permission to join college by the University. In 1880 Chandicharan Sen's daughter Kamini Sen (Roy) and Subarnalata Basu passed the entrance examination. They were followed in 1881 by six others. They were: Abala Das (Basu), Kumudini Khastagir (Das), Virginia Mitra (Nandi), Nirmala Mukhopadhyaya (Som), Priyatama Dutt (Chattopadhyaya) and Bidhumukhi Basu. All these women played an active role in women's emancipation in Bengal. All of them achieved eminence in this sphere. Kadambini went on to study BA as the only student in Bethune College and Chandramukhi did the same from Freechurch of Scotland. Results published in December 1882 showed Chandramukhi and Kadambini as the first two female graduates of the entire British empire. Chandramukhi later studied for an MA while Kadambini became a doctor. Kadambini had to cross a number of hurdles to qualify. She was declared unsuccessful by her examiners in India, though they permitted her to practice medicine. Dissatisfied, she went abroad and acquired medical degrees from both Glasgow and Edinburgh. Abala Das later studied medicine in Madras while Virginia Mitra and Bidhumukhi Basu did so in Calcutta. Thus the portals of higher education were opened for women by Chandramukhi and Kadambini. At that time crowds gathered to watch them pass. Especially women looked at them with reverence tinged with awe. It would have been fitting if Protiva's name had found a place alongside these two. But the women of the Tagore family never came to the fore in the field of degrees and diplomas. They went ahead in the world of art and culture.

Protiva opened the door to music for Bengali women. Disregarding orthodox norms Hemendra had arranged music lessons for his wife. Protiva was tutored both in Indian and Occidental music—she also broke with tradition and sang 'Brahmo sangeet' with her brothers in public on the occasion of *Maghotsav*. This pleased the cultured gentry of that time. Hemendra spared no pains in Protiva's musical training. Besides taking lessons from Ustad Vishnu Chakraborty at home, she also learnt European music and to play the piano. She could play many other musical instruments too. A letter of Hemendranath, written in 1882, shows him advising her about European music:

> 'Do not confine yourself to dance-music and a few songs. Try to master the works of German stalwarts like Beethoven and also the theory of music.'

Protiva was able to fulfil all her father's aspirations and she became an expert in music among women. Her performance on the sitar and the songs she sang at the Vidyatsahini Sabha prompted Raja Saurindramohan to gift her books on musical notation while Raghunandan Tagore presented her with an enormous tanpura. Apart from singing, Protiva broke with tradition in yet another field. Just as Chandramukhi and Kadambini paved the way for higher education of Bengali women, Protiva opened a doorway to music and dramatics. This daring example was no less courageous than horse-riding or the trips to England that were undertaken by her aunts. Her aunts had also participated in family productions where the audience comprised of near and dear ones. There was neither diffidence nor any fear of criticism. Protiva was the first one to appear on stage before the public. Any performance at the Tagore mansion attracted hordes of people. They would get to see and hear Bengali women belonging to an aristocratic family singing in public. Later these women came forward to act also in *Bidyatjan Samagam Sabha*. The first among them was Protiva as Saraswati in *Balmiki Protiva*.

The era of musical plays had begun among the Tagores when Rabindranath returned from England. *Basanta Utsab* and *Maanmoyee*, composed by Swarnakumari and Jyotirindranath respectively, had already been staged a couple of times before a family audience. Rabindranath composed a new musical play akin to opera, blending Indian and European music. He chose the story of the transformation of the robber Ratnakar into the sage Valmiki as depicted in *Ramayana*. The play had three female roles—Balika, Lakshmi and Saraswati. When the play was being rehearsed, Protiva's incomparable depiction of Saraswati prompted Rabindranath to incorporate her name into the play and call it *Balmiki Protiva*.

It was decided to stage *Balmiki Protiva* at the congregation of the Bidyatjan Samagam. It was the evening of Saturday, 16 Falgun 1287, according to the Bengali calendar, that *Balmiki Protiva* began. There was a light breeze blowing and the audience had assembled. The atmosphere was rendered sombre by the appearance of robbers on the stage. The audience was enthralled. There seemed no dearth of surprises. Depicting the two herons killed while making love were two real dead birds. The credit goes to Jyotirindranath. The staging of his younger brother's play so enthused Jyotirindranath that he went out bird-hunting. Unfortunately, he was unable to sight a single one. While returning home, after a day's futile search, he saw a peddlar with a number of cranes for sale. He purchased two, killed them and brought them home. Just like today, efforts were made even then to make the stage as realistic as possible. During the performance of *Kaal-Mrigaya,* a pet deer of Jyotirindranath had been let loose on the stage. These ideas of stage props originated from the play *Puru-Bikram* staged by the Bengal Theatre. Saratchandra Ghosh, belonging to *Chhaatubabu*'s family, acted as Puru. He would appear on stage riding a real white horse!

The novelty of *Balmiki Protiva* lay in the appearance of the actresses. A beautiful girl appeared in the role of Balika, with her hands bound. Many people in the audience recognized Protiva. This girl had enthralled them with her songs previously. Now they were charmed by her portrayal of Saraswati. The play left an unusual feeling of pleasure among the audience. Critics praised Protiva's acting when the news of this performance was reported in the paper *Arya Darshan*. According to one critic:

> Babu Hemendranath Tagore's daughter Protiva's portrayal of first Balika and then Saraswati was superb.

Protiva was fortunate that her first stage appearance generated only acclaim and not derision from society. Rajkrishna Roy wrote a poem in *Arya Darshan*, naming it *Balika Protiva*, mentioning Protiva's costume and appearance as follows:

> *Paroney gerua baas, alu thalu keshpash*
> *Ki ek apurba probha uthaley o barananey.*
> *Alankar boley karey, o balika janey narey,*
> *Prakritir alankarey alankrito ajataney.*

Dressed in saffron garb, with hair let loose,
Oh! What an ethereal glow emanates from her beautiful face.
This girl knows not the use of ornaments,
She has been adorned by Nature's ornaments.

The critic of the *Sadharani* magazine makes a special mention of Protiva's acting:

> The stage of the theatre has been embellished for the first time by a daughter of a genteel Bengali family. Protiva is the fittest person to adorn the coronation of the re-birth of Bengali theatre as its presiding idol. She has a melodious voice, is an expert singer, bright-eyed and graceful. Her songs and acting both pleased and astonished the audience.

There was another female character, Lakshmi, in *Balmiki Protiva*. According to Indira, the role of Lakshmi was played by Saratkumari's daughter Sushila in the first performance. It is curious that the critic of *Arya Darshan* did not mention the character of Lakshmi at all. It would have been natural to be charmed by Lakshmi's role at that time. Numerous actresses had appeared in the public theatres. Calcutta was agog with Nati Binodini's performance, but no girl from an aristocratic family could dream of acting before the public in those days. Perhaps Sushila's acting paled before that of others but her first attempt was certainly praiseworthy. Nothing has been heard about Sushila thereafter. They were four sisters. The other three were Suprova, Swayamprobha and Chiraprova. Though nothing much is known about the last two, this is not true of Suprova. Though brought up in the Tagore family, their education did not progress beyond *Charupath*. Nor is there any evidence of their inclination towards artistic pursuits. All of them were superb in housework and enjoyed being engrossed in a myriad domestic jobs. Among them Suprova was the liveliest and had a very good sense of humour. According to Sarala: 'She kept herself abreast of whatever went on in the mansion. From the servants' den downstairs to the rooms of the elders in the top floor, nothing escaped her notice. She was very good at entertaining and had an endless store of humorous anecdotes.' Though a Brahmo, in her later years she became a devotee of Lord Shiva. She was indoctrinated from a holy man and worshipped the idol daily. She was not cowed down by a sense of shame for having broken the traditions of her family. She just wished to have the right to follow a religion of her choice and there was no hint of awkwardness in her demeanour when she visited Jorasanko. She was the mother of the well-known artist Asit Kumar Haldar.

Like Sushila, Suprova had also appeared on the stage a couple of times in the home productions of the Tagores. This was probably during Hironmoyee's marriage when Suprova played the role of the hero's friend in Swarnakumari's *Bibaha Utsav*. At that time it was customary to have dances by nautch-girls or performances by professional jatra or theatre groups during weddings in wealthy families. At Maharshi Bhawan, dances by nautch-girls were never permitted. Instead, plays were staged at every wedding. The actors and actresses were all family members. There was a reason for this custom. Relations, including inhabitants of houses number 5 and 6, were unable to visit Maharshi Bhawan freely because of the dictates of orthodox Hindu society. The Maharshi's family, being Brahmo, would not attend a Hindu wedding where Lord Viṣhnu would be present in the form of 'shalgram shila'. On the other hand Gunendranath's family was unable to invite them since their other relatives would object, to share a meal with the Brahmos. Yet the wish to participate in such happy occasions was always there. So a play was staged either a day or a week after the wedding, when everyone was invited to Maharshi Bhawan. Since only sweets were distributed, the taboo of sitting down to a meal with Brahmos did not operate. It was in such a performance that Suprova appeared as the hero's friend. *Bibaha Utsav* was staged once again at the time of Suprova's wedding. The part played by Suprova was now performed by Swarnakumari's young daughter Sarala.

Bibaha Utsav reminds us of a few other ladies as well. One of them was Sushila who played the hero's role. She was the first wife of Dwipendra, Dwijendranath's eldest son. The other was Sarojasundari who was the heroine. She and Ushaboti were Dwijendranath's daughters. They were married to Mohinimohan Chattopadhyaya and Ramanimohan Chattopadhyaya, both of whom were descended from Raja Rammohan Ray's daughter.

Mohinimohan pioneered the Indian Theosophist movement and later lived in America for seven years. His ideas on philosophy, his poetic abilities and excellent command over the English language drew the attention of many. Apart from writing a number of books, he translated the Bhagwad Gita into English. Another of his brothers, Rajanimohan, married Sunayani, the younger sister of Abanindranath and Gaganendranath. After Sushila's death, Dwipendranath married Mohinimohan's sister Hemlata.

Saroja was a paragon of beauty with eyes shaped like lotus petals, a milk and rose complexion and long black hair comparable to dark rain clouds. Her granddaughter Surabhi writes: 'She always did up her hair in an ordinary bun which rested on her neck. She also sported sideburns imitating the Begums of Mughal Emperors. The sideburns looked lovely on her rosy cheeks.' Her face had a placid beauty all its own. She played the role of the heroine in *Bibaha Utsav*. Later she confined herself to the four walls of her home and became a housewife par excellance. When Mohinimohan decided to go to America, Saroja handed over all her jewellery to pay for his expenses. After he began to earn, a grateful Mohinimohan never went against any of her wishes. Yet Saroja's life centred round her family and their happiness. She was a very good cook and enjoyed feeding others. This is not to say that she spent all her time within the home. Every evening she would go for a drive along the banks of the Ganga in a landaulet. Ushaboti used to sing in the chorus. Once in *Kaal-Mrigaya* she and Indira acted as Banadevi. Perhaps their roles in the life of the Tagore family are not memorable but it is not possible to ignore their collective effect in brightening the andar mahal of the family. Moreover, if ever a search is made for all the actors and actresses of every Tagorean play, it will become clear that his plays and songs were popularized mainly by the family members.

Coming back to *Balmiki Protiva*, another performance was staged on a grand scale in 1893 to felicitate Lady Lansdowne. Prior to this, *Balmiki Protiva* had been staged a number of times during the decade 1881–92. Everytime, Protiva enacted the role of Saraswati and Rabindranath of Balmiki. This time, a number of well-known Englishmen were invited to see the performance. Dwijendranath's son Neetindranath was given the responsibility of stage décor. He tried his best to create a natural effect. Water sprayed down a metal pipe, from the verandah to the stage, depicting rain. The Englishmen were delighted. This time, the role of Balika, with her hands bound, was played by Protiva's third sister Avijnaya and that of Laksmi by Satyendranath's daughter Indira. Saraswati's role was enacted as usual by Protiva. Seeing the white-clad Protiva sitting on a snow-white lotus (made of pith while the veena was made out of ostrich-egg shell) everyone mistook her for a clay idol. Towards the end, when Protiva got up and handed over the veena to Rabindranath, singing in her melodious sweet voice, 'Take my veena, I present it to you. Its strings will strum whatever you wish to sing,' the audience was spellbound. The success of this performance proved the beauty and graceful culture of the Tagores. It was apparent that a play need not be based on devotional mythology or soft pornography.

Protiva strove a lot for music in her later years too. Fortunately marriage did not create any impediments. Like Saroja's husband, Protiva's husband was also a renowned figure. He was Rabindranath's friend Ashutosh Chaudhuri. Rabindranath first met Ashutosh during his second voyage to England. Ashutosh hailed from the well-known Chaudhuri family of Pabna. His background had been totally different from Protiva's. He never had the advantage of liberal, cultural surroundings in his childhood. Yet his achievements were unparalleled. All the seven brothers were stalwarts in their own fields, especially Ashutosh and Pramatha. Though Ashutosh never appeared on the literary scene of Bengal it was he who arranged and published Rabindranath's *Kori O Komal*. His greatest academic achievement was passing the BA and MA examination of the Calcutta University in the same year (1880). His trip to England was full of hurdles. According to *Purbakatha* by his elder sister Prasannamoyee, Ashutosh was the first person among the Chaudhuris to go abroad. Not just from his family, but no one from the district had ever done so either. Naturally orthodox society was aghast and proclaimed the Chaudhuris outcastes. Since they did not show any inclination to undergo the ritual penance, soceity came down on Ashutosh's widowed aunts—his father's sisters. Each one of them had to pay five *kahans* (a specific measure) of cowrie shells and shave their heads before they were accepted back into society. Prasannamoyee writes: 'They were child widows and had followed all the dictates of society since childhood. No one could comprehend why they were thus harassed.' This was the true picture of Bengali society. If a young man from a Hindu family went abroad, the entire family had to face social ostracism and harassment. Yet it was already 1881. Much before this, Jnanadanandini had been to England with two children, Chandramukhi had passed the entrance examination and was preparing to became a graduate, along with Kadambini. Protiva had already appeared on stage in *Balmiki Protiva*. Prasannamoyee's aunts were not illiterate either.

Though Rabindranath had to forego his trip to England this time, his friendship with Ashutosh continued. After his return from England, Ashutosh came in contact with other members of the Tagore family. His simple nature and love of literature endeared him to all. He met Protiva and it was considered by all that the brilliant young man would be an ideal match for the beautiful and accomplished Protiva. The wedding took place shortly thereafter. The Maharshi was especially pleased. He commented, 'Ashu is an asset to us. It is by great good luck that Protiva has been married to such a man.' An amusing incident occurred shortly before the wedding. Indira was accompanying Rabindranath to a meeting and Ashutosh happened to travel with them in the same coach. Though this was not preplanned, Neepamoyee was upset as she thought that Jnanadanandini might have been considering Ashutosh as a match for Indira. Jnanadanandini had irked many by her progressive ways and hence the suspicion. Jnanadanandini was highly amused. Her daughter was too young and she had no desire to get her married so early. Hemendranath died during this time and shortly thereafter Protiva was married to Ashutosh. Many had wondered at the time if Protiva's six sisters would ultimately make matches with Ashutosh's six brothers. Though three of Ashutosh's brothers later married into the Tagore family, none of the brides were Protiva's sisters. The marriage of Protiva and Ashutosh allowed the young men and women to mix freely with each other. According to many, this was due to the cultural ethos of the Tagore family while others opine that the real reason was their wish to be acquainted with the beautiful and accomplished young women of the family. Whatever the motive, it is clear that Bengali educated society had become conscious of the Tagore family, especially their young women. These women were not only well versed in literature but also accomplished in music. According to Indira, the interaction between the Tagore and Chaudhuri families was not always free from unpleasant repercussions. Such anecdotes also provide us a glimpse of contemporary Bengali society.

Protiva's greatest contribution in the field of music was to devise a simple way of writing notations. She not only rejuvenated the system of preparing notations and their application as devised by Dwijendranath and Jyotirindranath but also made it simple enough for general use. Before Protiva, no woman had ventured into the field of preparing musical notations.

The notations prepared by Protiva were regularly published in Jnanadanandini's *Balak* magazine. Protiva was also the first to prepare the notations for the songs in *Balmiki Protiva* and *Kaal-Mrigaya.* It has been mentioned that under Hemendranath's direction, she prepared the notations for numerous Brahmo sangeet and Hindustani classical music. Though it has not been possible to count their exact number but one of her brothers, Hitendranath, says in the Asaarh 1311 issue (15 June–15 July) of *Punya* magazine that it was about 300 to 400. However, it was not enough to prepare notations. Singers were necessary to sing these songs.

Protiva had already brought about a revolutionary social change by singing in public. She now took up the task of nourishing this movement. Along with preparing notations, she also tried to teach vocal music. Here again, the magazine *Balak* provided her with the means. In it she opened a music section called 'Sahaj Gaan Shiksha'. Since *Balak* was a children's magazine, first of all she tried to describe to its young readers what songs meant, while trying to define the essence of a song. Protiva said 'Songs are natural to human beings.' People's voices change when they laugh or cry. Thus we know that 'different moods have different tunes'. Songs evolved by a study of these tunes. This interpretation of music is entirely Protiva's own. In later years she propounded more original ideas on music.

Vocal music, as all other kinds of music, requires not only knowledge but regular practice. To facilitate the practise of music Protiva first opened Ananda Sabha and later Sangeet Sangha in her own home. Sangeet Sangha was well-known as a music school. She used to teach pure classical Hindustani songs, though she was also an expert in European music, having been tutored by Nicolini. Her expertise in Western music had so pleased the Maharshi that he had bought her a piano. He loved to hear Protiva's piano recitals. Now Bengali girls had an opportunity to learn classical vocal music properly. Along with Sangeet Sangha another familiar name is Sangeet Sanmilani. This was also a music school, established by Mrs B.L. Chaudhuri, i.e. Pramada Chaudhuri, the wife of Banwarilal Chaudhuri. These schools gave many Bengali girls the opportunity to learn vocal music. By then Protiva was Lady Chaudhuri, the wife of Justice Sir Ashutosh Chaudhuri, and a number of girls from aristocratic families were emboldened to join the school run by her. Instruments, especially the sitar and esraj (sarangi), were also taught, along with vocal music. Indira also joined Protiva in running the school. By then, she had also married into the Chaudhuri family.

Along with teaching music, Protiva also pondered upon a magazine dealing with various aspects of the subject. *Sangeet Prakashika* by Jyotirindranath had folded up many years ago. Thus there certainly was the need for such a magazine. To match *Ananda Sabha* Protiva named the new magazine *Ananda Sangeet.* She was always diffident about venturing alone and persuaded Indira to help her. Under their joint editorship *Ananda Sangeet* was published for eight years. In this magazine Protiva not only published musical notations regularly but she tried to rediscover long lost music, both vocal and instrumental. Protiva also began to write about old maestros who had gone into oblivion. Her biographies of Tansen, Sa Sadarang, Baiju Bawra Nayak, Maharaja Saurindramohan Tagore and many other musicians show her originality of thoughts on music. While studying any art form, it is essential to know about the artist as well as his creations. It is due to Protiva's efforts that the details of the lives and works of many musicians could be retraced. She never became a famous singer, but equalled her uncles in the theory of music. Her true achievement lay in the words spoken by her uncle Rabindranath during the prize distribution ceremony of *Sangeet Sangha* after her death: 'Music was not only in her voice, it filled her whole life. All her life's works were permeated by the beauty and sweetness of music.'

On the occasion of Protiva's death, her sister-in-law, poetess Prasannamoyee Devi wrote:

Eshechhile amader ghare
Chole gechho andhokar kore,
Kamala-rupini bodhu
Kantho bhora geet-modhu.
Sushomay alokiya geho;
Ki anando utsabe
Pratham ashile jobe
Shey katha bhulite nare keho.

You had come to our home
But have now departed, leaving all in darkness,
Dear sister-in-law who resembled the goddess Kamala,
With a honeyed voice full of music.
How our home was lit up with joyous celebration,
When you first entered its precincts,
Is indelibly etched in our hearts.

In the field of Rabindra Sangeet, Protiva's main achievement lies in preparing notations with swar sandhi of many songs. The best example perhaps is the notation of the song *Kon aloke praner pradip*. The idea of setting Sanskrit slokas to music and singing them was Rabindranath's. Protiva also made notations for the Ved-gaans set to music by Rabindranath. Maghotsav always began with a solemn and devotional Ved-gaan. It was sometimes '*Yademi Prasfuranniba*' or '*Twami swaranang*' or slokas from the Gita. Every time Protiva would prepare the notations and teach the others to sing. She herself also set the music for a few such songs. She set the sloka '*Twamadideva Purushapurana*' on the Kedara raagini. Though few, songs composed by Protiva herself are also available, especially *Saanjher pradip dinu jalaye* and *Deendayal prabhu bhulona anathe* which were popular as Brahmosangeet.

In Protiva's life an urge for knowledge and religion were mingled with her love of music. The Maharshi's spiritual endeavours and Hemendra's strong religious fervour, both influenced her life. In her advice on the occasion of New Year she said:

> Today wealth is adored, sought and it reigns supreme all over the world. But the seeker of true religion always needs you, oh Lord. The victory of religion lies with you. For you a religious man forsakes all and bears innumerable hardships. Wealth and fame are transitory but you are our eternal father, mother, teacher and friend all in one.

Though she did not go in for literary pursuits, Protiva had a good command of Bengali language and literature. She had not only learnt several languages like English, French, Latin and Sanskrit but was also interested in the study of history and geography. Unlike those of the other women of the Tagore family, Protiva's writings are rare. *Aalok*, a collection of her lectures, was published many years ago. A paragraph from her lecture is quoted below. It shows the unique character of her writing. She writes:

> Unless our heart is full of noble thoughts we cannot achieve nobility. The direction of our thoughts—good or evil—influences and directs our behaviour. If we are not restrained in thought, our lives become indisciplined and wayward. Who can help us control our thoughts and turn them away from evil? Who is the charioteer to help us? It is no one else but knowledge. We have to take refuge in knowledge to order our thoughts along the right path.

These few lines show Protiva's quest for knowledge and yearning for restrained thought. As *Nababarsha* greetings she sometimes composed short poems or couplets. Once she wrote *Barsho Probesh*.

> *Barsho elo barsho gelo niyati tomar*
> *Sumangal panchyajanya bajilo abar*
> *Prakritir ghare ghare naba anuragey,*
> *Bhariya uthilo biswa nabin sohagey.*

The year has come and gone, O fate,
Your benedictine conch-shell has sounded again.
In Nature's various abodes, in new modes,
The world is again filled with a new love.

While Protiva was dedicating herself to music and rediscovering the creations of old masters, her second sister Pragyasundari busied herself with another age-old but novel topic. Like her elder sister, she also began life with school, lessons in music and painting. Just as rivers originating from the same source often follow different courses, Pragya branched out on a new path. In the Tagore family every facility was provided to the women to practise various art forms. Pragya however was attracted by the culinary arts. This may not sound novel as all Tagore women learned to cook but the maximum marks were scored by Kadambari and Mrinalini. Saratkumari and Sarojasundari were also known for their proficiency. Pragya also learned to cook as a matter of course. Her mother Neepomoyee was a good cook. The Maharshi also encouraged them. Yet the daily menu was 'lentils–fish curry–*ambol*', '*ambol*–fish curry–lentils'. Apart from this, mashed potatoes, some fries like those of '*bori*' or vegetables dipped in gram-flour batter were also included. This was the general menu for the entire household. It was in the Tagore family that the custom of sweetening vegetable dishes originated. The Maharshi was very fond of such preparations. Various vegetable dishes and sweets were prepared at home by the daughters and daughters-in-law. Pragya's uniqueness lay in the fact that she was not content merely to cook the traditional dishes for her near and dear ones. Deflecting from the age-old customs of the Tagore family, she invented various dishes and served them to all and sundry.

The amount of thought and effort expended by Pragya over the kitchen and cooking was unequalled among women. While experimenting with various recipes at home she recorded them for the generations to come. This is the reason why her book *Aamish O Niramish Aahar* proved so engrossing. Numerous books on various aspects of domestic science have been written in this age and more are being penned; but the books written by Pragya about a century ago leave us spellbound. A few others merit mention: *Barendra Randhan* and *Jalkhabar* by Kiranlekha Roy, *Adarsha Randhan Shiksha* by Niharbala Devi and *Lakshmi-sri* by Banalata Devi also became popular as cookbooks, but that was much later. Men had also shown interest in this field. The Raja of Burdwan sponsored the translation of the Sanskrit *Pak-rajeswar,* and *Raannar Boi* by Bipradas Mukhopadhyay had also been published earlier. Pragya had researched much more on the subject and the prefaces to her two books on cooking may be considered a storehouse not only of various recipes but of home-making skills too. She took up this task well after her marriage as an experienced housewife.

Like Protiva, Pragya's husband was also a well-known personality. He was Lakshminath Bejbarua, the father of Assamese literature. Pragya had never met him before the marriage. In his autobiography Lakshminath says that a look at her photograph attracted him to this beautiful, accomplished and deeply religious girl of the Tagore family. He agreed to the match forthwith, though there was fierce opposition from his own family. In those days a son's marrying into the Tagore family was tantamount to losing him. In spite of a barrage of telegrams between Calcutta and Gauhati the course of fate remained unalterable. The spring evening of 11 March 1891 witnessed the *Shubhadristi* of these two after the *Saptapadi Gaman*. Lakshminath saw that Pragya took one look at him and smiled. A smile appeard on Lakshminath's lips too. Later, when he asked Pragya, 'Why did you smile so at the time of our *Shubhadristi*?' Pragya replied, 'I had seen you much earlier in my dreams'. Lakshminath's resemblance to the face she had seen in her dreams brought the smile to Pragya's lips.

Glimpses of such anecdotes penned by Lakshminath leave us in no doubt about the happiness of Pragya's married life. Marital bliss had made her sensitive to the duties of a wife, to make the home a haven of peace and happiness. Though she had acted in *Mayar Khela* and also learnt to paint, she forsook all this to make the oft-neglected kitchen her domain. Hemendranath considered cooking an art. He had thought of writing a book on the subject and had a notebook full of recipes and other details. He greatly encouraged his daughters in this matter. When Pragya began to devote her attention to cooking and ancillary topics, she was encouraged by Lakshminath too.

Pragya began to think about the kitchen while editing the *Punya* magazine. Hemendranath's children were the main sponsors of this paper. Pragya was the first editor and all her brothers and sisters used to write for this magazine. Right from the beginning recipes for various vegetarian and non-vegetarian dishes were published in this magazine. Being an excellent housewife, Pragya also quoted the current market prices—to avoid inconvenience to her readers. Today these pricelists evoke only nostalgia. Fish was unbelievably cheap. A half seer cut of rohu was three to four annas, a three-quarter seer cut of chitol cost six annas, eight or nine large-sized, egg-filled koi fish cost ten annas, an egg one pice, ghee was one rupee per seer, curd four annas per seer, tomatoes twenty for two annas. Prolonging the list will only cause heartache! All that we need to know is that Pragya—even as the wife of a wealthy man—had not checked these prices quoted by her servants. The actual prices may have been a little less.

Aamish O Niramish Aahar was published in three volumes. Pragya had also thought of writing a book on domestic science but unfortunately was unable to do so. This will always remain a great loss to the subject. It is doubtful if teachers of domestic science take as much care while writing books on the subject as Pragya did when writing her books. In the preface she has given essential directions on food, patients' diets, weights, measures, treatment of servants and cleanliness of the kitchen. Along with this she prepared a list with explanatory synonyms of terms commonly used in the kitchen. Many of the words are familiar yet such a list is certainly essential. The long list is an indication of Pragya's sincerity and earnestness. She used both colloquial and uncommon terms in her list. It is amusing to note that an unripe lime is *karai lebu* while an unripe mango is *kurui aam*. The term *daag deoa* which normally signified marking becomes synonymous in the kitchen with cooking spices in ghee (clarified butter). There are many other such terms, as, for example.:

bakhra	—	papri
chutput	—	sound of spices crackling when added to hot oil or ghee
haalshe	—	uncooked foul smell
rutitosh	—	toasted bread
pitni	—	a hammer used to flatten pieces of meat.
balikhola	—	items roasted in hot sand in a wooden dish
seena	—	chest/breast
chamkana	—	lightly frying on a dry dish
toi	—	an earthen vessel used to fry malpoa
tijel haandi	—	a wide-mouthed haandi for cooking lentils
tola haandi	—	a large haandi for cooking rice
khanda kata	—	chopping into small pieces
cheer kata	—	cutting lengthwise into two exact halves
chhunka	—	adding spices to hot oil or ghee

Before Pragya's list, how many were aware of such diverse terms used in the kitchen? If Bengali cooking is ever awarded a place in the folk arts, Pragya's name would certainly head the list. Her Indian recipes were mostly gleaned from rural Bengali life. The synonyms used in the Bengali kitchen were also typical of Bengali women's own language. These are going into oblivion fast. Her list also includes a number of utensils which are gradually becoming foreign to us. Thus Pragya's role in furthering folk art along with domestic science is appreciable.

Her books also contain other essential information for housewives—such as imparting the smell of onions to a dish without using onions or how to reduce the burnt smell of a slightly charred dish. How many know that hing (asafoetida) soaked in ginger juice imparts the smell of onions when added to a vegetarian dish? Or, if vegetables or lentils stick to the utensil due to slight charring, adding a few betel leaves considerably reduces the burnt smell. Details of preserving meat and fish as well as detecting their freshness are also there. 'A hilsa fish freshly caught from the Ganga is curved like a boat, and gradually straightens out as the day progresses.' She did not forget to mention the method of preserving vegetables by sun-drying. She even knew the methods of preparing *aluier bori* or pastules prepared by a vaid, with various ingredients to treat children's ailments. *Aluier bori* proves to us that women not only prepared a sick child's diet but were also involved in administering herbal medicines to them.

Pragya introduced a novel item in Bengali feasts. This was the use of a menu card or *kramani* as she termed it in Bengali. Just as sumptuous English feasts have menu cards, Pragya decided to have menu cards for her guests. She decided to write the menu and hang it on the wall of the dining room in case printing and distribution among the guests proved difficult. Pragya not only named the menu card *kramani*, she gave much thought over the probable items, the chronological order of serving them during the feast and modes of writing the menu that would add to its aesthetic value. A few of her *kramanis* will make this clear. First let us take up a vegetarian one:

Saffron bhuni *khitchuri*
Roasted dhundhul boiled beans

Boiled ripe mangoes
Salty malpoa from parbal
Fried ripe *kanthal*
Fried *kankrol*
Boiled rice
Khaja from arhar dal
Gourd curry
Brinjal and *bori* soup
Gram dhonka,
Brinjal Dolma
Moong dal with ground mango or alubokhara
Ambol of ripe parbal
Karhi from curd
Rammohan Dolma pillau
Kheer with litchis
Coconut toffee

It reads just like a poem and may be easily mistaken for one. Even though vegetarian, it is more than adequate to tempt the palate. This also gives us an idea of the feasts in those days. Pragya always tried out a recipe herself before including it in any of her menus. She had also invented a number of dishes and often named them after her near and dear ones, as, for example, Rammohan Dolma Pillau, Dwarkanath Phirnipillau, Surabhi kheer—named after her daughter who died young. On Tagore's fiftieth birthday she prepared a sweatmeat using cauliflower, milk, almonds, kishmish and saffron and decorated it with gold and silver foil. She named it kavi sambardhana barfi. None of the guests could make out that it had been made from cauliflower!

There are also many new and strange dishes, such as date pillau, curried chilli leaves, an *ambol* made from rasagollas, beetroot *hingi*, dalna from *paniphal*, gourd wrapped in leaves and roasted, mock fish-curry with curd, *ghanto bhog*, tender *puin* leaves fried in batter, *Saraswati ambol* from tamarind, boiled *amlaki*, kheer made from onions, *pat-tola* of koi fish, roasted crab, Bombay meat-curry and many others. Tutoring in the art of cooking is also in the book: 'When you learn to cook *hingi* it will be clear that it is a stage between a *dalna* and a *qualia*.' Let us look at a few more *kramanikas*. The non-vegetarian ones are not too elaborate.

Asparagus sandwich
Cucumber sandwich
Meat sandwich
Fish sandwich
Pound cake
Biscuit
Singara
Dalmot
Jhuri bhaja
Ice cream

Another one:

Bread croutons
Pickled lime
Almond soup
Bekti mayonnaise
Chicken haandi kabab
Mutton gravy cutlets
Vegetable and Tomato salad
Roast snipe
Potato sippets
Ufs alanaise
Dessert
Coffee

The vegetarian *kramanika* is much more elaborate and speaks volumes for the housewife's abilities.

Boiled rice,
Roast potatoes, roast brinjals mashed with milk, boiled radish, fried pineapple
Potato chops with banana flowers
Moong phampra
Stir fried figs, stir fried banana flowers
Moong dal with pumpkin
Spinach *ghanto*

Masur dal with bitter gourd
Oler dalna
Curried ladies finger,
Phupu pillau from cottage cheese
Vegetarian egg-ball curry
Dolma of pickled bitter gourd
Potato *dumpokta*
Curried raw tamarind with alum
Coconut *ambol*
Pakoras
Kheer from puffed rice
Kamali

Even banquets today do not have so many items. Vegetarian feasts have also gone out of fashion. At that time the accomplishments of a housewife were judged by the number of vegetable dishes, sweets and puddings she arranged around the thali. These feasts also reflect the calm and placid lives of affluent Bengalis. Bengalis were never prolific eaters but they were gourmets. Their artistic temperament sought fulfilment not only in permanent but also in transitory things. Bengali women converted the kitchen into an artist's studio.

Housewives of those days were familiar with most of the dishes mentioned by Pragya and were generally expert cooks. Unlike Pragya, none of them thought of writing down the recipes to ease the path of future generations.

Some of the menus show Pragya's aesthetic sense:

Fensa *khichuri* with peas
Palta leaves fried in batter
Batter-fried cauliflower florets
Peas fried in batter
Fried spring onions
Boiled rice
Gram dal malai curry with milk
Stir fried cabbage
Stir fried *teora saak*,

Ghanto of baby radishes
Ghanto of lal saag
Cabbage *ghanto*
Dalna of *gaach chhola*
Dhonka of *motor dal*
Orange kallia
Olkapi curry
Onion Dolma pickle
Cauliflower *dampokto*
Brinjal and plum *ambol*
Malai pillau with pineapple
Phulia

Such feasts were not everyday affairs. There are shorter *kramanis* too, though considering present standards they cannot be considered too brief.

Egg and mulligatawny soup
Boiled rice
Potato French stew
Chaun-chaun, fried rohu fish
Mutton Hussainy curry
Pillau
Fruit salad
Fruits

Or

Olive bread,
Coconut soup
Smoked hilsa
Boiled chicken, ham
Collar of mutton
Cold jelly and blancmange
Coconut toffee, candied ginger
Coffee

Consider a vegetarian menu:

Boiled rice,
Clarified butter, lemon, salt
Stir-fried green beans with neem leaves, boiled gram dal

Stir-fried *shulfa saag* with brinjal
Curried gram dal, batter fried pumpkin
Stir-fried punko saag
Bhartapuri
Stir-fried spinach
Ghanto from banana stem
Tile khichuri
Cottage cheese dalna
curried cucumber
Patol dolma
Ambol of *amra* with ground *til*
Ambol of ripe papaya
Lucknow *karhui* kheer of unripe mangoes

The *kramanis* make it clear that like French feasts one always had the option to pick and choose, otherwise so many dishes, along with boiled rice, pillau and *khichuri* would not have been served. Various condiments rolled in betel-leaves (paan) are an essential ending to any feast. Pragya mentions twelve different ways of preparing paan. 'Sweet paan pillau' was invented by her and she writes: 'When I served this to members of the Surhid Samiti they named it so.' She gives details of preparing slaked lime, catechu and other condiments for paan too.

We cannot help but wonder at Rabindranath's reaction to the culinary expertise shown by Pragya in her two books on cookery. Kavi sambardhana burfi must have pleased him. His enthusiasm for novel dishes is well-known as mentioned by a number of women in their reminiscences. Rabindranath never spoke to them about Pragya's culinary abilities, though he had her *Aamish O Niramish Aahar* in his library. When his daughter Madhurilata requested him for these books, he wrote to Subodh Chandra Majumdar: 'Bela has asked for the second volume of Pragya's *Aamish Aahar*. The book is in our library. Please look for it and send it to her.' We do not know if he encouraged her to prepare the *kramani*. He was known to use the word *rutitosh* for toasted bread. One would like to know if he coined the word or used it as named by Pragya as a sign of his affection. There is no one today who would be able to satisfy our curiosity.

Besides Hemendranath's daughters we have to consider another member of the Tagore family—Indira—the only daughter of Satyendra and Jnanadanandini. She was just a fortnight older than Hemendra's daughter Avijnaya who always called her 'Bon Didi'. Fortunately Indira lived to a ripe old age and thus provided us the opportunity to know another bright jewel of the Tagore family. She was the one to whom Rabindranath addressed his well-known *Chinna Patraboli.* Even if her contribution to all other walks of life been nil, there would still have been no doubt about the unique qualities of one who inspired Tagore to write these letters. However, this was only the beginning. Indira's exceptional personality was manifest in all her activities. The stunningly beautiful Indira was thus accepted affectionately as 'Bibidi' by all and sundry, in spite of her achievements. She was the type of person who made her home a haven of love and peace, just by her lifestyle.

Indira was born in 1873. The expectant mother Jnanadanandini had wished for a lovely daughter whom she could dress up to her heart's content. Her wish was granted. In Kaladagi, a town in Maharashtra, was born a daughter of the Tagore family. It was as if a star had strayed into this world. Her features were sharp, the eyes bright and complexion fair—like the Indian tube-rose. She was named Indira. The beauty of the Tagore women was acclaimed far and wide. A contemporary witness was Pramatha Chaudhuri. The year was probably 1884. On the day of Saraswati Puja, Rabindranath, along with niece Indira, went to deliver a lecture at Albert Hall.

Pramatha was then a student. He met his friend Narayan Chandra Sheel on the grounds of Presidency College after a long walk. Narayan informed him about Tagore's lecture and that he had brought his niece too. He also suggested that both of them go to Albert Hall which was just across the road. Pramatha was not keen at all. His friend said: 'Even if you are not eager to hear Rabindranath let us go and see his niece. I believe she is a beauty.' Pramatha lay down under a tree and said indifferently: 'I am not keen to see a little girl belonging to another family.' Many however were curious and eager enough to do so. Later the same Pramatha married Indira. Pramatha's mention of the incident in his autobiography *Atma Katha* gives us a glimpse of the curiosity evoked by girls of the Tagore family in contemporary times.

Not only was Indira beautiful but highly accomplished too. She had another achievement to her credit. Among the girls of the Tagore family she was the first to graduate. The Tagores had never set much store by school or college education. However the BA degree certainly had a value, especially at that time when people crowded the streets to have a glimpse of graduate women. Shortly before this, Kadambini and Chandramukhi had succeeded in their efforts to have the doors of the University opened. Women had slowly begun to crowd the university. Swarnakumari's daughter Sarala Ghosal had graduated before Indira, who was the first Tagore to do so. After passing the entrance examination from Loreto, Indira studied at home with Honours in English and French. She topped the list in the BA examination in 1892 and was awarded the Padmavati gold medal. Though a dozen women had graduated from Calcutta University before Indira, none of them had studied French at the graduate level. Eight years after Indira, Lillian Palit—the daughter of Taraknath Palit—again took up French. Lillian was the first Indian to file a suit for divorce, which created a furore in society. An examination of old records of Calcutta University shows that between 1882 and 1891 only twelve women graduated.

Indira was the thirteenth. Nirmalbala Sen was the only one among these women to obtain a double MA from the university. She received her MA degree in English in 1891 and in moral philosophy in 1894. The number was rapidly increasing, otherwise figures in 1910 could not have shown fifty-seven women graduates. Eight women passed the MA examination between 1884 and 1910, but none of them were related to the Tagores.

Indira knew French well. Fortunately her husband Pramatha Chaudhuri was also an expert in the language. His writings clearly show the French influence. In his letters, while courting Indira, he addressed her by the French term *mon ami*. Indira's letters also show the influence of the novelist Pramatha. Though she never tried her hand at short stories or novels, all her writings were brilliant in their humour and grace. 'When you think of me, do not imagine a French debutante—think of a homely Bengali woman, modern but certainly Bengali: one whom you would like to rule over your heart besides being the mistress of your home. I do not wish that any foreign traits, that are not inevitable and that cannot be blended with our Indian ways, should make their appearance in our home life.'

In another letter she says:

> The ways mentioned by you of transporting myself partly through letters—I think I understand them but I shall not adopt them, especially because a foreigner used to do so. If you are unable to imagine me without any sensory aids, then your pride as a Brahmin is in vain.

Or:

> You ask me if I can see you in my heart. If it means thinking about you then it is more difficult to answer. What else do I dream about? All twenty-four hours, during all my daily activities, whether I am alone or in company, I keep thinking of you, often I talk to you. Besides, so many divergent thoughts about you occupy my heart—I cannot write about them as they have no definite form. I hope I have been able to answer your query. You have not only entered my heart without permission but also show signs of conquering it in future—there is no doubt about it.

Pramatha Chaudhuri's forceful personality certainly influenced Indira but she also had the gift of the gab. Whatever the topic—

articles, music, criticism or reminiscences—her subtle personality has left its indelible mark on all of them.

Indira's achievements amazes us by their sheer vastness. Yet in our own interest we have to delve into the realms of reminiscences and oblivion to rediscover the fields in which she ensconced herself. It is not that she wrote a few books or prepared scores for music, her contribution in enriching the Bengali literature and music is almost unparalleled. Indira is one of the few Bengali writers who were able to write thought-provoking articles. It is surprising that Indira never tried her hand at short stories or novels, unlike her aunt Swarnakumari, in spite of both having magical pens. Her forte was articles, thoughts on music, reminiscences and translation. Her genius has been immortalized in these four branches of literature.

Translation is a difficult task. An unknown language may be translated into a known one but it is well-nigh impossible to infuse life into it. According to the poet Tagore 'translation is akin to a dead calf'. Indira was able to bring the 'dead calf' to life. She translated numerous poems of Rabindranath. The poet himself acknowledged that he had full confidence in Indira's translation. He wrote: 'All your translations are excellent. I have just shown them to Apurba. He claims these to be the best he has ever seen.' (6 January 1929). We also find the poet keen to entrust Indira with the task of translating 'Japan Jatri'.

When did Indira begin to translate? In 1885-86 (Bengali 1292) Jnanadanandini published an excerpt from Ruskin in *Balak* inviting a competition in translation. In the *Paush* issue (15 December–15 January), Jogendranath Laha received the prize. One more translation was also published along with that by Laha. The translator's name was given as 'Miss I'. The editor mentioned that it was by a young girl. 'Miss I' was undoubtedly Indira. Since then began Indira's attempts at concealing her identity. Let alone collecting all her articles from various magazines and publishing them in a concise volume, no list has still been made of all her writings.

Recently Rabindra Bhaban, Viswa Bharati, published the manuscript of her reminiscences as well as a collection of her published books based on her reminiscences, in three volumes under the title *Smriti Sampati*.

Apart from Rabindranath's works, Indira also translated Pramatha Chaudhuri's *Chaar Yarir Katha*. The work entitled *Tales of Four Friends* is notable. She also translated the Maharshi's autobiography—*The Autobiography of Maharshi Debendranath Tagore*—jointly with her father Satyendranath. These were from Bengali to English. Indira showed remarkable talent in her translations from French to Bengali. Pramatha Chaudhuri's companionship had further sharpened her abilities. Her four most remarkable translations are *Bharatbarsha* by Rene Grusse, *Kamal Kumarikashram* by Pierre Loti, *Bharat Bhraman Kahini* (Colombo to Shantiniketan) by Madame Levi and *Preface to the French Version of Geetanjali* by Andre Gide.

When did Indira first fall in love? She has narrated an amusing incident in her reminiscences *Jeevan Katha*, written towards the end of her life. She coaxed Rabindranath to take her and her brothers to Hazaribagh once. At that time it was customary for girls to fall in love with a nun from their convent school. Indira writes: 'This was probably a rehearsal for the future.' Her beloved was Sister Alaicee. This nun had been transferred to the convent in Hazaribagh and hence this trip by Indira.

Since love is being considered, it may be worthwhile to mention another episode in Indira's life. According to Purnima Tagore's biography of Indira, when she used to go to school a young man would wait daily in the park opposite their gate. They never spoke to each other but this gave rise to considerable amusement in the family. This was the basis of Rabindranath's song *Sakhi pratidin hai eshe phirey jay ke* (My friend, who is it that comes and goes back everyday). Though the girls of the Tagore family went out and also acted in plays, they never spoke to young men who were not related to them. This was noticed by Jasimuddin when he became intimate with the men of the Tagore family.

Indira and this silent admirer of hers met suddenly many years later, when both were above eighty. The gentleman had come to Rabindra Sadan in Shantiniketan to appeal for a job for his son. Truth is certainly stranger than fiction. This sounds like an incident from the pages of a novel. Many years had lapsed but the meeting proved awkward for both. Perhaps both were thinking of times gone by. Indira barely managed to go through the necessary formalities and left the room.

Indira had no dearth of suitors. Among them were Pramatha Chaudhuri and his elder brother Jogesh Chaudhuri. Indira fell in love with Pramatha as is evident from her letters to him before the marriage. There were quite a few obstacles to Pramatha and Indira's marriage but none of them prevailed. Pramatha proposed and Indira accepted. There was no objection from the Tagore family. The Maharshi was delighted.

Prasannamoyee writes in her *Purbakatha*: 'At the time of my brother's marriage into the Tagore family no new movement for ostracisation took place. My sensible aunts gladly acquiesced and their happiness knew no bounds when they saw the beautiful and accomplished bride. The advent of the bride has proved beneficial for the family in every way.'

This was written at the time of Ashutosh's marriage with Protiva, who faced no objections. Pramatha and Indira however had to face many hurdles though they overcame all of them. Since Indira's wedding had created some unpleasantness in Pramatha's family, and after the wedding she and Pramatha went to stay with his younger sister Mrinalini instead of with Pramatha's mother. Later, they shifted to their own house *Kamalalaya*. The saga thereafter is one of continuous effort and achievement.

Indira, who was one of the leaders of women's liberation in Bengal, did not have to face obstacles at every step as did her mother. Thus she had the opportunity to cogitate impartially about the overall role of women—comprising of education, liberty, licence, self-protection, working life, various conveniences and the lack thereof. Neither Jnanadanandini nor Kadambari or any other woman had had this chance. It is often difficult to separate the chaff from the grain and decide on the pros and cons of any matter until the initial excitement subsides. Just as the 'Young Bengal group' had to participate in some senseless acts just to go against superstition, the women of the early times had to show the same courage. There was a crying need for some self-sacrifice. Kadambari's horse-riding, Jnanadanandini's trip alone to England, Kadambini's study of medicine, education of Sarala Roy and Abala Basu, Chandramukhi's MA degree, coming out of the purdah to join openly in the prayers of the Brahmosamaj, use of shoes and Western dress while going out in the open coaches were all done to set examples before other women. These were absolutely necessary to break the age-old fetters of restrictions that shackled the mind and hearts of women. Indira belonged to the next generation. She was against both old conservation and blatant modernism. In every sphere of life, she was opposed to extremism and believed in following the middle path. Her own opinion:

> The women of today have to blend their courage with the patience and fortitude of the older generation. Alternatively today's intelligence has to be combined with the grace and gentleness of the older times. What Bankimbabu would say—a blending of the sharp with the tender. This successful intermingling is the mainstay of a woman's life.

Indira's style of writing was always direct and transparent; as her uncle, Rabindranath, said, 'bright and beautiful'. Even after reading her essays on non-fictional matters, he was unable to realize that this 'style' was Indira's own. The reason is not far to seek. Even today, men are presumed to be masters of non-fiction. Whatever the advances made by women, it is from the pen of men that the pearls of deep thought and incisive introspection have come. There is no point in denying this. Since this is true of world literature it is naturally the same in Bengali. However ours is a strange country where the term 'impossible' ceases to exist at times. Thus it is that men at times have been amazed by evidence of rare diplomacy from those behind the purdah. Similarly some women have shown such excellence in the field of introspection that they have been awarded the highest seat unquestionably. Indira was one of these rare ones. Her *Narir Mukti*, which comprises six essays on women's problems, is the best example of non-fictional writing in Bengali literature.

When Indira sat down to write her memoirs, she blended the art of storytelling into it. Her superb memory helped her to record many songs composed by Rabindranath in his early days. But for her, the tunes of many such songs would have been lost. She has detailed her reminiscences about Rabindranath's music, literature, plays, travels and family. This gives us a glimpse of Rabindranath's early life. When writing her memoirs, Indira always followed a particular code. She saw to it that when she wrote about someone, his true personality, as he was in his personal life, came through. She called this collection of small personalities her 'reverent bouquet of small flowers'. Her *Jeebankatha* reads more like a fairy tale or fable. It is mainly about herself, beginning with her birth and ending with the birth of Supriyo, her elder brother Surendranath's grandson. This book provides us with many anecdotes about both the Tagore and the Chaudhuri families.

A few excerpts along with Indira's summing-up illustrates this:

> My father's sisters, though born into rich families, were stingy whereas the daughters-in-law of that generation, though from poor families, never scrimped on spending. How does one explain such behaviour? To me the reason appears psychological. In our country, a woman's position is ascertained by her husband's wealth and social status. Since they along with their husbands were dependent on others, my *pishimas* (father's sisters) tried to count every penny. The women who came into the family as brides, mainly from Jessore, were generous and warm-hearted. They enjoyed entertaining and

acting as lady-bountiful. I remember though one aunt-by-marriage counting the stems of betel leaves to keep track of their number while one *pishima* would count the pieces of turmeric while giving out the daily stores. So the behavior of the two sisters-in-law cancelled each other out.

Jeebankatha has a number of amusing anecdotes too. While writing about her uncle Janakinath Ghosal, Indira says: 'His claim for being a good housewife is supported by the fact that while in England he used a quinine tablet to cook *suktuni* [a typical Bengali dish with a bitter taste] since the usual spices were not available.'

The anecdote about another uncle Jadunath (Kamal) Mukhopadhyaya is also hilarious. His elder brother Neelkamal Mukherjee had married into the family of Girindranath, the Maharshi's third brother. Girindranath's family lived in house number 5 while the Maharshi's family lived in house number 6. Therefore Jadunath, from his childhood, had had unrestricted entry in the Maharshi's house. 'Even after her marriage, my aunt would call him by name: Jadu. Hearing this *Karta Didima* (the Maharshi's wife) scolded her, saying, "Why do you call Jadu by name? Is Jadu your gardener?"'

Jadunath's daughter Suprobha was very witty with an excellent sense of humour. Indira has brought her to life with a few strokes of her pen. 'My cousin had a snub nose. Whenever her husband's taste clashed with her own, Suprobhadi would silence him by saying, "Don't talk about your taste. You chose me inspite of my snub nose!"'

Indira's comments about her own acting: 'Only once I played the role of Lakshmi in *Balmiki Protiva*. In one scene I was supposed to place my hand on my heart and say, "Do glance at me at this auspicious hour." My cousin Abhi always said, "Boudidi, your expression makes me feel that you have a stomachache."'

Thus Indira has preserved many a portrait of the andar mahal for us.

It is difficult to assess Indira's contribution in the field of Rabindra Sangeet. Her cousin Protiva opened the doors to the world of music for women while Indira helped recover the all-but-forgotten early compositions of Rabindranath. Abhignya, her cousin, had begun to give new dimensions to Rabindra Sangeet but was unable to leave any permanent stamp due to her untimely death. This is where Indira stepped in. From her childhood she had been tutored in Indian and European music, including instrumental. She took lessons in piano from Mr Slater, the organist of St. Paul's and in violin from Signor Manzato. She learnt classical Indian music under the guidance of Badridas Shukul. Hemendra's daughters were tutored in various branches of music but, except for Abhignya, none had delved much into Rabindra Sangeet. Thus the main burden was shouldered by Indira though all her cousins could sing Rabindra Sangeet. She would often comment humorously, 'Whenever I look back upon my life it appears like a desert of musical scores where the *ref* and *hasanta* appear as occasional thorny shrubs.'

It is well-nigh impossible to keep track of the musical scores made by Indira for songs. She preserved the tunes and notations by recovering the notations and teaching Rabindra Sangeet. Her articles on music helped enrich the context of these songs. One such booklet is *Rabindra Sangeete Tribeni Sangam*. In this work, Indira has shown how Rabindranath composed numerous new songs by setting his words to tunes composed by others. Moreover there are also examples of his setting creations by others to his own music. Compiling a list of such *Bhanga Gaan*, she has shown the tremendous achievement of Rabindranath with just a few alterations. This book is an invaluable addition to literature on music. Discussions on Rabindra Sangeet are numerous. Though the number of female critics is negligible, that of men is considerable. But none has gone into such details as Indira. For many, Indira's views have been the spring-board of their discourses. And why not? Rabindranath himself has left a blessing for her.

Amar e gaan jeno sudeergho jeeban
Tomar basan hoy, tomar bhusan.

Let my music be your
Attire and ornament all though
your long life.

From the details given by Indira we learn that out of 227 *bhanga gaan* (broken songs) of Tagore, the tunes of twelve are from Scottish and Irish tunes. The contribution of north Indian vocal music to Rabindra Sangeet is considerable. It amazes us to learn that the origin of the well-known song *Bidaye korechho jare nayan jaley* is 'Baaje jhanana morey payaliya', that of *Tumi kichu diye jao* is 'Koi kachhu kahare' or *Shunya hate phire hay nath* is 'Rumjhum barase'. There are examples of Tagore setting the words of other poets to music. Apart from the slokas by Vidyapati and the first stanza of Bankimchandra's 'Vande mataram' Tagore had provided the tunes for songs by Akshay Boral, Sukumar Ray and Hemlata Tagore.

Indira wrote innumerable articles on Rabindra Sangeet. She discussed its various aspects in a number of magazines. Notable among these are '*Sangeeter Rabindranath*,' '*Rabindra Sangeeter Shiksha*', '*Rabindra Sangeeter Baisishtya*', '*Rabindranather Sangeet Provat*', '*Swaralipi Padhati*' '*Shantiniketane Shishuder Sangeet Shiksha*', '*Harmony or Swar Sanjog*', '*Rabindra Sangeete Taaner Sthan*', '*Rabindranather Gaan*', '*Bisuddha Rabindra Sangeet*', '*Hindi Sangeet*', '*Amader Gaan*', '*Swaralipi*', '*The music of Rabindranath Tagore*'. All these bear testimony to the depth of Indira's thought and her command over music.

It is not possible to judge Indira only by the position she achieved. All her life she was associated with a number of women's organizations. For some time she also accepted the Vice-Chancellorship of Vishwa Bharati. Three universities honoured her with their highest awards—*Bhubanmohini Swarnapadak* from Calcutta University, *Deshikattam* from Vishwa Bharati and the first award announced by the Rabindrabharati Samiti.

Indira's near and dear ones knew how small these awards were when compared to her real achievements.

Herein lay the unique feature of Indira's personality. She had the rare quality of transcending emptiness not by doing anything actively but just by her very presence. When asked for blessings, she often penned short poems. Most have been lost. Only a few survive in the memories of some. She once wrote to Suchitra Mitra:

Ananda bilao tumi
Na kori karpanya,
Sudhukonthe sudhageet
Shune hoyi dhaya.
Mantramugdha srotribrinda
Kori nibedan—
Barey barey esho phire
Shantiniketan.

'You dispense happiness unstinted,
The songs from your beautiful voice charm us.
We, your enchanted audience, request you
Come back again and again to Shantiniketan.'

On the death of Surabhi, the five-year-old daughter of Pragya, she wrote:

Surabhi chhilo tomar nam
Tayi bujhi phuler matan
Sourav koriya bitaran
Dudine tyajile martyadham.
Shey sourav chiro din raat
Rohilo moder ghare
Tumi thako debatar torey
Amor amol parijat.

'You were named Surabhi,
Is that why like a flower
You left fragrance for a short while?
The fragrance lives in our home,
While you remain for the gods
The immortal parijat blossom.'

It was Indira who nurtured Rabindranath's ideals in Shantiniketan for twenty years after his death. There were others, but they were just helpmates, Indira alone was the prop and mainstay.

Indira's personality, which shone like a diamond, is what may be termed 'culture'. The influence of this charming culture pervaded every facet of her life, her toilette, conversation, aesthetics, love-letters, literature, home-management, *Sabujpatra, Kamalalaya* or the Ashram Cottage of Shantiniketan. This is her greatest contribution to society. For the Bengali, her life, which was a perfect blend of Indian and European education, was ideal. In her was personified the best of the unique culture of the Tagore family.

Let us return to Hemendranath's daughters. Protiva and Pragya had six other talented sisters. Their third sister Abhignya has been immortalized in numerous reminiscences. Comparatively few outsiders had a chance to meet her, but those who did, never forgot her. She was Rabindranath's favourite niece. She charmed even Rabindranath when she sang songs composed by him. While in Selaidaha, the poet often yearned to hear her sing. This is evident in his letters to Indira: 'I felt such a craving for Abhi's sweet songs. I then realized that among the many yearnings of my nature this had also been in the subconscious.'

What magic lay in Abhignya's voice? There is no one today to describe the indefinable beauty of this girl's voice, snatched away by untimely death. It has been heard that Rabindranath's earliest songs seemed personified when Abhignya sang them. Her rendering of Hindustani songs was equally poignant. Pramatha Chaudhuri was spellbound when he heard her sing *Thari raho mere aankhon aagay* in raag Chhayanat. This was the golden era of the Tagore family. Wrapped up in his joy of creation, Rabindranath was composing musical plays like *Balmiki Protiva*, *Kaal-Mrigaya*, *Mayar Khela*, one after the other.

Similarly Abhignya was bringing them to life with her tireless and melodious voice.

Abhignya had no equal in singing tragic songs. After *Balmiki Protiva* the poet composed *Kaal-Mrigaya*. In the cold and foggy evening of 23 December 1882, guests came again to Vidyatjan Sabha to view the performance of *Kaal-Mrigaya*. Protiva had made her maiden appearance on stage in *Balmiki Protiva*. This time it was Abhignya's turn. Her portrayal of Leela brought tears to the eyes of most of the audience. Rabindranath played the role of the blind Muni and Jyotirindranath that of King Dasarath but Abhignya's acting touched the heart much more than that of both her uncles. The critic of *Bharatbandhu* commented, 'Leela's songs were capable of melting even a heart of stone.'

Abhignya's matchless songs were again heard during the later performances of *Balmiki Protiva*. When she sang, 'Oh! What misfortune has befallen me' [*Haye, eki dasha holo amar*], according to Abanindranath's eye-witness account, 'The Bengali audience burst into tears.' Shortly after, Rabindranath composed *Mayar Khela*. By this time, Abhignya had grown older and her melodious voice had matured, with nuances of love and sympathy. The perfect blend of words and melodies in *Mayar Khela* gained life and beauty through Abhignya's voice. According to Indira and her husband Pramathanath, 'Abhignya could sing all the songs of *Balmiki Protiva* or *Mayar Khela* at one sitting. It was Pramathanath's opinion that he had never heard anyone else sing the lyrics of *Balmiki Protiva* with so much pathos as Abhignya. Much later Abanindranath, now an old man, on hearing the songs of *Mayar Khela*, wailed, 'The one who could sing these songs is no more. That little cousin with her bird-like voice has gone for ever . . . The bird that used to sing these melodies is dead.' Rathindranath writes about the evening-gatherings at Jorasanko. Jyotirindranath and Rabindranath attended regularly. The whole house was steeped in music. The literary nature of the sittings had made way for the musical. To quote Rathindranath, 'Strains of music could always be heard from every nook and corner of the house. Baba sang often. . . at times he requested the didis to sing. Avididi, the daughter of Shejojethamoshai, had the sweetest voice. Baba had great hopes of her becoming a renowned singer. Unfortunately, Baba's hopes were all dashed when Avididi died young.' The memory of Abhignya has thus never been relegated to the dark archives of the past. Whosoever heard her sing has always remembered her.

Abhignya usually played the role of Shanta in *Mayar Khela*. The melancholy character of Shanta was brought to life by Abhignya's voice, tinged with compassion and sweetness. Much later, in a performance at Birjitalao, Indira played the role of Shanta as the original actress had passed on. Abhignya's voice was quiet and solemn, touched with pathos and a hint of tears. To quote once again, 'She was an ethereal being, her face overshadowed by a pair of large eyes enlivened by sweetness and grace.'

Some cruel hunter's arrow seems to have pierced this loving heart. No one had any inkling of the fatal illness that had invaded this frail creature. On her wedding night, catastrophe struck. Just as the ceremony was completed, she came down with a high temperature. It showed no signs of abating. She was diagnosed to be in the last stages of virulent consumption, beyond medical help. Abhignya wasted away like the waning moon. She died in the Jorasanko house of the Tagores, giving her doctor-husband no opportunity to treat her or be able to cure her.

Abhignya's death dealt the greatest blow to Rabindra Sangeet. Had a talented songstress been available in those early days of experimentation, Rabindranath would have been able to establish Rabindra Sangeet even more firmly. This was not to be. Thus Bengal lost one of her jewels when this blossom faded away before reaching full bloom. After Abhignya's death, Rabindranath composed four sonnets: '*Nadiyatra*', '*Mrityumadhuri*', '*Smriti*' and '*Bilaya*'. He seemed to remember anew Abhigya with her beautiful deathless eyes and sweet voice of the birds at dawn:

Ankhi tar kahe jeno mor mukhe chahi
Aaj pratey shob pakhi udiyachhe gahi—
Sudhu mor konthoswar e prabhatbaye
Ananta jagat majhe giyechhe haraye.

Her eyes seem to glance at me and say
All the birds have risen singing this morning
Only my voice this dawn has lost itself
In the eternal universe.

Jagadish Bhattacharya, the author of *Kabi Manashi*, is of the opinion that these four sonnets are replete with memories of the poet's *Natun Bouthan*. This is difficult to accept. The diary of Kshitimohan Sen, in which he took down the discourse on the poem '*Chaitali*', mentions Rabindranath referring to these sonnets with the comment: 'These were written after the death of my niece Abhi'. Another person who was ecstatic in his praise of Abhignya after her death was Pramatha Chaudhuri. Normally he was not given to sentimentality. He considered Abhignya akin to Shakespeare's Ariel, i.e. an ethereal being. To him, Abhignya was an enigma and this girl of twelve or thirteen left a permanent impact on him. He said, 'Some people impress us so in the first meeting that the feeling is permanent. Abhi was one such rare being. The English say that those whom the gods love die young. Abhi was such a girl dear to heaven, because she never became a woman.'

Time waits for no one. Manisha, Abhi's younger sister, was also growing up. Her elder sister Abhi was an expert in Rabindra Sangeet, but Manisha chose European instrumental music. Like their eldest sister Protiva, she became an expert in piano and Western vocal music. Later she concentrated more on the piano and rose to be one of the best pianists of the country. Like her other sisters, she was also educated in Loreto along with ceaseless practise of music at home. The girls of the Tagore family appeared for the examinations conducted in Calcutta by the Trinity College of Music, Cambridge. Their success was also published in the local papers. Manisha always acquitted herself with great credit. She however had no inclination towards Indian music. Protiva used to sing Western classical songs and play classical music on the piano, but later she had turned to Indian classical musical, especially vocal music. Manisha however confined herself to the piano all her life. She did compose piano accompaniments to Rabindranath's *Padaprantey raakho sebakey* and a few others songs, but they never became popular. Similar was the fate of her piano accompaniment of *Tamishivaranang* from the Vedas. Thus Manisha remained practically unknown in the Bengali musical soirees. Moreover though learning the piano became quite a fashion among Bengalis—in an imitation of the West—the piano never found a place in most Bengali homes. Even in this era of popular Western instruments, the piano is confined to the drawing rooms of only a few rich families. This is mainly due to its large size and exorbitant price. Similar instruments like the piano-accordion and guitar have supplanted it. So pianists are still not well-known in ordinary society. Manisha's talent received its due acclaim abroad.

After Abhignya's death, her husband Debendranath Chattopadhyay married Manisha. He had tried his level best to cure Abhignya but it all proved to be in vain and she passed away. In the meanwhile her elder brothers had become very fond of the upright and broadminded young man. They proposed that Manisha should be married to Debendra. This would ensure his place as a family member and also compensate for the loss of their dear Abhignya. There was no objection from any side but a slight hitch arose. The Maharshi would give Rs 3000 as dowry to each granddaughter. The money was usually given to the bridegroom. This time he refused to give the sum to Debendra again. Probably he was testing Debendra's sincerity. Manisha's brothers—Hitendra, Kshitindra and Ritendra—were most embarrassed. They requested Debendra to agree to the marriage, promising to arrange for this sum later. Debendra had not even demanded dowry, so the wedding took place without any hitch. This so pleased the Maharshi that he gifted the money willingly. These facts are recorded in Kshitindranath's unpublished diary '*Maharshi Paribarey*'.

Manisha went abroad with her husband. Europeans were charmed by her flawless rendering of English notations on the piano. She also surprised them by the ease with which she could play Indian classical music in all its moods on the piano. Among those who formed her audience was the great Max Mueller. His letter to Manisha, full of praise, is still preserved in the Rabindra Bharati museum—a silent witness to Manisha's superb skill. This letter informs us that Manisha captivated the Western world not only with Western music but with her rendering of Indian, especially Hindustani, classical music.

Manisha was also in contact with the musical world in her own country. Just as Protiva and Indira were the life-blood of Sangeet Sangha, Manisha was intimately connected with Sangeet Sanmilani. Pramada and Manisha were great friends. Pramada's husband, Banoarilal Chaudhuri, was also a close friend of Manisha's husband. From Pramada's reminiscences we learn that, like Ananda Sabha, Sangeet Sanmilani was also a club to begin with. It was due to the interest and encouragement of its members that the Sangeet Sanmilani became a school of music. Pramada was in-charge but Manisha was also an active member. She often participated in the various programmes of dance and music, usually playing the piano or the violin. She wrote well but rarely. The old files of *Tattwabodhini Patrika* give us glimpses of Manisha's literary works. Apart from some essays she also wrote a play for children. Unfortunately, she did not preserve it. The language of her memoirs, written after Pramada's, death is lucid. She writes:

> It is impossible to write about Pramada and not mention Sangeet Sanmilani. My memory is not what it used to be.

> About forty years ago a few of us established a club. Our main aim was cultivation of music. My husband, Dr D.N. Chatterjee, Dr B.L. Chaudhuri and my brother Kshitindranath Tagore encouraged and helped us. The club would not have prospered without their help. Later we opened a school.
>
> When I moved to Shillong, my active participation came to an end though I used to advise them regularly through letters. At times Pramada thought of resigning from the Sanmilani but we never allowed her to do so. The Sanmilani had become a part and parcel of her. She was childless, but she treated all the young members as her own. She was addressed as Mithadidi, Mithapishi or Jethima by them. They were all near and dear to her. She was adept at proposing and arranging marriages.

Along with her literary activities, Manisha also tried to teach needlework through the pages of *Punya*. In those days beadwork curtains were a sign of aristocracy. This fashion was followed in the Tagore family also. Manisha tried to teach beadwork through graphic charts and drawings. Hemendranath's other daughters were also talented. The women of the Tagore family exemplified the building of a new social order by blending the old with the new. This was the reason behind their lasting influence on Bengali women. Lillian Palit, Ramola Sinha, Rani Nirupama, Suniti Devi, Sucharu Devi, Mrinalini Sen and many others had ushered in waves of new ideas into aristocratic society but they were unable to leave any impact on our society. This was because they appeared like figures on the distant horizon. Far greater had been the influence of Sarala Ray, Abala Basu, Kumudini Khastagir, Kadambini Ganguly and Chandramukhi Basu. Scores of girls were inspired by them and surged forward in the field of education. The girls of the Tagore family can also be cited with them.

Hemendranath's fifth daughter Shobhanasundari was always more interested in academics than music. While she was growing up, the tide of musical eminence of the Tagore family had begun to ebb. Her elder sisters were busy with music, painting and culinary arts. Perhaps her younger ones felt the same way. Yet Shobhana began to dream about writing like her paternal aunt Swarnakumari. The spontaneity and grace of those tales fascinated her. Meanwhile her studies in English progressed. Suddenly she was married to Nagendranath Mukhopadhyaya—a professor of English in faraway Jaipur. Nagendranath's family hailed from Howrah. There were four brothers. The title of Raybahadur had been conferred upon the eldest. Nagendra was the second. His third brother Jogendranath was later married to Shobhana's seventh sister Sushama. After her marriage Shobhana went to Jaipur. This seems to have been a blessing in disguise. In Calcutta women's emancipation was in full bloom. Durgamohan Das's daughters had also devoted themselves to social welfare. Sarala founded the Gokhale Memmorial College, Abala the Brahmo Balika Shikshalaya. The women of the Tagore family were the centre of attraction in society. Along with Protiva, Pragya and Indira, were Sarala and Hironmoyee. Besides Maharani Suniti, Monica and Sucharusundari came Hemlata, Priyamvada and many others. Among such a galaxy, Shobhana probably would not have dared to venture into new fields. She collected the choicest blooms from the deserts of Rajputana and her writing abilities blossomed amid new surroundings. Her material was from things strewn all around, yet unnoticed by anyone.

Shobhana was encouraged by her doting husband. Nagendranath also had a poetic bent of mind. He composed *Yakshangana Kavya* on the same lines as Michael Madhusudan Dutt. Many of his other compositions still exist as manuscripts, e.g. *Krishna*, *Menakanandini Kavya*, *Swargoddhar Kavya* and a collection of stories called *Sonar Dhaew*. But Shobhana's achievements far surpassed these. Rather than try her hand at novels like Swarnakumari did, she pondered on the possibilities of collecting folk tales and fairy tales which were slowly going into oblivion. Since she had never had contact with rural Bengal, she concentrated on Jaipur for her work. Thus a new vista opened up for Shobhana. On the pages of the *Punya* magazine appeared tales like '*Phoolchand*', '*Daalim Kumari*', '*Gangadev*', '*Luddhabonik Tejaram*', '*Dilip O Bhimraj*' and '*Lakkhya Takar Ek Katha*'. All these were based on legends from Jaipur. At first it appeared that, like Swarnakumari, Shobhana may have chosen *Tales from Rajasthan* by Todd as her source. This was not true. She had started collecting legends and folktales. Later, she also collected Jaipuri proverbs or Kahabats. She began researching on art and literature too. Her choice of topics based on folklore proved to be excellent. Considering the times, her interest certainly was a novel one. No lady until then had thought of collecting folktales, though Mrinalini had begun compiling fairy tales on the request of her husband Rabindranath. Treading the path of Jaipuri folk tales, Shobhana reached the world of ancient Indian fables and literature. The women of the Tagore family had taken the lead in many fields and Shobhana was not one to lag behind.

Along with Jaipuri folk tales Shobhana had begun compiling *kahabats*. In 1900-01 many people had become interested in this field. Reverend Lang and a few others had begun collecting Bengali proverbs. Shobhana, however, was the first to compile proverbs from a different province. She brought novelty into the topic by not only deciphering the meaning of these proverbs and translating them but also searched for similar ones in Bengali. The beliefs, satirical tendencies and reverence of the people of Jaipur and Rajasthan as well as some local peculiarities have been captured in these *kahabats*. Even today, almost a century after Shobhana's work, the number of such collections is insignificant. We may consider some typical examples:

Original	:	*Kaal ki jayori gadheri, parso ki geet gaawe.*
Translation	:	The donkey was born yesterday, but is singing day before yesterday's song.

Meaning	:	A donkey begins to bray immediately after birth—this is an inauspicious sign and is due to a reflection from its previous birth.
Bengali parallel proverb	:	*Rashbhabinindito swar* A voice which puts even a donkey's braying to shame.
Original	:	*Jaipur ki kamai bhaara balita khai.*
Translation	:	The income of Jaipur is spent on rent and cowdung cakes.
Meaning	:	In Jaipur, both house-rent and the price of firewood are exorbitant.
Original	:	*Sheetala kunsa ghora de, aap hi gadha charey.*
Translation	:	Sheetala herself rides an ass, how can she provide a horse?
Meaning	:	One who does not possess something himself, how can he/she give it to someone else?

Apart from its folklore, fairy tales and proverbs, Jaipur's local crafts also interested Shobhana. 'Domla Craft', which is the art of making daily household articles like utensils and containers as well as dolls using recycled paper, was taught by Shobhana to the readers of *Punya*. However all these activities were only preludes to her real achievement. Turning away from Bengali, she now began to write in English, stories from the *Vedas*, *Puranas*, ancient historical myths and folk tales. Shobhana was doubtful about her literary abilities and preferred translations to creative writing. Her first attempt was to translate Swarnakumari's popular novel *Kahake*. She named it *To whom*. It was not much of a success, since a translator hardly has any freedom of expression. When Swarnakumari herself translated *Kahake* as *An Unfinished Song* it was hailed as a new novel. Simultaneously, Shobhana began translating ancient Indian tales. Four such books were published by Macmillan Company of London.

The first one, *Indian Nature Myths*, written for children, was not a dry collection of rhetoric but appealed to one and all. Shobhana collected fifty tales from the *Ramayana*, *Mahabharata*, Puranas, Vedas, Upanishads and folk tales to write *Indian Nature Myths*. Most of these were based on stories of evolution as, for example, 'The origin of Tulsi Plant', 'The origin of Death', 'The origin of Volcano', 'The origin of Tobacco Plant', and so on. *Indian Fables and Folklore* is also written on the same lines. There are twen-tynine stories in all and they have been collected by Shobhana from epics, Puranas, *Kathasaritsagar, Panchatantra* and *Bhaktamaal*. Among these 'Mirage Bridegroom' (*Bhaktamaal*), A Rat Swayambar (*Panchatantra*), 'Eklabya and Drona' (*Mahabharata*) and 'Cow of Plenty' (*Ramayana*) must have astonished foreign readers. In almost every story Shobhana has been able to blend wonder with delight.

Shobhana's literary pursuit, which began with the collection of Jaipuri folktales, continues in *The Orient Pearls*, a collection of fairy tales. She has shown remarkable talent in collecting stories from ancient history, Puranas and folk tales in all these four books. Still there is a world of difference between translating anecdotes from Sanskrit literature and collecting fables and fairy tales prevalent in the villages of Bengal. She collected the latter from a blind servant of theirs. Had she published these in Bengali, it would have enriched Bengali literature enormously. Shobhana chose to write in English which was quite natural for her. At that time many women of aristocratic modern families had begun to write in English. Women educated in convents or brought up by English governesses naturally became anglicized in their ways. Taraknath Palit's daughter Lillian, Lord Sinha's daughter Ramola and the three Coochbehar princesses—Sukriti, Protiva and Sudhira—were more foreign than Indian in their lifestyle. Had they decided to write, they would certainly have done so in English. Similar was the case with Hemendranath's eight daughters and Indira. Again both Toru Dutt and Sarojini Naidu composed poems in English.

Sarojini, though Shobhana's contemporary, was much better known, especially for her unforgettable role in politics. Her three collections of poems, *The Golden Threshold*, *The Bird of Time* and *The Broken Wing*, were very popular. *The Golden Threshold* was reprinted seven or eight times between 1905 and 1920. Shobhana never reached such heights of fame, perhaps she lacked such genius. Still, her contribution is not negligible. *The Orient Pearls* ranks fairly high among the fables and fairy tales published upto 1925. Shobhana led the way among Bengali women in this field. Eight years later *Indian Fairytales* by Maharani Suniti Devi was published from London.

A glance at the names of collectors of folk- and fairy tales who preceded Shobhana shows the list was relatively short. It includes: Lalbehari De—*Folk tales of Bengal* (1883), Ramsatya Mukhopadhyaya—*Indian Folklore* (1904), Kashinath Bandopadhyaya—*Popular Tales of Bengal* (1905), Srishchandra Basu—*Folk Tales of Hindustan* (1907), Dakshinaranjan Mitra Majumdar—*Thakurmar Jhuli* (1907), Upendrakishore Roy Chaudhuri—*Tuntunir Boi* (1910), and Mac Kulak—*Bengali Household Tales* (1912). Shobhana's *The Orient Pearls* (1915) came just after.

There are twenty-eight fairy tales in Shobhana's book. Each one commences with 'Once upon a time' in the typical fairy-tale style. Some of the tales are fairly well-known, though quite a few are rare. The most fascinating seem to be 'The Wax Prince', 'The Golden Parrot', 'The Hermit Cat', 'A Nose for Nose', 'Uncle Tiger' and 'The Bride of the Sword'. Since there has always been an invisible link among fairy tales the world over, the contents of Shobhana's book may not appear unfamiliar to foreigners too.

The *Tales of the Gods of India*, though relatively less known, is novel in its portrayal of the loves and lives of gods. Recently, several such books about immortal love-stories from the epics and Puranas have been published under the title 'Prem Katha', e.g. *Bharat Prem Katha*, *Ramayani Prem Katha*, *Saswat Prem Katha*, and *Purana Prem Katha*. The authors of these are perhaps unaware that long before them Shobhana searched for love stories from the *Ramayana*, *Mahabharata*, Vedas and Puranas. For her book on the gods and goddesses of India, Shobhana chose thirty stories. In her book she mentions clearly the source of these stories. Her choice of names is also superb. There are five stories from the Rig Veda—'*Dyu O Prithibi*', '*Yama O Yami*', '*Rivoo Bhratridyay O Usha*', '*Aswinikumardyoy O Surya*' and '*Bibaswan O Saranyu*'. Fourteen have been collected from the *Mahabhatata*. All of them are well-known: '*Pururaba O Urvashi*', '*Sambaran O Tapati*', '*Ruru O Pramdwara*', '*Som O Tara*', '*Vasishtha O Arundhati*', '*Indra O Sachi*', '*Savitri O Satyavan*', '*Vishnu O Lakshmi*', '*Shiva O Sati*', '*Madan O Rati*', '*Arjun O Ulupi*', '*Bhim O taanr Rakshashi Bodhu*', '*Balaram O Rebati*' and '*Damayanti O Taar Dev Paniprarthi*'. From the *Ramayana* we have '*Ram O Sitar Galpo*' and '*Agni O Swahar Galpo*'. *Satapatha Brahmin* is the source of '*Chyaban O Sukanya*' and '*Mitra, Barun O Asir Akhyan*'. From the works of Kalidasa Shobhana has taken '*Kumar Sambhav*', '*Avigyan Shakuntalam*' and '*Meghdooter Galpo*'. The story of 'Yama and Vijaya' is from *Bhavishyapuran* while '*Behula O Lakindarer Kahini*' is from *Manasamangal*. She has also mentioned categorically the few tales that recur in more than one epic. '*Vishnu O Lakshmi*' appears both in the *Mahabharata* and the *Vishnu Purana* while 'Shiva O Sati' is both in *Mahabharata* and *Bhagavata Purana*. Shobhana's selection of stories as well as the meticulous care with which she mentions the sources is commendable. In later years, as the book became rare, the demand for such tales went on rising.

Shobhana came back to Bengali literature in the last years of her life. This was after her return from Europe. Many of her travelogues—'*Europey Mahasamarer Porey*', '*Londoney*', '*Ranakshetre Banga Mahila*' and '*Mahajudhher Par Paris*

Nagaritey' were published in various magazines. Besides, she became engrossed with Howrah Girls School. The Tagore progeny were all keen on establishing schools and Shobhana was no exception. A considerable part of her life was spent as a teacher of English in Howrah Girls School; childess herself, she found fulfilment in this work. Even today a silver medal in her memory is awarded to the best student every year. She had also founded a music school: Bani Niketan. She herself sang well and was a piano player. Like her elder sister Manisha, she was keen on teaching girls to sing. Life appeared to be happy when fate dealt a cruel blow.

A stroke ended Shobhana's life. *Premanjali*, a collection of heart-wrenching tales, was published by her devoted and heart-broken husband Nagendranath. Rabindranath wrote a small poem '*Shobhana*' as the Preface. Even today a marble plaque, with this poem engraved on it, stands in the burning ghat of Shibpur in Howrah where the mortal remains of Shobhana were consigned to the flames. Tagore's later poem '*Sphulinga*' is a slight modification of this poem:

Asta rabir kirane taba jeeban shatadal
Mudilo tar ankhi
Marame jaha byapto chhilo snigdha parimal
Marane dilo dhaki
Loye gelo shey bidaykale moder ankhijal
Madhuri sudha sathe,
Nutanloke shobhonaroop jagibe ujjwal
Bimal nabaprate.

The lotus blossom of your life has closed its petals along with
the rays of the setting sun,
The gentle fragrance that permeated the heart has been
enveloped by death.
She has taken our tears along with the nectar
on her departure,
To reappear in the garb of a new Shobhana—bright and lustrous
on a new morn.

Between the two busy sisters Shobhanasundari and Sushamasundari appears Sunrita like a small pause. She was the least known among Hemendranath's daughters. Like Abhignya her life was snuffed out early. Avigyna, however, lived in the memories of her near and dear ones. Sunrita on the other hand was forgotten even by her relations. Had she lived long she may have proved her talent in some field of life. Hardly any information about her is available today. Her husband Nandalal Ghosal belonged to the well-known Ghosal family of Baruipur. Later they had to shift to Shyamnagar due to reverses of fortune. Distance and penury were responsible for the severance of her contacts with her parental home. Her twin babies died at birth. However Sunrita and Nandalal live in the pages of the *Punya* magazine. They were both of a literary bent and contributed regularly to *Punya*. It is not known whether they had had a chance to meet each other before marriage. Like Pragya, Sunrita was interested in various aspects of housekeeping, especially cooking. She tried to familiarize the readers of *Punya* with the recipes of various mouth-watering pickles and preserves. She used to regularly publish methods of preparing pickles using mangoes, plums and tamarind. She took her first faltering step into the literary world with an article 'Shulinath of Burma'. The Shulinath Shiva is not very well-known even in Burma. One wonders how Sunrita came to know about him. Her interest in old temples rather than Burmese pagodas indicates her growing love for temple architecture. However she was able to author only one article.

Sunrita's younger sister Sushama was always a rebel. While her elder sisters studied in Loreto Convent she was coached at home and later admitted to the Diocesan school. Even at that tender age she felt an urge to surge ahead, breaking all shackles. Though Hemendranath's family lived in their own part of the Jorasanko mansion, with very little contact with the rest of the clan, Sushama's dreams centered on travelling, be it in India or abroad. To quote her, 'From my childhood I had always been keen on travelling . . .' Considering marriage to be an impediment to her dreams she decided to rebel against it. The traditions of the Tagore family, as well as her mother's firmness, stopped sixteen-year-old Sushama in her tracks. Not only that, Sushama was married before Sunrita. The girls of the Tagore family were reasonably orthodox in their views on marriage. Lillian Palit, the first woman Ishan Scholar and Sushama's friend, created a furore by filing a suit for divorce against her husband, barrister Sisir Mullick. After her divorce, she married Deep Narain Singh, the zamindar of Bhagalpur. Keshab Sen's granddaughters, Protiva and Sudhira, the Coochbehar princesses, married John Mandar and Henry Mandar. This naturally caused a good deal of commotion in society. We also have Hariprabha Takeda. In 1907 she married Wayman Takeda of the Bulbul Soap Factory. When she accompanied her husband to Japan in 1912 ignoring the protests of all her relations, society was startled. Yet the eagerness with which Bengalis read Hariprabha's *Bangamahilar Japan Jatra* is unparalleled. In comparison, the girls of the Tagore family were much more conservative. There were hardly ever romantic preludes even to inter-community marriage. Sushama was married to Jogendranath Mukhopadhyay on 7 March 1900. She had just stood first in the piano examination held by Trinity College, Cambridge. The examination used to be held in Calcutta and even European examinees could not hold a candle to her. Sushama, however, had no wish to restrict herself within the confines of music, literature or culinary arts, the beaten tracks treaded by her sisters. Her desire was to tread the path of women's empowerment. She felt shackled by marriage, though there was never any question of restrictions imposed by Jogendranath. A barrister by profession, his heart lay elsewhere. He was a keen mathematician and his *Modern Arithmetic* was a popular school-text. Still, Sushama felt uneasy. To quote her, 'My restless nature hardly allowed me to be contented with a quiet and peaceful home life.' She eagerly sought a path to go ahead.

The constant perturbation left her sleepless while her heart was heavy with sorrow.

At last a way opened for Sushama. She came across a copy of *Uncle Tom's Cabin.* Tears wet her lashes as she perused the book. She found that the writer was a lady Harriet Beecher Stowe. Sushama began to wonder about this lady. What was her life like? Did she have a home and family? How did she manage to author such a book? Settling down to read Madame Stowe's biography, a great sense of peace engulfed Sushama. She felt that she had found her true vocation. If Madame Stowe could do it, why could not Sushama?

Sushama turned her mind to writing. To touch women's hearts she decided to provide some concrete examples rather than raise slogans like 'Women arise' or 'Women have to be awakened'. If she could uphold women who had become independent as visible examples, it would become easier for others to emulate them. Since Madame Stowe was the one who enabled Sushama to overcome her misgivings, she decided to write about her first. It was certainly a novel idea at that time. Before this, Bengalis had not evinced much interest in writing biographies of well-known women. Of course, there were very few such women then. It was not possible for the contemporaries of those we eulogize today to assess their achievements. However, some work had been done on devout and pious ladies. Sushama began with foreigners. She planned to write about foreign women in Bengali and then about their Indian counterparts in English. 'Harriet Beecher Stowe', 'Harriet Martino', 'Madame de Stael', 'The Life of the Swedish Singer Linden' appeared one after the other on the pages of *Punya.* Sushama's mission in collecting and writing these biographies was to prove women's ability in all walks of life—literary, social, political and artistic (music). Apart from rousing the Indian women, Sushama also took up her pen to silence those who said that women did not possess the intelligence to perform any and every job and that they could only rear children, that they were not capable of achieving anything by their own intellect and judgment. People who refused to see the obvious, had to be jolted into doing so.

These Bengali articles by Sushama were published in *Punya.* Her travelogues in Bengali were published in the *Tattwabodhini Patrika*. Her writings on a visit to Kashmir, the scenic beauty of the valley and the descriptions of the journey were overshadowed by the details of the lifestyles and general poverty of the Kashmiris. At about the same time, she commenced writing *Ideals of Hindu Womanhood* in English. She chose Sati, Seeta, Shaibya, Savitri, Damayanti and Shakuntala as the ideals of Indian women. She showed an orthodox viewpoint in her choice of these Indian women. She was drawn by the self-sacrifice and dignity of these women, whose lives were shining examples of tolerance, sacrifice and conjugal fidelity. She did not write about Draupadi.

In 1927, Sushama, a housewife and mother of seven, visited the USA to familiarize herself with their educational system and women's emancipation in the West. Thus she seemed to come out in her true colours. Fifty years earlier, Jnanadanandini had sailed to England alone. That voyage, though adventurous, could not be compared to the one undertaken by Sushama. The latter's trip was akin to a lecture-tour or to that of a conqueror. Mohinimohan Chattopadhyaya, Pratap Majumdar, Swami Vivekananda and Rabindranath had already left their mark in the USA. An Indian lady, Rama Bai, had also preceded Sushama. Yet America was ecstatic over the visit of the niece of the 'Hindu Poet and Philosopher' Rabindranath. American newspapers had always described Rabindranath as a poet and philosopher, adding the prefix 'Hindu' without fail. So 'Niece of Tagore' evoked great curiosity and enthusiasm in the hearts of everyone.

Why did Sushama go to the USA? Her elder sisters Manisha and Shobhana had only gone as tourists but Sushama was cast in a different mould. She was keen to fulfill her childhood dreams.

She had been preparing herself to work outside the home. It was when her children grew up that she found time to look beyond the four walls of her home. In 1922 she opened a small school Balika Shiksha Sangha for girls. After she started her school, Sushama realized how vast was the number of illiterates in India. Till then she had known only the educated society. It now dawned upon her that ninety-nine per cent Indian women were illiterate. Yet the number of educated women in contemporary Bengal was not negligible. The era of Chandramukhi and Kadambini was long past. Abala Das's trip to Madras to study medicine was also old news. Bidhumukhi Basu and Virginia Mitra had joined the Medical College in Calcutta. Virginia stood first among all the students in 1888. Tatini Gupta (Das) topped the list among all the combined candidates of the Intermediate Arts examination of Bengal, Bihar and Orissa; Lillian became an Ishaan Scholar and Saralabala Mitra, a Hindu widow, went to England on a scholarship to train as a teacher. Sarala played a decisive role in the political arena and courageous women like Pritilata Waddedar, Kalpana Dutt and Bina Das had begun to come to the forefront. Nanibala and Dukaribala suffered prison sentences and inhuman torture by the police in the service of the motherland. Such feats were enough to dazzle anyone. Sushama's elder sisters were all well educated. Thus Sushama had no inkling about the vast numbers of illiterate girls, before she established her school. Apart from her school, Sushama also became deeply involved with the Women's Educational Society of India. As president of this society, she had the opportunity to ponder more upon the problems of women's literacy.

The US caught her eye because after World War I it had assumed far greater importance in world affairs than a destitute, impoverished and battle-scarred Europe. Moreover, the warmth and broad-mindedness of Americans, as experienced by Swami Vivekananda, was well-known. Sushama's uncle Rabindranath had also been there on a lecture-tour in 1916. Thus Sushama prepared to acquaint herself with the progress of women's emancipation in America. If Indian women could be influenced by the achievements and lifestyle of their American sisters, so much the better. For ease of recognition Sushama decided to use her maiden name in the USA.

Her visit certainly caused ripples among Americans. Contrary to their vague preconceived notions about Indian women, she appeared like someone from another planet. Rabindranath, the Hindu poet and philosopher, had moved their hearts and now his niece was on a visit to their land. The people of America were agog with curiosity, not so much to hear her but just to have a glimpse of her.

Sushama reached the USA in February 1927. To quote her: 'I felt I had gone on a pilgrimage to the New World.' Americans were amazed to see this women, endowed with beauty, purity, pride and courage. She seemed the embodiment of a burning flame. When she stood up on the dais effortlessly and cast her long-lashed, luminous black eyes on them, the audience was spell-bound. The foreigners saw 'a sari of purple silk with sleeves of green, embroidered in gold'. Their blue blood coursed faster in their veins and astonished praise flew from their pen. 'Miss Tagore is a charming bit of the orient in occidental setting; short of stature, quiet and demure, with lazy dark eyes that can flash fire when the occasion arises, it takes the native garb of India to really do justice to her Hindu beauty.'

Thereafter, when Sushama began her lecture in her melodious yet penetrating voice and impeccable English, the audience was enthralled. Such perfect pronunciation, faultless and clear! Most Indians failed to impress foreigners due to their defective pronunciation. Sushama blended her magnetic personality with her captivating voice. A foreign journalist wrote:

> She speaks softly, with never a trace of bitterness of her people, and her expression never changes, except when her deep dark eyes seem to smile.

Sushama's eyes had charmed people. One wrote:

> Her eyes are very large and very black.

After eulogizing Sushama's lecture, the reporter of *Daily Texas* admitted:

> Not only is Miss Tagore ably qualified to discuss this subject (The Ideals of India) through extensive study and experience, but she is also capable of presenting it in clear and forceful English, which none of the people of India can do.

American women found Sushama a novelty. They were startled to learn that Sushama had no intention of pruning her tresses but thought that long hair beautified a woman. Their amazement was unbounded on hearing that she neither used rouge nor lipstick, nor was prepared to smoke. Sushama considered all this 'most unladylike'. She smilingly answered the barrage of questions thrown at her. She certainly considered education essential and was here to observe the methods for imparting the same. However, she believed that 'Indian women should be tutored to prepare for married life, since helping them to be good wives and mothers was the best education for them'. This clearly shows that despite her aversion to marriage in her girlhood, she had accepted the traditional Indian views in later life as correct and beneficial. There was a time even in England when the best education for girls was considered to be one that taught them to become good housewives. Regarding solutions to the various problems that had beset the world, she put forth her views to the women of America thus:

> When women are united as wives, mothers and daughters, they have more influence on men than has a man on a woman. If we would only remember that we are all children of one God, our women united would establish world peace.

She also said:

> The supreme, traditional virtues of the Hindu women are fidelity, sincerity and self-sacrificing love. A wife subordinates her wishes to those of her husband.

According to Sushama:

> Real satisfaction lies in control and self-restraint. Let us enjoy the material side of life, but not lose ourselves in its glamour.

These lectures were published in the pages of reputed American papers. Unfortunately, the transcripts of her lectures are unavailable in India. Let us peruse some more of Sushama's words. She had no faith in the Western notions of marriage. Dressed in a crimson sari, she stood up in a meeting in New York, raised her eyes, bright as the evening star, and said:

'Your idea of marriage, companionate marriage and love seem very strange to us. Your divorces startle us. We believe in the sanctity of marriage, considering it a sacred and divine union of two souls. Our marriages are regarded as permanent; separation or divorce unspeakable, we stay married.'

There were doubts and whispers galore. People said: 'How is this possible? So long we have heard that women in India are but playthings in the hands of men. Respect for them is practically non-existent.'

Such questions from the American women brought a smile to Sushama's lips. She said:

> Our women exert much more influence. They help God in his creation. To you God is represented as father while in India we say *mother*.

Sushama also queried:

> If I did not have the ability to influence my husband how could I travel fourteen thousand miles away from home and be in your midst?

She also said that though she lived in purdah the Indian woman was not uneducated. Such customs would be abolished soon and women would be able to move about freely. She was eagerly waiting for that day which would perhaps be hastened by Western influence. She however refused to believe that a Western education could be the only ideal for an Indian woman.

Among Sushama's lectures in the USA, '*Bharatiya Nari*' (Indian Women), '*Nari Shiksha*' (Women's Education), '*Bharater Adarsha*' (India's Ideals), '*Bharater Darshan*' (Indian Philosophy), '*Vishwabhoginityabodh*' (Universal Sisterhood), '*Rabindranath Tagore*,' '*Mahatma Gandhir Darshan*' (Mahatma's Philosophy) and '*Baidik Sangeet*' (Vedic Songs) were very popular. Requests poured in for talks from various corners of America. Towards the end of her stay, she delivered two more lectures: 'My pilgrimage to America' and 'Advantage and Disadvantage of Intermarriage between Indo-Aryans and Euro-Asians.' Sushama returned home in July 1929 after having spent two years in America. She brought back important methods of teaching, valuable experience and unprecedented laurels. Sushama delivered lectures at thirty-eight places in the USA. Her honorarium for a lecture was fifty dollars. She needed to deliver lectures to meet her own expenses in the USA. The ladies' clubs where she spoke were always packed to capacity. American women paid great heed to her talks. These women had already won the battle for citizens' rights, civic amenities and education. However, the materialistic culture of the West had not been able to provide them with spiritual liberation. Swami Vivekananda had first shown the way and now these women looked to Sushama for guidance.

The main purpose of Sushama's voyage abroad was education. This is the reason why she represented India in the conference held by the 'World Federation of National Education'. She always believed that nothing in life was more important than education. According to her: 'The General Education for the masses is more important than any kind of agitation for political change.' Thus, like her uncle Rabindranath, she was unable to support Gandhiji's non-cooperation movement. She said: 'A word such as 'non-cooperation' is meaningless to the great majority in India, education being permanent and political conditions transitory.'

Unfortunately Sushama was unable to fully utilize her valuable experience after her return to India. The untimely death of her husband and a daughter, coupled with two of her sons renouncing the world and becoming ascetics, created critical problems for her. Sushama refused to be deterred. Her views on education and schools were published in newspapers. Her opinions and plans for education of the masses are commendable. The three main steps of her plan were:

1. A society called Bharater Nirakshsharata Doorikaran Samiti would be set up with twenty members from different provinces of India.
2. In every province a provincial committee would be set up.
3. Wherever there was a Union Board, a representative from every village under this board was to be chosen and a Village Education Committee to be opened by the provincial committee. It would be the responsibility of the Village Education Society to ensure the attendance of the village children in school. The essentials for the pathshala or village-school would be purchased by local contributions. Classes would be held in the open, under trees. If a voluntary teacher was not available, he would have to be paid a token honorarium—perhaps not in cash but with cereals and other necessities of daily life. Every zamindar would have to give five bighas of land. The financial requirement for each province would be between five to ten thousand rupees.

It is to be remembered that India was under British rule at the time, hence Sushama never thought of government help. Her plans are marked by the practical aspects of village life and spreading of education. One would have thought that Sushama would speak about the education, independence and women's emancipation in the West after her return to India. She did not do so as she was disheartened by the effects of women's education at that time. She says:

> When I see that women's education, i.e. the education of young girls, culminates in reading novels of *Bat-tala* shortly after they became literate, my frustration is boundless.

We have no means of ascertaining her views on the women leaders of the movement for women's liberation. One more word about Sushama needs to be said before moving on. In one of her articles—'*Americaye Bedanta Dharmer Provab O Samadar*'—Sushama had provided some information about Swami Vivekananda. Though the facts were not new, it is heartening to note that a lady of the Tagore family took time off in America to make enquiries about Swamiji. Sushama never alluded to Swamiji in her lectures but in her heart she was one of his followers. Moreover, she held the Ramakrishna Mission and its monks in deep reverence. Her eldest son also joined the monastic order of the mission. In the USA Sushama came to know Swami Abhedananda, Swami Paramananda, Sister Devmata and Sister Daya. Many Indians had been spreading defamatory rumours about Swamiji's sojourn in the USA. Some newspapers also showed a great deal of interest in such slander. The British government purposely encouraged such scandal-mongering; but most Indians were shocked and hurt. Sushama was one of them. So while she was in America she made enquiries about this holy man. Her queries were not in vain. Various Americans, especially ladies, informed her that all such rumours were nothing but mere fabrications. They also said that it was a conspiracy fostered by the British government. Thus Sushama was able to return home with her mission fulfilled and her heart at ease.

Among the eight sisters Sudakshina was the youngest. This was her pet name; her real name was Purnima. Having lost her father shortly after birth, Sudakshina was brought up under the loving care of her elder brothers and sisters. While she was growing up, she was eclipsed by her elder sisters. As she blossomed into a rare beauty, her near and dear ones seem to have been taken aback. They felt that she was not meant for an ordinary man but fit to partner a prince. The search for a suitable bridegroom was short. The fortunate one was Pundit Jwalaprasad Pande, a zamindar of Hardoi district. Jwalaprasad, a Kashmiri Brahmin, was a resident of Budhawan. Apart from being a zamindar, he also belonged to the Indian Civil Service. Sudakshina boarded a palki on her way to her husband's home in Uttar Pradesh. It was as if a spark from the Tagore family was blown into a far-off land. Sudakshina became well-known only after her husband's death.

Sudakshina is practically unknown in Bengal because her spheres of activity were Hardoi–Budhawan–Shahjahanpur in Uttar Pradesh. Like Sunrita, we find her mainly in the pages of the *Punya* magazine. She mainly wrote about 'Lucknow' recipes. Perhaps she was a good cook like Pragya or she may have taken up her pen to acquaint her own people in Bengal with the delicacies common in her new home. She certainly does not fit the role of a typical housewife—her head covered and the kitchen her domain.

Jwalaprasad had lovingly taught Sudakshina the details of managing property. She also learned to ride and wield a gun from him. Her English was flawless and matched that of the British. After her husband's demise, she would ride from village to village to inspect her zamindari. She had an elephant too and often rode out on it. She was widowed at the age of twenty-seven when Jwalaprasad succumbed to a carbuncle. The general consensus was that the days of the zamindari were numbered since the young widow, so far away from home, would never be able to manage. There was a commotion among the British personnel— after all here was a beautiful young widow and owner of great wealth to boot. However everyone was disappointed. It is rumoured that a highly placed British official requested her hand in marriage.

The proposal was honourable but Sudakshina declined. This is hearsay and there is no one left today to vouch for its veracity. Her nephew Basab Tagore writes:

> All eminent gentlemen who approached this young widow with proposals of marriage were politely refused by Sudakshina. Her husband was an absolute autocrat, she a befitting companion. Even the British official stood in awe of her.

How come Sudakshina was never scared of the English officials and stood up to them? It has been heard that Jwalaprasad's father had sheltered and helped some Englishmen during the Sepoy Mutiny. He was rewarded with special powers and a pledge that his zamindari would never be auctioned. The British kept their word, thus augmenting Jwalaprasad and Sudakshina's authority manifold. Though she gained full control of her husband's zamindari after his death, Sudakshina had no love for the English officials. She had to keep in touch with them to run her affairs but she never hesitated to complain to the higher authorities at the slightest sign of discourtesy or officiousness. The English officers seldom tried to cross swords with her.

It has been heard that Sudakshina was the uncrowned queen of her zamindari. The British conferred the C.I.E. on her. They also wanted to confer the title 'Maharani', not once but thrice! Every time Sudakshina declined. Her opinion:

> What purpose would such a title serve? My esteem would not be enhanced. It would only make way for more interference in my domain.

From Basab Tagore's writings, it appears that Sudakshina was awarded the Kaisar-e-Hind medal not as a zamindar but for her social service. A sugar mill was established in Shahjahanpur due to Sudakshina's efforts. She preferred to pass her days with her tenants who were more like her children. While dacoities and other atrocities were common in villages under other zamindars, Sudakshina's lands were free from such menace. Her subjects always said, touching their folded palms to their temple in reverence, that they lived in Ram Rajya.

She created a task-force comprising of hand-picked ex-dacoits. She regularly inspected the villages on horseback with a gun on her shoulder. People said her marksmanship was superb. In rifle-shooting competitions she beat even her rival Englishmen. Such firebrand and courageous women were rare in Bengal. Of course we know that Bengali women have always been competent in managing zamindaris. Rani Bhabani and Rani Rashmoni are well-known figures who ran their estates with tact and ability. Sudakshina, though not crowned queen, resembled one in terms of love and esteem, in the eyes of her subjects. She inherited her zamindari when still quite young and that too far away from home. Yet she had no problems in managing her affairs. She never accepted any help from her parents' side of the family nor from her in-laws. She adopted one of Jwalaprasad's nephews and spent her days in Shahjahanpur.

Apart from managing her estate, Sudakshina interested herself in public welfare and social service. As per the family tradition, she opened a school for the illiterate and backward people of Uttar Pradesh. The condition of the women there was akin to that in the dark ages. Sudakshina tried to spread the light of education among them. However she strongly objected to the 'Angrezi Hatao' stir during the non-cooperation movement. 'Angrez Hatao' was all right but certainly not 'Angrezi Hatao'. English was an essential language which had enabled us to sample the finest literary works of the world. She voiced her opposition strongly, threatening to close down her school if debarred from teaching English. Sudakshina, who was used to a Western lifestyle, was easily misunderstood by many. Yet all contemporary English officials knew that no one matched Sudakshina in her dislike of the British.

We have already mentioned that Sudakshina had also been

named Purnima. Under this name, she set the tune for a song. The song was called *The Indian Village Girl*. The records of this orchestra were quite popular though Sudakshina was apt to give the entire credit to her elder brother Hitendranath. She had a great love of music. Well-known artistes were paid honorariums regularly from her estate. Basab Tagore reminisces:

> The entire morning was spent in musical entertainment whenever Sudakshina visited Calcutta from Shahjahanpur. Sometimes, Shafiulla would play the sitar, on others Gopeswar Bandopadhyaya would sing. According to Pishima's request, there would be an incessant flow of classical ragas and raginis.

In Shahjahanpur also she would have musical soirées in her home regularly. Sudakshina's last years were not happy. It is easier to discipline one's own son than an adopted one. She was planning to leave Shahjahanpur and shift to Calcutta permanently when death struck. Sudakshina passed away suddenly.

Three other granddaughters of the Maharshi from his son's side still remain. They are the three daughters of Rabindranath. It may be better to talk about two others before moving on to Rabindranath's daughters. They are Hironmoyee and Sarala, the two talented daughters of Swarnakumari. They were contemporaries of Protiva, Indira, Saroja and Pragya. Though Hiranmoyee and Sarala actually belonged to the Ghosal family, they are better known as Tagore women. This is natural since Hiranmoyee and Sarala spent their childhood in the golden era of the Jorasanko mansion. Swarnakumari stayed in a portion of the second floor while the girls grew up with their cousins. Even after Swarnakumari and Janakinath had shifted to a separate house, they visited Jorasanko daily or someone from there visited them.

Hiranmoyee was the true helpmate and companion of her mother. After her death, Swarnakumari said, 'My daughter's death has left me motherless.' Be it the editing of *Bharati* magazine or running the Sakhi Samiti, Swarnakumari received the most support from Hiranmoyee. When the responsibility of editing *Bharati* fell on Hiranmoyee, she also persuaded Sarala to share the job. Sarala was involved in every endeavour of Hiranmoyee. In the early days of their working life, they had opened a pathshala for women in their own home at Kasiabagan. This may be considered as the forerunner of the present notion of adult education. The womenfolk of the neighbouring houses regularly came to fetch water from the pond in the Ghosal house. The school was started with about twenty unmarried girls and child widows from among these. The headmistress, Hiranmoyee, was then about fourteen or fifteen and her assistant Sarala barely ten. They both taught Bengali, English, music and needlework to the pupils. The school hours were from 4.30 p.m. to 6.30 p.m. Visitors from Jorasanko acted as examiners. Prizes were also awarded. Once Rabindranath was persuaded by his nieces to distribute the prizes.

Not much is known about Hiranmoyee. Her younger sibling Sarala's memoirs are full of fragrant whiffs of her 'love, devotion and affection'. At sixteen Hiranmoyee was married to Phanibhushan Mukhopadhyay. Sarala writes: 'Phanidada, along with Pishemoshay, was a regular visitor to our home in Shimla. He had cherished a desire to marry Didi since then.'

Hiranmoyee later became a member of the Ladies Theosophical Society but her real achievement lay in social service. After marriage, Hiranmoyee wrought a few changes in her mother's Sakhi Samiti, and transformed it into Bidhaba Shilpasram. The original Sakhi Samiti was almost defunct by that time. Prior to this, Hiranmoyee came to know about the activities of a Bidhaba Shilpasram established by Sashipada Bandopadhyay in Baranagar. This led her to remodel Sakhi Samiti into a Bidhaba Shilpasram for widows. She was deeply concerned about the inmates of this home. She herself always lived very simply. Her daughter Kalyani writes:

> Though my father was alive, I never saw her wear coloured sarees. A pair of gold bangles and *loha* (iron bangle denoting the presence of a husband) adorned her wrists. She put on a simple gold chain only when she went out.

During her last days, she was deeply worried about the future of her ashram. She lamented, 'Despite my life-long efforts and hard work for the ashram, I have not had any response from my countrymen. This work will not be permanent.' After her death, the ashram was renamed Hiranmoyee Bidhaba Shilpasram. Students were awarded medals for excellence in needlework and craft. Gaganendranath's youngest daughter Sujata also won a medal from here for her proficiency in handicraft.

An artistic temperament lay hidden under Hiranmoyee's social activities. She did not study further after passing the minor examination from Bethune School, yet she always maintained a link with literature. A number of her articles were published in *Sakha*, *Balak* and *Bharati*. They are still scattered in the pages of these old magazines. No one has made any effort to compile and publish them. As editor of *Bharati* she shouldered the entire burden practically alone. Sarala, who lived far away, was a notional co-editor. Hiranmoyee's articles in *Bharati* number nearly eighty. They comprise stories, poems, quizzes, criticism and non-fiction. Many of them are on Russia. These are translations, not original writings; yet her mastery of the language and choice of subject are commendable. 'Russia', 'Russian Prisons', 'Russian Trade', 'Russian Language and Trade', as well as 'Administrative System in Russia' are serious, thought-provoking and deserve a mention.

Hiranmoyee's original compositions were a few sonnets. To quote Sarala, one may say that though one may not become a well-known singer in spite of a melodious voice touched with pathos, similarly Hiranmoyee's poems are both sweet and poignant. Her devotion to *Bharati* was deep and sincere. This made her hesitant about assuming charge of the magazine. With a great deal of persuasion, she handed over *Bharati* to her uncle Rabindranath. She writes:

> I felt it would be better if we two cousin-sisters ran *Bharati* jointly instead of myself alone. Sarala approved the idea when I wrote to her. I was considerably relieved. Umeshbabu, Ramendrababu, Akshaybabu and Thakurdasbabu were of great help at that time. Dineshbabu and Jaladharbabu also contributed regularly. . . Thus we two cousin-sisters were co-editors of *Bharati* for three years. During this period, I did not cease my efforts even for a day to coax my uncle Rabindranath to take over the editorship of *Bharati*. A dripping tap wears away stone. Ultimately my uncle took pity on me and agreed to edit *Bharati*, i.e. he would write and select the articles for publication. As manager, I had to collect literary articles and correct proofs. I was very happy to hand over *Bharati* into his capable hands. Knowing my uncle, however, I was doubtful if this arrangement would continue for long.

Hiranmoyee's apprehensions were not baseless. Rabindranath accepted the responsibility only for a year. Hiranmoyee has expressed her views in a sonnet, on what was to happen after the year was out. She says: 'Even if the sun sets and darkness descends, still I shall be at hand.' She picked up the reins of *Bharati* again after Rabindranath. The association was a life-long one, severed only by death. To sustain *Bharati*, Hiranmoyee wrote poems, satires, quizzes, articles, and translations of Western literature. When the publication of *Bharati* ceased, Hiranmoyee had already departed from this world.

The budding political consciousness and patriotism observed in Swarnakumari blossomed out in her daughter Sarala. Such courageous and spirited women are rare. She was like a flashing sword freed from the scabbard, the 'Joan of Arc' of Bengal or the first Indian woman to bring patriotic songs to the masses. She was able to blend the three streams of literature, music and patriotism into a single course, though music and literature both followed her patriotic fervour. Sarala's childhood was spent in Jorasanko like that of her other cousins though she always nurtured a feeling of neglect. She felt that her mother, engrossed in literary pursuits, did not love her. This was not true though Swarnakumari hardly ever demonstrated her feelings. This was the norm in the aristocratic families of those days. In a large joint family, with at least one maid-servant per child it was not considered seemly for a mother to be involved in the daily care of her children. In the Tagore family, one or more servants were employed for each child. Male servants for boys, maids for girls and 'Doodh Ma' for infants—this was the norm. Sarala writes:

> . . . we had no contact with our mother since birth. She was distant like an unreachable queen. For us, the maid-servant's lap took the place of our mother's lap. We never knew the meaning of petting. Mother never kissed or stroked us. My aunts were the same.

In the wealthy aristocratic families of that time children were the most helpless. Sarala observed that the wives of her maternal uncles were not as indifferent about their children as her mother and aunts. These women came from other families, with other norms, and lavished a great deal of affection on their children. This was especially true of Jnanadanandini, who not only doted on her children but also celebrated their birthdays with splendour. Though her children had 'Doodh ma' and special servants, this did not affect the love demonstrably showered by Jnanadanandini on them. Sarala's heart felt heavy with hurt when she observed all this.

Perhaps the void created in her sensitive heart due to her mother's apparent indifference turned Sarala towards academic excellence. Passing the entrance examination from Bethune School when only thirteen, Sarala drew the interest of all those around her, including her mother. There was ample reason too. In the History paper of the entrance examination a question had been asked about Clive's conquest of Bengal. The question was based on the book *Lord Clive*, by Macaulay. Protesting against Macaulay's characterization of Bengalis as inferior, Sarala presented her answer with such logic, spirit and sincerity that the examiner N. Ghosh awarded her the highest marks. He also made enquiries about her family. Sarala stood first in History. She seemed to have matured overnight. She, whose looks were never comparable to those of her cousins, seemed to have overtaken them and forged ahead. No girl from the Tagore family had appeared in a public examination before her. Sarala passed not only the entrance but also the BA examination, with English Honours, in 1890 at the age of seventeen from Bethune College. Indira had not appeared for the examination till then. She was awarded the Padmavati gold medal by the Calcutta University for securing the highest marks. She was the first one to be awarded this medal and the seventh woman to graduate. She then decided to study MA in Sanskrit. She began attending classes but was unable to appear for the examination. Her choice of subjects gives us a glimpse of her grit and ability to change courses at will. Before studying for her BA degree, Sarala had studied Science. At that time, there were no arrangements for girls to study Science. Sarala persuaded her guardians to permit her to attend evening lectures along with her elder brothers. These were held in Dr Mahendranath Sarkar's Science Association. As Sarala was the lone girl-student, she had to wait in the staff- room, entering the class along with the professor. Her two elder brothers Jyotsnanath and Sudhindranath would sit beside her. Three chairs were placed in the first row for them. The other students would sit on benches. Pointing at Sarala's brothers, they would derisively whisper 'bodyguards'. Yet Sarala had no interest in Science for which she went to such lengths. Had she been keen on it, she would have wanted to be a doctor like Kadambini Ganguly or Abala Basu. Or she may have tried for admission into the medical college, like Bidhumukhi Basu or Virginia Mitra, recalling the unforgettable efforts of these two to study medicine. If she had been of a scientific bent like her mother Swarnakumari,

Sarala could have improved the development of scientific studies a great deal. Women of the Tagore family did not show any keenness for scientific thought. For a long time, they confined themselves to the pursuit of literature and arts. Sarala's interests lay elsewhere and she dabbled in various subjects searching for her true vocation.

Apart from academics, Sarala was also interested in vocal music. Since her childhood she had been able to create English 'pieces' using English chords in Bengali songs. She prepared the notations for some songs by Rabindranath and she also 'Westernized' a few of his songs. This pleased Rabindranath no end. When Sarala converted the song *Sakatare oi kandiche* into a proper English instrumental piece, it could easily be played by a band or on the piano. Rabindranath was delighted and requested her to compose a piano-accompaniment for *Nirjharer swapnabhanga*. This was also done. Sarala was then just twelve years old. Rabindranath presented her with a notebook to write down European songs in. He advised her to write them all down lest she forget.

Sarala's interest in music attracted the Maharshi's attention too. He asked her to set a poem by Hafiz to music. After a week Sarala sang the song while playing it on the violin. Debendranath listened enthralled. He seldom listened to music unless it was exceptional. From among his family members, he enjoyed Rabindranath's songs and Protiva's piano recitals. He was not only delighted to hear Sarala sing but he also arranged for a gift. A necklace set with diamonds and rubies was purchased for a thousand rupees. The Maharshi handed it to Sarala in a family gathering, saying, 'You are comparable to Saraswati. Though inadequate, I have this small ornament for you.'

Collecting songs and different tunes was an obsession with Sarala. She presented Rabindranath with a compilation of Baul songs and South Indian music. Rabindranath collated these tunes and composed many new songs. This incident has been mentioned by Indira in her '*Rabindrasangeeter Tribeni Sangame*'. Some of the songs composed by Rabindranath, by setting his own lyrics to the tunes collected by Sarala, are: *Anandaloke mangalaloke*, *Esho hey grihadevata*, *Eki labanye* and *Chirabondhu chiranirbhar*. We quote Sarala:

> My desire to give him a gift lay behind all my collection of music. The heart loves to give one who is able to accept gracefully. In our family, Rabimama was the best recipient. So all my gifts were concentrated on him.

While discussing music, few know that *Vande mataram* was first set to music by Sarala. Rabindranath had set the tune for the first two stanzas and then requested Sarala to complete the job. Sarala used to compose songs herself. Those patriotic songs created a great deal of fervour. We will get back to this topic later and concern ourselves here with Sarala's literary pursuits. In spite of all her preoccupations, Sarala wrote a great deal. She was awarded a prize from the *Sakha* magazine for a poem when she was only twelve. Her first article was '*Pita-matar prati ki byabahar kora kartavya*' [our duty regarding our behaviour towards our parents]. This was just the beginning. Thereafter she contributed regularly to *Bharati*. Though not very active as a co-editor, she wrote on numerous topics later, while editing *Bharati* on her own. This was just after her return from Mysore. A few years earlier, she had discontinued her studies for the Master's degree and gone to South India to teach in the Maharani Girls School in Mysore. This was certainly an epoch-making incident in the Tagore family. Society also frowned upon her decision to work. The *Bangabasi* magazine slyly remarked, 'Where was the need for this woman to go out alone in the world for a job? It is not as if she lacked anything here. Why then expose oneself to unnecessary pitfalls?' This was the general attitude of the times. As if food and clothing were all that mattered! Some people have always eyed with suspicion any move made by women to advance. The women of the Tagore family were always in disfavour for their activities. The general feeling was that these were done merely for bravado. However the women of the Tagore family surged ahead, buoyed by their emotions. Sarala, who had always been undaunted, could not stay at home. After all, she was not alone. Many other women had moved ahead. Women accepting jobs were no longer a novelty. Chandramukhi Basu as principal of Bethune College had proved that Indian women were no less competent than educated Englishwomen. Kumudini Khastagir had preceded Sarala to Mysore.

Sarala's taste for literature developed under the influence and companionship of Rabindranath. 'The one who opened the rich storehouse of Mathew Arnold, Browning, Keats, Shelley and others was Rabimama.' After her return from Mysore, Sarala settled down with *Bharati*. She advertized in the paper, 'Next month Shri Rabindranath Tagore will contribute a social satire.' Rabindranath was speechless. He had no inkling and the advertisement was already there! Though he scolded Sarala ('Why did you advertise without informing one? I shall not write it.'), he did write it. Sarala had just taken up the editorship and he did not wish to land her in trouble. Thus was written *Chirakumar Sabha*. Later, such advertisements by Sarala or her requests for literary contributions often displeased Rabindranath. In an impartial analysis, Sarala cannot be blamed over-much. She showed great astuteness as an editor. She was the one to start the practice of remuneration for writers. That *Bharati*—unlike *Balak, Sadhana* or *Punya*—did not remain just a magazine of the Tagore family was became of her. She embellished and improved *Bharati* in many ways. She would be on the lookout for talented new writers and give them a chance. An example is that of Saratchandra. He was then living in Burma. Having just started writing, he was still diffident about his work. At that time his uncle left the manuscript of *Bardidi* with the *Prabasi* magazine. After a while Ramananda Chattopadhyaya rejected the novel and returned it. Saratchandra's uncle Suren Gangopadhyay brought it as a last resort to the office of *Bharati*. The manuscript was handed over to Sarala.

She was in raptures after going through it, and said, 'Superb! Publish in three instalments in the issues of Baisakh, Jaistha and Ashar. Do not mention the name of the author in the Baisakh and Jaistha numbers. Everyone will think Rabindranath is the author. Our delay in publishing the name will be overlooked and the number of subscribers will rise. *Bardidi* will end in the Ashar issue and we will publish the name of Saratchandra as the author there.' Her advice was followed and all her predictions proved correct. Many readers asked Rabindranath about *Bardidi*. A surprised Rabindranath denied being the author but also considered it to be the work of a stalwart. His curiosity was aroused as was that of Gaganendra, Abanindra and many others. The interest created by the absence of the author's name in the first two instalments of *Bardidi* facilitated the acceptance of Saratchandra by the readers.

Apart from discovering new talents, Sarala enriched *Bharati* by having some rare works of reputed scholars translated from English. These were:

a) Nivedita: 'What every mother can do for her son' (*Pratyek Ma chheler janye ki korte parey*, Jaistha 1306) and 'The duty of Mother Bengal' (Sravana 1306).
b) Mahadev Govind Ranade—'Social rule in ancient times' (*Purba kaler samaj shashan*, Sravana 1307).
c) Mohandas Karamchand Gandhi: 'The Indian Colony in South Africa' (*Dakshin Africar Bharat opanibesh*, Sravana 1307)

It is rumoured that it was as editor of *Bharati* that Sarala first met the writer Pravatkumar Mukhopadhyay. Pravatkumar was a broad-minded widower with literary tastes. It is possible that a proposal for marriage with Sarala was mooted and Pravatkumar went to England to become a barrister and thus improve his career. Unfortunately, the wedding did not take place. The proposal had to be set aside due to tremendous opposition from Pravatkumar's mother, who was an extremely orthodox Hindu. Quite a few other names were also heard as would-be husbands for Sarala. Sister Nivedita had heard about Gokhle. The name of Dr Pyaramal was published by one newspaper. These were all idle conjectures. In our country, an unmarried woman past a certain age always attracts such comments. Sarala was a spinster till the age of thirty-three, certainly well past the accepted marriageable age even today. So rumours were quite natural. Not only was Sarala uninterested initially but Swarnakumari was also keen to keep her single. To quote Sarala: 'Mother always said: I won't get Sarala married. A child is akin to a blade of grass which flows along the course chosen for it by the parents. My feelings had also flowed along the course of remaining single and stood still on its shores.' Even the Maharshi had proposed: 'If Sarala vows to remain a spinster, I shall marry her to a sword.' Sarala had not agreed. When she did marry, her husband was certainly a fit partner for her. He was Rambhoj Dutta Chaudhuri, the rebel leader of Punjab, brilliant as an unsheathed sword.

Sarala contributed regularly to *Bharati*—lyrics, poems, short stories, novels, comedies, criticism and translations were all in the list. What remained then? Reminiscenes? Her *Jibaner Jharapata*, written during her last years, is an exceptional work. It would be no exaggeration to term it a mirror par excellence of contemporary times. Her articles discussing Sanskrit poems and epics: 'Ratibilap', 'Malati-Madhab', 'Malabikagnimitra' and 'Mritsha-katika' also merit attention. Bankimchandra, who was known as 'Sahitya Samrat', showed these articles to Shrish Majumdar and commented: 'Considering the writer's age, I am forced to admit that such penmanship would not have been easy for me at that age. After reading her criticisms I have begun reading these plays anew.' Unfortunately, no complete compilation of all Sarala's works has been published even today.

Sarala's first original contribution to literature was 'Premik Sabha'. Though the author's name had not been mentioned, it was acclaimed by all. Rabindranath personally congratulated her saying, 'It is well that you did not mention the author. Your article has been judged on its merit. It appears more to be the work of some experienced writer rather than that of an amateur. If readers had mistaken me as the author I would have felt honoured.' What could be a better compliment? Thereafter Sarala wrote several good stories.

As mentioned earlier, neither music nor literature was the focal point of Sarala's life. Patriotism reigned supreme. Literature and music helped her on her path of patriotic fervour. One might say that she was able to utilize these two means for political activity. No man from the Tagore family was so completely involved with extremist politics as Sarala. Soumendranath came into the field much later. The seeds of patriotism were sown in Sarala's mind by her parents. Janakinath was connected with the Indian National Congress whereas Swarnakumari was the first woman to participate in the 'Hindu Mela' and thus initiate feelings of 'Swadeshi' among women. Her Sakhi Samiti and 'Shilpa Mela' had latent seeds of patriotism. Sarala however entered politics directly. She tried, from 1895 onwards through *Bharati*, to foster the feeling of heroism among Bengali youth. Articles like 'Mrityu Charcha', 'Byayam Charcha' and 'Bilati Ghooshi banam Deshi Keel' awoke the somnolent pride and dignity of Bengalis. The idea of leading a healthy life and death in defence of one's honour began to enthuse people. Her article 'Ahitagnika' threw open the floodgates of fervour. Hordes of young men from schools and colleges approached her. She handpicked a few of them to form a band. She would place a map of India before them and make them swear to serve the motherland, body and soul. She would then tie a 'rakhi' on their wrists as a seal to their self-sacrifice. This society was not really a secret one, though it was forbidden to gossip about it.

The custom of tying a rakhi made of red thread was spread all over India by Rabindranath a few years later. In 1905, on the day Bengal was partitioned, he tied a rakhi on the wrists of Hindus and Muslims alike as a token of brotherhood and love. Sarala's use of the rakhi reminds us of Ela, the heroine of *Chaar Adhyaya*. The red mark she placed on their foreheads created tremendous fervour among young men. Such leadership was novel not only for the Tagore family but for the whole of Bengal. It was not common in England either, though this was the time of suffragettes in England fighting for voting rights. It is difficult to imagine a Bengali woman imbuing young men with heroic ideals.

The editorship of *Bharati* brought Sarala in contact with two more towering personalities—Swami Vivekananda and Sister Nivedita. The latter told Sarala that according to Swamiji, 'Sarala is a jewel among women, capable of great achievement. Her education was perfect. Every Indian woman should have such education.' Shortly thereafter Nivedita proposed to Sarala that she accompany Swamiji to England on his next trip. He wanted her to represent Indian women and preach the message of oriental spiritualism among the women of the occident.

Swamiji's wish remained unfulfilled as Sarala was unable to accompany him abroad. Became of reservations of the Tagore family and the Brahmo Samaj, Sarala was unable to maintain much contact with Swamiji and Nivedita. To quote her, 'Certain traditional superstitions and the diffidence induced by them were the reason for my lack of enthusiasm in this matter.' Sushama was able to realize Swamiji's dream, though partially.

In spite of Sarala's inability to fulfill Swamiji's hopes, the desire in her for a spiritual life was entirely due to the influence of Swami Vivekananda. Swamiji passed away, but his influence was at work. 'Just as a small seed blown into the crack of a wall slowly takes root, pushing through the crack more and more until it becomes a full grown banyan tree, so the desire for spiritual knowledge went tunnelling into my life.' Coming across a reference to Patanjali's Yoga Sutras in Swamiji's letters, she read these with the relevant Bengali translations. The reference to the Gita in 'Karmayoga' attracted her attention. 'I had not read a single sloka of the Gita earlier—Srikrishna had never been extolled in our family.' Sarala felt a great desire to learn the truth about the 'Hindutva' of the Hindus. 'My spiritual thirst was leading me away from the traditional Brahmoism of my childhood.' Of course this was much later, when Sarala had begun to write her memoirs. Before that, Sarala raised a storm not only in Bengal and Punjab but the whole of India.

She was suddenly requested to preside over a meeting. Sarala was hesitant. Though she had just been to Mysore, participating in a public meeting in Calcutta was beyond her wildest dreams. Even during her occasional trips to Swamiji's ashram, either her elder cousin Surendranath or Nivedita would accompany her. Nivedita was akin to a brilliant flame of light in Sarala's eyes. However Sarala ultimately agreed. On her request, the meeting was held on 'Poila Baisakh'. This was the day when Pratapaditya, ruler of Jessore, had been crowned. Young men discussed his life and demonstrated their skill in 'Lathi Khela', wrestling and boxing. The entire function was termed 'Pratapaditya Utsav'.

It was a sign of changing times that Sarala did not invite any adverse criticism. On the contrary, the newspapers showered unstinted praise.

> Oh what a spectacle! What a meeting! There were no lengthy speeches, no thumping of tables—only reminiscences of a valiant hero of Bengal, the wielding of arms by Bengali youth and their leader, a Bengali lady—has the goddess Durga herself descended on earth?

> Or

> We are thrilled to observe a lady presiding over a meeting of young men in the heart of Calcutta.

Another newspaper wrote:

'We are breathless in our efforts to keep up with Sarala Devi. Every morning one wonders—what next?'

Sarala had been able to gauge accurately the mental make-up of the Bengalis. Their hearts rule their heads and they are more influenced by sentiment than logic. To enthuse them one would have to touch their heart. Thus she began the observance of 'Veerastami' 'Rakhi Bandhan', 'Pratapaditya Utsav' and 'Udayaditya Utsav', also opening a gymnasium in her home.

The popularization of 'Pratapaditya Utsav' led to a confrontation between Sarala and Rabindranath. The latter was not prepared to accept Pratapaditya—whose character was not above reproach—as a national hero. In his novel *Bauthakuranir Haat* Rabindranath's portrayal of Pratapaditya is also along these lines. He was offended that Sarala was extolling the same man without judging the importance of his contribution to history. Sarala's argument was that she did not measure Pratapaditya according to a moral yardstick but by his political ideologies. 'It is undeniable that he—a lone zamindar—rebelled against the Mughal Emperor, declared Bengal independent and even had coins minted bearing his name.'

All in all Sarala initiated a tremendous movement. To cap all this was her music, which resembled the chords of a 'Rudraveena'. Her own composition 'Namo Hindusthan' was sung in the Congress convention of 1901.

Gao sakal konthey sakal bhashey
Namo Hindusthan!
Haro haro haro—joy Hindusthan!
Satshri Akal Hindusthan!
Allah ho Akbar—Hindusthan!
Namo Hindusthan!

Sing all ye in one voice
Namo Hindusthan!
Hara Hara Hara—victory to Hindusthan!
Satshri Akal Hindusthan!

Allah ho Akbar—Hindusthan!
Namo Hindusthan!

There was tremendous fervour all round. Mrs Saviour, in-charge of Swamiji's ashram in Almora, was so moved on hearing the song that she advised Sarala, 'If you just tour the cities and villages of India singing patriotic songs, you will be able to rouse the whole nation.' Sarala herself was unable to identify with the terrorists. She never supported murder or political robberies. She was keen to shape the young minds and infuse power in their veins. Jatindranath Bandopadhyay, later known as Swami Niralamba, came to Sarala from Baroda with a letter from Arabinda Ghosh, with the intention of setting up a secret revolutionary society. Sarala agreed to extend every help. The Bharat Uddhar society was established openly under the leadership of Barindrakumar Ghosh. Even a signboard was put up to this effect. Jatindranath lived in the premises of the society. He instructed the hordes of young men who came for riding, gymnastics and physical training. Soon differences surfaced with Sarala, when she heard 'that their party had ordered members to carry out robberies'. Unable to believe it, she journeyed to Poona and met Lokmanya Tilak after crossing a number of hurdles. When Tilak told her that he too did not uphold robberies, she distanced herself from the party. Another view is that a number of charges were levelled against her and she was removed from the party. Though no longer associated with the revolutionaries, Sarala was always involved in welfare activities.

Bengali women displayed unprecedented patriotism at this juncture. They may not have advanced noticeably in other spheres but all had answered the call to serve the motherland. Most of them came from ordinary families. Ladies from well-to-do aristocratic families were fewer in number. Sarala was a notable exception. Sarala opened 'Lakshmir Bhandar' to advertise and popularize the use of swadeshi goods. She was astonished to see that Surendranath Tagore's Japanese visitors carted practically everything from Japan, including writing paper! Once Sarala asked them: 'Why have you brought so much paper?' She was informed that the popular belief in Japan being that nothing was available in India, their womenfolk had packed in these papers. They felt that otherwise the men would not have been able to write letters home. 'Amazing!' thought Sarala. 'Japan considers India uncultured and under British rule, its people without any skills and incompetent.' She began using Indian-made goods. The cover of *Bharati* was henceforth of local yellow paper made from cotton. Apart from 'Lakshmir Bhandar' she opened 'Swadeshi Stores' in Bawbazar with the help of Jogesh Chaudhuri and a few others. These stores had been established before the partition of Bengal. Lakshmir Bhandar sold sarees collected from various districts of Bengal as well as other articles. The handicrafts prepared by the members of Hiranmoyee's Bidhaba Shilpasram were also sold here. Whenever she attended any public function, Sarala was attired from top to toe in swadeshi raiment. The medal she had received for running *Lakshmir Bhandar* had been fashioned into a brooch, which she always wore on her shoulder, when going out. Her matchless grace and unique mode of dress captivated everyone. To encourage appreciation of 'Swadeshi' she revived the fashion of placing a red mark (bindi) on the forehead and the use of 'alta' to adorn the feet of women. She even modernized the traditional Bengali festivals to make them acceptable to all and sundry. Thus 'Basantotsab' and 'Pous Parbon' were regenerated. During this time two magazines, Sarala's *Bharati* and *Bharat Mahila* edited by Sarajubala Dutt had taken up the task of imbuing women with the ideals of nationalism. They must have succeeded, otherwise how could women play such a glorious role in the freedom movement? Giribala Devi, the Maharani of Natore, Abala Basu, Sarojini Basu alias 'Banga Lakshmi', Nanibala Devi, Deshbandhu's sister Urmila Devi, Shri Aurobinda's niece Latika Ghosh—all came forward to pledge their allegiance to the fierce movement. Santosh Kumari Gupta led and directed the labour-movement among women. Pravabati Dasgupta directed the well-known sweepers' strike to raise awareness among them. Sarojini Basu swore not to wear gold bangles until the ban on chanting 'Vande Mataram' was withdrawn. Scores of women in a myriad Bengali homes, hidden from the public gaze, helped the movement. They may not have participated actively in the open but that in no way diminishes the value of their silent contribution. By this time Sarala was no longer involved in the active politics of Bengal. She had gone away to Punjab. Sarojini Naidu in Hyderabad and Bibhabati, wife of Jatindranath Roy, Magistrate of Madras, also caused considerable stir in these places. Sarala however created a storm in Punjab. She collected about five hundred young men in Lahore to arrange a protest meeting.

When World War I began, Bengali men were not allowed to join the army. When this restriction was removed in 1917, Sarala and other Indian leaders lectured all over, exhorting Indian youth to enlist in large numbers. Sarala had also composed marching songs which became popular. It appears that she encouraged Bengali young men to join the army to infuse courage and heroism in their hearts. She hoped that these trained soldiers would one day help break the shackles binding the motherland.

After her marriage to Rambhoj, Sarala's sphere of activity shifted to Punjab. In his political views Rambhoj was also as spirited and extremist as Sarala. The Bengal tigress had found a fitting mate. In Punjab, Sarala began with social welfare. She established 'Bharat Stree Mahamandal'. Her purpose was to cover the lacuna present in Sakhi Samiti and Bidhaba Shilpasram. This organization played an important role in the history of the establishment of women's rights. Its main aim was to educate women living in 'purdah'. Branches were opened first in Allahabad, and then in Lahore, Amritsar, Delhi, Karachi, Hyderabad, Kanpur, Bankipur, Hazaribagh, Midnapore, Calcutta and some other places. Krishnabhabini Das was in charge of the Calcutta centre. Almost three thousand women, confined within the four walls of their homes, were made literate within a few years by Krishnabhabini and her assistants. Krishnabhabini carried the lamp of literacy even to those women who had been denied education due to numerous family restrictions. A widow herself, she approached such families simply dressed and with bare feet. She thus identified herself with the traditional appearance of a widow and this helped her succeed in her efforts. When the widowed Sarala returned to Calcutta she established another branch of the Mahamandal and called it Bharat Stree Shiksha Sadan. It was due to their efforts that the custom of purdah was abolished to a great extent in Calcutta. With the increase in the number of schools for girls, students arrived in droves for admission. To facilitate the students, the Mahamandal also arranged to open baby crèches and hostels for girl students.

While in Punjab Sarala took charge of *Hindusthan* magazine. It has been said that according to the orders of the Chief Court of Lahore, Rambhoj's licence to practise as a lawyer would be cancelled if his name figured as the editor and owner of the magazine. As his fitting life-partner, Sarala suggested that her name should appear in the paper. This was done and Sarala brought out an English edition also. In it she began publishing inflammatory articles. When the Rowlatt Act was passed, *Hindusthan* was closed down, the press confiscated and Rambhoj exiled. Sarala alone helped steer the revolution in Punjab towards its culmination. The repression by the British reached its peak with the massacre in Jallianwala Bagh. Sarala's arrest was on the cards but ultimately it was not done.

Hereafter, Sarala swung wholeheartedly in favour of Mahatma Gandhi's non-cooperation movement. She was his right hand in the propagation of the 'charkha' (spinning wheel) and 'khadder'. The marriage of her only son Deepak to Mahatma Gandhi's granddaughter Radha forged a confluence of two families different in their outlooks. Pundit Rambhoj did not support the non-cooperation movement and this caused a rift between husband and wife. Sarala went away to the Advaita Ashrama in Mayavati for a while. When eyebrows were raised, Sarala put a question to the leaders of the Arya Samaj: 'Did women have no right to vanaprastha (renouncing worldly affairs in old age) which was advocated for men by religious texts?' She was told that there was no such bar. Sarala again went away to Hrishikesh, with Rambhoj's permission. News of his illness brought Sarala back, as a devoted wife, to nurse him. After her husband's death, Sarala's main role was as a social worker. She became the president of the All India Social Welfare Committee in 1925. However, she was gradually drawn towards a spiritual life and began to withdraw from social service. The exposition of the Upanishads by Acharya Binay Krishna Dev Sharma so touched her that she became his disciple.

The original reads:

Guro !
Chaitanye koro sampradan.
Gotrantar koro morey
Hey mangalnidan.

O Master, wed me to enlightenment,
Transform my life, oh my well wisher.

In spite of Sarala's diverse talents, Bengalis have cherished only the spirited and courageous side of her personality.

Along with the crowd of accomplished women in the Maharshi Bhawan, two sisters were growing up in the adjacent 'baithak-khana bari'. They were Gunendranath's daughters Binayini and Sunayani. By this time Saudamini's days of woe were over. All her three sons had grown up. Aban and Gagan's paintings had restored the prestige of the land. Binayini's wedding bells had sounded much earlier but under heartbreaking circumstances. Man proposes, God disposes. Gunendranath's life suddenly ended at the early age of thirty-six. As his granddaughter Pratima commented: 'No one knew what drove him so relentlessly towards suicide.' Her mother's grief must have influenced her since Pratima had never had a chance to see her maternal grandfather. Pratima had also heard another anecdote from Binayini. Boat trips were customary among aristocratic families. They were among the rare opportunities for their womenfolk to come out of purdah. Once Gunendra's two little daughters had accompanied their parents on such a trip. On their return after about a month, Binayini exclaimed, 'How one missed the open skies and the flowing river Ganga! The days spent on this trip seemed to disappear behind the walls of the aristocratic ancestral mansion.' Binayini's marriage had already been decided on with Seshendra Bhusan. After Gunendra's sudden death, a simple ceremony was held to solemnize the wedding.

Binayini passed her days in tranquility, in their double-storeyed house in Beadon Street, full of attendants, and a coach. In the Tagore family, it was customary for women to do up their hair according to the current fashion after an evening bath. Thereafter, they usually dressed in sarees dyed orange with sheuli or natkana. The main cosmetics used were *momrat*, a face cream made from wax, and kohl for the eyes. After completing their toilette, they generally went to the mistress of the house, who adorned their buns with floral garlands. This custom was prevalent in other families too. Binayini was an expert in hairstyles. She would tie the hair of her nieces into buns of different shapes and designs. The popular ones were *benebağan*, *manbholano*, *phansjaal*, *kalka* (paisley), *bibiana* and many others. Binayini would have probably remained hidden away from the public eye had not the manuscript of her autobiography been suddenly discovered. Her paintings also remain veiled. That Binayini could paint, perhaps not as well as Sunayani, is also not well-known. She also participated in family dramatics. Once she enacted the role of 'Raja' in the play *Ratnabali*.

Binayini called her autobiography *Kahini*. She began writing it at the age of forty-five. Though the date on the manuscript is 1916–17, she actually began her story *Kahini* much later, in 1918 (Bengali 1325) about five years before her death. The autobiography covers her life from 1873 to 1923 (Bengali 1280 to 1330). She says she does not know why she suddenly felt the urge to write about herself. The tradition of writing autobiographies was common among the Tagores. Not only men but even the ladies of Maharshi Bhawan had come forward to narrate their tales. Rassundari Devi however pioneered the path for women. She was not related to the Tagores. Her autobiography prompted Pramatha Chaudhuri to remark, 'Only women write their autobiographies in Bengali.' Another noteworthy book was *Atma Charit* by Keshab Chandra Sen's mother, Saradasundari Devi. A number of other autobiographies like *Pitrismriti* by Saudamini Devi, and *Sekele Katha* by Swarnakumari Devi had been published before Binayini penned *Kahini*. Any one of these may have inspired her, though she never tried to imitate their style. She just put down her feelings in her own way.

Binayini may not have had much to do with academics but her style of writing is simple and natural. It is just like seeing one's own reflection in a mirror, clear and unhindered.

An English lady used to come to teach them at home.

> The missionary lady Miss Smith's coach would arrive as soon as the clock struck two. She was accompanied by two other Christian teachers. My elder sisters-in-law would take out their knitting while some studied the English Royal Reader number one. I also sat down with the 'First book' to study A, B, C. I always looked forward to the time when they would go. After about an hour the missionary English lady (Mem) would speak about Christ for a while. Then they departed. I thoroughly disliked my English lessons, though the stories about Christ were quite interesting.

Her devout and religious nature overshadows all facts mentioned in the book. The seeds of religion and devotion had been sown in her childhood. According to their mother's instruction, the two sisters had to be up by daybreak and gather flowers from the garden. In the month of Kartik (mid-October to mid-November) the deity 'Sridhar' was worshipped. The two sisters had to be at the door of the thakurghar (the room of the deity) by six in the morning with the flowers. Their father's elder sister, Kadambini, was adept at decorating the deity. She would use different coloured flowers—yellow *kolke*, red oleanders or white tube-roses—on different days. Her nieces were then called to appreciate her handiwork. Binayini has provided us with this insight into the house number 5, especially a glimpse of Kadambini, in her diary *Kahini*. She also says:

> At home Akshaybabu would sing Brahma-sangeet at 9 a.m. My mother and aunts would listen, sitting in the andar mahal. Every evening, there were readings and expositions from *Shrimad Bhagwat*. 'Harinam Sankirtan' took place after dusk.

A comparison between the life led by Indira–Protiva–Pragya–Sushama and Binayini–Sunayani makes clear the wide difference in their lifestyles. Life at her in-laws, that is Prasanna Kumar Tagore's home, has also been described by Binayini in *Kahini*. Here the festival of Durga Puja was celebrated with great pomp and show.

> Four Brahmin priests sat before the goddess at the time of evening *arati*. Two of them chanted from the *Chandi* while the third read out the prayers to the eighty-year-old chief-priest. This old man bowed deeply before the goddess and stood up. Then began the *arati* with a tall, silver lamp-stand, holding one thousand and eight silver lamps, to the accompaniment of a silver bell. Wicks immersed in 'ghee' burnt in the lamps. Besides these, there were two other shining brass lamps—one on either side of the deity, on stands that were breast-high. Each held a *seer* of *ghee* and burnt for three days and three nights. While the lamps burnt, '*dhuna*' powder was sprinkled into two large '*dhunuchis*' filled with glowing embers. The entire *Thakur-dalan* was permeated with fragrance. The two large chandeliers—one on each side of the goddess and bearing

fifty candles each—were lit. Two young girls began to fan the deity with silver-handled '*chamars*'. The atmosphere was filled with the sound of drums and '*dhaak*'. All eyes, full of faith, were riveted on the countenance of the mother-goddess. The old priest performed 'aarti' with lamps, burning camphor, a large lotus flower and last of all with a white '*chamar*'. Then he blew the conch, garlanded the goddess and ended the ritual. For the womenfolk, a visit to the *Thakur-dalan* was like a pleasant outing. They never ventured there during the daytime. It was only for the evening 'aarti' that all members of the *andar mahal* trooped out to the *Thakur-dalan.*

A stroke of Binayini's pen has kept alive for us this picture of the womenfolk of Pathuriaghata:

> All of us dressed up to go to the *dalan* during 'sandhya aarti'. Decked in gold ornaments and Dhakai sarees worked with gold thread, with garlands in our hair, anklets and *alta* on our feet, and perfumed with *attar*, we would arrive there. We always found the idol of the holy Mother gorgeously decorated. It seemed as if the goddess had descended to this earth in person.'

Such coexistence of a placid, traditional lifestyle along with new ideas cannot be seen any longer. Binayini's narration is surprisingly simple yet touching. She has described her husband's death with great fortitude. Reading it, one is convinced that Binayini wrote just to unburden herself and not for others. We now follow her:

> Today is the saddest day of my life. My husband's condition had been deteriorating since yesterday. He requested me not to leave his bedside. He suddenly departed the next evening at 6 pm. During his last moments he placed his hand on mine and mumbled something. Despite my best efforts, I was unable to make out his last words. My days of happiness have ended. It was the 2nd of Baisak (1322 in Bengali). My grief knew no bounds. He left me within twenty days of falling ill . . . I am amazed at the patience granted to me then. I felt that all this coming and going was like blades of grass floating in a river.

> They are brought together by the waves and again swept asunder. Why then should I feel so much pain? My heart and mind became calm and I was able to prepare him for the funeral pyre.

Binayini is the second example of an ordinary woman realizing the transient nature of worldly feelings amidst heartrending sorrow. Earlier Prafullamoyee, engulfed in grief for her only son, had been able to overcome the loss of her precious son. Quite a few pages of Binayini's diary describe her spiritual experiences: 'My worship of my husband ended in the month of Baisakh but his place was taken by the lord of my heart and soul. I could sense his presence all the time and prayed to Almighty God. I would say, "What is happening to me? Lord, what have you done? Am I going out of my mind?"' Rabindranath had also noticed the mystic change in Binayini who had gone to Shantiniketan shortly before her death and met him there. On hearing that she was no more, he wrote to Pratima,

> When your mother came to Shantiniketan the other day, there was such an aura of devotion and depth of feeling about her, it amazed me. This time Binayini came very close to me spiritually. I felt a deep sense of peace and contentment when she would come and narrate her deepest thoughts to me. She had already experienced the upliftment of her soul which transcended death. She had already renounced the world in her heart. Observing her immersed in spiritual realization brought me great peace. It is certainly fortunate that she attained overwhelming peace and solace in her heart before departing this world.

Binayini's diary also inspired Abanindranath's '*Gharoa*', '*Jorasankor Dhare*', and '*Apankatha*' as well as Pratima Tagore's '*Smritichitra*'. Our memories come to the fore when we hear someone talking about bygone days. Binayini was the first one to reminisce about the old times and herein lies the importance of her autobiography.

Like her elder sister Binayini, Sunayani too liked to be absorbed in her household and religious activities. Her daughter-in-law Manimala says, 'She bathed at daybreak and wore a red bordered *garad* (silk saree) before sitting down for worship. Alongside my father-in-law, she performed '*Hom*' everyday. She would draw two footprints with sandal-paste in front of her and decorate them with flowers. After the '*Hom*' she touched her husband's feet in deep obeisance before taking up her daily chores as well as painting. In the dining room downstairs there was a wooden divan. On one side of it were piled paintbrushes, canvases, drawing paper and colours while on the other side were her household accounts-book and a cash box. She usually painted pictures of gods and goddesses like 'Radhakrishna', 'Haraparvati', 'Balgopal', 'Nanichora' (young Krishna stealing butter) and 'Krishna with Jashoda."

Sunayani never had any formal training in painting. Observing her two elder brothers absorbed in painting on the south verandah of their home, one day Sunayani took up the paintbrush. She was fairly old at that time and took to painting just as a hobby. In her memoirs Purnima, Gaganendranath's daughter, informs us:

> My father's youngest sister began to draw after shifting to her own home. She would come from time to time and show her work to my father. She had also taken lessons from Asit Haldar for a short while.

It was as if she was playing with her paints and brushes and not painting seriously. These playful brush-strokes sometimes produced a replica of baby Krishna, at others they seemed to depict the shy yet smiling eyes of a new bride. No influence of her artist brothers can be discerned in Sunayani's paintings. In the early days of modern Indian painting, the two brothers and their sister chose three different styles. Abanindra took up the Persian and Mughal technique, Gaganendra adopted the Japanese and cubistic style while Sunayani based her paintings on folk art or '*pata shilpa*', in a style all her own. The greatest attraction of a 'pata' is the manner in which the eyes are drawn. They are elongated, deep and dark. This characteristic of folk art by *patuas* is also present in Sunayani's paintings. She preceded Jamini Roy in such a depiction of the human eye.

Sunayani painted when the mood took her. She was the pioneer among Bengali women artists. It is not as if women did not indulge in painting at that time. For women brought up in the 'Western' fashion, painting was a sign of accomplishment, just like horse-riding, conversing in English or playing the piano. Hemendranath broke the orthodox traditions of the Tagore family when he arranged for his wife and daughters to learn to paint. A few paintings by Protiva had been published in *Punya* while two or three portraits by Pragya had turned out well. Thus Sunayani's dabbling with paints was nothing new. The novelty lay in her approach. Ladies who had learnt painting till then merely confined themselves to drawing just what appeared before the eye, whether it was a portrait or a landscape. This is true of Neepamoyee, Protiva and Pragya. Sunayani was an exception. Her pictures were a blend of what she saw as well as what she felt, lending them an indefinable beauty. Her paintings were the first to show originality. When she first began, she would take her work to her elder brothers and ask them, 'What do you think of my work?' They always encouraged her with words of praise and advised her to carry on. Sunayani persevered and slowly her home was filled with paintings. Like her mother and grandmother, Sunayani would sit on the divan in the dining-room and carry on with her daily chores. While she thus supervised the household or checked the accounts, suddenly a picture would appear before her mind's eye and her hand move involuntarily towards her brush and paint-box. Soon an outline would appear on the wet canvas. According to Monimala:

> She would sometimes apply a few brush strokes with a colour and then ask me to wet the canvas a few times. She would arrange all the wet canvasses with the pictures before her and

continue to gaze at them. She often asked me with a sweet smile, 'Can you see anything on the wet canvas?' I never could see anything but she would say, 'I can see the features of a bride and groom!' With soft colours and a flat brush, the beautiful couple then took shape. Often she would smear the canvasses with colours, leave them for a while, wash them gently and gaze at them as if charmed. Later, an enchanting portrait of Sri Krishna would appear with her brush strokes on the pale blue canvas.

One such painting she named *Ardhanarishwar*. Gaganendra was so impressed by it that he requested Abanindra—who was then connected with the Government Art College—to issue her a certificate. Abanindra, who had been observing Sunayani's work for quite a while, declined, saying, 'She does not need a certificate from me. The style she has adopted will win her one from our countrymen.'

This proved to be true. She won laurels both at home and abroad. The well-known sculptor Meera Mukherjee was struck dumb with amazement the day she first saw Sunayani's paintings. The experience was fresh in her mind even after thirty-three years. She said,

> She opened our eyes to a world that is simple and innocent. This world of innocence is mysterious in a strange way. Today in our world it will be very difficult to find an artist like Sunayani Devi. [*sic*]

But she had also expressed apprehension

> . . . it is sorrow that no one will know because the woman and the matriarchal in her subdued the artist in Sunayani. [*sic*]

The mistress of her own home, Sunayani had been married into the well-known Chatterjee family. Saroja and Usha had preceded her there as brides. Sunayani's husband Rajanimohan stayed in house number 5 for a number of years after marriage. Since she did not have to move to new surroundings after marriage, Sunayani was able to indulge in her hobbies: she played the piano, tried to learn English with the help of a dictionary, strummed the esraj while singing and, of course, painted. Sunayani often put up plays with the ladies of the family. Unlike in the Maharshi Bhawan, men and women never acted together in this house. Women enacted the roles of men as and when required. Once Jnanadanandini encouraged them to stage the play *Ratnabali*. Binayini was Raja, Gaganendra's wife Pramod Kumari was Rani, the part of the chief minister was played by Samarendra's wife Nishibala, Sunayani was Basabdatta and Abanindranath's wife Suhasini enacted the role of Chyutalatika. Sunayani would direct the little girls and put up plays like *Alibaba*, *Mrinalini* and similar ones.

Purnima has written about the play *Mrinalini*. Sunayani did not act in it herself but she taught all the players to sing. At the end of the work, Monorama becomes a widow. It was impossible to enact this scene on the stage since the in-laws of all the women would be present. So, according to Purnima, 'Pashupati took Manorama's hand and left for Benaras.' These ladies never experimented with plays written by Rabindranath, Jyotirindranath or even Abanindranath. This shows that life in the andar mahal of this house was tuned to traditional norms. Fortunately no one ever tried to dissuade Sunayani from painting. On the contrary, she was always encouraged by Rajanimohan. It was he who supplied her with brushes, canvases and paints. Rajanimohan realized that society was much more broadminded now. Moreover, Sunayani's paintings were of gods and goddesses, though she slowly evolved a style of her own. Gradually Sunayani's paintings attracted the attention of foreigners. The first one to show interest was Stella Cramrish. Her critical reviews enthuzed Madam Cocksheeter. This lady arranged for an exhibition of Sunayani's paintings by the Women's Art Club of London in 1927. The foreign viewers were charmed. Her brush strokes were firm without any hint of uncertainty. The most attractive features were the eyes of the models. They were elongated, and appeared immersed in some distant dream. Such a depiction of the eyes was certainly not according to the norms of Western art and yet it did not appear unnatural. It was as if Sunayani heralded a new style of art totally free from Western influence. Invitations for exhibitions came from both France and Germany.

It is surprising that Rabindranath never commented on Sunayani's paintings. This was the time when he himself had begun to paint and draw. He was also encouraging Gaganendra and Abanindra besides educating himself about the language of paintings. Is it possible that he never saw any of Sunayani's pictures? This seems improbable considering his interest in Indian art forms. He had also encouraged Abanindranath to paint a series of pictures of Radha-Krishna from the *Padabali,* while a major portion of Sunayani's work is taken up by Krishna and Shiva. Sunayani however seldom bothered about exhibitions and publicity, she painted because she loved to do so and gifted her work to her near and dear ones, right, left and centre. All the honour and recognition heaped upon her never had any effect on Sunayani's style. Her artistic world was taken up by the portrayal of fairy tales, folklore, stories from the Puranas, epics, *Arabian Nights*, the Bauls and Vaishnavas; folk art like 'alpana' and nakshi kantha, and pictures of Shiva, Krishna and Lakshmi predominate her work. There are several of Ardha Narishwar, Hara-Parvati and Radha-Krishna. Her innumerable drawings and painting all are touched with a simple innocence. In her work, some have noticed a resemblance to murals, some find a similarity with cave-paintings while others have looked for the first signs of the Bengal school. According to the sculptor Meera Mukherjee, 'Sunayani's paintings are devoid of high ambition, there is no play of skilled fingers and no preponderance of loud colours. Her works display just a simple innocent heart and clear vision.'

This becomes all the more apparent when we read Sunayani's poems. Like most women of the Tagore household, she could both sing and write poetry. Her poems were written secretly and like Binayini's autobiography, they lie hidden in the pages of her notebook. It has been possible to see two of her poems due to the courtesy of her daughter-in-law Monimala Devi. Both are touching in their lack of guile. Sunayani's poems resemble the works seen in children's textbooks of the time. Yet not only was she well acquainted with Rabindranath's works but had read those of other poets. Still her poems are simple, full of life, with a whiff of the earth about them and immersed in childlike contemplations.

Saradin boshi gaganer majhe
Aloker khela koriya shesh
Sanjher belay choley dinamani
Klanta shareerey apon desh.

Gramer pathti andharey dhakilo
Chhelera cholilo apon ghar
Pradip jaliya ke rekhey diyechhe
Alpona diye duar por.

Bodhuti cholechhe ghomtaye dhaki
Kolshi bhoriya loyia jal
Sopan bahiya chole dheere dheere
Charane tahar bajichhe mol.

Gagan sajilo natun shobhaye
Parane neel sari heerar phul
Jwalilo gagane hirak pradip
Ar nahi hobey pather bhool.

Kheya torikhani bahiya ekhoni
Ashibe je neye koribe paar
Bolibe kay jabi aay twora kori
Nahi kono bhoy bhabona aar.

After staying the whole day in the sky
And finishing the play of light,
The tired evening sun now departs for his home.
The village path is covered with darkness,
The boys tread homewards.

Some one has decorated her doorstep with 'alpana'
And left a burning lamp thereon.
A housewife, walks with her head covered
And carrying a heavy waterpot
Walks slowly up the steps while her anklets tinkle.
The sky dresses up anew in a blue saree
Studded with diamond flowers,
A diamond lamp burns in the firmament,
There is no more any risk of losing the way,
The boatman will soon arrive and call out
'O hurry, all ye who want to cross over,
There is no need to be scared any more'.

Or

Likhibo likhibo hotechhe basona
Ki katha likhibo bhebe na pai
Shobhitechhe giri sabuj baran
Megher bhitor dekhite pai.

Saradin hetha ekla boshiya
Cheye thaki oyi sudur paney
Nayan samukhe rashi rashi megh
Bhashiya jaye je apon monay.

Kotha hotey ashey jabey kon deshe
Pathiker kichhu thikana nai
Tobuo amar moner kamona
Amiyo sethay cholia jai.

I feel the urge to write,
Yet can't find the words.
I can see the green hills
Around the clouds.
Sitting by myself the whole day long,
I keep gazing before me.
Clouds go floating by before my eyes.
I know not whence they come nor where they go,
Just like a traveller without a destination
Yet my heart yearns to go there.

Sunayani's poems also appear as conglomerations of pictures—

nature, children, a room decorated with 'alpana' and lit by a lamp, a woman fetching water to the tinkling accompaniment of her anklets, the call of a boatman, green hills behind clouds, the clouds themselves, the traveller to an unknown destination—all these are typical of Bengal and may be the subject of paintings. Just the particular tone of the poems, the imagination behind them, the style and brush strokes akin to the *patuas* of Kalighat are peculiar to Sunayani. Leela Mazumder's daughter Kamala married Sunayani's grandson Manishi. Thus Leela Mazumdar had the opportunity to meet her a number of times. She says,

> One day I saw her in bed with her eyes closed. She was trying to move her right wrist from time to time. I was most curious. On questioning her, she opened her eyes, saying with a smile, "I am trying to draw in my imagination. My fingers can no longer hold a brush or palette.'

Sunayani was an artist of international stature, yet there was no arrogance or self-aggrandizement. She seemed to be like any other housewife. Her grandson's wife Geeta once accompanied her to the opening ceremony of 'Kala Bharati', a school for painting and drawing. Till the end, Sunayani was always interested in artistic endeavours and hence this trip. The well-known artist Jamini Roy was on the dais presiding over the function. Suddenly he spied Sunayani among the audience. According to Geeta,

> Jamini Roy immediately came down, held Sunayini by the hand and escorted her up, commenting, 'How could you think of me as president while Sunayani was there?'

Now we may move on to Rabindranath's daughters. Three daughters arrived like three lotus buds. They were Madhuri, Renuka and Atashi. The eldest, Madhurilata, was the darling of her father. Rabindranath was particularly fond of fragrant bel flowers, hence Jnanadanandini had nicknamed Madhuri Bela. Her father affectionately called her Bela, Beli or Beluburi. Debendranath Sen's collection of poems *Shishumangal* shows that Madhuri was the proper name. Debendranath had composed a sonnet on his friend's daughter since he felt that the girl was madhuri (a combination of beauty, sweetness and grace) personified. The last few lines of the poem are:

Hashi phullo Mrinalini, 'Aduri' boliya,
Sourabhe bhoriya dilo chumiya chumiya .
Ananda-madira kori piye ankhi bhori
Duhitar naam mori rakhilo 'Madhuri'.

The delighted Mrinalini, called her 'my darling'
covered her with kisses.
Intoxicated by joy she named the
daughter 'Madhuri'.

Bela was beautiful, with a fair complexion and chiselled features. Her arrival found varied expression in the imagination of her twenty-six-year-old father Rabindranath. Apart from some letters and memoirs, Bela's childhood has been immortalized through Mini in the short story 'Kabuliwallah'.

Madhurilata's upbringing was slightly different from that of other girls of the family. Unlike the daughters of Hemendranath or Satyendranath, she neither went to Loreto House nor to the Indian-style Bethune School. She was coached at home by several tutors. There were three English mistresses, Miss Parsons, Miss Elgi and Miss Lytten, besides Mr Lawrence, Shivvardhan Vidyarnab and Hemchandra Bhattacharya. Rabindranath had consulted Sister Nivedita about Madhurilata's education and taught her himself, besides all the other teachers. He did not leave any lacunae in Madhurilata's education just because she did not go to school. He had her coached in both Western and Indian music, literature and even nursing. Madhuri had to read *Shakuntala, Manusamhita* and *Vishnupuran*. Her father even encouraged her to read the novels of Bankimchandra. He had no reservation about these being fit for 'adults only'.

Madhurilata lived for barely thirty-one years. The history of her brief life is well-known since she was Rabindranath's daughter.

She was his first-born and he wove many dreams around her. His hopes and plans for her future were tinged with anxiety too. As the eldest among five brothers and sisters, Bela was the apple of her father's eyes. He always felt that she would be a very good girl when she grew up. She did because as soon as she was a little older Madhuri realized, 'Whatever I do, my siblings will follow it as an example. If I am not good it will be harmful for them as well as for me.' She knew that she was not talented like her cousin sisters, especially Indira, but she tried 'to be as good as I can'.

Like Mrinalini, Madhuri was bored by life in Selaidaha. She felt the days hanging heavily. Resentment began to rise against her father. No one else had the temerity to complain directly to Rabindranath but Madhurilata was her father's daughter. She wrote

> You do not feel lonely because you busy yourself thinking and discussing important topics. We are ordinary and often wish for the company of others. If you do not wish to stir out after coming here then please share with us the thoughts and topics that so occupy you.

It is astonishing to realize that Madhuri was not yet fourteen when she wrote this letter. It is obvious that she wanted to share her father's philosophic ideas from a tender age.

By the time Madhuri was fourteen Rabindranath was keen to get her married. One wonders why he was eager to marry off such a young girl. Not only Madhuri, he also wanted to give Renuka and Atashi in marriage while they were very young. Yet he had always supported the marriageable age to be higher. According to many, during the Maharshi's lifetime all marriage expenses in the Tagore family were met from the income of the zamindari. Probably this prompted Rabindranath to get all his three daughters married while the Maharshi was alive. He did succeed in the case of his two elder daughters. Besides, the question of a suitable young man was there. Eligible bachelors were certainly not easy to come by. Then, there would be a sizeable dowry to pay. Rabindranath entrusted his friend Priyanath Sen to be on the lookout. When talks did not seem to progress satisfactorily, Rabindranath consoled his friend, 'Do not tire yourself in fruitless search'. He again wrote, 'Just as a river flows on to join the sea, so will Bela reach her husband's shore in due time.' All these were consolations and of no help in arranging a marriage. At last an eligible young man was found. He was Sarat—the son of the poet Biharilal Chakravarti. A brilliant scholar of Calcutta University, he had been awarded the Keshav Sen Gold Medal for standing First Class First, with Honours in Philosophy in the BA examination, had again topped the list in the MA examination with Moral Science. At the time the proposal was mooted, Sarat had qualified as a lawyer and was practising in Muzaffarpur. He was in every way a suitable groom for Madhuri. Besides, Rabindranath had since his youth been attracted to the poet Biharilal. He brought back memories of the flower-garden on the second-floor terrace and literary evenings with Jyotirindra. He was Natun Bouthan's favourite poet, always amused by her and the author of 'Saadher Asan'. Biharilal had passed on but Rabindranath hoped that his son would be as good-natured.

Sarat's mother demanded a large sum of cash as dowry. Though the wedding would be solemnized according to Brahmo rites, the poet was not reformer enough to reject the demand. He was offended but acceded to the demand of ten thousand rupees as cash dowry, out of consideration for his daughter's happiness. Apparently, Sarat did not wish to go against the wishes of his elders. A mortified Rabindranath wrote to a friend:

> There have been many weddings in our family. It is only at my daughter's marriage that there was haggling over every aspect. Such a thing had never happened before and will be a source of everlasting distress to me.

The Maharshi usually gifted three thousand rupees on the wedding of every girl. This time he raised the amount to five thousand rupees. The balance five thousand was paid by Rabindranath. There were other hurdles even after the marriage had been fixed. Many relations frowned on the marriage due to fact that Sarat belonged to a Brahmin sub-caste not approved by them. However Rabindranath did not pay any heed to such objections.

After her marriage Madhuri came to Muzaffarpur. The people there had never set eyes on such a bride. Not only her exquisite beauty, tasteful clothes and jewellery but her charming behaviour won the hearts of the entire Bengali population in Bihar. Besides, her famous father had accompanied her. There seemed to be an unending stream of visitors. Despite the unpleasantness before and during the wedding, Rabindranath was happy to have Sarat as a son-in-law. He wrote to Mrinalini, 'You would never find such a dependable young man among a million.' He also advised Madhuri. She replied,

> 'I shall try my best to carry out your advice. Besides remembering he is superior to me in every respect and that I am not his equal, I shall also try to improve his home. He expects a number of good qualities in me—as I belong to the Tagore family—and my endeavour will be never to disappoint him'.

Madhuri's efforts were successful. Madhuri and Sarat were happy in their seventeen years of married life in spite of the difficulties Madhuri must have faced adjusting to life in Muzaffarpur. Madhuri struck up a friendship with the authoress Anurupa Devi. Anurupa's husband and Sarat were friends and this led to the friendship between their spouses. Anurupa had been away from Muzaffarpur at the time of Madhuri's marriage. On her return she met Madhuri on a bright summer afternoon. To her, Madhuri appeared like a divine creation who had charmed the entire town. Madhuri's capabilities as a housewife have been mentioned in her father's letters. Not only the girls from the Tagore family, Bengali girls in general are experts in housework.

Purdah was prevalent in Bihar at the time. Little education could reach the women due to this custom. It was not possible for Madhuri to remain contented just with running her own home well. She belonged to a family where women had stood by the side of their men in their efforts to spread knowledge. Sarat was not known to participate in any activities against social norms but he did not impose any restrictions on Madhuri. Madhuri had seen the advent of women's emancipation in Calcutta. Apart from the social services engrossing her elder cousin sisters, she herself had taught little boys in Shantiniketan while Sarat Kumar was abroad. Here at Muzaffarpur she found the women totally illiterate and their lives shrouded by purdah. She felt the need to sow the seeds of education among them. There was more than enough for her to do. She involved her friend Anurupa and together they established a Ladies Committee. Both were joint-secretaries. They then established a girls' school and named it Chapman Balika Vidyalaya. So far so good. Now came the question of students for the school.

Getting girl students in Muzaffarpur was a Herculean task. Conditions in Bihar were medieval as compared to Bengal. A contemporary of Madhuri, Aghorkamini Ray, had devoted much more thought on the condition of women in Bihar. Her unstinted efforts had wrought some change among women in Bankipore. She sheltered girls in her own home and gradually taught them. Thus she was able to make fifteen girls literate. Aghorkamini's daughters also helped her. To bring an end to the custom of purdah Aghorkamini walked the streets with her daughters singing devotional Brahmo Sangeet. The sight of these women singing in the open helped many others muster up the courage. Doors had begun to open slowly. There can be no comparison between a social worker like Aghorkamini and a young girl like Madhuri, who was in Muzaffarpur for only a short while. At this time another lady had tried to improve the condition of women in Bhagalpur. She was Begum Rokeya Sakhawat Hussain. She was a Bengali married to Khan Bahadur Sayad Sakhawat Hussain, who was then the deputy magistrate of Bhagalpur. He always encouraged his educated wife in her literary pursuits. Just before his death, he established a girls' school and left his wife in charge. Rokeya began the school with just five pupils and one teacher. The conditions in Bhagalpur, especially those of the Muslim society, beggar description. Countless girls and women were buried under the dark burqa. Once her marriage had been fixed, a girl was kept in a dark room for six to seven months. Such confinement round the clock brought about loss of health, eyesight and sometimes life itself.

But the restrictions were never eased. It was beyond Rokeya's means to improve, singlehanded, the lot of these hapless girls. All her efforts went in vain. To commemorate her husband's memory she was forced to shift the school to Calcutta. Deepnarain Singh's wife Lillian (Leela), Taraknath Palit's daughter, had been able to alleviate the misery of the women of Bhagalpur to a small extent. Muzaffarpur was practically next to Bhagalpur. How could two inexperienced young housewives hope to run a girls' school there? Anurupa despaired and thought of giving up. Madhuri's patience seemed inexhaustible. She began visiting the homes of the residents with her friend. They always travelled in a closed coach. This was necessary to win over the trust and confidence of the women. The custom of purdah was so rigorous that they never had even a glimpse of the sun. When Madhuri and her friend got off the coach, sheets would be held on either side of the path and walking between these they would enter a house. Though she was never used to purdah, Madhuri always tried to respect the social norms of a small town. She also had to get over the stigma of being anglicized and make herself one of those she wanted to help. Then only would these women open their hearts to her. Doors did begin to open. According to Anurupa:

> Madhuri brought about a change in Muzaffarpur. Fortunately she did not take it back with her. A girl from a wealthy family,

> beautiful, accomplished and cultured, had no qualms about meeting people, not half but all the way. This was totally alien behaviour to the Bengali aristocracy of Muzaffarpur.

Had Madhuri lived long enough she would certainly have carved a niche for herself. Unfortunately before the spark could turn into a full-fledged blaze there was a change of scene and Madhuri returned to Calcutta. After his return home as a barrister, Sarat Kumar began practising at the Calcutta High Court. Rabindranath was keen that he should do so and live in the red mansion in Jorasanko. Dwijendranath's grandson Ajeendranath says, 'They used to live in Rabidada's portion of the house and occupied a few rooms on the ground floor.'

Rabindranath had always supervised Madhuri's education. Her letters bear testimony to her powers of composition from an early age. Sarat Kumar also had literary tastes and was an avid reader. Madhuri's younger sister Mira has written, 'Before retiring at night, Didi and Sarat Babu would sit for a while in the hall downstairs and read Sanskrit plays. These included *Meghdoot* and *Shakuntala.*' Rabindranath handed over the unfinished manuscript of the *Ramayana* to Madhuri. Mrinalini had begun writing it and Rabindranath hoped that Madhuri would complete it. Not only her father but Anurupa also encouraged the diffident Madhuri to write. So far eight pieces of writing by Madhuri have been traced. Apart from translations, three of her short stories show her novelty of thought and her ability to write. Encouraged by her father, Madhuri wrote stories like '*Suro*', '*Mata Shatru*', '*Satpatra*', '*Anadrita*', '*Chor*', etc. These were published in *Bharati*, *Prabasi* and *Sabuj Patra*. The draft was always checked by her father. He once told Prasanta Mahalanobis, 'She had the ability but seldom wrote.' The truth of this comment is borne out by '*Mata Shatru*' and '*Satpatra*'. It is difficult to fathom how far these were altered by Rabindranath. It may have been that only the basic idea was Madhuri's. In the first edition of '*Galpa Gucchha*', Rabindranath's name was published as the author of '*Satpatra*'. He later informed the public that it had been written by his daughter. The portrait of the lascivious Sadhucharan with his predatory habits as depicted in '*Satpatra*' is as disgusting as it is horrible. The story ends with one comment: 'For Sadhucharan a wife was an expendable commodity. He discarded them as fast as he collected them!' The story and the last comment indicate Rabindranath's penmanship more than that of his daughter. The theme of '*Mata Shatru*' is also novel. It is about the unlimited greed of a hapless mother. This story bears an uncanny resemblance to Sarat Kumar's '*Sonar Jhinuk*'. Perhaps the basic plot was narrated by Rabindranath to both Madhuri and Sarat Kumar. In both the stories, an unbelievable tale has been made credible. Rabindranath once met Madhuri's friend Anurupa. He told her, 'Emulating you, she had begun to write. Had she lived she may have one day written like you.'

Unfortunately Madhuri's life did not end on the happy note on which it had begun. She and her husband lived in Jorasanko from 1909 to 1913. Minor differences began to crop up. These led to a great deal of unpleasantness. The real reason has never been clear. Rabindranath was abroad at this time and his youngest son-in-law Nagendranath was in charge of the household at Jorasanko. It has been said that Sarat Kumar was subjected to numerous pin-pricks and petty humiliations at that time. Though Sarat Kumar was not at fault, even a trivial matter like who should read the newspapers first led to altercations. Madhuri and Sarat Kumar moved out into a rented flat in Dihi Serampore. Going by what is known about the situation, one may assume that deteriorating relations between the arrogant Nagendranath and the sensitive Sarat Kumar prompted the move. It seems that there were other undisclosed reasons. Rabindranath had sent his second and third sons-in-law abroad almost directly after marriage but not Sarat. Sarat Kumar and Madhuri must have been hurt by this behaviour. As an outcome Sarat Kumar and Nagendranath went abroad about the same time. There is no satisfactory explanation for why Rabindranath suddenly decided to send Sarat Kumar abroad after so many years. It is probable that he did so to assuage the feeling of hurt in the hearts of his daughter and son-in-law. Rabindranath paid the passage money to England for all his three sons-in-law and used to send ten pounds per month to cover their expenses. It was at this time that Madhurilata wound up her home in Muzaffarpur and shifted back to the Tagore mansion. All Rabindranath's efforts could not heal the breach. When he drew up his will in 1912 Rabindranath arranged for Madhurilata to have fifty rupees per month and Atashilata (Mira) one hundred rupees. There were problems galore in Mira's married life and Nagendranath was not well-off. Madhuri's financial condition was better, her needs fewer and presumably this prompted Rabindranath to make the above arrangement. This again further estranged the two sisters. A letter to Satyaprasad from Rathindranath at the time indicates this:

> It is unfortunate that Didi and Mira are still quarrelling over trivia. They are not children. If they refuse to see reason nothing can be done.

By the time Surendranath apprised Rabindranath of the situation, matters had reached the point of no return. Sarat and Madhuri left Jorasanko for Dihi Serampore. Before Rabindranath's return Madhuri was pregnant but the child died prematurely. This further upset Madhuri. The poet tried his best to convince Madhuri and Sarat of his love and sincerity. He wrote:

> What is the use of dwelling on what is past? Bel, I am not accusing you. I only request you to wash away from your mind whatever feelings of hurt you bear us—even if they are valid ones.

To Sarat Kumar he wrote:

> If you have felt that there is lack of love and concern for you in my heart you have misunderstood me. Even if you have noticed any such shortcoming in me, is it impossible for you to forgive me?

Nothing succeeded in overcoming Sarat and Madhuri's resentment and no reconciliation was effected. Sarat and Rabindranath never met after this.

What about Madhurilata? Apart from an untimely death, will nothing more ever come to light? Who stood by her at the time of the heartbreaking rift with her revered and renowned father? Who consoled her? It was from this time that she gradually wilted and was soon bedridden. When she was a little better, after about a year, she wrote to her friend Anurupa, 'I live in despair in my closed room, shut away from friends.'

Lying on her sickbed Madhuri felt,

> A curtain has been raised. I am learning to view people anew. Had I not suffered such a great blow perhaps my perceptions would never have been roused. This hovering between life and death for the past one year has forged new bonds between my soul and heart. This has enlightened my vision, strengthened me and my life seems to have acquired some meaning.

This perception of Madhuri, that her life had been futile until her soul and heart came to know each other well in her sickbed, and only when she was hovering between life and death, made it impossible for her to come back to the mundane affairs of daily life. Apart from Anurupa, Madhuri had corresponded with another friend Induprova at that time. Her letters to Induprova bear no trace of her new perceptions nor any hint of sadness. Could it be that she was trying to forget? She wrote,

> When graduating is the only examination a woman has to successfully clear for marriage, what is the point in having a long memory?

Madhuri had been keen to visit Induprova in her Hazaribagh home. She was able to make the trip as is evident from Jyotirindranath's diary, 'Sarat and Bela arrived suddenly this morning . . . by car from Hazaribagh. They will be leaving tomorrow.'

Shortly thereafter it was learnt that the summons had come for Madhuri. The illness, tuberculosis (pthysis), that had already snatched away her younger sister Renuka, had attacked the ethereal Madhuri. It appeared to her near and dear ones as if it was not an illness but a test by the Almighty. Rabindranath wrote to Rathindra,

> I know the time for Bela's departure is close at hand. I do not have the strength to go and see her.

However when the time really drew near, Rabindranath had to go to his daughter's bedside. Madhuri was by then a shadow of her old self, her body ravaged by illness. She would put out her pale hands, cajoling him as she did as a child, 'Father, tell me a story!'

The father's heart seemed about to break. It was only the other day, his once-lively second daughter Rani had clung to him with her thin hands and made the same request. He had not realized that he would be met with a similar request so soon. All the tales in the storehouse of this master of storytellers seemed exhausted. His voice choked. Still he went on telling tales. He had tried to amuse Renuka with poems from *Shishu* since she herself had barely stepped out of childhood. To Bela he would narrate the story of Binu from *Palataka*, and others like 'Mukti' and that of the lost Bami. This also came to an end eventually. Prasantachandra Mahalanabis has described the day thus:

> When we reached Jorasanko, the Poet invited me upstairs as usual. After a short silence he said, 'I had known for a long time that she would go away. There was nothing that I could do, still I used to go every morning and sit by her bed holding her hand.'

Though he tried to accept Bela's death calmly, it was obvious that the father's heart was broken. Lady Ranu Mukherjee's memoirs give us as inkling of the depth of his loss. 'After the cremation, he came to our doorstep calling out, "Ranu, Ranu, where are you?"'

It would have been clear to those who knew Rabindranath well that it was at this moment of profound grief that he wanted to see Ranu as an alternative to his own daughter. A few days later he wrote to Ranu,

> You came to me at a very heartbreaking juncture . . . my daughter who left this world was my eldest child. I had nurtured her myself. Rarely does one come across such beauty and loveliness on this earth. You arrived just when she left me. I felt as if the departing glow of affection lit up a similar one before being extinguished.

In his collection of poems *Palataka* there is one poem: '*Shesh Pratishtha*'. In this the poet says:

> *Eyi katha sada shuni, 'Gechhe chole, gechhe chole'.*
> *Tobu rakhi bole*
> *Bolo na 'Shey nai'.*
> *Shey kathata mithya, tai*
> *Kichhute sahey na je*
> *Maramey giye baje.*
>
> I always hear, 'She is no more, no more',
> But I want to say, 'Never say she is not there'.
> This is not true and hence it is unbearable,
> Hence it wounds my heart.

There are quite a few factual misconceptions regarding Madhuri's death. Most of them concern Sarat. It is true that the unpleasant situation created in Jorasanko was not overcome even by Madhuri's tragic death. According to Pravatkumar Mukhopadhyaya, Rabindranath's biographer, Sarat and Rabindranath never met after the former left Jorasanko. 'When Bela was on her deathbed, Rabindranath used to visit her in the afternoon. Sarat would be in Court at the time.' On the other hand Maitreyi Devi has quoted Hemlata Devi. Therein we find Hemlata saying,

> He ignored all insults to go and see Bela on her deathbed. She was the apple of his eyes. Sarat would be smoking with his feet propped up on the table. He did not even have the courtesy to

lower them on seeing his father-in-law. He would overlook all such indignities and go to his daughter's bedside. She would also turn her face away.

Both the statements appear to lack credibility. Both Rabindranath and Prasanta Mahalanobis mention going to visit Madhuri in the morning. Prasanta used to give Rabindranath a lift daily, so the chances of his making a mistake were negligible. On the other hand Pravatkumar, Tagore's biographer, says 'Afternoon'. If this is construed as after 10 a.m. then it is possible to reconcile the two statements. The poet had also written to Kadambini Dutt about being busy with his daughter during the day. The chances of his meeting Sarat Kumar at this time of the day were slim. It is also not possible to accept Hemlata's statement as unequivocal. Rabindranath himself said that his daughter would say, 'Father, tell me a story.' In his letter to Ramendrasundar Trivedi, written after Bela's death, Rabindranath laments that he was unable to alleviate her suffering. It was not possible and yet, 'she had full confidence in her father right till the end.' Thus it is not possible to accept that the daughter turned her face away from the father.

Moreover, Prasanta Kumar Pal has shown that money was spent for appointing nurses for Bela, buying flowers as well as medicines for her. This was taken from the family kitty and is recorded in the books of accounts. So it is difficult to believe that at this time Sarat and Madhuri behaved discourteously. The day the two could have met, that is when Bela passed away, Rabindranath turned back from the staircase after hearing the news. After his wife's death, Sarat returned to Muzaffarpur. He bought a property belonging to an old indigo planter and settled down to the life of a recluse. His main recreation was his garden. Many people are of the opinion that Madhurilata's married life was not happy. It is also said that her frustrated life was the source of Rabindranath's short story 'Haimanti'. Despite a resemblance between Madhuri and Haimanti, the former's married life does not appear to have been frustrated.

Indira has written, 'Sarat had been devoted to Madhuri during the short span of their life together.' However neither Rabindranath nor Sarat ever tried to bridge the wide gulf of resentment and hurt pride.

Among Rabindranath's daughters only Mira or Atashilata lived long. Renuka or Rani, the poet's second daughter, who was older than Mira, died a young girl, before having a chance to blossom. Most of what we know about Renuka is from Mira's *Smriti Katha*. Renuka was always strong-willed, obstinate, and whimsical. She seemed uninterested in things normal for a young girl. Dressing up never interested her and she disliked tying her hair into a bun. Renuka was married when only eleven, just a month after Bela's wedding. Rabindranath told his wife, 'I have fixed Rani's marriage . . . Chhoto Bou, the boy is very good-natured as well as good-looking. I liked him very much. Rani is so strong willed, her husband ought to be a gentle person.'

The marriage took place accordingly though Rani did not accept her new role happily. She was relieved to learn that her husband would be going abroad directly after the marriage. She thus did not object to any of the rituals during the wedding. Two disasters hit Renuka hard—her mother's death and her husband's return from America after being unsuccessful in his studies there. Her brooding ultimately led to her contracting tuberculosis. Rabindranath would recite to her poems from *Shishu*. Perhaps his own childhood peeped into his mind while he tried to amuse his daughter.

The breeze of the pine forests in Almora were reputed to be beneficial for tuberculosi patients. Rabindranath took Renuka to Almora for a change. Towards her end Renuka would plead, 'Baba take me home.' Rabindranath brought her back to Jorasanko. When medicines failed, he read out to her regularly from the Upanishads so that her departure may be eased. This is probably why during her last moments Renuka clutched her father's hand saying,

Everything is becoming dark. I can't see anything. Baba, please read out *Pita Nohasi* to me.

In Renuka's life, her father stood above everything. So, when she had to surrender to death, she had wanted to cross over the last barrier holding on to his hand.

Mira's proper name was Atashilata but she was better known by her nickname. As the youngest of the family, her life began on a very happy note. She was surrounded by the loving care of her parents as well as elder brothers and sisters. Unfortunately these happy and carefree days were soon lost. One death after another in Rabindranath's family forced Mira to spend her time either with Jnanadanandini or Madhurilata and at times under the care of Rajlakshmi Devi. Towards the end, her permanent address was 'Malancha' in Shantiniketan.

Like her elder sisters, Mira's education also began at home. Mr Lawrence coached her in English while Kartikchandra Naan gave her lessons in art. Rabindranath himself encouraged her to correspond in English. At one time he was also on the look-out for an English mistress to teach Mira needlework. Mira was a great favourite of Tagore's friend Jagadishchandra Bose. He was very keen to marry her to his nephew Arabindamohan. Jagadishchandra would tease Mrinalini about the possible dowry. Rabindranath also enjoyed such discussions.

Alas, the happy event never took place. One wonders what would have happened had Mrinalini lived longer. After her death, Rabindranath looked for a Brahmin groom for Mira. There was a proposal of Mira's marriage with Tarunram Phuken of Assam. Rabindranath was deluded by the handsome young Nagendranath Gangopadhyaya and made a grave error of judgement. Nagendranath belonged to the 'Sadharan Brahmo Samaj'. He was looking for ways and means to go abroad. Rabindranath decided to marry him to Mira and send him to America. The lure of a passage to America prompted Nagendranath to agree to a marriage according to the norms of the Adi Brahmo Samaj.

However, trouble and disagreements erupted from the day of the wedding. According to the tenets of the Adi Brahmo Samaj it was essential for a Brahmin groom to wear the sacred thread, while that of the Sadharan Brahmo Samaj was to discard it. Nagendra was given a new sacred thread just before the ceremony. But he threw away the sacred thread 'given by Baba' in presence of all the guests. So wrote Madhurilata while describing the wedding to Rathindranath who was away. Thereafter, during every ritual—wearing a 'topor', being smeared with turmeric paste *(gaaye halud)* and exchanging of garlands—Nagendra's behaviour crossed all bounds of decency. To quote Madhurilata again, 'The groom's ill-mannered behaviour shamed us. Nagendra's shamelessness seems boundless.' Even though the Maharshi had embraced Brahmoism he had adhered to the prevalent rituals, especially during such functions. This had been the norm in his family so far.

It is not easy to say if these incidents on Mira's wedding night were an indication of her future. To begin with, there seem to have been no fissures in her life with her husband. Mira belonged to the most cultured family in Bengal. Rabindranath always taught his daughters to accept that the husband was superior in every way. This has been observed in his letters to Madhuri. Mira also followed her father's instructions. In her letters to Nagendra, she refers to herself as an, 'uncultured, shy village girl' and says 'I am not capable of doing any work so you will have to bear a lot. My only hope is that however ignorant I may be, you will have patience and teach me.' Such a polite and innocent confession had no effect on Nagendra. Probably he took it to be true and chose to treat her with disdain. Even after the birth of their two children, a son Nitindra and a daughter Nandita, there was no change in Nagendra's behaviour. The couple began to drift apart. After Nagendra's return to India, Rabindranath had entrusted him with numerous responsibilities. Nagendra misused this trust: he spent lavishly, got into debt and behaved atrociously with the other members of the family. Thus he brought unhappiness and strife into everybody's life. Madhuri's relations with Mira were also soured. The death of the elder sister, who had heaped upon her only love and care until Mira was married, does not seem to have left any mark on her. At least, this is what one feels after reading Mira's *Smriti Katha*. Madhuri is hardly mentioned there.

Mira's separation from Nagendra became inevitable. This hurt her father who had tried to educate her in every field. He told her, 'I have tried my best to protect you from the frivolous attitude prevalent among women, their narrow-mindedness which warps and distorts their views on practically every important aspect of life and the way they fritter away their days in idle gossip, ignorant about the important worldly affairs. I hope my efforts will not have been in vain.' Though this was written in a different context, it clearly shows the lofty ideals to which Rabindranath wanted to attune his daughter's mind.

Initially Rabindranath may have tried to discuss matters with Nagendra. He tried to explain a man's disrespect for and cruelty towards a woman thus:

> One reason for lack of respect and harshness towards women is that we have had scant help from them in broadening our mind. Since their role is confined to looking after us and caring for our physical needs, their worth is devalued in our minds.

It is doubtful if Rabindranath really believed this. The women of the Tagore family could never be classed as ordinary or common. He himself had always received adequate mental support from Mrinalini as was evinced by his feelings after her death, 'There is no one left to whom I can unburden myself.'

Mira returned quite a few times to Shantiniketan to help and relieve Rabindranath. Sir Ashutosh Mukhopadhyaya appointed Nagendranath to set up the Agriculture and Agricultural Research department of the Calcutta University. When Nagendranath wanted to forcibly take Mira to Calcutta, Rabindranath expressed his views unequivocally,

> I certainly do not wish for even a hint of a separation between you and Mira. It is well-nigh impossible for me to accept the responsibility for the same but I have to do so with great sorrow. In Madras I saw that Mira was scared of you and was apprehensive of being insulted by you in public. I then realized that your basic natures are not compatible.

It must be said that as a father Rabindranath showed surprising firmness and grit at this juncture. 'The very idea that she may have to accept a lifestyle against her wish, is unbearable for me.' Again he wrote,

> The differences that have cropped up between the two of you are not superficial. It is beyond me to try and heal the breach by threat or force. I cannot imagine anything more cruel and demeaning.

From this time Rabindranath tried to help Mira stand on her own feet. 'I want you to be capable of supporting your own family independently and permanently. Otherwise my heart will never be easy.' About this time Nagendra had to go to England to work for and obtain a Ph.D degree. This was as per a stipulation of the Calcutta University. Rabindranath sent him the passage-money, the other expenses being borne by the University. A few years later, Nagendra and Mira were legally divorced. Probably there was some suggestion of a reconciliation. Rabindranath's reply to Nagendra was,

> The present alienation of the relations between the two of you is heart-breaking for me. Had there been any chance of a revival I would certainly have tried. The situation is such that no coercion is possible. Moreover I do not consider it correct to enforce any such method in such relationships. Under these circumstances I consider it my bounden duty to do whatever is needful to release both of you.

As his daughter's trials and tribulations increased, the sight of her misery made her repentant father write to Rathindra,

> I was the one to hand her the first punishment of her life. On her wedding night, when Mira had gone to the toilet, a cobra was lurking there. I feel that if the snake had bitten her then, it would have meant deliverance for her.

It is easy to imagine the depth of Rabindranath's grief that made him pen such words. Towards the end, he showed the firmness expected of a father.

Henceforth, Nagendra and Mira's lives coursed along separate paths. Mira's days were spent in her own home 'Malancha'. Nitindra and Nandita often came to stay with her. Nagendra and Mira met just once again. It was in Germany by their son's deathbed. Even overwhelming sorrow was unable to bring together two hearts brimming with hurt pride. In Mira's *Smriti Katha*, written during her last years, there is no mention at all of Nagendra. It was as if he had been completely erased from her heart.

The self-effacing Mira spent her lonely days in 'Malancha'. Her only consolations were her two children. Unfortunately, they predeceased her. Nitindra's death was most untimely. The culprit was the same fatal disease—tuberculosis. Nandita passed away much later. No outward manifestations of grief were ever visible in Mira's behaviour. Tagore always said, 'To bare one's deepest sorrow before the world demeans it and is humiliating.' With a similar attitude Mira also concealed her overflowing cup of grief from the world at large.

One wonders why she never wrote about herself even towards the end. Did she feel, 'How long can I guard what will be lost eventually?' Was that the reason behind her writing at all? It does not seem so. One whose entire life has been a waste and full of loss, what could she wish for? She wrote *Smriti Katha* 'to while away the long hours spent in the sickbed.' Thus there is neither continuity nor any glimpse of her own life in this narrative. She has only written about those whose company brought a ray of light into the darkness of her heart. She captured them in her heart but remained unrevealed herself.

The pages of *Smriti Katha* are tinged with Mira's feelings. It is difficult for any one to conceal one's feelings completely. When the plants in her garden flowered, all her grief seemed to disappear and her heart calmed down. Her style of writing and language are both simple.

> Bel and juin blossoms covered the trees, in the morning I saw sheuli flowers wet with dew strewn on the red earthen road and the fragrance of chameli blossoms wafted in the breeze. All my heartache disappeared. I felt that I had been amply rewarded. When I was unable to concentrate on anything, it was love of gardening that kept me going.

Long before she wrote *Smriti Katha* Rabindranath instructed Mira to write summaries of some Indian and English articles. Eight of these were published in *Prabasi* and three in *Tattwabodhini*. Apart from these, Mira did not contribute practically anything of literal value during her long life and stay in Shantiniketan.

Along with Mira ends the saga of the Maharshi's granddaughters.

Now we come to women who entered the Tagore family as brides. Just as the daughters carried the culture of the Tagores to different families, similarly some others entered the family with characteristic traditions from a different environment. Though all of them were not equally talented, it has been possible to learn about those who were exceptional in their accomplishments. The best-known among the women who entered the Tagore family as brides at this period are Hemlata, Pratima and Sangya.

Hemlata was the second wife of Dwipendranath, the eldest son of Dwijendranath. Dwipendra's first wife Sushila and her younger sister Charushila both entered the family by marriage. They hailed from a village in present-day Bangladesh and both were short-lived. Sushila was a good singer and adept at acting. In her short lifespan she left her mark on the members of the andar mahal. In her reminiscences Prafullamoyee has said that Sushila could sing with great feeling. Her songs always charmed the listeners. This characteristic was present also in the voice of Sushila's son Dinendra. Sushila had also participated in dramatics during the golden era of the Tagores. In the play *Bibaha Utsav* she enacted the role of the hero. Her acting as a man was so good that Saudamini had narrated it to the Maharshi.

The song *O keno choori kore chai* was very popular among the members of the Tagore family. Neither her acting nor singing ever reached the world outside. Blessed with a sweet disposition, Sushila enjoyed company. It was observed that she had the power to mesmerize people. Had she lived longer, one would have seen another talented woman.

After Sushila's death, Hemlata came into the family as a bride. She was descended from the daughter of Radhaprasad Ray. Radhaprasad was the son of Raja Rammohan Ray. Since three girls from the Tagore family were already married to three of Hemlata's elder brothers, she was no stranger to the andar mahal. Now she entered the family. From the day sixteen-year-old Hemlata became Dwipendra's wife, she became the mother of her two stepchildren. Since that time she became 'Barama' (elder mother) to everyone. Childless herself, she was revered and loved by all. Apart from the qualities of caring for the sick, supervising and managing a large family, she had the rare gift of penmanship. She was the first lady acharya of the Adi Brahmo Samaj. In between looking after the family, social service and religious discourses, she carried on with her literary pursuits.

From her childhood, Hemlata had shown a keen interest in academics. Her father Lalitmohan had had her coached in astrology besides English and Bengali. For Hindus, the study of astrology is forbidden to women. Perhaps this was because a woman's entire existence depended on a man, so what would she achieve by a knowledge of her fate? Hemlata's mother was also against her studying astrology. Lalitmohan would nullify her arguments, saying with a smile, 'My daughter is a Brahmin.' Probably he felt that Hemlata, like a Brahmin, had great powers of perception, so it would not be difficult for her to master astrology. It is not clear how far her pursuance of astrology progressed though a few of her stories clearly indicate the influence of such study. Her elder brother Mohinimohan also helped her read Kali Singhi's *Mahabharata*. Observing her interest, Dwipendra appointed Miss Maescoll to coach her. Andrews Pearson taught Hemlata English poetry for two years. Besides, Rabindranath also helped her with her studies. He would select good articles in English from Indian as well as foreign magazines and ask Hemlata to translate them. It was his encouragement that led to Hemlata's interest in Bengali literature. Not only literature and language, she was interested in religion and spiritualism too. Her father was a direct disciple of Troilangaswami. Her elder brother Mohinimohan had been associated with the Theosophist movement and later came in contact with Shivnarain Swami. Hemlata also considered herself a disciple of Paramhamsa Shivnarain Swami. Thus she had leanings towards various spiritual ideas and religions. To the traditions of Raja Rammohan Ray were added the life work of the Maharshi. To quote Hemlata, 'About six to seven years after my marriage my husband's grandfather, Maharshi Debendranath Tagore, told Pundit Hemchandra Vidyaratna "This granddaughter-in-law of mine has a right to *Brahmogyan*. Please teach her the ten Upanishads." I studied the Upanishads for three years under his guidance.' Rabindranath gave her some books on the Sufi cult which she read avidly. She also translated the article 'Islam in Africa'. After reading this, the poet commented while coaching her, 'Are you planning to convert to Islam? Your heart and mind become so enlivened when discussing the Sufis.'

By then Hemlata was no longer a shy new bride. She replied,

'The Sufis are great saints. But I cannot convert to anything. This is Rammohan's influence. How can I enter the confines of one single religious thought?'

Her answer pleased Rabindranath no end. He said,

That is right! The blessings of Raja Rammohan Roy are obviously on you.

Later when she saw Arabia from the ship while on her way to Europe, Hemlata was overwhelmed with a yearning to touch its soil. She felt,

> This is where the Prophet Muhammad was born. This is the land where he spent his life. He was interred here and his remains are perhaps still intermingled in this soil.

She thus accepted every religion with deep reverence.

The Maharshi had also given his blessings to Hemlata. After Balendra's death, arrangements had been made for the family to participate in religious discourses. It was during one such session that the Maharshi heard about Hemlata's interest and pursuance of religious studies by herself. He then began discussing various aspects of religion with Hemlata for an hour every afternoon. This went on for seven long years. Hemlata's interest and arguments had persuaded the Maharshi to permit her to perform *'hom'*. This was not just fire-worship. This was an oblation performed to experience the presence of the omniscient and omnipotent God.

The Maharshi bequeathed to Hemlata the ring he had received when being initiated into Brahmoism. This was in appreciation of her religious belief and devout nature. Hemlata knew nothing about it. After the Maharshi's death, his khajanchi (treasurer) handed over the ring to Hemlata. He said, 'The master asked me to give this to you. He said that you deserve it the most.' Hemlata wore the ring for a number of years. It has been later preserved in the Rabindra Bhawan of Shantiniketan. This incident proved that Hemlata was different from other women and the most deserving heir to the Maharshi's lifelong efforts at self-realization. About this time the women of the Tagore family were achieving success in many walks of life. Hemlata, however, was quietly rendering religious advice and tenets. A collection of these was published as a booklet. The prices included *Paramatmaye ki Prayojan* (What is the need for the Almighty), *Sristi O Shrasta Kahar Naam* (What is Creation and Who is the Creator), *Chaitanyamaya Purna O Sarbashaktimaan Ishwar Kahar Naam* (Who is the Almighty God Full of Consciousness), *Satya Laaver Upay ki* (What are the Means of Attaining Absolute Truth). In these gems of advice lie hidden the essence of Brahmoism. Hemlata revered every religion and had no bigotry about any particular one. The monks of the Ramakrishna Mission enjoyed her lectures. She participated in the centenary celebrations of Shri Ramakrishna Paramhansa Dev. There she described Ramakrishna as an incarnation of the Lord Shiva—a source of a childlike joy and happiness.

Along with her pursuit of religion, Hemlata also interested herself in literature and social service. By this time, the social restrictions for women were gradually slackening. Thus Hemlata never faced any hassles in her various activities. Moreover she was known to be deeply religious, educated and the mistress of a wealthy home. Despite all her activities, her care and concern for her home never waned. One wonders how she managed to fit in so much, so successfully. Stories, poems, articles, plays, children's books, reminiscences, lyrics—Hemlata wrote all these. Over and above, she edited the magazine *Bangalaksmi* and was in charge of Sarojnalini and Basanta Kumari Homes for widows. She was also responsible for looking after the young students of Shantiniketan. It may be best to deal with her literary achievements first. A number of women began to write after coming into the Tagore family. With Hemlata it was an inborn gift. She never lost her individual touch and thus her stories are on a different note. However, when writing articles or reminiscences, she embraced the typical style of the Tagores.

Only three collections of Hemlata's poems have been published. They are *Jyoti*, *Akalpita* and *Alor Pakshi*. Numerous poems are still scattered in the pages of different magazines. Rabindranath and Jyotirindranath had set some of Hemlata's poems to music.

The ones by Rabindranath are *Ohe sunirmal sundar ujjwal subhra aloke*, and *Balak praney alok jwali*. Jyotirindra set to music the poem *Ami aar kichu na jaani*. Indira and the well-known singer Surendranath Bandopadhyaya has also set some of Hemlata's poetry to music. The name Jyoti was given by Rabindranath and Akalpita by Jyotirindranath.

Most of Hemlata's poetry is imbued with a love for God. Small compositions bear a depth of thought yet are neither complicated nor difficult to comprehend. There is no conflict of form and metaphor, no play of symbolism and analogy, and neither the faintest indication of visual imagery. Yet there is something indefinable. She has tried to express knowledge of the outside world together with the feelings of the soul. This vision also indicates her own perceptions.

Antarey chetana anubhave
Bahire shey dhare
Nanamato roop,
Antarey bahirey nehare je tara
Ghuche tar bhaba—
Bandhaner dukh.

The heart only feels, the whole manifests
itself in many outward forms,
When one can see the same omnipresent
both in the heart and outside,
All his griefs come to an end.

The language and context of Hemlata's poems show the influence of Rabindranath who enjoyed reading her poems. In his book *Kavya Parichay* he included the following poem by Hemlata.

Shekhane phutile prem, rahi sheikhane
Shugandhe bhorilo pran akul
Karile sabar chitto, taba samatul
Nahi e dharay. Mrityu hori loye jaye.
Lakho lakho pran, lupto kori tamashay.

Jekhane phutile tumi, rahi sheikhane
Mrityure karile kolay, anander doley
Diley je tahare dola; gupto dwar kholay
Amriter; deen marta paye taar swaad.
Prem taba svarnakanti nitya shobha paye.
Apon asane boshi shubhro sushamaye
Mrityu o amrito majhe ja ache bichchhyed
Purnatar majhe tar ghuchayechho bhed.

I wish to remain where love you blossom
The fragrance fills my heart,
Joy brims over every being,
There is none equal to you.
Death robs millions of lives, enveloping them in darkness.
You remain where you blossomed,
Embracing death, you rock it with joy,
Whence the secret door concealing eternity opens,
The impoverished world is thus able to taste it.
Love, your dazzling vision appears, eternally
steady in all its pristine beauty;
You have dispelled the difference between
Death and eternity within yourself.

Duniyar Dena and *Dehali* are two collections of stories by Hemlata. The stories in the former show an influence of Tagore's *Lipika*, and are full of philosophical views. Kamini Roy was not only surprised to read these stories but also felt that in Hemlata's literary work her life's experiences have had more influence than have conjectures and imagination. This is very true. In the case of women, their literary characters often do not acquire reality. Basically it is due to a lack of practical experience. Hemlata was never so handicapped. In the course of her social work, she came across people from different backgrounds and observed them with her unusual insight. Thus she was able to impress even the literateur Rabindranath. He normally did not like to read literary works by women, yet *Dehali* so entranced him that he wrote Hemlata a unique letter.

> I enjoyed reading your short stories. The portrayal of the characters and the surroundings are absolutely true to life. Your varied experience, acquired during your sojourn in numerous villages—both large and small—of Bengal have been enlivened by your powers of perception. Your stories are but an exhibition of pen-portraits of such experiences.

Dehali entranced the writer Tarashankar Bandopadhyaya also. He commented,

> The authoress, though from an aristocratic family, is closely associated with a number of welfare organizations of the times. In the course of her social work she has had to move among, and mix with, people from various levels of society. She collected the plots of these stories during this work. These have been touched up by her imagination and brought to life by her pen. Thus these are not aspects of society as imagined by someone far removed from reality, but the true reflection of her insight and gentle heart.

After Swarnakumari, Hemlata was the only one among the Tagore women to achieve so much acclaim by creating original works of fiction. Calcutta University honoured her by awarding her the first 'Leela' prize. Hemlata's stories resemble those of *Laharini* by Saratkumari, rather than Swarnakumari's work. In both cases, their simple yet humourous outlook to life is reflected in their stories. Like her poems, Hemlata's short stories are devoid of complications. The characters, events, surroundings and dialogues are all simple, natural and without any effort to gild the lily. Most are the products of Hemlata's real experiences. While managing the Widow Homes she learnt about the joys, aspirations and griefs of many women and gained many unusual experiences. Otherwise she would have never been able to portray the heroine of 'Chandramoni'. The idea of poverty forcing a family to declare their unmarried daughter a widow, and sending her to a widow home, was beyond the wildest dreams of the authoresses of that time.

Perhaps the best description of Hemlata would be as a social worker. Women of the Tagore family had carried on social service along with their achievements in the field of literature and music. However, women's welfare was Hemlata's main objective. Her maximum activities were connected with Sakhi Samiti, Widow Homes and Bharat Stree Mahamandal. Besides, she had also accepted the charge of Sarojnalini Nari Mangal Samiti and Basanta Kumari Widow Home in Puri. The organizing ability shown by Hemlata in managing and running these institutions is comparable only to that of Krishna Bhabini Das of Bharat Stree Mahamandal. For women belonging to aristocratic and educated families like the Tagores, social service had both pros and cons. However when educated women of the nineteenth century came forward to further the cause of women's welfare, those of the well-to-do families did not lag behind. Since the queen and empress of India, Queen Victoria, herself was interested in such work, the women of the Tagore family never faced any obstacles. One may wonder about the nature of their social service. Their prime object was to alleviate the lot of widows. They realized the most important aspect of women's welfare—only education and economic independence could help women take charge of their lives. With their natural aptitude for leadership and unerring judgment of the main problem, they soon found themselves at the helm of affairs. This is also the reason why the Tagore family became trendsetters in fashion, culture, literature and the general attitudes of Bengal at the time. Beginning with Swarnakumari's Sakhi Samiti, numerous women of the Tagore family—having migrated into numerous families all over India—are even today intimately connected with women's welfare.

Sarojnalini Ashram was founded in 1925. Shortly thereafter Gurusaday Dutt requested Hemlata to look after it. Later Hemlata saw that Nari Shiksha Samiti had Abala Basu, 'Hiranmoyee Shilpasram had Swarnakumari and Bharat Stree Mahamandal had Sarala but there was no one to manage Sarojnalini Ashram after the death of Sarojnalini Dutt. So she had perforce to assume full charge herself. Dedicating herself body and soul to the ideals of women's education and welfare, she strove to find out the spheres where their rights had been curtailed.

Nari ki sudhu narer bhogya?
Nahe ki janani, nahe ki bhogini
Nahe ki biswahiter yogya ?

Is woman only a plaything of man?
Is she not a mother, a sister
And worthy of universal welfare?

Though strictly adhering to the norms prescribed for orthodox Hindu widows, she showed a surprisingly liberal outlook in considering the main problems facing women. She explained succinctly the true meaning of women's independence. She refused to call the liberty of free mixing between the sexes independence.

> A woman who wishes to mix with a man just because he is a man is uneducated. A truly educated women is one who considers a man a human being above all else.

She spared no pains to disabuse those who looked at Bengali women's desire for independence with a jaundiced eye. Bengali women were never prompted by a desire for free mixing. Their real grievance was that they had no right to share responsibilities equally with men.

The women's liberation movement of Europe greatly motivated Hemlata. Inspired, she visited various European countries to assess the success of this movement and also discern the actual extent of such freedom. On her return, there was no noticeable change in her views on the subject. To her the ideals for a woman were self-sacrifice, patience, discipline and welfare of others. She always tried to inspire women along these lines in real life as well as through her articles. Hemlata never used high-sounding principles about love. Her view:

> Steadfastness is the prime criteria without which one can never be called human, be it love for another person, country or the Almighty. These are not different but manifestations of the same emotion.

She was a welcome visitor to all institutions, especially those concerned with social welfare. This was mainly due to her ability to identify herself spontaneously with such organizations. Mahatma Gandhi called her 'sister' and had invited her to Sabarmati Ashram. To all others she was universally known as Bara-ma.

Today however Hemlata is remembered not for her social service but for her *Smritikatha.* Contrary to the traditions of the Tagore family, she did not write her autobiography. She wrote some articles in her imitable informal style. These reflect her delightful personality. Hemlata could have easily written about her long and active association with social and women's welfare work, as well as her unusual ability to direct such work. *Bangalakshmi* was originally a mouthpiece of the Sarojnalini Ashram. It was transformed into a literary magazine by Hemlata. Along with her own numerous compositions she helped publish those of other women. When the publication of *Sabujpatra* ceased, Indira handed over to Hemlata *Sadhumar Katha*, the autobiography of Mohit Kumari Devi. Thus was published the tale of woman belonging to the Pathuriaghata Tagores. Hemlata's nieces Geeta and Deepti were actively involved in women's welfare too. Deepti was also a scribe and her articles were regularly published in *Bangalakshmi.* None of this inspired Hemlata to pen her autobiography since she was not keen to chronicle the various experiences of her life.

She however tried to capture on paper the personalities of people whose proximity had enriched her life. To her they were like the philosopher's stone which turns to gold whatever it touches. These articles demonstrate shades of reminiscences—still, her detachment and objectivity while writing these are commendable. Articles like '*Rabindranather Bibaha Basar*', '*Baisakher Rabindranath*', '*Sansari Rabindranath*', '*Ascharya Manush Rabindranath*' and '*Rabindranather Antarmukhin Sadhanar Dhara*' are of great help in understanding Rabindranath. He himself said, 'They are enjoyable.' These articles are a veritable goldmine for biographers of Rabindranath Tagore.

Hemlata writes:

> Mrinalini once had some gold studs made as a birthday gift for Rabindranath. He refused to wear them saying, 'What a shame! Men do not wear gold. What sort of taste is this?' Mrinalini had the jeweller turn them into opal-studded buttons. The Poet wore them reluctantly on a few occasions.

Another quotation from Hemlata:

> Before the establishment of the school, we often stayed with Rabindranath and his family in the old 'Kuthibari' of Shantiniketan. His wife ran the household and I helped her. My husband was in charge of all necessary purchases including groceries and other expenses . . . The Poet would often comment to his wife, 'As I was writing downstairs I hear you ordering ghee, semolina, puffed rice, flour and sugar daily for making sweets. You seem to be having a good time as every demand is fulfilled.' Naming my husband he said, 'He will never refuse you and supply whatever you ask for. Heaven help a family with a master and a mistress like the two of you. It would go bankrupt in no time.' Mrinalini would refer to my husband saying, 'He understands the requirements of a family and it is a pleasure to run a home with him. Why must you interfere?'

There are numerous incidents about the sage Dwijendranath. Though an erudite scholar, he was very absent-minded and childlike. There was usually some commotion or other during his mealtime. The smell of spices in a dish cooked with banana-flowers made him create a furore. He was convinced that the ingredients of a shampoo had been added to the dish!

Another amusing incident about Dwijendranath reads as follows:

> He was served with freshly fried *loochees* in the evening. Touching them he said, 'What kind of *loochees* are these? They are dripping with ghee, even my fingers are smeared.' He handed over the entire plate to me saying, 'Go fry some with water for me. Whoever heard of *loochees* being fried in ghee?' Hemlata went away quietly. She rolled out some dough into *loochees*, dusting with flour instead of ghee, and then fried them. When she served these, they met with Dwijendranath's approval since there was no trace of ghee on them. He commented, 'See how well they came out fried in water!' After the meal, when Hemlata related the truth about frying the *loochees* Dewijendranath burst out laughing. His rueful comment, 'Of course, adding the dough to hot water would make a mess. I seem to have taken leave of my senses. I am sorry to be such a bother. You had better do whatever you think fit . . .'

Had Hemlata not been there, many such intimate pictures of the Tagores would have been lost to us. Would it have been possible for a man to portray such informal pictures of a family?

Apart from Sushila and Hemlata, many other women entered Dwijendranath's family by marriage. They were Charushila and Sushovini, the two wives of Arunendra, Nitindranath's wife Sarojini, Sudhindranath's wife Charubala as well as Sukeshi and Sabita, the two wives of Kritindranath. Like Sushila, Charushila, Sushovini, Sarojini and Sukeshi did not live long. Their contribution, within the family or outside, hardly merit detailed mention. Charubala could sing well. Though she was never involved with any movement, she always tried to inspire her children with feelings of patriotism. The child Soumyendranath first heard patriotic songs and tales about the freedom movement from her. He says, 'Mother used to read the newspaper daily. She would tell us all about the nationalist movement.' It was on his mother's lap that Soumyendranath had his first lessons in patriotism. Sukeshi spent a lot of time in Shantiniketan. She was not only jolly and good-natured but very affectionate too. She brought up Arunendra's motherless children as her own. In one of Rabindranath's letters to Mira he says, 'I hope to reach Calcutta by the end of the month and take you to Bolpur. Till then you will stay in the care of your *Bouthan* Sukeshi.' At this time Rabindranath stayed mostly in Shantiniketan. The glory of the Tagore mansion in Jorasanko was fading gradually. This was but natural. In the nineteenth century, the members of this mansion had been at the helm of events. In the twentieth century one member achieved world renown. His individual personality transcended those of the others. He however chose Shantiniketan and not this mansion as his sphere of work. It is in Shantiniketan that the informal atmosphere of the Tagore family blossomed afresh. The women of this family founded Alaapani Sabha and Anandamela. They also published magazines like *Sreyashi*, *Gharoa* and many more. These magazines were handwritten and managed by the women themselves. Hemlata, Kamala, Indira, Pratima and Sukeshi were all there in Shantiniketan. She often participated in plays with the other ladies. She was adept at tricking people with various mock dishes. Once she fooled Kritimohan Sen with champak flowers made from sliced pumpkin! Once Sukeshi, Shanta and Seeta opened a dress-stall during Paus Mela. It was in front of Hemlata's room in Neechu Bungalow. Seeta writes,

> . . . The sale was quite heartening. We wrote on a placard 'Come quickly, come quickly to *Bouthakuranir Haa*.' This was hung round the neck of Lakshman, Sukeshi Devi's boy servant, and he was sent to tour the entire ashram . . . The mela went on until dark with a great deal of noise and gusto.

Unfortunately Sukeshi succumbed to an attack of influenza. A few months after Sukeshi's death, Kritindra remarried. His second wife Sabita was a very good artist. The familiar and well-known fresco in the Jorasanko Tagore mansion is her handiwork. Later she completed a course in art under Nandalal Bose in Shantiniketan and joined the Design centre in Patna. Sabita was more a craftswoman than an artist. Though a painter himself, Nandalal had given great attention to various handicrafts in the curriculum of Kala Bhawan, Shantiniketan. Many of his students neither painted nor sketched in later life but showed extraordinary talent in designing. Sabita was one of them. It was after her husband's death that she left Shantiniketan for Patna. She won acclaim as a designer and once travelled to Japan to learn wood and bamboo craft. Though she accompanied Hemlata on her European trip and was good friends with Mira and Sreemati while she was in Shantiniketan, she hardly maintained any ties with the Tagore family later on.

Jnanadanandini was bent on securing a paragon of beauty as a bride for her only son. Whenever she saw a pretty young girl, she would put forth a proposal for her son. She would even bring her home for a while. Unfortunately Surendranath would not agree and his mother was forced to send her back home with toys! This often brought her to tears but her son was adamant. Once there was even a proposal for a marriage between Surendranath and Sukriti, who was the daughter of Maharani Suniti Devi of Coochbehar. Though the two families were lifelong friends, the Maharshi objected. He was dead against inter-caste marriages. Later Surendra's bosom-friend Jyotsnanath Ghoshal married Sukriti. Jyotsnanath was Swarnakumari's son and there was stiff opposition from his family too. A portion of a letter written by Jyotsnanath to the Maharshi has come to light in a copy of the *Tattwabodhini Patrika*. He writes, 'Even my parents have refused to be involved in any way with this marriage.' Fortunately, the relations of the newly-married couple were not severed from their respective families.

Surendra's marriage was fixed suddenly. Priyanath Shastri was one of the Maharshi's favourite disciples. His granddaughter

Sangya came one day to Satyendranath's residence at Store Road. The reason: to invite the family for her brother's 'upanayan'. She was a good-looking girl with sharp features. Every one liked her. Nalini's husband Surhitnath was there at the time and suggested to Jnanadanandini, 'Here is a suitable girl, why don't you arrange a match between her and Surendra?' Jnanadanandini agreed without further ado. Since he was cajoled by his mother into marrying, Surendra refused to see Sangya before the wedding. The Maharshi was overjoyed. He even had an extra spoonful of rice in delight! He ordered, 'During the marriage all Devi's wishes must be complied with.' Devi was the nickname of Sangya's mother Indira. Actually Indira was also descended from the Tagores. Dwarkanath's brother Radhanath was the grandfather of Indira's father Shrinath Tagore. It was the Maharshi who had arranged the marriage between Indira and his favourite disciple Priyanath.

It may not be inconsequential to pen a few lines about Indira here. Every branch of the Tagores has produced talented girls—though their number may have been fewer than those from Jorasanko. In Radhanath Tagore's family, Indira was one such person. Even as a child she showed a love of learning, a sense of humour and an aptitude for writing. She began her autobiography *Amaar Katha*, but this comprised her childhood memories only. She used to take her lessons with her Gurumoshai and the day she was able to rhyme words and compose a few lines of poetry her joy knew no bounds. She came running to her tutor. He was pleased and commented, 'You seem to have stolen my thunder!' He then showed the poem to Srinath Tagore with great pride saying, 'See, the teacher has no such abilities but his disciple has surpassed him.'

After her marriage, Indira went to her in-laws' place at Hridaypur. Hearing the palki-bearers, the village boys came running, shouting, 'There go a bride and groom'. Indira writes, 'They observed me from head to foot. Observing my red saree, one of them said, "There goes the bride." Another one had seen the shoes on my feet and exclaimed, "Oh no! It can't be the bride. Don't you see the shoes? It must be the groom!" Had Indira written more she could have presented us with many such anecdotes and pictures of rural life. Her *Amaar Katha* makes enjoyable reading. Her other two books are *The Life of Priyanath Shastri* (*Priyanath Shastri'r Jeeban Katha*,) and *Prabandha Kusum*.

Surendra's wedding with Sangya took place with considerable pomp and show. Since Sangya was much younger than him, Surendra had asked his sister Indira, 'Is she a mere infant?' A difference of nineteen years did not affect Surendranath's love for his child-bride. Apart from an English mistress from Loreto for the twelve-year-old Sangya, Surendranath himself began to coach her. He was an excellent translator. He was so adept in translating spontaneously while reading a text from English to Bengali that one could not be blamed for mistaking the translation for the original. Gradually Sangya also became an expert in this work. She translated several Japanese stories. These were published in *Punya* magazine. Even today in some old and faded copies lie hidden *The Mirror of Matsayana* or *Eurishima*. Surendra must have helped her since he had also translated Japanese works of fiction. He translated a Japanese historical story '*Ekti Basanti Prater Prasphutita Sakura Pushpa*' (A Sakura Flower that Bloomed One Spring Morning) and dedicated it to Sangya. Had Sangya been a trifle more enthusiastic, there may have been more translations of Japanese literature at that time.

Like many other women of the Tagore family Sangya had a flair for acting. Though Rabindranath had shifted to Shantiniketan, he was heavily dependent on the ladies of his family whenever he wanted to stage a play, not only for their legendary dramatic abilities but also because the budding artists of Shantiniketan were still in their infancy. Once he decided to stage the play *Bisarjan* in Calcutta. It would not be a family affair in the courtyard of the Jorasanko mansion. The play would be staged three evenings at the New Empire Theatre as a commercial show. Defying his advancing years, Rabindranath himself enacted the role of Jaisingh. Manjushree, one of Sangya's daughters, was entrancing as Aparna. Sangya played the part of Gunabati. Soumendranath, who was one of the audience, wrote, 'My aunt was incomparable as Gunabati.' Despite all her aptitude for literature or dramatics, there was a curious detachment in Sangya's nature. Jnanadanandini often complained, 'Sangya is not interested in dressing up. She does not supervise Surendra's meals'. Yet Surendra always indulged her every wish. Sangya writes,

> When we were married I stood in great awe of my husband. Perhaps this was due to the wide disparity in age and I was too young. It is astonishing how he managed to dispel all my qualms within six months. He did it with great affection, tact and love.

Surendra took Sangya to visit many places. Once he took her to Sister Nivedita.

> Sister Nivedita welcomed us with sweets. She showed me a good deal of affection. Later we returned home.

As the years passed, Sangya felt curiously detached from worldly affairs including her family. Perhaps the reason was the spiritual inheritance from Priyanath Shastri. Yet she herself wrote,

> On my marriage I was blessed with everything that a woman can ask for: a handsome, educated husband with an excellent character, great wealth and the incomparable dignity of my father-in-law, a palatial home and innumerable attendants.

When her first child—a son—was born just nine moths after the Maharshi's death, the women of the family considered him to be a reincarnation of the Maharshi. In all she bore six children. Sangya spent her days surrounded by the loving care of her family. Still, when she wandered about in Satyendranath's huge mansion on twenty-two bighas of land, with two lotus-filled ponds and a huge garden, Sangya felt an indefinable yearning. 'What do I lack, what do I want?' At times she felt a whispering in her heart, 'What have you deluded yourself with?'

The change in Sangya's mental attitude has been chronicled in detail in her *Sevikar Kaifiat*. It is actually a memoir of her spiritual life. In her younger days, Sangya never realized what she was yearning for. Later, she felt nirvana to be the ultimate goal of human life. This conciousness became clearer when she went to Diamond Harbour with her youngest son for a change of air. While gazing at the river she had a supernatural realization. It was as if a celestial glow enveloped her and showed her a glimpse of the blissful eternal being.

> I felt as if a current of incredibly delicious music was flowing all round me.

Sangya confided her feelings to her elder sister. This lady had already taken diksha (initiation) from a guru. This was the norm advocated by traditional Hindu scriptures. She naturally wanted to take Sangya to her guru. It took Sangya a while to overcome her strong Brahmo beliefs. When she went ultimately, her sister's guru had left this world and she met his disciple. In her own words, 'As soon as I saw him I was overcome with joy and stood transfixed.' This gentleman gave diksha to Sangya and her heart seemed to quieten down. Sangya did not take Surendranath's permission before her diksha but he made all the arrangements for Sangya's trip to Kashi. Even this could not dispel Sangya's melancholia. After all, it is not possible for the mundane affairs of home and family to tie down one who is about to set out on a search for the divine. At about this time, she came across the book *Sadhan Samar*. After reading this she seemed to have been at peace, albeit temporarily. Before her quest in the spiritual world was over, both Satyadev Thakur, the author of *Sadhan Samar*, and Sachchidananda Swami passed away. Sangya considered both as her gurus—the former one who taught her about spirituality and the latter as one who gave her diksha. To quell the unrest in her heart, Sangya went to many others for spiritual guidance. Her mental agony was such that she would often close the door and beseech the Almighty.

> Lord, do not let me forget myself by the lure of material wealth. Let not the glamour of clothes, jewellery and money make me forget you. Help me remember you at all times.

After Surendranath's death, Sangya decided to sever her ties with home and family and she proceeded on a pilgrimage. In Hardwar she met Mata Anandamoyee who initiated her into *sanyas*. It was twenty years after she had taken diksha. The last tie with the world—her name—dropped like a withered leaf from Sangya's life. The adored daughter-in-law of the Tagore family was now Swarupananda Saraswati. In her interview with Amiya Bandopadhyay, Sangya had said that she was originally given the name Swarupananda Parbat. Clad in saffron with her head shaven, she set out to tour the pilgrim centres of India. In Kashi she met Aseemananda Saraswati. She was by then popularly known as Sadhuma. Aseemananda came to her unasked. The mantra he gave her astonished her. It was the same that she had received at the beginning of her spiritual quest. Receiving it again towards the end of her days left her speechless. This was her last diksha. At long last, her heart and mind were at peace.

Though Sangya was never keen on literary pursuits, some of her poems portray her deep yearning for the sublime. The poems have been collected in *Kripakana*. Every one of her poems is tuned to spiritualism. 'Purnama' appeals to us as it portrays an entreaty straight from the heart :

Narir dehe e bhabete hey
Labhiya janam ajike ami,
Matritya je ki taha to jenechhi,
E deho sarthak hoyechhe swami.

Rekho na morey khudra ma kore
Dharanite karo go parichito,
Sabari je ma hobo go hetha
Shey rope hoye purna bikoshito.
Kalyankami mangalkami
Matrirupini amay heri
Dharar anya putra o kanya
Charipashe mor dandak gheri.

Being born as a woman
I have tasted motherhood
My life has been worthwhile, my master.
Do not keep me restricted,
As just a mother for my own,
Help me to be known
As the universal mother on earth.
Observing my benevolent motherly look,
Let all the sons and daughters of the world
Come and stand all round me.

In her interview Sangya told Amiya Bandopadhyay:

> My children always nurtured a sense of hurt. They felt that they were denied the care and attention that was their due. I tried my best to look after them, nurse them in illness and do whatever else was necessary but in my heart I always felt I must not occupy myself only with them. There was much more to be done.

Perhaps Swarupananda Saraswati's constant travels from one pilgrim centre to another, her life in the ashram as well as her association with other ascetics would have always remained unknown but for a chance meeting with Kalyani Dutt. Hearing about Sadhuma in the Nimbark Ashram, Kalyani went to meet her. To quote Kalyani's words about Sadhuma's abode in Bhubaneswar,

> It was an old cowshed which had housed cattle in the past. Even now one room was piled high with cow-dung cakes and straw, while *Sadhuma* sat next to this room. Her tranquil face and calm demeanor attracted me immediately.

Kalyani already knew about Satyendra's palatial mansion. Acceding to her request Sadhuma told her about her previous life and handed over the notebook containing her autobiography. Hitendranath's wife Sarojini, Kshitindranath's two wives—Dhritimayee (Dhritikumari) and Suhasini—and Aloka, who was Ritendranath's wife, had all come into Hemendranath's family by marriage. None of them were ever involved in any progressive activities. The three sons of Hemendranath appear to have become unusually conventional. Unlike their father, none of them seem to have been keen on women's education. The reason for this attitude is not known.

In comparison, Balendranath's wife had some chance of education after her marriage. Her original name was Sushitala. She was a granddaughter of the Pathuriaghata Tagores and had been brought up outside Bengal. Married at thirteen, her name was changed to Sahana. Balendranath was a good husband, but Sahana's happiness lasted only three years. Widowed at sixteen, she returned to her parents in Allahabad. Her father was a man who had kept pace with the changing times and decided to get her remarried. Unfortunately, not only was the Maharshi dead against widow remarriage, none of the members of the so-called broad-minded Tagore family agreed. Under the Maharshi's direction, Rabindranath himself went to Allahabad to coax and persuade Sahana to return to Jorasanko. Such conduct appears strange since only a few years later, he changed his views regarding widow remarriage. Sahana, convinced by Rabindranath, came back to her in-laws. He wrote to Mrinalini:

> . . . I have met Sushi and her mother. Sushi has agreed to return. Her mother has also given her permission. I had anticipated a great deal of opposition, but both of them consented after I explained the situation.

On her return to Jorasanko, Sahana concentrated on her studies. Earlier she had been tutored in English by Mr Lawrence.

This was during her stay at Selaidaha. There she and Madhurilata used to read *Bisarjan*, *Mayar Khela* and *Balamiki Protiva*.

On Sahana's return to Calcutta, Prafullamoyee admitted her to school. She says, 'I felt her heart would find peace if her mind was engaged in studies.' After her schooling was complete, Sahana went to England to get a degree in teacher's training. She had wanted to gain some practical experience also. Sahana had been keen to study science. She had written to Rabindranath in Shantiniketan for help. After all, she had left Allahabad for Jorasanko trusting his word implicitly. Unfortunately, Rabindranath completely discouraged her. His letter said, 'Science is taught in our school but for experimental work in the laboratory you will have to be exposed to all and sundry and work with them. Would it be possible?' It is difficult to comprehend such an attitude. Surely the women of the Tagore family had not reverted to purdah? Prafullamoyee tried her best to fulfil all Sahana's requests and wishes. Sahana loved to travel. Prafullamoyee sent her to visit Kashmir, nor did she have any qualms about sending her to England for higher studies. Then why this restriction for her in Shantiniketan? Ill-health compelled Sahana to return from England after a short while. Except for Prafullamoyee, no one in the Tagore family, not even Rabindranath, spared a thought for Sahana. Prafullamoyee lamented, 'I was the only one to support her.' An untimely death ended Sahana's unhappy life.

Pratima was a descendant of the Tagores and also married into the Tagore family. This was nothing unusual. Being Piralis, marriages between men and women of different branches as permitted by the blood relationships were common. Besides, aristocratic families are always loath to dilute their blue blood. So the practice of selecting brides from among the girls of the extended family was always prevalent among the Tagores. Such examples abound among the families in Pathuriaghata–Chorbagan–Koilahata and house number 5 of Jorasanko. Since the Maharshi's family embraced the Brahmo faith, it was not possible for the others to be related to them by marriage. That there was no dearth of willingness was obvious at the time of Sangya's wedding. Pratima was Binayini's daughter, the niece of Abanindranath, Samarendra and Gaganendra and thus a granddaughter of house number 5. Her father was related to the Tagores of Pathuriaghata. She may be considered to form a link among three families. This did not come to pass but Pratima certainly knit together the neighbouring houses number 5 and number 6 of Jorasanko. Entranced by this pretty grandchild of Saudamini, Rabindranath's wife Mrinalini had confided to her intimate ones, 'I would like to have this pretty little girl as my daughter-in-law. I hope her grandmother (Chhotodidi) will consent to give her to us.' Incidentally it may be remembered that Saudamini was very fond of Mrinalini because they both hailed from the same place—Jessore. Mrinalini had expressed her desire to her husband, who had agreed. Pratima's parents, maternal uncles and grandmother all knew about it.

Mrinalini had an untimely death. Pratima also grew up. At that time it was customary in a Hindu family to marry a girl by the age of ten or eleven. Possibly this prompted Pratima's guardians to raise the proposal first suggested by Mrinalini. There was also a rumour that Rabindranath was thinking of getting his son married in the month of Phalgun 1904 (Bengali 1310). However, Rabindranath was against marrying off his adolescent son and sent the same reply to Pratima's guardians. They construed it as his opposition to the proposal. Pratima's wedding was fixed with Nilanath who was the grandson of Kumudini, Gunendranath's younger sister. Pratima was just eleven at the time.

Pratima was married in the same month of Phalgun. In the month of Baisakh she went to her in-laws on an auspicious day. Who can alter destiny? Within a few days of Pratima's arrival, Nilanath was drowned while swimming in the Ganga. Pratima returned home with the stigma of being inauspicious. Five years later, on Rathindra's return from abroad, Rabindranath proposed Pratima's marriage to his son. The Maharshi had passed away by then and Rabindranath knew all about Mrinalini's heartfelt desire. He had also been cogitating on the miserable conditions of child widows. To cap it all, Labanyalekha of Dacca's Guha Thakurta family returned home as a widow. She was more like a daughter to Rabindranath and he was keen to re-establish her in life. Rabindranath prepared himself to overcome old traditions and marry Rathindra to Pratima. If he did not marry his son to a widow, how could he expect others to do so? He confided in Gaganendra,

> You should get Pratima remarried. Persuade Binayini to agree. Her life is barren and it is difficult to overcome temptations at this young age. Do you want her to be dependent on her brothers' charity after her parents' demise? Would it not be better to remarry her? Please consider carefully.

The broad-minded Gaganendra was more than willing. Binayini was worried about the social repercussion. They were not Brahmos. Vidyasagar had had a law enacted in 1856 legalizing widow remarriage. In the wave of social reform, some widows were remarried but in general did Hindu society accept such remarriages? Binayini felt, 'I shall be ostracized by society. I have to consider my other children and their marriages later on.'

Gaganendra was unperturbed. He told her:

> Do not be scared. I shall back you. If society ostracizes you and makes you an outcaste, I shall sever all my relations with society. We cannot allow a young girl's life to be ruined thus. Rabi-kaka is proposing marriage with his own son, not an outsider. Our niece will be close to us. Please do not disagree. We have to persuade Pratima.

To begin with, Pratima was unwilling. It is not easy to overcome shackles of age-old traditions. She may have had apprehensions too. However, Gaganendra had to use all his powers of persuasion to bring her around. He said, 'Think of the past as a bad dream. Now you have to start life afresh.'

Jyotirindranath commented in his diary,

> Had a discussion with Samar and Gagan about Rathi's marriage. They have shown a great deal of grit and determination this time.

There was a great deal of opposition too. Kumudini's family members were loud with their protestations. Later on too, if they ever saw Pratima present at any family feast, they would promptly depart.

Ignoring the protests of society, Gaganendra himself had Pratima remarried. He knew full well that Hindu society at that juncture was not strong enough to discredit them. However this cannot be considered to be the first widow remarriage, if we consider the Tagores as a whole. A few months earlier, Chhaya of the Pathuriaghata Tagore family had been remarried.

We might just as well spare some lines for Chhaya or Chhayamoyee. Her father Satindramohan was descended from Harimohan, the son of Darpanarayan Tagore. Satindramohan's family and Rabindranath's family were fairly close even though there had not been much intermixing between the two families.

Five years after Renuka's untimely death, Rabindranath had her husband Satyendranath married to Chhaya. Satyendra had remained close to Rabindranath's family and to Shantiniketan even after Renuka passed away. His marrying into a Pirali family may have been a contributing factor. The wedding took place on 18 June 1908. Rabindranath had made several visits to Satindra's house to arrange the wedding. He not only attended the wedding but put them up in his Jorasanko home. This is evident from his letter to his son who was out of Calcutta. He wrote, 'The wedding is over and Satya has come to us today with his new bride.' He even directed that Renuka's jewels be passed on to Chhaya. A short while after Satyendra's marriage, the wedding of his brother Sachindranath Bhattacharya took place with Madhavika, Samarendranath Tagore's daughter. Rabindranath had put forth the proposal for this marriage too.

Satyendra's woes did not end. A few months after the wedding (25–26 October) death claimed him. Rabindranath was heart-broken and lamented in a letter to Manoranjan Bhattacharya, 'I arranged his marriage barely a few months back . . . Satyendra succumbed to a fever after suffering for just three or four days. His wife has been left all alone. Such are the ways of death.' He also wrote to Satyendra's uncle Narendra Bhattacharya, 'When I think of Chhaya's grief my own knows no end.' Chhaya's widowhood had affected Rabindranath deeply. Death is unpredictable but the poet was unable to accept Satyendra's death as a cruel quirk of fate. He had mooted the proposal and got Chhaya married and now was unable to evade a sense of responsibility. He encouraged Satindramohan to get Chhaya remarried. It is worth mentioning that many people think Chhaya was a child widow and was remarried to Satyendra. This was not true. It was her first marriage.

Chhaya was remarried in 1909. This was the first widow-remarriage in the Tagore family. It is possible that Rabindranath helped in the search for a suitable groom. Chhaya was married to Nalinikanta Chattopadhyaya, whose father Nabakanta was a well-known Brahmo of Dacca. Nabakanta's daughter Charubala was married to Sudhindranath Tagore. Nabakanta was a devout Brahmo, with a progressive outlook and a firm belief in women's liberation. He passed away in 1904. During his lifetime he played an active role in the founding of the Eden Female School in Dacca. He was also connected with various welfare organizations like Dacca Subha Sadhini Sabha, Dacca Yuvati Vidyalay, Antahpur Stree Siksha Sabha, Dacca Subhosadhana Sabha, and Balyabibaha Nibarani Sabha. These organizations helped create a healthy and progressive social atmosphere in Dacca. His son also showed considerable courage in agreeing to marry a widow.

When Satindramohan informed Rabindranath that the marriage had been fixed, the poet was very pleased. He offered to act as the 'acharya' and solemnize the ritual himself. It is not known if there was any commotion in the family over this event. Satindra was of a bold and independent temperament. He neither agreed to wed his daughters young nor baulked at getting his widowed daughter remarried. Rabindranath's active participation had also minimized the possibility of social ostracism.

Chhayamoyee's second marriage turned out to be happy. The women of the Pathuriaghata Tagore family were seldom active outside the home. Thus Chhaya never played any role in the progressive movements in Dacca, though she had opportunities galore. She however made her home a haven of joy and led a full life with her husband and children. Pratima was also connected to the Tagores. Prasannakumar Tagore was the maternal grandfather of Seshendrabhusan—Pratima's father.

Rathindra and Pratima's wedding was the first instance of a widow remarriage in the Jorasanko Tagore family. Later, Rabindranath had Labanyalekha married to his favourite student Ajit Kumar Chakravarti. Gaganendra's son Gehendra had died, leaving his wife Mrinalini a widow. Gaganendra was keen to get Mrinalini remarried. Mrinalini however objected strongly and the proposal had to be shelved. Widow remarriages at the time depended largely on the broad-mindedness and courage of the groom. Most were not as fortunate as Pratima.

Thus Pratima entered Rabindranath's family despite all social impediments. She was very good-looking and people said that even Madhurilata's beauty paled before her. Her calm, quiet and pleasant expression so charmed Rabindranath that he wrote,

> It is my sincere wish that the eternal divinity may manifest himself unhindered amidst you and my family. When his light will set your being aglow, its lustre will shine bright and lovely through your transparent and pious nature. I am sure of this because of the purity of your heart. You have appeared to light the sacred lamp of my home. By your piety my home will be transformed into a holy temple—this hope turns stronger in me daily.

Rabindranath always addressed her as Bouma (bride-mother) or Mamoni. In his later years, she was the apple of his eye. For thirty-two years she looked after him with great devotion. This was a charge she had accepted willingly and with love.

What about Rathindranath? After marrying Pratima his happiness knew no bounds. This is evident in his letter to his dear friend Nagendranath, who was Mira's husband:

> Dear Nagen, I hope you will understand the reason for my long silence. I was far too busy due to the wedding. I sit down to write to you with a heart brimming over with joy. Pratima is now my wife and adorns my home. She is such a charming person. I have no words to describe her. If I began narrating her virtues you would never believe me and call me a lunatic into the bargain.

Pratima's formal education began after she came to Shantiniketan. Unlike the Maharshi's family, where considerable emphasis was laid on women's education, in Pratima's parental home, girls were married off even before they completed the primary level. Rabindranath had thus given considerable thought to Pratima's education, especially in choosing a governess for her. According to him, 'The lady who will be a companion for Pratima must be well versed on points of social etiquette.' Pratima had Miss Burdet as her teacher for a while. Rabindranath also supervised her progress even when he was away in Shantiniketan. Once he wrote to her from Selaidaha:

> I hope your lessons are proceeding according to schedule. I had requested Ajit to coach you before I left. You must have completed the first book in English. I had suggested another book for you. I hope you are able to understand the contents. The text is much easier than the English book that you have read. Ask Hemlata to help you study some Bengali prose and poetry daily. Try to improve your spelling.

This letter gives us an idea of the extent of Pratima's education at the time of her marriage. With amazing intelligence she overcame her lack, becoming proficient in a number of topics within a few years. Her style of writing was simple yet penetrating. In 'Smritichitra' when beginning to write about herself, she says,

> At the time of our marriage I was sixteen and my husband twenty-one. My maternal grandfather's house was number 5 while that of my in-laws number 6. Though I did not feel much of a change in moving from one house to another, the change in view-points and attitudes was enormous. Both my parents' sides of the family were orthodox Hindus. Their lifestyle, culture and opinions reflected a traditional outlook. Whereas the atmosphere in my in-laws' home was liberal and modern.

This observation by Pratima makes it clear that the sixteen-year-old girl had no difficulty in discerning the differences between the two homes and their culture. With her tremendous powers of adjustment, she had no problem adapting herself to the new culture. Coupled with her intelligence, Rabindranath's teachings attained new dimensions.

Pratima's contribution to art and literature is considerable. Not only could she write and paint well but her *Gurudever Chhabi* is the standard for judging Rabindranath's paintings and sketches. To quote her,

> Just as the essence and rhyming of his poems have a character of their own, so have his pictures a totally different style. From no angle can they be termed as imitations. Had the Poet chosen to pen the characters of the people he drew, there would emerge Sandip, Bimala, Nikhil, Sharmila, Gora, Madhusudhan and others. These were the principal characters of his various novels. As soon as he put aside his pen for the artist's palette, the same faces appeared on the canvas. Normally, artists have the idea of their picture in mind when beginning a painting. They decide on the interplay of the various aspects, background and the colour-scheme before commencing work. As they progress, they begin to meditate upon their creation. With the Poet, his painting originated in his meditation on the

> topic. The colours, lines and composition of the work seemed to flow spontaneously from his brush with hardly any planned movement of his conscious mind. Thus Gurudev's paintings and sketches seemed to begin with that level of imagination where other artists completed theirs. He himself said, 'When I sketch and draw I have hardly any conception about the character of my composition. The interplay of various lines and the joy I derive therein have made me an artist.'

In truth, just as he did not follow Kalidasa or the Vaishnava poets in his language, similarly he did not borrow from the Ajanta, Kangra or Mughal schools of art while painting. When he sang all he thought of was the flow of his rhymes. He told stories through the colours of his paintings. His many-spendoured talent overcame all shortfalls.

Dividing Rabindranath's art into three categories, Pratima has shown that while the poet's paintings of natural scenes and animals attracted the attention of the French, his portraits of human faces draw effusive praise from the Germans. Yet it is difficult to analyse these pictures. They express an eternal truth of creation which beggars description.

> It is discernible only to one possessed of a rare insight. Otherwise it remains unseen like the rays of a pure gem deep down in the mines.

The urge to paint was Rabindranath's 'lady love' of his sunset years. Naturally such a 'love' is most demanding. He painted over two thousand pictures during his last years. It was as if a new world had begun to appear before his vision, which his fingers portrayed on canvas. According to Pratima,

> Just as Tagore portrayed all facets of creation in his poems, so he painted the history of the full repertoire of evolution of beings in his pictures. The forms of this man-made world as well as those of animals are being moulded in stages by the ebb and flow of the tremendous force generated by the movement of the various stars and planets. The waves of the same current

must have touched the heart of the artist. His brush, imbued with this perception, poured forth unique portrayals, not only of humans but of animals and natural scenery too.

Apart from art criticism, Pratima herself was a good artist. Her mother, aunts and maternal uncles all painted and sketched. Her first source of imitation was her maternal uncle Abanindranath Tagore. After marriage she took lessons for a while from the Italian teacher Gilhardi. Later she added to her knowledge while working with Nandalal Bose. Quite a few of her paintings bear testimony to the high quality of her artistic ability. Pratima had always been deeply interested in handicrafts. Her travels with Rabindranath took her all over the world. Whichever country they visited, she always tried not only to familiarize herself with the local handicrafts but also to import the know-how to Shantiniketan. Thus she had the technique of Indonesian Batik work included in the curriculum of Kala Bhawan. She herself trained in ceramics while in France and made arrangements to have it taught in Sriniketan. She often incorporated foreign designs and motifs which she had observed abroad into Rathindranath's wood and leather craft. This symbiosis helped create novel trays, flower vases, vessels and lamp shades. The 'Shantiniketan style' observed on leather bags, prints, cane or leather stools and many other decorative articles is almost entirely due to Pratima.

Along with painting, Rabindranath encouraged her to pen her thoughts. He named her Kalpita Devi. Under this pseudonym Pratima composed a number of poems. Every time she wrote a poem, she would take it to the poet. She was always apprehensive of his reaction but could not rest easy until he had seen her creation. Rabindranath paid great attention to her work, though he sometimes used his pen to embellish her efforts. Quite often he would keep the thought intact and yet create a new poem to impress upon her how it was possible to change the entire poem with a play of words. In the poem '*Smriti*' Pratima wrote:

Eyi grihe eyi puspabithi
Jare gheri ekdin tomar kalpana
Gorechhilo imarat deepti garimar,
Uttapta kamona tobo jar prati dhulir kanay
Jeebanto koriyachhilo taba muhurtere.
Je basana mone chhilo purilo na
Abasanna pran
Gelo chole chhaya phele angane prangane.

Around which your imagination
Built a mansion of pride,
Your burning passion
Infused into every grain of which
Had enlivened your moments,
The heart's desire remained unfulfilled
The wearied life left leaving a shadow on the homestead.

Rabindranath changed the language:

Eyi ghar eyi phuler keyari
Eke gher diye tomar kheyal
Baniyechhilo paristhaner imarat.
Tomar tapta kamana
Rangiyechhilo tar pratyek dhulikanake.
Tar pratyek muhurtake korechhilo tomar aabeg diye asthir.
Tumi chole gele,
Akritartha akangshar chhaya bheshe bedachchhe
Angane prangane.

This room, the flower beds,
Your fancy had encircled it to build a
Fairy palace,
Your burning love had imbued even its dust,
Your passion had excited its every moment.
You are no more
Only the shadows of unrequited desire float
Around every nook and corner.'

Such poetic encounters were common between Rabindranath and his Kalpita. Kalpita's prose shows a clear influence of

Rabindranath's *Lipika* and is more akin to poetry in prose form. Memorable creations are '*Nati*', '*Mejobou*', '*17th Phalgun*' and '*Sintala Durgo*'. Charmed by Pratima's '*Swapna Bilasi*', Rabindranath wrote '*Mandirar Ukti*'. He requested Pratima to write '*Naresher Ukti*' in the following chapter, thus he would write '*Narir Ukti*' and Pratima '*Purusher Ukti.*' This would end the novel, with Kalpita competing with Rabindranath! Kalpita gave up the unequal battle, declining to compete with him.

Pratima also wrote several memoirs. Based on her mother's diary ,'Kahini', she wrote *Smritichitra*. In this Pratima describes the way the women of house number 5 dressed on various occasions. Idol worship had ceased in Debendranath's family but in the adjacent house, all traditional Hindu festivals like 'Durgapuja' and 'Dol Jatra' were celebrated with the usual pomp and grandeur. This was the custom in every aristocratic Bengali family of the day in Calcutta.

Pratima writes:

> For every festival women had typical dress codes. For Saraswati Puja or Basant Panchami we wore black-bordered sarees dyed orange, flowers in our hair and a *catechu* mark on our forehead. Durga puja was the time for various bright-coloured sarees, floral ornaments and decorating our foreheads with various designs made from sandalwood paste. Dol Purnima meant fine muslin sarees, floral ornaments and garlands scented with atar or 'rose essence'. The red *abir*, when sprinkled on our white muslin sarees, enhanced their beauty. Perhaps this was the purpose of such a dress.

There is no mention of jewellery in Pratima's description. Gaganendra's youngest daughter Sujata has informed that at that time it was customary to wear gold during the day time, pearls in the evening and diamonds and other gems at night. This was the mode for weddings and other festivals. Maybe the idea was that gold shines better in daylight, and the lamplight reflecting from diamonds and other gems gives them added lustre and glamour.

The reason for choosing pearls for evening wear is not very clear. Was it because pearls look best in the shadowy, half light of dusk when the sun is setting?

Recently Pratima's *Smritichitra* has been published again. The second part contains her reminiscences about herself, a few non-fictional articles and two works of fiction. The editor Sunil Jana says,

> I came by these hitherto unpublished manuscripts by the merest chance . . . On my earnest request Sunanda Babu searched through their home 'Chhayaneer' in Shantiniketan. He found two old files which belonged to his father, the late Giridhari Lala. He handed them over to me and among the various papers I suddenly came across these manuscripts of Pratima Devi. It is unbelievable and amazing.

Among the stories 'Galpa Ek' should be of special interest to the readers though the editor has not chosen to discuss it. One wonders if the plot was suggested by her Babamoshai Rabindranath. He often provided his near and dear ones with ideas for fiction. Apart from Charuchandra, Saratkumari and Madhurilata there may have been many such others. Moreover, Pratima was very close to Rabindranath. They engaged in playful competition in writing stories or in altering each other's poems. There is a striking resemblance between Pratima's '*Galpa Ek*' and '*Badnaam*' written by Rabindranath almost towards the end. '*Badnaam*' was published in Asarha 1348 (June-July 1941). Pratima's manuscript is undated and there are certain differences. In the story by Pratima, Sadu tells her husband, 'I shall not stay back but go along with you. Will you have the courage to declare in court, "This is my wife's lover?" The papers will go to town about the exploits of your wife Saudamini Devi! Will you be able to bear it?'

In '*Badnaam*' Sadu neither threatens her husband nor entreats him to save Anil. She just says, 'I know the infamy that will threaten my relationship with society shortly . . . I shall always follow him till the last stage of his punishment. I wish you all happiness. Do not be worried. You will have no difficulty in finding a new companion . . . I just want you to know that I cared for you as best as I could out of love and deceived you utmost out of a sense of duty.'

The refinement discernible in this part is obviously due to Rabindranath's pen. One wonders if Pratima first wrote the story or whether both she and Rabindranath wrote separately and Sadu's statement reflects their different temperaments? Sadu as portrayed by Pratima is a human being with all her attributes while Tagore's Sadu is an ideal woman. '*Badnaam*' is Rabindranath's last story published during his lifetime. It was written about three months before he passed away. Perhaps that is why it has remained outside the realm of criticism.

The second story by Pratima is just titled '*Galpo Dui*' and has no other name. According to the editor, it is incomplete, 'Either she did not write further or the end has been lost.' This story is written with World War II and the famine of Bengal as its background and is totally different from the first.

> . . . Just then a Bengali woman along with a few uniformed Europeans got into the car. I suddenly realized that this was my old friend Sheila. We were together in college. I was amazed at her dress. She wore a khaki coat studded with brass buttons over her saree. A khaki cap was set at an angle on her head. A bag hung from her shoulders. Her eyebrows and lips were both painted.

Sheila's transformed looks were unrecognizable. In college she never wore anything other than khadi sarees and was a staunch 'swadeshi'. We hardly realized the change being wrought by the war in the general culture of the country except when confronted by some scenes on the streets of Calcutta.

Pratima's most memorable contribution lies not in painting or as an author but in propagating dance as a part of the curriculum in Shantiniketan. Formerly, dancing was absolutely taboo among

Bengalis. It was preposterous to take even a few steps on the stage along with music. *Balmiki Protiva* or *Mayar Khela* involved acting though some efforts were made to bring about a semblance of dance by moving the hands a trifle. Pratima felt that times were changing and women were coming forward in all fields. So why should they lag behind in the sphere of dance, especially when it would be convenient to carry out the experiment in Shantiniketan?

Pratima's stage appearances were few. She enacted the role of Khiri in the first staging of the play *Lakshmir Pariksha* by the ladies of Shantiniketan. This was shortly after her marriage. Thereafter, though she never acted again, she was the inspiration behind all Tagore's dance dramas. Rabindranath himself had no plans of composing dance dramas of *Chitrangada* or *Parisodh*. He became conscious about this new art form only when Pratima presented him with a rough draft. Divakar Kaushik writes, 'The dance-drama, with its opera-like origins, would be just a poet's dream, on paper or in his mind, if Bouthan does not pick it up in its infancy and nourish it with a feminine flair.' People were not used to seeing ladies of quality dancing on stage. How would it be taught in Shantiniketan and by whom? Undaunted, Pratima began her arduous endeavour. She was not a dancer herself, never having taken any lessons in this art form. She only had her unusual sense of beauty and artistry to guide her. Moreover Udayshankar's occasional appearances indicated that Bengalis were becoming dance-conscious. Of course Udayshankar's dance partner was no Bengali girl but the Frenchwoman Simki. Reba Ray was the first to open the doors of dance to Bengali women. Soumendranath and his friends had arranged to celebrate 'Rituchakra' at the University Institute. As the last song began, *Je kebol paliye beraye, drishti eray, dak diye jaye ingitey* (one who is elusive, avoids our eyes and beckons with hints), Reba suddenly dashed out of the choir like a comet and began dancing on the stage to the rhythm of the song. The audience was thunderstruck.

Snide comments like 'whoever heard of gentlewoman dancing in public' filled the air. Soumendranath gave an apt reply a few days later. In a performance held in the courtyard of the Jorasanko Mansion, three girls—Chitra, Nandita and Sumita—danced to the tune of *Nupur beje jaye rinirini* (the anklets tinkle away). About a year later Rabindranath staged *Natir Puja*. Around this time Keshab Chandra Sen's granddaughters eased the path for other gentlewomen. The play *Shrikrishna* was staged to raise funds for the Victoria Institution. Nilina portrayed the child Krishna while Sadhana played the adult role. Sadhana was a good kathak dancer. She later married Madhu Basu and appeared as a danseuse several times both on the stage and in cinema. *Alibaba*, *Rajnartaki* and *Dalia* bear testimony to her acting abilities. Reba Roy not only began to teach dance in *Sangeet Sanmilani* but also started staging elaborate dance dramas. But that is another story.

What Pratima began to teach at Shantiniketan should perhaps be called *Bhav Nritya*. After a few dance sequences in *Barshamangal* she requested Rabindranath to compose a dance-drama based on his poem *Pujarini*. She was keen to have girls perform it on Rabindranath's birthday. Thus was written *Natir Puja*. Pratima worked round the clock to make the performance a success. In a later-day performance, Nandalal Bose's daughter Gauri gave a sterling performance as Sreemati. Her unforgettable acting and dancing is remembered even now.

Pratima was able to give a concrete form to Tagore's dance style, after fourteen years of tireless effort. The play was *Chitrangada*. *Shaapmochan* came just before it. Pratima's book *Nritya* is proof of her researches on dance forms. The distinctive style of *Chitrangada* became even more pronounced in *Chandalika*. By then the audience had seen performances by Udayshankar, Reba Ray and Sadhna Bose. Even Sreemati had begun to stage *Bhav Nritya* set to Rabindranath's poems, albeit in the style of modern dance, on an experimental basis. *Chitrangada* was first staged in

1936 in the New Empire Theatre. From this time upto 1940 there were forty shows. This account is from Santidev Ghosh who was both in the dance troupe and the music choir. The roles of Arjun, first and second Chitrangada were played by Nivedita, Jamuna and Rabindranath's granddaughter Nandita respectively. Pratima always managed behind the scenes. Every costume was approved by her and she held onto the traditions of Shantiniketan even in the matter of stage decor. Pratima always adhered rigorously to the codes of decency and beauty inherent in the scenes and costumes of Tagore's plays and dance dramas. She will always be remembered for the superb taste observed in the graceful mode of dressing and make up of the female characters. Towards the end of Rabindranath's life he would instruct her to make sketches of the various stage decors.

It has already been mentioned that Rabindranath first planned the dance dramas due to Pratima's eagerness. He also composed *Mayar Khela* in a new format. Pratima would also transform poems like 'Samanya Kshati' from Rabindranath's *Katha O Kahini* or pieces like 'Dalia' or 'Kshudita Pashaan' from *Galpaguccha* into tableaux to be performed before the poet. In such performances there was more of dancing than acting.

What is there in the characters of Rabindranath's dance dramas that distinguish them from others? According to Pratima, it is the blend and amalgamation. The dance form of Shantiniketan did not follow the style of any particular dance school. The distinction was achieved by permutation and combination of steps and postures. Thus the dances of *Chitrangada*, based on the Manipuri school, cannot be observed anywhere in Manipur. Similarly *Chandalika*, composed in the styles of south India, is unrecognizable in any south Indian dance. This was blending and combining at its best. This mixed mode of dance was now set on firm foundations of music. She said, 'This was the new contribution by Shantiniketan. Such display of dance with music is not seen in our old dance forms.'

Pratima had expended considerable thought on preserving the beauty, distinctive style and character of the Rabindranath dance form. She had considered notations for dances on the same lines as notations and scores for music. She felt that the artist might pass away but not the art. Art to her was immortal. The characteristics of the dance style that blossomed as an art before Rabindranath's eyes had to be sustained. Otherwise those graceful movements would be lost.

Thus Pratima held dance classes to train the new girls of the ashram to dance and perform before Rabindranath. Until he approved, she would not be satisfied and the practice would go on relentlessly. At that time, it was the essence of the ideas inherent in the songs that were portrayed in the dances. She herself showed the students the various movements, and often composed dances synchronizing beautifully with the songs. She instructed her students to write down the notations of the dances. She also tried to have the various dance postures sketched by the artists of Kala Bhawan preserved.

No one understood Rabindranath as completely as Pratima. He often had ideological differences with his son Rathindranath but never with Pratima. Thus the article '*Nirban*' by Pratima, detailing the events of Rabindranath's sunset years, became so vivid. The detached manner in which she has portrayed the last episode in a few words, like the delicate brush-strokes of a master painter, has to be read to be appreciated.

In Shantiniketan she also supervised the aspects of women's education and welfare. She founded Alapini Samiti with Indira, Hemlata, Sukeshi, Kamala, Mira and many other ladies as members. Sometimes they would hold shows amongst themselves. These were away from the public eye and meant only for women. The members would sing or enact various dance postures, often they would sit on small stools under the tamarind tree (*tentultala*) and hold storytelling and music sessions for the girls of Bolpur.

Rabindranath always encouraged the *ashramites* to engage in welfare-work in the villages around Bolpur. Pratima had arranged for the girls from the Ashram to take turns in visiting the nearby villages. They went either on foot or by bullock-cart. They tried to educate the illiterate village women in elementary health and hygiene, preparation of wholesome meals and simple handicrafts that would help them earn some money. As Pratima says 'When I first began visiting Goalpara to popularize various handicrafts with Gouri Devi and Sukumari Devi, the village women did not know how to hold a needle properly. Moreover, traditionally orthodox views always created a barrier between us. Many village women were loath to allow us entry into their homes since we did not believe in the caste system and the restrictions imposed thereby.' Pratima's two students, Gauri and Basanti, helped her in this work to their utmost ability. Sukumari Devi was more touchy and often commented, 'Why must Bouma go to such trouble for those who are unwilling to learn?'

Pratima was not one to give up. She would visit every household, and fetch the girls for her classes. Better acquaintance gradually alleviated the reticence of the village women. Originally when the women came to learn needlework they were very conscious about touching their teachers. Gradually this taboo was overcome. According to Pratima, 'Our love and concern seemed to touch their hearts just like the natural rays of the sun and fresh air. Perhaps one of the best students was Suva Devi. Suva, a child-widow from Goalpara and a student of Sukumari and Gauri Devi, became an expert needlewomen. Her artistry was such that a shawl embroidered by her matched those from Kashmir.' In 1930 Mr Elmhurst came to Shantiniketan and his wife Dorothy, as the first president of the village women's organization, not only awarded Suva Devi the first prize for needlework but also bought the shawl which had been awarded the pride of place. She paid a special price for this to encourage the students. This is but an example of Pratima's tireless endeavours to realize in practice all Rabindranath's dreams.

Rathindranath had some differences of opinion with the Vishwa Bharati's mode of functioning in later years. As a result, he decided to leave but Pratima did not. She lived in Shantiniketan till the end of her days.

In due course of time three girls entered Gunendranath's family. Saudamini, by dint of great austerity and suffering, had succeeded in saving her family from utter ruin. Her three sons were devoted to her and she had them married young. The three brides, Pramodkumari, Nishibala and Suhasini had been chosen from well-known families. The stunningly beautiful Pramodkumari was only nine years old when she entered the family as Gaganendranath's wife. Pramodkumari's father Mrityunjay Bandopadhyay was a sub-judge in Gazipur (and grandson of Kukilmoni, whose father was Peary Mohan Tagore of Pathuriaghata) while her mother Surasundari was the granddaughter of Dwarkanath's elder brother Radhanath Tagore.

Samarendra's wife Nishibala was the daughter of Ahindrabhushan Chattopadhyay while his brother Bhujagendra Bhushan's daughter Suhasini was married to Abanindranath. Both the brothers were the grandsons of Prasannakumar Tagore of Pathuriaghata. Abanindranath's sister Binayini had already been married to Seshendrabhusan, the younger brother of Bhujagendra and Ahindra.

Suhasini was older than Nishibala, but after marriage she always addressed the latter as 'Didi'. This was because her husband Abanindra was younger than Nishibala's husband Samarendra. This was as per prevalent family norms where relationships and not age determined seniority. All these girls had been brought up according to the traditions of aristocratic families of the time. A wooden divan covered with a cane mat and a cushion served as a seat for Saudamini. She supervised the household and taught her three daughters-in-law all the necessary domestic skills. This included the daily worship of the family deity, care of various guests and numerous other chores including paring vegetables. Like fancy cooking, this was the regular routine followed in all well-to-do households of the day. Maids would wash and skin potatoes and Saudamini would instruct her daughters-in-law to pare these into different shapes and sizes for the various dishes. Potatoes for frying had to be cut differently from those for curries. Saudamini sighed with relief when she saw the expertise of her daughters-in-law.

These ladies also participated in the functions held at home. They would listen to music from behind reed curtains or even put up plays themselves. Once the play *Ratnabali* was staged. Apart from Pramodkumari, Nishibala and Suhasini, their sisters-in-law Benayini and Sunayani also took part.

It was customary in house number 5 to have a theatrical performance whenever a wedding took place. This was considered an essential part of the celebrations since it was not possible to invite everyone to the wedding or feasting. The situation of the residents of Jorasanko's house number 5 was rather unusual. Culturally they were more akin to their cultured next-door neighbours, Maharshi Debendranath's family, but were socially more closely connected to their relations in Pathuriaghata, Chorbagan and Koilahata. The Brahmos would never come to any function where the 'Shalgram Shila' was worshipped. On their part, the non-Brahmos would never sit down to a meal with the Brahmos. A theatrical performance was an event to which everyone could come. It was also possible to serve various snacks to everybody since there was no question of sitting down to a meal. Neither house in Jorasanko ever had the tradition of performances by professional dancing girls. Usually there would be a theatre and a musical soiree. Though the ladies of Gunendra's family never appeared on a public stage, there was no bar on acting before the numerous relatives.

Among the three ladies, Pramodkumari was the most daring. Nishibala and Suhasini always turned to her in any crisis.

Gaganendranath's daughter Purnima has provided us with glimpses of her mother. Pramodkumari was an expert cook and Purnima tells us how she augmented her culinary skills.

> When Didi from Kasi [Varanasi] came to Calcutta she would always cook a Bengali version of mutton curry called *Bangla pantha*. My father was very fond of this dish cooked by her. She was a superb cook and my mother learnt a lot from her. My father's maternal aunt taught mother a speciality of Jessore—curried 'koi fish' with *choi* (a creeper with pungent roots). I was fond of curried 'ol'. Whenever my mother cooked this dish, she would send the coach to fetch me from my in-laws' place. She was also adept at cooking meat and fish dishes. I have yet to taste meat kababs and *ambol* of tiny prawns as tasty as made by her. She was very fond of feeding people. One just had to mention a dish and she would cook it. In her old age she had difficulty moving around. She would ask the maids to place all the ingredients before her and then cook while sitting on a chair.

This in spite of having a cook, bawarchi and a number of servants. Theirs was a large family. Not only could Pramodkumari work hard, she knew the exact amounts of the ingredients necessary to cook any dish. This was something that every mistress of a wealthy family had to learn. They always personally weighed out the rations and stores for the daily cooking from the store-room. Mohanlal remembers an incident from his childhood. During some function Pramodkumari had weighed out the required quantity of ghee and flour to the cook for frying a large number of loochees. After a while the man came to her and asked for more ghee. She said, without batting an eyelid, 'Fry the remaining loochees with water! If you can't then go away at once. I shall get an expert cook from Singhibagan.' Mohan was amazed to see that the cook fried and brought the total number of loochees. All of them tasted the same—the ones fried in ghee and the others in water! As Pramodkumari knew the exact amount required, the cook was unable to fool her.

Saudamini became greatly dependent on Pramodkumari. She would often admonish the latter for not having her meals on time. Pramodkumari's stock reply was, 'Mother, if I eat now I shall not be able to work. Let all the jobs be over, then I shall have my meal.' She was the prop and the mainstay of the entire household. Whether it was a confinement, nursing a sick person or bandaging a wound, everyone looked to Pramodkumari. Though the old midwife Sultana was there, an adolescent girl about to bring forth a new life would want her 'Bara-ma' or Pramodkumari. Sometimes Tripurasundari, the widow of the Maharshi's younger brother Nagendranath, would come for a visit. She was paranoid that everyone wanted to poison her for her property. She always asked Pramodkumari to taste whatever was served to her. When there was a proposal to sell the ancestral house (house number 5) Tripurasundari objected violently. She said, 'I shall never allow this property to be sold. How can one think of selling Dwarkanath Tagore's home that has housed seven generations? This will not happen in my lifetime.' How many people are able to prevent the inevitable?

Coming to Suhasini, Aban's wife, a memorable event in her life was her meeting with Shri Ramakrishna Paramhansa Dev in her childhood. After her marriage she usually depended on Pramodkumari in domestic matters. Abanindranath once told his daughter Umarani, 'Your mother was so timid that I could never think of leaving her on her own. Thus I refused numerous invitations.' Later Suhasini became very fond of going out almost every evening. Her grandson Sumitendra says, 'Every evening our driver Mishir would bring the Buick convertible to the portico. Didimoni with her grandchildren would go out towards Chowringhee. After driving along the Strand and taking a few turns round the maidan in the fresh air she would do some shopping or visit one of our relations.' A perusal of the above lines indicates the phenomenal changes in our society and social life. Time was when women could only go out in covered *palkis*.

Their lives were restricted by the four walls of the home. Their evenings were spent in futile dressing-up as a pastime. Then came the era of going out in the evening. The joint families had begun to split up and these evening-outings were an excellent means of keeping in touch with various relations. This is also past history now. The graceful golden evenings seem to have been lost to us. Working women merely anticipate it as a time to return home. Distance and alienation amongst the various branches of a family are on the rise. This becomes more perceptible if we view a large family like the Tagores.

Abanindranath took Suhasini to several places like Puri, Konarak, Darjeeling and Mussoorie. Bitten by the travel bug, she also went to pilgrim centres with her son Alok and son-in-law Manilal. No one ever considered it necessary to pen her opinion about her husband's art. It may be that she never gave it much thought. This is lent credence by her taking her son-in-law Nirmal shopping during the time fixed for a sitting by her husband. Once on her return from a trip to Agra, Jaipur, Delhi and Lucknow she asked her husband with naïve astonishment, 'How did you manage to paint such pictures? The scenes I visited were exactly similar to your paintings!'

Abanindranath replied with his usual humour, 'Well, you see, my piety is much greater than yours. I have visualized what you saw in reality.' Similarly Suhasini's portrait was enlivened by Abanindranath's brush and choice of shades.

Let us return to Maharshi Bhawan. The women of the Tagore family carried their culture wherever they went. Since they are scattered far and wide it may be best to proceed chronologically. Considering Dwijendranath's family, his grandson Dinendranath—Dwipendranath's son—was first married to Sunayani's daughter Bina. Glimpses of this wedding can be found in '*Parinaya Sangeet*', published on this occasion. The event took place on 29 *Magha* at Salikha. The poem was written on 23 *Magha* by Harishchandra Haldar who probably was in charge of the decorations. According to Gaganendranath's daughter Purnima they learnt the art of alpana from Harishchandra, who was good at sketching.

Below is a description of the décor of the bridal chamber:

Bilati asane pasham ganthone
Pranganey bichhano ranjite baas
Koto chitra anka nahi lekha setha
Bohichhe paduka hoiye daas.
Kasther asan satin shovan
Basa, shoa, khara sovichey sarey
Khachito deyale sona, rupa chhaley
Jogjoga jhokay bhiter dharey.

Foreign carpets woven in red wool,
Are spread in the courtyard.
They are decorated with innumerable paintings
And serve for repose of shoes.
Wooden seats with beautiful satin covers,
And cushions strewn around in rows.
The walls and floors ornamented with
Mosaic, gold and silver work,
Shine like the sun.

The outer 'Mahal' had also been decorated, perhaps under the supervision of Harishchandra himself.

Gaser toran crown shovan
Baari, thaam, toru nishan anka,
Patar khilaney urichhe nishaney
Sari sari tham shovichhey haanka.
Chiner line jholey aganan
Kagajer doom jharey jharey jivalay
Haanki darbari juri gari chori
Jaichhey chatake phatake galey.

The gas lamp on the main gate
Embellished with pictures of a crown,
The whole house
Decorated with flags,

Arches made of leaves
Rows of pillars ornament the scene.
Chandeliers and paper-domes are alight,
Guests in phaetons enter the main gate with great fanfare.

Though the house had been decorated for Dinendra's wedding, no *nahabat* was played. The absence of *nahabat* is described thus:

Dinendrar bor-besh tai sabha samabesh
Anander kolahal e Dwarkapurey
Nahabat bina tai bajitechhe surey,

Dinendra is dressed as a groom.
Thus this gathering
The tumultuous joyous noise at this Dwarkapur
Is still melodious without a *nahabat.*

Maharshi Bhawan of Jorasanko has been referred to as Dwarkapuri probably because the Maharshi was still there. Other arrangements had also been made in plenty,

Dadhi, matsya bharekbar asitechhe barebar
Daley daley bahakera prabeshe agar.
Ghrita, kheer, mishtannadi goney sadhya kar.
Polao, kalia, kofta kheye holo loke tripta
Nibritta korilo jathar anal
Nimantrita rabahuta nara nari dal.
Pola laddoor thala subhro sandesher dala
Ketuma swajan grihe jai saaey saar.
Daas dasi choleydalay katare katar.

Loads of curd and fish come again and again,
Numerous bearers surge in,
It is impossible to keep track
Of ghee, sweets and kheer.
Invitees and gatecrashers.
All have not only satiated their hunger,
But have had in plenty
Pillau, *qualia* and kofta.
Trays of pillau and laddoo

Wicker baskets filled with snow-white *sandesh*,
Are being sent to the homes of all friends and relatives,
By hordes of servants moving in long files.

After Bina's untimely death, Kamala became Dinendra's second wife. There are some people who are able to touch the hearts of those all around them without actually doing anything. Kamala was one of them. Her compassionate and generous nature coupled with a sense of humour was incomparable. She and Dinendra spent most of their time in Shantiniketan. Being the eldest granddaughter-in-law of the family she received Rabindranath's affection in great measure. As she was his *Naat Bou* he would often tease her to the point of embarrassment. In the midst of company he would make her sit next to him and say, 'Kamal, sit next to me. I am enamoured of you. It matters not if others see us thus and carry tales to Calcutta.' 'Others' meant Seeta and Shanta, the daughters of Ramananda Chattopadhyaya. Another incident witnessed by Seeta: the poet often teased Kamala about the relations between 'Rabi and Kamal'. He wondered why the word 'kamal' appeared again and again in his lyrics. Once he was told that Dinendranath had objected. This was because every time the word 'kamal' appeared in a song in his music class the students would smile. Rabindranath was aware that Dinendra and not he was the object of banter. With mock gravity he said, 'The fault lies with the womenfolk. They have been gossiping all over.'

Kamala was a member of the Alapini Sabha. This organization had its own magazine *Shreyashi*. It was rumoured once that Kamala had written a story for the same. Rabindranath's enthusiasm and curiosity knew no bounds. He wanted to know all about the tale. On being told there was no marriage in the content he queried if there were any divorces! His comment to Kamala, 'What were you about? You couldn't even arrange a single wedding in your story?' When Pratima informed that the hero was a poet, Rabindranath pretended to be enraged and said,

'You must have fashioned this character on me. I refuse to speak to you!'

Very few copies of *Shreyashi* are available today. The above-mentioned story by Kamala could not be traced in any of the numbers available. There is just a small article by her titled 'Gaan'. Probably Dinendranath revised this article. Not only did he have a marvellous repertoire of Rabindranath's songs—he may be called their treasurer—but he composed poems himself. His first volume of poetry *Nirab Been* (the silent Bina) was dedicated to his first wife Bina. Suresh Chandra Samajpati reacted with a cynical comment: 'The grandfather and grandson are playing their "Silent Bina" so loudly that soon there will be no need for the band on the maidan.' A mortified Dinendranath hid away all his literary creations. After his death Kamala published a collection of all his works. The language of 'Gaan' is simple and touches the heart. To quote:

> It is through music and songs that we can perceive our sentiments of joy, pleasure, pain and reconciliation. The inexplicable strains of music blend with these feelings, lending them an indefinable beauty and heighten our perception of unity in diversity and happiness in the midst of separation.

Dinendranath's sister Nalini also sang well. On the occasion of her marriage to Surhitnath, the younger brother of Ashutosh Chaudhuri, Rabindranath composed the song, 'Illumine this delightful evening O Lord.'

Arunendranath was the second son of Dwijendranath. Not much is known about Arunendra's three daughters Latika (Lalita), Sagarika and Kanika. They not only lost their mother at a young age but were themselves short-lived. All three were reputed to have been accomplished and good-natured. Like her aunt Pragyasundari, Latika's husband was an Assamese. Jnanadaviram Borua, the youngest son of Rai Bahadur Gunabhiram Barua, married Latika in 1906. It appears that Latika was known in the Tagore family as Lalita. After her marriage, her in-laws may have preferred Latika.

Both Latika and Jnanadaviram were good at dramatics. Latika and her sisters are not as well-known in the field of music and acting as the other ladies of the Tagore family. However once Latika surprised everyone by her superb portrayal of Khantamoni in the play *Goraye Galad*. It was as if the character had come alive. The two younger sisters Sagarika and Kanika were keen on their studies. Kanika also acted, sang and played the sitar well. She portrayed Indumati in the same performance of *Goraye Galad* whence her elder sister was Khantamoni. She is also believed to have played the role of Neerabala in a staging of *Chirakumar Sabha*. Kanika was married into the Tagore family of Chorbagan. Apart from Rabindranath's daughters, Sagarika was the first girl from the Tagore family to go to Shantiniketan for her studies. She studied in the Balika Vidyalaya with Mira and Shamindra and stayed with her aunt Hemlata Devi in the neechu bungalow.

Amita was the wife of Arunendranath's son Ajindra. According to some people his name was Ajinendra. Amita was the daughter of Labanyalekha, the child widow whose remarriage Rabindranath had arranged. The poet looked upon Labanya as his daughter and thus his links with the family went back many years. So Amita occupied the place of Rabindranath's granddaughter and granddaughter-in-law all in one. Besides, he called her his 'Mahishi'. In the conducive atmosphere of Shantiniketan Amita mastered both dramatics and music, but she was shy. It took all Dinendranath and Rabindranath's powers of persuasion to get her on the stage. In one of his letters to Nandita, Rabindranath writes, 'After a great deal of coaxing we have been able to persuade Amita to act in the play *Sudarshana*. I hope it will last.' Amita acted well and later played the role of Malati in *Natir Puja*. She was dressed in a saree held a little high with a garland of *akanda* flowers round her hair in a bun, and another garland of *kunch* fruits round her neck. Thus attired, when she wound the end of her saree round the waist, raised her hands to heaven and wailed, 'The one who called my brother away, the one who called . . . ,' and burst into tears, the audience was spellbound. Rabindranath himself coached her.

Later, after Amita had entered Jorasanko as a bride, the play *Tapati* was staged. None of the ladies available in Shantiniketan were able to portray Tapati the Queen to Rabindranath's satisfaction. Disheartened, he decided to drop the idea but Dinendranath intervened. He said 'Rabidada, why don't you send for Amita? I am sure she will be able to play the role of Tapati just as you want.' Rabindranath was rather hesitant saying, 'This is a difficult role. Will she be able to manage it?' Anyway he agreed to Dinendranath's suggestion and sent for Amita. All his doubts were dispelled once he saw her act. The rehearsals went on for three months before the final staging. Rabindranath played the role of Raja Vikram and Amita that of his queen. Her performance was unforgettable. Abanindranath was one of the audience. He was as overwhelmed by *Tapati* as he had been by the acting of Nandalal Bose's daughter Gauri in *Natir Puja*. He commented, 'Amita entering the fire as Tapati was unique. It touched the chords of one's soul.' He also said that none of the latter-day shows could match this one.

Of course there was a flipside to all this. Tagore had to bear the brunt of adverse criticism whenever he attempted anything novel. It had happened when *Raja O Rani* was staged the first time and occurred once again. Even in this later day and age, a critic charged Rabindranath directly and wrote, 'The poet Rabindranath took the role of Raja and had his grandniece played his queen. The others are just following in his footsteps.' Another comment, 'He still dyes his hair and beard to appear young and acts with adolescent girls.' In spite of the changing times Amita had to face the same situation as Jnanadanandini so many years ago. Fortunately neither Amita nor anyone else in the Tagore family ever paid heed to such adverse criticism.

After she enacted the role of *Tapati*, Rabindranath addressed Amita as 'Mahishi'. He would send her letters thus:

Mahishi,
Tomar dooti haater seba
Janina morey pathalo keba
Jakhan holo belar abasaan—
Deebos jakhan alokhara
Takhan eshey sandhya tara
Diyechhe tarey paras sanmaan.

Mahishi,
At the end of my day
I know not who sent me the tender touch
of your caring hands.
When the day has lost its glory,
The evening star has
Honoured it with its touch.

3 Baisakh 1346 'Paramvikram'
(April 1939).

Apart from her caring nature Amita had the rare ability to write. Her mother often reproached her that so many people had their compositions corrected by Rabindranath, why did not Amita? Perforce she overcame her diffidence and went to Rabindranath. He asked her, 'You write, don't you?' She replied, 'Not very often. Sometimes poems are formed in my mind. Some I write, others get lost.' The poet said, 'Yes, this is an obstacle especially for girls. I am sure you will succeed—you have inherited the gift from your father.' On Amita's request, 'Won't you help me by correcting my work?' Rabindranath read her poem. He was pleased and said, 'Your language is so lucid that I do not wish to alter it.'

Thus encouraged, Amita began to write in earnest. '*Anjali*' and '*Janmadin*' were published. They were simple and lucid poems which touched the heart.

Jobey shudhaye shokoley morey tumi ki peyechho
Koi dekhalena aji?
Mouna nata mukhe thaki, ki dibo uttar—ki peyechhi ami?
Antaheen paona sheje ritutey ritutey

Barne gaane bichitrota majhey,
Shunya patra purna kori rakhi shey sadar
Tai mor dukhya kichhui nai.

When everyone asks me,
You never showed us today what you have received.
I bow my head in silence, what can I reply
What have I got?
It is an endless gift
Which in the music, the shades and variety of every season
Fills all emptiness, thus I have no grief.

Like poetry Amita's style of writing prose was also good. Her non-fictional articles take one along the realms of reminiscences, paintings and storytelling automatically, one after the other, leaving us with a sense of nostalgia. Amita had the knack of drawing pen-portraits of a character in a few lines. Reminiscences neither overshadow the contents nor ideologies confuse the mind. A great deal of information about Tagore's dramatization of characters and playacting in general is gleaned from Amita's article. Rabindranath laid great emphasis on voice modulation and insisted that the end of the dialogue should not be too low or indistinct. He often forgot his lines so his co-actors always had to be on their toes. They also had to remember his dialogue. Otherwise he often began composing new lines, making it very difficult for others to keep track. To quote the article:

> He laid great emphasis on the voice of the main actors and actresses. If someone's voice was shrill or did not come up to his standards he would drop the person forthwith. There were no microphones and everyone had to speak loudly so that their voices carried right to the last row. Rabindranath checked that the voice did not drop towards the end of a dialogue or become indistinct. He was also particular about the body movements of the players. Often a player would move his or her hands and feet to express motion yet keep the head rigid. Tagore would never allow that. He said that movement of the head and neck were essential in emphasizing sentiments.

Amita also tells us that Rabindranath could alter his voice to suit different characters. She says, when reading out the part of Suman's mother in the play *Muktadhara* the way he called out 'Suman baba, Suman,' in a voice trembling with emotion is unforgettable. It often brought tears to the eyes of the listeners. Similarly, when reading aloud *Crescent Moon* he altered his voice so successfully for the mother and the child that one would think two different people were reading out the piece.

> His normal voice was rather soft and reedy but I have often heard him speak in a loud baritone. Thus he was able to alter his voice as required while continuing to read out normally.

Amita confined herself to small articles but she could have given us a great deal more information had she so desired. She was equally reticent about her music. She just recorded one song—*Tomar mohan rupe ke raye bhoole*—in a long-playing record titled, '*Panchakanyar Gaan*'. This too was done after much persuasion by others.

Dwijendranath's fourth son was Sudhindranath. His family also boasts of three daughters and an accomplished daughter-in-law. The eldest daughter Rama had an extraordinary voice. Rabindranath loved to hear her sing his lyrics. Her brother Soumendranath said,

> The songs sung by our elder brother Dinendranath, elder sister Rama and myself in the functions at 'Bichitra' are innumerable. Hearing didi Rama sing *Ei je kalo maatir basa*, *Naago ei je dhoola aamar naa e*, *Ebar rangiye gelo hriday gagan sanjher rangey*, *Sandhya holo go—o ma sandhya holo booke dhoro*, was a bewitching experience for the audience—never to be forgotten.

Rabindranath himself remarked that hardly anyone could bring to life his lyrics as well as when Rama sang them. Rama and her sisters were educated in Shantiniketan, so their training in vocal music continued unhindered. Apart from Dinendranath,

Rama also took lessons regularly from Radhika Goswami and Ustad Shyam Sundar Mishra.

The song *Deshe deshe nondito kari* was composed by Rabindranath to mark the Congress session in Calcutta in 1917. Soumendranath recalls, 'Dada Dinendranath, Ramadidi and I first learnt the song at home. This song was sung for the first time in public during the Congress session.' Apart from Soumendra, others have also mentioned Rama's unusual voice. Sarojasundari's granddaughter Surabhi writes,

> We went with Mother to a performance of *Barshamangal* at the 'Bichitra' hall. There have been numerous performances of *Barshamangal* and *Rituranga* later on. To me this particular one was memorable since this was the first time I heard Rabindranath recite . . . Also I remember Ramapishi's rendering of the song *Aaji jharer ratey tomar abhisaar, paran sakha bandhu hey aamar*, in her melodious voice.

It is a great pity that such a golden voice was never recorded. Only those who actually heard her sing can describe the wonderful mingling of sweetness and depth of feeling in her voice.

Rama was not only interested in singing but also encouraged others to do so. Similar was the case with literary pursuits. She took part in dramas a couple of times. Once she played the role of Kumar in *Mayar Khela* and that of Shanta on another occasion. Both the performances were good. Had there been no Rama no one would have known about Prafullamoyee's *Aamar Katha*. Day in and day out Rama would sit with her and cajole, 'Nadidi, please tell me about yourself, please.' It was her coaxing that made Prafullamoyee traverse back to her childhood through tears and open the doors of her memory. This was no mean achievement! Rama herself also wrote. In *Sreyashi*, the women's magazine in Shantiniketan, she published a few translations. These were from English and her language was simple yet lucid. One of them, '*Sapurer Galpo*' (The Snake-Charmer's Tale), was translated from a tale by Snehalata Devi.

Indira was very keen to collect together Rabindranath's works on women. She mentioned to quite a few people, 'If someone would search through the entire works of Rabindranath, collect together all his writings about women and publish them, it would be a major achievement.' Rama had taken up the task mainly to indicate the position of women in Rabindranath's literary works. She published quite a few such collections under the heading 'Rabindra Sahitye Naari' in several numbers of *Sreyashi*. Unfortunately, lack of time prevented her from maintaining a proper sequence.

According to family traditions Rama had established a school, Savitri Shikshalay, in Bagbazar. She spent a lot of time and effort in collecting subscriptions to set up this institution. The author Pravabati Devi Saraswati had cooperated with her at this time. Later on Rama quietly withdrew herself from this school. Mental worries and anxieties led her, in later life, to seek solace in the ideals and teachings of Lord Buddha. She associated herself with the Mahabodhi Society, dedicating herself to Lord Buddha. For them she published a collection of articles: *Lord Buddha and his Message*. Though she herself did not contribute, she managed to include articles by Rabindranath, Indira, Asit Haldar, Surendranath Tagore and Ramananda Chattopadhyay. Much of Rama's later life has been described by her younger sister Ena. She has also preserved carefully her sister's sketches and literary efforts. Possessions are preserved but the owners depart.

Sudhindranath's second daughter Ena did not have a voice like her elder sister, but she was adept at playing the flute and the sitar. She also participated in the tableaux enacted at 'Bichitra'. Once she played the role of Shakuntala. Ena broke the traditions of the Tagore family when she married Rajendrachandra Ray. To quote Surabhi, 'Since the marriage was registered according to civil marriage rites it did not take place at the Jorasanko Tagore mansion. Both my grandfather, himself a son-in-law of the Tagores, as well as Maharshi Debendranath Tagore, were violently opposed to this form of marriage.' Sailasuta Devi has given details of this marriage in her book *Parinaye Pragati*. This is a book about emancipated women and is full of sarcasm and ridicule of the modern society. Sailasuta Devi (on page 213 of this book) writes about Ena and Rajendra: 'Ena Devi belongs to the Tagore family of Jorasanko. Mr. R.C. Ray's forefathers were Hindoos and Baidyas by caste. Mr. Ray's father Gopal Ray is a believer in Christianity . . . Ena is well educated and accomplished. Mr. Ray was charmed on meeting Ena. She also was attracted to him. They both discussed about their marriage and decided to keep their separate religious beliefs. Even after marriage each would follow his/her own faith.'

After the wedding Ena went away to Dacca. The social atmosphere was totally different. Though there was ample scope for her to establish herself as a queen of high society, she preferred to concentrate on building a happy home. Surabhi always enjoyed her visits to Ena's Lower Circular Road House since: 'there was never any scandal mongering or gossiping here.' Rabindranath was very fond of Ena and her husband. On Rajendra's death he composed a few lines of consolation to Ena. The lines were written by Rabindranath both in Bengali and English.

Matite mishilo mati
Jaha chironton
Rohilo premer swarge
Antarer dhon.

Dust returns to dust
Which is imperishable
Dwells in love's heaven,
treasured by the Eternal.

Both the poems were written on the same page.

Sudhindranath's youngest daughter Chitra spent some time in Shantiniketan. Dance, music and dramatics were in her blood and she mastered them easily. Her brilliance however lay in dancing.

At that time training in dancing had just begun in Shantiniketan. This had been planned by Pratima Devi and a Manipuri guru Navakumar had come as the teacher. A number of girls besides Chitra, Nandita and Nandini from the Tagore family formed the first batch of students. Among them were Sreemati Hathi Singh, Gauri Basu, Nivedita Devi, Amita Chakraborty, Malati Sen, Uma Devi, Amala Raychaudhuri, Jamuna Devi and many others. Sreemati and Amita later married into the Tagore family. Chitra had been in the forefront from the very first performance held to break the taboo against gentlewomen dancing on stage. The performance was held in the courtyard of Jorasanko where Chitra, Sumita and Nandita danced to the accompaniment of the song, *Nupur beje jaye*. Later the song *Sabar rangey rang meshate hobey* in the play *Rituranga* had Chitra dancing to the tune. Quite a commotion was created when Chitra played the role of Maya Kumari in the play *Mayar Khela*. This was directed by Sarala Devi and staged at the New Empire theatre on 28 August 1927. The *Englishman* wrote,

> . . . an entirely novel Indian dance by Miss Chitra Tagore and another by Miss Reba Roy . . . were greatly appreciated by the larger audience.

A similar view was expressed by the representative of the *Forward*:

> The dances formed a salient feature of the play. It was a sheer delight to watch Sm. Reba Ray and Sm. Chitra in their movements . . . In the magic of Chitra's feet was revealed the enchantment of first love.

A few days after the show of *Mayar Khela* directed by Sarala Devi was over, the play was staged once again by the members of the Tagore family. This time Chitra performed a solo Japanese dance. This was reported by the reporter of *The Forward* on 13 September 1927 as follows:

Srimati Chitra, who excelled in her Japanese dance, came in for the largest share of the claps. Her quick and 'jumpy' steps, though an adaptation from the west, seemed to have a fascination all their own.

Apart from dancing Chitra played the role of Basabi in *Natir Puja* and that of Manjari in *Tapati*. She also sang in the choir of the second play. In *Chirakumar Sabha* her portrayal of 'Nripabala' astounded everyone. Later on, however, she withdrew from such activities.

Sreemati had met Rabindranath long before she became a bride in the Tagore family. She belonged to the aristocratic Hathi Singh family of Ahmedabad. She left college during Mahatma Gandhi's Non-Cooperation Movement and came to Shantiniketan, probably in 1921. At the time Kala Bhawan and Sangeet Bhawan were grouped under the same head and the students learnt both music and painting. Sreemati may be considered to be the first student of Kala Bhawan since she came specially to study art, painting and drawing. She left a government college to join Kala Bhawan but her main forte proved to be dance and not art. Her real name was probably Suhasini but it has been completely eclipsed by the name which Rabindranath gave her—Sreemati.

In Shantiniketan Pratima had begun her efforts to teach 'Bhav Nritya' to express the essence of poetry. A dance teacher Naba Kumar had arrived from Manipur and Sreemati joined the troupe. She also continued with her art classes. The various dance postures found new expression in her. Unlike Nandita, Nivedita, Jamuna and Gauri it may be incorrect to call Sreemati a student of Shantiniketan in the truest sense. Her style of dance was one created by herself. Though her training had started in Shantiniketan, her ideas on dance did not find expression in any one style of dancing. She created a new technique by imbuing dance with new expressions. It is amazing to think how she managed such a feat, when dance was almost looked down upon by gentle society. Even today her dances appear exceptional.

Completing her education in Shantiniketan, Sreemati went to Germany to study methods of child education. What she really learnt there was dancing! She toured the various countries in Europe. She not only observed the various dance forms but also held performances herself. What she showed abroad was 'Indian dancing', a style entirely her own. It was based on the Manipuri dance school but had been developed into a unique representation. In Germany she did not take much formal training but observed innumerable dance forms. She took some lessons in the techniques of modern dancing in Mary Wigmann's School of Dance.

On her return to India Sreemati danced to the accompaniment of a recitation of Tagore's poetry. It was a novel idea and pleased the poet no end. She also performed to the accompaniment of songs but somehow this never satisfied her. The wealth of her rhythmic movements found its ultimate culmination when dancing to the lyrical rhymes of poetry. Her heart seemed to dance involuntarily to express the ideas inherent in these poems.

Her first such effort was to dance to the recitation of the poem '*Jhulan*'. The audience was charmed. Sreemati's ability to give expression to the essence of a poem sans any music was amazing. After '*Jhulan*' she chose '*Shishu Tirtha*'. This was a much more difficult proposition but Sreemati was not one to be deterred. Her choice excited Rabindranath. Accompanied by his recitation Sreemati exhibited the 'Bhava Nritya' of 'Jhulan' and 'Shishu Tirtha' in her own technique. This was a synthesis of Manipuri, kathakali and Hungerian dance forms. Even today this seems like an extremely modern idea.

The artist represented the idea of awakening of a new life with great verve and simplicity through her movements. Apart from the recitation by Rabindranath there was no musical accompaniment. It was not easy for all to comprehend such simple yet sincere and vigorous dance postures, but Rabindranath was thrilled. He immediately realized the true potential of dance as a medium for expressing moods and sentiments. Charmed by the grace of Sreemati's dance, Rabindranath wrote:

> She takes delight in evolving new dance forms of her own in rhythmic representation of ideas that offer scope to her spirit for revelling in its own ever-changing creations which according to me is the proper function of dance and a sure sign of her genius. It has often caused me great surprise to see how with perfect truth and forcefulness she has harmonized her movements with my own recitation of my poems—a most difficult task requiring not only a perfect fluency of technique but sympathy which is creative in its adaptability. Her dance is never languid and suggestive of allure that cheapens the art. She is alert and vigorous and the cadence of her limbs carries the expression of an inner meaning and is never an exhibition of skill, bound by some external canons of tradition.

The only other person whose name is worth mentioning along with Sreemati's in the field of Bhav Nritya is Haimanti. She was the wife of Amiya Chakravorti and presented a dance with a recitation of the poem '*Dusshamay*' from *Kalpana*. Till date no successor to these two has emerged.

Sreemati married Soumendranath in 1937 and thus became a member of the Tagore family. This was the first instance of a wedding between a Tagore and a Gujarati lady. Though both were involved in politics, their paths had deviated. Sreemati joined the Non-Cooperation Movement and even went to prison. Soumendra had also joined the Non-Cooperation Movement, but later he became an extremist. After her marriage Sreemati dissociated herself from politics. She now involved herself in social welfare, experiments with Tagore's poems, and art. A competent organizer, she was associated with Rachana, a women's organization in the forties. She also interested herself in welfare schemes like vocational training for women, training them in needlework and marketing the products. During Partition, she arranged to collect old sarees, have kanthas stitched from them, and have them sold.

She examined, audited and experimented with Rabindranath's poems constantly for her dance forms. She gave performances in many places like Madras and Srilanka. Everywhere her dancing won her unusual acclaim. She herself enjoyed watching Rukmini Devi dance. Her own creations *Vishwachhanda*, *Leela Baichitra* or *The Road to Freedom Ballet* were also novel conceptions. In 1950 a dance-drama *Basabdatta* was held in the New Empire Theatre. This was based on Tagore's poem '*Abhisaar*'. In this Sreemati presented a dance to the accompaniment of Soumendranath's recitation. The choice of the poem was exceptional. No one before or since has had the courage to represent the poem '*Dur hotey ki shunish mrityur gorjankey*' from *Balaka*, through dance. She had a melodious voice, and the Mahatma always enjoyed her bhajans. Later she recorded a few bhajans too. She founded a dance school Nrittya Kala and one for music—Baitanik—in her own home. Unfortunately, the former had to close down for dearth of enthusiastic students. Sreemati abhorred trite repetition.

As for paintings, pictures, the 'Society of Oriental Art' is an example of her ability in this field. An anecdote recounted by Surabhi provides an insight into her genuine earnestness and zeal regarding viewing and collection of good paintings. Surabhi wrote:

> One day aunt Sreemati told me that she was keen to visit the art collection of Maharaja Prabirendra of Pathuriaghata. The relations between the women of the Maharshi's family and those of Pathuriaghata had been severed many years ago. The men were the perpetrators but the brunt had to be borne by the other sex. Let alone visiting each other, even when there was a marriage between a near relation and a member of one of these families—this occurred regularly—the ladies of the other house were not allowed to participate in the wedding.

On the horns of a dilemma Surabhi suggested that Sreemati talk to her mother-in-law Charubala first. Sreemati retorted, 'I refuse to be embroiled in those old disputes. I am determined to go, so please make the necessary arrangement.' It was her genuine interest in art that helped Sreemati rise above past dissentions and strained relations. Her action pleased both the families. After all time is a great healer and blunts the edge of old jealousies and disagreements. Thus every branch of art that Sreemati engaged in was enriched by her.

Both the daughters of Dwijendranath were married into the Chatterjee family. The elder, Sarojasundari's husband Mohinimohan, went to the USA. So she stayed in the Tagore mansion for quite a while. Later, on his return, Mohinimohan rented a house in Raibagan and moved his family there. After a couple of years he purchased a house in Macleod Street and began to live there. It was built in 1832, most probably by John Parks. Built in the colonial style this mansion with a lovely garden was considered a premier centre of art and culture of Calcutta for many years. This heritage building has been lost mainly due to the indifference of Calcuttans.

Saroja and Mohinimohan had three sons and four daughters. Among them the youngest son, Tapanmohan Chattopadhyay, and the two younger daughters Geeta and Deepti are well-known. The two elder sons Mohimohan and Nayanmohan married Prakriti and Mamata respectively. Both these were related to the Tagores of Pathuriaghata. They were descended from Kadambini and Kumudini, the two daughters of Girindranath Tagore. At the time of Mohimohan and Prakriti's marriage, old religious conflicts came to the fore.

According to traditional Hindus, the presence of the 'Shalgram Shila' as a witness to the marriage rites was absolutely essential. The Brahmos were against this belief. Mohinimohan had converted to Brahmoism in his youth but later accepted certain features like *hom* and sacred fire of the traditional faith. On the wedding day, ten-year-old Prakriti was dressed up in all her bridal finery, ready for the ritual. She was in a red Banarasi saree, her hair, coiled into a beautiful bun with golden zari ribbons, studded with gold hairpins and combs. Her forehead and cheeks were decorated with motifs drawn with sandal paste. She was decked with ornaments from head to her ankles—*tikli*, earrings, nosering, bangles and tinkling anklets. She also had the traditional *Lakshmir Chubri* in her hand and appeared to be the goddess incarnate. This was the traditional dress for a bride. Just before the wedding was about to begin, a member of the groom's party was seen entering the room with his shoes on. One of the girl's family requested him, 'Please do not come in with shoes. The 'Shalgram Shila' is here. It was as if a matchstick had been held to a keg of powder. The bridegroom's party objected, saying the precondition was that '*hom*' would be performed but no 'Shalgram Shila' would be present. Accusing the girl's family, the groom's father, relations and the Tagores prepared to leave. Only the groom sat unperturbed. As news reached the ladies inside, the bride's mother Pranayini fainted. After a great deal of altercation, Mohinimohan told his fourth brother Rajanimohan, 'I do not wish to ruin an innocent girl's life. You stay back and have the marriage solemnized.' Rajanimohan had married Sunayani, Abanindranath's sister. Thus it was a case of 'all's well that ends well'. Prakriti entered her husband's home as a new bride. Saroja blessed her with the traditional gold-covered 'loha' while Mohinimohan presented her with a pearl necklace. Neither Saroja nor Mohinimohan showed any hint of the unpleasantness that had taken place during the wedding. Prakriti appreciated this and kept rigorously to all the norms of Mohinimohan and Saroja's household. Her daughter Surabhi notes that her mother never maintained any relations with her parents or maternal uncles. She only went once every year to touch the feet of her elders on Vijaya Dashami. Surabhi once said to her 'Ma, you have the permission to visit Pathuriaghata and Koilaghata for the Vijaya dashmi pranam. If you go a day earlier you can easily see the *baran* of the goddess.' But Prakriti never agreed to do so. Her stock answer was, 'That would be insulting my father-in-law. I cannot imagine doing something that he does not approve of.'

Prakriti's father Jaladhichandra Mukhopadhyay was an artist. He had taken lessons from James Archer. An oil painting of Prakriti by him adorned the sitting room of Saroja's Macleod Street home. Prakriti herself could also draw well. Saroja's relations with both her daughters-in-law were extremely affectionate and cordial. In their spare time they often played *Dash Panchish* with cards or went to Satramdas Dhalamal's jewellery shop together. Like the Tagores they were also fond of reading and listening to music. Soumendranath writes, 'Intoxicated with the melodies I would sing song after song. Bara Bouthan and Mejo Bouthan (i.e., Prakriti and Mamata) would always sit there with me.' After her marriage Prakriti had her youngest brother-in-law Tapanmohan not only as a companion but also as a tutor. Mohinimohan was very strict in certain matters. He did not approve of co-education. Though his two daughters Geeta and Deepti graduated with honours he never allowed them to study for their Master's degrees. Prakriti's daughter Surabhi was not permitted to join art school. Asit Kumar Halder, the artist, was Mamata's first cousin and Tapanmohan's friend. He was a frequent visitor to Macleod Street but there is no record of Prakriti having taken any lessons in painting from him. Though at that time many women of aristocratic families, including those of the Tagores, learnt to paint and draw at home, Surabhi does not mention anything about her mother's painting. All the same, Prakriti was a good artist. Her water colours based on 'Krishnalila', 'The Life of Buddha' and Rabindranath's '*Kavya O Kahini*' show her consummate skill. Her paintings were printed regularly in *Prabasi*, *Bichitra* and *Bangalakshmi*. She was influenced by the modern Bengali style and was also an expert in Jesso painting, painting on silk and crafts like Minakari and work on shellac. Her pictures received awards both from the Sarojnalini Women's Welfare organization as well as Calcutta University Institute. A collection of her 'alpana' motifs and examples of needlework under the title *Chitran* was published at this time. The preface of *Chitran* was written by Mukul De. Prakriti was associated with his school of art.

Mohinimohan may not have believed in coeducation but he certainly did not keep his family confined within the four walls of his house. Every evening Saroja went for a drive in a landaulet. She never approved of motor cars. However, whenever she went to Jorasanko on her monthly visits to her parents' house, it was always in a closed phaeton. Even the two green glass windows above the door were raised by the syce. Saroja also attended parties with her daughters and daughters-in-law, particularly those thrown by Protiva. Ashutosh Chaudhuri was by then a judge of the Calcutta High Court. The parties at his place were lavish and Surabhi gives us a glimpse of the dresses and accessories common for these.

> The sarees were usually light Banarasi or Dhakai Jamdani. The blouses always matched the colour of the saree. Hair was done up in a bun. Rouge and lipstick were not used. The ladies usually were a sindoor mark on their forehead. 'Attar' was the favourite perfume. Since sandals were forbidden in parties attended by the Governor's wife, ladies wore stockings and high-heeled shoes. An ostrich-feather fan was high fashion. This was obviously a custom from the Victorian Era.

There were variations in taste also. Foreign perfumes held a tremendous attraction for Surabhi.

The same ladies of this family began to spin yarn from cotton and weave it into khaddar on a spinning wheel or charkha, during the Non-Cooperation Movement. This sea change was brought about by Soumendranath. He used to peddle khaddar from door to door. Prakriti would buy the stuff from him, dye it in pale lemon or saffron and gift it back. Prakriti was also a good actress. Once Sunayani staged the play *Biraha*, enacted by the ladies of the family. It turned out so well that she decided to enact it before Rabindranath. He was then in 'Bichitra'. The entire performance delighted him. Prakriti's portrayal so pleased him that he not only blessed her but admonished Mohinimohan saying, 'Your wife is such a good actress, yet you have confined her only to housework!' Thus Prakriti had identified herself totally with the culture of her in-laws. Nayanmohan's wife Mamata was the granddaughter of Kumudini's son. Such marriages between the various branches of the family were common among the Tagores. One reason certainly was that they were Piralis and looked down upon by other Brahmins. Even otherwise, in wealthy families it was the normal practice not only to have a 'ghar jamai' (a son-in-law living with his wife's parents) but also to choose daughters-in-law from among relations. A prime factor was the security of the girl concerned. After all, women have always been soft targets for social persecution and injustice. The Maharshi and Rabindranath did try to marry daughters outside the circle of relations but this was uncommon.

Mamata's father worked in Punjab and her childhood was spent there. Later she joined Protiva's Sangeet Sangha where she took lessons from Ustaad Enayat Khan in sitar and in vocal music. After her marriage she was coached by Dinendranath Tagore in Shantiniketan. Once Rabindranath told her, 'If you come to me I can also teach you.' Later he demurred saying, 'Well you had better learn from Dinu. You may not like my way of teaching.' Mamata was an expert cook and needlewoman. She once cooked 'cheese rice' for Rabindranath and it was an instant hit. Hemlata was an aunt of both Prakriti and Mamata, being their father's cousin. Herself deeply involved with the Sarojnalini women's welfare organization, Hemlata had drawn both Prakriti and Mamata into this work. Cutting, tailoring and needlework were a few of the means of livelihood open to destitute widows. This is what Mamata trained them in at Sarojnalini. After Nayanmohan's untimely death, she dedicated herself heart and soul in ameliorating the lot of hapless widows.

Geeta and Deepti were the youngest of Saroja and Mohinimohan's daughters. They proved to have been two bright stars in the crown of the Chatterjee family. Saroja and Mohinimohan had two older daughters, Shakuntala and Sumana. These two as well as Ramanimohan and Ushaboti's daughters Murala and Karuna had been married with a good deal of pomp and show. Unfortunately three of them died young and one was widowed. These mishaps convinced Mohinimohan that the girls of his family were not destined to lead happy married lives. He thus decided against Geeta and Deepti's marriage and began educating them. Whether it was this or the dearth of suitable young men, both Geeta and Deepti never married. They enjoyed long lives and were well-known in the sphere of social welfare. All the girls of this family studied in the Diocesan School and College. This institution, like Loreto House, was gradually gaining popularity among the aristocratic Bengali families. The affectionate behaviour of the nuns was a special factor in attracting the girls. The daughters of Protiva, Pragya, Saroja and many others of the Tagore family were students of Diocesan. Geeta and Deepti were always together and they even dressed alike. Both graduated with flying colours. Since Mohinimohan did not allow them to join the University, both the sisters took their Bachelor's degree in Teachers' training (B.T.) from Diocesan. Thereafter they began teaching in the same school. Although Mohinimohan had decided against having his two younger daughters married, he had never thought that they would earn their own living. This was a mindset common to all wealthy families of the day. The tendency in aristocratic families had been to segregate academic qualification from its inseparable corollary—earning money—where their women were concerned. Thus Geeta and Deepti soon chose social service as their sphere of activity. They became associated with the All Bengal Women's Association, Jyotirmoyee Shishu Bhaban and other such organizations. Whatever little time was left was utilized by their aunt Hemlata for the school run by Sarojnalini Association.

Both the sisters sang well and Deepti also played the violin. The difference between the two sisters was that Deepti also wrote well: stories, novels, reminiscences, non-fictional articles, travelogues, plays, translations—her works are scattered in the pages of various magazines. During the last few years she translated nursery rhymes. These are untraceable today mainly because of indifference and negligence. No attempt has been made to collect her available works and to publish a compilation of the same. Inevitably, her non-fictional articles deal with women's problems. During her involvement with social service she was witness to the injustice meted out to women both within and outside the home. She saw, 'The responsibilities of women are increasing manyfold as compared to the few rights they are gaining.' She felt that, 'the prestige that is being won for them is just to keep them engaged in the service and care of others.' Thus a woman is not awarded any dignity for being a woman, but is being duped into performing service with the lure of respect and honour. When writing the article 'Marriage customs in the Bali Islands' Deepti's pen was like a rapier thrust,

> The fathers are the ring leaders of the persecution of their daughters. For them their daughters do not count. Sons are the be-all and end-all of their existence.

This attitude is not restricted to the Bali Islands alone but prevails in all eastern countries. Deepti further says,

> God has been generous in bestowing this land with scenic grandeur. Yet God's most beautiful creation—a woman—is considered a tradeable commodity. The shameless bargaining over a woman's body is nauseating to say the least.

Her article '*Path chalateye ananda*' covers her visit to Europe. In 1934 the two sisters first went to England and then visited France, Italy and Germany. This was before the advent of World War II. There was a specific purpose behind their trip to Germany. They had heard of the Passion Play of Oberamergau and wanted to see it. This theatrical spectacle is staged once in every ten years. It is considered a great privilege to witness this drama, based on the life and personality of Jesus Christ. The tri-centenary of the play was in 1934. In her article, Deepti gave a detailed description. She was spellbound by the play and says:

> Oberamergau is a small village on the banks of the river Yamar . . . One can see the Alps all around . . . This small sleepy village wakes up once every ten years. Then people come from Germany and abroad to witness their Passion Play . . .

From her article, we learn that there is a history behind the origin of this theatrical tradition. In 1634 the survivors of the plague in the village took a pledge that they would enact, once every ten years, the Passion of Christ or the suffering that He underwent to redeem mankind. The actors all belong to the village and, during the ten-year period, are examined carefully before being chosen to participate in the play. Deepti wrote:

> I am unable to describe what I have witnessed. It seemed as if I was turning the pages of the Bible, one by one. Not once did the thought cross my mind that this is only acting.

In this context, it may be recalled that the incomparable Bengali work *Jishu Charit* was written by Deepti's elder brother Tapanmohan.

Ever since they could remember, Geeta and Deepti had been told that they 'have two maternal grandfathers in Shantiniketan. One was our own grandfather and the other Rabidada.' They came to know Rabindranath intimately in 1939. The memory was unforgettable. Deepti says:

> After grandfather's death we had not been to Shantiniketan for a number of years. In Phalgun (February-March) 1939 we went for about ten days and put up at Uttarayan.

When they met Rabindranath in the evening he queried, 'Don't you collect autographs?' Both the sisters said, 'Oh yes! Will you write a few lines and autograph it?' The poet agreed and the two requested him to write in English. They were keen to show his message to their non-Bengali friends.

Geeta and Deepti bought autograph books and sent them to Rabindranath. The next evening when they went to see him, he said, 'I have addressed the lines to you. I hope you will like my message.' What Rabindranath wrote was: 'You have risen late, my crescent moon, but my night bird is still awake to greet you.' Deepti said, 'As we were reading his words, he said, "It is meant for you, you have come to me too late."' Baro-ma (Hemlata Devi), who was there, said, 'Kakamoshai (uncle), why have you written in English? Do you consider them memsahibs (foreign ladies)?' The poet replied, 'This is as per their request.' At this point of the conversation between the poet and Hemlata Devi, Deepti remembers saying, 'You know Rabidada, had you written anything in Bengali, Mejopishi would have had it published immediately in *Bangalakshmi*.' Rabindranath smiled and replied, 'You are quite right. That is why she is annoyed.'

Many such small anecdotes, full of the loving banter between an affectionate grandfather and his granddaughters, appear in Deepti's reminiscences. Deepti's style of Bengali writing is rather anglicized. Rabindranath had noted this and told the sisters, 'Education in an English medium school has made your English impeccable but your ways have become alien. Stay with me for a while, I shall put all that right.' According to Deepti,

> In spite of all his achievements Rabindranath could mix easily with young people. With an erudite scholar he would behave as one yet the same man would become the traditional Bengali grandfather with his grandchildren. The transformation was so swift that it astonished all of us.

In Shantiniketan, Rabindranath's feet were massaged with oil every evening. Once Geeta and Deepti turned up with the request to be allowed to perform this chore. The poet said, 'That is impossible. You are here for a few days, how can I let you do such a job?' Not to be outdone, the two retorted, 'Where do we get a chance to massage your feet? We would consider it a favour.' Rabindranath agreed with a smile.

Rabindranath was rather finicky about the people who did such physical chores for him. However Geeta and Deepti met with his approval. He did demur saying, 'I never knew modern women were keen to massage anyone's feet. Your dresses are so dainty. If they get stained with oil, will it be possible to have them cleaned here? Perhaps you will have to send them to Paris!' Geeta and Deepti were not to deterred. Once, as Deepti held his hand to massage it he said, 'Oh! You are determined for my *pani piran* (taking one's hand in marriage). Well go ahead.' Later as she sat down to massage his feet he said 'Dear me! Now she is going to wring my feet!'

Soon the visit drew to a close. The two sisters approached Rabindranath with a photograph of his. Though he pretended to be annoyed at first, he later relented, saying, 'All right, leave it behind. I am going to write something really nasty. That will serve you right.' In the evening the photograph came back with the inscription:

> *Aloker smritichhaya buke kore rakhe, chhabi bole takey.*
>
> A photograph is that which treasures the memory of light in its heart.

During the leave-taking he said, 'Do come again. I know you will come even if only to massage my feet.' That year when writing to them after Durga puja he wrote,

> My two granddaughters, Geeta and Deepti, accept my blessings for Vijayadashami. My feet are yearning to meet your graceful palms.
>
> Vijaya Dashmi 1346 (1939), Rabidada.

They met again at the foundation-stone-laying ceremony of Mahajati Sadan. Rabindranath greeted them with, 'Oh! I wondered why my feet were refusing to move.' He again invited them to Shantiniketan saying, 'No one else will be able to tutor you as well as I. There is so much I can teach you.' Geeta and Deepti were unable to take up the invitation. Probably it was not possible for them to leave Calcutta. Rabindranath teased them,

> Is it just the lure of Calcutta or is there a deeper reason? Does it involve young men? If it is modesty, why doesn't each of you whisper to me about the other?

When Rabindranath was brought to Calcutta towards the end of his last illness, the two sisters rushed to see him. Deepti gives an account of their conversation.

> As we touched his feet he queried, 'It is quite some time since I saw you last. How are you?' Before we could reply he continued, 'Don't ask me the same question though.' On our telling him that he looked well he countered, 'When have I ever looked unwell?' Death was knocking at his door. Yet his manner was as jovial as ever. Pain and physical suffering had not diminished his joyfulness. Impending death had not been able to conquer his spirit. Death itself stood defeated.'

This visit was on 29 July 1941, just eight days before Rabindranath left this world.

Deepti's reminiscences allow us a glimpse of the witty Rabindranath in informal surroundings. Geeta and Deepti's social service brought them in contact with Netaji Subhas Chandra Bose too. He once visited them, along with a Polish lady, Miss Marilla Folk, at their Macleod Street residence. Unfortunately it has not been possible to ascertain any details of this meeting.

Though Deepti was a prolific writer, her works were never published as a book. A detective novel by her, *Lakshmididir Kalo Chasma*, was once chosen by Radha Films for a movie. Some scenes had been shot at Macleod Street, but the project was abandoned halfway through. Quite a few of her stories and novels still lie hidden among the pages of various magazines. In some of them their house serves as a background, in some there are glimpses of their family and times. In Deepti's novel *Jaya Parajaya* Sarojini says, 'My dear, we never learnt to depend on our own powers of judgement. I try my best to move according to the norms of the family I entered as a bride. I never had any opinion of my own, to me your father's views were supreme.' Today Deepti is remembered for her social service while her literary role seems to be lost forever.

Dwipendranath's granddaughter Purnima was also Surendranath's daughter-in-law. Such marriages between among close relations was common among the other branches of Tagores but in the Maharshi's family this was the first instance. Dwipendranath's daughter Nalini was married to Surhit Chaudhuri. Among her three daughters two were married into the Tagore family. The second daughter Aparna was married to Nabendranath Tagore. Nabendranath was Gaganendranath Tagore's son and thus a resident of house number 5. Now Purnima came into the Maharshi's family in house number 6. In the atmosphere where Purnima grew up, every girl could sing and perform on the stage. Purnima was no exception. She played the role of Balika in *Balmiki Protiva*, that of Amar in *Mayar Khela*, Lakshmi in *Lakshmir Pariksha* and Purabala in *Chira Kumar Sabha*. After she graduated, Rabindranath requested that she be allowed to teach English in Shantiniketan. Teaching was in the blood of the Tagores; so Nalini agreed readily. Purnima taught English in Shantiniketan for a year and a half. It was here that she struck up a friendship with Leela Majumdar. In her autobiography Leela writes, 'Purnima joined a week after me. Her job would be an honorary one since her guardians held the view that unless women were dependent on them, the social status of their menfolk was lowered.' Such social taboos prevented Bengali women, especially those from West Bengal, from gaining economic independence in spite of having opportunities. Decades ago Sarala took up a job outside her home to encourage Bengali women in their quest for independence. Yet the ladies of the Tagore family were unable to continue this tradition. They always considered teaching a form of social service. It was only after the Second World War and the partition of India that the scenario changed slowly.

Indira Devi has given a fairly detailed account of Purnima and Subir's marriage in her autobiography *Jeeban Katha*: 'Since Subir and Nalini were second cousins Subir decided to have the marriage registered according to the 'Gour Bill'. Our friend Shri Atul Gupta, an authority on Hindu law, had advised this. The Maharshi did not approve of registration for any marriage of the members of the Adi Brahmo Samaj. This was because according to the Law of 1872 one had to declare during registration, "I am neither a Hindu nor a Muslim, etc." The Maharshi was keen that marriages conducted by the Adi Brahmo Samaj be considered Hindu marriages minus the idol worship. In the Gour Bill one does not have to make such a declaration now. Suren too may have had his reasons against registration but he was never one to object to his son's wishes.'

Indira's humorous running commentary continues about Subir and Purnima choosing each other. '. . . He was extremely handsome and well built. His looks certainly entranced one person—the one whom he later married. At the time Surhit and his family had rented the first floor of Lal Bungalow so there were opportunities galore for them to meet and get to know each other.' In a few simple words Indira Devi has described a delightful love story.

When the marriage of Purnima's elder sister Aparna had been arranged with Gaganendranath's son Nabendra, Rabindranath had not approved of this wedding between the two closely related families. In an undated letter to Rathindranath he wrote, 'I shall certainly not accept the invitation to Apu's wedding. Why is Dipu so worried about this since he was the one to arrange the match?' Thus it is safe to assume that he did not approve of Subir and Purnima's marriage—perhaps because of their decision to have the event registered. Indira writes, 'None of the regular priests of our Adi Samaj being available, we were forced to get Hemlata Bauthan and Saraladidi to officiate.' Indira does not elaborate on the reasons for non-availability of the priests from the Adi Brahmo Samaj. This incident however brings to the fore the fact that the ladies of the Tagore family never held back from any task.

In her later life Purnima lived permanently in Shantiniketan. After her husband's death in 1953 she began to teach in Patha Bhawan. She was also an active member of the Alapini and Nari Kalyan Samity. Her greatest pleasure lay in the company of her 'namaa' Indira Devi. Indira was also very fond of her and encouraged her in all her endeavours. Purnima had begun to write a biography of Indira Devi. This was something she always wanted to do, though it is a difficult job to write about a dear one. More so when the writer herself is a character in the narrative. Purnima's language is graceful. Her descriptions are not unduly burdened with unnecessary details but help us to understand Indira. There is an amusing anecdote about the time Indira was the vice chancellor of Vishwa Bharati. Once a professor brought a case against the university and in due course the police turned up to enquire about the case. Indira commented with her usual dry humour, 'Due to my long life I have had numerous experiences but this certainly is an unprecedented situation. I hope I won't be imprisoned and have to subsist on *lapsi*.' Unfortunately the book has not been published so far.

Thakur Barir Ranna by Purnima is a popular book on cooking. It is not an extensive work like Pragyasundari's *Amish O Niramish Aahar*. Purnima has chosen just the dishes favoured by the Tagore family. Indira was a gourmet although she never cooked. According to Purnima, 'Whenever a dish served in any function or otherwise pleased her she made it a point to write down the recipe.' This notebook she later passed on to Purnima. Purnima's mother Nalini was also a superb cook and had taught Purnima a number of dishes. All these have been compiled in this book. Items like 'tomato fish', 'mutton Bengali', 'mutton with khus khus', 'brinjal chutney', 'cauliflower with eggs' and 'cabbage with rice' are sure to appeal to connoisseurs of good food.

Subir's brother Prabirendra's wife was Anima, Mihirendra's wife was Leela and Sunritendra's was Satirani. Leela did her bit between her domestic engagements for the Widow Shilpasram.

Like Purnima, Satirani also came from a branch of the Tagore family. She was the great granddaughter of Dheerabala and connected to the Pathuriaghata and Koilahata Tagores. Her elder sister Shibrani was married to Samarendranath's son in house number 5. Satirani was well-known as a singer and she also acted well. Once when *Chirakumar Sabha* was staged in Shantiniketan she played the role of Nripabala. In Saharanpur she organized the play *Rituranga* with the domiciled Bengalis. Satirani's reminiscences are also lucid. She says,

> When I start thinking about the days gone by, so many events crowd together. It is difficult to pen them systematically. Some I witnessed while others are hearsay but they are all memories now. Talking of mementos, I have a wine glass used by Dwarkanath Tagore. There was also a chair used by Rabindranath, I donated it to Rabindra Bharati, and a manuscript of *Bisarjan* that I donated to Viswa Bharati. All that remains with me is the Poet's music. My mother taught me to sing Rabindra Sangeet from the time I learnt to lisp a few words. My aunt Surupa Devi taught me numerous songs by Rabindranath. Later I had the immense good fortune to learn from Indira Devi. I was brought up in an atmosphere of Rabindra Sangeet and even now it is the prop and mainstay of my life. At every moment, in every situation of life some songs of his come to my mind.

Of Surendranath's two daughters Manjushri and Jayashri, the elder Manjushri had been closer to Rabindranath. She was one of the first two girl-students of Shantiniketan. She possessed an exceptionally melodious voice and she participated in various functions of the Vishwa Bharati Shantiniketan. She not only sang but also played the veena. She accompanied Rabindranath on one of his trips abroad and returned home after spending a year in London's Clifton Boarding School. While in London the sculpturess Miss Bower sculpted a lovely statue of Manjushri. Manjushri was a versatile actress. In 1923 the play *Bisarjan* was staged in the New Empire Theatre for three evenings. Rabindranath had initially chosen Manjushri for the role of Aparna but it was later decided that Ranu Adhikari would play the role. Rabindranath wrote to Ranu, 'If you do not come there will be problems. I had requested Gagan to train Manjushri for the role but that does not seem feasible.' Ranu came but was unable to act on the first evening. Manjushri portrayed Aparna with grace and verve. Rabindranath, despite his advanced years, brought to life the young Jaisingha with unusual expertise. Sangya had been chosen to play the role of Gunabati. Unfortunately she fell ill after the second evening and it was Manjushri who stepped into the role. It was no mean feat for an amateur artist to portray two different roles in the same play on two consecutive days. Though she had had no time to rehearse, Manjushri captivated the audience with her effortless acting. This was not a performance in the informal atmosphere of Jorasanko or Shantiniketan. Tickets had been sold for the public show. Yet Manjushri had no bouts of nervousness. Her dramatic abilities came to the fore as Sumitra in the public performance of *Bhairaber Boli* in 1929. Rabindranath had dramatized his novel *Raja O Rani* as *Bhairaber Boli*. Many years ago Manjushri's grandmother Jnanadanandini had turned in a sterling performance as Sumitra. In the show staged in 1929 the part of Raja was played by Manjushri's husband Kshitishprasad Chattopadhyaya. Rabindranath was abroad and thus he was unable to see the performance.

In later life Manjushri involved herself with the political movement. Her husband Kshitishprasad was a front-ranking leader of the Congress party and one of the chief initiators of the Non-cooperation movement. Manjushri's involvement with the Non-cooperation movement was more from an all-consuming feeling of sympathy and compassion rather than from any keen political consciousness. It was this sense of compassion that later drew her to the Communist Party.

During the disastrous famine of 1943 Manjushri was in Krishnanagar. She had no inkling of the unimaginable misery faced by the famine-stricken people and the conditions prevailing in Calcutta. She chanced upon a newspaper published by the communists. Glancing through it she came across Somnath Lahiri's article 'Queues of Death in Calcutta'. As she read the article in shocked disbelief, tears streamed down her eyes. Filled with remorse and pity she was unable to swallow even a morsel of food herself. After a sleepless night Manjushri was determined to help these starving people. She arrived in Calcutta the next morning and collected some money with the help of her husband and relatives. She consulted Dr Bidhan Chandra Ray, purchased some essential drugs and returned to Krishnanagar. She opened a relief centre in her house to combat the epidemics inherent in famine. At this juncture the members of the local Communist Party came forward to help her. Till then the party had no women's cell. Manjushri founded the Mahila Atmaraksha Samity with a few others. *Gharey Bairey*, edited by Manjushri, was the mouthpiece of the Samity. Its purpose was to fight for the rights of those women who had no footing in society, at home, in political or economic fields. She had observed that such women were the most deprived and thus she decided to fight for them. She said,

> Atmaraksha Samity is meant for those women who have not been able to find a foothold in any sphere of life, be it social, domestic, political or economic. They are deprived of all their rights. Our movement is for their just rights. A society and government that denies a woman her basic minimum rights and allows her potential to be frittered away is unacceptable as impartial or just by the Atmaraksha society, nor will it ever do so. *Gharey Bairey* has vowed to carry this message to every home.

The publication of *Gharey Bairey* was stopped after a few issues. Manjushri then brought out another magazine called *Jaya*. In March 1949 the Communist Party was banned in West Bengal and the government proscribed the magazine. Manjushri had been elected president of Mahila Atmaraksha Samity just about a month earlier. Along with Manikuntala Sen and many others, Manjushri was imprisoned. Writing about her, Manikuntala says,

> Till now we knew Manjushri Devi as an affectionate and silent worker. In prison we saw her quiet spiritedness . . . Our jail visitor one day suggested to her, 'Why must you involve yourself in all this? After all, you can go home whenever you wish.' Perhaps he had heard about her husband's position. Manjushri was furious at the hint and rushed out of the room with a loud 'No'. Her whole countenance seemed to burn with anger and humiliation. She was a very reserved yet determined person and never spoke much.

All the Communist workers went into a fast at this time. The women joined in five days after their male colleagues had begun. Manjushri also fasted for fifty-three days along with the others. Considering her age, the others had tried to dissuade her but she was unshakeable. She spent about a year in prison and was released in 1951 when the ban on the Communist Party of India was withdrawn. In 1952 she went to China to participate in the First Asian and Pacific Peace Conference. The delegation consisted of Saifuddin Kitchlu, Dr Gyanchand, and others. Manjushri had been chosen as 'Rabindranath's granddaughter'. In China she did not get much chance to acquaint herself with the political and social life of the common people. Such delegations seldom offer one an opportunity to do so. All of them had a tremendous curiosity about the new regime. Just as Tagore had been fascinated by the new Russia in 1930, so was Manjushri when she saw an ordinary coolie of the Canton rail-station reading a novel by Li Sun. She was pleasurably surprised by the education and literary taste of an ordinary worker. She later wrote a book *Naya Chiney Ja Dekhechi*. It dealt mainly with her experiences in China. Her style was absorbing but she seldom wrote. During the first two general elections she worked as a publicity agent for Manikuntala Sen and Somnath Lahiri. When E.M.S. Namboodiripad organized the meeting of 'Hands of Kerala' in Calcutta, Manjushri sang the opening song, *Sarthak janam amar janmechi ei deshey*. However, her involvement with politics was gradually waning. She severed all relations with politics after the split in the Communist Party.

Manjushri's younger sibling Jayashri has preferred to remain behind the scenes. Besides being educated along with her sister, she participated in a few shows. She acted as Saraswati in *Balmiki Protiva* and Rituraaj in *Rituranga*. In the latter production, Sahana Devi provided the vocal music. Jayashri chose Kulaprasad Sen as her life partner. Since it was an inter-caste marriage there was considerable opposition from the family. The Maharshi never approved of marriages between Brahmins and non-Brahmins. He had refused the proposal of the princess of Coochbehar for Surendra on these grounds. Times however had changed. Surendra supported Jayashri saying,

> We proclaim loudly that we are all the children of the same motherland. Then how can I object if my daughter chooses to marry someone from another caste? Our grandparents and parents deviated from the traditions of their forefathers. We are now going against their customary ways. In effect we are doing just what they did.

Rabindranath himself officiated as the acharya in this marriage. Even though it was inter-caste, there was no registration. When Rabindranath was in Allahabad, Jayashri requested him to write a few lines since he had not done so at the time of the wedding. He wrote,

> *Tomader biye holo Phaguner Choutha*
> *Akshay hoye thak sindurer kouta.*
> *Saat chade tobu jeno katha mukhe na phote*

Nasikar doga chhede ghomtao na othe.
Shashuri na bole jeno 'Ki behaya bou-ta . . .

You were married on Phalgun the fourth.
May your sindoor box be ever-full,
You must never answer back
Even if slapped seven times,
Your saree-pallau should never rise
above the tip of your nose.
Your mother-in-law must
Never be able to say,
What a shameless hussy
Is my daughter-in-law . . .

Hemendranath had eight daughters and three sons. All were devoted to music and education. Protiva was the eldest among them. All her children loved music. Her eldest son Arya Kumar was more interested in photography and painting. His wife Leela was the only child of Ranendramohan Tagore and Sulajini. Sulajini again was the elder sister of Abanindranath's wife Suhasini. Despite her modern education Leela was interested in Sanskrit poetry and ancient traditions of India. She liked to compose poems. After reading her verses Rabindranath wrote, 'Leela's imagination and style of composition have both pleased me.'

Aryakumar used Leela as his model in many of his photographs. Though his work was appreciated by all, Ranendramohan's family disapproved. Aryakumar later went to Paris to study further developments in photography and returned after a number of years. Leela had also been to the United Kingdom with the Chaudhuri family shortly after her marriage.

A collection of Leela's poems was published in the form of an album. It was named *Kishalaya*. All the pictures of Leela published in her book had been taken by Arya Kumar. Melancholia is a characteristic of all Leela's poems. The apple of her wealthy parents' eyes, a paragon of beauty, accomplished, married into an aristocratic family, a handsome talented husband and children—

although her daughter died young—yet the air of gloom and sorrow prevalent in her poetry leaves the reader perplexed. She wrote about Urmila who has been ignored by Valmiki in his epic *Ramayana*.

Hey chiro birohini hey priyo pujarini
Nirobe upasana emon kar?
Rajar bodhu botey kahar heno ghate
Kahar bhale eto bedona bhar . . .
Patite tanmay tumi je chinmoy
Paoni pratidan kachhete tar
Dekheni sanyasi shey byatha binyashi
Sri Ram moy hridoy chhilo tar.

Oh you eternally separated from your lover,
Oh dear worshipper,
Whom do you worship so quietly?
You are the daughter-in-law of a king
Yet who is so fated
To be fraught with so much pain.
Totally devoted to your husband
You are conscious only of him
He has not reciprocated your love
The Sannyasi never observed
That pain in your being.
His heart was full of only Rama.

Another poem:

Tomar shukher diney
Utsab miloney
Bhuley jodi jao morey kshati nahi taye
Sangihin jobe tumi
Nitanta nirjane
Smariyo amaye Sakha e minati paye.
Basanta kusum chhaoa
Madhabi bitane
Nahi shono kshati nai amar e gaan
Duranta jhoder ratey
Shayan shithane
Mor gaane kshonotare dio Sakha kaan.

During your days of joy,
Celebrations and union with friends
There is no harm if you forget me.
But when you are without friends,
Alone and desolate,
Remember me my love, I beseech you.
If in your garden decked with spring flowers
You do not listen to my song
There will be no harm done.
But in a stormy night,
With your head on the pillow
Dear love pay heed to my voice for a moment.

Or else:

Amar ja kichhu haraye giyachhe
Phuraye giyachhe daane
Chhadaye giyachhe nikhil bhubane
Hajar hajar prane.
Amar ja kichhu bilaye diyachhi
Bhiksha kator kare
Subasher moto ubiya giyachhe
Samabedonar jhare.
Tai aj ami kangal hey Swami
Sunya amar shob
Sabar majhare amar praner
Payi aj anubhav.

Whatever I had is gone,
It has ended in charity.
It has spread over the whole world
Unto millions of hearts.
I have given away my all
To begging palms.
It has evaporated like fragrance
In a storm of compassion.
Thus I am destitute today my Lord,
Everything of mine is empty.
However it is amidst all
That I can feel my soul.

Apart from poetry Leela also wrote fiction and short stories: '*Nabaghana*,' '*Jharar Jharna*', '*Dhruba*', '*Sinchon*' and '*Roop-heenar Roop*'. In her social novels Leela has dealt with the complexities of love. In the story '*Chhabi*', Chameli the heroine is a Christian while the hero Naba Kishore is a Hindu and a teacher by profession. His wife Sutara on the other hand is in love with Chameli's brother. By a quirk of fate Leela's talent was lost forever before it had a chance to blossom fully. After her death, her heartbroken father arranged for the Leela Prize and the Leela Lectures at Calcutta University in her memory. Hemlata Tagore was awarded the first Leela Prize. Anurupa Devi in 1945 delivered the first Leela Lecture. Her topic was 'The place of women in society and literature'.

Protiva's second son Aswinikumar's wife was Felicita. Aswini had gone to the UK to study law. There this strikingly handsome young man met the ballerina Felicita Lodetti of Milan's La Scala Theatre. Felicita had been in the third position in Anna Pavlova's troupe and came to perform in England. A certificate shows Felicita being requested to accept the position of the prima ballerina by the La Scala Theatre after she had been associated with ballet from 1904 to 1914. The Chaudhuri family was considerably westernized and Aswini was charmed by Felicita's dancing. The attraction was mutual and they fell deeply in love. Felicita decided to give up the glamorous life of a Prima ballerina and spend her life as Aswini's wife. Protiva welcomed Felicita warmly as a member of her family and sent her a pair of gold armlets as a gift. These had originally belonged to Neepamoyee, Protiva's mother. Though it is not possible to determine the feelings of Felicita's family after all these years, there certainly were certain impediments. Felicita was a Roman Catholic and it was normally not permissible for her to marry someone who was not even a Christian. This was more so because she was so well-known in the world of ballet. However love triumphs over all impediments. Aswini and Felicita appealed to the Pope and a special dispensation was granted to them. In 1920 Aswini married Felicita and brought his bride home to India. As they met for the first time Protiva put a pearl collar studded with rubies and diamonds round Felicita's throat and welcomed her in the traditional manner. Felicita was overwhelmed with joy.

The next forty years witnessed Felicita's spectacular efforts to become a typical Hindu wife and daughter-in-law. She captivated all her husband's near and dear ones by her loving and sweet nature. She learnt to wear the saree, always covering her head in the traditional style and considered her husband's family as her own. She was associated with the Calcutta School of Music and played the piano. Aswini himself was also a connoisseur of music. Aswini had taken charge of '*Sangeet Sangha*' after his mother's death. Thus the husband and wife enjoyed similar tastes. Felicita had adapted herself so well to her role as a housewife that it was difficult to visualize her previous life. Aswini's sister Asoka's daughter-in-law Smita says, 'She [Felicita] never gave an inkling of the glamourous life she had left behind or of ever having been a reputed ballerina. She wore a saree, covered her head with the pallu pinned in place and spoke Bengali fluently. She also cooked Indian dishes and had integrated perfectly with the Bengali way of life. Once she and her husband took me to see an English movie about famous ballets. It was the only time I saw her deep involvement and appreciation of ballet dancing.'

Asoka was Protiva and Asutosh's only daughter. She had inherited her mother's love of music. She not only sang well but also prepared notations. The musical score for a number of Rabindranath's songs were made by her. The atmosphere in her father's house was steeped in music. His parties were often attended by artists and musicians besides other luminaries of society. Asoka often played the piano or sang in such gatherings. In 1911 Protiva threw a party to welcome Lady Hardinge. The family members put up the play *Balmiki Protiva*. Asoka played the role of Saraswati while her aunt Shovana acted as Lakshmi. Asoka's piano recital in the congregation held during the visit of King George V in 1912 was acclaimed by all. She later joined the Sangeet Sangha. Along with her mother and Indira she took up the task of creating musical scores and notations. Along with Indira, she regularly contributed to the magazine *Ananda Sangeet*. Her notations include Tagore songs like *Bara asha niye*, *Shanto harey mamo chitta nirakul*, *Khanchar pakhi chilo*, and *Tomari grihe palichho snehey*. She had considerable command over classical music. This was evident in the notations she prepared for tunes like Iman Ragini, Khambaaz Ragini, etc. Sangeet Sangha opened up a path for girls from good families to learn music and its student strength rose continuously. Asoka used to teach both vocal music and the piano. However Western classical music was always her first love.

The last thirty-five years of Asoka's life were spent in Ranchi. Many Tagores, apart from Jyotirindranath and Satyendranath, had built houses in Ranchi. Asoka's husband W. Chowdhury built a house next to Satyendranath's 'Satyadham' at the foot of Morabadi Hill. She visited England with her father before her marriage and went to her husband's home in Sylhet twice after her marriage. However, she was never able to accompany her geologist husband on his prospecting trips. Her physical disability was partly responsible. Her days in Ranchi were spent in the pattern set by the ladies of the Tagore family. Every morning she would supervise the weighing of daily rations, draw up the list for provisions with the servant in charge of marketing, measure out the milk for the family members—everything followed a strict routine. Every girl of the Tagore family was meticulously trained in household management. Modern education made no difference to this tradition. Besides this, painting, literary pursuits and needlework were also popular. Nothing was ever wasted. Old pieces of material were joined with hand-crocheted lace to form table mats. The wealth of her parents or husband had no effect on these habits. There was no scope for Western classical music in Ranchi at that time and slowly Asoka moved away from her music. She usually spent her time reading. She accepted the change from Calcutta's aristocratic society to a quiet life in Ranchi with equanimity. This ability to adjust oneself to one's surroundings was a characteristic of the Tagore family. In general Tagore girls carried this culture with them while daughters-in-law were trained accordingly. Asoka's religious tolerance and broadmindedness are worth a mention. She had no religious bigotry. Her youngest son was married according to Hindu rites, with 'Shalgram Shila' and all other details. She not only accepted this but never objected later to her youngest daughter-in-law's observance of Hindu rituals like Lakshmi Puja and various other functions.

Hitendra's family also had three talented women. Two were his daughters Gayatri and Medha while the third, Amiya, was the daughter-in-law. There were others equally talented among the Tagores before them but a choronological order is being followed for fear of losing track. Change was taking place rapidly in the world outside. Yet there was no effort to move with the times in the Thakurbari. Gayatri was an excellent pianist though she had also been trained in vocal music. Her accomplishments remained confined within the family circle and never came before the public eye. At that time, education and other accomplishments were considered to be a mere means of self-expression. A close watch was kept to note if they helped in improving the well-being as well as the social status of the family. Fortunately such attitudes have undergone a sea-change today. A talent in any field is nurtured by parents and every effort at acieving excellence in it is made. This certainly has been a step in the right direction. Formerly many a creative faculty withered away because of hindrances and frustrations. It was because of the above-mentioned viewpoint that many educated and talented women of the Tagore family were denied the opportunity of being the best in many fields. Those from other families, unburdened by such attitudes, were able to forge ahead.

Medha was a superb singer. According to Basab Tagore, 'At the time Bara Jethaima was alive. She was my mother's elder sister and the most beautiful among the daughters-in-law. Her younger daughter Medha's beauty matched her mother's. Medha had her training in vocal music from Gopeswar Bandopadhyaya. Her aunt Sudakshina loved to hear Medha's melodious voice and often took her for a visit to Shahjahanpur. There Medha increased her repertoire of Hindi songs. Rabindranath also enjoyed hearing Medha sing. When the king and queen of Belgium visited Jorasanko, the younger members of the family staged a dance-drama in their honour. Medha participated in that dance-drama *Nataraj*, directed by Rabindranath himself. Her exquisite beauty charmed everyone.'

Meanwhile Sudakshina arranged a match for Medha. The young man, Rajnath, was an extremely handsome Kashmiri Brahmin. He had just returned from England after training as an engineer. The proposal was approved by everyone and Sarojini went with Medha to give Rabindranath the good news. One of the ladies present commented, 'Is there such a dearth of eligible Bengali young men that one has to import one from Kashmir?' Tagore smiled and said, 'After seeing me how is it possible for her to fall for anyone else?' Since Medha was his grand-niece it was quite in order for Rabindranath to joke that she could never approve of any Bengali except himself.

Medha's husband was in the Railways, in a transferable job. Thus Rajnath and Medha travelled a good deal. Off and on, Medha came to Rabindranath with her repertoire of songs. Rabindranath often composed new Bengali songs based on the Hindi lyrics he had heard from Medha. Medha sang Ab to mere kaan. Rabindranath altered it and composed *Kaar banshi nishi bhorey bajilo rey*, which Medha sang during a performance of

Shesh Barshan. Due to her self-effacing temperament, Medha's music remained known to only a few. She was generally very shy, gentle and good-natured. Childless, she devoted herself to social work. This has always been a tradition of the Tagore women. Almost all of them have been involved in social service at some time or other. When Mr Rajnath was posted at Kharagpur some members of a political party were so impressed by Medha's social service that they requested her to contest the election as their representative. Always averse to publicity, Medha declined. Her social service was meant for the poor and needy. She never once agreed to appear in the limelight of publicity. After retirement Rajnath and Medha settled in Lucknow. She continued to stay there even after her husband's death and never returned to Bengal.

Amiya had won recognition as a singer much before she entered Hintendra's family as a bride. She says, 'I was about six or seven when I first started taking singing lessons. I cannot even recall the name of the Ustadji, but I remember he taught me to sing while he played the sarangi. A portion of *Balmiki Protiva* was performed in school once. I sang, *E ki e sthir chapala* and *Jao Lakshmi alakaye*, as Valmiki. On another occasion I played the role of Saraswati and recited *Deenheem balikar saajey esechinu*.' Being an only daughter, Amiya was brought up with great love and care. The well-known Dhrupad singer Yogendra Kishore Bandopadhyaya coached Amiya for many years in his school of vocal music. It was a concert organized by the Sangeet Sangha that brought Amiya in contact with the Tagore family. She remembers, 'The first day when I went to Protiva Devi's place with my father she wanted to know what I had learnt in school.' Amiya sang the song *Aaji dakhin duar khola* with action as she had been taught in school. Protiva, Nalini and Indira were all pleased with her. She joined the Sangeet Sangha. She was awarded a number of medals including the Ashutosh Mukhopadhyay gold medal. She won the last for singing Dhrupad in Raag Puria, beat

Chautal, in a music competition among the students of Bethune School and College.

Sarala requested Amiya's father's permission for her participation in *Mayar Khela*. He acquiesced gladly and the rehearsals began. During this time Rabindranath happened to visit Jorasanko. Sarala took Amiya to him and said, 'I have taught Amiya all Pramada's songs. Please show her the actions to be performed with the music.'

Rabindranath's surprised query was, 'What! She has picked up all the songs?'

Sarala replied, 'Oh yes! You just show her the actions.'

Amiya says,

> He was very busy, yet he agreed. I was so nervous. I was not sure of myself and the Poet was going to direct. He was so loving and gentle that all my nervousness evaporated. He showed me the necessary actions with Pramada's songs, *Delo sakhi de*, *Olo rekhey de*, *Key dakey?*, *Aami kobhu phirey nahi chai*, *Okey balo sakhi balo*, *Doorey danraye achey*, *Ami hridayer katha bolitey byakul*, *Aar keno aar keno*. He acted so well even in the feminine role, it was difficult to believe one's eyes.

This performance of *Mayar Khela* paved the way for Amiya's marriage into the Tagore family. Her detailed description helps us know about the rituals of the Tagores. She says,

> We were Hindus but the marriage took place according to Brahmo rites on 17 Maagh, 1335. Before the wedding there was an 'ashirvad' ceremony. Sudhindranath Tagore came to bless me along with Suresh Sankhyatirtha who officiated as the priest on the boy's side. Our family priest was also present. When we alighted my mother-in-law put a loha bound in gold on my wrist. She also put some honey and sweets in my mouth. The entire wide path from the car to the big covered verandah was covered with red *shalu*. The two acharyas sat one on either side of the dais. The two of us sat next to them. My father-in-law's younger brother and Sureshbabu chanted

> the *mantras*. The *Saptapadi Gaman* was followed by *Sindoor Daag*. In a paddy measure were some grains of paddy and a small box containing *mete sindoor*. After the sindoor had been put on my forehead and hair-parting, we went up the red *shalu*-covered staircase to our room. A *kajal-lata* was stuck in my hair and a paddy *rek* was on my head. My husband had a small mirror and a *jaanti*. He was behind me and went on snipping the paddy until one reached the bedroom. The room had been furnished with carpets and cushions. After we sat down, all the elders came and blessed us. Later, there was the customary rite of *stree aachar*. All the necessary accessories were placed in a *kula* and brought in. I still have the crown shells used for the traditional *kari khela*. Thereafter I was taken down to dip my feet in a mixture of milk and aalta held in a shallow tray. During the time some milk had been put on the boil in a small vessel. If it boiled over the new bride was considered to be a harbinger of wealth.

Since Amiya's husband was not keen on her participating in public, be it acting or singing, she chose the life of a typical housewife. However there was no bar against music lessons. Rather, Hridindranath encouraged her. Amiya had been a student of Gopeswar Bandopadhyay before her marriage. Since he also taught Medha, Amiya was able to continue her training in Jorasanko. Whenever Rabindranath came to Jorasanko he would send for her either in the morning or evening. Amiya recalls,

> Whenever I had time, either I would sing to the Poet or he would teach me songs. This gave him the greatest pleasure. I learnt so many lyrics at that time. I specially remember *Ki ragini bajalo*, *Boro bismyaya lagey*, *Ogo kangal aamarey kangal korecho*, *Aakul keshey ashey*, and *Mori lo mori*. He usually preferred songs with a playful tune. He would continue to teach a song for days until I mastered it perfectly. He also liked to hear me sing. I sang all kinds like Dhrupad, Dhamar, Khayal and Bhajans.

Amiya sang again in public on Rabindranath's seventieth birth anniversary. Before this she had probably sung in a performance of Barshamongal the song *Barshan mondrita andhakarey* and *Srabana akashey oi*. Rabindranath had been present on that occasion too. On the first day of the function held at the University Institute, she sang *Mori lo mori amaye banshitey dekechey kay*. Dinendranath accompanied her on the esraj. The audience was spell-bound. Amiya was presenting a song before Rabindranath that he himself had taught her. Her melodious voice reminded one of bird song. Sudhindranath's second daughter Ena had heard that Amiya's voice resembled Abhignya's. Since Ena had never heard the latter, she only listened entranced. Amiya received proof of Rabindranath's approbation soon. She says, 'On the second day of the function the poet called Dinudada and said "Ask Amiya to sing *Ogo kangal amarey*." I was not scheduled to sing that day. I realized that Rabi-dadamoshai must have enjoyed my song. He never expressed his preferences. It was impossible to guess even from his face.'

After this function Amiya began appearing in public. There were performances galore within the family. Notable were *Shaapmochan* and *Natir Puja*. Amiya says, 'Dinudada was preparing me for the role of Sachi when Rabidada said Amiya will sing *Sakhi andharey ekela gharey*. Nababarsha—the Bengali New year—was an informal affair but Maghotsav was always on a grand scale. There were three kinds of invitation cards. The ones for select male guests were white and issued in Rabindranath's name. Those for select ladies were pink and in Jnanadanandini's name while those for the public were yellow and issued again in Rabindranath's name. The whole garden would be decorated with marigolds. The shehnai would be played from dawn. An organ was hired from Dwarkins. The whole house turned gay with the celebrations.' Amiya always sang on such occasions. Once she sang the song *Kee dhwani baajey*. There is a small history behind this song. In Amiya's own words, 'Till the end Rabidada loved to hear Hindi songs. He was very fond of the song *Boley Boley*

Jaaorey, based on the raga Bhairavi though I don't know if he composed any Bengali song based on this.' Another day Amiya sang *E Dhani Dhani Charan Parasat* based on the Purabi raga. She had learnt it from Gopeswar Bandopadhyay. Within a short while, the Poet composed the extraordinary lyric *Kee dhwani baajey gahana chetana majhey*. Amiya was overwhelmed and says, 'The most morable event was his composing a Bengali song based on a Hindi lyric that I had sung.' Remembering this, Amiya called her memoir '*Kee dhani bajey*'.

Rabindranath was very keen to have Amiya and her husband settle in Santiniketan. But since her mother-in-law preferred to live in Jorasanko Amiya was unable to move out. Amiya herself usually picked up a song merely by hearing it sung. Apart from occasional appearances, she always helped in teaching others to sing. They had landed property in Cuttack and stayed there occasionally. There she coached local girls in music for performance of *Barshamangal* and other functions. Amiya recorded two songs *Hey Nutan* and *Sanmukhe shanti parabar*. Sailajaranjan Majumdar had taken great pains to teach her these two songs. She was unable to cut discs regularly due to the rather conservative attitude of her husband. She told Sandhya Sen, 'They did not approve of the idea of my records being played at street corners and every Tom, Dick and Harry listening. However my mother-in-law was very liberal. She would remonstrate with my husband, "Your *pishis* appeared on stage and there were no objections. It is most unfair that Amiya should be prevented from singing on the radio or cutting records just because she is a daughter-in-law."' Though preferring to remain behind the scenes, Amiya later became a member of the audition board and a judge in the music competitions held by Akashvani. For a number of years she was tied up with bringing up her children and making regular trips to Orissa to manage the zamindari there; times were also changing. With Rabindranath's death the typical musical atmosphere also was lost. Amiya and her family had to move out of the Jorasanko mansion. Fortunately Amiya's voice was not lost to us. Ena's daughter Krishna Ribou had settled in Paris. On one of her visits to Calcutta, she taped Amiya's songs for her friends in Paris. Amiya was rather hesitant. She was growing old and was not sure whether the songs sung without any accompaniment would appeal to the French. Letters from France extolling her songs came, dispelling all her qualms. Amiya's melodious voice had touched the hearts of the French people transcending the language barrier. Next came Satyajit Ray for his film *Kanchanjangha*. The scene was Karuna Bandopadhyay sitting quietly by herself on the Mall, Darjeeling, and singing. Amiya found recording very tiresome. To quote her, 'The people in the studio are never satisfied and are always finding fault.' Her cousins Monica and Leela Desai were well-known film actresses and had often tried to persuade her to sing in films. Their arguments, 'If you sing thus not only will you be famous but earn a lot too.' Amiya never paid any heed. Satyajit Ray managed to persuade her and she recorded the song *E parabasey robey key*. The song was much appreciated by the public. In another long-playing record *Panchakanyar Gaan* she sang *Baro bismay laagey* and *Tobu mone rekho*. Even in her old age, when she sang the consummate artistry of her voice and mastery over the various techniques like Taan, Mir and Laya were exemplary. Amiya herself never believed it. She believed, 'People who want to hear me now do so because of their interest in the older style, taught by the Poet himself. No one hearing me today will be able to recall the erstwhile Pramada of *Mayar Khela*.' To disprove Amiya we may quote Debabrata Biswas. In his *Bratya Janer Ruddha Sangeet* he wrote, 'Amiya Tagore is now over seventy years old. She still sings and the natural artistry and interplay of notes in her voice are beyond the so-called authorities. None of them are capable of reproducing them let alone prepare the notations.'

It will not be out of context to write about Satyabala and

her daughters at this juncture. The two sisters, Satyabala and Surendrabala, were the daughters of Tarasundari. Tarasundari's father Troilokyamohan was descended from Darpanarayan Tagore. However their connection with the Pathuriaghata branch is not very clear. Amiya was Surendrabala's only daughter. We learn from Amiya that after Satyabala was widowed in her childhood she was remarried to Umedram Lalbhai Desai, a resident of Rampur. The nawab of Rampur was a great patron of musicians. It was from his veena maestro that Satyabala had her training. She also learnt classical music from an ustaad. Even in those days Satyabala's performance on the veena had been recorded. She also participated in several musical functions in the USA and helped found a music school in Bombay. Satyabala's eldest daughter Shanti was married to Bratindranath Tagore. Her other two daughters Monica and Leela were both well-known film actresses of their time. Leela was the better known of the two. Born in New York, she joined films after graduating from Lucknow University. For a woman of her calibre with exceptional looks, who was also highly educated, an expert dancer and belonged to an aristocratic family, the reason for joining films was a desire to tread new paths. A career in films as a means of self-expression had then just begun to attract men and women from wealthy families. Leela's first appearance before the camera was in 1937-38. Quite a few other women from different families, albeit related to the Tagores, had also joined films at this time. Notables were Devikarani, Ramola Devi, Monica Gangopadhyay and Sudha Mukhopadhyay.

Leela acted in films like *Didi*, *Jiban Moron*, *Kapalkundala*, *President*, *Dushman*, *Nartaki*, and *Vidyapati*. In 1942 she shifted to Bombay and began to act in Hindi films. The hero of her first Hindi film *Tamanna* was Radhamohan Bhattacharya. *Geet Gobinda* was one of her most popular films. Audiences of yesteryear still remember Leela's films like *Sharafat*, *Nagadnarayan*, *Bichar*, *Mujrim*, *Kalia* and many others. A keen danseuse, she toured the whole of India with her dance troupe. She often thought of penning her memories of those golden years but never actually got down to it.

Leela's younger sister Monica also acted in a few films. In *Nemai Sanyas* she was teamed with Chabi Biswas as Bishnupriya, and with Radhamohan Bhattacharya in *Aparadh*. Monica's film career was much shorter than Leela's.

At about the same time there appeared three accomplished ladies in Kshitindra's family. Like Hitendra's family, two were daughters and the third a daughter-in-law. By this time the joint family in Jorasanko had broken up into separate units. To Kshitindra's two daughters Gargi and Bani, singing came naturally. Gargi could pick up any song after hearing it just once. She confined herself mainly to her home and family but managed to create an atmosphere of music wherever she was. In between her household chores she tried her hand at literary ventures. Some of these were published in the hand-written magazine *Kishalaya*. Unfortunately copies of these are unavailable now.

Bani was brilliant in her own way. Apart from being an accomplished singer she was an excellent pianist. She was awarded a doctorate degree for her research on vocal music. As Dr Bani Chatterjee she is equally well-known abroad and at home. The main hurdle against foreigners enjoying Rabindranath's lyrics is language. Realizing this, Bani took up the task of translating Tagore's songs. She translated a number of them keeping the tune and rhythm intact. These became very popular abroad. One example is her composition and translation of Tagore's *Anandalokey mangalalokay* into 'In the realms of joy and good'. Rabindranath himself was keen to hear Bani's works. Bani's composition and translation of *Jay bharatir jay* was widely acclaimed. Hearing this Rabindranath had thought of requesting Bani to convert his *Janagana mana adhinayaka jayo hey* into a Western harmony. Unfortunately this never came to pass. One stanza of this song is now our national anthem; yet Bani remembered that in the Congress Session held during the Non-cooperation Movement the organizers had requested the Poet's permission to leave out a few lines of the song. This was mainly due to paucity of time but Rabindranath did not agree. So the song was sung in its entirety. Bani was one of the chorus.

With her natural flair for music Bani also wanted to delve into music from an artistic as well as scientific view point. After consolidating her knowledge of Western classical music during her stay abroad with her husband Dr Sachi Kumar Chattopadhyaya, she began to analyse music from a psychological angle. The topic was a novel one. Later her work gained recognition and she was requested by the Asiatic Society to deliver quite a few lectures.

Questions may be raised about the exact topic of her research. Actually she tried to analyse music from various angles. 'Was it possible in a practical and scientific manner to bring about psychological or any other change by the effect of Indian or Western music?' this was Bani's query. She has sought to find the answer also. We are often told that music has tremendous powers of exciting emotions. It is said to have the ability to melt a stone and mesmerize wild animals. The human mind is certainly not harder than stone. The question is whether such change is really possible. If it is, can it be analysed as a scientific phenomenon? If it cannot, then how could Indian music-maestros give human forms to the various ragas and raginis? How could they assert, 'Deepak Raga is capable of creating fire while Megha raag can bring down showers.' According to Bani, various physical changes are brought about by the waves generated in the air due to the sounds of music. Ancient Indian musicians were aware of this and based their philosophy of ragas on this. To quote her,

> This encourages us to look forward confidently to the time when the truths underlying the Science of Raga-music should be further unearthed and extricated by scientists from the heap of accumulated debris of ignorance and colourful interpolations perhaps, the hieroglyphics of the Raga-music deciphered and

the sublime philosophy of the Raga-music, in all its purity, to its pristine glory restored. [*sic*]

Bani believed that tremendous scope for research in oriental sciences lies hidden in the various ragas and raginis of Indian music. It is probable that a critical study of raga-music and its detailed analysis may open the door. There is no end to the experiments, arguments and counter-arguments in this respect. Ecerpts from some of Bani's important articles were published in the journal of Indian Science Congress. She had earlier delivered lectures on these topics during her visit to Europe. The main themes were, 'Psychology and Music'(1934), 'Psychomusic in war and after'(1944), and 'Music in Basic Education Psychology' (1949). The years indicate the time of publication of these lectures. The actual lectures were delivered shortly before the time indicated.

The records of the Asiatic Society in Calcutta also show some lectures delivered by Bani. They are 'Diversional Therapy and music', 'Tagore and Music', 'Applied Music', 'Cultural Contact and Music', 'The Vedic Songs and Tagore', 'Western Music and Raga Raginis', 'The West and the East, in music they meet,' 'Indian Music and Simultaneous Harmony', and 'Comparative Studies of Music'.

Bani researched extensively on the last mentioned topic, hoping to find the influence of Indian ragas and raginis on Western music. She felt that since there were similarities in human nature everywhere the same should be true of music. Tunes, unhindered by language, should show some resemblances. She found the existence of 'harmony', considered to be solely a Western feature, in Indian music. In her last years Bani had begun to write a comparative history of oriental and Western music. Unfortunately she was unable to complete it.

Bani's translations of Rabindra Sangeet keeping the tune, rhyme and mood of the original intact, have been highly appreciated by foreigners. Professor Edward Deemock of the Department of Asian Languages in the University of Chicago

Jnanadanandini Devi

Svarnakumari Devi

Protiva Chaudhuri

Pragya Sundari Devi

Indira Devi Chaudhurani

Sushama Devi

Sarala Devi Chaudhurani

Sunayani Devi

Hemlata Tagore

Sangya Tagore

Protima Tagore

Amita Tagore

Sreemati Tagore

Madhurilata Devi

Felicita Chaudhuri

Bani Chattopadhyay

Amiya Tagore

Menoka Tagore

Kalyani Mallick

Nandita Kripalani

Purnima Chattopadhyay

Krishna Ribou

Supurna Chaudhuri

Rita Devi

Smita Chowdhry

Devika Rani

Milada Gangopadhyay

Sheila Chattopadhyay

Jayashri Bandopadhyay

Eiko Tagore

Asmita Trivedi

Aleena Basu

was overwhelmed on hearing Bani's translation of Tagore's songs. His congratulatory letter reveals the importance of Bani's research. Prof. Deemock felt that these translations would benefit the whole world since till date it had no clear notion of Tagore's poems and lyrics. To quote him:

> This is just a note to express appreciation for the work you are doing in translating Rabindranath's song into English. In the first place, anything at all that is done to make the work of that genius more known to the non-Bengali-speaking people of the world is that much for the good. Your work, however, goes one step further. The world seems to have some idea, however vague, of Rabindranath's greatness as a poet, and perhaps somewhat less, of his greatness as a lyricist and musician, even though he towers as high in these fields as in the others . . .
>
> This gap you will be helping to fill by giving the English-speaking world the opportunity to hear Rabindranath's words in translation, sung in his original music. For as you have shown, songs are meant to be sung and heard and not read. I am grateful to you for your work and when your work becomes known, I will not be alone.

Kshitindra's daughter-in-law Menoka was Abanindranath's granddaughter. Her mother Umarani has not been mentioned so far. She will come later in chronological order. Umarani's husband Nirmal Chandra was fond of music and arranged to train his daughter from an early age. She trained under Gopeswar Bandopadhyay and Ustaad Bachchan Mishra. One day Dinendranth happened to hear her sing. He was highly impressed. Menoka had a deep baritone rarely heard these days. Dinendranath was so charmed that he said to Menoka's father, 'Let me teach your daughter. She is an uncut diamond of the first water. I shall polish her and you will see how dazzling she will become.' Menoka's father agreed and Dinendranath, finding a fit pupil, handed over to her his entire rich store of music. Menoka did not fail him either. She poured her entire being into acquiring whatever was being given to her. Her music pleased Rabindranath who encouraged her saying, 'Keep practising, you will be able to scale great heights.' Rabindranath's looks, his poetry and music, everything had a great attraction for Menoka. She always prayed, 'I want to be in this atmosphere forever. Let me not be removed from here.' The Almighty heard her and granted her her wish. Menoka's songs on the celebration of the eleventh day of Maagh charmed Kshemendra. Thus Menoka came as a bride to Kshitindra's family. Her musical training continued and on completion came the record *Esho Esho Aamar Gharey* and *Shesh Belakar Shesh Gaaney*. Dinendranath accompanied her on the esraaj. Then there was a second record, *Tomar Bina Aamar Manomajhey* and *Tomar Surer Dhara*. Thereafter history repeated itself. Menoka's mother-in-law Suhasini, though broad-minded herself, was unable to oppose the traditions of the family. Later in the long-playing record *Panchakanyar Gaan* Menoka sang the old song *Esho esho aamar gharey*.

Menoka had regretted her inability to learn music from Rabindranath. This had been alleviated by Dinendranath. Menoka felt his loss very keenly. Menoka always felt distressed at the readiness with which Dinendranath's name was erased from public memory. Yet, not only did he hold the key to the entire treasure-house of Tagore songs in his heart but he was also a leader in training others. Menoka named her school of music 'Dinendra Shikshayatan' to assuage her feelings. There was an amusing incident behind the opening of this school. A young girl in the neighbouring house used to practise Rabindra Sangeet daily but she sang out of tune. Kshemendra became so sick of hearing her morning and evening that he requested Menoka to teach this girl. Thus Menoka had to open a singing-class primarily to ease their own life!

Gradually her school of music flourished. She also became associated with other music schools like Baitanik and Parani.

Encouraged by the enthusiasm of her students Menoka began to teach lyrics composed by Tagores other than Rabindranath. Satyendranath, Jyotirindranath, Dinendranath, Soumendranath, Swarnakumari, Indira, Protiva and many others had composed lyrics. Unless these were practised regularly, all these would be lost. Menoka won many honours in her life.

Another important contribution of Menoka was her effort to teach students Rabindra Sangeet in her home 'Tagore Bhawan' in Orissa. The Tagore family had property in Cuttack and Bhubaneshwar. When Menoka was there her enthusiasm and encouragement inspired quite a few Oriya and Bengali students to learn Rabindra Sangeet. Over a period of ten years Menoka taught at least forty students. She lost count of the number that these forty then went on to train, but the enthusiasm among Oriya students to learn Rabindra Sangeet gave her a great deal of satisfaction in her old age. She had been honoured on a number of occasions but her greatest effort was to ensure that the lyrics composed by other members of the Tagore family did not go into oblivion. In Calcutta she taught a number of students songs composed by Dinendranath. Later on this responsibility has been taken up by the Indira Shikshayatan.

The ladies who entered Ritendra's family by marriage were Subho Tagore's wife Nirmala and, after her death, Arati, Sidhindranath's wife Parul and Basab Tagore's wife Smriti. Subho Tagore was a happy-go-lucky person who enjoyed life. A good storyteller, he was not amenable to any discipline, especially economic. Whenever he came by some money he would squander it away in princely luxuries, quite indifferent to the future. His wife Arati's days were spent in perpetual uncertainty. Surabhi mentions an incident in her memoirs which speaks for itself. Once Subho had gone to Bombay to prepare for a trip to Egypt with samples of Indian art and handicrafts. He and Surabhi held an exhibition and collected some funds. Some more was received by way of advertisements. Suddenly Surabhi's husband asked her for three hundred rupees. Surabhi refused saying that she did not have so much cash as it was the end of the month. Without a word Sudeb opened the almirah, took out three hundred rupees from the cash collected from the exhibition. He handed Subho a postcard and prepared to leave for his office. On Surabhi's remonstrating that it would be impossible for her to account for the sum, Sudeb calmly replied, 'Both you and your uncle had better go to prison.' Then Surabhi saw that the letter was from Arati requesting for some money. Subho kept absolutely mum during the incident.

That evening Sudeb returned home early. He may have felt a twinge of repentance. Subho was his uncle-in-law but, as Sudeb was older, he addressed Subho by name. He asked Subho, 'We are at our wits' end after marrying once. How did you have the courage to marry twice?' Pat came Subho's smiling reply, 'Saheb, Arati's father was a literateur and the editor of an Assamese magazine *Abahan*. He was a friend of mine, I never imagined that his daughter Arati would fall in love with me and threaten to jump to her death. So I had to marry her.' No one knows whether the story was true or a figment of Subho's fertile imagination. Talking about the hardships faced by her mother, Arati's daughter Chitralekha says, 'Such hard work must have been very tiring for my mother. But she always said, "I wanted to lead an active life and that is what I have done."'

Arati herself wrote, both in Bengali and Assamese. Apart from sundry articles in the *Sundaram* magazine her *Chhayaranga* is a modern novel written in a spontaneous style. In this there are episodes from her own life too. She translated Lakshminath Bezbaruah's *Aamar Jibansmriti* and Lakshminandan Bara's *Gangchiler Dana* from Assamese to Bengali. The translation is excellent and effortless, it is impossible to guess that it is not the original. She wrote features on art, culture and films both in the *Times of India* and in *Link*. She not only sang on the radio but was also the editor of *Akashi*, the Assamese version of *Betar*

Jagat. She became a member of the film censor-board too. Had she lived longer, we might have been introduced to some more of excellent Assamese literature though her translations.

Siddhindranath's wife Parul was the daughter of Dhirendranath Gangopadhyay or D.G., one of the earliest film directors. Parul's mother Premikadevi was related to the Tagores of Pathuriaghata. Premika's mother Protiva was the great-great-granddaughter of Kanailal Tagore. Premika was a paragon of beauty. Her husband Dhirendranath was the younger brother of Rabindranath's son-in-law Nagendranath. Moreover Sarat Kumari's granddaughter Protiva, Chiraprova's daughter, had married Jnanendranath, another brother of Dhirendranath. Films—the latest medium of expression of art—had attracted the brilliant Dhirendranath. He decided to take up film-making and to prove to the world that the entry of women from good families into films would greatly improve the industry. At the time it was unimaginable for any respectable family to allow its women to act in films. A friend of Dhirendranath's jokingly told him that there was a most competent actress in his own home. There was no point in his not considering her and trying to persuade others. D.G. thought over the suggestion and approved of it.

His wife Premika Devi was not only an exceptional beauty but talented too. A film could easily be made with her as the heroine. Dhirendranath himself had studied in Shantiniketan under the guidance of Rabindranath. The deterioration of relations between Mira and Nagendranath had not affected Rabindranath's affection for D.G.

Ignoring the storm of opposition, D.G. brought Premika Devi to films under the screen name Ramola Devi. He told his wife, 'If you are worried about opposition from the family, I shall not be deterred though I may have to lose you. You have to choose between my work and myself on one side and family obligations on the other.' Premika chose to be with her husband. She stood by her husband, ignoring tremendous opposition from the family. Contemporary magazines and newspapers described her as 'overbold and daring'. This was the time of silent movies and she acted in only a few films like *Flames of Flesh*, *Panchasar*, and *Hidden Treasure*. Her untimely death at the early age of twenty-two snuffed out a budding genius. Premika's full name was Premikamoyee but after her death in 1930 it was misprinted in papers as Premlatika. She had no time to realize the impact of her actions upon Bengali ladies of respectable families. She opened for them a door to a career full of new opportunities.

Premika's two daughters Parul and Monica also appeared in films as child artists. Eight-year-old Parul faced the camera in *Maraner Porey*. This was a silent movie based on the *Arabian Nights*. She acted in two more films: *Takaye Kee Na Hoy* and *Panchasar* in 1931. Parul hardly remembers anything about the films or her acting. The appearance of a girl from a respectable Bengali family was an epoch-making event at the time. It was akin to five-year-old Saudamini's admission to Bethune School nearly a century ago. Neither Devikarani nor Sadhana Basu had appeared till then. Parul's acting career came to stop with her mother's untimely death. Shortly thereafter Mira tried her hand at matchmaking and Parul was married into the Tagore family. In the atmosphere prevailing in her in-laws' house Parul could never think of acting in films, nor was she keen on doing so.

Parul's younger sister Monica was also a well-known film actress. While a child, she was dubbed the Shirley Temple of Bengal. Monica's advent into films sounds more like fiction. On a visit to Metro cinema with her father she was enchanted by the performance of a young girl, more a child. Her father asked her in jest, 'Will you be able to act like her?' Monica agreed immediately. Her first film was *Pathabhuley* by her father D.G. Unlike her elder sister, Monica was keen on a film career. She acted in *Nemai Sanyas*, *Epar Opar*, *Nari*, *Daabi*, *Pashan Devata*, *Bandita*, *Dashiputra* and many others. Many an audience of yesteryear will remember her spontaneous acting as Kaberi

Basu's younger sister in *Shyamali*. Her last movie was the musical hit *Asha* with Kanan Devi. In Monica's case, marriage did not interfere with her career. Married to Patanjali Guha Thakurta in 1946, she had two daughters. The silver screen was never able to cast its shadow on her happy home.

Premikamoyee's younger sister Mamatamoyee was the wife of Hemchandra Gupta. Like D.G., he was also associated with the film industry. Their son is the well-known film producer and director Dinen Gupta. Dinen Gupta's wife Kajal was able to influence the audience on her first appearance in *Antarikshya*. Later she specialized as a character artist. Many people may still remember her performance in Ritwik Ghatak's *Ajantrik*. Kajal's daughter Sonali played the role of Satyabati in *Pratham Pratishruti*.

Let us return to Parul. A few months after her marriage came the wedding of Nandita. They were cousins and so Parul came to Shantiniketan from Jorasanko. Mira took her to meet Rabindranath. The poet was delighted to see this new great-niece-in-law (*naat bou*) and said, 'What beautiful eyes! Stay here. I will draw your portrait.' Mira objected 'How can that be? She is a new bride and has to stay with her in-laws.' Rabindranath's rejoinder was, 'She is so pretty. Keep her well dressed and adorned at all times.' Unfortunately, Parul had to return to Jorasanko before the portrait could be painted.

The situation—both financial and otherwise—of the Tagores had begun to change with the times. Parul chose the proper upbringing of her three children as her main task. She also decided to do so by earning a living. She shifted to Shantiniketan with her family. Things may have been easier had she put them in the hostel. She preferred to take up a job. She became the warden of the students' hostel of Patha Bhawan. She and her children lived with Mira in 'Malancha'. Both her daughters Sukriti and Prakriti were excellent singers. They acted well and participated in every function held in Shantiniketan. Parul always laid the greatest emphasis on education but music was in the blood of the girls of Hemendranath's family. It is worthwhile to mention an amusing incident in this context. Satyajit Ray came on a visit to Shantiniketan. At the time he was about to start work on a movie based on three short stories from Tagore's *Galpaguccha*. On meeting Sukriti he felt she would be ideal for the role of Mrinmoyee in *Samapti*. He requested Parul for her permission. Parul, who had herself acted in films so many years ago, refused. Satyajit Ray was perhaps displeased but Siddhindranath approved of her decision. Parul's refusal did not stem from any false prejudice. She just felt that her daughter at that age did not possess the grit needed for a career in films. Being D.G and Ramola Devi's granddaughter, Sukriti might have become a great actress but she was not interested.

Parul always put her duty to her family above everything else. Her constant endeavour was that neither the family name nor her personal image should ever be tarnished. All her children are well educated and successful in their chosen fields. Parul often spends her time in quiet surroundings, at others she stays in the midst of her family. She feels both to be necessary for appreciating life. All in all Parul's viewpoint is certainly modern.

Smriti joined Ritendra's family much later. Basab was an artist and had roved all over. By the time he married, the family had left the Tagore mansion of Jorasanko. Ritendra's family was the first to dispose off their share and move out of the family mansion. Smriti, Basab's wife, used to write a column regularly in the *Jugantar* paper under the heading *'Aain achhay athacho'*. She also wrote poetry and fiction. In the pages of the monthly *Basumati* magazine lie several of her stories. One such is *'Ekti Phutkir Janya'*, a humorous story. Such stories by women writers are few and far between. In this story, Bimal in futile search of a job suddenly inherits his *pishi's* property valued at Rs 50,893. In the nineteen-sixties, fifty thousand rupees was a considerable sum. Bimal is able to land a job since the head-clerk is keen to get his sister-in-law married to Bimal. Bimal had been in love with Nandita. Nandita's guardians now withdraw all their opposition to the match. Bimal is amused to perceive how a small piece of news could alter everything. When his *pishi's* property came to him after some days, it was only Rs 508.93. The decimal system had come into use a short while ago. Just a decimal point (*phutki)* changed Bimal's life! Smriti's other story '*Pratigya*' is a love story and not off the beaten track. Smriti always preferred to keep herself away from the public gaze. She was a stranger to many due to her love of solitude.

Pragyasundari and Lakshminath Bezbaruah had four daughters. The eldest, Surabhi, died at the tender age of five and a half. Though not a great deal is known about the other three—Aruna, Ratna and Deepika—they matched their cousins of the Tagore family in education as well as in other accomplishments. Lakshminath and Pragyasundari were in Sambalpur for many years, but the girls stayed with their aunt Protiva Devi. They studied in the Diocesan school and learnt music at *Sangeet Sangha*. All three sang well. Aruna prepared the notations and musical scores for a number of lyrics. These were published in *Ananda Sangeet*. A thorough grasp of music is essential for such a task. Among the songs are *Mori sei roop*, written and set to music by Ritendranath Tagore, *Naache bhalo nache madan gopal* and *Jayjay jagajana tarana karano* possibly composed by the poet Madhavdev and set to music by Hitendranath Tagore. Aruna most probably taught in Sangeet Sangha too.

The tradition of dance, music and drama of the Tagore family held a great deal of interest for Lakshminath Bezbaruah. References to the staging of *Balmiki Protiva* are found again and again in his writings. He himself had participated too. Between 1912 and 1914, *Balmiki Protiva* was staged quite a few times. It was performed at Sir Ashutosh Chaudhuri's residence to felicitate Lady Hardinge. The actors and actresses were all family members and Aruna played the role of 'Banadevi'.

The ladies of the Tagore family generally created an artistic and cultural atmosphere wherever they went. Sambalpur was no exception and the credit goes to both Lakshminath and Pragyasundari. Inspired and encouraged by Lakshminath, *Balmiki Protiva* was staged twice in the local Victoria Town Hall. Lakshminath acted the part of the first dacoit while Pragya and her three daughters rendered the songs. In another performance in 1914 Aruna acted as Saraswati while Ratna and Deepika played the roles of Banadevi.

After her marriage Aruna went away to Baroda. Her husband Satyabrata Mukhopadhyay was employed there and later became the dewan. Baroda was not only a princely state but it was also conservative and orthodox. In keeping with the prevalent atmosphere Aruna was never seen participating in music soirées or stage performances in Baroda. According to Aruna's daughter Rita, despite all her entreaties, neither Aruna nor Satyabrata permitted Rita to learn dance as a child.

It has been possible to unearth an article written by Aruna on the birth centenary of Lakshminath Bezbaruah. A small part is quoted below:

> In 1914 or thereabouts when Rabindranath's operetta *Valmiki Protiva* was on the stage in aid of our Day Fund, my father was selected, out of many, by Rabindranath himself to act the part of the First Dacoit. This was a great honour, because Rabindranath was a strict judge of histrionic abilities. After my father's death, he wrote a very moving obituary. The famous artists, Gaganendranath and Abanindranath, who were cousins of my mother, were also very fond of my father. Particularly Abanindranath who had a great sense of humour and wit, would laugh heartily, cracking jokes whenever he met my father at Jorasanko.

This is the only reference available regarding the staging of *Balmiki Protiva* with Lakshminath as the First Dacoit. In the performance held at the residence of Sri Ashutosh Chaudhuri this role was played by Jnanadaviram Barua.

Pragyasundari's second daughter Ratna spent her early years in Calcutta. At Sangeet Sangha, she learnt to play the esraaj from Kakuv Khan besides her training in piano. She participated in a few musical and dramatic performances before her marriage. Her husband Rohinikumar Barua belonged to an aristocratic Assamese family. At the time of her marriage she did not know much Assamese. Her parents were in Sambalpur and she stayed with her aunt Protiva Devi, studying in Diocesan School. Even after marriage she and her family spoke Bengali and English at home and Assamese when conversing with her husband's side of the family. Thus she was adept in all the three languages. She probably wrote her autobiography in Assamese. Her childhood memories include an incident involving Rabindranath. This was in 1923. Ratna and her sisters came to spend the weekend at Jorasanko every Saturday with Ritendranath and his family. Ratna's maternal uncles, despite being landlords, did not have a car and horse-drawn coaches were the means of transport. After their school examinations were over and they were preparing to leave for Sambalpur, the news came that Lakshminath had been bitten by a dog. The mishap occurred in the house of his friend Nagen Chaudhuri. Lakshminath was taken to Shillong. Though she was not too well, Ratna accompanied her father. Lakshminath's treatment began at the Pasteur Institute in Shillong. Rabindranath was also in Shillong at the time, in Monisha's house 'Jeet Bhumi'. As Ratna's fever began to rise Lakshminath got worried.

Fortunately Dr Bidhan Chandra Ray was staying in the room behind them. Lakshminath went to request him to have a look at Ratna and found Rabindranath there. The latter immediately said, 'Lakshminath, I also know some remedies, so let me try those and then you can consult the doctor.' He immediately came to Ratna with his box of homeopathic medicines and gave her some. Unfortunately his treatment failed and the fever showed no signs of abating. Dr B.C. Ray examined her tongue and diagnosed it to be a case of typhoid. Within a week Pragyasundari reached Shillong with a few relations from the Tagore side. Ratna has narrated this in her memoirs. She also wrote an article in English, 'Lakshminath Bezbarua and Pragyasundari Devi'.

After their marriage Ratna and Rohini Kumar spent some years in Calcutta and then shifted to Dibrugarh. There Ratna involved herself in numerous social and cultural activities. During the World War II, when many refugees were forced to migrate to India, Ratna and her husband gave yeomen service. They not only escorted the homeless Indians to the various relief camps but extended all necessary assistance. These grateful families maintained contact with the Baruas till many years later. Many members of Drobomoyee's family also had to flee to India from Burma, but the barriers of ignorance about each other prevented the members of the two branches of the Tagores from establishing any links with each other. What a quirk of fate!

There was a large army cantonment in Dibrugarh during World War II. Ratna often took food and snacks for the Indian Army-men stationed there. In addition to her social work she considered it her duty to help the Indians during the 'Quit India' movement. Rohini Kumar was associated with Mahatma Gandhi and Jawaharlal Nehru. Ratna always tried to do her best to improve the conditions of women and children. She shouldered the responsibility of touring the tea-gardens of Assam to inform the Government of India about their plight.

Deepika was the youngest of the three sisters and the apple of her parents' eyes—Lakshminath and Pragyasundari. Like her sisters, she also studied in Diocesan School. She must have been trained in music, but there is no record of her performing as a singer. In a presentation of *Balmiki Protiva* in Sambalpur she participated with her sisters in the role of Banadevi. Deepika was a great favourite with the nuns of her school because of her gentle disposition and loving nature. Though away from her parents, she lived in Calcutta with her near and dear ones, surrounded by love and affection. However, times change and with that human relationships alter. An unexpected blow hurt Deepika beyond measure and she felt alone and unloved. Four years earlier, Deepika had gone to Shantiniketan. The purpose was to spend the Christmas holidays with her dear 'Rabidada'. A few days prior to that the Viceroy, Lord Irwin, had visited Shantiniketan. This was a memorable event for a small town like Bolpur and preparations had been afoot for many days. This may have been another reason for Deepika's trip. She not only attended the Poush mela but also took an autograph from Rabindranath, on 25 December. He had penned a few lines along with his signature. He wrote:

Jwalo nabajibaner nirmal deepika,
Marter chokhe dharo swarger lipika.
Andhar gahane racho aloker bithika,
Kolokolahale ano amriter geetika.

Light up the pure lamp of a new life,
Unfold the heavenly message before mortal eyes,
Create a path of light in the deep darkness,
Bring the song of eternity amidst the babble of noise.

Rabindranath's benedictions proved to be surprisingly true in Deepika's life. She made up her mind to embrace Christianity and she became a nun. Her aim was to spend her life in service of the poor, thus making it akin to a lighted lamp expelling darkness on earth. She considered the nuns not only her ideal but her near ones. Her decision hurt her father Lakshminath grievously. Several letters were exchanged between the two. In one of them, Lakshminath says, 'My dear Deepika, you mention about my elder brother's conversion to Christianity in both your letters. You are unaware of the reason behind it and therefore mention this. The matter is extremely painful to us and hence we did not tell you earlier. Doctor Bezbarua became a Christan due to poverty and not lack of love for his own faith. Your wish to convert to Christianity is not due to any lack of money. Your mind and heart appear clouded by a frightful hallucination. Surrounded by the ocean of love of your near and dear ones, you are unable to discern the truth and are running after a mirage. My dear Deepika, what a terrible mistake, a terrible mistake.'

Lakshminath wrote the letter on 14 July 1932. There must have been other letters between him and Deepika, as well as meetings, but no records are available. In November of the same year Deepika embraced Christianity, joining the Anglican Church. In January 1935 she became a nun and went to England. After spending a few years in the convent of St. John the Baptist she returned to Calcutta in January 1938.

Being in the preaching order of the Church of England, Deepika used to teach. Women of the Tagore family have always liked this job, schools being in their blood. Deepika also enjoyed her work. Perhaps her life would have continued along this path but fate intervened. Problems cropped up with the closure of the Indian branch of the Church of England. The nuns were requested to leave the convent and go back to family life. Those who renounce the world and family willingly do not do so to return eventually. Sister Deepika chose the path of service to the poor. It was not within her powers to grant life but surely she could help the sick and destitute or perhaps get them to hospital for expert care. Her willing service and sweet demeanour are still fresh in many hearts. Saroja's granddaughter Sujata saw Sister Deepika trudging barefeet along dusty roads to care for an ailing orphan. The sight of such privation hurt Sujata. Yet Deepika was untouched, like a flower growing in slime. If anyone remonstrated with her about the hard work, she would smile and say 'My soul is hungry.' There is an article by her 'Lakshminath Bezbarua, the Man and Father.'

Following the conventions of her order Deepika never discussed her previous life, though she kept in touch with all her relations. She would visit them regularly, have a chat and then return to her humble abode. She had neither any complaints nor regrets. Her one wish was to be cremated after death. Perhaps it is easier to change one's religion than traditional beliefs. Every religion has strict injunctions for monks and nuns. It was not possible to carry out the last wish of the protestant Sister Deepika. Despite all requests and efforts of her relations, she was buried.

Bharati was Sushama's daughter and thus Hemendranath's granddaughter. She was a good sitarist and had played at public shows. While studying in Bethune College she got married. Her husband was also descended from the Tagores on his mother's side. Thereafter Bharati withdrew from the public gaze and confined herself to her home and family.

Saudamini's grandson Suprakash was married to Tanuja. Tanuja was from the family of Kumudini that is from the Tagores of house number 5 of Jorasanko and Girindranath Tagore. Suprakash was the curator of the museum in Baroda and Tanuja went there after her marriage. She was a superb cook. The cooking in her parent's home was quite different and she began to record them. Her main purpose was to bring a variation in the daily menu and to make it more appetizing. She was encouraged in this task by Rabindranath. The poet had been invited by the maharajah to deliver a lecture in Baroda. Though a royal guest, Rabindranath made it a point to visit Suprakash and Tanuja. She offered him various types of sandesh she had prepared. Charmed by her sincerity, the poet composed a poem and presented it to Tanuja.

Kalyaniya Tanu,
Antare taba snigdha madhuri punjibhuta,
Bahire prakash sundar hatey sandeshe.
Lubdha kabir chitta gabheer gunjita,
Mugdha madhur mishta raser gandhe shey.
Rabidadare je bhulale tomar natitwey
Prabashbasher avakash bhori atitthey,
Shei kathatuku ganthi dilo eyi chhande shey.

Dear Tanu,
The accumulated sweetness of your heart,

Finds expression in the *sandesh* from your hands,
The tempted poet's heart begins to hum,
Enchanted by the fragrance of its sweet syrup.
You have charmed Rabidada by your *Naatitwa*
Honouring his stay away from home with your hospitality;
This emotion he has woven in this rhyme.

Later Rabindranath changed the above poem slightly, added three more stanzas and included it in his book of verse *Prahasini*. This particular poem was named '*Naatbou*'. Later Tanuja published her book on cookery, *Paanchmisheli*. This book has helped ease the culinary burden of many a housewife. One such person is Madhumita Haldar. Her comments, 'The culinary tastes of my husband's family are so different. Garlic and vinegar are a must in every dish, even arhar dal. When cooking moong dal just ginger, salt and sugar are added. Sometimes of course vegetables are also added. For fish curry, sour curd is used while there is a dish called Bangla mangsher jhol. Had *Paanchmisheli* not provided these recipes I would have landed in trouble.' Tanuja's book has other unusual dishes like cottage-cheese *ghanto*, pudina chutney, fish *moulie* and corn cutlets. Tanuja gave a lot of thought to the problems faced by housewives. Her view was, 'No one likes to have the same dishes every day.' She also felt, 'Changing the daily menu so that appetites are not jaded is a perpetual worry for a housewife. So I give here the list of dishes for a week. It is not necessary to cook all of these. One can pick and choose at will. I hope this list will ease the burden of housewives to some extent.' The weekly menu though elaborate by today's standards is certainly very useful. Apart from cooking, Tanuja was a good needlewoman. She was an expert in creating new designs in knitting. She wrote a book *Boonooni* mainly to teach women the art of needlecraft and knitting.

Aditi's name has now faded into oblivion but the memories of those who knew her still show us the endearing personality of this granddaughter of Saratkumari. Among the least-known descendants of the Tagore family are Saratkumari's daughters. In spite of having had the rare opportunity of growing up in the cultured atmosphere of the Jorasanko mansion, they always held themselves aloof. Sushila and Suprobha were observed in the limelight occasionally but Swayamprobha and Chiraprova were never. Swayamprobha is mentioned in a few letters written by Rabindranath to Indira and later published in *Chhinnapatra*. It arouses our curiosity to find Prasanta Kumar Pal commenting, 'This niece was especially close to Rabindranath. He mentions her several times in his letters . . . ' Perhaps Rabindranath said something in this context in a letter written after Swayamprobha's marriage. Indira Devi replied with a caustic comment that men tended to view certain aspects of life like marriage more theoretically. Rabindranath accepted the criticism in his reply, 'My philosophizing about Swayamprobha's marriage was quite useless.' Neither Rabindranath's earlier letter nor Indira's letter have been found. However, at the end of his reply to Indira, the poet took a dig at women or at those who are not overburdened by sentimentality. Among these he included both Swayamprobha and Indira. He said, 'Swayamprobha and her husband are happy. Gradually these passions will subside. Then life will flow gently, bound by ties of love, affection and habit.' It has not been possible to learn anything more about Swayamprobha thereafter.

Aditi was Swayamprobha's youngest daughter. She had a beautiful singing voice and every delicate art-form like painting, music and literature attracted her. She had a sweet and sympathetic disposition. While quite young a match was arranged for her from amongst a related family. Aditi's husband Neelanjan was the son of Nabinprakash Gangopadhyay. His mother Traankumari was descended from the Pathuriaghata Tagores and the youngest sister of Mohitkumari. Neelanjan's stepmother was Indrani, the granddaughter of Saudamini, the Maharshi's eldest daughter. Thus the two granddaughters Indrani and Aditi, of the two sisters Saudamini and Saratkumari, were now related as mother-in-law and daughter-in-law! This was a common feature among the Piralis, particularly the Tagores, since marriages took place among three or four families only. To avoid complications, the members of the Tagore family had decided on a norm to adhere to the new relationship once a marriage took place.

Indrani welcomed Aditi with open arms and spared no pains to make her happy, but fate willed otherwise. Soon she lost her husband and she returned to her parents in a widow's white garb. In the twinkling of an eye, her life came to a standstill even before it could begin properly. She sang well and had exceptional artistic abilities but it was unheard of to engage a male tutor to teach a young widow to sing and paint. Aditi herself was so crushed by this cruel blow that she found it difficult to concentrate on anything. Our society is always against granting the least opportunity to a widow. Aditi was taken back to her in-laws to look after her husband's ailing sister. Perhaps the idea was to keep her engaged. Aditi was not only very tender-hearted but loved to nurse sick people and to alleviate their pain. She decided to train as a nurse and to dedicate herself to the care of the sick and destitute. Unfortunately even noble intentions have to face the strongest objections. During the early days of the twentieth century, lady doctors and nurses had no status in Bengali society. Members of respectable families not only looked down on the nursing profession with contempt but nurses were relegated to the category of untouchables! Only the helpless or destitute considered this as a profession. Aditi's father Aswinikumar Bandopadhyaya refused point blank to allow her to study nursing. He felt that a widow's needs were meagre enough to be met easily by either her in-laws or her brothers. It is true that Aditi was loved by all her relations. Her tenderness touched even the most hard-hearted person. Yet the joy of achievement and freedom attained by the sweat of one's brow is no less than the gratification of the love of one's own. Other women also can have feelings akin to Florence Nightingale. Aditi had wanted to find a release from her grief amidst the noble job of service to the sick but it was of no avail.

During World War II, when the members of the Tagore family were moving out of Calcutta due to the fear of bombing, Aditi's in-laws also decided to do the same. Aditi decided to come to Shantiniketan, though her family moved elsewhere. Aditi must have met Rabindranath earlier but when she came to stay in Shantiniketan for good, Rabindranath was no more. Had he been there, perhaps he would have been able to guide her. However Aditi seemed to have found peace in Shantiniketan. She used to live alone in a mud house with a pet dog. Amid the ochre-hued surroundings she appeared like a white marble statue, very similar to the sheuli flower moistened by dew at dawn. Her pet dog's 'samadhi' is still there.

The poverty and the simplicity of the Santhals' spurred Aditi to do something for them. She put in a lot of effort in educating Santhali children. Since she had neither the backing of any organization nor the training to teach, her service was restricted to financial help and donations. She spent all her resources to help these children buy the books necessary for their schooling. The murmur of Santhal children in her courtyard probably reminded her of Vrindavan. She became eager to see the young goatherds there. This is mere conjecture because Aditi suddenly left everything in Shantiniketan and departed for Vrindavan. She even severed all connections with her family. As far as it has been ascertained, the Onkarnath Ashram in Vrindavan was her new refuge. It is nothing new for women to renounce home and family under the magnetic pull of spiritualism. We know about two such daughters and a daughter-in-law of the Tagore family. Not everyone is able to tread this path with success. Aditi did not possess the mental firmness requisite for a nun, along with love for the Almighty. Her brother's son Arani—a journalist—found her counting her days half-starved and sick. Very fond of his pishi, he more or less forced her to return home and cared for her till she regained her health. On hearing about her return, Neelanjanprakash's nephew Niradhiprakash persuaded her to come back to her in-laws' home. This just goes to show Aditi's ability to endear herself to others without achieving any greatness.

There was no dearth of erudite women in Swarnakumari's family. All her three children were highly educated and eminently successful. Her granddaughter Kalyani set an example by showing her grandmother's strength of character and literary ability in her own achievements. Hiranmoyee's only daughter refused to toe the usual line followed by the Tagore women. In spite of playing the role of Banadevi in the staging of *Balmiki Protiva* at Sir Ashutosh Chaudhuri's residence, Kalyani's interests lay elsewhere. Married before her graduation, she kept up her studies, along with sitar and violin lessons. Her sixth child was born a few months after she graduated with honours in 1932. Ramananda Chattopadhyaya, the editor of *Prabasi,* published a photograph of Kalyani with her children under the caption 'Creditable Achievement by a mother of six'. Kalyani passed the MA examination in 1936 as a non-collegiate candidate of Calcutta University. She stood third among all the candidates and first among the women, winning the Kamala Rani gold medal. Though her subject was Bengali, she taught Sanskrit in Loreto School. She also began to consider doing research work. Initially she decided on women's education in the nineteenth century. Later, inspired by Gopimohan Kaviraj, she chose the complex topic involving the religious beliefs, history and philosophy of the lesser-known Naath sect. The 1901 census in India showed the presence of 45,463 Naath yogis. They have never been clearly identified in any census thereafter. Akin to Shaivite yogis, the 'Naath' religion also has some similarities with Buddhism. Many of the names of the eighty-four Buddhist yogis and their writings found in *Charyapada* are also found among Naath yogis. All these were saints who had attained salvation.

Topics like 'Goraksha Vijay', 'Sanyas of Gopichand', or 'Songs of Mainamoti' that we come across in Bengali literature are more related to folk literature. The ascetic practices of Naath yogis have shades of various popular religious cults like Tantra, Hatha Yoga, Shaibachar, Dharmapuja, Bajrajaan, and Sahajiya. The influence of Naath yogis is found in religious sects all over India. This was the complex and unusual subject of Kalyani's research. She visited all the important monasteries of the sect in India. Though she was helped by some, most monks refused to divulge to a woman their secret modes of worship and penance. It was with great perseverance that Kalyani succeeded in her task. There has so far been no further substantial research in Bengali literature on Naath yogis or their literature.

Both the books authored by Kalyani are rare now. Though the topic was serious, her language was simple. A few examples from her *Naath Panth* are quoted below. Kalyani writes:

> . . . I would like to discuss about certain characteristics of the austere penances followed by the Naath yogis as well as their deductions. The fundamental principle of all ascetic practices is eternal salvation. Human beings believe in renouncing the world and strive to be released from the cycle of birth and death. In the 'Naathpanth', eternal salvation, though considered essential, is not the goal. Their ideal is to attain divine grace with special powers and transform this mortal body into an immortal one and thereby become free of earthly attachments. Thus they consider the body not as a hindrance but an aid in achieving such freedom. The release obtained by death is not considered to be a true one by the Naath yogis since it is obstructed by the loss of the human body. They consider it a bounden duty to strive to make the physical body, wherein it has been possible to attain heavenly bliss, imperishable and immortal. There is no certainty after death. Since a yogi who has attained salvation and freedom from worldly attachment is able to leave the mortal body at will he is able to master time and wander about as he desires.

Naath yogis also placed importance on vanquishing worldly desires as a means of removing ignorance and acquiring spiritual knowledge. This is a common feature of all religions. The Ultasadhan of the Naath yogis meant turning the mind inwards for contemplation. Kalyani researched to find links of the Naathpanth with other religions and succeeded. A further proof of the accuracy of her work was in the Naath sect honouring her with the title 'Mahamohopadhyaya'.

The apparently hard-headed Kalyani had a sympathetic and benevolent heart. Just as Swarnakumari always maintained friendly relations with other women-writers of her time so did Kalyani interact with the poetess Nistarini and many others. She kept in touch with the *Bharatstree Mahamondal* as well as with Hemlata's *Bangalakshmi*. She always tried to share her mother's concern about the inmates of the widow home. Her mother's plight had left a deep impression on her. Perhaps this lay behind her friendship with Nistarini who lived in Kashi. Kalyani wrote both in Bengali and English. She did not confine herself to Naath yogis but wrote several articles on Swami Vivekananda, Shri Ramakrishna and Sarada Devi. Her other articles like 'Mayer Katha', 'Didimar Katha', 'Jnanadanandinir Katha', 'Rabindra Smritibarshiki', 'Bhratrismaraney' and 'Pramotha Chaudhuri' are also equally relevant along with those on more serious topics. She wrote articles on women's education, some poems on contemporary topics, her travels to Kashmir, Sikkim and Shatapanth in various magazines. She took 'Diksha' from Swami Hariharananda Swami of the Kapil Muni Math. She never alluded to the honours heaped upon her. However she treasured the poem conveying the felicitations of the Kashi Mahila Mandal on her acquiring the degree of MABT. This was composed by the poet Nistarini. Below is an excerpt:

. . . Prabaser nidarshan,
bisuddha pranayadhan,
Pradanichey tava karey ogo subadani.

Kshudra shakti kshudra asha,
Akapat abinasha,
Anabil swachchhotoya swarga Mandakini,
Madhumakha bhalobasha,
Janena maukhik bhasa,
Kavya alankar nahi janey e ramani,
Nitanta saralabala sati prabasini . . .
Esho mor priyo sakhi
Abar abar dekhi,
Tomar o snehamakha saral bayan.
Sikshar adarsha jodi
Raksha koro mirabodhi
Dhanya hobey Aryanari abar Bharatey
Ghuchibe andhar kara
Ujalibe chandra tara
Alokey alokmoy sundar jagatey . . .

. . . A token from afar,
A pure and simple gift of love
Is being presented to you
Oh beautiful one,
Small abilities, small hopes
Guileless and eternal
Like the clear heavenly Mandakini,
Whole-hearted devotion
Knows not the gift of speech
This woman knows neither
Poetic nor ornate words.
She is a simple, devout soul
Living away from home
Come O my dear friend,
Let me glimpse again and again
Your candid and affectionate face.
If the ideals of education
Are upheld by you always
The women of India will
Be blessed again.
The darkness of a prison
Will disappear,

The moon and stars shine again
In a bright and beautiful world.

Mira's daughter Nandita was Rabindranath's only granddaughter. He had numerous grand-nieces and nephews. Quite a few others, though unrelated, occupied a similar position in his heart. Thus his role as a grandparent was wide and all-pervading; yet Nandita stood out amongst the others. This was due to her exceptional qualities. She was involved in practically every function at Shantiniketan and was the brightest star of Pratima's dance school. Though Nandita was very fond of her father but the unhappiness of Mira and Nagendranath's life had had its effect on their children. Nandita initially studied at Gokhale Memmorial School in Calcutta. Later she joined the Kala Bhawan and Sangeet Bhawan and became an integral part of Shantiniketan. She had gladly participated in all Rabindranath's new experiments with dance forms. When *Chitrangada* was staged for the first time in 1936, Nandita appeared as the second Chitrangada. Nowadays this character is named Surupa but Rabindranath himself never separated Chitrangada into Kurupa and Surupa. In the first show Nandalal Bose's daughter Yamuna played the role of the first Chitrangada. We know from Shantidev Ghosh that *Chitrangada* was staged forty times between 1936 and 1940! The first time Rabindranath himself took his dance troupe to various cities in western India, Patna, Delhi, Allahabad, Lucknow, Meerut, Lahore—*Chitrangada* proved to be a roaring success everywhere. Rabindranath himself would be on the stage in every show. Every member performed well. One day Yamuna came down with high fever. Though Nandita normally danced in the role of the second Chitrangada, she enacted both the roles with aplomb and thus averted a crisis. There were times when the opposite also happened.

Along with *Chitrangada* a few other dance-dramas were composed. They were *Chandalika*, *Shyama* and *Tasher Desh*. In all of these Nandita played the main role. Not only was her acting superb but every character she portrayed was brought to life by her excellent postures and wonderful expressions of the various moods. The other memorable names are Gauri Basu, for her superb acting in *Natir Puja*, Shrimati in her solo performances and Queenie or Amala Raychauduri as 'Haratani' in *Tasher Desh.* Rabindranath always felt at ease with Nandita on the stage and would send for her at odd times. He wrote to Mira, 'I am in trouble. I have suddenly been informed that a Japanese group is coming to see and examine our dance forms. If *Buri* does not come the entire show will be a farce that will be far reaching enough to cross the ocean.'

Nandita always obliged with her usual liveliness. Once it was decided to stage *Arupratan.* Amita was to play the role of Sudarshana. Rabindranath had thought of appearing as Surangama himself but was persuaded by others to give the role to Nandita.

In 1936, Nandita was married to Krishna Kripalani—a man of her own choice. The handsome, erudite and humorous Krishna was a general favourite. Rabindranath said that Krishna was one of the two real gentlemen he knew. In Shantiniketan Nandita and Krishna's friendship ripened into love. Their friends were all aware of this. Rama Chakraborty writes, 'After Miradi went for her siesta in the afternoon, *Buri* would cross the garden, vault over the small gate and walk up to *Ratankuthi.*' The young professor Krishna Kripalini used to live in *Ratankuthi* at the time. There is no inkling of Rabindranath's feelings when Krishna Kripalani asked him for Nandita's hand in marriage. The readiness with which he consented surprised Krishna. He was overwhelmed by the poet's support in spite of his being a non-Bengali, non-Brahmin and non-Brahmo. The incident had astonished Pravatkumar Mukhopadhyaya too. He says, 'Since it was an inter-caste marriage, it was registered in Suri according to the "Teen Ain" of 1812, i.e. the Civil Marriage Act. Again the auspicious day for the traditional ceremony was fixed for the twelfth of Baisakh 1343 (1938). It is amazing that Rabindranath, who was not only opposed to marriages according to the "Teen Ain", but had always severely criticized the religious custom of fixing auspicious days according to the almanac, accepted all this without a murmur.' All arrangements for Nandita's wedding had been made by Rathindranath. The bridegroom rode a decorated elephant! Nandita, dressed in traditional bridal finery, was given away by Mira while Pundit Kshitimohan Sen acted as the priest. Rabindranath presented them with a house *Patrapoot* hoping that it would always be filled to the brim with beauty and love of their new life together.

When Rabindranath was ill another facet of Nandita's character was revealed. During his serious illness Nandita nursed him as she did others. She would be there by his sickbed every day, without a break, from morning till noon. Amita, who used to be with her said, 'Nandita had a tremendous ability for hard work and nursing. Rabindranath seemed to derive a great deal of comfort from her care and wrote:

Didimoni,
Aphooran santwanar khani
Kono klanti kono klesh
Mukhe chinha deye nai lesh
Kono bhoy kono ghrina kono kaje
Kichhumatro glani, sebar madhurje chhaya
Nahi dey ani.

Didimoni, unending mine of consolation
No fatigue or distress.
Puts any sign on your face.
There is no fear or aversion for any task,
No shade of weariness
Dims the graciousness of your care.

Alas this care too came to an end.

After Rabindranath's death Nandita got involved in politics. She and Krishna Kripalani joined the All-India Non-cooperation movement of 1942. The freedom movement had greatly inspired the womenfolk. Women from almost every family, educated or illiterate, came forward casting aside all thoughts of personal safety. It may be said that the complete emancipation of Bengali women was a consequence of this movement. One wonders why the call for freedom touched the hearts of women who had been forever denigrated and persecuted. Both Nandita's cousins Aruna Gangopadhyaya and Purnima Bandopadhyaya were involved in politics. Purnima's husband Pranab was the son of Saudamini's granddaughter Shanta. Purnima was associated with the Congress for many years. Aruna later became well-known as Aruna Asaf Ali. By this time the fervour of terrorist politics had begun to abate. The daring deeds of Shanti, Suniti, Bina, Kalpana and Preetilata had become legends. Along with a large number of women who joined the August movement, Nandita also courted arrest. She was sentenced to six months in prison. Shrimati and Rani Chanda were also with her. Rani Chanda says, 'Nandita often sang *Jodi tor daak shuney keu naa aashey* .' She listened to others singing too. They had been sent to Rajshahi jail and the women decided to unfurl the Indian flag within the jail on 26 January. The flag was stitched carefully from three pieces of khaddar procured by dyeing a gamchha in saffron, tearing off a saree-pallu and a corner off a bedsheet. The flag was attached to the branch of a neem tree at dawn. The entire jail reverberated with Nandita and Maya's voice as they sang *Joy hok, Joy hok, naba arunoday* as the day was just breaking. Her letters from prison bear testimony to her amazing command over language.

Nandita was as self-effacing as her mother and always tried to remain hidden from the public eye. Thus most of her qualities remain unknown and there is very little record of her considerable accomplishments. While at Shantiniketan she learnt batik work, leather craft and block printing on textiles. She took lessons in painting from artists like Nandalal Bose, Benodbehari Mukhopadhyay and Ramkinkar. A fresco on the wall of 'China Bhawan' bears testimony to her aptitude and competence as an artist. There is only one record of Nandita and that too with

Shandidev Ghosh, Sudhin Dutt and Amala Dutt. The two songs are *Jana gana mana adhinayaka* and *Jodi tor daak shuney keu naa aashey*. Yet when India became independent Nandita joined Sucheta Kripalini in singing the national anthem at midnight. This shows that Nandita shied away from publicity not out of diffidence but from a natural disinterest.

She always came forward with a smile whenever asked to represent her country. Her trip to South America in 1950 with Mrinalini Sarabhai's dance troupe and to the USSR in 1960 on their governments' invitation are two such instances. In the latter instance she was deputed by the Indian government to teach the dance-drama *Chitrangada* to the 'Kuibyshev on the Volga' ballet. When Krishna Kripalani was appointed the cultural secretary at the Indian Embassy in Brazil, Nandita not only was of great help to him but also acquainted herself with the cultural life of Brazil. At this time she also wrote in the Bengali *Desh* magazine about some of her experiences in South America. To quote her, 'During our stay Rabindranath's *Daakghar* was staged. Cecilia Meireless translated it and was the main inspiration behind the stage performance . . . her youngest daughter Maria acted as 'Amal'. I could not help feeling how happy Rabindranath would have been, were he here.' Nandita's abilities as a creative writer are scattered in her letters and travelogues. A short story written by her about a case while she had been in prison bears a strong resemblance to Rabindranath's 'Shasti'. Nandita's tale is titled 'Nirdosh'. It is about a young woman Lali who is in prison serving a twenty-year sentence. Her six-year-old daughter Zia is also with her. It is a strange tale. Convinced that her unfaithful husband had killed his mistress, Lali accepted the blame. The actual culprit was the murdered woman's husband. Lali says, 'A voice seemed to whisper in my ears, "Say you committed the murder. Otherwise your husband will be hanged." I stood up and shouted, "I am guilty. Let my husband off." Everyone was surprised. I was sentenced to twenty years in prison. Zia's father said to me, "Do try to forgive me. You have accepted the blame and punishment to save me but I did not commit the murder."' The story ends at this point.

Nandita took up a job with the Delhi Cloth Mills primarily to help her parents. Besides that, she used to teach in a dance school. This aspect of Nandita's life is almost unknown. She once thought of resigning after her father's death but decided against it, out of consideration for her mother. She wrote to Rama Chakraborty, 'It is essential for women to be economically independent. Life becomes much easier if one is able to fend for oneself without having to look to parents, brothers, sisters or husband for support. I am very fortunate to have landed this job since I have hardly any qualifications.'

This letter is a proof of the change that was taking place in the attitudes of the women of the Tagore family along with time. Many people were of the opinion that the women of this family were unable to keep up with the times and the advancement in women's conditions. This was not quite true. Circumstances, family traditions, an aristocratic upbringing and a characteristic educational atmosphere often prevented the women of the Tagore family from mingling with the masses. However it is obvious from Nandita's letter that they had begun to adapt themselves to contemporary socio-economic conditions, though in a family with members scattered far and wide it is difficult to discern such changes.

Nandita was deeply hurt by the changes taking place in Shantiniketan. She felt,

> ... The ashram was built on such high ideals, for which grandfather worked so hard. His life's work is being ruined before our very eyes. I feel none of us can escape the blame. Today one hardly comes across idealists. Those of yesteryear have also deviated from the straight and narrow path. I can't think anyone worthy of the job in the whole country. Some days back I felt like retiring to my upstairs room in the ashram and doing whatever my heart wished. Alas there is no freedom

> for human beings. None of us is independent. It is just a fallacy.

An incurable illness caused Nandita's untimely end. Perhaps that is why most of her accomplishments appear incomplete or half done. Dance, music, recitation, acting, writing and her views, nothing came to fulfilment. Another addition to the list is a film. It was most probably *Chandalika*: Nandita acted as the mother of Prakriti but the film could not be completed due to lack of funds.

Rabindranath wrote a lot about his 'Didimoni' and she is remembered by many as his granddaughter. Few have however tried to gauge her potential as an individual. The towering personality of the man whom Nandita had as one of her nearest relatives did overshadow her to a certain extent. It nevertheless infused certain sterling qualities in her. The day Nandita breathed her last, bearing all her suffering in silence, the last ray of Rabindranath from the Tagore family was wiped out.

Nandini, alias Poopey, was not born into the Tagore family but Pratima brought her up as her own. Poopey's father, Chaturbhuj Damodar, was a Gujarati businessman. An admirer of Rabindranath, he had settled in Shantiniketan. Seeing him troubled with an ailing wife and a small baby girl, Pratima decided to adopt her. Nandini later wrote,

> I was very ill and the doctors had given up all hopes of my survival. My mother, Pratima Devi, took me in her arms, and brought me to my grandfather Rabindranath, requesting his permission to adopt me.

Poopeyrani was thus installed in Uttarayan. Rabindranath named her Nandini. From the age of three began sessions of listening to stories. To amuse her Tagore composed any number of rhymes and short stories. Thus Nandini's contribution to Rabindra-literature is considerable. The story of 'Shey' and the rhymes of *Khaapchhara* all originated with Poopey's demands for storytelling.

Nandini was a gifted writer. In her adulthood she wrote *Pita Putri*. There are anecdotes about both Rathindranath and Rabindranath. An incident about the poet losing his temper has been described by Nandini in her own words,

> . . . I had never seen Grandfather so angry. It happened when his beard was snipped during his illness. Dr Nilratan Sarkar, Dr Bidhan Chandra Ray and others had come from Calcutta for Grandfather's treatment. They were unable to diagnose the cause of the pain from his head down to the neck. They decided to administer a sleeping drug to Grandfather and examine the area covered by his beard. A sleeping drug was given to him with his dinner and after he fell asleep the doctors cut away some hair near his ear and some of his beard covering his cheek. They were thus able to examine him thoroughly, diagnose and prescribe the necessary medicines. They were apprehensive of Grandfather's reaction when he woke up and so they left for Calcutta the same night. As soon as Grandfather woke up, he realized that something was amiss. He was furious when he saw his face in a mirror. He summoned Banamalidada and asked him how such a thing could happen. Banamalidada was almost in tears and pleaded ignorance saying that he had gone off to bed. Grandfather refused his morning coffee. When Banamalidada went to request him he scolded him and asked for Father. On being informed that Father had gone to Sriniketan early in the morning due to some urgent business, Grandfather fell silent and sat quietly in a huff. Every time Banamalida went to request him to eat, he got a scolding. No one else dared to approach him. Ultimately Ma went up to him and said that no one else would be able to eat anything if Grandfather did not. Grandfather kept silent. When Ma went to request him a second time he burst out in great distress saying, 'Don't any of you have any sense of courtesy? Wasn't it necessary and proper to at least ask me once before tampering with my beard?' Finally he relented and had his meal but Father was so scared that he kept away from Grandfather for quite a few days.

The entire episode is narrated like a movie. It had made such a lasting impression on little Nandini's mind that she presented this impeccable account when writing about her grandfather in later years. Had she made time from a full family-life to present a few more such pen portraits, they would have been invaluable. Averse to publicity, she wrote very little.

We now not only go back to house number 5 at Jorasanko but also revert to earlier times. Saudamini had a number of granddaughters. They were Gaganendranath's three daughters, Sunandini, Purnima and Sujata, Samarendranath's five Madhabika, Malabika, Kamala, Supriya and Anima, and Abanindranath's three who lived long enough to be mentioned—Uma, Karuna and Surupa. Their accomplishments varied but Saudamini had trained all of them to be excellent housewives. Though the girls of this family were educated like those of the other branches of the Tagores, they were never brought into the limelight. Uma, Abanindranath's daughter was the eldest with Sunandini a few months younger than her. The girls were usually educated at home. Indubala Devi, a Brahmo lady, used to teach the elder girls as well as instruct them in needlecraft. Uma however had studied in Bethune School. She had been awarded a prize for general proficiency but her grandmother forbade her to go to school to collect it. This was because her marriage had just been fixed with Nirmal Mukhopadhyay who lived next door. No one considered the hurt feelings of a ten-year-old. Uma remembered the incident all her life. We often do not appreciate that a trivial action can cause grievous anguish to the young mind.

Like the other girls of the Tagore family, Uma too was highly gifted. Apart from participating in family performances she acted twice in large shows. One was as Marzina in *Alibaba* and the other as Golapi in *Viraha*. Rabindranath had seen the performance and was highly impressed by her dramatic abilities. He wanted to take Uma along on his trip to Java. Her in-laws agreed but Abanindranath objected saying, 'Uma will not be able to stand the strain.' Most people at the time considered women incapable of enduring physical hardships. The desire to protect women from the rigours of outdoor life was cited as a reason for confining them indoors, as also for the efforts to ensconce them in comfort and easy living. This attitude was not always conducive to women's happiness or self-esteem and they were often chided in later life for their timidity and shyness. No one had anticipated the sweeping changes in society so soon. Gunendranath's family still had shades of the old conservatism.

Uma was an expert needlewoman. Even in her old age, with shaking fingers, she embroidered beautifully. Her delicate handiwork, like a spider's web, brought to life various motifs, like stem, leaves and paisley, on cloth. At this time it was customary for all young girls to be taught needlework before marriage and quite a few took it up as a hobby even afterwards. It seems probable that girls in aristocratic families took to needlework after the advent of English governesses. Though needlework, especially making and embroidering kanthas was common among village women, our society had evolved a new norm: no stitched dress could be worn for any auspicious occasion! In many wealthy families, torn sarees could never be darned and worn. They either had to be given away to maidservants or recycled as kanthas. The women of East Bengal were especially proficient in this craft. It is not known whether they adopted it as a means of livelihood but their habit of embroidering their names on the kanthas indicates their pride and pleasure in creating these embroidered nakshi kanthas. Though the Tagore women were expert needlewomen, Uma was the first one among them to turn to this craft. Kanthas were not popular in Calcutta, quilts and *balaposh* were in vogue and this may have been the reason for the lack of interest of these women. Uma also remembered listening to stories, on winter evenings, covered by a *balaposh*. However, kanthas could not have been unknown among the Tagores. Most Tagore brides hailed from Jessore and their relations often visited them during festival time. The women would bring along various culinary dishes, dolls and other gifts crafted by their expert fingers. Any form of art or craft attracted Abanindranath and he was a great appreciator of the naksi kantha. Moreover this was a period when folk arts were being revived. Abanindranath would collect samples of 'nakshi kanthas, embroidered borders and various stitches. Uma, a worthy daughter of an artist father, would replicate on the kanthas designs like boyka, baanspatta and terashi. Some family members still have a few of these. Impressed by her expertise Abanindranath would also sketch various designs, matching them with the colours of the available threads for Uma to embroider. Uma also invented numerous new stitches but she never kept any records about these. Some ladies had published books on cutting, tailoring, knitting and needlecraft. Notable among them are: *Adarsha Suchishilpa* by Sushila Devi, *Adarsha Suchichitra* by Kananbala Devi, *Suchichitra Shiksha* by Aparajita Devi, Gayatri Devi's *Suchi Likhan*, Sulekha Devi's *Suchirekha* and Tanuja Devi's *Bununi*. None of these however deal with lessons in nakshi kanthas.

Uma created a dramatized version of her father's *Khirer Putul*. This was a folktale which Abanindranath got from Mrinalini's collection. Though the effort received praise, Uma never gave any thought to such ventures later on. In her old age, when her eyesight had dimmed and she could no longer stitch kanthas, Uma began to write her memoirs. It was not her autobiography but all about her father. She named the book *Babar Katha*. There is no other work that affords such a close look at Abanindranath. Intertwined are anecdotes about herself and their house at 5, Dwarkanath Lane. She never planned to write, it was just a sudden inspiration. She says,

> My father used to draw and paint pictures. I shall write about the pictures of old days . . .

I was then a little girl. Early in the morning father would come down to the first floor. Father and Mother lived with us in the second floor of the Jorasanko house. Father would have a wash and stroll in the round garden. After a while he would sit on an iron bench there. I would also get up early and go to the garden with Gupidashi. Father would tell me a lot of stories. As soon as the second-floor windows opened Father would say, 'Nelli, your mother is up, go to her and write the name of the goddess Durga.' Everyday, I had to sit where my mother worshipped and fill a whole page with the name of the goddess, using 'alta' and a reed pen. After this we had to drink our milk. The summons came from my grandmother. She sat on the divan in the verandah, reclining on a cushion, with my Chhoto pishi next to her. Ballav our milkman used to bring the milk in three or four brass containers that shone like gold. Our servant Srinath would measure out the milk into a huge *kara*, which shone like silver, with an equally bright ladle. Srinath boiled the milk, brought it back to the verandah and poured it into our bowls after cooling it. The cooling was done by pouring the milk a couple of times from one bowl to another. Avinash would bring Father's and my uncles' silver cups and saucers. Grandmother would pour the foaming milk herself into these cups and have them sent outside to the south verandah. By this time father and his two elder brothers would be there. I often followed Avinashdada. Baba always drank his milk holding the cup with both hands. He always had this habit. When drinking water, he would pour it into both his hands folded together and drink . . .

At eight o' clock our bawarchi Navin would bring toast and boiled eggs on a tray and place them before the three brothers. They fed the crows first and then had their breakfast. Bishwambhar bearer would come with *albolas* containing smoking tobacco for the three masters.

Thereafter began their working session. It was either writing or sketching and continued till midday. At about noon the three brothers would have their bath and sit down to lunch in front of Grandmother. After lunch they went to the outer quarters to rest. This was in a small marble floored room. In summer a bearer would pull the *tanapakha*. When this room was later converted into a study for the boys, Father and the uncles rested in the library. At 3 p.m. our servant Nilu would serve all the three brothers with *daab* (green coconut) water. At 4 p.m. Father always went up to Grandmother's hall. He would have a paan, chat with her for a while and then come to my mother's room. At this time he would play the esraj and teach me to sing. At 5 p.m. he would come down to the verandah downstairs. My grandmother also came and sat down in Chhoto pishi's verandah. Barama would arrange various sweets, savouries and fruits on marble dishes and send them downstairs through Avinash and Nilu. This was the teatime menu for father and his brothers. After having the snacks they went down to the garden. All the children also congregated there. The menfolk or 'babus' from the neighbouring houses would also come.

We often sat on the terrace near our grandmother on moonlit summer evenings. There is no end to the stories we were told. Sometimes everyone met on the second-floor terrace of the large house (the Maharshi's house). Robidada would sing and Father would play on the esraj . . . Every evening we all had to visit our grandmother in her room. Then we went to Father's room. Hearing him tell stories was an important daily routine for us.

In winter all of us cousins would cover ourselves with *balaposhes* and sit around our Didi from Simla. She would tell us stories. Sometimes father would also wrap a *balaposh* around himself and join our storytelling sessions.

At 9 p.m. we all were called for dinner. After dinner, the three brothers would sit in their sitting room in the outer quarters and smoke. At the time it was customary not to smoke in the 'andar'. After their smoke the three brothers would get up and retire to their bedrooms. This was the regular daily routine of my father. Most of his days have been spent thus.

The reason for this lengthy quotation is the vivid picture this book provides about life in house number 5. This is what may be termed as 'writing a picture'. There are so many such pictures that it is difficult to choose. Uma has also portrayed the agony of the artist Abanindranath.

> . . . Father had suffered a great deal in his family life but his life as an artist was also full of agony and despair. I often stood behind Father when he painted. One day he immersed the painting in water, lightly stroked it with a flat brush and put it in the sun. When he brought it out of the sun his face had a melancholy look. He said, 'I was unable to capture with my brush the shades my mind had visualized.'

Another day Abanindranath sat down to paint a portrait of Uma's husband. After completing the sketch the first day, Abanindranath told him to sit in the same pose the next morning. He would put in the colours and complete the painting. Uma recounts,

> The next morning Ma took all of us to New Market. She persuaded my husband to accompany us saying that the sitting could be done after our return. When we returned from shopping we found Father sitting glumly in his painting chair. He was very annoyed and scolded Ma roundly saying, "I spent the whole night planning the colour scheme and in the morning found that everyone had disappeared." We all requested him to paint but he refused saying that both the time and mood had passed. He never painted that portrait. I often feel that had we not taken my husband shopping that day, Father's painting of him would have been there.

A great man, when viewed by a near one, seems to be looked at with fresh eyes. Hemlata noticed so many mundane details in Rabindranath's family life, like his differences with Mrinalini over gold studs, his experiments with cooking and his singing in his *Basar Ghar.* By recording these incidents she may have caused Rabindranath occasional embarrassment or displeasure, yet it is safe to say that no man would have noticed such details while writing about Rabindranath. Uma's pen portrait of Abanindranath gives us a similar taste of a delightful personality.

The uncle Rabindranath refused to wear gold studs and compromised with opal-studded ones. The nephew was no less in his idiosyncracies. He always drank water from a bell-metal *ghoti*. Suhasini once presented him with a silver one, on the fulfillment of her *Savitri-vrata*. Uma recalls,

> Father refused to drink water from this silver *ghoti*. I coaxed him saying, 'Ma will be very hurt. Drink from it for a few days and then put it by.' After Ma's death, Father said, 'Put that *ghoti* away. Otherwise it is sure to be stolen. It is beyond me to look after it.' Thereafter he never drank water from that *ghoti*.

Herein lies the success of reminiscences recounted by women. Only they can paint such informal pictures. They are able to see the infinite in small things and treasure them in their memory like pearls in an oyster. Shattered by her husband's death, Uma went back to her loving father. Abanindranath was then in Gupta Niwas. To quote Uma again,

> I went to father. He said, 'Come sit here. Will you stay here?' I replied 'Yes.'
>
> Father continued slowly in his usual affectionate tone, 'That is good. Stay here for some time. Do not give up your home and family. When your mother died I went away to Shantiniketan. I had to return, unable to stay there.' He was quiet for a while and then said, 'Everything is an illusion but death is real. No one knows about rebirth after death, but once you are born death is a certainty.'

After writing *Babar Katha* Uma had hoped to write about herself. Had she done so it would surely have been another incomparable book of pen-portraits. So much that is unknown would have come to our knowledge. But it was not to be. The saga of a woman's life, her aspirations, achievements, pleasures and agony were lost forever in the inexorable movement of time.

It would be best to write about Uma's cousins at this juncture. Chronologically Gaganendranath's eldest daughter Sunandini came just after Uma. Her marriage had been fixed with Pravatnath almost at her birth. At the time many guardians, including the Tagores, arranged matches in this fashion. Moreover Sunandini's marriage was arranged among distant relatives. When she was barely a week old, Pravatnath's aunt Surendrabala came with the proposal. Sunandini's in-laws lived next to Jorasanko Tagore mansion. Dwarkanath Tagore's elder sister Rasbilasi had been married into this Chatterjee family. Five or six generations later another daughter from the Tagore family came in as a bride. Sunandini's mother-in-law, Mohitkumari, came from another branch of the Tagores. The daughter of Atindranandan Tagore of Pathuriaghata, she had also been married when barely nine. In her old age Mohitkumari renounced the world to become a sanyasini and was known as Sadhuma. Sunandini herself never wrote anything but her mother-in-law wrote an autobiography which gives us a lot of information. Sunandini was a lively and mischievous little girl. Once she conspired with her brothers and cut off the '*tiki*' of the Pundit while he slept. Her grandmother Saudamini retaliated with, 'She has had enough education. Get her married off.'

Though Uma was a few months older, Sunandini was married earlier. The two cousins were married to two young men descended from two nephews of Dwarkanath Tagore. Their houses were divided just by the narrow Singhi Bagan Lane. From their parent's home they could see their in-laws' place, or it would be correct to say that it was the other way round. Sunandini's wedding was celebrated with great pomp. In marrying off Sunandini, Gaganendranath performed what is known as 'Gauri Daan'. Just before the wedding Amarendranath Chattopadhyay, the groom's uncle, said, 'Sampradaan is not possible if the bride wears stitched clothes.' Though times were changing the Chatterjee family was still very conservative and bound by strict traditional norms of old. The purdah system was pretty stringent in the Pathuriaghata Tagore family too, yet it was not as rigorous as in the Chattopadhyay abode. After her marriage Mohitkumari observed that in her parental home it was permissible for women to go for a dip in the river Ganges.

They were carried in palanquins covered on all sides but in her in-law's place, 'No one can go for a dip in the Ganges.' There was no question of women going anywhere by train or by horse-drawn coaches.

Gaganendranath did not show any annoyance over the comment by Amarendra. He told them, 'The bride is not wearing any stitched clothes. You can see for yourself.' This was true. The saree had been draped so skillfully that it appeared as if the girl was wearing a blouse. Everyone present praised Gaganendranath's artistic taste and the way the saree was draped. Gaganendranath had his daughter painted in her bridal attire with a *kajal-lata* in her hand—it was a beautiful picture that would always remain with the father though the daughter would go away to her new home.

It was customary for professional dancing girls to perform in the andar mahal during any wedding. Though debarred from the Brahmo Maharshi family, two such women called Nagen and Kusumi went to all the other Tagore homes. They would take booking money in advance, come on the particular day, entertain the ladies and take 'bakhsheesh'. Purnima recounts, 'All the ladies would dress up in jackets with *Punjabi asteen* or *rumal asteen*, take small feather fans in their hands and assemble in the hall on the second floor. Nagen, Kusumi and other dancing girls said, "It was like a collection of fairies."' Such descriptions show that the cultured atmosphere prevalent outside had not permeated fully into the andar mahal. Their contact with the outside world was mainly via the dancing girls, singers and other women of the poor working classes, like gardeners and weavers. It was a while before dancing girls became debarred from respectable society.

The inhabitants of the andar mahal, with their minds clouded by orthodoxy and conservatism, sometimes created a great deal of mischief. Purnima tells us about an incident that she heard from Sunandini's mother-in-law Mohitkumari. Gaganendranath had gifted his eldest daughter some diamond jewellery. At

Sunandini's in-laws' place an argument began among the invited ladies. One group said that the stones were white sapphires and not real diamonds while the other insisted that the stones were genuine diamonds. Neither party was prepared to concede defeat and a bet of one hundred rupees was placed. A few days later, the ladies sent their old manager for the set. Since the case bore the name of 'Cook and Kelvy' it was sent to the same shop to ascertain its genuineness. The shop suspected the jewellery to be stolen and refused to return it. Thereafter they were told the name of the master of the house. The English owner of Cook and Kelvy came personally and said to the gentleman, 'I made this set for a wedding in Gaganendranath Tagore's family. From where did you get it?' The master of the house kept the shop owner waiting and learnt about the entire episode from the ladies of his family. He immediately signed a receipt for the jewellery, and sent the retrieved set back to Mohitkumari. The ladies involved came in for a good deal of rebuke. Later sweets and other dishes worth a hundred rupees were sent as atonement.

Though she does not specify, it appears from Purnima's account that she thought the ladies of house number 6 were involved in this altercation. She says, 'Those who had maintained relations with us said that the stones were diamonds while the others said that they were white sapphires. Since Debendra embraced the Brahmo faith the women of his family never visited us though the menfolk did.' The truth seems to lie elsewhere. No Hindu family ever invited any Brahmo to any socio-religious function. This was mainly because of the problems that would arise when people sat down to eat. Orthodox Hindus flatly refused to sit down to a meal with any Brahmo. Purnima herself mentions this. Since the women of the Maharshi's family were absent on this occasion, the question of the genuineness of the jewellery may have been raised by the ladies of some other family. Purnima's comment in the very next chapter is, 'Since Debendranath embraced Brahmoism, the Pathuriaghata Tagores descended from Darpanarayan had severed social relations with us.' It is thus possible that Purnima did not have any knowledge of all the members of such a large family. Despite certain factual errors, Purnima's *Thakurbarir GaganThakur* is the best description of the andar mahal of number 5, Jorasanko. She has been able to depict the mannerisms and even the voices of the inhabitants with astonishing lucidity.

We learn about Sunandini mainly from Purnima's account. She has also portrayed the agony of a child-bride. She writes, 'At first, Didi took her marriage to be a kind of game. Her in-laws' place was very close to our house. When she saw us playing in the garden and was unable to join us, she was just like a wild bird that had been caged. Whenever she came over, she would howl the place down, refusing to go back.' Grown-ups hardly realized the misery of the child-bride. Mohitkumari felt offended at Sunandini's behaviour. Yet not only had she been married at the age of nine but she had written in her memoirs, 'From today I shall have to change all my ways, eating habits, mode of dressing, behaviour, everything. From today I become dependent on the wishes of others. Those days of going for coach rides, singing or chatting whenever the mood took me—or eating whatever I wanted to—they are all a thing of the past.' She never sighed while writing all this because, according to her, 'I was not worried as at that time I had not even learnt to do so. Moreover, never having seen any girl going away to her in-laws' we never knew the heartache associated with it.' Perhaps this was why Mohitkumari wanted to mould her nine-year-old daughter-in-law in the same way.

Men had however begun to realize that times were changing. Gaganendra was vehemently opposed to sending his daughter to her in-laws' place by force. Sunandini's father-in-law, Priyonath Chattopadhyay, also shared the same view. He would say, 'Let her grow up. As she matures she will come of her own accord. Why do you have to force her into submission?' Pramodkumari and

Mohitkumari had accepted the old, orthodox rules as normal. Yet when we are told that Mohitkumari's guardians took her on an outing around Calcutta on the eve of her wedding, just because the nine-year-old was going into a family where girls were not allowed to go even in a covered palki for a dip in the Ganga—the helpless and miserable lives of numerous young girls rises vividly before our eyes. Mohitkumari recalled,

> Before the ritual of smearing me with turmeric, my father took me to see the fort in the morning. We also went up the monument. In the afternoon we visited the museum and the zoological gardens. In the evening we went as usual for a drive to the Maidan and returned home after listening to the band. Only that day father hardly even glanced at me. Whenever our eyes met I found his brimming with tears. I remember all this clearly.

Even in this so called broad-minded family, where a daughter was taken all around town on the eve of her marriage, Mohitkumari's mother always spent her days confined within doors. To quote Mohitkumari again,

> The women of today are able to learn and practise music, move about freely out of doors, but my mother could never even go out into the verandah outside her room. She spent her days suffering in silence. If my grandmother went out of the house, my mother would fulfill her desire to have a glimpse of the courtyard from the verandah. There was no question of watching the public road or the traffic thereon. What was there in the courtyard? Two wells, one of them derelict, verandahs on three sides of the large courtyard and a four-storey-high wall on the fourth side. When I think of Ma's longing to just see such a sight my heart fills with sorrow.

The saga of these three child-brides shows us the change in times and attitudes.

Mohitkumari's autobiography is an important document for various reasons. It certainly gives us an insight into the traditional norms of her parents and her husband's family. It is quite probable that many women living in the andar mahal had literary leanings. This would be especially true for those from wealthy families who were not only taught to read and write but also had a lot of time on their hands. Their diaries were seldom preserved due to a lack of awareness. Thus intimate pictures of numerous families have been lost forever. Mohitkumari was descended from Darpanarayan Tagore. We get a glimpse of the existing conditions of her parental home when she says,

> I was the first girl go to her in-laws' after marriage. So far it had been the norm in my father's family to choose handsome 'Kulin' boys for their daughters, marry them and keep them as 'ghar jamais'. I would be treading a new path, living with a new family and adjusting to strangers. All this was unknown and my habits, demeanour and lifestyle—everything would change.

After marriage, Mohitkumari came to her husband's family. Her husband was descended from Rasbilasi, the elder sister of Dwarkanath Tagore. Thus she has created glimpses of this family too. In spite of living practically next door to the Maharshi's family, no influence of the latter was discernible in Rasbilasi's descendents. In this house the men lived in the outer quarters and the women in the andar mahal. Mohitkumari's widowed father-in-law also lived in the outer mahal. Quoting Mohitkumari, 'My father-in-law never came inside. He and my husband both had rooms in the ground floor of the outer mahal. I would raise the wooden window shutters of my room in the first floor and watch my father-in-law strolling about.' Mohitkumari ardently wished to have her father-in-law live with the family in the andar mahal. This wish was fulfilled after the marriage of her daughter. She writes,

> After my daughter's wedding we persuaded my father-in-law to move into the andar mahal. Both of us were very happy. My husband and I often discuss how well everything had turned out for us. Our daughter is married. Babamoshai is near us.

He is more like a son, and most of his conversation is with me. He often spoke about my mother-in-law, her views, her way of doing things, her food habits, etc. Such conversation always cheered him. When I first came as a bride Babamoshai not only had all his meals and slept in the baithak khana but also carried out his daily worship and meditation there. So there was no chance of my meeting him.

This description of Mohitkumari depicts accurately the general situation in well-to-do Bengali families. Jnanadanandini's writings also give us similar indications but the Maharshi's family was changing rapidly. Neither in Gaganendranath, Samarendranath and Abanindranath's families, nor in Mohitkumari's father's house were the delineations so rigid. Mohitkumari's widowed sister-in-law Surendrabala was at the helm of affairs in this house but even she never thought of persuading her father to move into the andar mahal. It was Mohitkumari who brought this about.

Every member of Mohitkumari's husband's family was of a devout nature and Mohitkumari herself was no exception. However, her autobiography *Sadhuma's Katha* indicates that unlike Sangya Tagore's quest for spiritual truth, Mohitkumari turned to God the way ordinary human beings do when in distress. She would pray to the family deity 'Gopal' installed in the second floor of the house. She said, 'Someone seems to whisper in my heart, "Pray to Madhusudhan and keep reciting his name, this crisis will pass, the slander levelled against you will disappear". As I went on doing so my heartache slowly abated.' After her husband's death she renounced the world. Taking the name of Mahanandi Bharati she took to wandering as an ascetic. Unfortunately the last pages of *Sadhuma's Katha* were not printed and so there is no way of ascertaining anything more about her.

Moved by Sunandini's tears, her distressed father Gaganendranath vowed, 'I shall never marry off a daughter at the age of nine.' This despite the fact that a proposal for his second daughter came just two days after Sunandini's marriage.

Kalikrishna Tagore's youngest daughter Prabhaboti was charmed by the seven-year-old Purnima. She said to Pramodkumari, 'I want to request you for your younger daughter. This is for Mejodidi (Sarojini's) youngest son Nishanath'. This was the usual way in which marriages were arranged in large families. A girl from outside the family circle was chosen by the Tagores only if no one suitable from the various branches was available. Though Purnima's marriage was fixed, it was decided not to hold it until she was twelve. One day Sarojini sent word that she would like to bring the girl over to show her to Kalikrishna Tagore. In Purnima's own words, 'I immediately began to cry. I thought that I would be kept there by force just like Didi was at her in-laws' place.' She was persuaded after much coaxing and came back loaded with toys. She continues, 'Since then they would take me often. I also felt braver. These visits stopped a year before the wedding. My grandmother said, "She must not go anymore. The boy and the girl should see each other at the time of *Shubha Drishti*. The girl is grown up and they should not see each other." I was twelve at the time of my marriage and even then my grandmother said "She is quite old now".' These were the usual practices in aristocratic families, to acquaint a girl with the customs and norms prevalent in her husband's family home.

Reverting to Sunandini and her accomplishments—though she was not of a literary turn, she was a superb craftswoman. She was adept at making rag dolls. These were known as *guria putul*. She was instrumental in that early era of patriotism in diverting people's taste from foreign dolls to home-made Indian ones. Her dolls in the guise of a snake-charmer and a betel-seller were enchanting. The snake-charmer doll was awarded a prize by the Hitakarini Sabha as well as the Calcutta Exhibition. Handmade toys and dolls crafted by women fetch a high price nowadays. It was from the Tagore family that appreciation of such cottage handicrafts began. Sunandini had a beautiful voice and was a good actress. Once she played the role of Giribala in the play *Mrinalini*, charming everyone by her singing and acting. Mohitkumari never barred Sunandini from such varied means of self-expression. Her heartache for her own mother must have been assuaged by Sunandini's spontaneous lifestyle. Along with her happy temperament Sunandini was very good at fooling people. Numerous people were taken in by her '*charchari*' made of grass. At that time it was a favourite pastime of women to fool a new bridegroom. Whenever such a young man visited his wife's parental home, Sunandini was summoned to lend a hand. She joined whole-heartedly in what was to her another art form. Countless sons-in-law of the Tagore home have been fooled by her 'rabri' made of blotting paper, 'beguni' of cotton wool and stir-fried bits of straw.

Purnima was as artistic as Uma. Her expertise as a needlewoman, especially the designed kanthas embroidered by her, have to be seen to be believed. She was also very good at making paper houses, dry fruit dolls and pictures by arranging various coloured lentils on paper. Artist daughter of an artist father, she never ignored even that which could be created from simple and insignificant materials. What was the utility of such creations? Such paper houses were used in decorating the 'tattwa' sent during weddings. These were real showpieces among the wealthy homes in Bengal even in the last century. The 'tattwas' sent during weddings of the Tagores were elaborate affairs. About a hundred to a hundred and fifty bearers and maids would be sent carrying trays and baskets laden with gifts. Apart from all the well-known sweets and savouries of Calcutta, there were various special items of Jessore. These comprised coconut-kernel sliced in the shape of flowers, cumin seeds and puffed rice cooked in sugar. There would be 'batasha' covering a whole tray, 'kadmas' filling a wicker-basket and khoya dolls. Along with these eatables were sent trays laden with dry-fruit dolls or various pictures made with lentils. Such articles were perishable and were lost after giving transient pleasure but the tradition of sending an elaborate 'tattwa' still persists in Bengal. Many women today have adopted the decorating and arranging of 'tattwa' as a profession, unaware of Purnima's name and the fact that such work was made into an art form by Gaganendranath's daughters.

Like Uma, Purnima also wrote about her father and her home. A perusal of this brings back the lifestyles of those times vividly. She says, 'Once *Daakghar* was staged. The stage was erected in the hall of Rabidada's *Lal Bari* (red house). Baba played the role of Pishemoshai and Chhotokaka that of the village headman. There was a great rush for tickets, people nearly came to blows in their eagerness to buy them. Even hundred-rupee tickets were bought at the last minute. All the three brothers acted well. I stood at the window in Baba's room and watched the performance. Due to the disapproval of my husband's family I could not go to Rabidada's house to see the play.' The andar mahal of the Pathuriaghata Tagores was still separated from the Maharshi's family by a wide gulf. Changes were taking place but at a very slow pace. The year Purnima was married an All India Exhibition was held in Calcutta. To quote Purnima, 'At the time the women of our family did not go out of doors.' Gaganendranath requested Purnima's mother-in-law for permission to take Purnima along with his family. He was keen that Purnima should see the exhibition and promised that no one would come to hear about it. Purnima continues, 'My father-in-law was considerably liberal. He told my father, "Take her with you. This is the chance of a lifetime. These women will neither go themselves nor allow others to do so."' The sequel is rather amusing and gives a glimpse of the impending social changes. 'At that time my husband's maternal grandfather Kalikrishna Tagore had expired. Prafullanath Tagore was still a minor and the Pathuriaghata Tagore family ran on the dictates of Jatindramohan Tagore. My mother-in-law was very keen to see the exhibition but was rather hesitant. My father said to her,

"Why are you so worried? You are not committing any crime. If you are afraid of public criticism, I shall take you along with the ladies of my family. No one will be any the wiser." . . . My father took me to see the exhibition first and then he took my mother-in-law. My elder sister-in-law went with her father. It was only then that Prafullanath Tagore was emboldened enough to take the ladies of his family to the exhibition.'

After completing *Thakurbarir Gagan Thakur*, Purnima had begun to write about herself and her family through an allegorical tale. It was meant for her grandsons. The incomplete manuscript was titled *Chander Bari* and in it Purnima, her husband and others were portrayed as inhabitants of heaven. Purnima was depicted as a beautiful girl who had descended to earth. Unfortunately the tale did not progress far.

Gaganendranath's youngest daughter Sujata, though highly accomplished, always shied away from publicity. She learned to sing just by listening to her elder sisters but would never agree to sing before anyone. Purnima tells us, 'She would stand near me and listen to the music and songs. That is how she picked up music. One day while she was repeating the song standing on the verandah downstairs, our grandmother Saudamini heard her.' Though Saudamini summoned Sujata to her and asked her to sing again. Sujata was too shy to do so. Saudamini told Gaganendranath, 'Your youngest daughter has a lovely voice. Get Shyamsundar to teach her.' Purnima gives us an account of Sujata's mellifluous voice. 'Once Father threw a big party. Many Englishmen were among the invitees. Haashi (Sujata) was not married then and father made her sing Rabidada's *Jeeboney jato pooja holo na sara*. The audience was spellbound and appeared not conscious of the fact that the drinks' glasses were slipping from their hands!' The last line not only gives us a glimpse of the party but reveals Purnima's sense of humour.

Like her elder sisters, Sujata was also of an artistic bent and interested in handicrafts. Many people may still remember the cottages made by the various ingredients of preparing 'paan'. Sujata's artistic vision was blended in these cottages and they formed an essential part of wedding 'tattwas'.

Sujata's husband Saroj Mukhopadhyay was descended from Ishwarchandra Vidyasagar's son. Her home was near Park Circus and Gaganendranath had decorated it with some of his own paintings. This was ransacked during the 1946 riots of Calcutta. Sujata had to refurnish and decorate a new home. She used *paan mashla* not only to depict cottages but also musical instruments like the sitar, tabla and harmonium. On the occasion of Sharmila's wedding she made an entire cricket team! Sujata was always keen to create dolls or other ornamental articles from discarded things and herein lay her achievement. It is easy to prepare dolls and decorative articles from new ingredients but not so from leftovers. As a child Sujata saw her uncle Abanindranath utilizing all such material. He transformed pieces of wood into 'kutum katam' and also decorated his manuscripts with pictures created out of newspaper cuttings, labels from sarees and bottles, pictures of actresses, advertisements and cartoons. A very good example was the manuscript of *Khudur Ramayana.* He pasted Hitler's head on Ravana's shoulder! He believed that nothing was too insignificant for an artist. Sujata also used ice cream popsicles to make dolls houses and small discarded bottles for pincushions, salt cellars and dolls. Today numerous women have earned credit by making decorative dolls out of leftover material. This art of transforming the insignificant into something beautiful was a characteristic of the Tagore women. Apart from their own artistic temperament, association with Japanese artists helped them develop an eye for aesthetic beauty in seemingly insignificant things. Besides, village women of Bengal had been experts for ages in their creative genius. The most common example involves the recycling of old sarees and other materials into beautifully designed kanthas with thread drawn from those very saree borders. Sujata's sisters were very good at making kanthas and she may have picked up handicrafts from them.

Sujata, unlike her sister Purnima, never wrote much. However, on request from the members of the Gaganendranath Centenary Committee, she wrote a small article. It is a very informal piece of work and gives just a glimpse of her unending memories of her father. She says, 'At Darjeeling, Baba would keep gazing at Kanchenjunga enraptured. He taught us to see the vision as it appeared to his artistic eye. We could plainly see the features of a reclining Mahadev with the lines of his face clearly discernible. Until then we had only perceived it as a snow-capped peak.'

This ability to help people see beyond the apparent was characteristic of Abanindranath and Gaganendranath. Sujata also found satisfaction in creative handicrafts. She also won a couple of awards for her 'alpana' and needlework. Abanindranath had taught her the art of bonsai. Even in her old age she would show people her fifty-year-old banyan tree which still lived.

Like most ladies of the Tagore family Sujata was very good at bridal make-up. Such was her expertise that even a homely girl looked beautiful after Sujata had made her up. When Latika's daughter Ira's wedding was fixed she wanted Sabita to dress and make her up on her wedding day and Sujata to perform the same job on the day of her *bou-bhaat*. Due to unavoidable circumstances none of these wishes could be fulfilled. Sujata was always in great demand for this job, not only in her family circle but also among friends. Even in her old age, when her hands were no longer steady, she never refused to dress a bride. She had noted with amazement that however modern otherwise, a girl always preferred the traditional bridal dress and make-up on her wedding day. Sujata's granddaughter Shinjita had also asked for her grandmother's artistic touch to make her up on this most important day.

Bridal make-up reminds us of another lady who was superb in this art. The lady was Samarendranath's daughter Madhabika, one of five sisters. Besides Madhabika's twin Malabika there were Supriya, Kamala and Anima. Madhabika's husband Sachindranath Bhattacharya was the younger brother-in-law of Renuka, Rabindranath's second daughter. Apparently every aristocratic family had its own characteristic make-up for brides and the Tagore family was no exception. Nowadays the usual method is to dip the end of a clove in sandalwood paste and dot the bride's face with various designs. In the Tagore family the entire forehead would be covered with sandalwood paste and then a fine comb would be drawn over it. These combs were a specialty of Jessore. When the fine lines of sandalwood paste from the eyebrows to the hairline had dried up, designs would be made on them with vermillion and other ingredients.

When Indira decided to collect and publish details of the various *stree aachar* during a typical wedding she turned to Madhabika for help. Not only had Madhabika been present in numerous weddings in the large joint family, her keen interest in all such matters had helped her remember the minutest details. It is from her account that we learn about the *stree aachar* during weddings in the Tagore family. Even after embracing Brahmoism, the Maharshi had not done away with this aspect of a wedding. In house number 5, the traditional customs were all followed. Madhabika remembered all the rituals or *reet* as they were called. Beginning with the *gaye halud*, they continued for nine days after the wedding. The description given by Madhabika is by and large the same as those observed in West Bengal. To quote her:

> After *baran* the mother accepts *kanakanjali* from the son. In a small round dish is placed a small quantity of *atap* rice and a one rupee-coin. This is given to the bridegroom while his mother stands before him with her saree-pallau outspread. She asks him thrice 'My son, where are you going?' The son replies, 'Mother, I am going to get a daughter-in-law for you.' After repeating this thrice he pours the rice and the one rupee into his mother's saree-pallu. He then makes his obeisance to the god Narayan and to his mother and then he leaves. After

the *sampradaan* the news has to be conveyed to the mother. She then boils the *kanakanjali* rice and breaks her day-long fast with this cooked rice, milk and sweets.

There were rules and rituals governing the nine-day-long wedding festival of the Tagores. Madhabika writes,

> On the third day after the wedding, the bride and groom go to the bride's place and come back together. This is known as *dhulopaye gaman*. Then on the ninth day is *jor bhanga*. The bride and groom go to the bride's house. The bride's mother welcomes them into the house after performing *baran*. Then the red thread tied round the wrist is untied, conch-shell bangles are removed and the girl wears a black-bordered saree. The *gaant-chhara* is also untied that day. The groom returns home while the bride stays with her mother. This is called '*jor bhanga*'. For eight days one has to keep *dari sindoor*. On the ninth day the *dari sindoor* is shortened and vermillion is applied over a short length of hair-parting by the bride.

Among the Tagores taking off the conch-shell bangles and jewellery was known as shithlano. Probably the phrase 'taking-off' was considered inauspicious and *shithil kara,* which means 'loosening', was used instead. This colloquially became *shithlano* or *shitlono*. Even in Mohitkumari's autobiography we came across the phrase 'My jewellery was *shithlayeed*'. She further mentioned,

> For eight days after the wedding, the bride has to eat fish and rice for both lunch and dinner. During these eight days, she cannot touch a widow or use a black ribbon for her hair. The hair must not be plaited but coiled into a bun.

Madhabika, with her eye for detail, has recorded practically all the rituals. She appears simply as Madhabika Bhattacharya in the book.

Madhabika's twin Malabika had been an expert at composing rhymes and limericks since her childhood. Once she chose a relative as her subject and was suitably reprimanded by her grandmother

Saudamini. However the limerick amused Saudamini. There is no record of this humorous lady indulging in such compositions later in her life as well. Another sister, Kamala, wrote poetry and quite a few of her unpublished poems still exist. She was also associated with a few women's organizations. In a poem written after her daughter's death she seems to have adopted the style of prose rhythm:

Amar hritpindo chinre kede
Niyechhe ke takey, shob shunya kore diye
Tar porey tar bondhu duti eshe
Boshlo amar kachhe, ekbar
Amar dike cheye matha royilo
Nichu kore, chokher jal nile
Shamle amar kachhe, Mashima
Bole dakle amay tara;
E janmer moto shey gelo chole, rekhe
Gelo bujhi, eder amar kachhe
Bholate amay.

Tearing my heart apart, who
has taken her away,
Turning everything barren.
Then her two friends
Came and sat near me, once
They glanced at me, then
remained with bowed heads,
Their tears they did not shed, Mashima (aunt)
They called me.
She has left me forever, perhaps
Leaving these two near me
To console me.

Uma had two siblings—Karuna and Surupa. A third died in her infancy. Karuna was married to Manilal Gangopadhyay. Unfortunately she died young, leaving three small children. The youngest, Surupa, was married to Dheerabala's grandson of the Koilahata Tagore family. She is mentioned here to avoid confusion.

As a young girl Surupa charmed the audience as Sudha Malini in *Daakghar*. Once Rabindranath requested Abanindranath to bring a small girl from his family. Until then no one had dared use child actors and actresses on the stage though every child in the Tagore family could sing reasonably well. Rabindranath was the first person to point out the ability and sense of responsibility shown by children when on the stage. Abanindranath brought Surupa along. Though slightly scared, she read out a small portion of *Daakghar*. Rabindranath approved saying, 'Aban, prepare her for Sudha's role. Do not drill her too much. Let her act naturally.' Surupa writes, 'Father would dress me in a red saree worn tightly, my hair in a bun on top of my head, a bead necklace, anklets, a basket of flowers in one hand and a doll under the other.' Sudha's reminiscences give us other details about the staging of *Daakghar*. Chairs had been placed just in front of the stage for Lord Carmichael and other distinguished guests. Samarendranath had arranged red roses in a flower vase placed on a table. Surupa immediately asked for a red rose to put in her wicker basket. Samarendranath refused saying, 'Your basket should be empty since you are supposed to go and pick flowers.' But since Surupa was adamant, Rabindranath intervened, 'Let her have one. After all a "malini" may have a garden in her own home and this may have come from there.' In that particular show of *Daakghar* Asha Mukul Das played the role of Amal. The play was staged for five days with everyone turning in an excellent performance. After every show the two child artists were warmly felicitated by the audience. According to Surupa, 'Though no medals were awarded everyone was so affectionate. Rabidada was pleased, he gifted a lovely green silk zari-bordered handkerchief for my doll.' Later whenever there was a suggestion of staging *Daakghar* Rabindranath would sigh, 'My Amal and Sudha have grown up, who will enact these roles?'

Rabindranath was very fond of Surupa and always addressed her as 'Malini'. Perhaps he composed the poem *Daarey keno nara diley ogo malini* with his 'Malini' in mind. Surupa did not continue with acting. Once she played the role of Malati in *Natir Puja*. It was not preplanned and happened by mere chance. Referring back to Surupa's account, '*Natir Puja* was to be staged in the wide verandah of the Maharshi's house. A group of girls had come from Shantiniketan to enact the various roles. Just a day before the show the girl who was to portray Malati came down with high fever. Rabidada ordered Dinudada, "Go, bring my Malini." Dinudada rushed in like a portly barge, took hold of me and presented me to Rabidada. Turning a deaf ear to all my pleadings and excuses about lack of time he said, "You have to act. I shall tutor you myself." Rabindranath had taken great pains and the show passed off well. Later he called Surupa to the verandah upstairs, garlanded her and said, "This is your prize."'

Though she did not act much Surupa wrote fairly regularly, mainly poetry and articles. Her articles covering her memories of Abanindranath, Somendranath and 'Sudhasmriti' from *Daakghar* are scattered over the pages of various magazines.

Every girl in this family was made proficient in all the household arts, especially cooking and kantha stitching. The last was a speciality of the girls of house number 5. Needlework was certainly taught to young girls of other families but there is no record of their proficiency in making nakshi kanthas. A needy Brahmin, Harish Chandra Haldar lived in this house. Apart from doing stage decorations and being a general factotum, an important job of his was to draw various designs of nakshi kanthas to be made and to teach the girls the various stitches needed to embroider them. Uma and Purnima were masters in this art while the others were passable. Like her father, Surupa was adept at creating artistic objects from seemingly insignificant things. She prepared *kutum katam* from sea shells. To encourage the literary aptitude of the younger members of the family, Abanindranath asked them to write down their dreams. He bought 'Srirampuri paper' which could be rolled up as horoscopes. This novel dream book has the writings of many members, both young and old. There are two by Surupa. One of them goes as follows, 'One day Shovanlal and I were standing in the outer verandah. Kalu was making ghostly noises from the schoolroom to scare us. Suddenly he called out, "Shovanlal, come and see." Both of us ran and saw Tukuni with a number of pigeons perched on a rod. Baba was sitting and the head-gardener stood nearby. I wanted a small white one from among the pigeons and requested Baba to buy it. Baba refused saying, "It is a ghost pigeon." Our head-gardener also said, "Don't take that one. A black pigeon roams about here, catch it." Just then a black pigeon did pass by. We caught it and went back to our room.'

Dreams may not have any meaning but Surupa's account of her dream certainly backs her father's theory that these can suggest good plots for fiction. Surupa was only twelve at that time. Had she kept up the habit she may have been able to create more besides the meagre number of reminiscences and articles.

Quite a few girls entered house number 5 of Jorasanko as daughters-in-law. Gaganendranath had celebrated his eldest son Gehendra's marriage with great splendour. Purnima tells us, 'On a long strip of yellow satin resembling a horoscope was written in red ink the date, time and names, like a zodiac. The entire strip of satin was rolled on to a small piece of sandalwood and tied with a silk thread having zari tassels at both ends.' This set the fashion for having wedding invitations shaped like horoscopes. This was the first marriage in Gaganendranath's family. He had wanted to invite all his relatives and friends and have what was termed *dhala nimantron*. Purnima further narrates, 'There was a lot of factionalism in society so it was decided to have the *dhala nimantron* apart from the social functions. On the day of the theatre there would be no sit-down meal but snacks and sweets served buffet-style and everyone would be invited.' In spite of such a lovely wedding, Gehendra's marriage did not turn out to be happy. He died within a year. Gaganendranath was keen to get Gehendra's widow Mrinalini remarried since Pratima's remarriage had already taken place. Mrinalini refused and she too passed away soon after.

The match between Gaganendranath's second son Kanakendra and Suramasundari was fixed when Surama was barely three years old! Surama's mother Sarajubala was the sister of Gaganendranath's daughter Sunandini's husband. The pretty little girl would visit the Tagore family-garden to watch fireworks and she was chosen for her beauty. She was very fair with cheeks as red as pomegranates. The flush deepened when she smiled. She had been brought up by Mohitkumari who observed, 'The child has a quaint charm of her own and was able to captivate all those around her. Her bewitching looks and innocent gaze made everyone love her.' Surama was good in dramatics and often participated in the various performances held at *Bichitra*. Once *Shakuntala* was staged as a tableau. Surama was Dushyanta and Sudhindranath's daughter Ena portrayed Shakuntala. On another occasion Surama played the role of Pashupati in *Mrinalini*. Her ability to impersonate male characters well prompted the jovial Gaganendranath to dress her up as a 'durwan'. The plan was to fool an elderly lady who was a regular visitor to their house as well as to that of Maharaja Jatindramohan Tagore. Surama, impersonating a 'Bhojpuri durwan', with a huge turban and a formidable moustache, entered the courtyard. She banged the stick in her hand and informed the elderly lady concerned that she had been sent to escort her to Jatindramohan Tagore's place. The lady was completely taken in and stood up saying, 'Come, let us go'. The assembled ladies burst into laughter. Pramodkumari came and said, 'Barama, that is Surama. The girls have dressed her up as a durwan to trick you.' The lady was furious and it took a great deal of tactful apologizing and coaxing to pacify her. Such jokes often enlivened the atmosphere of the andar mahal. Gaganendranath of course solemnly remained behind the scene.

Gaganendranath's third son Nabendra was married to Aparna, the daughter of Nalini and Surhit Chaudhuri. We have come across Aparna's younger sister earlier. The match was probably arranged by Dwipendranath but Rabindranath refused to accept the wedding invitation. Nalini had objected strongly when told that the ceremony would have to be held according to Hindu rites. It appears that Rabindranath mentioned this as the reason for his refusal. Indira believed that the marriage rituals in the bride's home should be according to *their* religious beliefs. After marriage, when living with her husband's family, the girl should observe the norms prevalent there, provided she had no objections. Indira's comment was, 'In our society girls are considered so easy to come by and helpless, that the groom's family is able to exert unjust pressures and impose their views on the girl's family.' It is amusing to note that in this case the groom's party was none other than Gaganendranath's family who had always been very close to the Maharshi's family. Indira did not spare the Brahmo families from her caustic comments:

> The only objection that Brahmos can have to a wedding performed according to Hindu rites is if there is any idol-worship involved. As far as I know in a Bengali Hindu wedding the 'Shalgram' or 'Narayan Shila' is there just as a witness. Not only is the Shila not worshipped, no obeisance has to be made either. If that is the case, what objection can a Brahmo groom have in having the wedding rites in a room where the 'Shalgram Shila' is present? Nothing stops one from considering it as an inanimate object like the furniture in a room.

She had of course hit upon the crux of the matter—the helplessness of the bride and her family. As she continues,

> It is difficult to give up rituals which have been handed down through generations. It hurts one's ingrained superstitions and family pride, particularly if it has to be for a woman. The general notion is that all the sacrifices should be on her side. Yet such trivial differences of opinion are leading to so many

good proposals being nipped in the bud and causing a great deal of unhappiness.

Marriages in the Tagore family—of both men and women—often led to unpleasantness: one of the main reasons was the difference in the rituals followed by the Brahmos and Hindus. This was however not the only reason. Nagendra and Mira were both Brahmos, yet considerable unpleasantness had arisen during their wedding.

Aparna had practically all the accomplishments common to the girls of the Tagore family. She not only played the violin well but also sang well. Her rendering of two songs *Danriye achho tumi aamar* and *Jodi prem diley na praney* were unmatched. She acted very well as Ila in *Bhairaber Boli* as well as in a few other plays. Later she became totally involved in daily family life. The name 'Aparna' was also rather unusual at the time. Indira says,

> We named her Aparna as it was uncommon, of course it has become very popular now . . . I had gifted her a brooch showing her name—a gold leaf with an 'A' before it and a straight line after it. In Bengali 'parna' stands for leaf and the A before and short straight line after the leaf signified 'Aparna'.

Among the young girls who entered Samarendranath's family about this time, Umashashi and Shibarani were from related families. Umashashi was the granddaughter of Nirajini, the eldest daughter of Kalikrishna Tagore of Pathuriaghata. Nirajini's younger sister Sarojini's son was already married to Gaganendranath's daughter Purnima. The marriage could not be held on the scheduled date as Umashashi came down with measles. There was quite a fracas over this. The day before the wedding Sunayani came to her mother and said, 'You appear to have everything ready for the wedding. I have just been to the girl's place. They are also busy with preparations but it will be impossible to make the girl sit on the *pinri* tomorrow and have the *gaye halud*.' On being questioned by Saudamini, Sunayani continued, 'The girl is down with measles. She is running a high fever and her face is swollen with rash. She is unable even to sit up. Her family is trying to suppress the attack with medicines and she may die. Either you postpone the date or stop the wedding altogether.' Saudamini was very annoyed and said, 'Summon Gagan and Samar. Ask the coachman to harness the horses. I want to go and see for myself. If necessary I shall have the wedding solemnized with some other girl on the same date.' On her return from the girl's place. Saudamini opined, 'Had I known about this earlier, the wedding date could have been postponed. Now with this last minute hitch I want to solemnize the marriage with another girl on the same date and time.' She called their old barber Chandra and said, 'Go to Chhoto Raja's residence. My niece's daughter is there. She is very pretty. Tell them I want her as a bride for Surindra. Fix up the match, you will be handsomely rewarded.'

'Chhoto Raja' was Saurindramohan Tagore. As the barber was getting ready to leave, Gaganendranath intervened. He told his mother, 'Cool down and then we will think of another bride'. Saudamini replied, 'Then go and fetch Kakima from Koilahata. Let us hear what she advises.' Kakima was Nagendrabala, the daughter-in-law of Ramanath Tagore. The Tagore mansion of Koilahata was the residence of Dwarkanath's stepbrother Ramanath. It was very close to the former's house and was identical to the Maharshi Bhawan in design. The entrance was from Ratan Sarkar Garden Street. It was where the Venkatesh Temple now stands. The members of this family have been scattered all over Calcutta since the forties of the last century. Nagendrabala was the mistress of the Koilahata house and soon came in her palki. She said, 'It may be better not to proceed with the wedding since there has been a hitch and you are also in doubt.'

Gaganendranath patiently explained to Saudamini why such a decision would be wrong. 'If we cancel the wedding now it will be very difficult for the girl's father to find another suitable groom. I am sure you realize his predicament. It was not correct on our part to have fixed the match so early.'

Saudamini was convinced by the logic of Gaganendranath's words. After all, what would the girl's father do and where would he find another suitable groom? It was sheer helplessness that had forced him to risk a sick child's marriage. However, bent on not retreating from her notions and determination, Saudamini compromised by saying, 'All right, I will have the wedding solemnized with the same girl but not from Kumud's house. If they agree to bring the girl to Sarojini at Pathuriaghata, only then will the ceremony take place.' As soon as Purnima informed her mother-in-law, she agreed with pleasure. After all, the girl was her late elder sister's granddaughter. Thus Umashashi entered the family as a bride in the month of 'Asaar' and not 'Maagh' as had been decided earlier.

The entire incident has been presented to us by Purnima. Noteworthy is the trivial reasons that led to a marriage being cancelled at the time. Any hitch was always considered inauspicious and worried the womenfolk. If the cancellation was at the last minute, it could lead to considerable loss of face and money. All these considerations may have prompted Saudamini's reaction. It is also obvious that in such matters the decision of the mistress of the house was final. This was one instance where the last word was not by the master of the family. It is true that Gaganendranath's sound advice prevailed but that did not diminish the dominance of the andar mahal. Perhaps 'dominance' is too strong a word, 'authority' might be a better choice.

Bratindranath's first wife Santimoyee was the daughter of Satyabala Desai. Apart from being well-liked by everyone for her sweet temperament, not much is known about her. Bratindranath's second wife Vina was a film actress. She appeared in a few Hindi movies. Nothing else could be ascertained about her.

Jayindranath's wife Shibrani was a good singer, like her sister Satirani. She had been tutored in Rabindra Sangeet by her aunt. However, her talent did not spread beyond her home and was lost in the darkness of oblivion.

Parul was Saudamini's granddaughter, and the youngest daughter of Irabati. There were two Saudaminis living in the two adjacent houses number 5 and number 6 at Jorasanko. One was the daughter of the Maharshi and the other the wife of Gunendranath. Both were great friends and each became *soi* for the other since they had the same name. Originally they had decided to marry Irabati's daughter Indrani to Abanindranath. The close relationship however prohibited such a match. Many years later when Irabati gave birth to another daughter, Abanindranath's mother Saudamini came to see the baby. She was so taken by the three-day-old child that she chose her then and there as the future bride for Abanindranath's eldest son Alokendra. The baby girl Parul was later married to Alokendra, though by then Saudamini was no more. Her family had honoured her word.

Parul's mother Irabati was the daughter of Saudamini and the granddaughter of the Maharshi. Parul, her youngest daughter, was thus a grand-niece of Rabindranath. Parul had been coached in vocal music and the sitar by Surendranath Bandopadhyay before her marriage and thereafter by Shyamsundar Mishra. She also learnt painting from Nandalal Bose but she was always diffident about appearing in any public performance. This was perhaps due to her preference to stay behind the scenes. Rabindranath however persuaded her once to accept a role in *Varshamangal*. She only agreed when assured that she would not be required to sing or speak on the stage. She appeared as 'Sharat Lakshmi', with her lovely tresses flowing, and the song *Hey kshaniker atithi* heard. Her role consisted of entering the stage silently, with the song, and then walking out backwards. Unlike modern times, no one was allowed to turn his or her back towards the audience while leaving the stage. One always had to walk backwards slowly.

Parul would often attend the sessions by Rabindranath in *Bichitra*. She had the privilege of hearing him recite *Shesher Kabita*. She had observed that when Rabindranath read out an amusing anecdote he never laughed himself but observed the reactions of those present. Many among the audience were hesitant about giving vent to their feelings. Parul, being his grand-niece, did not stand in awe of Rabindranath. She would burst out laughing whenever the occasion arose. Rabindranath would stop reading and question, 'Why are you all laughing?' This often silenced the others but Parul would retort, 'You are narrating such funny anecdotes, why shouldn't we laugh?' The answer obviously pleased Rabindranath because whenever there was a reading session in *Bichitra*, Parul would be summoned.

Saudamini, Abanindranath's mother, had passed away by the time Parul was married. The old traditions and customs however remained unaltered. Every morning the daughters-in-law had to sit down to prepare the vegetables for the various dishes. Suhasini would sit on a bare wooden divan. Porters would bring in their wicker-baskets laden with vegetables and fish. The old cook Basanta would come for instructions. Suhasini would dictate the menu for lunch in detail from start to finish. The daughters-in-law would sit with a *bonti* and a huge brass bowl full of water before each one. The maids would pare the skin off the vegetables and wash them. The daughters-in-law would then slice the vegetables into different shapes and sizes for the various dishes to be cooked. By the time Parul was married, the size of the kitchen had begun to shrink. But not so the daily menu. Thus Sumitendra's memory mainly comprises his mother,

> I can still see my mother, with her head covered by one end of her saree sitting in front of her mother-in-law. She would be cutting vegetables and putting them into large troughs full of water. The maids washed them and arranged them separately on large round metal trays or thalas.

Since there was a definite pattern for cutting the vegetables, their very shape and size enabled the cook to understand whether they were meant for a meat dish, a curry, a *qualia*, a stir-fry or deep frying.

The culinary excellence of the Tagore family was well-known. The members were gourmets who not only enjoyed good food but also loved to treat others to it. In those days, cooking was an art-form for women. It was one of the main modes of expression of their artistic abilities. Every girl had to learn the art, though daily spells in the kitchen may not have been necessary. A great deal of time was also spent in various crafts associated with the kitchen. Preparing *bori* was one of them. Sumitendra remembers,

> Ma and Didimoni would have sessions of preparing *bori* almost the whole year round, in the room where the vegetables were pared and sliced. Little cots made by binding flat pieces of fine wire-mesh in a wooden frame were placed before Ma and Didimoni. As each such cot was filled with *boris* it was taken away by the side of the inner courtyard either to the terrace above the Thakur ghar, to the verandah in the inner house or to the terrace beside the kitchen in the north. As each little cot was filled it was taken away to be sunned and immediately the maids would put another one before Ma and Didimoni. This went on for almost a fortnight every morning during winter. Various types of *boris*, small and large, were thus created by Ma and Didimoni.

Parul was also an expert at making paan. In those days this was a major task allotted to the daughters-in-law. A few hundred paans had to be prepared daily, not only for themselves but for others too. Usually after the main meal everyone had a paan, even those who were not addicted to it. Every guest was always offered a paan. Parul generally prepared paan using betel leaves, lime, catechu, finely sliced betel nuts, cinnamon and aniseed. The betel leaves with the condiments were folded in different shapes. According to Sumitendra,

> Ma folded the betel leaf into a triangle with a clove pinned in the centre. It reminded one of a nose-pin. Ma would count and

arrange the paans in the various small containers before her, close them and have them sent to the different rooms.

When Abanindranath's second daughter Karuna died, leaving three young children, Parul brought them up as her own. Sumitendranath told us about what he heard from Karuna's daughter Reba.

> Until her marriage, she used to address my mother as Ma. When her marriage was fixed, Ma called Didi aside and said that if her in-laws heard her addressing her aunt as Ma there may be some misunderstanding. Since that day Didi converted 'Ma' to 'Mamima'. This however had no effect on their relationship which always remained that of a mother and daughter, not an aunt and niece.

After she left the Jorasanko house, Parul was often inconsolable. She would wonder, 'Why was the house demolished?' The baithak khana house of Dwarkanath Tagore had been built forty years after house number 6, known as the Maharshi Bhawan. Had it been there next to the Maharshi Bhawan Parul would have been able to go and visit the lovely site occasionally.

Namita, the wife of Abanindranath's youngest son Manindranath, also came from a related family. Sumitendranath says, 'This match was arranged by my father's youngest sister.' That means Surupa. Surupa's husband and Namita were first cousins. Namita sang very well, especially classical songs. Her talent was restricted within the family circle. While reminiscing Sumitendra wrote, '*Kakima* had a melodious voice, classical songs rendered by her were most enjoyable.' Her daughters also sang well. At one time practically every girl was taught to sing. This custom was prevalent in many branches of the Tagore family.

Binayini's daughter Pratima has already been presented while discussing the members of house number 6, Dwarkanath Lane, Jorasanko. As the Tagore family expanded so did the complications of relationship among the members. Sometimes two people were related to each other by four or five connections!

Both the marriages of Pratima took place within the family circle. She and her first husband Nilanath were both descended from Girindranath Tagore. His daughter Kumudini was Nilanath's paternal grandmother while Pratima's mother was the daughter of Gunendranath who was again Girindranath's son. Similarly Binayini's daughter-in-law Chandrima was the daughter of Kadambini's grandson Jaminiprakash Gangopadhyay. Apart from being a paragon of beauty Chandrima was highly accomplished, though these never came before the public gaze. Educated at Loreto School, she was also a good cook like the other ladies of the Tagore family. Her real interest however lay in painting. Her father, a well-known artist, had also painted a portrait of his daughter. Chandrima's interest probably originated from her father and it is possible that she took her first lessons from him. During this era we come across numerous women painters. Painting was considered an essential accomplishment for girls of aristocratic families and most of them had teachers for this. Thus these girls were familiar with paints, canvases and brushes. This applies to the women of the Tagores too. Bound by numerous edicts and inhibitions, the world of painting provided them with full freedom of self-expression. The division of art into two categories—fine arts and handicrafts—and considering women as craftswomen, was a monumental error. This is clear when we observe the paintings by the female members of the Tagore family. They learnt to sketch and paint because they wanted to do so. It had nothing to do with designs in needlework or alpana. Unfortunately most such ladies have remained unknown since they never thought of exhibiting their work or participating in any art competition. Chandrima was one such person. Like her mother-in-law Binayini she painted in the privacy of her home. A few of her paintings still adorn her son's collection.

Sunayani had four sons and four daughters. For a number of years after marriage she lived in Jorasanko with her family. Later she shifted to her own home at Beniapukur. Here also the number of residents neared a hundred, comprising relations, various underlings and servants, besides her immediate family. Her eldest daughter Bina was married to Dinendranath Tagore but died of diptheria while still young. Among the others both Pravati and Anuja were married into well-known aristocratic homes. Pravati's husband belonged to the Roy family of Bowbazar. Their palatial mansion was the cynosure of all eyes. Anuja was married into the Koilahata Tagores. Her husband's grandmother Nripabala was the daughter of Kadambini. Kadambini on the other hand was Gunendranath's elder sister and thus she was Sunayani's aunt. This was again a marriage within the family circle.

As Sunayani's family expanded, her work-load grew. Gradually, four daughters-in-law came to share her domestic burden. The eldest among them was Kalyani, Anuja's husband's sister. Kalyani was only ten when she was married to Ratanmohan. Since the two families were already related Kalyani entered her new home on a tide of happiness and assurance. She loved to write and paint, apart from running the home well. Her father Jagadindranath Tagore was also a painter. Kalyani was an only daughter and both parents doted on her. Her father encouraged her to paint while her mother tried to shield her from all the vicissitudes of life. As per the prevailing tradition they had to marry off Kalyani at a tender age but she was fortunate in having found a conducive atmosphere at her husband's home. Sunayani was an artist herself and other women in her family had also taken lessons in painting. Not only were Kalyani's pictures selected for art exhibitions in Calcutta but they won prizes too. Kalyani was closely associated with the Calcutta branch of All India Radio. She had a melodious voice which stirred listeners and she was often summoned by the authorities for reading sessions. She usually read short stories, poems and skits that she had composed. Thus she became well known as a writer. Kalyani never mentioned herself in these literary compositions. However every work by an author is in some measure an autobiography. People who write their autobiographies are seldom able to express life in its entirety. A perusal of Kalyani's fiction convinces us that she drew upon her own experiences to write these. This comes to the fore when we read about Ranu, the heroine of 'Gauri Daan'.

> Ten-year-old Ranu was to be married. The proposal was from a wealthy family. It was always wise to get a daughter married if a suitable groom from a good family was available. This was the reasonable view of Ranu's father though her mother had not been very keen. Ranu's father was fulfilling his wish.

The character of Ranu's mother shows shades of Kalyani's mother Mahaprabha.

> She came as a stranger to her husband's family but soon became good friends with her sisters-in-law who were by her side though thick and thin. She had to put up with a lot of travail and whenever there was a moment to spare her heart would yearn for her dear parental home. Those days passed like water under the bridge. The memories of that restricted life within the walls of an aristocratic home have also disappeared like a dream.

This is not just an imagery of Ranu and her mother but also describes Kalyani's feelings. Had it not been so, her amazement on seeing a rose-shaped bulb or longing for a *ghagra*-clad doll would not have been so lifelike. Actually 'Gauri Daan' is a detailed description of weddings in the Koilahata Tagore family. The characteristic features of a bride's dress, hairstyle, make-up and toilette as prevalent in the Tagore family appear in this story too. 'The entire forehead was smeared with sandalwood paste, a fine ivory comb run over it and then a small dot drawn on it.' This has also been heard to be a speciality of the Tagore family. It is obvious that the members of the Tagore family, though scattered far and wide, had kept up the same customs and norms in every home. Another special custom: 'According to the prevailing norm an iron bangle bound in gold was put on the wrist next to the red conch-shell one.' Usually, the mother-in-law puts an iron bangle on the left wrist of a new bride, perhaps as a throwback to a woman's imprisoned state after marriage in ancient times. This bangle is never taken off during the husband's lifetime and often is not discernible among the other bangles. In the Tagore family, the girls wore iron bangles on both wrists. This was a special family tradition. One was from the parent's side while the other was given by the in-laws. Being bound in gold and alike in design, they often escaped notice. Though the custom of wearing iron bangles is on the decline, this tradition is still maintained in most Tagore families.

In 'Gauri Daan' Kalyani writes,

> The bridegroom's sisters have come with a box full of jewellery and sarees. They will dress up the bride in the clothes and ornaments belonging to their mother and grandmother before taking her away. The jewellery varied—pearl necklaces with seven strands, diamond tiaras, ornaments covering the ear, bangles, armlets and many others. This custom of dressing up the bride, though not common, is prevalent in Ranu's husband's family.

This was also a typical custom of the Tagores. Jyotirindranath had gone with a box full of ornaments for Prafullamoyee. At the time of Gehendra's marriage, Saudamini had sent her own jewellery to dress up the new bride. She felt that heavy ornaments were absolutely essential for a bride though the weight of gold used was being slowly reduced for convenience's sake. Again Mohitkumari, who was later Sunandini's mother-in-law, has narrated the story of her sisters-in-law coming with a casket laden with jewellery for her during her wedding. A detailed study of Kalyani's literary works gives us not only an insight into her own life but also a picture of contemporary society.

Only one of Kalyani's books *Mounarekha* was published after her death by her family. She wrote several other plays and novels. Though listed in the foreword of *Maunarekha* they are still unpublished. Works like '*Smriti*', '*Ekti Din*', '*Ashrujal*', '*Dotana*' and '*Panchashar*' are about characters she knew and about familiar surroundings. She never stepped out of her own experiences. There were two world wars during her lifetime, yet they did not influence her writings. Similarly she did not write anything about Independence or the Partition of India. But she did manage to paint an excellent picture about the cruel waste of a woman's potential. The heroine, Anju, of '*Ekti Din*' was married into a wealthy zamindar family. She lived with them in a palatial mansion in Calcutta. To quote from the book, 'Their lunch is not over till 4 p.m. and dinner at 1 a.m. Morning tea is at 10 a.m., when their day begins.' Visiting Anju to invite her for a wedding her friend saw,

> The car stopped before a palatial house . . . the way to the 'andar mahal' was indicated . . . a very long dark corridor. I stumbled and then somehow went ahead in the darkness. Ultimately I saw a staircase with a dim bulb above it. The steps were as narrow as they were steep. I never knew such houses existed in Calcutta. There was a verandah around a square courtyard. The whole house was full of ornate mirrors, marble tables, huge bedsteads, couches, armchairs, marble figurines and many other articles of furniture. It was obvious that these people were old aristocrats and did not belong to the nouveau riche.

A girl married into this family did not have the freedom to go out. She was only permitted to visit relations on the occasion of a wedding. To continue from the narrative,

> Anju's mother-in-law appeared. She said, 'I never go anywhere but I shall send Anju if my husband allows it. I do not think he will have any objection.' Thereafter she observed me for a while and asked several questions about my family. In the course of our conversation a distant link with us was also discovered. I of course hardly understood the tenuous relationship.

It is obvious that this description is based on Kalyani's own experience.

She has also written about the modern women of her time. Although the acknowledged beauties of society flitted like butterflies from musical soirees to tea parties, their marriages followed the traditional norms. Such girls often wove dreams around their tutors or some poor young man in the family. Kalyani never depicted marriage between such characters. This was because such marriages never took place in real life. This was because at that time girls believed, 'Bengali girls should not have an opinion of their own. It would not be correct.' Kalyani has tried to analyse the women's feelings. About one of her heroines Mili she says, 'Her quiet acceptance surprised many people but it was unnecessary. Sandip's good looks and wealth had attracted Mili towards him.'

Family and wealth were the criteria that determined the eligibility of a young man and often the girl herself helped in this choice, though she may have sighed over the poor boy who had touched the chords of her heart. Sometimes the girl's father would give preference to a young man's education over his finances but the mother would disagree. 'She is our only daughter and naturally we want a suitable son-in-law. Tarun is unable to satisfy any of the prerequisites for moving about in Calcutta society. He may be a good boy but that is not enough.' Kalyani's heroines are girls whose dreams touched all the colours of the rainbow but who lacked the determination to convert these into reality. One of her heroines, Ruma, agrees to marry an England-returned engineer sporting a diamond ring which dazzled the eyes of every prospective bride's mother. She did not like him but was too scared of her mother to refuse his suit. There had been several women already in this eligible young man's life. Yet Ranjan cannot be blamed either. He had taken Ruma's permission before presenting his suit to her guardians. This is why Kalyani's heroine Mili says,

> My husband spends every evening with his friends in revelry. Since I refuse to join in he has 'rewarded' me amply. My body

> is witness to these 'rewards'. I have to spend my whole life repenting the mistake I willingly made.

These sketches are strewn in the stories of *Mounarekha* and have considerable social significance. The resentment that accumulated in the minds of the poor against educated, wealthy and beautiful girls found expression in the writings of many authors. We have to search the works of women writers of the time to get a glimpse of the various shades of women's feelings in an era when they were still timid and did not stand on a firm footing. Kalyani's short stories have to be appreciated in this light.

Apart from short stories, Kalyani also wrote plays, especially humorous ones and skits. She staged *Ek Pashla*, with the help of her family members. The audience also comprised of the Tagore family and other relations. And two sons Rashmohan and Lokmohan played the part of the two widowed Pishis. Lokmohan's cousin Monishi enacted the role of Lokmohan's wife Geeta's husband. Kalyani directed the play herself. This has been narrated by Geeta's granddaughter Asmita. She heard it from someone else. It was the influence of the Tagore family that prompted Sunayani to have plays staged in the Chatterjee family. Kalyani kept up that tradition. The women of the Tagore family have always been known for their interest and participation in social service and education. As a child Kalyani had come in contact with Krishnabhabini Das. The latter had told Kalyani, 'To be a true partner of an educated man, the wife must be educated too.' Kalyani remembered this and also felt,

> Under the present circumstances every woman has to be independent. To achieve this, education and common sense are essential. If necessary women should be able to earn a living and stand on their own feet. Many become helpless after the husband's death or due to other complications in family life. If she has the necessary educational qualifications, the mental strength and the ability to depend on her own judgement,

> then it is possible for her to combat such odds and emerge victorious. It is far more honourable to earn one's own living than to depend on the charity of others.

This was in a radio talk delivered by Kalyani fifty years ago. Yet it is amazingly modern. She should also be remembered for her social service. She established the Kalyani X-ray fund with her own money. This is an important asset of the Bengal Tuberculosis Association and is used for the welfare of needy patients.

Manimala, the wife of Sunayani's second son Manomohan, belonged to the well-known Goswami family of Serampore. Though from outside the Tagore family circle, she entered Sunayani's household at the age of twelve as a bride due to her exceptional good looks. Among the Tagores, as in many others wealthy and aristocratic families, young brides were educated and made cognizant of the family traditions. This was especially true if the girl was from outside the related family circle. Manimala's husband went abroad for higher studies and Manimala was first coached by an English lady and later admitted to Diocesan School. Kalipada Ghosal instructed her in painting at home while another English lady was appointed to teach her the piano. Sunayani spared no efforts in training the young bride to be a befitting wife for her husband. Training in running a home was routine. All Sunayani's daughters-in-laws could paint and draw. Though she encouraged all of them, she never tried to instruct them. Manimala did not join college after passing the Senior Cambridge examination. Though she adapted herself well to her new home she never approved of the zamindari atmosphere prevalent with the aristocratic traditions therein. Fully aware of great waves of social change in the offing, her main purpose in life was to educate her children and to make them self-sufficient. To achieve this she sent her sons to Doon School. This was the first instance in the family of sending young boys so far away to study. It only came about Manimala's untiring efforts. Later she sent her daughters to study in Gokhale Memorial School and

Brabourne College, again going against the existing traditions. Manimala never neglected the traditional customs because of her modern outlook. She was a superb cook and an expert beautician, especially when it came to bridal make up. Her caring and charming behaviour captivated everyone around her. She had painted a large number of pictures but there were never exhibited. She never had any wish to do so since to her it was something she did for pleasure. One of the founder members of Sarada Sangha she later became its vice-president. Sunayani was so taken up with her loving nature that she preferred to stay with Manimala in her old age. Manimala took great pleasure in arranging and preserving Sunandini's paintings. When she wrote it was about Sunayani and not about herself. She had painted a portrait of Sunayani along with many others including one of Thakur Sri Ramakrishna Paramhansa Dev.

Binapani, wife of Sunayani's third son Sumohan, belonged to the Tagore family of Pathuriaghata. It was for this reason that no one from the Maharshi's family or from that of Mohinimohan Chattopadhyaya's attended the marriage. Even later, they refused to sit at the same table for a meal with members from Bina's parental side. It was not because they did not approve of Bina but because there was an unwritten rule in the two families. Perhaps the reason was that one branch was Hindu and the other was staunch Brahmo.

Bina was a very good singer. Rabindranath and his Shantiniketan rose above all the dissensions among the various branches of the Tagore family. Bina once composed a poem about Rabindranath.

Bahukal agey ek boishakhi dinete
Bhirechilo gaaner tori janhabi kuletey
Aaj jodi elo sei Panchishey Baisakh
Ore tora khol dwar baja re sankh.

Many years ago on a Baisakh evening
The boat of lyrics tied up on the shores of the Janhabi,

Now that the twenty-fifth of Baisakh is here again,
All ye open the door and blow the conch shell.

She wrote this much later in life though literary activities always interested her. The atmosphere in her parent's home was conducive too. Her elder brothers—especially Prabodhendunath—all wrote, sang and painted. Bina began writing when she was quite young. Her elder sister Subrata was a very good painter. Their maternal uncle Hiranmoy Raychaudhuri was a well-known artist. Both Prabodhendu and Subrata learnt painting and drawing from him. Bina was coached mainly after her marriage. She was however more interested in tapestry work than in painting pictures. At one time pictures made with wool on carpet material were very popular. It was the vogue to have such pictures—be it of the family house, or the goddess Annapurna—framed and hung on the walls of almost every Bengali home. Sunayani always encouraged Bina, saying that tapestry was also an art form. The medium of expression need not be the same for everyone. Bina also learnt batik from Kalipada Ghosal but she was more interested in writing, especially her experiences on visiting a new place. She wrote mainly poetry and some short stories, but she never thought of publishing them. One of her poems titled 'Beejmantra' goes as follows:

Pratham jedin elam aami
ei dharanir bookey
Matrinamer beejmantra
Uccharinu mookhey
Sedin thekey aaj abodhi
Daakchi ma ma boley,
Anya name diksha newa
Aar ki amar sajey.

The day I first came
To this world,
I uttered the 'Beejmantra'
of Ma.

Since that day I have
Been calling Ma, Ma,
How does it behove me
To take 'deeksha' in any other name?

Now we come to Sarojasundari's two granddaughters. Related by birth to two well-known families, they also had the misfortune of seeing two joint-families break up. A great deal would have remained unknown had Surabhi not decided to write down her memoirs in her old age. Her *Nana Ranger Dinguli* is a huge canvas portraying a wealth of varied experiences. They include Surabhi's family as well as the Tagores. The change that was wrought in women's psychology with time is obvious when the first thing Surabhi says is, 'At the age of ten I used to go to school dressed in a frock, yet my mother was married at that age.' This ability to express a great deal of sentiment in a few simple words is characteristic of Surabhi's style. Her adherence to truth and facts may have embarrassed quite a few but it has certainly brought to life the large mansion of Macleod Street and its inhabitants. Connected to the three main branches of the Tagores—Jorasanko, Pathuriaghata and Koilahata—she never had any interest in their internecine conflicts. As a child she often felt miserable due to the restrictions imposed by such differences of opinion.

One wonders if the quarrel between the two brothers, Nilmani and Darpanarain, over property and Nilmani's shifting to Jorasanko with his family, were the only reasons behind the permanent embittered feelings and strife. The families related to both the branches also became embroiled in this controversy. Why did the Chatterjee, Mukherjee and Ganguly families that were connected to both the branches by marriage have to keep up the estrangement? Yet on the surface everything appeared normal as the men-folk would meet each other and invitations were issued on all social occasions. During the marriage of Sunayani's granddaughter Rachana with Prasantanath—the third son of Prafullanath Tagore—Surabhi noticed, 'None of the ladies from the Jorasanko Tagores and our family went to Prafullanath Tagore's house for the wedding. Even the marital relationship was unable to bring about social acceptance. Even at my grandmother's place we never sat down to a meal with these people.' Sunayani seems to have been able to rise above such inhibitions since she chose two of her daughters-in-law from the Koilahata and Pathuriaghata Tagores. The Jorasanko Tagores did not maintain any connection with the family of Maharaja Jatindramohan Tagore. His grandson Jaladi Mukhopadhyaya's daughter was Surabhi's mother Prakriti. As mentioned earlier there was an altercation at the time of Prakriti's marriage to Mohinimohan. Furtunately Mohinimohan resolved it with his calm good sense. However Surabhi remembered her mother going to her parental home only once every year. The reason is there in Surabhi's narration, 'Jaladi Mukherjee could never forget that his grandfather was Maharaja Jatindramohan, nor could my grandmother that she was descended from the Koilahata Tagores and married into a royal family.' This pride was there in Prakriti as well. Observing the norms of her husband's family and those of her mother-in-law's family, i.e. the Jorasanko Tagores, she had no qualms about practically severing all relations with her parents. This exaggerated sense of pride no doubt made them continue with old family, feuds but it also endowed them with exceptional qualities: a blend of aristocracy with modernization, delicate and refined aesthetic taste, unusual artistic sense and the ability to transform their surroundings for the better, whatever be the circumstances; these qualities appear to be natural and inborn for them.

Surabhi was a student of Diocesan School along with her cousin Sujata. She was strong-willed and told her mother, 'I want to join art school to learn painting.' She had had artistic leanings since childhood. Both her mother and grandfather were good artists as was her paternal grand-aunt Sunayani. Painting was a common hobby of many women of the time. Sunayani had appointed teachers to instruct her daughters-in-law in painting and quite a few women of the Jorasanko family also indulged in this pastime. So Surabhi's desire to join art school was quite natural. Every year she would go to grand-aunt Sunayani's house during Saraswati Puja—no puja was allowed in her own home—and pray to the goddess with folded palms: 'Please bless me so that I am able to paint with a brush and paints. This is my earnest wish, please grant it to me.'

It is not known whether Surabhi's mother Prakriti ever encouraged her daughter in her artistic aspirations. Surabhi has just mentioned, 'Ma painted very well,' about her artist mother. She could have told posterity so much: were her first lessons in painting from her mother? There is no mention. Surabhi just mentions Prakriti telling her, 'Complete your studies first. Then we will engage a tutor to coach you in painting and drawing at home.' The main reason behind this decision according to Surabhi was, 'Mohinimohan did not approve of co-education. He had strong objections to my joining art school.' Surabhi did join art school ultimately. 'Because I felt that in a brush and paints lay my real vocation. I often dreamt about becoming a renowned artist.' All this happened much later. By then Prakriti had died and Surabhi came to know that Mohimohan had lost a great deal of money in the gold-mining business. To quote her:

> Within forty years the joint family nurtured by my grandmother broke up. Though we all remained in the same house our kitchens were now separate . . . The splendour of that huge mansion seemed to disappear in the twinkling of an eye. Not only did wealth and grandeur vanish but so did quite a few of the people therein.

Faced with the harsh realities of life Surabhi took up a job. By then Sarala had returned to Calcutta and opened a school in Scott Lane. She took Surabhi there and said, 'Try teaching for a while. You may feel better.' The work helped Surabhi regain her balance. The dark days showed no signs of abating. Mohinimohan's death left the three of them—Surabhi and her two brothers—orphaned and helpless. While Prakriti was there, she and Surabhi were regular visitors to Mukul De's art school. Surabhi had thus struck up a friendship with Mukul De's wife Bina. When a Women's Section was opened in the art school, Mukul De requested Bina and Surabhi to join. There they began to sketch and paint under Jainul Abedin. As Surabhi says, 'After my mother's death it was playing with paints that gave me some happiness.' Unfortunately, due to the advent of the Second World War, whose shadow had been looming large for a while, their lessons did not progress much further.

Rabindranath appears again and again in the writings of the women of his family. Various informal aspects of his may be seen in their memoirs. Though Surabhi had seen Rabindranath a couple of times earlier, no one had introduced her properly. After Prakriti's death, and the sudden demise of Rajen Ray—Ena's husband—Surabhi, Ena and her son Ranen went to Shantiniketan, probably in search of peace. Rabindranath was waiting for them in 'Punascha'. Surabhi says, 'We all bent down and touched his feet. Ena-pishi pointed to me and said, "This is Sarojapishi's granddaughter Surabhi." Thus my long cherished wish was fulfilled. Every evening we would go and sit with "Kartababa". When we returned after hearing him talk, I always felt as if we had come back from a devotional prayer meeting presided over by him.' One day Rabindranath told her, 'I want to sketch you.' He did so and showed it to her. As Surabhi kept quiet he said, 'Can't you recognize yourself? I told you that I shall paint you as you appear to me.' Though Rabindranath never told Surabhi what he saw, he told Krishna Kripalani, 'She has been badly hurt and is unable to conceal it. Her countenance is branded with the signs of some heart-breaking grief. I have visualized that in her portrait.' Later Surabhi asked Ena, 'Did you ever tell your Rabidada anything about me?' Ena replied, 'No, I never had the chance.' Surabhi realized, 'Only a person who has suffered pain can fathom another's heartache. Rabindranath had suffered several heart-rending bereavements. Thus my grief was apparent to him.' Surabhi had requested Rabindranath for her portrait. He refused, saying, 'Why should I give it to you? I have drawn it, so it is mine.' Though Surabhi was not upset, the actual picture for which she modelled was never identified. Later, her only photograph with Rabindranath was also lost from her collection.

Thereafter, Surabhi went to Simla with her brother. There she took up a job as a translator with a newspaper. To quote her, 'At that time news about the war would come in Bengali from Berlin, Rome and Tokyo. These were taped. I would go in the morning, play the tapes and translate the text from Bengali to English. Thereafter I would hand over the translations to my boss and return home in the afternoon. Surabhi mentioned two memorable incidents of this time. The first one is about Subhas Chandra Bose. Her two pishis Geeta and Deepti were acquainted with him and he had visited their Macleod Street house also. Surabhi writes, 'During the war Subhas Chandra Bose managed to give the armed and alert police force of the British the slip and escape to Germany. Later he created the Azad Hind Force/ Indian National Army abroad. One morning my boss summoned me and said, "You have to come to the office tonight. Subhas Bose will be speaking on the radio. You must not write down anything or discuss it with anyone.' I gave him my word and he was reassured. 'Subhas Bose travelled to Japan in a submarine from Germany. After landing in Japan he thanked the German officers. He spoke in Hindi, Bengali and English. He ended every speech with Jai Hind.'

The other incident was during Mahatma Gandhi's fast while he was interned in the Aga Khan Palace at Poona. 'That day his condition was critical. I had headphones attached to my ears but did not write down anything. All the while I thought, if Mahatma Gandhi dies I shall leave this office for good.'

These two incidents give us an idea of the variety of Surabhi's working life. No other woman of the Tagore family had ventured into such jobs before her. Later Surabhi decided to marry. She had certainly crossed the normal marriageable age for Bengali girls. Girls remaining unmarried was nothing novel in Mohinimohan's family. Two of his daughters never married. Surabhi's husband Sudeb Bhattacharya was her eldest pishi Sumana's stepson. Surabhi says, 'We first knew him as my pishi Sumana's stepson. All of us brothers and sisters used to call him "Dada". I was not in love with him at the time but we were good friends.' Sudeb proposed twice. She refused him the first time as she was worried about the social furore this marriage would create, in spite of the fact that no blood relationship existed between the two. Later she changed her mind, returned to Calcutta and informed Sudeb, 'All my connections with Macleod Street have been severed. If you want to marry me it will have to be at the Marriage Registrar's office in the High Court. I do not intend appealing to anyone for help.' Sudeb agreed and they were married forthwith. Sudeb's cousins on his mother's side stood by them at this time. A perusal of Surabhi's memoirs leaves us amazed at her grit and mental strength. With what ease she narrates, 'The news of our marriage was published in *The Statesman* the next day. I was mentioned as Mohinimohan's granddaughter. There was an uproar among the relatives all round Calcutta. Everyone was dismayed and began to look for us everywhere.' The first to accept the marriage and invite Surabhi and her husband over were Suprakash and his wife Tanuja. Suprakash was the grandson of Debendranath's daughter Saudamini while Tanuja was descended from Girindranath's daughter Kumudini. Rabindranath's daughter Mira was also there to bless the newly married couple. Nayanmohan's wife Mamata came when she learnt the whereabouts of Surabhi from Tanuja and took the couple to Macleod Street. Later other members of the family also came. Surabhi was relieved. 'My apprehensions disappeared completely. I felt delirious with happiness.'

A greater part of Surabhi's life after marriage was spent away from Calcutta, in Bombay. Though deeply involved in all family affairs she found time for other pursuits too. In 1953 she held an exhibition titled 'Hobbies and Handicrafts'. With her artist's vision and keen sense of aesthetics she purchased various earthenware pots of various shapes and sizes from the potter's colony at Dharavi. These were mainly used as receptacles for water. After Surabhi touched them up with her brush and paint they became beautiful articles for decoration. About this time she also began her literary pursuits. She started contributing articles on handicrafts in the Stanvac House Magazine, *Femina*, *Illustrated Weekly* and the *Times of India*. The handicrafts she discussed included the Bankura horse, Baluchari and Dhakai sarees, combs, etc. To quote her, 'From 1953 to 1965 I wrote a great many articles. It is impossible for me to list them now but I do remember this as a happy period in my life, writing for various magazines. I enjoyed my personal income, however meagre.' She was also associated with quite a few well-known advertising agencies. About this time she was appointed the chairman of the Museum Society and later became one of its principal trustees. Her selection to this high office amazed her. She opined, 'Usually it is the well-known and acclaimed who become the trustees of museums. I am just a housewife.' Surabhi's phenomenal success in this job proved that the selectors had not erred in their choice. She proved once again the inherent ability of the Tagore women to improve their surroundings and to bring beauty in to mundane affairs. She succeeded in arousing public interest anew in Indian art and Indian dancing. When she settled down to write her memoirs during the last years of her life, she had suffered numerous bereavements. Yet the writing bears no trace of bitterness. She says, 'The dark clouds of sorrow have dispersed, leaving my heart aglow with the rainbow colours of happiness.'

Surabhi's cousin Sujata was the only child of Nayanmohan and Mamata and was thus Sarojasundari's granddaughter. Apart from losing her father in childhood the pattern of her early life was no different from other girls of her time. She attended Diocesan School with her cousins and learned singing. Her handwriting was very good, and so she always copied out whatever her 'Baroma' Hemlata Devi wrote for *Bangalakshmi*. She however never thought of writing anything herself. After marriage she left Calcutta for Serampur. This was where her husband worked and later this became her field of social work. All the Tagore women were interested in social service.

Deepti and Geeta, two of Sujata's pishis, were well-known social workers while her 'Baroma' Hemlata Devi was associated with numerous such organizations. She had managed to interest other ladies of her family in *Bangalakshmi*. Sujata opened a school for adult literacy in her home at Serampore. Many years back Dinendranath had bought an autograph book and requested Rabindranath to write a message for Sujata. The poet had composed a two-line poem in accordance with her name and signed it. It read,

Samsarer kharataape rikta jaar pran
Sujata, amrita patrey koro tare daan.

To one whose life has become destitute
By the harsh glare of the world.
Sujata, bestow on him
A bowl full of nectar.

It was dated 4.10.1929.

This was exactly the task that Sujata took up. She spent many years in educating women who were withered by the blaze of misfortune and in making them self-reliant. She began this in Serampore. Her daughter Rita says, 'When I was growing up I remember Ma holding adult education classes every afternoon. These were held on one side of a big room behind our rear portico. On the other side, the women of the "Samiti" would be engaged in stitching and needlework. The students had names like Chanchala, Kiranshashi, Nayantara and one was known just as "Kurer Ma". Once there was a chance of some government aid. An inspector was to visit the school and the students were specially tutored to face him. It was a Herculean task. This was during the nineteen forties when there was very little awareness and consciousness among such women about themselves. As Rita continues, 'I always heard Ma say, "Chanchala, say B, A, G, H, is *baagh* (tiger)." Chanchala would shake her head and reply with the greatest aplomb, "Yes, Ma. B, T make baagh." Ma would sometimes lose her patience and say, "If she spells like this before the school inspector not only will there be no grant, they may abolish my school itself." Fortunately the school was granted aid. Sujata once arranged an exhibition to sell the handicrafts made by her students. The girls arranged embroidered tablecloths, handkerchiefs, sweets, savouries and various other knick-knacks in stalls. A gate resembling the Sanchi 'Toran'—built with banana stems and tinsel paper—was erected by Sujata in front of the stalls. This was admired by everyone and all the wares were also sold. The poor women seemed to realize anew the value of their handiwork. This encouraged them to try and become self-reliant. Though women labourers had always existed, every poor woman could not go out to work. Sujata's efforts showed them a small but effective path of earning a living.

During the great Bengal famine and thereafter, Sujata's work-sphere grew. Rita was too young to comprehend but she noticed, 'Ma bringing in powdered milk, rice, blankets, etc., and distributing them standing on our back verandah.' Involved in famine relief Sujata trudged from village to village on foot. At first her feet would swell up but she later became accustomed to the rigours of such work. After Independence she was associated with other welfare organizations too. As the representative of the AIWC she came to the Joka-Bishnupur project. Her other companions of Serampore also spread far and wide. Wherever she worked Sujata was always in the forefront. Apart from Joka-Bishnupur, she also worked in the Kalikapur-Pratapnagar Project, South Garia, South twenty-four paraganas, Anganwadi and in villages like Andharmanik. Apart from educating women and teaching them handicrafts, Sujata and her team also tried to train the midwives. The efforts of Sujata and her companions helped bring down the high rate of child mortality in these areas. These projects later wound up.

On a later visit Sujata found that the houses built for the 'Samiti' with great effort had been ruined by neglect and disuse. Non-government projects appeared to be gradually coming to naught rather than showing any improvement when taken over by the government. As president of 'KarmaKutir' Sujata toured Bengal villages at one time, to rouse a sense of awareness among women. A play based on the removal of the chains of foreign rule from Mother India was staged at Serampore College shortly after Independence. Rita remembered, 'Ma played the role of Bharatmata. She was clad in rags and her hands were bound with chains.' Sujata spent the greater part of her life trying to break the bonds shackling women and replacing their ragged dresses.

Another daughter of the Tagore family, Smita, was the daughter of Amita and Ajin Tagore. Her childhood coincided with the period just before the Jorasanko mansion was converted to the Rabindra Bharati University. Since the time she opened her eyes she saw dramatics and dance and heard music in the very atmosphere of her home. Smita was keenly interested in dancing. 'I believe as a child I began dancing whenever a record was played. As I grew older we all used to enact plays. There also I would compose dances and perform them,' she said. She had a chance to acquire further training while living in Shantiniketan. By this time girls from the Tagore family and others had begun to learn dancing. When Pratima staged the dance-drama, *Lakshmir*

Pariksha at Shantiniketan in 1942–43, Smita had her chance of performing.

Smita also had a good opportunity of learning and observing dance recitals while she was a student of 'Baitanik' which was run by Saumendranath. The dance performances presented by this organization were always directed by Sreemati. In the nineteen fiftees Smita danced to the time of *More bhawanerey ki howaye matalo* at the New Empire Theatre. The programme was directed by Sreemati. Smita felt that this was her chosen vocation because it filled her with unalloyed pleasure. She participated in *Sheshbarshan*, *Samanya Khati*, *Rituranga* and *Tapati,* besides playing the role of Arjun in a college performance of *Chitrangada*. Seeing the tall girl, Madhu Bose was impressed and wanted to cast her as Labanya in his film *Sesher Kavita*. Ajin Tagore refused permission. Smita was barely eighteen and came to know about this incident much later. It upset her but a decision of her mother grieved her even more. While Smita was still a student, Udayshankar came as an examiner of dance. He had just been elected dean in the Rabindra Bharati University.

Smita appeared for the test, full of trepidation, and she was selected. Since her childhood she had dreamt of choosing dance as a vocation and having a troupe of her own. She felt that she had arrived at the threshold and would be able to fulfill her dream. Unfortunately at this crucial moment Smita's mother objected. She would not allow her daughter to learn dancing. Shortly thereafter Smita was married. Luckily her husband Mihir Sinha had no objections to her dancing or acting. Thus Smita was able to join the 'Roopkar' group of Sabitabrata Dutt. The lapse of time in the interim period stood in the way of her returning to the world of dancing. However her acting in the role of Bansari caught the eye of everyone. She never had to look back; she appeared in the role of Mrs Lahiri in *Byapika Vidaye* staged at Rangmahal after rehearsing for just four days. Later she also enacted the role of Mrs Roy in the same play. She toured extensively with the group, thus enriching her storehouse of experiences. *Sheshraksha* was the last play to be enacted in the wide verandah of the Jorasanko mansion. Smita played the role of Indumati.

While play-acting on the stage Smita was offered roles in films. Since it involved a different kind of acting, she was rather hesitant to begin with. When Tarun Majumdar offered her a role in his film *Palatak*, she found that it was similar to the various ladies she had seen as mistresses of wealthy homes. Thus she no longer had any qualms about setting foot in the film industry. After *Palatak* came Satyajit Ray's *Mahanagar*. Her consummate acting drew everyone's attraction, though the role was a minor one. In Purnendu Patri's *Streer Patra* she played the role of Bindu's elder sister. It was a perfect portrayal of the eldest daughter-in-law of a large joint family. Another memorable role was in Tapan Sinha's *Atithi*. Apart from *Jatugriha* and *Adalat O Ekti Meye* Smita has also acted in Tarun Majumdar's *Sajani O Sajani*, Dilip Mukherjee's *Byabadhaan*, Ajay Kar's *Barnali*, Pravat Mukherjee's *Devatar Deep*, Dinen Gupta's *Rajani* and *Sathey Sathyan*, Pravat Ray's *Sedin Chaitramas*, and many others like *Chotobou*, *Bahadur*, and *Shatarupa* to name a few. She has been widely acclaimed as a character artist. She was invited by the Calcutta Doordarshan to enact various roles in serials. Smita acted in *Sonar Sansar*, the first Bengali serial telecast by them. Since then she has acted in various serials like *Kolkata Kolkata*, *Charitraheen*, *Grihadaha*, *Sreyashi*, *Sinhabahini*, *Ratnadeep*, *Kichu Kanthey Katoroop*, *Lajjya* and *Saatkahan*. In each one of these her performance has been flawless. Smita herself feels bored at times. Had she joined films earlier she may easily have come in as a heroine. This would not only have been more glamorous but also provided her acting talent a wider scope. She had always enjoyed dancing and presented a dance performance at Rathindra Mancha. The occasion was Abanindranath's birthday, the time was the nineteen eighties and the dance—the same one that she had performed on her first appearance at New Empire under the direction of Sreemati Tagore. This was the last time she danced on the stage and that too because of a special request by Abanindranath's granddaughter Menoka.

Like her mother, Smita too writes well though she has never thought of writing an autobiography. All her literary efforts are articles based on reminiscences. Notable ones are '*Nrithyer aanginaye meyera*', '*Tapatir pratham obhinaya*,' or '*Jorasankor laal bari ba bichitra bari*.' Her article '*Ekti abohelito manush: Dinendranath Tagore*' did not get the attention it deserved. Smita was the first one to write about this sensitive man and the reasons behind his leaving Shantiniketan. Much has been written about this man but Smita was the first one to do so. Perhaps her contribution would have been greater had impediments not delayed her advent. The audience was denied the pleasure of seeing a girl from the Tagore family in the role of 'Lavanya'.

Ena and Rajen Ray were in Dacca when their daughter Krishna was born. She turned out to be a jewel of Sudhindra's family. Rajen and Ena later shifted to a house at Lower Circular Road in Calcutta. Their house was well-known for hospitality and had another characteristic. According to Surabhi, 'There was never any gossip or scandal-mongering here.' Krishna studied in Loreto and during her adolescent years the atmosphere of her home became charged with the freedom movement as her uncle Saumendranath was directly involved in active politics. About this time the Second World War broke out and Rajendra also passed away suddenly. Shortly after the war ended Krishna was awarded the Madame Chiang Kai-shek scholarship for study in the USA. She was admitted to the Wellesley College in Massachusetts to study Russian language and philosophy. Her professor for the Russian language was Vladimir Nabokov while Albert Einstein unfolded the mysteries of Western philosophy to the students. The latter happened to be a friend of Saumendranath. He not only took great pains to explain the philosophy of Kant and Hegel to Krishna but would often play the violin for her. Other friends proved helpful too. Louis Kellog looked upon her as a daughter and took her to Swami Pravabanando while Henri Cartier-Bresson introduced her to Jean Riboud.

The scion of one of the most aristocratic families of Lyon, Riboud was working in New York at the time. To the man, tired and depressed by the bitter experiences of war, Krishna's friendship and company proved a healing balm. Though descended from one of the wealthiest families in France, life had made him a reformist. He and Krishna soon found a great deal in common and fell in love. When he proposed marriage Krishna went to Swami Provabananda for advice. His blessings and encouragement helped disperse the vague disquiet in her heart. To conform to Riboud's mother's wishes they were married by a Catholic priest, thus uniting two aristocratic families of the East and West.

They first settled in New York. The couple's hospitality and love of art drew artists, painters, photographers, film directors and other well-known personalities of France and Italy to their flat. However, the presence of leftist persons among their guests began to give rise to suspicions. The unpleasant experiences of the war prompted the couple's decision to return to France. Back home, Riboud not only began to develop his business but he also began to think about setting up a centre for artists and authors to express their views freely. Krishna helped him achieve this dream. Their Paris flat, the palace at Lyons and the mansion in the deserts of Arizona became pilgrim centres of art. A large garden behind their Paris flat was converted by Krishna into an oriental paradise.

Rarely does one come across a woman like Krishna, with her fine artistic sense. Her friends included not only the French President Mitterand, Indira Gandhi, Satyajit Ray, Roberto Rosselini, other artists and writers from all over the world but also numerous ordinary people. She remained basically unknown to people in India because of the geographical distance. Her interest in India and Indian handicrafts never waned. On a visit to India in the nineteen fifties she came across some fine sarees—probably Balucharis. This was the time when Suvo Tagore, Ajit Mukhopadhyaya and a few others had begun their efforts to revive the old weaving arts of India. Suvo, who was also Krishna's maternal uncle, encouraged her to study about the various forms of textile weaving. Any art form always interested Krishna. She threw herself into this project heart and soul. All her acquaintances have testified to her indomitable will and her determination to achieve a goal. Getting down to research about weaving textiles, she realized that not only would it be necessary to collect various samples of textiles but also to preserve them. Woven cloth normally does not have a very long life. Visiting various museums Krishna became an expert on the different methods for weaving cloth in the orient. The ancient history of this art form lies in China. Krishna visited the country about ten times. Her first research paper was published in 1970. The topic was 'Textiles of Tung Huang of China'. She later decided to delve deeper into the textile-weaving industry of China since Indian designs, weaving techniques of central Asia and numerous other aspects were blended into this. After all, weaving is not bound by geographical limits.

In 1979 was established the AEDTA or *Association Pour l'Etude et la Documentation des Textiles d'Asic* in Paris. This comprised of the huge collection of woven material of the Ribouds. Whatever Krishna had acquired for over twenty years is here along with books, a library and other facilities. Gradually AEDTA has become a global village. It provides full facilities for research in the textile Industry of Asia. It is open to scholars from all over the world—American, Indian, Chinese, British, Russian and others. There are provisions to help research laboratories about to close down for lack of funds as well as publication of research papers. This is the largest collection of oriental clothes and a focal point for interested visitors to Paris. Continuous research is helping to discover lost historic links as well as the quiet picture of the spread of our culture. Quoting from a research paper by Krishna, 'While working on twelve pieces of material collected from different monasteries in Lhasa we have come across some astounding facts.' On arranging the data thus obtained it becomes apparent that the pieces have been woven in some secret code. As far as it has been possible to ascertain these pieces originated among the Vaishnav community, but the designs are full of Islamic decorations. Another mystery is that the looms on which these pieces were woven were never in use in India. Krishna writes, 'No one knows how these pieces of material came to Lhasa and probably the puzzle will never be solved. At least not until it is possible to ascertain by research the technique used in weaving these materials.'

Krishna won honours galore. These include the Legion of Honour and Chevalier d'Arts and Lettres from France. She lectured in universities all over the world including the Archeological Institute of Beijing. She was the only non-Chinese to be invited to a special seminar in Manchuria. She is considered the most erudite specialist on Chinese textiles. No one has yet produced anything akin to her research on the Chinese textiles produced between the fourth century BC and the tenth century AD. The above narration may give the impression that Indian textiles did not interest her too much. This is not the case. The collection of Indian textiles and woven cloth of the AEDTA is unparalleled. There are eighty Baluchari sarees, innumerable Jamdani sarees and nakshi kanthas. The designs of the Balucharis show a clear influence of the Mughals and Portuguese. In the pallu of these sarees have been woven images of the daily lives of the aristocrats as well as of foreigners. There is a diamond-and-pearl-studded turban from Lucknow awaiting any interested researcher. The Indonesian collection includes an eight-inch wide cummerband belonging to a Japanese prince and woven from the hair of women! There are also examples of batik work in gold. There is a Japanese kimono made of banana leaves! Among the 3,500 items in the museum is a very rare dress of a Manchurian emperor—it is made of yellow silk and has dancing dragons woven in threads of gold and silver. It is difficult to tear oneself away from the cotton coat embossed with gold and made for a samurai soldier of Japan or the coloured block print on a white gown from Masulipattam. The collection of rare Jamevars from Kashmir beggar description.

Krishna's private life was not free from tragedies. Shortly after the death of her husband, her only son was killed in an accident. Though shattered by these blows, the cultural queen of France did not pause. Her well-known friends were also of great help at this juncture. Thus ended her life one day. She had been able to pass on her love for textiles to her descendants. Her grandson Thomas has taken up the tasks left by her. Thus Krishna will live forever in the continuity of her work.

Ushaboti's granddaughter Chitra had heard so much about the Tagore family in her childhood that she decided to study in Shantiniketan after her schooling was complete. Indira, Pratima and Hemlata were in Shantiniketan at the time. Chitra enjoyed the years she spent there. She learnt the art of 'alpana' from Nandalal Bose's daughters and loved to use this form of decoration during weddings and other festivals. Since her husband moved all over India it was never possible for her to have a settled existence. While in Delhi she did take part in some plays but basically played the role of a good housewife. However she always took pride in her descent from the Tagores and felt an affinity with them.

Supurna, the eldest daughter of Satyendranath's grandson Subir and Purnima, participated with Smita in practically every performance of music, dance and drama that was held in Shantiniketan. Later she became totally absorbed in Rabindra Sangeet. A look at the smiling child had prompted Rabindranath to say, 'Name her Salila.' For reasons unknown she was not named Salila. A new name Supurna, combining Su of Subir and Pu of Purnima was chosen. Indira probably had a hand in this as she loved experimenting with new names. Rabindranath also approved. For children of the Tagore family, music was always considered a part of daily life. The child Supurna's first singing lessons were from Indira who was very close to her. As she says, 'Nadidi first taught me to sing. Since she was part of the family I never considered her my guru.' In school also she not only continued these lessons along with her studies, but stood first thrice in the Dinendra Memorial competition. To quote Supurna again, 'About this time Ma requested Prafulladada to arrange for some special coaching for me.' Supurna was a student of Patha Bhawan at the time. Prafullakumar Das began a special class with Supurna and Chitralekha Chaudhuri. In Supurna's words, 'There was a table at Sinha Sadan for playing table-tennis. I would sit on that during my singing lessons. Prafulladada taught very well. The first song I learnt was *Tumi daak diyecho kon sakaley*. I often teased him but he was never annoyed . . . He always followed the musical notations scrupulously.' Supurna learnt from many others. Professor Chinu Choubeji of Sangeet Bhawan gave lessons in classical music. According to Supurna, 'Besides his classes at Sangeet Bhawan we would also go to his house. He took great pains over us. Often he would ask us to sing solo, one after the other. If the first student began off key the others would follow suit. This infuriated him. He would say, "You are like rotten potatoes. If one begins on a wrong note all the others do the same." It was mandatory to pass the examination in esraj-playing before one could be awarded the diploma in Rabindra Sangeet. I could hardly hold the instrument straight, let alone play it. The examiner was Asheshda and I was scared stiff. I somehow managed to play a piece from the raag Yaman. Ashesda awarded me forty marks. He must have taken pity on me; otherwise I did not deserve to pass in esraj-playing.'

Thus Supurna completed the Sangeet Bhawan course. Had Supurna written more she could have provided a picture of the Shantiniketan of her days in more detail. She is rather diffident. Probably her only memoir till date is *Dinguli more*.

Supurna really belongs to music heart and soul. Even on holidays she always carried a copy of *Swarabitan*. Once the whole family went on vacation to Shimultala. Supurna remembers, 'There Nadidi taught me the song *Baro bedonaar moto*. Nadidi was sitting on a chair darning while I sat on the floor singing. Later I sang this song on numerous occasions in various places. Whenever Nadidi went anywhere to lecture on music, she would take me along to sing the songs taught by her.' Supurna did not learn from Indira only. Every year the family would come to Calcutta from Shantiniketan during the summer and puja vacations. Subir Tagore stayed on the second floor while Rabindranath stayed on the first floor towards the front side.

Quoting Supurna once more: 'In the back portion of the Jorasanko house, Amiya Jethaima lived on one side and Amita Kaki on the other. Every evening I would go to Amiya Jethaima's place. Buri (Smita) would come and Snigdhadi would be there too. There was an open paved courtyard in front of Amiya Jethaima's room. She would sit there on a cane stool and all of us sat on the ground, with a *Geetabitan* in our hands. As she began to sing we would locate the page in the book and join her. After singing a song a few times we never needed to look at the book. Her style was such that she never repeated a particular line or a difficult stanza specially, but sang each song in its entirety a couple of times. Since we heard her every day it became quite easy for us to pick it up. The songs we learnt from Amiya Jethima are *Ogo kangal aamarey*, *Swapan jodi bhangiley*, *Koto katha taarey*, *Aakul keshey* and many others.

Shantidev Ghosh was also one of Supurna's tutors. Every year a troupe would visit various places to enact dance drama like *Chitrangada*, *Natir Puja*, *Tasher Desh*, and *Shyama*. Supurna was a permanent member of this group and visited Delhi, Bombay and Madras. She was also in the last cultural troupe that visited Pakistan and staged *Shyama* there and participated in the musical broadcast of *Shyama* by Dacca Radio. Akashvani Kolkata often aired songs by the students of Shantiniketan and Supurna was one of the regular singers. She has lost count of the songs she sang. Her marriage to Subhas Chaudhuri took place in 1956. Since he was himself associated with the world of music it became easier for Supurna to find a footing as a singer. She also began to emerge as a teacher of music, the Womens' College Ranchi being her first assignment to teach Rabindra Sangeet.

Supurna participated in the first convention of Rabindra Sangeet arranged by 'Dakshini'. Her style of singing attracted the listeners. Hiran Kumar Sanyal commented in the *Parichay* magazine: 'Supurna Tagore's style of singing, with a deep voice and clear pronunciation, shows how it is possible to express both the grace and vigour inherent in Rabindranath's songs.' In spite of such praise it was quite some time before she cut a disc. Her first record with the songs *Poob hawatey deye dola* and *Kaar jeno ei moner bedan* in 1963 was appreciated by the public but it was a full ten years before her second record came out. This was mainly due to her shying away from the public gaze. The two songs in her second disc are *Deen abasan hole* and *Kone se jharer bhool.* Later she recorded some more but these were a mere drop in the ocean compared to her abilities. She has however tried her best to train her students. Her view, 'With my limited resources if I can create one or two groups of artists proficient in Rabindra Sangeet I shall have nothing more to ask from life.'

Like the other women of the Tagore family Supurna also participated in drama. Beginning with *Lakshmir Pariksha* directed by Pratima in Shantiniketan, Supurna played the role of Lakshmi in *Valmiki Protiva* a number of times there. Once when *Natir Puja* was staged by 'Geetabitan' she acted as Malati. In *Mayer Khela* produced and staged by the Ashramik Sangha of Shantiniketan in New Empire Theatre in 1965, Supurna's characterization of Shanta was appreciated by the audience, both for her acting and songs. Supurna however has always put her students before herself. Her main efforts have been to create an awareness about music amongst them and amongst people at large.

While teaching music at Patha Bhawan School in Calcutta the Chaudhuri couple conceived the idea of 'Indira Sangeet Shikshayatan'. Here they teach not only vocal music but also help release cassettes and publish books related to music. Supurna and her husband have brought to light not only songs by Rabindranath but also many forgotten lyrics by other members of the Tagore family. Supurna has also recorded a song by Jyotirindranath: *O hridayanath eso hey*. She has no interest in all the experimentation and commotion about modernizing Rabindra Sangeet. She believes in the pure style that she heard and learnt from Indira, Amiya and other teachers who had received it from Rabindranath and Dinendranath. Their only daughter Srinanda has also followed in her mother's footsteps and is a Rabindra Sangeet artist.

Supurna's younger sister Ishita is the absolute antithesis of her sister. Though her childhood was also spent in Shantiniketan she has no recollections of having ever wanted to immerse herself in the world of music. Her main interest lay in academics. In that aspect she is certainly unlike most women of the Tagore family but she does resemble them in another aspect. She not only enjoys teaching but also has the ability to run a school. In Shantiniketan the seniors were always put in charge of supervising the younger children. Ishita acquitted herself well in this job, showing early her capabilities in management. After obtaining the master's degree in Philosophy, Patha Bhawan School and its students became her life work. Thirty years passed in a flash, preparing students for their role in a wider world. She had begun some research work but gave it up due to the exigencies of service. After all, the job of a school principal does not involve just teaching but also running the school administration smoothly.

Along with this Ishita is associated with 'Shishutirtha'. This is an organization on the lines of an SOS village. A young student of Shantiniketan, Gunjan, used to come from the SOS village. His tale encouraged Ishita and some others—including her sister-in-law Subhra Tagore—to start 'Sishutirtha' in 1989. It is still a small organization, caring for ten orphan children. They are being looked after and educated and will perhaps make the nation proud some day. Ishita gets a great deal of pleasure working for this organization.

Subhra Tagore is descended from the Tagores and also married into the Tagore family. Her mother Anubha was the granddaughter of Gaganendranath and the daughter of Kanakendra and Surama. Just as Protima has been discussed before Binayini, and Namita before Uma, so Subhra comes before Anubha. Subhra's father Ramendranath Mukhopadhyay's sphere of work was outside Bengal, in UP. However the cultural influence of the Tagore family is a part of life for its members. Thus Subhra was also drawn into it. Her first lessons in singing were from her mother. Anubha herself was a good singer and had had the rare opportunity of being taught by Dinendranath Tagore. In spite of such opportunities to learn Rabindra Sangeet Subhra's interest lay in dancing. She learnt kathak especially since it was the most popular dance form in Uttar Pradesh. Another ambition of Subhra's was to study in Shantiniketan. Perhaps distance made the heart grow fonder. Subhra felt drawn towards Bengal and her relations. After all, our subconscious mind always pulls us towards our roots. With the decline of Jorasanko, Shantiniketan became the focal point of such attraction. Though not many did so in Rabindranath's lifetime, many members of the Tagore clan turned later towards Shantiniketan. Some came as visitors, but many have settled there permanently.

Subhra's dream came true in 1956. She took admission in Sangeet Bhawan to learn dancing. Kathakali and Manipuri were the two dance forms taught here. She also studied at

Binaya Bhawan simultaneously and took the teachers' training. This was to prove of great help. In 1958 Subhra participated in *Vasantotsav* for the first time. Her happiness was aptly reflected in her performance. Later she played the roles of Arjun in *Chitrangada*, Uttiya in *Shyama* and Haratani in *Tasher Desh*. In the Tagore centenary year celebrations Santidev Ghosh entrusted her with the role of Malini. Her marriage to Supriya, the eldest son of Subir Tagore, was again within the family circle. She continued her dancing along with household chores and also took up teaching. She taught in wide-apart places like Dehradun, London, Calcutta and Shantiniketan. She has always enjoyed teaching dance. In Dehradun *Natir Puja* was staged in Hindi under her direction. About this time she began to think about preserving the purity of Rabindranath's dance-dramas. To gain further experience in this field she would perform a dance-drama every year with the students of class ten of Patha Bhawan. After getting her master's degree in Education she accepted charge of the Ananda Pathshala. She seemed to find pleasure in every sphere of work. Apart from being a superb cook, she became an expert in handicrafts, especially batik work. The atmosphere of Shantiniketan provided her full scope for self-expression and hence her continuous efforts in various fields. Fond of dressing up, she also enjoys dressing others. While dressing the various actors and actresses she felt that the costumes for the various dance-dramas and other plays of Rabindranath should reflect the contemporary times. The heroines of *Chirakumar Sabha* were certainly advanced for their times but their dress has to be in accordance with contemporary styles. Similarly, while staging dance dramas it has to be remembered that the dress and make up of Haratani of *Tasher Desh* or Pramada of *Mayar Khela* must follow that of the first performance. Just as Pratima thought about dance scores and pictures to preserve the purity of expression as approved by Rabindranath, similarly Subhra laid emphasis on the dress codes.

Manju, the daughter-in-law of Surendranath's daughter Manjushri, is not only a professor of History but also involved in active politics. For Manjushri, joining the communist movement was more of an accident but Manju was associated with leftist politics from her student days. When her role changed from a student to that of a professor, she became involved with the teachers movement and NFTW. She was the secretary of the Indian History Congress for three years running. She has always had the advice of support of her husband Gautam Chattopadhyaya. Gautam not only belongs to the same profession but also shares her views.

Manju's research paper, 'Petition to Agitation', is a documentation of how the Bengali's devotion to the British gradually changed to a yearning for freedom. To do this she has taken the help of various articles published between 1857 to 1885 in different newspapers and magazines.

Manju's greatest achievement was in introducing anew to the present generation the oft-forgotten women labour-leaders of yesteryear. She first thought of writing about these women while working for *Chalar Pathey*, the mouthpiece of the Communist Party. At Bangiya Sahitya parishad she came across a few thought-provoking articles by the labour leader Santosh Kumari Devi. These had originally been published in the *Sanhati* magazine. Her curiosity aroused, Manju met the editor Jnananjan Pal, the son of Bepin Chandra Pal. Gathering some more information Manju wrote an article on Santosh Kumari for publication in *Chalar Pathey*. This was in 1970. About ten years later Chinmohan Sehanabis informed Manju that Santosh Kumari was keen to meet her. Manju met her and Santosh Kumari handed over her unpublished reminiscences in English and some other material to Manju. Thus was written *Labour Leader Santosh Kumari*. The first woman labour leader of the labour and trade union movement, Santosh Kumari was well-known in the twenties of the last century. When she stood by the poor jute-mill workers no man, let alone woman, came forth to help her. From Manju's book we learn about Santosh Kumari's struggle to establish the rights of women. She had suggested that society rehabilitate women who were victims of various social inequalities and injustice.

We also owe our thanks to Manju for writing about Pravabati Dasgupta, another woman labour leader, and about the sweepers' strike. She has discussed the communist leader Sudha Ray who was involved with the port workers' strike and Dukhmatdidi who belonged to a different order of society and was the leader of many workers' movements.

Manju wrote various articles on women's education and emancipation, especially about labour movements and the role of women therein. If these articles, now scattered across various magazines, were to be collected and published they would enhance our knowledge about such women. Unfortunately a hectic schedule still prevents Manju from getting down to this task.

Most women of the Tagore family have taught at some time or the other. Mihirendranath Tagore's daughter Mitra always enjoyed this task. She began her teaching career at Hyderabad and is at present the vice-principal of the Army School at Secunderabad. Indrani and Pranati are married to Mitra's two elder brothers. Indrani teaches English at Gokhale Memorial School in Kolkata. Pranati on the other hand is well-known in another field—as a newscaster of Doordarshan. She has been associated with Doordarshan since 1976 and before that, listeners were familiar with her melodious voice in innumerable advertisements of Vividh Bharati. Hers was also the first voice that announced the names of the various stations of the Calcutta Metro Railway. Apart from all this Pranati is well established in the world of drama, and poetry recitals. Pranati belongs to the Mitra Mustaphi family of Hooghly. She learnt to recite all by herself and still believes that recitation is a question of feeling and cannot be taught. The importance of regular practice cannot be denied but the devotion must come from within. Her mother Nilimadevi and maternal uncle Kalicharan Ghosh always encouraged and inspired her. After obtaining her master's degree in History Pranati also studied for the B.Ed. degree, but her exceptionally melodious voice drew her away from teaching in to another field. She has been experimenting on the ways and means of drama and poetry recitals via various media. She is very keen to arouse public interest in these topics. She has been invited to various places in India for her poetry recitals. It has become clear to her that listeners not only in India but even abroad, like the Nehru Centre in London, Ireland or Sweden, have a yearning for good poetry. While working with students in different workshops, she has observed that everyone has a characteristic mode of expression. Even those who do not know Bengali show an interest in it after poetry recitals. She also writes occasionally, her main aim being to attract children towards poetry.

Pranati also participates in the recitation of dramas or play-reading. Her rendering of the role of Sisi in *Shesher Kavita* as well as that of the Sutradhar in *Chirakumar Sabha* has been appreciated by many. Such play-readings are also becoming popular. Besides all this, Pranati also has her advertising agency, Manson Films. She tries to give quality time to her family. Her aim is to instill traditional family values in her only child Suprabho. She thus bears the age-old convictions of the Tagores: family before a personal career.

Sunritendranath Tagore worked in Saharanpur, UP, and both his daughters—Surashri and Shyamashri—grew up there. Their mother Satirani was apprehensive that they may even forget Bengali. Thus she and her husband took great pains to coach their daughters in music and encouraged them to read Bengali. Though the girls studied Hindi in school and college and conversed with their friends in the same language, they also visited Calcutta every year in summer. Surashri was able to recite the entire *Chitrangada* when she was only six. This showed that the cultural heritage of the Tagore family was inherent in every member. Sunritendra was so pleased by his daughter's recital that he arranged to have it recorded. At that time such personal recordings were possible. These were not sold in the open market but were meant for individual collectors. Sunritendra loved to travel and drove around all over India with his family. Those memories are still treasured by his daughters.

Once the Bengalis of Saharanpur requested Sunritendra to help raise funds for a permanent Durgabari. He organized two functions. On the first day was staged *Rituranga* and on the second, the Hindi version of *Daak Ghar*. Surashri's portrayal of Amal was widely applauded. The money collected paid for laying the foundation of the Durgabari.

Surashri and Shyamashri both graduated from Agra University. Surashri also sang well and obtained the 'Sangeet Visharad' from Lucknow. After marriage she moved to Calcutta. Having a Master's degree in Hindi helped her teach the language in many schools. She is also fond of experimenting with various culinary recipes. This seems an inherited trait since most members of the Tagore family were interested in cooking. Sunritendranath had a dish called 'Tagore Special'. Surashri took to naming the various popular dishes among the Tagores according to the family members. Notable ones published in *Sananda* magazine are 'Dadar daal', 'Dheerabala's patal', 'Dheerabala's aamkheer', 'Babar lemon rice', 'Maar ilish-roast', and so on and so forth. One may wonder about Dheerabala. She was the daughter of Kadambini and Jnagnesh Prakash and she lived in Entally. Residents of this area of Calcutta comprised mainly of the daughters and sons-in-law of the Tagores and their progeny. Not all 'ghar jamais' lived in the Tagore mansion. They were often bequeathed separate houses where the daughters lived with husband and families. Most of the sons-in-law belonged to the legal profession and made considerable contribution in protecting the property of the Tagores. Dheerabala was a cook par excellence. She invented numerous new dishes whose taste the family has remembered for five generations. Surashri introduced the general public to these specialties of her family.

Shyamashri learnt Manipuri dancing at Shantiniketan, though her first love always was the sitar. Like her elder sister, she taught Hindi to innumerable youngsters. While at this job she often felt the lack of a writer like Sukumar Ray in Hindi. It distressed her that no efforts to translate Sukumar Ray in Hindi had been made thus far. Recalling the pleasure of reading '*Pagla Dashu*' it saddened her that Hindi-speaking children were unable to enjoy such works. Knowing her feeling, all her friends encouraged her to start translating the works of Sukumar Ray. She had first thought of '*Aabol Tabol*' but then she thought it would be difficult to capture the humour in poetry. She decided on '*Pagla Dashu*' and '*Haw Jaw Baw Raw Law*'. After completing the translations she had the book published at her own expense. It was widely acclaimed but what gave Shyamashri the greatest pleasure was '*Pagla Dashu*' being enjoyed by non-Bengali children.

When Suhita came as a bride into Hemendra's family the Tagores had spread all over Calcutta. Suhita's childhood was spent in Germany. Her father Kanailal Ganguli, though a scientist, had a deep love of literature. He translated *Faust,* keeping intact Goethe's style. After returning to India he settled in Lucknow, but sent his daughters to Shantiniketan lest they lose touch with Bengal. Their association with the Tagore family was a close one but Suhita found it difficult at first to adjust to the changed surroundings as well as the mode of education. Among the four sisters she was the most shy and sensitive. Her elder sister Geeta Ghatak, and younger one Rita Gangopadhyay, are well-known in the world of vocal music. The third sister teaches science.

When Suhita returned to Shantiniketan later to join Kala Bhawan she seemed to have found her desired place. While in Lucknow she had started taking painting lessons from Asit Halder. It was on his insistence that she joined Kala Bhawan. Here she had well-known artists like Nandalal Bose, Suren Kar and Ramkinkar Baij as her teachers. She learnt various styles of painting and sculpture like tempera, water colour, fresco, wood cut, etching and clay modelling. She also took lessons in the typical handicrafts of Shantiniketan—batik, bandhani and leather-work. Though good at all of these, she particularly enjoyed her lessons in sculpture from Ramkinkar Baij and was his favourite pupil. She also excelled in music and dance. Santidev Ghosh included her in his group of vocal musicians. With him she sang a duet *Choley jaye, mori hai, basanter din*, besides her numerous individual performances.

Her days seemed to flit away in a world full of music and art. Enchanted by this beautiful and accomplished girl, Amiya—another well-known Tagore—chose her as her daughter-in-law. Hemendra's family witnessed the entry of another star full of possibilities. She was offered a job by Vishwabharati after completing her course at Kala Bhawan but she was unable to accept it, bowing to the unwritten norms of the family. Though Amiya had been able to continue her practice of music despite domestic limitations, Suhita was unable too do so. Summoned by some domestic chore in the midst of clay modelling, the idea would have deserted her by the time she came back to the job, leaving only the clay behind. She found it impossible to work under such conditions and a lot of time flew by. She did try her hand at small tasks but was unable to conceive anything on a large scale. After all these years she has begun to dream anew. Her mother-in-law and husband are no more, the other members are busy with their own lives. Times have changed and she now finds herself with a fair amount of time on her hands. Perhaps it is too late to go back to artistic endeavours since concepts have changed, but surely it is still possible to teach art and handicrafts. Whatever she learnt is still fresh in her memory and she is imparting it to children. It gives her immense pleasure to see guardians sending little children to painting schools, girls are also taught various handicrafts. A sense of grace and art is so essential for keeping our environment beautiful. Children also have to be taught that their inheritance lies in creation and not in destruction. These are the lessons that Suhita wants to teach young minds.

Kshitindranath had named Bani's daughter Gitanjali. Before going abroad, Bani had gone to visit Rabindranath with her daughter. The little girl appeared fascinated by the poet's white beard! When asked her name, she replied, 'Gitanjali'. Rabindranath queried, 'Really? Who named you?' Bani told him that it was Kshitindranath. The poet said to the little Gitanjali, 'I hope you will be able to live up to your name.' Bani insisted that Gitanjali spend an hour daily practising music. Apart from vocal music, she also learnt to play the piano and violin. Educated both in India and abroad, most of Gitanjali's working life has been spent in Calcutta, teaching mathematics at the Modern High School for Girls. Though she deviated from vocal music, her love for the same has always been there. She is always called upon to direct all musical functions in school.

Subho Tagore's daughter Chitralekha is another member of Ritendranath's family. Most members of her father's family, including the women, were artists. Subho himself was not only a good painter but very knowledgeable about art. His articles on the subject were often published in *Sundaram*. Thus Chitralekha grew up in an artistic atmosphere, though her childhood was fraught with grave uncertainties due to her father's apathy in worldly affairs. She had also seen her mother's struggle to carry on their day-to-day life. She inherited both her father's artistic temperament and her mother's capabilities. Following the family trend she joined the Art College and went away to Canada after completing her course. Engrossed in a happy family life with husband and children, she managed to keep up her artistic pursuits. Water-colours are her favourite but she has tried her hand at acrylic paints too. She is also interested in the abstract style of painting. In 1992 she held a group show in Calcutta with paintings and sketches of the old houses of the city. Each of these historical edifices bears testimony to our culture and styles of architecture, yet they are fast disappearing from our midst. Chitralekha has tried to immortalize them on canvas with her paints and brush. Some art critics feel that there is a touch of the spiritualism prevalent in Chitralekha's paintings. She is now keen to hold an exhibition in Vancouver. Her plans include establishing an art gallery with her father's collection and publishing a collection of her mother's writings. She is however unsure when all this will be possible.

Prakriti and Sukriti, the two daughters of Parul and Siddhindranath grew up in the unique cultural atmosphere of Shantiniketan. Originally they lived with their mother at Mira's house, though later Parul built a place of her own. Prakriti and Sukriti had Sailajaranjan Majumdar, Kanika Bandopadhyaya and Santidev Ghosh as their teachers. Both the sisters not only sang well but participated in dance recitals and plays too. Prakriti once won the 'Dinendra Memorial Prize' for vocal music. Her delight was all the more as Indira Devi was the head examiner. Apart from functions in Shantiniketan, Prakriti also went abroad with the troupe to sing during Rabindranath Tagore's centenary celebrations. Sukriti also participated in *Kaal Mrigaya*, recorded by H.M.V. under the direction of Kanika Bandopadhyaya. Later, she did not show any interest in such performances. This was akin to her indifference regarding acting in Satyajit Ray's film *Teen Kanya* or discontinuing her painting despite having an aptitude. Like numerous other talented women of the Tagore family Sukriti preferred to live quietly behind the scenes, avoiding the public gaze. Teaching was the one activity that Sukriti never gave up. This was also a characteristic of the Tagore women. Sukriti found time to teach despite the demands of a home and family and teaches at Patha Bhawan. When Pravatkumar Mukhopadhyaya was writing *Rabindrajeebani* Prakriti helped him. She now spends a great deal of her time in Texas. In accordance with the traditions of her family, she has built up a cultural and musical atmosphere there.

Subhashri entered Ritendra's family upon her marriage. Her father, Niharendu Dutta Majumdar, was a close associate of

Subhas Chandra Bose and was involved in the movement for Independence. He was also a noted barrister and Subhashri is a worthy daughter. While she was a student, she learnt music and dance at Baitanik. After her masters in English literature, she has been teaching for the last quarter of a century. Her mother-in-law, Parul, took up a job in Shantiniketan to bring up her children; hence there was no question of her wanting to confine Subhashree within the four walls of a home. The women of the Tagore family never neglected the home even when they stepped out of its boundaries, either from necessity or urged by their latent yearnings. Though many women have changed with the times and have little time for the home due to excessive involvement with academics, dance, music and sports, Subhashri was unlike them. She moulded herself into the model of the Tagore family. Her family is a successful blend of the modern and the traditional. Her children place great store by traditional values, unlike many of the younger generation who are adept at brushing such norms aside. This certainly is a gift for Parul and an achievement for Subhashri.

Shubashri considers all members of the vast Tagore family as her own. This was perhaps the reason for the close bond of affection that grew between her and Basab Tagore's wife Smriti. Used to spending her days alone, Smriti hardly thought of anyone as her own. During the last years of her life Subhashri was able to penetrate this barrier.

In the midst of her teaching, Subhashri found time to carry on her research and take the M.Phil degree. She is a reputed professor, respected by her students. Her literary oeuvre consists mainly of translations. In the collection of stories by women writers published by Anustup she has translated Protiva Bose's *Dukul Hara*.

Protiva's daughter Asoka had three sons. The youngest, Aniruddha, was married to Smita. Smita's father was an officer in the Indian Railways and her childhood was spent in Rawalpindi and Lahore. A year before Partition their family moved to Delhi.

Due to her father's transferable job Smita moved from place to place like Lumding in Assam to Gorakhpur in UP. Her college and university education was mainly in Lucknow. She studied organic chemistry for her master's degree and stood first class first in the university. Shortly thereafter came marriage. Aniruddha was also an officer of the Indian Railways. His father Woopendranath, a geologist, chose Smita for her knowledge of German, among her other qualities. Woopendranath was not only fluent in the language but he also wrote the Gothic script with ease.

Smita lost no time in acquainting herself with the norms of the Chowdhury family—which had been initiated by Protima Devi. A trip to Shillong with her husband gave her the opportunity to meet quite a number of family members there.

Smita also continued with her academic pursuits amid her numerous domestic chores and social obligations. When Aniruddha was posted in Allahabad, she began research work under Professor Nil Ratan Dhar. After completing her thesis and getting the D.Phil degree she was awarded a Commonwealth scholarship to the UK. She carried on research as a post-doctoral fellow at the Imperial College of Science and Technology, London, for two years. In 1972 Aniruddha was posted to Calcutta and Smita joined the Birla College of Science and Education, now known as Acharya Jagadish Chandra Bose College of Science and Education. After Aniruddha's sudden death in 1976 began Smita's days of arduous and lonely struggle. Near and dear ones, relations from far and near, all offered their help but she chose to take up the responsibility of her daughter herself. Her daughter Anuradha was also brilliant like the mother and graduated from Presidency College with Honours in History. Anuradha is associated with the Rotary Club of Calcutta and loves to keep herself busy with social welfare projects. After her retirement from service, Smita also became involved with different welfare organizations. She enjoyed working for Anandan and Nabanir with her daughter. Working for social welfare has been a characteristic of the women of the Tagore family. Smita also put her mind to another important task. She is preparing the genealogical tables of her parents and in-laws. She has recently published a book, *Kay, Kobe, Kothay*, about the history of her father's family. She is also working on the genealogical table of Ashutosh Chaudhuri's family. If there were more such daughters and daughters-in-law around, the family tree and history of many other families would come to light. This is not a task to be shouldered by one person alone but by everyone.

Besides all the reverence and respect showered on the women of the Tagore family it has been observed again and again that they all had a clear field for the flowering of their talent. There was usually a sympathetic and understanding family environment which was of tremendous assistance in their endeavours at self-expression.

However there is one example where a member had to struggle against the gravest odds to forge ahead. This was Rita, one of the brightest jewels of Hemendranath's family. Her dedication and devotion to various dance styles will evoke respect forever. Rita was the granddaughter of Pragyasundari and Lakshminath Bezbarua, the only daughter of Aruna and Satyabrata Mukhopadhyay. While Satyabrata was a student at Oxford, he came to know Maharaja Sayaji Rao of Gaekwad. It was at the Maharaja's insistence that Satyabrata accepted the post of dewan of Baroda. Though Rita's mother Aruna was well educated and a good singer, she seemed to have gone into oblivion in the ultra-conservative and old-fashioned atmosphere of Baroda. In Baroda she was never seen in any other role except that of a housewife. Among all her brothers Ritendranath was the closest to Pragyasundari. When a daughter was born to Aruna and Satyabrata in Baroda they decided to name her Rita, remembering Ritendranath. Born and brought up in an enlightened family, Rita's interest lay in a new form of art. Udayshankar presented the 'Nataraj' dance at a function in Baroda. Rita watched spellbound. Belonging to an orthodox Brahmo family she had never visited a temple, neither did she know anything about 'Nataraj'. On returning home from the show she expressed a wish to learn dancing. Needless to say, nobody paid any attention. Within a few years and after a great deal of effort Rita managed to get an idol of Nataraj and a *pata* of Jagannath. Touched by her yearning, her parents bought her a gramophone and some old records. To quote Rita, 'This magic instrument came into my life with its promise of strange, wonderful vistas where I could give free rein to my dreams. Behind closed doors, I let my fancy run wild.'

Rita's parents paid no heed to her interest in dancing. They told her in unequivocal terms that she would be allowed to learn dancing only after completing her studies. This urged Rita to devote herself wholeheartedly to her studies and her intense desire to learn dancing helped her race through school and college. She graduated when she was only seventeen and she enjoyed studying English and Sanskrit. However her parents refused to keep their word. They raised various arguments like, 'You are growing up and have to be married,' 'What will people say', 'How is it possible for a girl of our family to dance on stage?', etc.

About this time Satyabrata retired and moved from Baroda to Shillong to settle there permanently. It was here that Rita first had the opportunity of learning dance from a Manipuri master. She had a few army officers' wives as her fellow students. Within a few days, Rita's father came to know and rebuked Rita saying that she was wasting his money on dancing. Rita decided to fend for herself and began giving dancing lessons to children. The money she earned by teaching such 'action dancing' helped her to pay for her lessons in Manipuri dancing. From now on, she never accepted any financial help from anyone for her dancing training.

In the midst of all this, Rita was married. Before the wedding she had been assured that there would be no impediments to her dancing. She presumed that her husband liked this art form. While on their honeymoon in Sri Lanka, Rita suggested they visit a performance of 'Kandy Dancing'. Her husband's displeasure at the proposal shocked and dismayed her. She felt that she would have to sacrifice dancing at the altar of domestic peace. Fate willed otherwise and probably it was in Rita's stars to become a danseuse. One evening in Calcutta on returning from a party Rita found her old Manipuri dance-master at her doorstep. He informed Rita that he had managed to get her address and had come to Calcutta from Imphal to open a dance school. When Rita realized that the old man had come this far depending on her help she did not have the heart to refuse him. She writes, 'Thus dance came back into my life. Friction at home had to be endured stoically as the price for the joy I felt in dance.'

Sometime later Rita's husband was transferred to Madras, now known as Chennai. This was a golden opportunity for Rita and she began training in Bharatnatyam. She observed that this dance form had nothing in common with what she had learnt earlier. With incredible hard work and diligence she mastered a great deal within a few months. As had been the case with her Manipuri dance-master, Rita became the favourite of her Bharatnatyam teacher. Her days of happiness seemed to end too quickly. Her husband managed a transfer to Bombay. Undaunted, Rita decided to learn a totally new dance form.

The way Rita advanced on her chosen path to success, overcoming every adverse circumstance, amazes one. Hardly any other girl of the Tagore family has had to surge ahead completely on her own. Every step to success has to be taken on one's own but often there are others to encourage and inspire or guide one along the correct path. Dance has been Rita's inspiration and her encouragement has come from her dance teachers. Her tremendous love of dance and keenness to learn it commanded their affection.

In Bombay, when Rita decided to shift from Bharatnatyam to other styles, fate seemed to lend a hand. At that time the poet Vallathol had sent the dance maestro Asan Karunakaran

Panikkar to Bombay to teach kathakali. Rita began to train as a kathakali dancer. This training proved to be of tremendous help. She had not been taught to express her feelings through facial expressions in Manipuri dancing while Bharatnatyam gave her only rudimentary ideas of abhinaya. This lacuna was filled with her training in kathakali. During this time, she also learned kathak. Dance is an art form which cannot find full expression in the confines of a home. The time came for Rita to present her art before the public. She went to Kerala to prepare the item 'Putana Mokshom', with the help of her guru. Demoniacal expressions are much more difficult to portray and this dance was at the time strictly meant for men. Undaunted, Rita learnt to express demoniacal feelings through her kathakali. Slowly her dance began to bring Putana, Nakratundi and Sinhika to life. Among these 'Putana Moksham' became so popular that all Rita's dance shows would end with this item. It was in Bombay that Rita had an appreciative audience. Her only son was also born here. Unfortunately her domestic life was never free from strife. Though she came to Shantiniketan in response to an invitation by Protima and she had heard that Indira always talked of her as 'our Rita', she never had much connection with the Tagore family. Despite that she often longed for love and appreciation from her near and dear ones.

Rita was invited to visit Europe in 1958. It was mainly due to the efforts of Pandit Ravishankar that her first trip abroad came about. By then she was already established as a noted danseuse at home, like Indrani Rahman and others. Rita performed in England, France, Denmark and Germany. The only accompaniment to her solo performance was provided by taped music, yet she enchanted her viewers. On her return to India she concentrated on mohiniattam. This eagerness of Rita to master different dance styles is extraordinary. Normally an artist concentrates on any one particular dance form. Rita, however, learnt Manipuri, Bharatnatyam, kathakali, kathak,

Mohiniattam, kuchipudi and last of all Odissi. In between she had been abroad once more.

Yamini Krishnamurti's rendering of Odissi charmed her. Odissi appeared to personify all her dreams about dancing. She learnt that Yamini was trained in Odissi by Guru Pankajcharan Das, who was considered the father of modern Mahari dance. Enchanted by the incomparable wealth of this dance form, Rita not only invited Pankajcharan to Bombay but also became his disciple. She says, 'Since that time I have been devoted to Odissi, almost obsessed with it, gradually giving up all the other styles that I had acquired with so much effort and joy. I made up my mind to dedicate myself to the resuscitation and worldwide projection of this dance tradition of the Mahari of Orissa, which had long been a victim of social stigma.'

It may not be out of context to say a few lines about the Mahari dance with reference to Rita's writings. The dance form popularly called Odissi is known in the Jagannath Dev temple at Puri as Mahari dance. The 'devdasis' were known as maharis. At one time temples all over India had 'devdasis' and they had their own characteristic style of dance. They were looked down upon in society and later many people began to agitate for the eradication of this practice. Along with 'devdasis', dance had become taboo for woman of polite society. However in the last century a new consciousness about dance grew among many artists. On one hand there was the arrival of Udayshankar and on the other hand dance began to be taught at Shantiniketan. In Orissa, Guru Pankajcharan Das began to train students in the neglected Mahari dance style. He was himself the son of a Mahari. At the time men did not train in this dance style. Young boys were taught the 'Gutipoa dance'. Pankajcharan and his students re-established the stigmatized devdasi dance in cultured society. Among his well-known disciples are Kelucharan Mahapatra, Yamini Krishnamurti, Sanjukta Panigrahi, Priyamvada Mohanti, her daughter Ahalya and many others. Among these, only three have followed his style in toto. They are his daughter Vijayalakshmi, Ahalya and Rita. Certain characteristics of the Mahari Dance distinguish it from other styles. Rita learnt these from her guru Pankajcharan who in turn had been taught by his maternal aunt, Ratnaprabha Devi. This characteristic is that to the Mahari, dance is not a fine art but a form of worship. Thus they never felt constrained by any purity of ritual or convention. Guru Pankajcharan often presented the same dance with different postures, musical beats and tempo. Rita was the first to present the 'devdasi' dance in its proper form to the world.

While in Assam in 1965 for a dance programme Rita came to know about the 'satriya' style of dance. In Assam, ascetics learnt this dance at the 'satra' or places of worship. This dance was only meant for men but two of them agreed to teach Rita. This was because she had Assamese blood in her and her maternal grandfather, Lakshminath Bejbarua, was a patron of the Kalambari Satra. After her training Rita presented this dance both outside Assam, in India and abroad. She also mastered the 'Deonati' and 'Deodhani' dance styles of Assam. Their names suggest that they are forms of 'Devdasi' dance. Her training in various dance forms advances the view that in ancient India all dance styles evolved and developed around a temple. Whenever Rita learnt a dance style she also mastered the temple art associated with it. She later set herself the task of re-establishing the Mahari dance style by bringing it from the Jagannath Temple to the modern public stage.

Had Rita been content to rest on her laurels at this stage she would still have been known as a superb dancer. She however was set on inventing new dance styles. The exposition of drama through dance has been observed with Rabindranath's *Chitrangada*, *Shyama*, *Chandalika* and other dance dramas. Though there was no apparent link between Rita and this new style, she must have had unseen links with the genius and cultivation of fine arts by the members of the Tagore mansion.

These were accidental since Rita's main aim was the revival of the fine arts of ancient India. Her guru Pankajcharan Das was of immense help in this task. Rita's first dance-drama was most probably *Panchakanya: Kunti, Draupadi, Tara, Ahalya and Mandodari*—the five unforgettable characters of *Ramayana* and *Mahabharata* were brought to life by Rita in a solo performance of Odissi, lasting over three and a half hours. It had taken her six years to prepare it. The performance was widely acclaimed and Rita had her desired reward: a special award by the Sangeet Natak Academy for her work on Mahari dance. The academy had the entire performance filmed in video to preserve it. Last but not the least were the blessings of her guru. To reach the pinnacle of success one often has to sacrifice a great deal. This has been true in Rita's case. At this time her domestic life became unbearably disturbed and it was impossible to avoid a split. Along with divorce the course of Rita's life changed. By this time she had returned from her fourth trip to the USA. *Panchakanya* had been widely appreciated there and she was invited by the University of New York to join the faculty to teach dancing. She accepted it because the need for a steady income was paramount, as she had been granted the custody of her son. However she had to forego the position she had acquired as a danseuse in India. She did return after completing her contract, but the wide gap of ten years did not permit her to get back to the world of Indian dance.

Undaunted, Rita again concentrated on dance-dramas. She staged Kalidasa's *Kumar Sambhavam*, *Meghadootam* and *Ritu Sambharam*, and followed up with Sudrak's *Mritshakatikam*. Her *Lavanyavati* in Oriya and *Khana,* based on a Bengali story, as well as *Mahadurga* based on *Chandipuran* earned enviable accolades. She picked up certain anecdotes from the Bible and Greek mythologies and tried to present them through Indian dance styles combined with Western background music.

This experiment she named 'Prak Pratichi'. She was the first Indian dancer to make such an attempt. Her efforts earned her a choreography fellowship from the public service programme of Public Artists of New York in 1979. In 1982 and 1984 she was again awarded fellowships for choreography by Washington's National Endownment for Arts. *Mary Magdalen*, *The Song of Solomon*, *Delilah*, *The Garden of Eden*, *Bathsheba* and *Liliath* were produced one after the other. The video tapes of all these have been preserved by the two organizations mentioned above. All this praise did not please her as much as her 'Gati Bilas Pallabi', where she enjoys performing amidst her own cultural environment. In 1994 the Sangeet Natak Academy again filmed on video-tape the flawless rendering of Mahari dance. Rita was happy that she had succeeded in her mission of getting Mahari dance its deserved stature. Even today dance is her life and not just an art form. To quote her again, 'My dance is my total life. The prospect of a time when I will not be able to dance is unthinkable.'

Rita visits Orissa every winter and generally takes back some new styles of dance. She has also wrtten articles on dancing and has just completed her autobiography *The Eternal Flame*. Here the story of her life is entwined with almost every dance style of India. She still teaches her students and holds the view that there is no age for dancing, it can be learnt at any age. Such a statement is only possible from one whose every waking moment is occupied by dance. She says that she has no time for anything else, and 'I think dance, I live dance, I dream dance.'

Among Ratna's daughters, Ira taught in various places. Women of the Tagore family enjoyed teaching and Ira was no exception. She has now joined a number of social welfare organizations. Like her grandmother, Ira is a superb cook. Apart from editing and publishing her grandmother's books, Ira herself is about to bring out a cookery book in English.

Saudamini, the Maharshi's eldest daughter never went to her in-laws but continued to live at Jorasanko even after marriage. Her daughters however were distanced from the Jorasanko house after marriage.

Saudamini's eldest daughter Irabati was related closely to the Pathuriaghata Tagores. Two of her three daughters were married into the Tagore family. Her youngest daughter Parul was married to Abanindranath's eldest son Alokendra. Irabati's second daughter was Indrani. Her daughter Shefalika was married to Prabodhendunath, the son of Prafullanath Tagore while Prabodhendu's sister Subrata became the wife of Indrani's son Niharprakash. Subrata and Shefalika were great friends.

Prafullanath Tagore was a talented man and a connoisseur of the arts. He had a love of music and was a collector of paintings and sculpture. His wife Amiya and Rabindranath Tagore's wife Mrinalini were first cousins. Amiya's brother Hiranmay Raychaudhuri was a well-known sculptor. Prabodhendhu and Subrata had their first lessons in drawing and painting from him. It was soon obvious that Subrata had a gift for painting and sketching. Even today her paintings adorn their house, though it has not been possible to save many of the large canvasses painted by her. A huge work in the Ajanta style was considerably damaged by water. A perusal of her paintings indicates that if Subrata had kept up her training the world would have had another excellent painter. However Subrata did not paint much after marriage. Her son Niradhiprakash does not remember seeing his mother paint. In those days men seldom spared a thought as to how their womenfolk spent their time. Unlike Sunayani, Subrata did not have much spare time to indulge her hobby. She was very fond of nature and scenic beauty. Later she painted some scenes of Dehradun, Mussoorie and Darjeeling. Her style here is quite unlike the one observed in her work on Ajanta cave's paintings, but both are pleasant and appealing. Apart from painting Subrata played the sitar well and had been trained in vocal music by Radhikaprasad Goswami. Her father, Raja Prafullanath, had a large portrait of his daughter decorated and framed from abroad. It adorns the living room of the Gangulis' even today. In many Tagore households we come across such portraits or photographs. It has been heard that at one time there were no photographs of girls of the household and even if there were some, they were never kept in the living-room. However in the Tagores, especially in the main households, large framed photographs of girls can be seen. These most probably formed a part of the trousseau, since such portraits still exist in the families where these girls were married. It is quite possible that a large portrait formed an essential part of home décor, especially if the girls' father happened to be an artist or an art lover. It is noteworthy that such portraits were highly appreciated by the groom's family and displayed in the main room.

Maya, one of Subrata's daughters-in-law, was at one time a regular contributor to the *Sandesh* magazine. She wrote mainly poems and rhymes for children.

Indrani's daughter Shefalika was married to Prabodhendunath Tagore, the elder brother of Subrata. Her son Sandip has recorded his mother's beauty in the following lines,

> My maternal grandmother was fair, with tawny eyes and hair while my mother had black eyes and hair. Her features were sharp and her long hair fell beneath her knees. Whenever she sat with her hair loose I would stare spell bound at her face which resembled the moon looking out of dark clouds. Like the other women of the family she had studied at home and had a good command over English and Bengali. Later she helped her erudite husband in his writing.

Shefalika's elder daughter Padma remembers,

> Since our childhood there was an atmosphere of music all around us. My mother sang very well. She had been taught by Radhika Goswami. Dinendranath had trained her in Rabindra Sangeet. My mother's melodious voice matched her exquisite beauty. At that time it was not customary for women to sing in public they only did so in intimate circles or within the family. This was particularly true in our branch of the Tagores.

This narrative by Padma gives us a glimpse of the atmosphere prevalent in the Pathuriaghata Tagore family. This becomes more explicit when Sandip writes, 'Ma was slim and slightly built. She disliked ostentation of any kind. She usually wore hand-woven cotton sarees and only a few pieces of jewellery. The saree was always worn low to cover her feet. Yet I remember the same Ma in Mussoorie. She would ride out with my father wearing Jodhpurs, coloured shirt, and riding boots with a whip in hand. We would stare at her awestruck.' It is obvious that given the chance the women had the ability to excel in every aspect of modern behaviour. However the time for them to override the prevalent family traditions even when they were in Calcutta came much later. Shefalika had learnt to play the esraj from her uncle Dinendranath and was fond of reading the *Ramayana* and *Mahabharata* aloud. When her children were small she took the responsibility of not only teaching them the three Rs but also trained them in music. Along with all this there was the job of looking after the family. This is something every mistress of a Tagore home had to do. Amiya had handed over the keys of the store-room to Shefalika which was tantamount to putting the reins of the family in her hands.

Prabodhendunath spent quite a few years translating the Rig Veda. Unfortunately he suffered from acute rheumatism and was often unable to write. During this time Shefalika was a great help to him. He would dictate for two hours every morning and evening and Shefalika would write it all down. Her own health was also delicate and she suffered from asthma. Yet, year after year the husband and wife sat in the arbour of their garden, carrying out their literary pursuits.

Saudamini's younger daughter Indumati lived in south India after marriage and did not have much connection with the Tagore family. One of her daughters, Leela, was married to Manmatha Chaudhuri, a younger brother of Ashutosh and Pramatha. Another one, Stella, was married to Swarnakumari's grandson

Ajitnath Ghosal. She had a couple of other daughters. The brightest jewel in Indumati's family was Devikarani, the daughter of Manmathanath and Leela. Sarojini Naidu called her 'The Nightingale of Indian Films'. Devika Rani was sent to England at a young age for studies. It was rumoured that when the small girl visited Rabindranath Tagore with her parents the poet had noted her exceptional abilities in music, acting and dancing. It is only a genius who can spot another budding one. Rabindranath was enchanted and requested Devika's parents to send her to England. He felt that only there could she get proper training and the environment necessary for shaping her personality properly. It was in London that the budding genius inherent in Devika was able to bloom fully. Heeding Rabindranath's counsel, Leela and Manmatha sent Devika to the UK. Manmatha was keen that she specialize in architecture while other family members wanted her to study modern textile designing. Devika herself wanted to be an actress. While a schoolgirl in South Hampstead School, she won a prize for her superb portrayal of Cleopatra in class. Wining a scholarship to the Royal Academy of Arts in London to study dramatics helped Devika take a decision. She took admission to the class in applied arts to study textile designing, decor and architecture. This helped her advent towards the film world. When only eighteen, she got the job of a textile designer in a reputed studio. Her beauty and gracious personality slowly began to unfold. While working here she met a brilliant young Bengali—Himangshu Ray. Ray had begun his education at the Brahmacharya Ashram in Shantiniketan. During the First World War he came to London for higher studies. He began to study law in order to become a barrister. His tremendous attraction for acting and the world of art made him give up his legal studies. He decided on the film industry as the best medium for expressing his talent. This was then the latest medium of art form the world over. Many men in India, like Dhiren Gangopadhyay alias DG, had also begun experimenting with this mode of expression. In

England Himangshu Ray was joined by Bepin Pal's son Niranjan Pal, Madhu Bose—the son of Pramathanath Bose, the artist Charu Ray and many others. Himangshu Ray's film *The Light of Asia*—a biography of Buddha—caught the imagination of the audience. Sarojini Naidu's sisters Sunalini and Mrinalini had acted in this film. In 1928 Ray started on his famous film *A Throw of Dice*, based on the *Mahabharata*. He met Devika Rani and requested her to join his production unit.

Devika Rani accepted with pleasure. Perhaps she thought that this would help her ambition of becoming a film star. She has never mentioned anything much about her personal life anywhere. Her parent's reaction to their daughter's eagerness to become a film actress is not known. One wonders whether they encouraged or tried to dissuade her.

Himangshu Ray and Devika Rani were married shortly thereafter. There is no record of the reaction of the Ray or Chaudhuri families to this event. The couple left England for Germany for filmmaking. They took training in film production from Erich Palmer. Devika also approached Max Heinhardt for training as an actress. He asked her to learn German first. Devika agreed and surprised Max by her rendering of a dialogue in German within a short while. Her flawless pronunciation as well as her controlled and natural rendition charmed Max. Twentieth Century Fox was filming *The Snake Charmer's Daughter* and they invited her for the role of a gypsy girl. It was a fantastic opportunity, but Himangshu Ray did not agree. He felt that Devika Rani's rare genius should be for the films made in her own country. Devika Rani acquiesced, though numerous people said later that she should have accepted the role.

Devika Rani made her public appearance in films after another two years, in 1933. The film was *Karma*. Himangshu Ray produced it and was also the hero. This was the first film in English with Indian actors and actresses. It was greatly appreciated by the public abroad and Devika Rani's superb acting won her accolades from all. She was named 'The First Lady of the Indian cinema'. The film was made both in English and Hindi. In India the film faced a lot of criticism as there was a long kissing scene. The other female character of this film was played by Sudharani, the princess of Burdwan. The BBC invited Devika Rani to lecture in their first television show.

On their return to India, Himangshu Ray and Devika Rani established Bombay Talkies. The contribution of Bombay Talkies to the Hindi Film Industry is enormous. Along with film production, new Indian artists were trained here. These included Ashok Kumar, Kishore Sahu, Dilip Kumar, Madhubala, Khwaja Ahmed Abbas and many others who became famous later. Devika Rani also began to act. Her first film in India was *Gagan ki Ragini* followed by *Jawani ki Hawa*. The one after that was *Jeevan Naiya* with Ashok Kumar as the hero. Ashok Kumar had given up studying law and came to train as a technician. Films at that time had roused a tremendous curiosity, especially in young men to whom it represented a peep into forbidden territory. Film actors and actresses were outcastes in society. When Himangshu Ray offered the hero's role in *Jeevan Naiya* to Ashok Kumar he was on the horns of a dilemma since he worked in the same studio. He told Ray, 'Sir, the film actors and actresses come from the lower rungs of society. I have no wish to act in films.'

Ashok Kumar writes in his memoirs, 'Himangshu Ray's expression became grave. He said, "My wife is Rabindranath's grand-niece. Do you mean to say that she comes from a lowly society?" I tried to shout a refusal but he interrupted and continued, "Sudharani is the daughter of the Maharaja of Burdwan. Gyan Mukherjee has secured record marks in the University. Do you consider them to be lowly people?"'

Ashok Kumar had no more to say. Incidentally it should be remembered that many men of aristocratic families had begun an effort to erase the stigma associated with films. Dhiren Gangopadhyay, Madhu Basu and Himangshu Ray persuaded their wives to act in films. They thus set an example. Earlier most actresses came from the families of dancing girls or prostitutes.

Devika Rani was in a class of her own since she herself was keen on an acting career. She appeared in the maximum number of films with Ashok Kumar. To quote him, 'She was not only an exquisite beauty but her demeanour, deportment and even her complexion resembled that of an Englishwoman. Having been brought up in London she was far more fluent in English than Hindi. To cap it all she was my boss's wife. I was tongue-tied with shyness, let alone able to rehearse properly.' The pair caught the public imagination. Films like *Acchut Kanya*, *Janmaboomi*, *Izzat*, *Savitri*, *Nirmala* and *Vachan* were produced in quick succession. In all these Devika Rani appeared natural and at ease. She had learned to differentiate between acting on the stage and in films. Her natural acting in the first 'talkies' of the day leaves us astonished. *Acchut Kanya* was a superhit. The popular song *Mai ban ki chiriya* of this film showcased her talent as a singer. It was a beautiful blend of her gracious personality and melodious voice. In *Nirmala* she portrayed an unfortunate old woman and then she acted in *Durga*.

Himangshu died in 1940. Thereafter Devika produced quite a few successful films like *Kangan*, *Bandhan*, *Punarmilan* and *Kismat*. She also acted in *Anjaan* and *Hamari Baat*. Unfortunately these two films did not do well at the box office. Himangshu was an excellent organizer, though not extraordinary in acting. He had vision, foresight and a rare ability to transform his dreams into reality. Forty-three years after his death, during the last years of her life, Devika Rani said in an interview, 'It was he who made me what I am. It was he who trained me, directed me and taught me.'

In 1945 Devika Rani left the world of films for good. Running the Bombay Talkies had begun to prove difficult for her. Also, by this time the Russian artist Svetoslav Roerich had entered her life. He first met her as a model. Their relationship deepened and Devika decided to remarry. She had wanted to film the *Mahabharata* on a grandiose scale like Cecil B. De Mille, and Himangshu may have dreamt about it but it was not to be. She felt the call of another world—that of the fine arts. The rest of her life was spent as a patron of art, literature, music and drama. In 1958 she was awarded the Padmashri. The then Prime Minister Jawaharlal Nehru made it a point to attend the ceremony despite a heavy schedule. According to him, 'Who can resist the charm of Devika Rani?' She was also the first recipient of the Dadasaheb Phalke award. She divided her time between her five hundred-acre experimental farm at Bangalore and the picturesque house at Manali. She lived like a queen till the end and always said, 'I have no time to look back.'

Asit Halder's mother Suprabha was the daughter of Saratkumari. Asit Halder was originally associated with Kala Bhawan at Shantiniketan and his daughter was born there. Rabindranath himself named her Atashi. Before she was old enough to appreciate the greatness of Rabindranath or the unique atmosphere of Shantiniketan, Atashi shifted to Lucknow with her father. Asit Kumar was the principal of the Maharaja Art School there and later that of the Government Art School. From her childhood Atashi loved to paint. Losing her mother at an early age she turned to her brush and paints to alleviate her loneliness. She always showed her father whatever she drew or painted. She remembers, 'Baba never taught me painting but approved of whatever I showed him.' This helped build up her self-confidence. She was educated at the La Martimere School for Girls, but there was no provision for separate training in art. While still quite young, she was married to Arabinda Barua. Rabindranath blessed the young couple with the following words:

Purnata asuk aji tomader tarun jeeboney
Anandey kalyaney premey shubho logney subho sanmilaney.

Let fulfilment come to your young lives,
In love, in joy, in prosperity in this union,
In an auspicious moment.

The Baruas belonged to Calcutta and were Buddhists. Atashi also loved the Buddhist atmosphere. Her pictures are based on religions inspiration and she always preferred line drawings. Though a lot of her time was taken up looking after her erudite husband and four children, domestic chores were never able to completely engross her. She continued with her painting, albeit slowly. After a lot of experimentation she sent her work for an exhibition. The picture was awarded a prize by the Academy of Fine Arts. This helped disperse her diffidence. Her husband was not only an intellectual but also the leader of the Buddhists in Bengal. A great deal of his time was taken up in social welfare. All the impediments that hamper a woman's entry into the world of art were there for Atashi, including the ill-health of two children. Yet she dedicated herself heart and soul to Lord Buddha and immersed herself in painting. Most of her well-known pictures are related to the life of Buddha and the cave paintings of Ajanta. In 1950 she had the opportunity to visit Ceylon, now Sri Lanka, to participate in the world convention of Buddhists. She thus had the golden opportunity to make pencil sketches of all the eminent guests there. She also sketched and drew numerous pictures of the various Buddhist shrines of Sri Lanka.

The Mahabodhi Society of Calcutta published a set of ten picture-postcards called 'The Life of Buddha'. Later, the Bengal Buddhist Association published twenty-one picture-postcards on the life of Buddha. All these were drawn by Atashi. These came to the notice of some members of the Digambar Jain Trust. They were fascinated and contacted her. They were keen to depict the life of Parsanath in the marble friezes of the Parsanath temple at Belgachia, Calcutta. Buddhism and Jainism had coexisted for centuries; so the inspiration to have Parsanath's life painted after seeing that of the Buddha was not only natural but also an expression of broad-mindedness. Thus the beauty of art triumphed over religious orthodoxy. Atashi drew the various phases of Parsanath's life and these were carved and painted on the walls of the Parsanath temple by sculptors and artists from Jaipur. It took about a year and a half to complete the work. This gracious temple is still one of the main tourist attractions of Calcutta.

In 1956 Atashi travelled to Nepal to participate in the world conference of Buddhists. This trip helped her enrich her sketch-book. On her return she again took up her paint box and brush. Her visual impressions found life in her paintings and she was able to depict the Lord Buddha in her sensitive choice of colours and lines. In 1958 an exhibition was held with one hundred and fourteen paintings and it drew notice and praise from many quarters. Akashvani requested her for her reminiscences of her father. The artist father had helped his artistic daughter in forming her original style. He had never restricted her with his direction, but only encouraged her. This encouragement and inspiration from the ideals of Buddha's life were all that Atashi needed to go ahead in the field of art.

Returning to the main household of house number 5 at Jorasanko: time had wrought numerous changes in the old mansion. Its family members had scattered far and wide. A number of new faces appeared in Gaganendranath's family. The six daughters of Kanakendra and Surama—Anubha, Gauri, Bakula, Karabi, Subhra and Seema—were all talented. They made their mark in the fields of music, needlework and batik. Among them Anubha merits special mention as she recorded two of Rabindranath's songs in the early days of the gramophone. These were, *Dekho dekho shuktara*, and *Nai elay jodi samaya nai*. The record is not available any more. Anubha was tutored by Dinendranath and took part in Varshamangal. She also acted in a number of Tagore's plays. In *Bisarjan* she was Haashi and in *Bhairaber Boli* she portrayed Ila's friend. Her musical career was hampered when she moved to her husband's workplace at Roorkee. She however turned her talents to social service and set up a childcare centre there. Later, in Bombay, she opened a school to teach batik and also started the 'New Work Centre'. Anubha's love for the fine arts came to the fore when she encouraged the dancing talent of her daughter Subhra and arranged for her training in kathak.

In the Tagore family it was customary for the name of the eldest son to begin with the same letter of the alphabet as the father's. Girindranath's two sons were Ganendra and Gunendra. As Gaganendra's eldest son Gehendra died childless, the eldest son of Kanakendra was named Geetindra. Kabindra, the other son's name, matched that of Kanakendra. Geetindra was married to Arunendranath's granddaughter Ira Barua. Though Ira was descended from house number 6 of the Tagores of Jorasanko, she had not been brought up there. Her mother Latika (also known as Lalita) was married to Jnanadabhiram Barua of Assam. After Pragyasundari and Lakshminath, this was the second inter-provincial marriage in the Tagore family. Ira's mother Latika was a grand-niece of Rabindranath.

There have been rumours and hints from many sources about a marriage proposal between Rabindranath and Swarnalata, the eldest daughter of Rai Bahadur Gunabhiram Barua, though nothing definite was known. It may be recalled that Rabindranath always jested about his marriage saying, 'There is no story behind my wedding.' Among the various young girls seen by his elder brothers and sisters in-law there is the story of there being even a south Indian girl. This incident was related to Maitreyi Sen and Seeta Devi by Rabindranath himself. Though she was from a wealthy family and was an heiress to seven and a half lakh of rupees, the general disapproval of the Tagores for this lady was evident in Dwijendranath's well-known poem:

Anindita Swarna Mrinalini hok
Subarna tulir tabo puraskar/Madrajar kare
Je porey se poruk khaiya chok.

Let the incomparable golden lotus
be the reward of your golden paint brush,

If anyone else wishes to be enticed
by the south Indian let him do so
with his vision gone.

These lines were composed about six months before Rabindranath's wedding. While writing the poet's biography, Krishna Kripalani mentions a girl from Orissa rather than Madras. The Tagores had a zamindari in Orissa; so there seems nothing unnatural in another landlord of the state wanting the handsome Rabindranath as his son-in-law. Kripalani also mentions Jyotirindranath and Rabindranath visiting the zamindar's place to meet the girl. On the other hand, there is a line in Jnanadabhiram Barua's autobiography *More Katha*, which translated into Bengali reads, 'Strange are the ways of fate. The marriage of my elder sister to the Poet never took place; yet Latika, the eldest daughter of Arunendranath and granddaughter of the learned philosopher Dwijendranath, was wedded to me on the 1 July 1906. How opinions and views change! This match was arranged by my elder sister Swarnalata. Now many widow remarriages are taking place in the Tagore family.' Based on this statement by Jnanadabhiram, Usha Ranjan Bhattacharya in his book *Rabindranath and Asom* says that, according to Jnanadabhiram's *More Katha*, there was a proposal of marriage between Rabindranath and Swarnalata. The proposal was negated when Debendranath heard that Swarnalata was a widow.

An affectionate bond grew up between Rabindranath and Jnanadabhiram. The latter has written that the Poet often joked about this possible relationship. Moreover according to Shri Bhattacharya during a proposal to photograph Rabindranath he teased Ira, 'I missed your pishi but if you are with me I do not mind being photographed.'

Next comes determining the time when this proposal was mooted. According to Bhattacharya, Debendranath, in spite of his initial approval, turned the offer down since the girl was a widow. Lakshminath Bezbarua in his memoirs informs that

Swarnalata was widowed on 31 March 1890 and remarried on 15 February 1899. Lakshminath was one of the main witnesses to her remarriage. Moreover, Rabindranath's wife was alive during this time. She was married on 9 December 1883 and passed away on 23 November 1902.

Ira has shed light on this controversy. According to her the proposal of a match between Rabindranath and Swarnalata was mooted in 1883, many months before the latter's first marriage.

Rai Bahadur Gunabhiram Barua was the founder editor of *Assam Bandhu,* and a very broadminded person. He was close to Pundit Ishwarchandra Vidyasagar and attended the historical widow remarriage in Sukia Street. He embraced Brahmoism in 1869 and after the untimely death of his wife Brajasundari, married Vishnupriya. Vishnupriya at the time was a widow with two children. Swarnalata was the daughter of Gunabhiram and Vishnupriya. Exceptionally beautiful, Swarnalata was a student of Bethune School and later became a well-known writer. She is also acknowledged as the first woman journalist. For sixteen years she reported to the Associated Press. She came to the Tagore mansion with her father to attend some function and it was then that a match between her and Rabindranath was proposed. It is probable that Dwijendranath penned the lines, 'Let the golden Lotus (Swarna Mrinalini) be the reward for your golden brush' sensing Rabindranath's approval. On hearing that Swarnalata's mother had been a widow before her marriage to Gunabhiram Barua, Debendranath turned the proposal down. Thereafter, when Rabindranath's sisters-in-law went to Jessore in a party on the lookout for a suitable bride, there is no record of Rabindranath's going with them to see the girl, though he accompanied them to Jessore. Prasanta Pal has commented, 'It is difficult to believe that Rabindranath would willingly choose as his life partner a girl not yet ten and practically illiterate. This gets credence from other sources. Abanindranath has mentioned about Rabindranath's reluctance to marry. He says, 'Rabikaka's marriage just did not seem to take place. In spite of everyone's entreaties he would just keep silent and look down. Later the family persuaded him to agree.' It is possible that the main pressure came from Debendranath who called Rabindranath to Mussoorie in September. It was shortly thereafter that marriage preparations were underway and word was sent to Abhoy Charan Ghosh, an employee at the Tagores' *seresta* in Jessore. Rabindranath's wife Bhabatarini was renamed Mrinalini in accordance with the lines penned by Dwijendranath earlier.

The proposal of a match between Rabindranath and Swarnalata had hardly been mentioned even within the family circle. This is perhaps because Rabindranath himself preferred to keep it a secret. It was only after Swarnalata's death in 1932 that he mentioned it in jest to Jnanadabhiram and Ira. Jnanadabhiram was very fond of his elder sister. Thus he felt keenly the rejection of his elder sister's hand for that of Rabindranath, especially when his own marriage took place to a member of the same family. Naturally the change of attitude and view-point also struck him. It was Maharshi Debendranath who was against widow remarriage. The wedding of Jnanadabhiram and Latika took place after the Maharshi's death, at the insistence of Swarnalata. Rabindranath also had his son Rathindranath married to the widow Pratima.

Latika died prematurely. Her children were brought up by her sister Kanika in Varanasi. Since Kanika's husband held orthodox views Ira never had a chance to learn music or dancing. On a visit to Calcutta in 1933 she heard that Rabindranath had come from Shantiniketan with a troupe for his dance-drama *Shapmochon.* Tagore had never met many of his grand-nieces and nephews and their progeny and Ira was one of them. She approached Ajindra's wife Amita to introduce her to Rabindranath. Though it was difficult to find the poet alone, Amita had carte blanche to see him during his meals. Wearing a saree with her hair in two plaits Ira got ready with her autograph book. Collecting autographs had always been her hobby. Amita introduced her to

Rabindranath. He had just sat down to his meal and asked her to leave the autograph book with him promising to sign it later on. Rabindranath told Amita to give Ira a part in his *Shapmochon* and also said to Ira, 'Come on, you have to act now!' Though delighted, Ira was worried since she knew nothing of acting. As there was no time for her to memorize a role, the Poet gave her the part of fanning Lord Indra in his court. She did not have to utter any lines but just be present on the stage. In the evening when she got back her autograph book she found that the Poet had penned a lyric for her.

Shuno Srimati Ira
Ki bisheshane miley tomar naam
Sakalbelay anek bhabilam
Janina tumi adhira kina
Athoba tumi dhira.
Shuno Srimati Ira
Namer meel kon rattan sathe
Bhabinu tai kalam niye hatey
Noyo to nila noyo to chuni
Tumi kamal heera.'

Listen, dear Ira,
Searching an attribute for your name
I spent the whole morning.
I know not if you are Adhira (restless)
Or Dheera (serene),
Listen, dear Ira,
What gem resembles your name,
Thought I with pen in hand:
Not a sapphire, not a ruby,
You are a diamond.

He had not only signed the lyric but also put down the year and place—Jorasanko 1933. Her heart brimming with joy, Ira returned to Varanasi. She had some freedom after joining college. Her acting talent found full scope there. She had another chance to meet Rabindranath in 1935. Hearing about his visit to

Allahabad she went there to meet him at the Krishnasram of the Theosophical Society.

When Rabindranath had met her earlier Ira had two plaits and he had named her 'Dwibeni'. This time she had tied her hair in a bun, and looked quite different. Seeing the change Rabindranath wrote another short poem:

Prayagey jekhaney Ganga Jamuna
Milayechhey dui dhara,
Taari tiradeshey sekhaney tomar dekhechinu ki chehara.
Dwibeni tomar naam diyechinu dui beni sojasuji
Pithey nemechhilo achal jharna bujhi...
Aji eki dekhi khonpaye tomar bandhiya tulecho beni
Chander sango chanderey magia jomeche megher shreni
Ebar tomar namer badal na korey upaya nai,
Bolibo Khonpa garabini khobani dakibo tai.

Where the currents of Ganga and Jamuna
    have met in Prayag
On that shore I saw you first,
I named you Dwibeni
Your two plaits had descended
    down your back like a frozen cascade;
What do I perceive today?
You have coiled your plaits into a bun,
Hailing the moon for company,
    clouds have gathered upon cloud.
I have to change your name
And shall call you proud of
Your bun—'Khobani'.

This poem was published in the *Probasi* magazine. After reading it a lady actually came to Ira's home to see her tresses.

Rabindranath was very fond of Ira. Apart from joking about her aunt he often coaxed her to come and stay at Shantiniketan. 'You will be able to learn music and drama and be accomplished all round.' Ira was also tempted to agree. At the time she had joined college and begun to read *Gora* as a textbook in Bengali.

Rabindranath not only autographed her book but also took pains to explain various chapters to her. He would tease her saying, 'You are sure to put on airs and tell your friends that Rabindranath has taught you *Gora*'. He asked her which character she liked best. On Ira's comment that he had criticized the Brahmos in *Gora* he just smiled. He was curious to know if she could cook like her mother.

Ira was in the group photograph of Rabindranath with Dwijendranath's family. Ajindranath suggested the group and the poet teased Ira, saying, 'I was denied your pishi, but I do not mind being photographed if you are near me.' Jnanadabhiram was also in Shantiniketan at this time. In 1943 Ira passed the MA examination in English literature. Her meeting and marriage to Gitindranath took place about this time. Abanindranath was very fond of Ira. At the time he was busy composing *Jatra Palaas*. He had wanted to cast Ira as the honeybee in his Jatra.

Ira came in contact with other well-known personalities too. In Lucknow she met Jawaharlal Nehru and Vijayalakshmi Pandit. The former gave her his autograph along with a few lines of good wishes. Ira later met Gandhiji. He usually liked autograph hunters to be clad in khaddar. Moreover five rupees had to be donated per autograph. This money went to Gandhiji's ashram. Complying with all the above norms, Ira deposited her autograph book. When it was returned to her with Gandhiji's autograph, she found that the page containing Jawaharlal Nehru's signature and message had been torn away! She later wrote about this to Nehru who immediately sent her a fresh one.

Ira travelled far and wide with her husband. Moving in high society she was unable to further her talents. Though very good at drama, her acting talent did not get a chance to flower even in Shantiniketan. However all her three daughters inherited it. Her second daughter Tinku was discovered by Tapan Sinha and Sharmila became well-known as a discovery of Satyajit Ray before crossing her teens. Ira's youngest daughter Romila might have been a discovery of Aparna Sen who wanted to cast her as Jennifer Kapoor's pupil in *36 Chowringhee Lane.* However, though she was a successful model, acting did not hold any attraction for Romila.

It may be best to write a few words about Rekha here, though very little is known about her. Samarendranath's daughter Malabika was married to Pradoshchandra Mukhopadhyay. Pradoshchandra's father Jaladichandra was descended from Kadambini. Malabika's youngest daughter was Rekha, whose husband Dr Narayan Menon was associated as a director with the Sangeet Natak Academy and Akashvani. Rekha was also known in the field of music and dance but she merits special thanks for her role in collecting details about Rabindranath from abroad during Rabindranath's birth centenary. She went to Europe with Krishna Kripalani, Kshitish Ray and others. Some rare records and films were collected by them for the Audiovisual Section of Rabindra Bhawan. Rabindranath had recited *Ami paraner saathey khelibo aajikey* from *Jhulan* in Bengali in Sweden. This had been taped by the Swedish academy and recorded and preserved in the Rabindra Bhawan. During this trip some films were collected from Germany. A few scenes from this film collected from the UFO studio were probably used by Satyajit Ray for his documentary. The efforts of Rekha and her husband Narayan Menon in collecting films, pictures and transcripts of lectures by Rabindranath have greatly enriched the Rabindra Bhawan.

After the death of Abanindranath's second daughter Karuna, her children were brought up in Abanindranath's family. Karuna's daughter Reba addressed Alokendra's wife Parul as 'Maa' till her marriage. Though Reba often penned down her thoughts she never thought of publishing them. In the Tagore family children were encouraged to write. Writing not only helps widen the imagination but also improves language. It also encourages one's self-expression, clarity of thought and ability to pen one's thoughts rationally. If there is enough talent this may lead to a place in the literary world also. Everyone may not became a literary figure but the habit of writing is useful in passing examinations and also helps to build the foundations of life. Abanindranath always encouraged his grandchildren in this respect. When they entreated him for suitable plots he said, 'Don't you dream? Start writing them and the plots will follow.' Reba also wrote down her dreams a couple of times. One went as follows:

> One day I was going for a drive in our phaeton with Kokomama, Baradada, Chhotodada, Khukimami, Khepu, Kori, Mintu and Baba. When we had gone a short distance Baba and Kokomama got down. The rest of us drove on to our big garden. We found Kokomama plucking flowers. Baradada asked Kokomama, 'Where is Baba?' Kokomama replied, 'He is upstairs.' We went up and the phaeton drove away.

Reba was just eight years old when she wrote this.

Karuna's eldest son was Mohanlal Gangopadhyay. His *Dakshiner Baranda* was an effort to preserve the saga of Dwarkanath's original garden house—better known as House number 5 Jorasanko—before it was demolished and lost forever. Mohanlal was a well-known statistician. While in London, he met a Czechoslovakian lady—Milada. It was a winter evening and both were at a musical soirée. Mohanlal was the only Indian student in the gathering. On being introduced to him Milada mentioned reading Rabindranath Tagore's *The Gardener* and *Geetanjali* in Czech translations. Mohanlal informed her with a smile that he was related to Rabindranath, her favourite author. Their friendship deepened and in 1935 Milada realized that she was in love with Mohanlal. On hearing her decision to marry him her friends were shocked. Comments like, 'You must be crazy to think of marrying an Indian. How will you adjust to the Indian way of life?' were showered on her. This failed to deter the two young lovers and they got married secretly. Thus the Tagore family acquired another accomplished daughter-in-law.

By this time clouds of the World War II had begun to gather over Europe. Apprehending Germany's attack on Czechoslovakia Mohanlal requested Milada to come back to London in 1938. There they decided to complete their studies and return to India as soon as possible. Due to unavoidable circumstances they were unable to return together. Since Milada, after her marriage, was a citizen of British India she needed a special permit to visit her parents in Czechoslovakia. Mohanlal accompanied her to the Nazi office in London. After a great deal of pleading, she was granted permission to visit her motherland for a month. Milada describes a part of the proceedings thus:

> I said, 'My mother is very ill, and if she cannot see me before I go to far off India, she is going to die. She will not be able to bear it.'
>
> Then the officer-in-charge asked me, 'Are you sure she is going to die if you do not see her?'
>
> I said, 'Yes, I believe she would die if I do not see her before going to India.'

World War II started just two days after Milada left her homeland for India. She had no news of her family until 1947. She lost a great deal due to the war. As she says,

> I never saw my mother after 1939. At the height of the war, my mother tried to get news of India—about me really—on the radio. Someone heard her listening, which was banned, and reported her. She was arrested by the Nazis and taken to a concentration camp. She never returned.

Milada travelled to India alone. She came from her native city to Marseilles via Trieste and from thence by a British ship. This was the last ship from Europe to India before the war. All Europe was on tenterhooks about the impending war and the window-panes of the ship were painted black. When the boat docked in Bombay, Milada found a gift-packet from her husband awaiting her. It contained a saree, blouse, petticoat and a pair of beautiful slippers. With the help of an Indian shipmate, Milada stepped onto Indian soil attired in Indian dress. Mohanlal was overjoyed. His younger brother Shovanlal welcomed his sister-in-law with a bunch of lotus-buds instead of roses. Though the house at Jorasanko had lost a lot of its old grandeur, the womenfolk welcomed her in the traditional style, blowing conch shells. Abanindranath had been painting at the time and commented, 'I am sorry for the parents who have lost you forever.' During the war, most members of the Tagore family had shifted to Shantiniketan. Milada was also one of them. She met Rabindranath, but he was not too well. For three months Milada learnt various handicrafts. Observing some Santhals during Basant Utsav she first thought of working among the adivasis, though she found her true vocation a few years later.

In Shantiniketan Milada met Binodini Devi, the princess of Manipur. On her invitation Milada visited Imphal. While there she expressed a desire to visit the neighbouring Nagaland. The princess of Manipur helped her get an inner line permit. According to Milada, 'I entered Nagaland in a mail-bus escorted by a convoy of 120 military trucks.' The beauty of the Naga hills enchanted Milada and she became curious about the lifestyle of the Nagas. During her second trip Milada was fortunate to meet Nivisa Chasie, an Angami Naga youth. He was a teacher in the High School in Kohima and helped Milada's entry into Naga society. For over twenty-five years, from 1963 to 1988, Milada took permits to visit Nagaland eighteen times. She met various Naga tribes to acquaint herself with their lifestyle, observing them at close quarters. She was able to win their unstinted love and able to see the perfect blending of their talent and artistic ways. She first wrote a book in Czech about the Nagas. Later came *A Pilgrimage to the Nagas* in 1984 and *Naga Art* in 1993. Both were in English. Naga society had never before been observed from an anthropological and historical viewpoint. Since she was an excellent photographer, Milada's books are full of rare pictures.

Milada chose teaching as her profession. She has been associated with South Point School—specially its nursery section—since its inception. Her spare time was spent writing. In Czech she wrote *In the land of Jewel*, and *Pictures from Bengal*. In Bengali she published a collection of fairy tales, *Baaro Masher Baaro Raja*. With Mohanlal she jointly translated the Czech short story, 'Blue Chrysanthemums'.

Amitendra's wife Arundhati was another lady to enter Abanindranath's family by marriage. Her father Prafulla Chandra Chakravarti was the first Indian engineer employed by the Bengal Nagpur Railway. Since his job was a transferable one Arundhati studied mainly at home under the guidance of private tutors. Later she went to London for higher studies. After her marriage she came to Shantiniketan. It was customary for everyone to join some course or other there. Arundhati enrolled in Kala Bhawan to train in handicrafts. She had always been interested in needlework and particularly in knitting. Later she won prizes at international knitting competitions. Amitendranath says that Arundhati and a few others revived the old 'Karusangha' an organization for handicrafts. To quote him,

> Once my brother put up a coffee stall in the Mela premises. My wife said, 'Those of us who have qualified from Kala Bhawan will exhibit our handicrafts within the coffee stall.' This was the first Karusangha.

Arundhati left for America soon after, so Shantiniketan never became her field of work. She and Amitendra were there for twenty-five years. While working in the library of Oakland University in Roberta, Michigan, she studied MA in Applied Developmental Psychology. Later she began research on the unusual topic, 'Concern with Fear of Death among Three Religious Ethnic Groups' (1977); these three religions were Hinduism, Buddhism and Christianity. The main purpose of this work was to associate with the thoughts and feelings of a dying man and help him. There is no denying the importance of this topic from the psychological point of view. Moreover this help has to be based on practical experience to be sincere and useful. It is possible to fight with an incurable disease till the end if there is proper counselling and guidance. Similar support is needed by those hapless families who have to watch helplessly a dear one slowly ebbing away. Arundhati attended the workshop of Kubla Ross regularly and watched quite a number of such incidents. In India no work has been done on this topic yet. Arundhati did think of setting up an organization utilizing her experiences abroad, but in our country grief is still treated as an entirely personal problem. There is hardly any concerted effort to deal with it in a larger social context. Thus such efforts are not very fruitful here. However Arundhati always counsels if approached by individuals.

She is also adept in translation and has translated Alokendranath's *Abanindranath Tagore* into English.

According to the conception of the Tagores, Sumitendranath's wife Shyamashri was '*Gharer meye*', i.e. she hailed from another branch of the Tagores. She was descended from Dwarkanath's sister Rasbilasi's daughter's side. Her father Mohan Ghosal was well-known in the film world. Shyamashri was a student of Calcutta Girls High School but her main interest lay in sports. Table tennis, badminton, basketball—she was not only a superb player but also the school captain in all these games. She won innumerable cups, medals and prizes and was the first girl from the Tagore family to show such proficiency in sports. Had she not belonged to the Tagore family, it is quite possible that she may have achieved a place in the sports world rather than remaining confined to a small circle. After her marriage, she dissociated herself from the world of sport. She learnt vocal music from Ashoktaru Bandopadhyaya but was never interested in it as a career. She much preferred to see the depiction of cultural atmosphere in various functions. This led her to think of producing cultural shows. She may be easily called the first Indian woman impresario. Even today it is men who are common in this role. Such impediments never deterred Shyamashri. Ability to direct others, courage and a clear concept of the artistic world are essential to succeed in an impresario's job. Shymashri had all these attributes in full measure. The job of film production was already known in her family and her captaincy in school and college sports helped her develop the other necessary qualities. Thus the shows organized and produced by her were not only successful but also bore the stamp of superb taste. She produced shows with Ali Akbar, Yamini Krishnamurti, Vilayat Khan, and Nikhil Bandopadhyaya. The latter's daughter Mita later married Shyamashri's son.

Shyamashri also tried her hand at film production. Normally it is not necessary for a producer to have knowledge of film direction. Shymashri had a thorough knowledge of the film world. The well-known Radha Films belonged to her father Mohan Ghosal and numerous Bengali films had been produced by this film company. However, before she entered the world of film production, Shyamashri took training in film direction under the renowned Polish film director Christoph Janucci. She now produced a documentary—*Graven Image*—based on the life of the famous sculptor Chintamani Kar. Not only did it captivate the audience but won the highest presidential award, 'Swarnakamal'. Shyamashri produced two more documentaries. *Sculptor Speaks* was based on the sculptures of Chintamani Kar while *Glimpses of Bengal* dealt with the terracotta temples of Bengal. Her choice of topics for the documentaries gives us an idea of her refined taste and fine artistic sense. In spite of all her success Shyamashri does not like restricting herself to any one particular subject. The only exception is her school 'Aban Nursery Nook', which takes up a lot of her time. This is an old trait of the women of the Tagore family. She has thus been able to utilize her B.T. degree. Shyamashri's characteristic is that she does not believe in attempting anything before she is fully cognizant of all the aspects involved.

Binayini's granddaughters were all accomplished women. Kalidas and Chandrima tried to educate all their children well and also encouraged them to pursue any subject in which they showed a special aptitude. This attitude bore excellent dividends. A woman's genius flowers best in a conducive atmosphere. All four of Chandrima's daughters had the chance to spend a great deal of time in the sylvan surroundings of Shantiniketan. Chandrima's eldest daughter Manasi was a keen painter like her mother. She passed her MA in English literature and had the good fortune to come in contact with Rabindranath Tagore.

Chandrima's second daughter Sunanda played the sitar well. She also took her masters' degree in Geography. Madhabi and Pranati's interests lay in dancing. Had they kept up with music and dancing, the trend of teaching dance introduced by Pratima would have continued unabated even after Gauri and Nandita. Madhabi taught dancing in 'Dakshinee'. She participated in the programme of dance held in New Empire in 1950. Her flawless dancing as Krishna in *Bhanu Singher Padabali* enchanted the audience. When Tinku Tagore played the role of Mini in Tapan Sinha's film *Kabuliwalla* it was Madhabi who taught the little girl to dance to Rabindra Sangeet.

Just as Chandrima's daughters excelled in music, dance and painting, her daughter-in-law Manjari also wanted to be an artist. She came to Kala Bhawan in Shantiniketan from Darjeeling. Not only did she take lessons in drawing and painting, she also appreciated the beauty of nature. Nature shows tremendous restraint and grace in decking herself beautifully. Painting is often but an imitation of nature and in some cases an effort to seek the truth from its heart. In Shantiniketan Manjari was a batch junior to Suhita. She thus had the good fortune of being trained by eminent artists. Due to unavoidable circumstances

Manjari was unable to establish herself as an artist later, but she continued to teach drawing and painting in between her domestic commitments. Teaching youngsters in Beltala Girls School or in 'Chitrangshu' often took her back to her own days as a student of art. She now teaches in 'Rupam' in her own house. This helps her relive the golden days of her youth.

Binayini's youngest daughter Aparna was married into the Majumdar family. Her daughter Bela, known as Sudha after marriage, took her master's degree in French literature, standing first class first. Sudha used to teach in Burdwan University and took a keen interest in the fine arts and literature. She was an excellent sitarist, having been trained under Vilayat Khan. At one time she became the secretary of the Oriental Art Society. During the last few years of her life she became associated with the Chinmay Ashram of Pune and preferred to keep herself occupied with various welfare projects.

Padma also was married into the Majumdar family. She was descended from the Pathuriaghata Tagores, being the daughter of Prabodhendunath Tagore and Shefalika. Shefalika herself was the great-great-granddaughter of Saudamini—one of the Maharshi's daughters. Padma should have come later chronologically, but is being mentioned here due to her relationship with the Majumdar family. Padma's mother was a very good vocalist; so she and her siblings had all been brought up in an atmosphere steeped in music.

Padma's training in vocal music began under Bacchan Mishra. Later she began to learn 'Dhrupad' from Acharya Jogindranath Bandopadhyaya. He taught all the young members of this family. Padma sang very well. To quote her domiciled brother Sandip Tagore, 'Padma later became an expert in the 'Dhrupad' style of vocal music. I always listened to her songs entranced; she was accompanied on the pakhawaj by our music master Jogindranath Bandopadhyaya of Andul. When her trained voice reverberated among the sculptured pillars of our *Chandi Dalan* I always prayed that her song should never end.'

Though the ladies of Padma's paternal family regularly learnt music well in advance of their contemporary times, they never appeared in public. Padma was an exception. Not only was she able to appear in the world of music but she also participated in a number of plays in college, like *Chirakumar Sabha* and *Bisarjan.* Prabodhendunath's friend, the poet and swimmer Shanti Pal, taught swimming in the tank at Hedua in north Calcutta. Every morning Prabodhendu took all his four daughters there to learn swimming. During the Second World War the family shifted to Bhagalpur. There Padma continued her singing lessons with Bibhutibhusan Gangopadhyay. Later she trained under Krishnadas Ghosh and Damodar Mishra, also participating in the All Bengal Music Conference and the shows held by Baitanik.

Saumendranath's songs had a characteristic melody. These were sung in 'Parani'. Padma was attracted by the political, or rather distinctive-tunes that were heard only in Saumendranath's songs. He loved listening to Padma and always wanted her to sing the songs composed by him. Though exceptionally good in the 'Dhrupad' style Padma never presented any songs in this style on Akashvani or Doordarshan. However, when performing in a group with Baitanik she did so occasionally.

At the time of Padma's marriage some objections had been raised because her mother-in-law—Aparna's sister Pratima—had been remarried after being widowed. These were however overruled. Pratima was on intimate terms with the Majumdar family and always stayed with them during her visits to Calcutta. It was Pratima who performed the traditional Badhubaran when Padma first stepped into her husband's home. Shibani Ghosal once requested Padma to visit Shantiniketan and interview Pratima. She did so and from this we are told that when Pratima went to the Maharshi's house (number 6 Jorasanko) from house number 5, Jorasanko after her remarriage, she did so in a horse-drawn, flower-decorated brougham. Jnanadanandini performed the *badhubaran* and, in Pratima's own words, 'She put my mother-in-law's "loha" on my left wrist, and welcomed me into the home. It was customary to keep the "loha" of a woman who predeceased her husband for the daughter-in-law.' Padma's interview tells us that this tradition was followed in the Tagore family too. This interview was taken on 10 September 1968. Padma's husband Amit has also written about his maternal aunt Pratima.

The atmosphere of the Majumdar family was conducive to Padma's interests in music and literature. In her parental home these two ran side by side. Padma herself has written poems, reminiscences and sketches. In an article she says, 'In Indian society women had no dignity in the field of arts. Women exponents of music and song were known as *baijis* and were treated as social outcastes. In spite of being equal to male musicians in every respect they were never awarded the same honour and respect. The contribution of the members of the Tagore family of Jorasanko in earning social acceptance and dignity for women in the field of music today is unquestionable. The ladies of this family participated in Rabindranath's plays and sang songs, utterly disregarding the prevalent social norms.'

Padma has been able to keep up the tradition of music in her family. Her daughter Bhaswati sings well and has been a pupil of Krishnapada Ghosh. Not only is she fond of listening to music but she also has an enviable collection of bhajans and 'Dhrupad'. She has been associated with the English department of La Martiniere for a long time.

Padma deserves a mention for her contribution in another field. At a time when there was not a single coffee-shop in Calcutta, she opened Caffetree in her own house. In 1997 Padma's son returned from America full of praise for the excellent coffee-shops there. Padma and Amit decided to provide coffee to their neighbours. They wanted to prove that one did not need to go abroad or to a five-star hotel to taste excellent coffee. Thus began their experiments to blend their resources and wishes. Padma had inherited her love of cooking from her father who was very keen on this. Unfortunately Shefalika was never able to spend much time in the kitchen due to ill health. The brownies made according to Padma's recipe are an added attraction for coffee-lovers. Today quite a few good coffee-shops have come up in Calcutta; but to taste various blends of coffee excelling both in aroma and taste a visit to the small coffee shop in Ray Street is a must.

It is time we turned again to Sunayani's family. Down the generations, Sunayani, her daughter-in-law Kalyani and her daughters-in-law Sheila and Geeta have all been painters. This certainly is an uncommon and unique characteristic for any family. Sheila of course is better known as a writer. Her translation of Rabindranath's *Shyamali* was published by the Vishwa Bharati almost fifty years ago. Sheila's father Satyendramohan Bandopadhyaya was a class-fellow of Subhas Chandra Bose in Presidency College. He stood first class first in Philosophy while Subhas Chandra secured the second position. Satyendramohan later joined the Indian Civil Service. Sheila's mother not only sang well but also accompanied her husband on his hunting trips. Sheila was brought up by an English governess from the age of two and spoke English as well as her mother tongue. As a child she lived in England and studied in Woodstock. On her return to India she joined Gokhale Memmorial School. While in England she had began to learn painting from Carl Sara. Her forte was water colours. At the age of seventeen she was married into the Chatterjee family. The atmosphere here was totally different from the one in which she had been brought up. In the Tagore family a new bride was always trained in modern etiquette. This involved schooling, lessons in singing and a musical instrument—usually the piano or sitar. Time was also allotted for painting and conversing in English, besides literary pursuits. Along with all this the girl was trained in housekeeping. This meant supervising the servants and making them work properly. It was not an easy task. Unless one is proficient, it is not possible to detect the laxity and thieving of others. The cooks and servants were always kept on their toes by the expert housewives of the Tagore family. Sheila had never had a glimpse of these affairs in all her seventeen years before she landed into a wealthy family, used to the zamindari traditions. Rajanimohan was a well-known attorney with a large income. Sunayani also had a great deal of streedhan of her own. Though Sunayani's household in Beniapukur was at a considerable distance from Jorasanko, the norms of the latter were prevalent here. These were the zamindari traditions. It was here that Sheila's domestic training began. Every morning Sunayani would come and occupy her divan. Just as her mother Saudamini would, reclining on a divan, supervise the household, Sunayani did the same. She would simultaneously paint pictures. Sheila had seen numerous people living in the house besides those who dropped in regularly. All of them had their meals here and food was cooked for about a hundred people daily.

The role of an expert housewife was vital for the smooth running of such a household. Sheila had to be with Sunayani every morning; her job was to look after the store-room. Sheila not only had no previous knowledge of this chore, she was also not very keen on it. She often spent the time sitting with Sunayani, taking lessons in painting or listening to reminiscences. Sunayani had a vast amount of jewellery. She gave Sheila a pair of gold bangles handed down from the time of Dwarkanath. These bangles, looking like solid golden rays of the sun, adorned Sheila's wrists till the end. Sunayani also had a seven-strand necklace of large pearls which she divided among all her granddaughters-in-law. There was a twenty-one-strand necklace, the strands cascading from the neck to the feet. This Sunayani gave to Srimohan's wife Arati. Saudamini had also given Sunayani some jewellery belonging to Jogmaya.

In the meantime Sheila carried on with writing. She always wrote in English. There are no Bengali works by her. She also did a large amount of translation. She began with the poems of Rabindranath Tagore's *Shyamali*. Her main inspiration and encouragement came from her father. She decided to translate *Shyamali* because the poems appealed to her. She always needed to be emotionally involved before taking up any job. Sheila's *Green Beauty* has won acclaim as the best translation of *Shyamali*. The book is still available, but under the heading *Shyamali*. It was first published in 1955 by the publication department of Vishwa Bharati. A literal translation of poetry is a difficult task but Sheila achieved this successfully.

The following is the actual Bengali version of the lines from '*Shesh Praharey*' also titled 'At the Late Watch':

Bhalobashar badaley daya,
yatsamanya shei daan,
seta helaphelari swaad bholano.
Pather pathiko paarey ta biliye ditey
Pather bhikhari key.
Sheshey bhuley jaye bank perotei.
Taar beshi asha karini sedin.

'Pity, in place of love,
That pettiest of gifts,
Is but a sugar coating over neglect.
Any passerby can make a gift of it
To a beggar on the street,
Only to forget the moment the first corner is turned.
I had not hoped for anything more that day...'

Sheila also translated the last stanza of '*Shyamoli*'. The Bengali lines are :

Jabo aami
tomar byatha bihin bidaye dine
aamar bhanga bhiter porey gaibe doel lej duliye
ek sahanai baaje tomar banshitey, ogo shyamali,
Jedin ashi abar jedin jai choley.

I will go,
The day you part from me with no pain,
The *doyel* will sing swinging its tail
On my forsaken homestead,
There is but one tune of Sahana that plays on your flute.
Oh green Beauty,
On the day I came and the day I go away.

Along with her writing Sheila continued her studies. She took her master's degree in English literature and was a regular contributor of fiction in the *Amritabazar Patrika*. Her stories were published regularly almost every Sunday. In the Puja, Annual and Tagore issues were published her translations of Tagore's stories. The first to be published was 'The Buried Treasure' in 1952. It was a translation of 'Guptadhan'. After that it became a regular annual feature.

In 1954 came 'Dalia'. In 1955 it was 'The Garlanding'—a translation of '*Malyadan*'. '*Pratihimsha*' was translated as '*Revenge*' in 1956. Then came 'Punishment' or '*Shaasti*' in 1958, 'The Girl Ascetic' or '*Tapaswini*' in 1959, and '*Debt and Dues*' or '*Dena Paona*' in 1960. Shiela translation of two stories. 'Taraprasanna's Masterpiece' from '*Taraprasannar Kirti*' and 'Gift and Return' from '*Daan Pratidaan*'. In 1962 came 'The Editor' or 'Sampadak'. The last two were in 1963: 'The Artist' or '*Chitrakar*' and 'Failure' or '*Fail*'. After this Sheila did not publish any more translations. During this time she had also translated stories by Bibhutibhushan Bandopadhyaya and some other authors. In the sixties she also contributed to the *Illustrated Weekly of India*. Satyendramohan's death on 24 December 1961 hit Sheila very hard and she gradually withdrew from the literary world.

Rather than force herself to continue writing, Sheila now tried her hand at painting. She always had an interest in archaeology and travelled far and wide to places of archaeological interest. Her paintings are a blend of what she saw and what she imagined.

Quite a few of these were published in the *Masik Basumati* magazine.

Neither her literary work nor her paintings were ever collected and published in the form of a book or album. She however had carefully preserved the typed copies of all her literary efforts. On being questioned she said, 'My father had all these typed and arranged, they are still there as such. I never thought of publishing them as a book. Had I considered the possibility perhaps it would have been done.'

Besides possessing all the characteristic qualities of the Tagores and their relations, which set them apart, like culture, personality and artistic taste, Sheila appears to stand apart, adorned by a unique halo all her own.

Geeta belonged to the Mukherjee family of Uttarpara. She was married when she was only thirteen. Thereafter the education of this pretty and unusually lively girl began in Loreto School. Kalipada Ghosal taught her painting at home. She used water colours mainly. Geeta acted in the plays written by her husband and also loved to write. These included poems, nursery rhymes and memoirs. Though small compositions, these give us glimpses of a person or a period in time. In one of her nursery rhymes Geeta wrote:

Tumi amar chhutir diner galpa bola pishi,
Ghumer samay hao je tumi ghoomparani mashi.
Tumi amar achin desher pakshirajer ghora,
Toma bina hoina amar parir deshey ora.

You are the pishi who tells me stories during holidays
At bedtime you are the mashi who puts me to sleep
You are the winged horse of my unknown lands
Without you I cannot fly to the land of fairies.

Geeta's reminiscences read like fairy tales, especially when she talks about her childhood or of even older days, as mentioned by her mother. Geeta's paternal grandfather, Sanatkumar Mukhopadhyay of Uttarapara, was old-fashioned, conservative and dead against women's liberation. His view was 'If the womenfolk of the family read plays and novels, especially works of Sarat Chandra and Bankimchandra—like *Anandamath*—they would become far too independent and aggressive.' Geeta's mother had studied in the Brahmo Balika Vidyalaya before her marriage and, since she was on excellent terms with her mother-in-law, her literary and musical pursuits were unhindered even after marriage. To quote Geeta, 'Ma would get numerous good books—Rabindranath's *Chayanika* and Madhusudan's *Meghnad Vadh Kavya*—and keep them in the wall-almirah in her room. As soon as lunch was over, my mother, Jethaima, a nieghbour Kamalapishi and my paternal grandmother would be busy reading and discussing these books. This literary pursuit went on usually till four p.m. However, as soon as my grandfather's footsteps were heard in the evening, Ma and my aunt would put the books away, draw the small curtains before the glass panes of the wall-almirah and sit down with a piece of needlework or knitting.' The winds of change unlocked most locked doors.

Another narrative by Geeta gives us a glimpse of the various ways and means devised by the daring womenfolk of her family to get a taste of independence. Time was when women submitted to spending their lives behind four walls, but when these restrictions were not relaxed with the passage of time, subterfuge was inevitable. During the time mentioned by Geeta, whole night theatre shows were held in Calcutta during Shivaratri. This was because devotees had to keep awake all night. Many men and women also broke their fast in the evening, after lighting a lamp at the Nakuleshwartala in Kalighat. Once Geeta's mother, grandmother and aunts decided to do the same. When Geeta's grandfather was informed, he called his son Duldul and said, 'Look Duley, tomorrow the ladies all want to go to Kalighat. You will accompany them and see that they return home safely in time.' Thereafter Duldul was summoned to the andar mahal. The ladies told him, 'We will leave by 2 p.m. and go straight to

Rangmahal Theatre to see the play *Sati.* Thereafter we will go to Nakuleshwartala by six p.m., light the lamp and have some sweets and snacks in the coach. Again we will see the nine p.m. show of Ahindra Chaudhuri's *Shahjahan* and leave for Uttarpara at midnight.' Geeta's grandmother raised a slight objection, 'How will we explain such a delay to my husband?' Geeta's mother said, 'Why, we will say that the pontoon bridge at Howrah over the Ganga had been opened and so we got delayed.' Due to such meticulous planning the visits to the theatre by the ladies of his household never became known to Geeta's grandfather.

In another instance, the ladies went out to a wedding invitation at Khiddirpur one evening. Though they were supposed to have dinner, they just tasted some fish fry and sweets, proceeding straight from there to the Star Theatre for the 6 p.m. show of Sisir Bhaduri's *Alamgir*. The women were all decked up in expensive Benarasi sarees and jewellery. Fortunately they were well covered with shawls; but still they attracted a fair amount of attention. The three-year-old Geeta and her maid Radha were also in the party, complete with bedding, milk bottle and hand-fan! Geeta tells us,

> Duldul uncle managed to arrange for a small space where I could be put to sleep. The management had insisted that I should not cry loudly during the show. When everyone returned home late at night they found Grandfather pacing up and down in the sitting room! As they entered the house and began to go upstairs, Uncle began to berate the Calcutta Port Trust.
>
> 'It is disgraceful. There is no parity between what they publish in the papers and the actual situation about traffic on the pontoon bridge. Three ships passed before the bridge was joined together for through traffic, we had to wait so long.' Grandfather just said, 'Well, I hope my little darling was not inconvenienced—'

. . . his little darling being his beloved granddaughter Geeta. Many such anecdotes are stored in Geeta's memory. If penned down, they are sure to form an imminently enjoyable book. It would also preserve for us glimpses of the combined efforts of a mother-in-law and a daughter-in-law: prompted by love, as well as snippets of happenings in ordinary day-to-day life.

There were numerous well-known ladies among Geeta's in-laws. She had the good fortune to know Sunayani intimately. Geeta's memoirs give us glimpses of Sunayani also. She was then over eighty, unable to walk properly and almost blind. Remembering her daily rides every evening to the Maidan and the Strand with the grandchildren, Lokomohan suggested one day, "Come Grandma, let us go for a drive. It is a low car, you will have no problem getting in."

Sunayani demurred, 'Let it be.' Geeta felt that Sunayani did actually want to go; so she insisted, 'Please, Grandma, you will feel much better.' Sunayani still said, 'Why bother? I am sure it will inconvenience you.' Geeta writes,

> This was characteristic of her. She would never request anyone for anything and did not like any special arrangements for herself. However we managed to persuade her. As she entered the car she said, 'It has been so long since I sat in a car.' My husband asked, 'Where would you like to go?' She replied, 'Let us go to the Strand by the side of the Ganga.' As the car entered Circular Road, she recognized it and exclaimed, 'What is this road? Many years ago, when I used to come for a drive with your grandfather from our Beniapukur house, we used to come this way. It was such a long time ago.' As we drove past the Victoria Memorial her eyes seemed to be lost, turned to the past. Turning her head from side to side, she said, 'We used to come to the Victoria Memorial on every full moon night. The old trees are still there.' So many memories seem associated with the memorial of Queen Victoria even now . . .
>
> As our car passed along the banks of the Ganga and turned in front of Eden Gardens, Grandmother said, 'A band used to play here every day and the garden would be aglow with flowers all the year round.' She smiled and continued, 'It is so

> bare now.' When asked about the return-route, she said, 'Let us go back along the Strand.'

Perhaps Geeta will also give us some fairy tales from her reminiscences.

Geeta's second daughter Supriya seemed to have inherited Sunayani's talent. Even in her childhood she used to paint and draw like her great-grandmother. Sunayani always hoped that this child would be her worthy successor. Supriya kept up her practice of painting and was associated with the Kala Bharati. However, she is not very well-known as an artist. She concentrated more on painting cards and this clearly shows all the magic of Sunayani's skill.

Some other members of Sunayani's family merit a mention. Manimala's two daughters-in-law came from two different families. Kamala, the daughter of the writer Leela Majumdar, has published a book on cookery jointly with her mother. Maitreyi, the other one, is a granddaughter of Hemendra Kumar Ray. She is closely involved with the women's liberation movement and is a well-known human rights activist as well as a freelance journalist. She has not only pondered on the various problems faced by women but has also striven to raise public opinion against their cruel exploitation. She has been associated with the Naari Niryatan Pratirodh Mancha from its very inception. She has also detailed her opinion of feminism clearly: 'Literally feminism is an ideal which claims equal rights for all women. Those who make these claims are known as feminists. However this is a very narrow interpretation. The claim for equal rights hardly describes this ideal. Feminism is a much wider social movement whose origin cannot be traced to any one particular event. This movement was born during a doubt-ridden time in history. The main purpose was not just getting some privileges for women but to bring about a change in society based on equality. In this movement of 8 March 1857 the demands of the women workers were : better wages, congenial and healthy environment in the work place and reduction of hours of work from sixteen to ten. With this movement as its foundation, began one in the nineteen-sixties. The main demands of the latter were: right to birth control and abortion, better job opportunities, equal wages for equal work and economic independence. To this has been added a protest against use of women as symbols of consumer goods and sex and abolition of all types of discrimination.'

Maitreyi's views are certainly very different from the long-standing ideas of the Tagore family. However much the Tagores may have participated in women's emancipation and their women's active participation therein, there is a wide gulf between their ideas and Maitreyi's view point. From another angle it may be said that they have helped Maitrayi in formulating her views. In spite of such differences, Manimala was very fond of Maitreyi. She always said that after all, her son Kishore was different from the others. He was an artist with an interest in music. So where was the harm if his wife did not wish to mould her life according to the prevailing norms? Maitreyi has presented us with a small anecdote, based probably on her own experiences: 'There was a table in one corner of the room with a flower-vase. Flowers had been arranged to blend tastefully with the shape and colour of the vase. The hostess' friend and his wife were overwhelmed. There were more surprises waiting for them. On the dining table were arranged their favourite vegetarian dishes. Replete with the excellent food, they commented before leaving, "You are so accomplished and cook so well. We cannot comprehend how you became a feminist."' Maitreyi noticed that the general opinion regarding feminists was, 'They are ugly, not good housewives and devoid of all womanly charms and graces.' She has also observed, 'The problems and values of women of wealthy and upper-caste families are totally different from their persecuted sisters belonging to the lower castes.' In spite of all these hindrances they are trying to awaken consciousness in women. Real improvement will be achieved only when one woman will understand the problems of another who is not her sister. Apparently the time has not come for such a view-point but a consciousness has been created. Maitreyi and other human rights activists are naturally not satisfied by this slow progress. She will always be remembered as a feminist trying to 'produce crops on barren soil.' The decision to strive for and earn the right to control one's life, rather than to beg the Almighty, has already become the basis of many a woman's character. It is still not clear whether their sisters have an equal importance in their heart. To achieve such a goal not only Maitreyi but every woman will have to strive.

Manimala's daughter Jayashri is also something of an exception in her family. It never even occurred to me to ask this Reader in the Genetics Department of Ramakrishna Mission Seva Pratishthan about her interest in singing or painting as a child. Passing from Gokhale Memorial School, she later joined the Science College with honours in anthropology. She specialized in physical anthropology and the topic of her research was 'Growth and Development of Newborn Babies'. It seemed more appropriate to discuss her work than to ask questions about fellowships and scholarships won by this busy woman. Attached to the mobile health unit of the Seva Pratishthan, she worked for twelve years in various villages. Her writings give us an inkling of the shocking conditions of the girl child.

> During pregnancy the male embryo far outnumbers the female. As no scientific explanation is known so far, this has been considered as a natural phenomenon. However the chances of death according to its physical condition are more for the male embryo. So an examination of the sex ratio at the time of birth shows a slight tilt towards the male. In developed and many developing countries, the number of girl babies increases within two years of birth. Our country however is an exception to this rule. A baby's growth is very rapid from two to twelve months and maximum care is needed during this period. Our mentality being oriented towards the son, a baby

> girl is purposely neglected. As a result the death rate of female babies is 21% more than that of males between the ages of two months and one year.

Not only this, Jayashri quotes the experimental evidence culled by Dr C. Gopalan, an expert on nutrition,

> Though the number of malnutritional babies is five times greater for female babies as compared to the male, hospital records show this ratio to be 50:1. This is because any ailment of a male child, be it malnutrition or otherwise, is immediately attended to whereas the female child is often neglected . . .

Jayashri has also had unusual experiences while working on behalf of the Ramakrishna Mission in ten underdeveloped villages of South 24 Parganas. She says, 'Durga of Panchagram is an ordinary illiterate woman bowed down by poverty and family responsibilities. Her husband Panchanan is a share cropper working as a daily labourer for farmers. Due to the seasonal nature of his employment he has regular work for just six months a year. The remaining six months he barely manages. A greater part of his earning goes towards country liquor. They have two sons and two daughters. Durga is unable to alleviate the poverty of her family even after toiling from dawn to dusk. Approaching the mobile health unit for treatment, she met Jayashri and other health workers who told her about family-planning. She ultimately decided to go ahead and came to the hospital under the pretext of visiting relations. On her return after the ligation operation, she faced inhuman torture. Her husband starved her for a week.

> Tears came to my eyes seeing her misery but when I said, 'You have suffered so much because of us,' she replied, 'No Didi, when my husband realizes that I have acted for his and his children's well being he will come round. However much he beats me I shall not leave my home. You will see, finally I shall win.' Durga has won. Peace has been restored in her home. Poverty is still there and Panchanan still beats her when he is

> drunk. However, he looks after his home and family. When his daughter Lakshmi fractured her arm, he regularly took her to the hospital thirty miles away until the arm was set right. Though they often go without a meal, still they bring us papayas from their trees. A few health centres, proper treatment, sympathy and a helpful attitude can bring about so much change. An illiterate woman—with barely a roof over her head, who goes hungry most of the time and is cowed by grinding poverty—managed to become educated in the truest sense of the word, developing her inherent potential.

As Jayashri's narration was about rural Bengal she has perhaps named an unknown woman Durga. This of course is a most fitting name for such a courageous person. It is about such 'Durgas' that 'Agamani' songs have been composed by poets in Bengal, depicting the trepidation of Himalaya's wife Menoka.

Jayashri has had such varied experiences while working in rural Bengal that it is difficult to pick and choose. A quote from one of them:

> Once a village woman came to see us. She wore the saree in a non-Bengali style and her language was a mixture of Bengali and Hindi. She told us that though this was her native village she was married in Ayodhya. On our questioning her she said that one day she had gone to visit her grandmother in Garia. There a friend became bought her some *sandesh* from a nearby shop. She passed out and when she became conscious, she found herself in a police station in Ayodhya. A gentleman turned up soon after and brought her from the police. She was married to the younger brother of this man. She was her husband's second wife and very well cared for. Theirs was a joint family with her husband's parents and his elder brother's wife. She was well treated and she had no problems adjusting with them. She had four sons and was now the mistress of the house. A few days ago, her husband's younger brother was coming to Calcutta and offered to bring her along. Thus she was able to visit her native village once again. She had learnt after her marriage that numerous girls from her village as well as neighbouring ones were married in Ayodhya and leading happy lives there.

It was amazing. Jayashri took up her pen to write about one among the 38,024 villages of West Bengal. She particularly noticed,

> The girls in rural villages are slowly being educated and are against early marriages. In these villages, women deserted by their husbands sustain their families. They often engage in small-scale cottage industries like spinning, weaving or making joss-sticks but the income is negligible when compared to the needs of these homes.

In her experience, spread across ten to twelve years, Jayashri observed,

> 'The women of Panchagram have begun a silent battle against the male-dominated society. They may not be revolutionaries but they can certainly be called fighters, considering their battle against the daily problems besetting their lives. Unfortunately society seems oblivious to this day-to-day struggle.'

On her numerous visits to Panchagram with the mobile health unit of Seva Pratishthan Jayashri observed another positive change. 'The children of Panchagram initially had no interest in listening to stories, they would just wait for the bell to ring at mealtime. The same children are now not only being educated but they are also participating in sports and painting competitions. In 1990 China sponsored a World Art Competition. Sasthi Mandol from this village came first with a painting of Panchagram.'

Jayashri is associated with the Vivekananda Institute of Medical Research along with the Ramakrishna Mission Seva Pratishthan. In her department of genetics, research is undertaken on 'chromosome mapping'. This work helps cure gene-related diseases. It has been possible to help thalassemia patients also. Along with the rising importance of gene-related treatment and the effect of heredity on various ailments, there has been an increase in Jayashri's research. Though she combines social welfare with her work, her family has never been neglected. Every one of the four members is educated and gainfully employed.

It would be in order to mention a few descendants of Kadambini and Kumudini now. It is quite difficult to trace everyone in such a large family and some may not have been portrayed properly. An example is Jeenprakash's daughter Tilottama who not only painted well but was peerless in handicrafts. Unfortunately, it has not been possible to ascertain anything further about her. Kadambini's daughter Nripabala was married to Harindranath Tagore. Their grandson Arabindanath was the husband of Anuja, Sunayani's daughter. It is not known if any of Sunayani's daughters painted but Anuja's daughter Shibani stands out among her family members. She showed exemplary competence in social welfare. The wife of Asit Ghosal, Shibani always treasured the memory of her meeting with Rabindranath Tagore. Once Shibani and her husband had gone to Bankura with Sunayani. Rabindranath had also come there to lay the foundation stone of a local school. Sunayani visited her 'Robikaka' with her granddaughter and grandson-in-law. In her old age Shibani described the meeting thus,

> . . . We arrived at the residence of the magistrate Mr Haldar. Crossing the gate and verandah we stood before the poet's room. Grandmother opened the door gently. We saw the poet reclining on an arm-chair with his eyes closed. All the windows were shuttered and the panes were of blue glass. The room was full of the fragrance of 'champak' flowers. It was an unearthly feeling. I was thrilled with joy. I had read his poems and knew his songs practically since I learnt the alphabet; but I had never imagined meeting him in such unusual surroundings.

A musical soiree was held at the magistrate's bungalow that evening. Shibani's husband Asit sang well. The poet was charmed to hear him sing two Rabindrasangeets; *Dukhero barashaye* and *O haar manaley go*. Later he recorded both the songs. The poet asked Shibani to sing. Encouraged by her grandmother's enthusiasm and the poet's eagerness, Shibani was at her wit's end. She however decided to sing the song *Chander haashir baandh bhengechey* because the tune was quite simple. The only problem was that the word 'Shashi' appeared in the song. This was the name of Asit's grandfather. In those days, women did not utter the name of their father-in-law or husband's elder brother. So Shibani substituted 'Shashi' with 'Bookey'. When she explained this to the poet, '. . . he first frowned but later asked me to sing. I sang with as much feeling as I could muster. The poet listened with his eyes closed. Then he commented, "You have done a good job."' Thereafter, Shibani would go everyday and sit at Rabindranath's feet. People from far and near came to pay their respects. As his great-grandniece Shibani was emboldened to ask him one day, 'Dadabhai, did you ever fall in love?' The smiling rejoinder of the poet was, 'Yes my dear, but it was only a fall, I never could get up.'

Shibani's true abilities came to the fore later. During the Second World War, the ground floor of the Ghosal's palatial mansion was taken over temporarily to house the famine-stricken multitude that was pouring into Calcutta. The plight of these hungry and helpless creatures horrified Shibani. Daughter of a wealthy family, married into an equally wealthy one, she had never seen such misery. She was particularly concerned about the women. Most of them had no educational qualification or training for jobs that may be found for them. Suddenly she came across an exquisitely crafted nakshi kantha in the possession of one of these women. Though the women of the Tagore family were acquainted with this craft, it—like many other handicrafts of Bengal—had practically disappeared from public memory before the Partition. It was only in vogue in East Bengal. When Shibani asked the woman how long it would take her to make such a kantha, she replied, 'In summer when the days are long, I can make one in twenty days. Otherwise it takes me a year.' Shibani begun to discuss the possibility of helping these hapless women by selling their handiwork. The state Social Welfare Board and some other people who appreciated art and craft encouraged her.

Thus in 1953 was established Ganganagar Mahila Shilpasiksha Mandir in Ganganagar village on the outskirts of Calcutta. Women and girls were trained in child-education, needlecraft, kantha-stitch, batik, and weaving. Arrangements were also made to sell their work.

Shibani's effort has popularized the nakshi kantha to a great extent. Though one should remember Abanindranath's efforts in this matter, as well as Subho Tagore's interest, these efforts to revive the art of nakshi kantha were from an artistic viewpoint while Shibani exploited the commercial potential. The craft that was mainly used to make a coverlet in East Bengal, was also used to make cushion covers, bedcovers, shawls, tea-cosies, table-cloths and ultimately sarees. Such embroidered sarees are known as kantha sarees. Now the same work is being done on sheets and kurtas as well as on chadars. In Bangladesh also various experiments are being carried on now with the kantha stitchery. This had not been done in earlier times. The artists of Ganganagar have also been able to popularize kanthas abroad as items of home decoration. Thus an old art form was revived by its tremendous popularity among women in West Bengal and many women became involved with this as a business. As the secretary of her organization Shibani always gave voluntary service. She was also associated with Akashvani.

Meenakshi, the wife of Arunendranath Tagore, left her familiar surroundings in Calcutta for Pondicherry many years ago. Her husband belonged to the Koilahata branch of the Tagore family and was closely associated with the Aurobindo Ashram in Calcutta. He took a keen interest in the activities of the Ashram and often helped supervise their work. Meenakshi first visited Pondicherry with Arunendra. At that time many Bengali families had settled there and had dedicated themselves to service of the Ashram. It was like a large happy family with the Mother at the helm. With her sincerity and keenness to realize Shri Aurobindo's dream she had touched everyone's heart. Meenakshi decided to stay on in Pondichery. Arunendranath agreed, though their three sons were in Calcutta. Meenakshi approached the Holy Mother with her heart's desire. She wanted to stay on as an Ashramite working for the same. The Holy Mother agreed. Meenakshi was first put in charge of the garden, then the kitchen and last of all the children's section. The children of the Ashram found their lost homely environment in Meenakshi's gentle care and motherly love. She has been in charge of the children's department since 1956 and considers them as her own. Arunendranath and his three sons went to Pondichery much later. Though they did not stay with Meenakshi there was no dearth of communication. Even today they keep abreast with all her news, especially her devoted grandson Manav.

Meenakshi finds great satisfaction in this work. So many children grew up under her care and then scattered all over the world, only to be followed by new ones. The Holy Mother herself had entrusted Meenakshi with this task, having full confidence in her abilities. Meenakshi has been able to do full justice to the confidence reposed in her and this overrides even her sense of joy. With her advancing years, she is able to care for only a few children. They stay with her and looking at their cheerful appearance, it is impossible to realize that this is not their own home.

Kumudini's family has been mentioned earlier. A permanent rift between her family and that of the two Tagores of Jorasanko occurred from the time of Rathindra's marriage to Pratima. The latter's first husband had belonged to Kumudini's family. Such an attitude did not find favour with the members of the other branches of Tagores. Times were changing and they did not consider the remarriage of a girl-widow an offence. However this rift continued for many years.

Tanuja, the daughter of Kumudini's grandson Naranath, was married to Saudamini's grandson Suprakash. Tanuja has been discussed much earlier. She had three other sisters. Manuja,

Shibani and Malabi. Malabi's husband Purnendunath was the eldest son of Raja Prafullanath Tagore of Pathuriaghata. The wedding had taken place with great pomp and show since Raja Prafullanath was very wealthy and a big landlord. His family owned nearly a thousand villages in the Bakharganj area of East Bengal. Apart form other treasures, there was a vast amount of heirloom jewellery. These did not belong to any one female member individually but anyone could use them, whenever she wished or the occasion demanded. This probably was a tradition prevalent in the royal families and among the big zamindars. Whatever a bride brought from her paternal home at the time of marriage or received as gifts, was considered to be her own property.

Malabi was married when she was only twelve. Before that she had an English governess and studied in Diocesan School. Besides, she had learnt dancing, music, needlework and painting. At that time efforts were made so that girls had as many accomplishments as possible. Their main aim and that of their guardians was to see them established as mistresses of well-to-do homes. The women of this family were not allowed to move out of doors alone or whenever they wished. Malabi sang very well and had been coached in 'Khayal' and 'Thumri' by Gopeswar Bandopadhyay. It is probable that she kept up her singing after marriage. She learnt to paint from her governess and cards painted by her were sold in exhibitions. There is no news of her keeping this up later though many members of the Pathuriaghata Tagores painted. Painting was certainly appreciated by this family. Malabi once wrote an article on Sunayani's paintings in Subho Tagore's magazine *Sundaram*. She was also interested in writing, though most of her work remains unpublished and the manuscripts are also missing. The creations of many a woman have been lost similarly.

Kumudini's granddaughter Neeraja was married to Saradindranath Tagore of Koilahata. Neeraja's twin sons Sujanendra and Sajanendra were married to two sisters—Suchitra and Ira. Sujanendra was the elder of the brothers by a few minutes, though his wife Suchitra was younger to Ira. Ira and Suchitra's mother was the granddaughter of Maharaja Saurindramohan. Though sisters, and married into the same family, they were quite different in their tastes. One was an excellent housewife while the other was gifted with superb artistic sense. Ira managed the household while Suchitra loved to write and paint. She had been born with a rare gift of artistry but never had the chance of any formal training in drawing or painting. No one ever drew even a few lines to teach her the basics of sketching the human form. Widowed at an early age, she had the responsibility of bringing up three young children. Yet she painted because she loved to do so. Durgapuja was celebrated annually in the house. Suchitra painted several pictures of Durga and Jagaddhatri. Her portrait of the poet Rabindranath was absolutely flawless, only a minute scrutiny reveals it to be a painting and not a print. Her main inspiration came from pictures by famous painters published in various magazines and calendars. Shortcomings in her work never bothered her. Thus she was able to portray Abanindranath's *Shahjahan* perfectly.

She showed the same devotion when decorating the deity 'Gopal'. Often asked to dress up a bride, she told her own granddaughter, 'The Banarasi for the wedding should be red but have the one for the "bau bhaat" in turquoise embroidered with silver flowers. It should remind people of an evening sky full of stars.' These few words give us an idea of Suchitra's artistic sense.

Suchitra loved to travel, especially to places of scenic beauty. This was not very easy but once her children were settled, Suchitra was able to indulge herself. Since she loved to write, she recorded the memoirs of these travels in her note-book. Some have been published in different magazines but many others have accumulated as manuscripts. The following excerpt is from one such manuscript and provides a glimpse of her visit to the Vivekananda Rock before the present temple had been built.

> . . . The steam launch anchored near the Vivekananda Rock and we slowly stepped onto this holy spot. This is where lie the foot prints of that great man. Beyond the wide courtyard rise a flight of marble steps. On the other side there is a small temple housing the piece of rock carrying the imprint of Vivekananda's foot. This piece of stone lying in a glass case placed atop a low platform is lit up by the dim yellowish rays of an electric lamp . . .

Neeraja's sister Suraja was the wife of Maharaja Pradyotkumar of Pathuriaghata. It needs to be mentioned that Maharaja Jatindramohan had no son and so he adopted Pradyotkumar. History repeated itself when Pradyotkumar adopted Prabirendramohan. Prabirendra was the youngest son of Pradyotkumar's stepbrother Shibkumar and Snehalata, Suraja's younger sister. Though they represent the Pathuriaghata Tagores, Kumudini of the Jorasanko Tagore House was Suraja's paternal grandmother. Prabirendra's wife Suriti belonged to the well-known Pakrashi family of north Bengal. Her father was closely associated with the dramatic world of north Bengal while her mother traced her descent from Devi Chaudhurani. All her accomplishments have been overshadowed by her incomparable beauty. At that time every young girl in an aristocratic family was taught to play the piano. Suriti also leant to play the guitar along with her piano lessons. Most of her training in instrumental music was from Dakshinamohan Tagore. She had an excellent command of French and began her painting lessons with Anil Bhattacharya.

The following is an anecdote about Suriti's beauty. She was commonly known as Durga because of her ethereal beauty resembling that of the goddess. Saroja's granddaughter Surabhi had tried hard to bridge the rift between her family and the Pathuriaghata Tagores. Surabhi's mother was born in the same Raj family though she did not keep up much communication after her marriage. Surabhi's memoirs lead us to believe that her efforts had been partly successful. Anyway, one day Lady Ranu

Mukherjee told Surabhi that she had heard that the Maharani of Pathuriaghata was a paragon of beauty and would like to meet her. Surabhi arranged for the two beauties to meet at her place. To quote Surabhi:

> . . . Durgadi came to our house. The first thing one noticed was her glowing, flawless rosy complexion. Her brownish hair was knotted into a simple bun, her doe-shaped eyes had a calm look. Her smile was bewitching—the teeth resembling a row of perfectly matched pearls. Durgadi was not very tall and was dressed simply in an expensive Shantipur sari with a zari border. She wore a pair of pearl tops, a gold chain, gold-encrusted 'loha' and conch-shell bangles. The two ends of the pair of gold bangles she wore, were shaped like a fish-head. Apart from a round red vermilion mark on her forehead, her face was free of make up. Her feet were in a pair of ordinary sandals and her entire demeanour was dignified, calm and quiet.

As Surabhi waited to see the two beauties together Suriti asked her, 'Why is your Ranudi so keen to meet me?' Surabhi replied, 'Why, don't you feel any desire to meet her?' Though Suriti gave no reply she must have been curious, otherwise she need not have accepted the invitation. Ranu came on time. According to Surabhi, 'Ranudi was tall and slim. She wore one of her favourite light-coloured Banarasi saris, and a pair of long earrings. She was faultlessly made up and had on high-heeled shoes. Both were beautiful but their beauty was of two entirely different kinds.' Later, these two ladies came to know each other well.

Coming back to Dwijendranath's family, Surabhi's two daughters, Supriya and Sumitra, made honourable contributions in the field of education and social service in Maharashtra. Supriya's childhood dreams centred around music, dance and painting. Thus she may be called an artistic daughter of an artist mother. Despite all this, she loved to be with children. So after her husband's death she chose teaching as a profession and is now based in Nagpur. An added bonus has been the pleasure of teaching Rabindranath's dance-dramas to non-Bengalis and also presenting them with performances of the same. To encourage children she taught them Rabindra Sangeet and helped them portray the essence of a poem with paint and brush. In consequence of this work she directed *Chandalika*, *Barashey Rimjhim* and *Krishnakali*. She also put up a street show—*Sher Bachao*—with her students. This was an appeal to the public for tiger preservation during Wild Life Week. Apart from all this, every year she directed the 'Spirit of Shantiniketan' in her school, holding classes in music, dance and art in an open courtyard. Supriya's sphere of activity is not restricted to her role as the principal of her school but is spread widely in social work. This has won her the 'Abantika Shakuntalam' award from the country. One hopes that she will present us with a collection of the varied incidents of her busy life, perhaps a reminiscence like *Nana Ranger Din* by Surabhi.

Supriya's younger sister Sumitra was also interested in social welfare. This prompted her to take up the job of teaching hearing-impaired children in a Central School. Hearing impairment makes many a child helpless. With great persistence it is possible to teach a three-year-old child his mother tongue. Due to her exceptional aptitude in this field Sumitra was able to attend the 'Instute Voor Doven' in Holland. To quote her:

> . . . I learnt a great deal on the job—how to elicit conversation from a child who can only gesture and produce some sounds, how to use every possible opportunity to give language . . .

Sumitra dedicated herself heart and soul to her work. She observed that a hearing-impaired child learns to speak by observing lip movements. Thus it is often necessary to repeat the same word several times. She says,

> As the children grow older I have to be prepared to discuss any topic under the sun! With no text books to guide me at the early stage, I teach by instinct, thinking on my feet, talking

endlessly and repeating until at last the child says a word or phrase.

The work is back-breaking but gives Sumitra immense satisfaction. She considers her life blessed, being able to make hearing-impaired children speak.

Sujata's daughter was named Rita. This seems a favourite name among the Tagores. Though keen on social work, she was hindered by illness, accidents and death. In her childhood she saw her mother engrossed in social work. She herself also became associated with many voluntary organizations. At present Rita is involved with 'Vivek Chetana' at Keyatala. Rita's real forte is writing for children. She writes well but has never felt like doing so for adults. Few people write only for children these days. Rita is one of them and has penned the golden days of her childhood for them. Here is an excerpt. 'We were interested in drama. Once it was decided to stage "*Abaak Jalpaan*" from Sukumar Ray's *Jhalapala*. Burnt cork was used to draw moustaches and beards by my elder brothers. I wore a dhoti and kurta, tucked my plaited hair inside the kurta, put on a pair of rimless spectacles with the glass replaced by cellophane paper, took a stick and sat down on a cane stool to recite Rabindranath's "*Kanai Master*". Just as I said "The kitten is my pupil", an awful commotion took place. My pet cat Buchu who had been sitting on my lap with a bell on a green ribbon tied round her neck, miaowed loudly and jumped off my lap, despite my restraining hands. She ran by the side of the stage and disappeared in a trice. I was flabbergasted but somehow managed to complete the recitation. Buchu had been a model of good behaviour all through the rehearsals.'

Rita's childhood was spent in Serampore, away from both the Tagore mansion and Macleod Street. Yet these two places exerted their influence on her family atmosphere. They often staged Tagore's *Daakghar* with the students of Sujata's adult education class. During the Second World War they spent some time in Shantiniketan. On her return to Serampore, Rita had to move to Calcutta as there were no good schools for girls in Serampore. Rita has not penned anything about her later life, yet she spent some time in Uganda and had thought of writing about the folk culture of Africa. The local residents of Uganda also loved her. They often said, 'Mama, you call us and talk to us but here no one addresses us.' On the eve of her departure they requested her for a photograph saying, 'Please give us a photograph. Even if you are unable to do so your memory will be engraved in our hearts in letters of gold.' All this was over thirty years ago; yet the memory of the bright smiles of these people remains undiminished in Rita's heart.

Chitra's daughter Radha is a very good painter. Her mother was Ushaboti's granddaughter. Radha studied at the Government College of Art and also learnt to play the piano from the age of eight. Her father enjoyed playing the violin and, pleased with her progress, bought her a baby-grand piano. After marriage Radha shifted to Punjab where she has been described as 'Piano Lady'. She says, 'I was eight when I began learning it at a convent in Calcutta. Later, my father, who used to play the violin, admitted me to the Calcutta School of Music.'

Radha enjoys teaching. This is a trait common to many members of the Tagore family. Many of Radha's students have won gold medals for painting. Others have learnt the piano and revived piano playing in their homes. Rather than strive for any individual acclaim, Radha finds greater pleasure in teaching a multitude of people.

Shefalika's eldest daughter-in-law and younger daughter Srilekha come under Saudamini's family. Music and painting form an integral part of life for every member of Shefalika's family. Eiko is the wife of Shefalika's eldest son Sandip. He used to teach at Otemon Gaikun University and has been associated with the Arizona State University since retirement. Sandip has been living in Japan for the last half a century. He is a well-known artist and has been endeavouring to popularize Rabindra

Sangeet in Japan along with teaching Tagore literature. He writes about his first meeting with Eiko, 'I met her while on holiday in Tokyo. After about a week I realized that I had found my life partner.' Eiko was from an aristocratic family and a student of English language and American Literature. Eiko demurred initially; the marriage had to be deferred for a year since Eiko had not completed her studies. Finally they were married in 1958. Sandip further informs us, 'The Japanese society is like a huge python, it squeezes and exploits women for its self-interest. Many Japanese women marry non-Japanese men not out of love but to get away from their menfolk.' Though this was not Eiko's reason for choosing Sandip, the shadow of Japanese society must have clouded her feelings. Since marriage, she has shown a great love for Indian culture, trying to get acquainted with it and integrate herself into it.

Along with her teaching, Eiko has written five books in Japanese about Indo-Japanese culture. These include collections of Indian stories, folk tales and translations of fairy tales. Sandip has translated the titles into Bengali—'*Gadhakey manush kara gelona*', '*Dol Dol Dolani*' and '*Bharater pakhi Hiramon*'. Besides these, Eiko has described her experiences during her travels in India and also penned *To India as a Japanese Bride*. She has written articles about Indian culture, but as her sojourn was a brief one it is not clear how close she is to India. However a letter from their eldest daughter Maya to Sandip clearly underlines Eiko and Sandip's efforts to imbue their children with love and respect for India. Maya writes, 'You and Mother always strove to impress upon us the culture of India. The traditions of your motherland have certainly influenced my life. I am proud of my descent from an Indian and hope to imbue my children with the same ideas.'

Sandip's sister Padma has been mentioned already. They have three other sisters, Srilekha, Chandra and Srirupa and a younger brother Sudeep. Painting and vocal music have influenced the lives of all of them. They all sing well. Chandra is an expert needlewoman and could have added new dimensions in the artistic world with embroidered pictures. Her daughter Kaushiki also sings well. Srilekha is a well-known vocal singer. She began at the early age of two. Jogendranath Bandopadhyaya used to teach all the young members of the family to sing. The two year old would toddle into the room and try to imitate them. This is how her lessons in 'Dhrupad' began. Had her elder sister Padma devoted more time to her music, she would have been an exceptional 'Dhrupad' singer. Srilekha's interest lay in Rabindra Sangeet. Later she also specialized in Atulprasad's songs and acquired a permanent place in the world of vocal music.

Srilekha studied in Rabindra Bharati University and learnt vocal music alongside. Rabindra Bharati had as its teachers many eminent vocalists. Srilekha took honours in Rabindra Sangeet and stood first-class first in the BA examinations. Later she also took her master's degree. In the undergraduate course she also had to study Philosophy and Sanskrit. It was here that she met Professor Dr Samiran Chandra Chakraborti, a brilliant man revered by all for his profound knowledge of Sanskrit. Srilekha was charmed and finally decided to marry this great scholar and accept him as her life partner. There was nothing impulsive about Srilekha's decision. Tastes differ and so do lives and choices. Though born into a wealthy family she had wanted to marry someone from a middle-class background rather than a rich man. She felt that modesty follows learning while wealth is accompanied by arrogance. She chose a learned man unhesitatingly, thus showing her strength of character.

After marriage, initially she found the going hard. She who had never had to lift a finger before marriage now had to do all the housework herself. Srilekha had great strength of purpose. She would say to herself, 'I have had all the pleasures of wealth. Now let me see the hardships. This also is a new experience.' She slowly learnt the ropes and along with looking after her home, she carried on with her music. For twenty-five years she was a regular artist with Akashvani, singing the songs of Atulprasad. She also travelled to Japan on an invitation from the Friendship Society there to present vocal music. Her brother Sandip was also there at that time. Professor Chakraborti has been to Germany and other countries on lecture trips several times, but it has not been possible for Srilekha to accompany him. She, however, has no regrets and is happy with her home and family. In the nineteen sixties, women of West Bengal became very keen on working outside the home. Srilekha was no exception. She was interviewed thrice and selected but she was unable to take up the job as her husband did not agree. Though there is no dearth of activities at home, still . . .

A centre for Vedic studies has been established in Calcutta due to the efforts of Professor Chakraborti. Swami Vivekananda had also dreamt of founding a school for Vedic teaching. Students from all over the country and abroad come to Prof. Chakraborti. German students are the most enthusiastic about ancient India, especially its literature. Indian students are also evincing an interest in ancient Indian literature. It is not possible to exist for long without roots. One is inevitably drawn towards one's own culture and literature. This comprises Prof. Chakraborti's mission in life. It is a matter of great pride for his wife too. Srilekha's daughter Jasodhara is also a good vocalist.

To keep alive the songs of the Tagore family is the main aim of Srinanda, daughter of Supurna and Subhas Chaudhuri. The practice of Rabindra Sangeet flowed uninterrupted in Satyendranath's family. Purnima and Supurna were both taught by Indira herself. Srinanda has lived amid the world of music since her childhood. She learnt Rabindra Sangeet from Suchitra Mitra, Hindustani classical from Sukhendu Goswami and old Bengali songs from Chandidas Maal. Passing out from 'Indira' with flying colours, Srinanda's music training has been occasionally hampered. This is because of her academic excellence. A first-class first in her master's degree examination in Geology followed by scholarships and the lure of higher studies and research did interrupt her musical career from time to time. Employed by the Geological Survey of India, however, she spends her spare time practising music. Today she is widely popular as an artist of Rabindra Sangeet. Like her mother, Srinanda is keen to preserve the purity of Rabindra Sangeet. She has had invitations to perform from the State Sangeet Academy to the Tagore Centre in London. Srinanda's association with Radio and Doordarshan dates back to her childhood. Her melodious voice has been captured in numerous cassettes. Some of them are '*Shishu Bholanath*', '*Ekti Rangeen Morichika*', '*Puja O Prem*', '*Gaan Amar*', '*Rituranga*' and '*Bhorer Aalo*'. Her individual cassettes include, '*Ogo Antaratama*' and '*Pather Shesh Kothaye*'. Srinanda's songs have been heard in various serials like *Chaturanga*, *Seemana Chhariye*, *Vijaya* or the short stories of Rabindranath.

Along with all these lie the responsibilities of a home and family. Following the traditions of the Tagore family, she gives equal importance to both her home and her life outside.

Srinanda has no desire to experiment with Rabindra Sangeet. She is keen to hand over to her daughter Srimanti the musical tradition that has passed from Indira Devi to Supurna and has thence been inherited by Srinanda. Srimanti is still a student. She is keen both on music and academics. No one knows yet which course her life will take.

Atashi's daughter Kalpita traces her descent from Saratkumari. Though describing her as an artistic daughter of an artistic mother may be a misnomer, she is interested in handicrafts. Asit Kumar Haldar, his daughter Atashi and her daughter Kalpita—they have been painting for three generations. She has mastered the craft of batik by her own efforts. Her main interest was doing batik on leather, which brought her praise from many quarters. An MA in Geography and a teacher by profession, she often dreamt of opening a boutique. Her dream has now come true. She has named her boutique Kalpanik and specializes in creating sarees with a blend of batik and bandhni. Her handicrafts are just as good as her proficiency in painting, music and cooking. Her work, mainly a product of her own imagination, makes it difficult to believe that she is completely self-taught. Her daughter Swarnila in interested in modelling and acting. She appears occasionally on Doordarshan in small roles. Kalpita's smiling comment, 'I neither hinder nor abet her.'

The face that stands out from the row of talented women of house number 5 in Jorasanko is that of Sharmila Tagore. From *Apur Sansar* to *Missisipi Masala* and *Devi*, *Aradhana*, *Amar Prem*, *Nayak*, *Safar*, *Mausam* and *Shesh Anka,* among other successful films, her unforgettable appearance is fresh in the public memory. Sharmila is Ira's daughter and has been acting in films since the age of fourteen. Ira herself showed considerable acting ability during her college days. This talent has been inherited by her daughters. Sharmila's younger sister Oindrila appeared in Tapan Sinha's *Kabuliwallah* as Tinku Tagore and won every heart. A few years later it was advertised in the newspapers that Satyajit Ray was looking for a new face for *Apur Sansar*. Sharmila's family teased her saying, 'Will you apply?' Before she could do so, Satyajit Ray himself rang Geetindranath.

Geetindranath queried, 'Where did you see my daughter?' Satyajit Ray replied with a smile, 'I had posted men before every school. One of them saw your daughter, followed her and thus gave me your address.'

Geetindranath agreed after some hesitation, but Sharmila still maintains 'Nobody asked me for my opinion!' With the release of *Apur Sansar* the film-world found a new heroine. Geetindranath never wanted Sharmila to take up films as a career. Sharmila also wanted to continue with her education and joined Loreto College with History honours. She wanted to be a painter or a danseuse. Born into an artistic family, the great-granddaughter of Gaganendranath Tagore, it was not unnatural for her to want to be a painter. All the same, she had learnt dance since childhood. Many people had observed her dancing in performances of C.L.T. (Children's Little Theatre). Satyajit Ray may have selected Sharmila from such a function. Sharmila has repeated what he said to Geetindranath.

Sharmila possessed every prerequisite of being an actress. Her rare facility of expression, eloquent eyes and guileless look as well as the dimple in her check—all these helped establish her as a heroine. She also possessed the ability to adjust herself to any situation. Her versatility in turning out flawless performances in widely different films like *Apur Sansar* and *Devi* on the one hand and *Kashmir ki Kali* and *An Evening in Paris* on the other, coupled with their commercial success, has also helped her. Sharmila has been able to bring to life divergent characters like the mother in *Aradhana*, the journalist in *Nayak*, the heroines of *Mausam* and *Amar Prem*—both dogged by misfortune but representing different facets of life—and the doctor in *Safar*. In films like *Chhaya Surya*, *Nirjan Saikatey*, *Aranyer Dinratri* and *Shesh Anka* her presence is noteworthy.

Sharmila married the nawab of Pataudi. Entering an aristocratic Muslim family did not interfere with her film career. Neither did she neglect her family. In an interview she said, 'Today's young generation are learning to consider their personal interest while we were taught to consider the family first.' Perhaps this is the reason behind her success, both within and outside the home, both as a housewife and in her career. Her son Saif married Amrita, also an actress of the silver screen. Though taken aback and initially hurt by her son's sudden decision, she had no qualms about accepting her daughter-in-law. She even decked Amrita in all her own bridal finery. Her two daughters are busy in their own sphere of work. The elder—Saba—has influenced the world of art by her jewellery-designing while the younger—Soha—is seeking her inheritance in the film world. They all belong to the twenty-first century.

Oindrila alias Tinku never acted after *Kabuliwallah*. She will always be remembered as a child artist for her superb performance. She brought to life Rabindranath's 'Mini'. Later she made occasional appearances in the world of sport. She was practically unparalleled in playing bridge. She played chess and also wrote articles on card games. Had she not departed untimely she might have contributed more in these two arenas.

Abanindranath's daughter Uma's daughter-in-law Shanti is a well-known singer. At one time she presented 'Raga Sangeet' regularly over Akashvani. Today her school 'Gaur Mallar' is one of the chief institutions teaching 'Raga Sangeet'. Manindranath's daughter Sthira was also interested in vocal music. She took lessons too and Menaka was very keen about her training as a singer. However, later Sthira never tried to take her place in the singing world.

Let us return to Kumudini's descendents. Writing about Malabi's daughters Ratna and Champa invites mention of the Pathuriaghata Tagores. Both Ratna and Champa were contemporaries of Padma, Srilekha and Shyamashri, besides being their cousins. Padma's father was the younger brother of Ratna's father. To quote Champa, 'All told, we were twenty-one (cousin) brothers and sisters about the same age. We were great friends and as children never felt the need for other friends. Thus we never had time to think whether there was any unwritten rule against mixing with outsiders.' Moreover, occasionally musical soirées were held on Sundays and their mothers and aunts also participated. A 'Bhai Bon Sangha' was established anew in this family. Earlier there was a 'Bhai Bon Samiti' at the Jorasanko Tagore-house. It was established in 1886 and Dwijendranath describes the founding members thus:

Hitu, Nitu, Kshitu, Kritu, Suren, Bibi, Bolu, Sudhi
Jyotsna, Sarala—kee aar bolbo—Sarvya gune gunambudhi.

Hitu, Nitu, Kshitu, Kritu, Suren, Bibi, Bolu, Sudhi
Jyotsna Sarala—Oh what can I say,
Possessing every accomplishment, they are oceans of virtue.

The 'Bhai Bon Sangha' of Pathuriaghata was of much more recent origin. One of the main founders was Champa's husband Nilendra Halder. He was also a distant cousin and the preponderance of such marriages has already been mentioned.

Though from a zamindar family, Purnendunath qualified as a barrister himself. He encouraged all his children to go for higher education, especially equipping oneself for a career. This certainly shows his farsightedness. Ratna and Champa were also keen on a career. In the nineteen fifties and sixties many women had begun to think about earning one's own living. The eagerness to have a career and to stand on one's own feet was no longer a whim but a right earned by women. Fifty years later, it is difficult to comprehend their feelings and their surroundings.

Two examples may be quoted.

In Ratna and Champa's family, every girl attended school and college, learnt to sing and participated in games. Like Shyamashri, Champa was good at table tennis, badminton, billiards—the greatest backing coming from the 'Bhai Bon Sangha'. Yet Ratna and Champa never had the liberty to go out alone. Everyday they were escorted to college and back. Not that they always travelled by car, but even on a bus a durwan would always be there. Ratna always wanted a career and did a secretarial course from the YWCA In 1958 all the students were to be sent to Ooty for training. Purnendunath agreed but sent a durwan along. Ratna held her peace in Calcutta but after reaching Madras, she bluffed the man, managed to leave him behind at the railway station and went off to Ooty. Later she worked as the programme secretary of the YWCA with great competence for a number of years. She had to resign in 1986 because of eye trouble. At that time many women were not permitted to work outside the home after marriage. Ratna had taken up a job before her marriage and when her would-be mother-in-law queried, 'How will you manage to work living with your in-laws?' Ratna replied without the slightest hesitation, 'In that case I shall not marry.' Fortunately, her in-laws were broadminded and Ratna never faced any problems. After resigning from her job, she has opened a vocational training centre in her own house as she loves to be occupied and busy.

Like her elder sister, Champa also studied in Loreto School and then in Lady Brabourne College. Later, she joined Gokhale Memorial School for her teacher's training course. She was also keen to take up a job like Ratna. Before she could start job-hunting, she was requested by the authorities of Gokhale Memorial School to join there. At that time, before appointing a teacher the school committee always checked the family background. They approved of Champa because, apart from academics, she was proficient in music, dramatics and sports. They were sure that the children would enjoy having such a teacher. Frantic with worry, Champa asked her father's permission. Purnendunath agreed but had a durwan accompany her on her way to and back from school. After about a year the school authorities asked Champa, 'We have heard that you are about to be married. Unless we are assured that you will continue afterwards we do not wish to make your services permanent. We must have the permission of your father-in-law.' Champa knew her in-laws well as she was a *gharer meyey* (daughter of the Tagores). She approached her would be father-in-law—Neerajchandra. He was already acquainted with the school and gave the necessary permission readily. Champa retired in 1997, after teaching for thirty-seven years. Originally she taught English but later became the head of the junior section. Ratna and Champa were the two first women of the Pathuriaghata Tagore family to have established themselves as working women.

Bani was another notable member of Koilahata Tagore family. She is also descended from Kumudini and is the youngest daughter of Sujanendra and Suchitra. Her father was interested in music while Suchitra's mind was attuned to every branch of fine art—painting, singing as well as writing. Bani, who is a well-known Rabindra Sangeet artist today, has been interested in this branch of music since her childhood. Even at that age she was fond of listening to records of Suchitra Mitra, who could always impart a touch of her personality in her songs. Bani's early training in music began under Ramkrishna Mishra, well-known as a strict disciplinarian. She lost her father early and thereafter the family moved from Koilahata to South Calcutta. Thus they were distanced from the families at Pathuriaghata and Jorasanko. Seeing Bani's interest in Rabindra Sangeet one of her cousin brothers, Adrijanath Mukhopadhyay, had her admitted at 'Dakshini'. Thus began Bani's arduous endeavours in the realm of music. She was a pupil in 'Dakshni' for three years. After she earned her diploma Shubho Guhathakurta trained her in Rabindra Sangeet based on different Ragas. In 1962 Bani had the chance to learn from her ideal—Suchitra Mitra. In an interview Bani told Sandhya Sen,

> Suchitradi initiated me in the art of losing myself in the world of music. She also moulded my viewpoint regarding voice-modulation and expression. Had I not come in contact with her I would never have had any conception of how a change in volume can change the very meaning of a song.

She had begun recording earlier but started singing in public about this time. During Rabindranath's centenary year, the Rabindra Jayanti celebrations of the Congress in various Indian cities like Delhi, Patna and Lucknow were inaugurated with Bani's songs. In 1962 she went to Burma—Myanmar today—to participate in the Bengal Literary and Cultural Conference. In 1964 she went to Nepal as a cultural representative. As a radio artist she has been all over India and appeared on television in Dacca. Kanika Bandopadhyaya herself introduced her to Mr P.K. Sen of the Gramophone Company. Her first record was, *Hey Madhabi dwidha keno* and *Deep nibhe gechhey momo*. In 1972 she held a solo programme of Rabindra Sangeet at Max Mueller Bhawan. Her fame as a noted singer was slowly spreading like the delicate fragrance of a flower.

In the course of her career Bani met Kalyan Roy. He was a good singer, an expert commentator and a senior official with the Publicity Department. When they decided to marry, many in the Tagore family objected, though some family members stood by Bani.

Bani entered her new life, her heart brimming over with dreams. She had always been a good at socializing and full of life. Her singing, and teaching music, seemed to continue unabated. Several records were made. They include, *Sakhi pratidin hai*, *Aaji jharer ratey*, *Aamar na bala bani*, *Momo antara udashi* and many others songs. Apart from training under Suchitra Mitra, she also trained in Raga sangeet—her bugbear in childhood—from Jnan Prakash Ghosh and Prasun Bandopadhyay. Unfortunately, the sudden death of her husband ended the happy days for Bani.

Bani took refuge in music. Now she became associated with various musical organizations, especially teaching and producing musical programmes. Besides the ability to teach, she showed a decided competence in organizational work. She was also helped by numerous other artists. At one time she was associated with groups like 'Sura Sanchayan', 'Gandharvi', 'Raagini', 'Suratirtha' and so on. Now she looks after her own group 'Kingshuk'. Associated with it since 1969, this organization has also become, like music, an inseparable part of her life.

Before writing about Suchitra's daughter-in-law Gauri it would be best to remember that the Koilahata Tagore family had not been able to rid itself of orthodox and conservative views for quite awhile. Loss of his father at a young age had made Sovendra realize the importance of education but this had not touched the outlook of others. Gauri belonged to an educated and enlightened family. Her father, Narendranath Roy, was interested in literature. Her elder brother, Sachin Roy, and his wife were both students of Anthropology and associated with the Indian Museum. They were the main architects of the Anthropological Gallery in Calcutta. Gauri herself was a good student and studied for her master's degree in History. Though she continued her classes after marriage, she was unable to appear for the final examination. She was expecting her first child and her guardians did not allow her to sit for the examination. She also hesitated out of consideration for her unborn child. This was also the reason for her never taking up a job. However, while bringing up her daughters, she always impressed upon them that education and being able to support oneself were the most important goals in life. With this modern outlook, she educated every illiterate person who came to work for her and encouraged him/her to save money in a bank. Thus she insisted that education, an income of one's own and thrift were the essentials of life. Without these one is demeaned at every step. She always encouraged her mother-in-law Suchitra to paint, providing her with paints and brushes. Her own two daughters are educated and self-supporting besides each having a family of her own.

Jayashri was another member of this family. She was Ira's daughter-in-law and Swapanendranath's wife. Her husband was a well-known painter. Jayashri herself trained as a dancer under Prahlad Das though she never appeared in any public function outside school or college. At that time, as even now, women mainly preferred teaching as a profession. Jayashri was no exception and taught in South Point School. Her daughter Srinayana's interest lay in vocal music and she was a student of Bani.

While discussing the Koilahata Tagores it would be in order to mention Ramanath Tagore's sister Drobomoyee and her family. They had practically no connection with the main Tagore family as the later generation had migrated to Burma, today's Myanmar. Suchitra Goswami belonged to this family. Her childhood and adolescent years were spent in Burma. When only thirteen she joined the Azad Hind Fauj. Apart from becoming a member of the Rani of Jhansi Brigade, she was attracted as much by the dreams of Indian independence—the country she had never seen—as by Netaji Subhas's ideals. Her father himself took her to enlist for the IMA Suchitra trained simultaneously as a nurse and in military warfare. Apart from nursing in hospitals she spent time in the jungles of Burma during the bombing of that country. Her father's sudden death proved disastrous. Suchitra had to take up a job for the sake of her family. In 1948 she came to India. Though unable to continue with the INA Suchitra's struggles went on. Today, the military training imparted by Manvati Pandey or Vijayalakshmi in the distant past appear like a long-lost dream down memory lane. That life is forever a thing of the past.

Among Shibani's daughters, Gopa is a doctor. Few women in the Tagore family have shown a tendency to study medicine. Gopa herself was also not very keen on a medical career but her father wanted to make his bright daughter a doctor. Thus Gopa entered Medical College and in due course specialized as a gynaecologist. In the beginning, she did not like her job overmuch but slowly she was impressed by the look of relief evident on the pain-wracked faces of her patients by her visits. She never realized when the responsibility of caring for them became a pleasure for her. Her nursing home in north Calcutta is always full of anxious people. Along with bringing a new life into the world, she also brings the mother unspeakable joy. Though a doctor's life is fraught with occasional strife and is often misunderstood, Gopa believes that honesty, sincerity and devotion to one's job can overcome such misconceptions.

Amrita, one of Shibani's granddaughters, deserves to be mentioned too. Her mother Rekha was Shibani's eldest daughter. As a child Amrita observed Shibani's involvement with the 'Ganganagar Mahila Samiti'. Amrita was always interested in textiles, especially those of Bengal. While moving though the markets of Lagos in Nigeria, she found a preponderance of

Indian textiles there. Finding textiles worked with typical Indian floral motifs in sequins and mirrors, she enquired about the name of the material. She was told that all the material was known as 'George'. Some were 'fancy George' while others just 'plain George'. She again came across similar George material in the 'Oven Dreams' exhibition in Malaysia, though no one could enlighten her about the country from whence this material came. Undaunted, Amrita contacted Ms Rosemary of the Victoria and Albert Museum while she was in London. From a perusal of a paper by Jayen Aika, a researcher at the University of Minnesota, Amrita learnt about the Kalabari village in south India. The cloth woven by the inhabitants of this village was known as 'George' in Nigeria. Amrita's interest in textiles found in another country proved gainful for India. Along with Rosemary, she attended a textile conference in Madras and also visited Kalabari. She found forty thousand weavers engaged in weaving cloth for Nigeria. Thus she was able to locate the birth-place of 'George' textile. Amrita feels, 'The original name of Madras was Fort St. George and so this material was called George'. Along with her studies in Indian textiles, Amrita also began research on these topics. The textile industry of Bengal gradually became an obsession for her. As a member of the World Craft Council she toured South-East Asia. Covering a textile exhibition in Bali, she wondered why no exhibition of textiles was held in India. After all, there was no denying the popularity of Indian textiles abroad. She established an organization—Sutra—with the help of Shilpa and Praful Shah of Bombay and Darshan Shah of Calcutta. The purpose of the organization would be to revive the lost textiles of India. Kamaladevi Chattopadhyaya had begun the handicrafts Movement fifty years ago and now Sutra took up the same work. Thus Amrita also accepted the responsibility of completing Shibani's unfinished work.

Gopa's advent into the medical profession has already been noted. Somehow medical and engineering options seem to go hand in hand. Debaprasad Tagore's daughter Aleena graduated in electrical engineering from the Bengal Engineering College, training in computers as well. She is the first woman from the Tagore family to have joined the Engineering College. Aleena however is in no way related to the Jorasanko Tagores. Her father Devaprasad Tagore was Chhayamayee's nephew, and descended from Harimohan, the son of Darpa Narayan Tagore. Due to certain domestic responsibilities, she was unable to work for long as an engineer. After marriage, she moved to Hong Kong with her husband. Initially she took up a job there, but gave it up after a while to look after her daughter Malini. The girls of the Tagore family never ignored their domestic responsibilities in spite of all their activities outside. Aleena also followed the tradition. Though an engineer, she had inherited artistic tendencies from the Tagore side of her ancestors. Her paternal grandmother Anita was also interested in handicrafts. A miniature '*Barandaala*' made by Anita for dolls' weddings still occupies pride of place among the possessions of Aleena's mother. Aleena also had the same urge for fine arts and handicrafts. Her artistic inclinations now came to the fore. As soon as her daughter began attending school, Aleena began to learn pottery and porcelain-painting, along with the Japanese art of 'Bonsai' and making artificial flowers. Her latent genius began flowering in a conducive atmosphere. With encouragement from friends, she began conducting 'hobby classes' at home. It is after all a characteristic trait of the Tagore women to add grace not only to their own lives but to their surroundings too.

Aleena now lives in Seoul, South Korea. She has found a world of her own despite the change in her husband's place of work. Her porcelain paintings are purchased from the 'hobby centre' by the local people to decorate their homes. It is impossible to detect that the artist is a foreign woman. Aleena has also become an expert in paper tole and parchment craft. Her competence seems to find new avenues of expertise. At present she is learning Hanzi Korean paper craft.

Geeta's granddaughter Asmita appears to have inherited Sunayani's talent and love of painting. While she was in class nine her main preference for astronomy became evident. She specialized in geography, but carried on studies in astrophysics simultaneously. As ISRO's amateur observer, she has satisfied numerous queries about Halley's comet. Married into the well-known Trivedi family, she has not only been able to nurture her dreams of painting and playing the piano but also her interest in astronomy. She enjoys watching the movement of stars through a telescope as well as her job as an honorary lecturer for the Astronomy Awareness course conduced by the Birla Industrial and Technological Museum. She is also working on the relation between astronomy and Indian metaphysics. There have been many wrong interpretations of this aspect but now most of it has been found to be correct. Asmita's topics for painting centre on astronomical objects. This certainly is a novel outlook.

Sanjukta and Saswati belong to the Koilahata Tagore family and are Bani's nieces. Their mother Gauri always impressed upon them the value of education and self-sufficiency in a woman's life. Along with academics both the sisters showed an aptitude for dance. They first began lessons under Amala Shankar at the Udayshankar India Culture Centre. Later they toured various parts of the world as members of Mamata Shankar's ballet troupe, presenting dance programmes. Their efforts to build up a career proceeded simultaneously. Sanjukta is an MA in History while Saswati graduated with honours in Geography. As she enjoyed teaching, Sanjukta joined the Nava Nalanda School after getting her B.Ed. degree. She has been actively associated with all the cultural programmes presented by this school since 1987. She also dabbles in painting, music and writing poetry. The history of art and Indian philosophy also interest her. Besides all this, Sanjukta has mastered another one of her grandmother Suchitra's accomplishments—that of dressing up a bride. Like many another member of the Tagore family, Sanjukta enjoys dressing and making up a bride. She herself prefers the traditional style though the preferences of the brides always comes first. She has received every encouragement from her family. Her husband Alakesh Bagchi is keen on drama and music. He has held musical performances in many countries. Sanjukta's son Arjun is also experimenting with 'taal instruments'. There is no doubt that as a worthy representative of the Tagore family Sanjukta has succeeded in creating a graceful domestic atmosphere brimming with happiness.

Saswati has kept up her contact with dancing, though her role has changed to that of a teacher. She is associated with the 'Udayan' school of dancing. Her contacts with Mamata Shankar's Ballet Troupe remain unbroken despite her job with the school of dancing. Suchitra's granddaughters have both inherited her talent for painting, perhaps Saswati more than Sanjukta. Saswati is also fortunate in having a family sympathetic to her aspirations. Her husband Nirmal Tagore is interested in music while both her children are proficient in instrumental music. As a member of Mamata Shankar's Ballet Troupe, Saswati along with her elder sister has toured England, Sweden, Germany, France, USA, Canada, China, Japan, Thailand and Malaysia. Now she teaches young ones to dance. Surely one day these children will participate in dance programmes all over the world and bring her fulfillment and renown.

Saumya, Suriti's daughter-in-law, was married at a comparatively young age. Later, she joined college and took her master's degree in English. She first learnt to dance under Ram Gopal Mishra and later turned to bharatnatyam. At present she is associated with 'Kutambalam' (Nrityamandir) as a dance teacher. Her daughter Sauraja is an exponent of bharatnatyam and one of the rising artists of 'Kutambalam'. Sauraja has already won a national scholarship and dreams of becoming a well-known danseuse one day. Saumya is also keen to see her daughter's hopes fulfilled. She herself has retired from the stage in order to care for her son and daughter's education. Since academics and dance keep Sauraja busy, Saumya is kept busy too.

The story of the andar mahal has perforce come to a halt now, because in the twenty-first century, the distinction between *sadar* and *andar* has disappeared. Few today know about the old 'Ram Bhawan'. The andar mahal of house number 6 of Jorasanko was once known as 'Ram Bhawan' after Ramlochan–Rammani–Ramballav. Even today the elderly members of the Tagore family refer to the portion adjacent to the Maharshi Bhawan by the same name. All the members of this house have shifted elsewhere. A number of them have been discussed, quite a few others remain unmentioned since they are scattered far and wide and it has not been possible to locate them. Radhanath Tagore's family no longer uses the surname 'Tagore.' They have reverted to the original 'Bandopadhyay'. The family traits like love of music and drama, however, persist among them. It has not been possible to write about them individually.

The women of the Tagore family are today all gainfully employed. Sushama's great-granddaughter Sumana has done her master's degree in Economics, standing first-class first. Similarly Gaganendra's daughter, Purnimadevi's great-granddaughter, Mahasweta Chattopadhyay has just finished training in bharatnatyam as well as Odissi. Both have vast spheres of activity before them. The extensive family of Jairam has fragmented and scattered all over. Their sphere of work, economic situation and social standing have all undergone a sea change. The feud between Neelmoni and Darpanarayan now sounds like fiction to their descendants. Relations between the two families were never severed. Neelmoni also helped in getting his nieces married. However, rumours of dispute were rife for a long time. It is possible that Debendranath's embracing Brahmoism was the cause of the gradual distance arising between the two main branches. Today neither that society, nor that pomp and splendour or hair-splitting over religion or any eagerness to follow history exists. What persists is the dazzling memory of a brilliant cultural heritage. At the centre of the Tagore family stands Rabindranath, who belongs not just to the Tagore family, Shantiniketan or Bengalis alone but to the whole of India. In 1998, when Nafisa Joseph became Miss India, her first comment was that she belonged to the Tagore family and was connected to Rabindranath. Nafisa is actually descended from Darpanarayan Tagore and not from the Jorasanko branch. Still, she considers herself a daughter of the Tagores. Her comment shows that among the widely spread members of the Tagore family, reminiscing has not lost its value even in the twenty-first century. Anyone connected to this family—by birth or marriage—inherited its cultural heritage. Story after story has sprung up. In the design woven between history and the future will be an account of the achievements and failures in the long and rugged path trod by women's emancipation. Abanindranath said, 'People are not interested in dry accounts. What they want are tales.' The verdant sojourn down memory lane has often tried to draw us towards tales and fiction. The main effort of this book has been to portray the various facets of women's struggle for self-acceptance and present a picture of their changing mental make up.

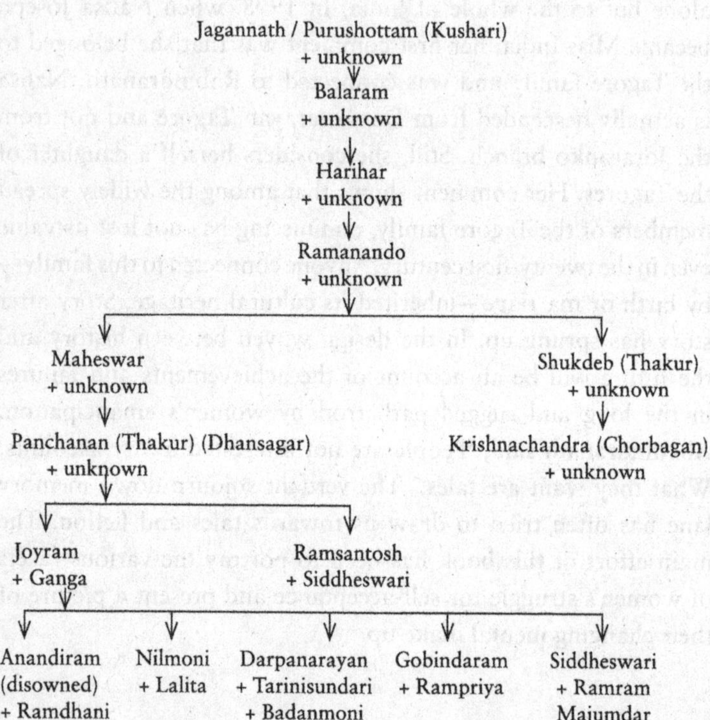
Bangshalatika
Thakur Family
Jagannath / Purushottam (Kushari)
+ unknown
Balaram
+ unknown
Harihar
+ unknown
Ramanando
+ unknown
Maheswar
+ unknown
Shukdeb (Thakur)
+ unknown
Panchanan (Thakur) (Dhansagar)
+ unknown
Krishnachandra (Chorbagan)
+ unknown
Joyram
+ Ganga
Ramsantosh
+ Siddheswari
Anandiram
(disowned)
+ Ramdhani
Nilmoni
+ Lalita
Darpanarayan
+ Tarinisundari
+ Badanmoni
Gobindaram
+ Rampriya
Siddheswari
+ Ramram
Majumdar

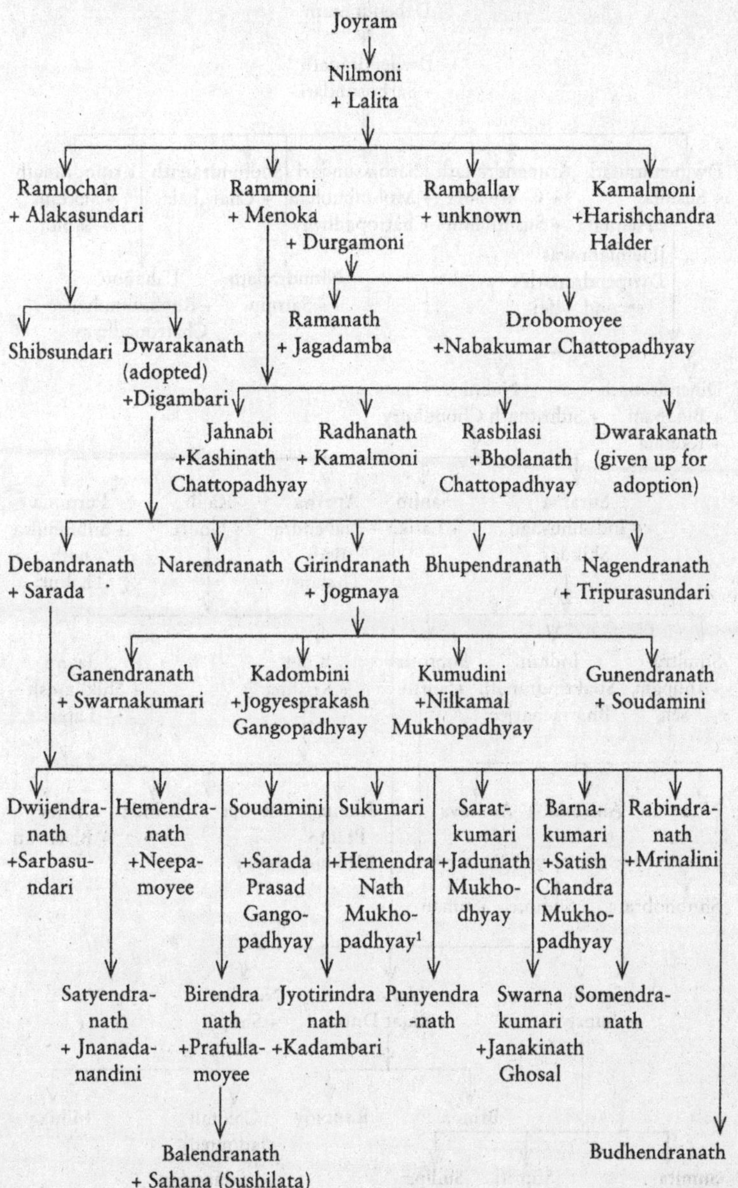

1 Ladlimohan Thakur family

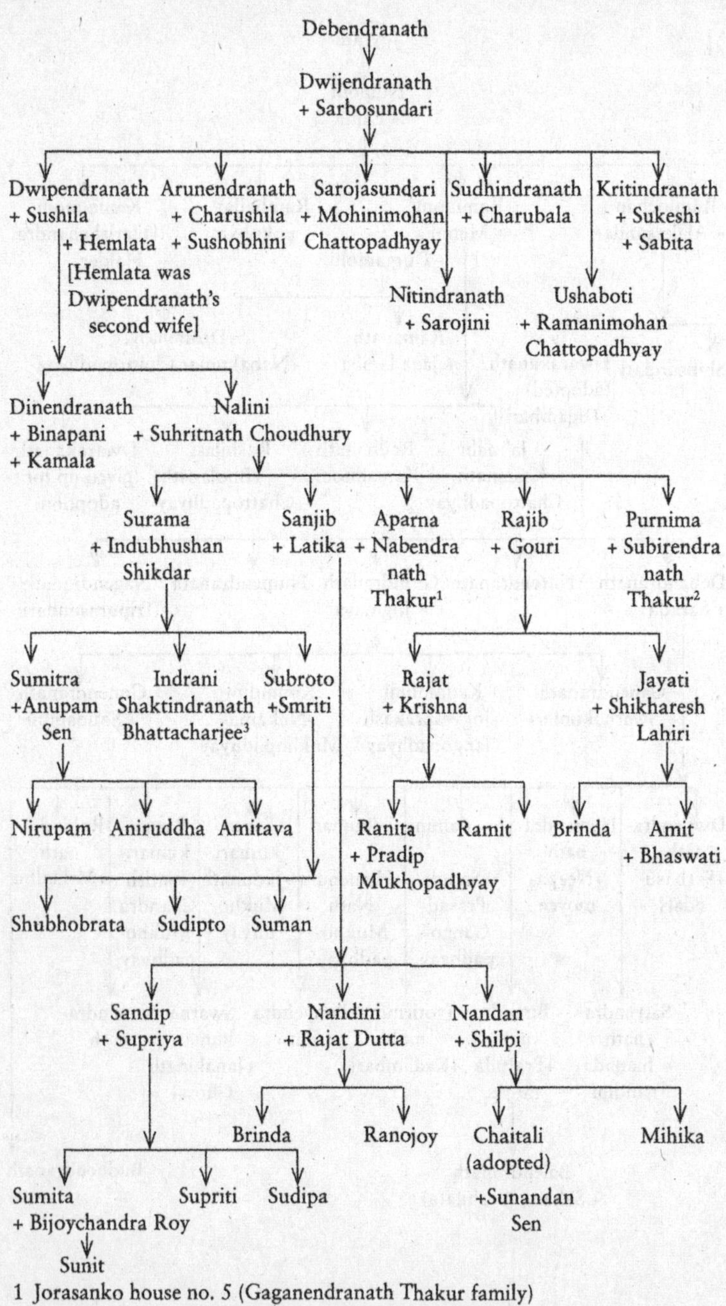

1 Jorasanko house no. 5 (Gaganendranath Thakur family)
2 Jorasanko house no. 6 (Satyendranath Thakur family)
3 Jorasanko house no. 5 (Samarendranath Thakur family)

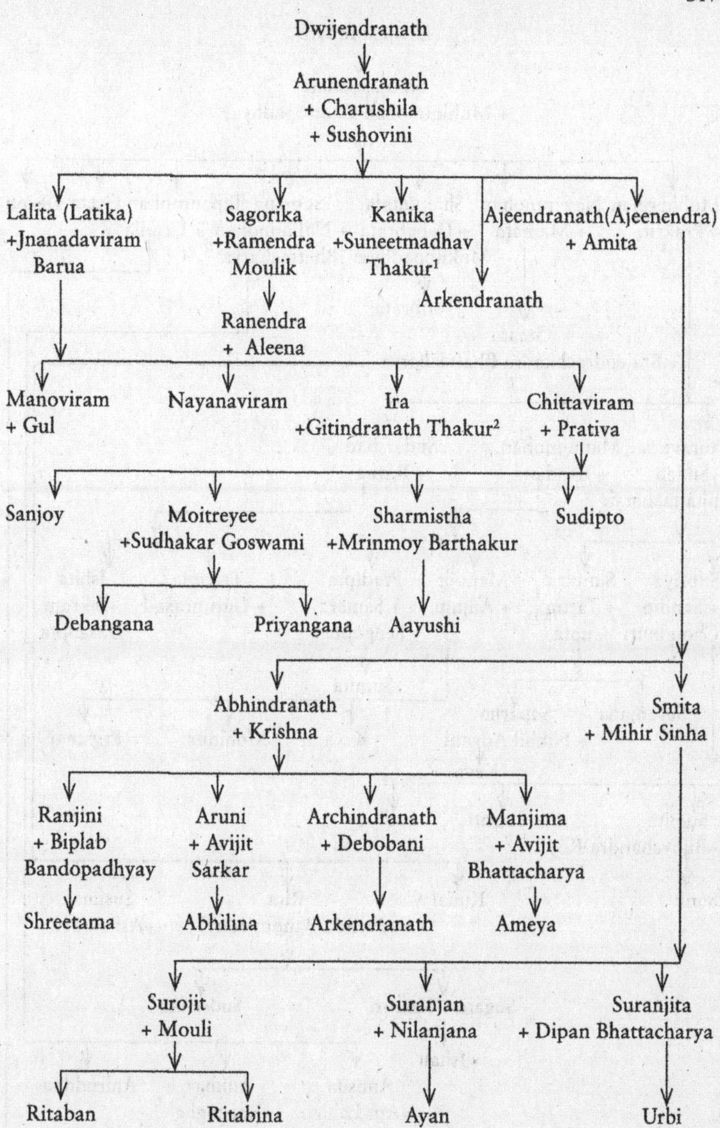

1 Chorbagan Thakurbari
2 Jorasanko house no. 5 (Gaganendranath Thakur family)

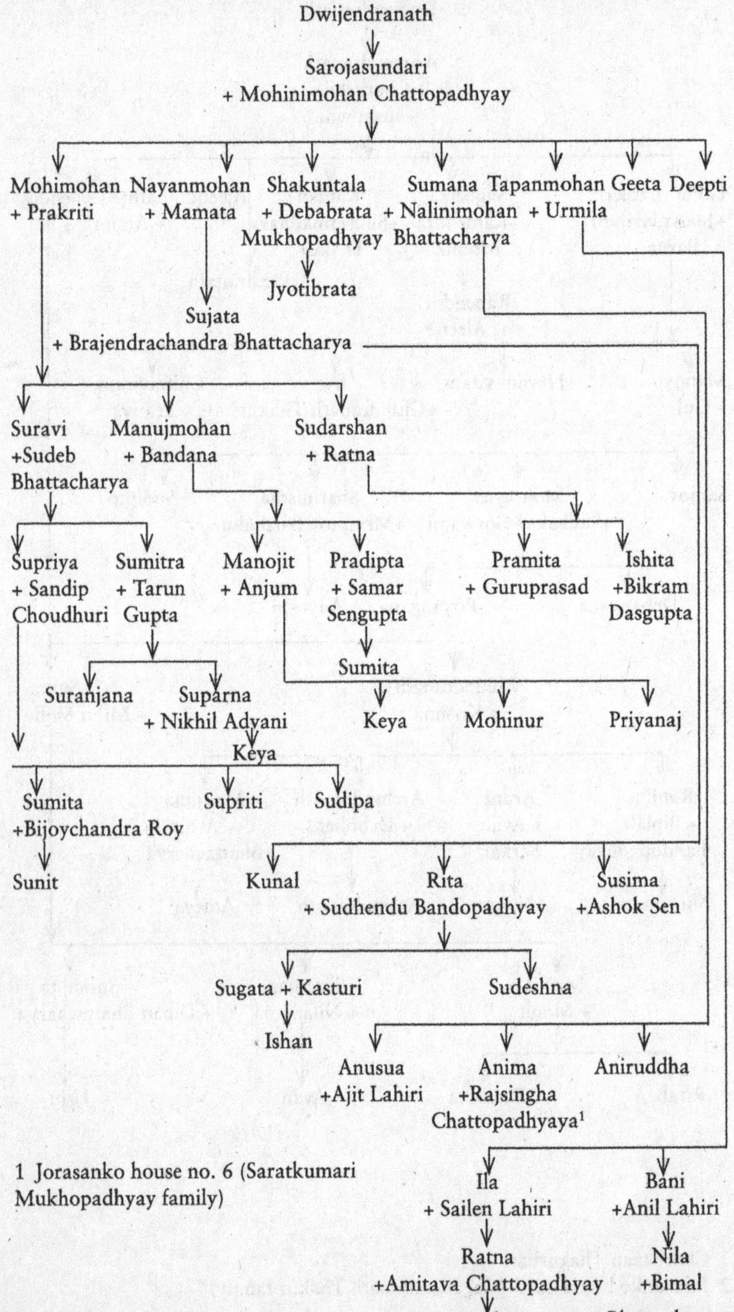

1 Jorasanko house no. 6 (Saratkumari Mukhopadhyay family)

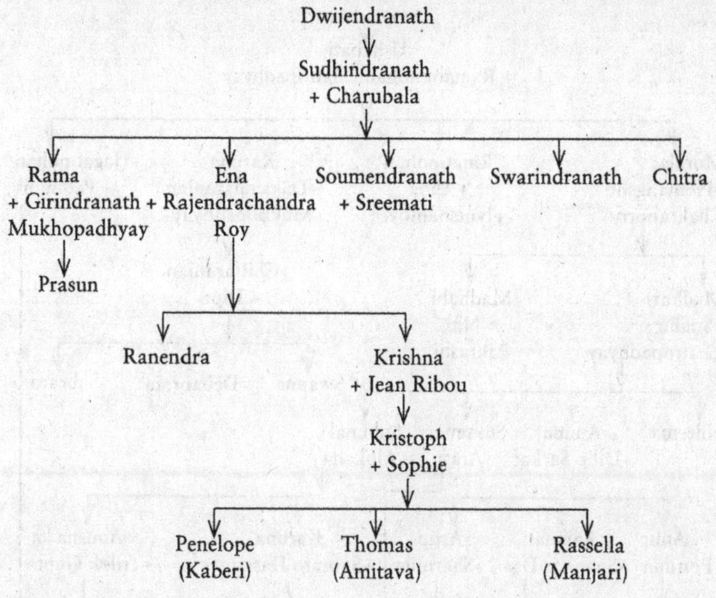
Dwijendranath
Sudhindranath
+ Charubala
Rama
+ Girindranath
Mukhopadhyay
Prasun
Ena
+ Rajendrachandra
Roy
Soumendranath
+ Sreemati
Swarindranath
Chitra
Ranendra
Krishna
+ Jean Ribou
Kristoph
+ Sophie
Penelope
(Kaberi)
Thomas
(Amitava)
Rassella
(Manjari)

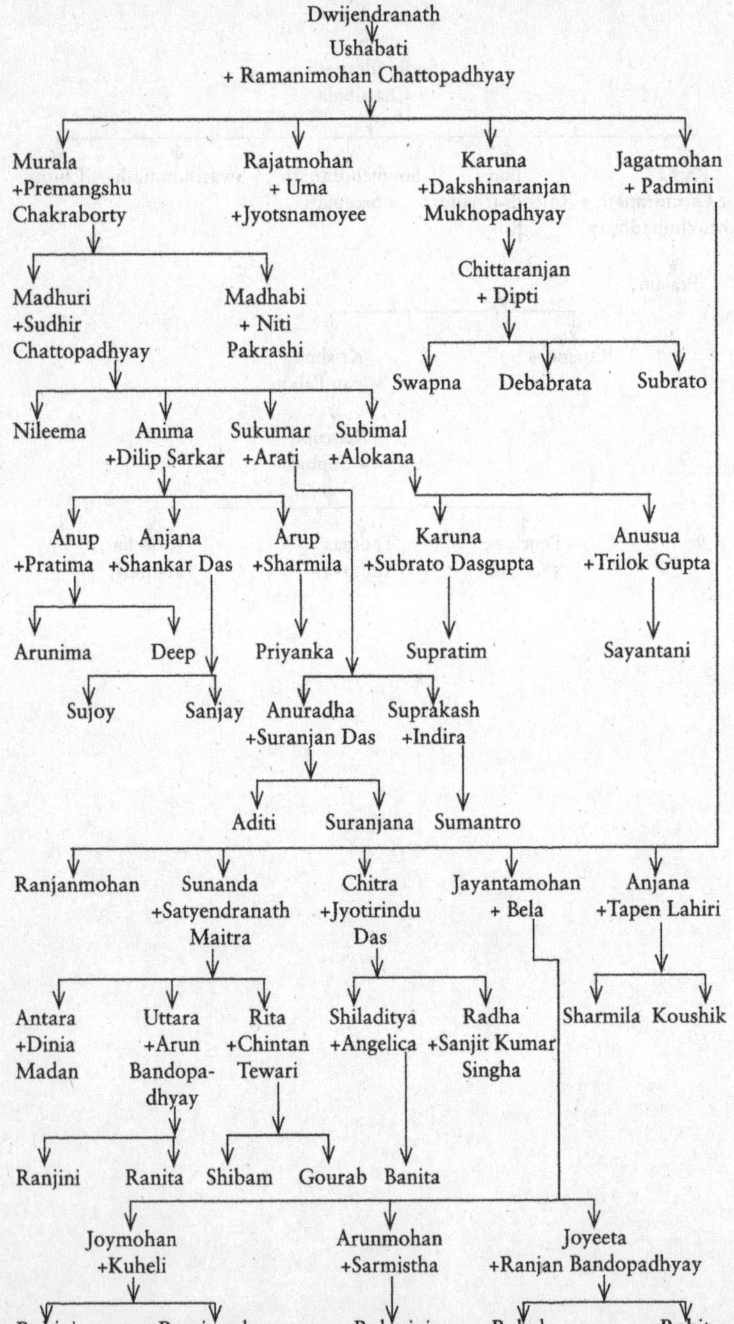
Dwijendranath
Ushabati
+ Ramanimohan Chattopadhyay
Murala
+Premangshu
Chakraborty
Rajatmohan
+ Uma
+Jyotsnamoyee
Karuna
+Dakshinaranjan
Mukhopadhyay
Jagatmohan
+ Padmini
Madhuri
+Sudhir
Chattopadhyay
Madhabi
+ Niti
Pakrashi
Chittaranjan
+ Dipti
Swapna
Debabrata
Subrato
Nileema
Anima
+Dilip Sarkar
Sukumar
+Arati
Subimal
+Alokana
Anup
+Pratima
Anjana
+Shankar Das
Arup
+Sharmila
Karuna
+Subrato Dasgupta
Anusua
+Trilok Gupta
Arunima
Deep
Priyanka
Supratim
Sayantani
Sujoy
Sanjay
Anuradha
+Suranjan Das
Suprakash
+Indira
Aditi
Suranjana
Sumantro
Ranjanmohan
Sunanda
+Satyendranath
Maitra
Chitra
+Jyotirindu
Das
Jayantamohan
+ Bela
Anjana
+Tapen Lahiri
Antara
+Dinia
Madan
Uttara
+Arun
Bandopa-
dhyay
Rita
+Chintan
Tewari
Shiladitya
+Angelica
Radha
+Sanjit Kumar
Singha
Sharmila
Koushik
Ranjini
Ranita
Shibam
Gourab
Banita
Joymohan
+Kuheli
Arunmohan
+Sarmistha
Joyeeta
+Ranjan Bandopadhyay
Rohini
Romitmohan
Rukmini
Rahul
Rohit

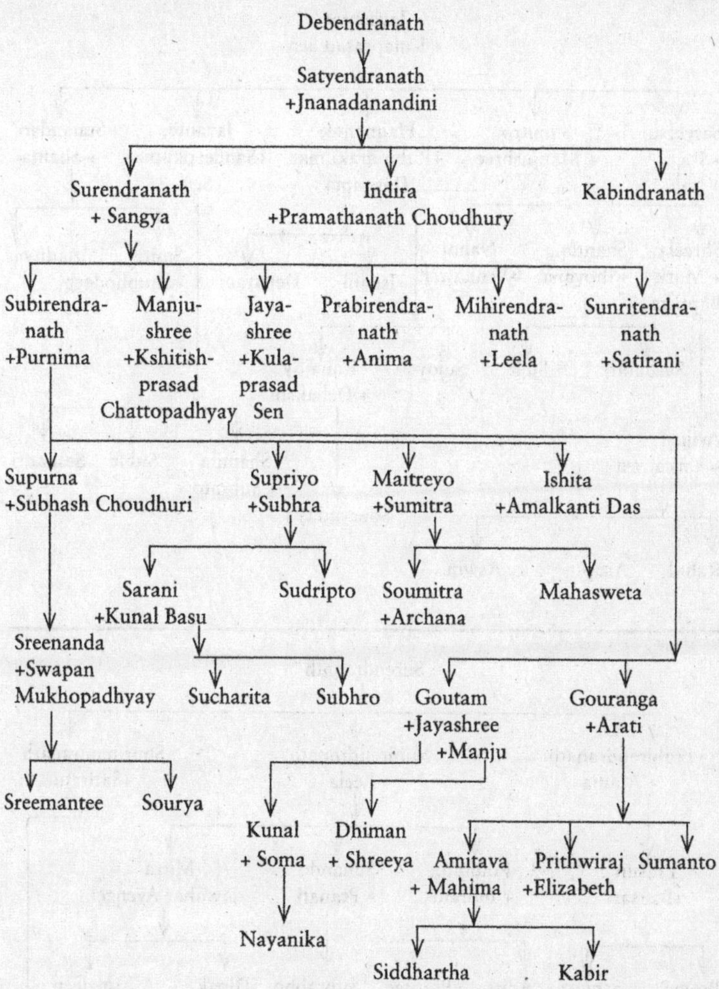
Debendranath
Satyendranath
+Jnanadanandini
Surendranath
+ Sangya
Indira
+Pramathanath Choudhury
Kabindranath
Subirendra-
nath
+Purnima
Manju-
shree
+Kshitish-
prasad
Chattopadhyay
Jaya-
shree
+Kula-
prasad
Sen
Prabirendra-
nath
+Anima
Mihirendra-
nath
+Leela
Sunritendra-
nath
+Satirani
Supurna
+Subhash Choudhuri
Supriyo
+Subhra
Maitreyo
+Sumitra
Ishita
+Amalkanti Das
Sarani
+Kunal Basu
Sudripto
Soumitra
+Archana
Mahasweta
Sreenanda
+Swapan
Mukhopadhyay
Sucharita
Subhro
Goutam
+Jayashree
+Manju
Gouranga
+Arati
Sreemantee
Sourya
Kunal
+ Soma
Dhiman
+ Shreeya
Amitava
+ Mahima
Prithwiraj
+Elizabeth
Sumanto
Nayanika
Siddhartha
Kabir

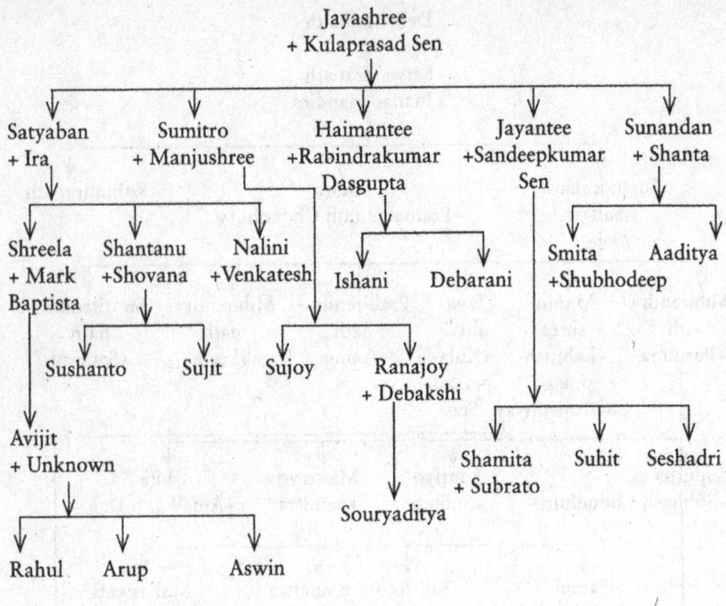
Jayashree
+ Kulaprasad Sen
Satyaban
+ Ira
Sumitro
+ Manjushree
Haimantee
+Rabindrakumar
Dasgupta
Jayantee
+Sandeepkumar
Sen
Sunandan
+ Shanta
Shreela
+ Mark
Baptista
Shantanu
+Shovana
Nalini
+Venkatesh
Ishani
Debarani
Smita
+Shubhodeep
Aaditya
Sushanto
Sujit
Sujoy
Ranajoy
+ Debakshi
Avijit
+ Unknown
Shamita
+ Subrato
Suhit
Seshadri
Souryaditya
Rahul
Arup
Aswin

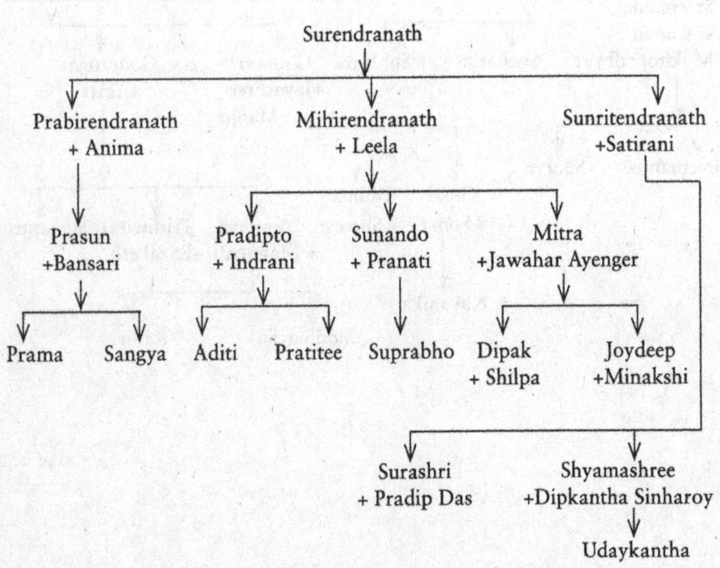
Surendranath
Prabirendranath
+ Anima
Mihirendranath
+ Leela
Sunritendranath
+Satirani
Prasun
+Bansari
Pradipto
+ Indrani
Sunando
+ Pranati
Mitra
+Jawahar Ayenger
Prama
Sangya
Aditi
Pratitee
Suprabho
Dipak
+ Shilpa
Joydeep
+Minakshi
Surashri
+ Pradip Das
Shyamashree
+Dipkantha Sinharoy
Udaykantha

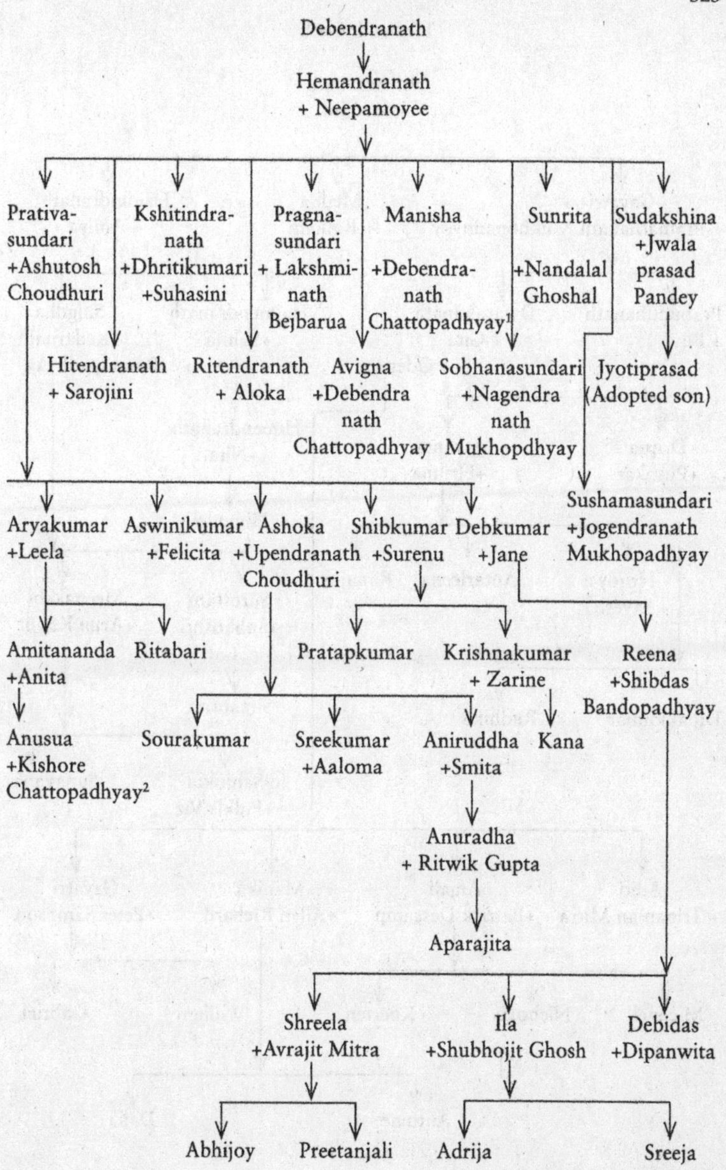

1 Debendranath Chattopadhyay married Manisha after the death of Avignya
2 Harimohan Thakur family

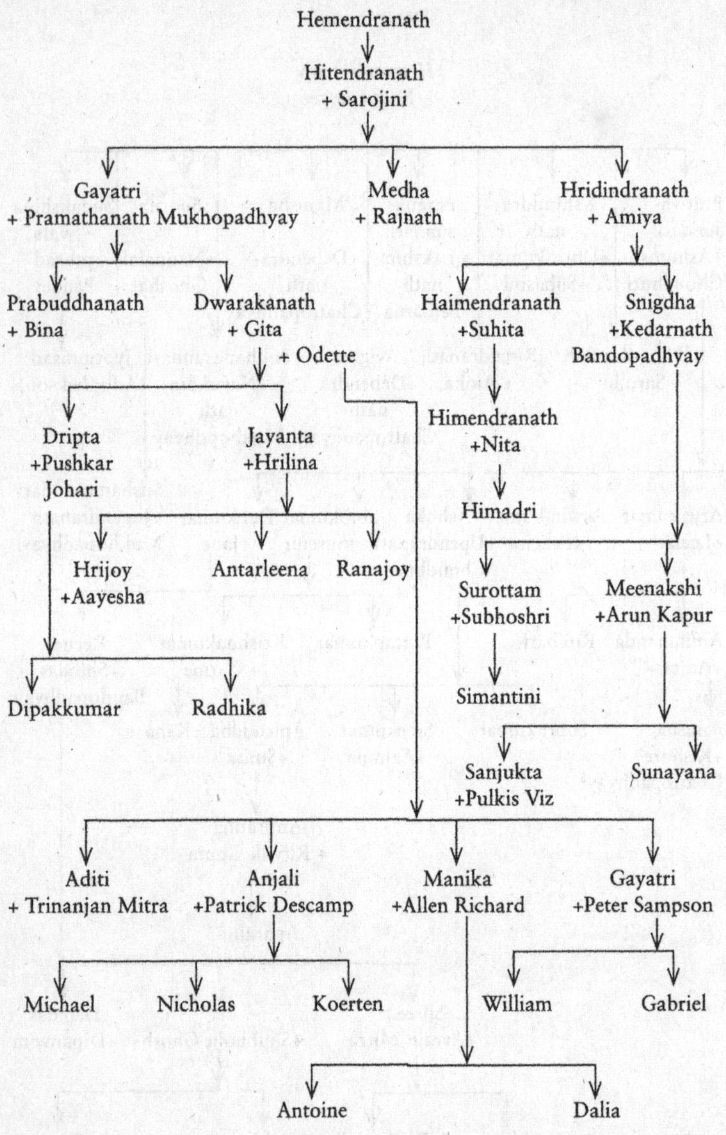
Hemendranath
Hitendranath
+ Sarojini
Gayatri
+ Pramathanath Mukhopadhyay
Medha
+ Rajnath
Hridindranath
+ Amiya
Prabuddhanath
+ Bina
Dwarakanath
+ Gita
+ Odette
Haimendranath
+Suhita
Snigdha
+Kedarnath
Bandopadhyay
Himendranath
+Nita
Dripta
+Pushkar
Johari
Jayanta
+Hrilina
Himadri
Hrijoy
+Aayesha
Antarleena
Ranajoy
Surottam
+Subhoshri
Meenakshi
+Arun Kapur
Simantini
Dipakkumar
Radhika
Sanjukta
+Pulkis Viz
Sunayana
Aditi
+ Trinanjan Mitra
Anjali
+Patrick Descamp
Manika
+Allen Richard
Gayatri
+Peter Sampson
Michael
Nicholas
Koerten
William
Gabriel
Antoine
Dalia

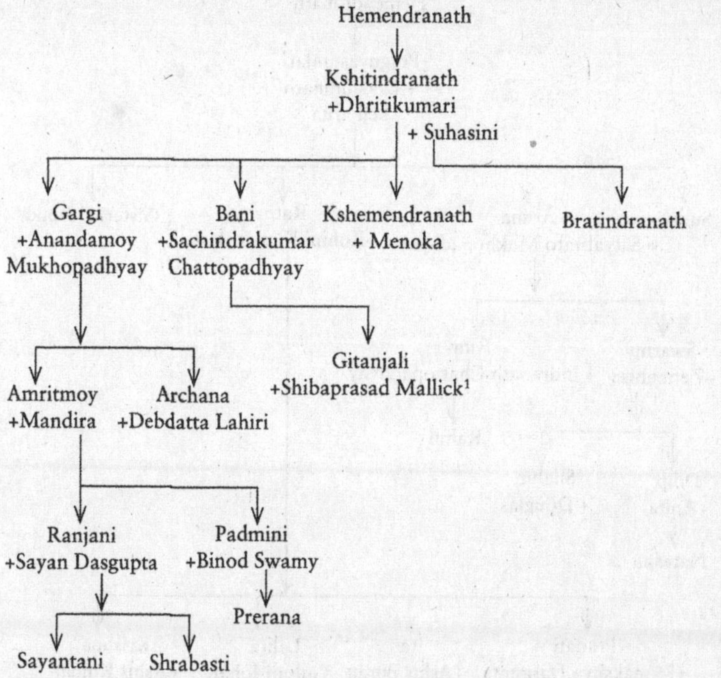

Hemendranath
Kshitindranath
+Dhritikumari
+ Suhasini
Gargi
+Anandamoy
Mukhopadhyay
Bani
+Sachindrakumar
Chattopadhyay
Kshemendranath
+ Menoka
Bratindranath
Amritmoy
+Mandira
Archana
+Debdatta Lahiri
Gitanjali
+Shibaprasad Mallick¹
Ranjani
+Sayan Dasgupta
Padmini
+Binod Swamy
Prerana
Sayantani
Shrabasti

Ritendranath
+ Alaka
Riddhindranath
daughter
Subhogendranath (Subho)
+ Nirmala
+ Arati
Siddhindranath
+ Parul
Basabendranath
+ Smriti
Chitralekha
+Prithwiraj Sen
Siddhartha
+Mina
Sundaram
+Kelly
Rigindranath
+Subhoshri
Prakriti
+Sujit Roy
Sukriti
+Indrajit
Chattopadhyay
Surojit
Adhiraj
Surya
Prarthana
Priyanka
Shamitendranath
+ Shubhra
Ranitendranath
+ Debarati
Rajeswari
Jashojit
+ Helen
Barota
+Charles
Hallis
Kumar
Julia Sujata
Ana Sujaya
Maya

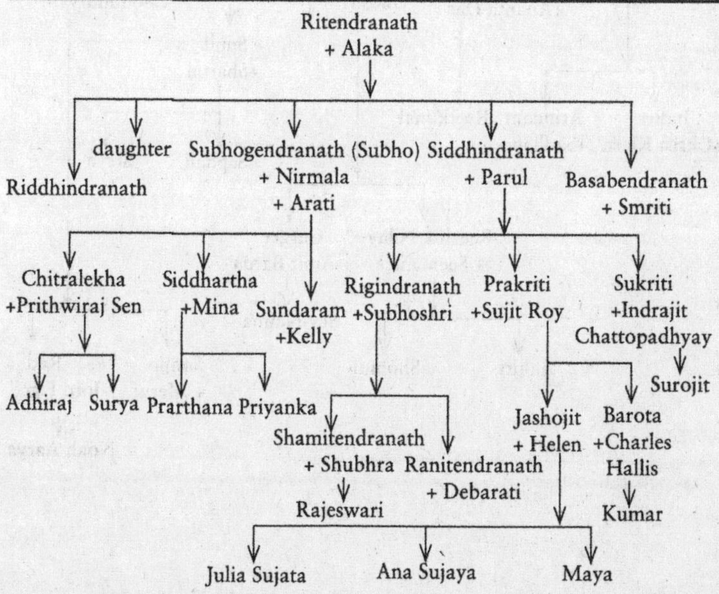

1. Anandiram Thakur family

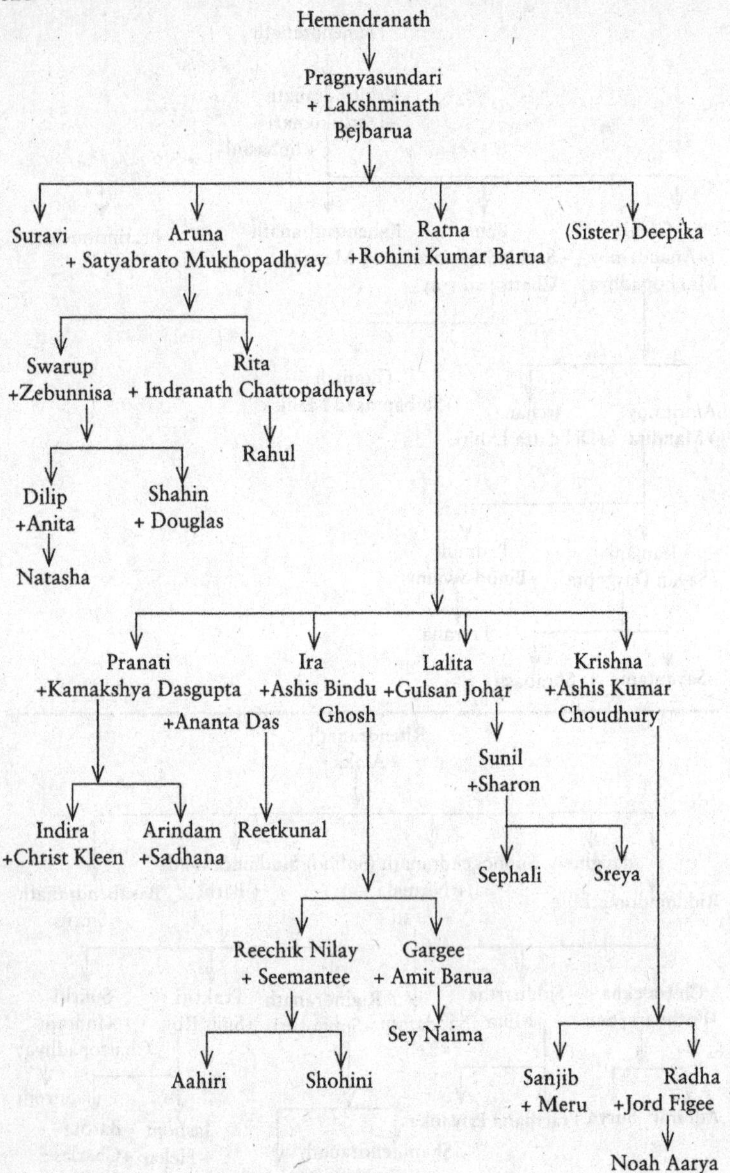
Hemendranath
Pragnyasundari
+ Lakshminath
Bejbarua
Suravi
Aruna
+ Satyabrato Mukhopadhyay
Ratna
+Rohini Kumar Barua
(Sister) Deepika
Swarup
+Zebunnisa
Rita
+ Indranath Chattopadhyay
Rahul
Dilip
+Anita
Shahin
+ Douglas
Natasha
Pranati
+Kamakshya Dasgupta
+Ananta Das
Ira
+Ashis Bindu
Ghosh
Lalita
+Gulsan Johar
Krishna
+Ashis Kumar
Choudhury
Sunil
+Sharon
Indira
+Christ Kleen
Arindam
+Sadhana
Reetkunal
Sephali
Sreya
Reechik Nilay
+ Seemantee
Gargee
+ Amit Barua
Sey Naima
Aahiri
Shohini
Sanjib
+ Meru
Radha
+Jord Figee
Noah Aarya

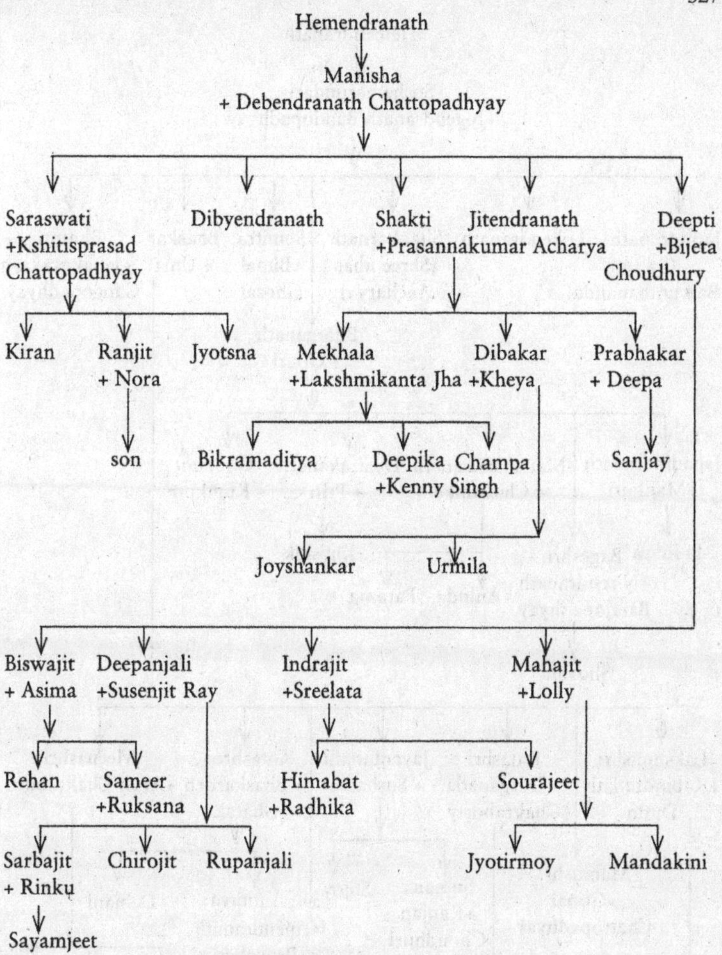
Hemendranath
Manisha
+ Debendranath Chattopadhyay
Saraswati
+Kshitisprasad
Chattopadhyay
Dibyendranath
Shakti
+Prasannakumar Acharya
Jitendranath
Deepti
+Bijeta
Choudhury
Kiran
Ranjit
+ Nora
Jyotsna
Mekhala
+Lakshmikanta Jha
Dibakar
+Kheya
Prabhakar
+ Deepa
son
Bikramaditya
Deepika
+Kenny Singh
Champa
Sanjay
Joyshankar
Urmila
Biswajit
+ Asima
Deepanjali
+Susenjit Ray
Indrajit
+Sreelata
Mahajit
+Lolly
Rehan
Sameer
+Ruksana
Himabat
+Radhika
Sourajeet
Sarbajit
+ Rinku
Chirojit
Rupanjali
Jyotirmoy
Mandakini
Sayamjeet

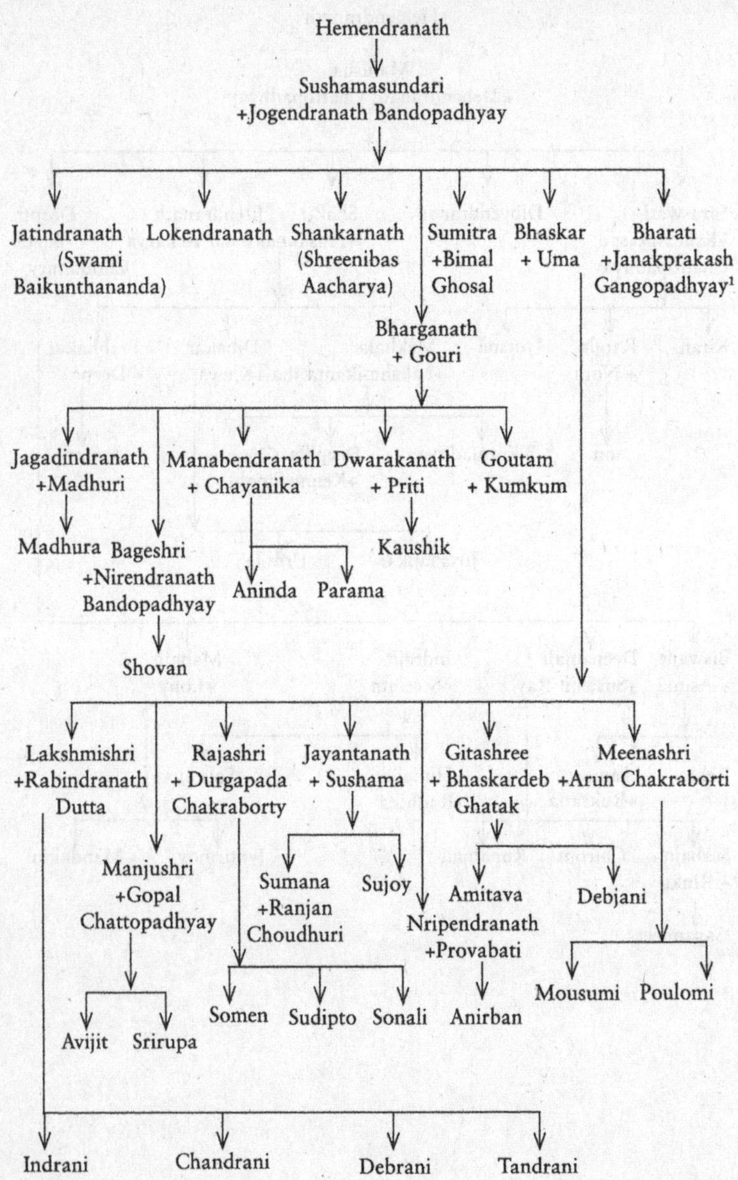

1 Jorasanko house no. 5 (Kadambini Gangopadhyay family)

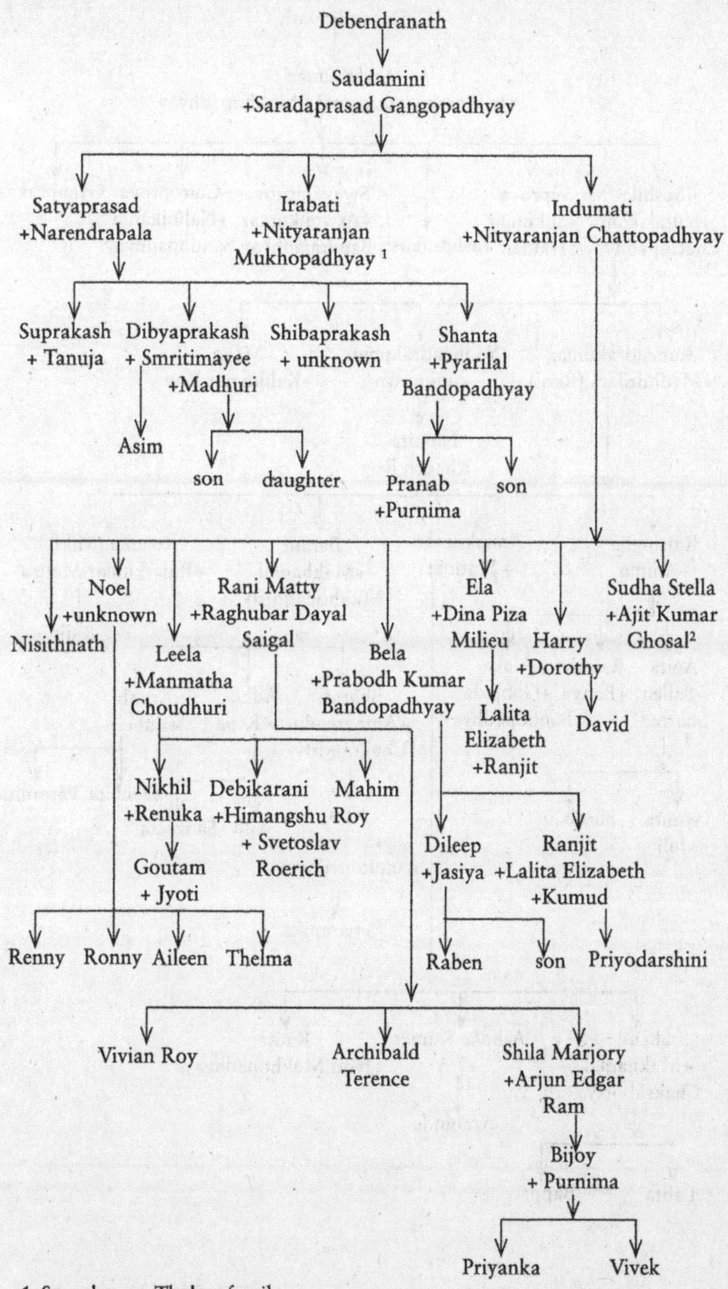

1 Suryakumar Thakur family
2 Jorasanko house no. 6 (Swarnakumari Ghoshal's family)

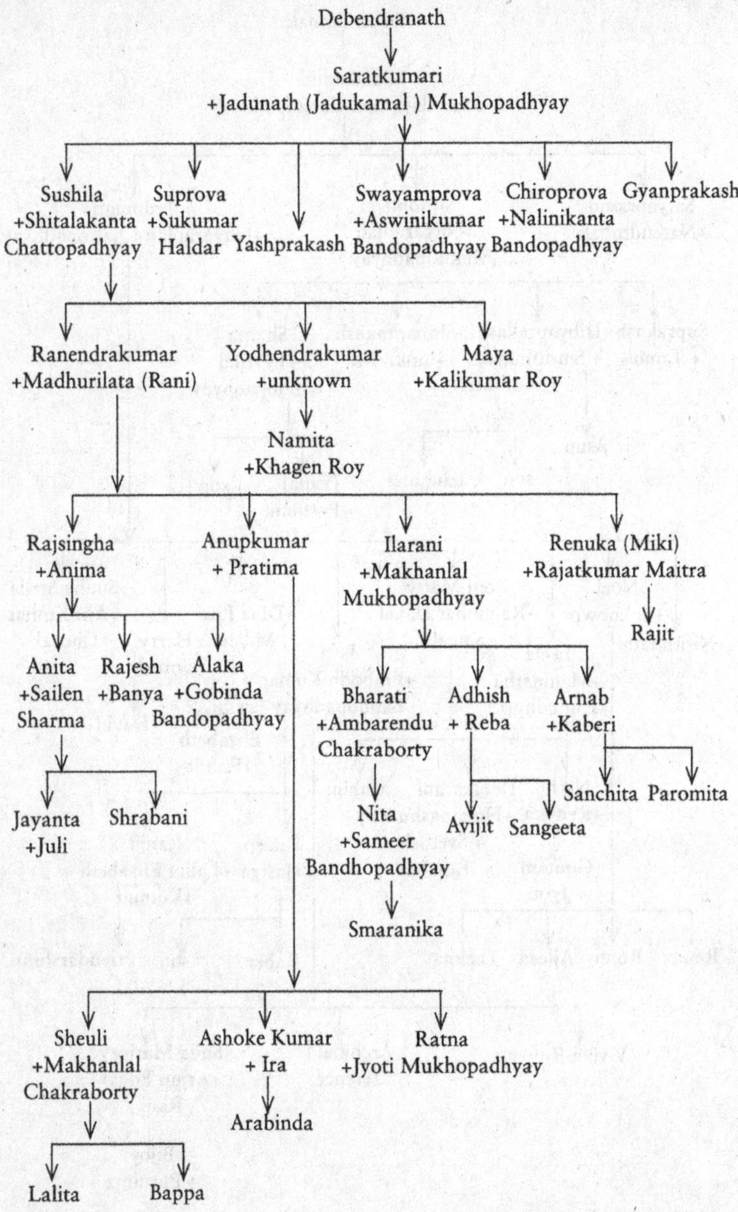
Debendranath
Saratkumari
+Jadunath (Jadukamal) Mukhopadhyay
Sushila
+Shitalakanta
Chattopadhyay
Suprova
+Sukumar
Haldar
Yashprakash
Swayamprova
+Aswinikumar
Bandopadhyay
Chiroprova
+Nalinikanta
Bandopadhyay
Gyanprakash
Ranendrakumar
+Madhurilata (Rani)
Yodhendrakumar
+unknown
Maya
+Kalikumar Roy
Namita
+Khagen Roy
Rajsingha
+Anima
Anupkumar
+ Pratima
Ilarani
+Makhanlal
Mukhopadhyay
Renuka (Miki)
+Rajatkumar Maitra
Rajit
Anita
+Sailen
Sharma
Rajesh
+Banya
Alaka
+Gobinda
Bandopadhyay
Bharati
+Ambarendu
Chakraborty
Adhish
+ Reba
Arnab
+Kaberi
Sanchita
Paromita
Jayanta
+Juli
Shrabani
Nita
+Sameer
Bandhopadhyay
Avijit
Sangeeta
Smaranika
Sheuli
+Makhanlal
Chakraborty
Ashoke Kumar
+ Ira
Ratna
+Jyoti Mukhopadhyay
Arabinda
Lalita
Bappa

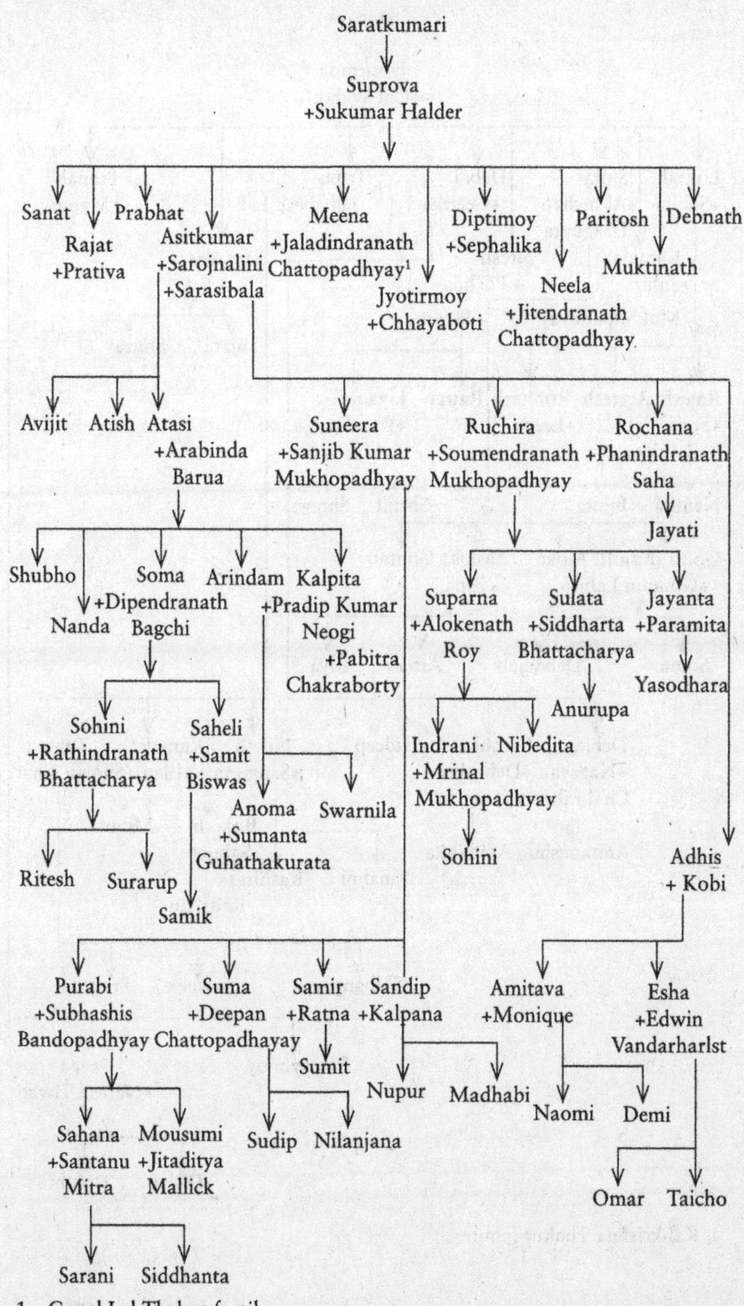

1 Gopal Lal Thakur family

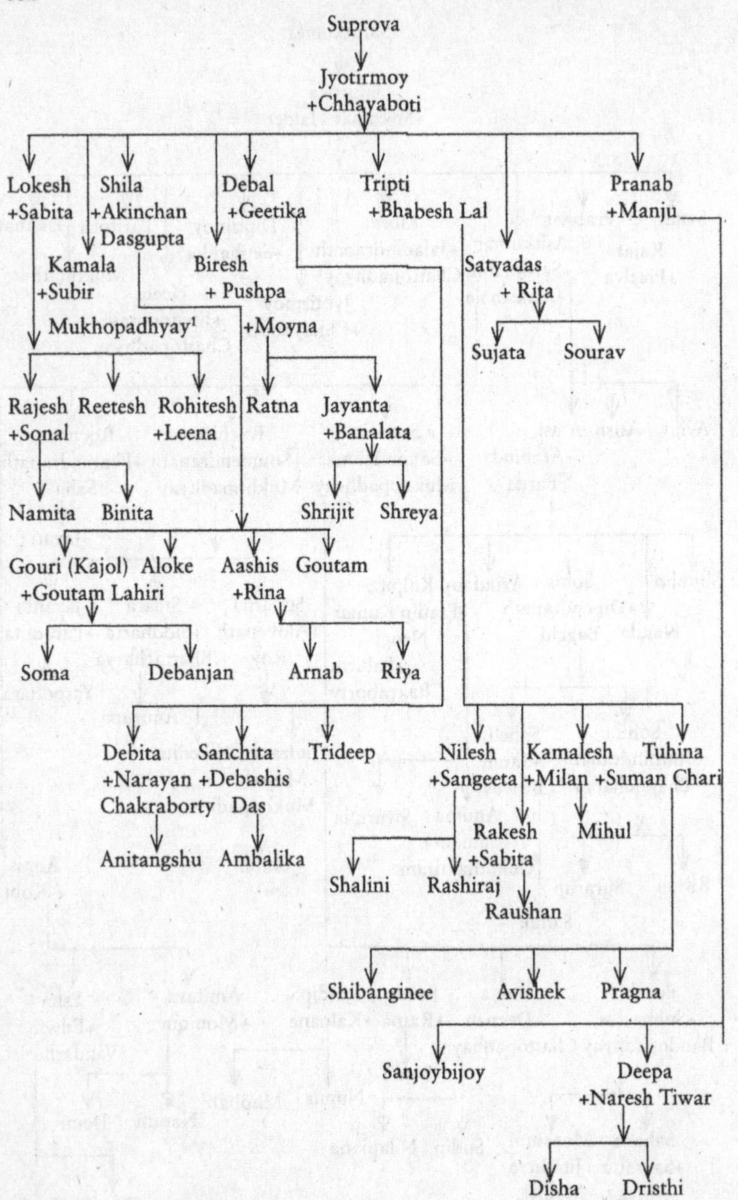

1 Kalikrishna Thakur family

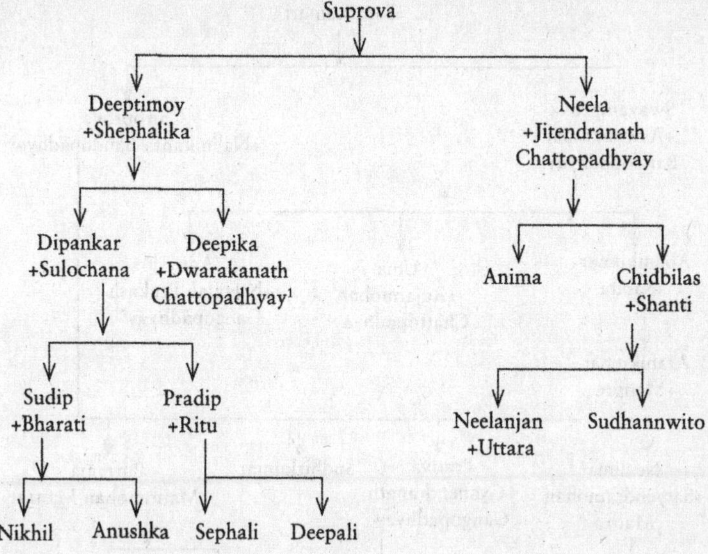

1 Rasbilasi Chattopadhyay family

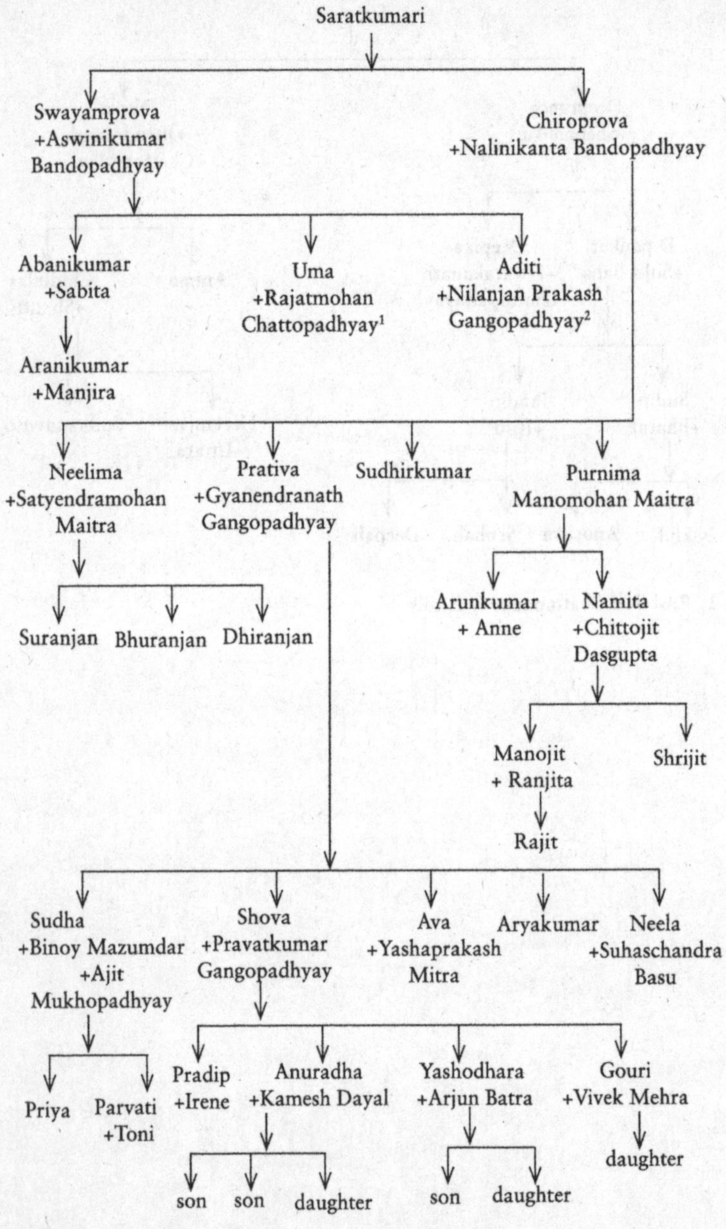

1 Jorasanko house no. 6 (Dwijendranath Thakur family)
2 Jatindramohan Thakur family

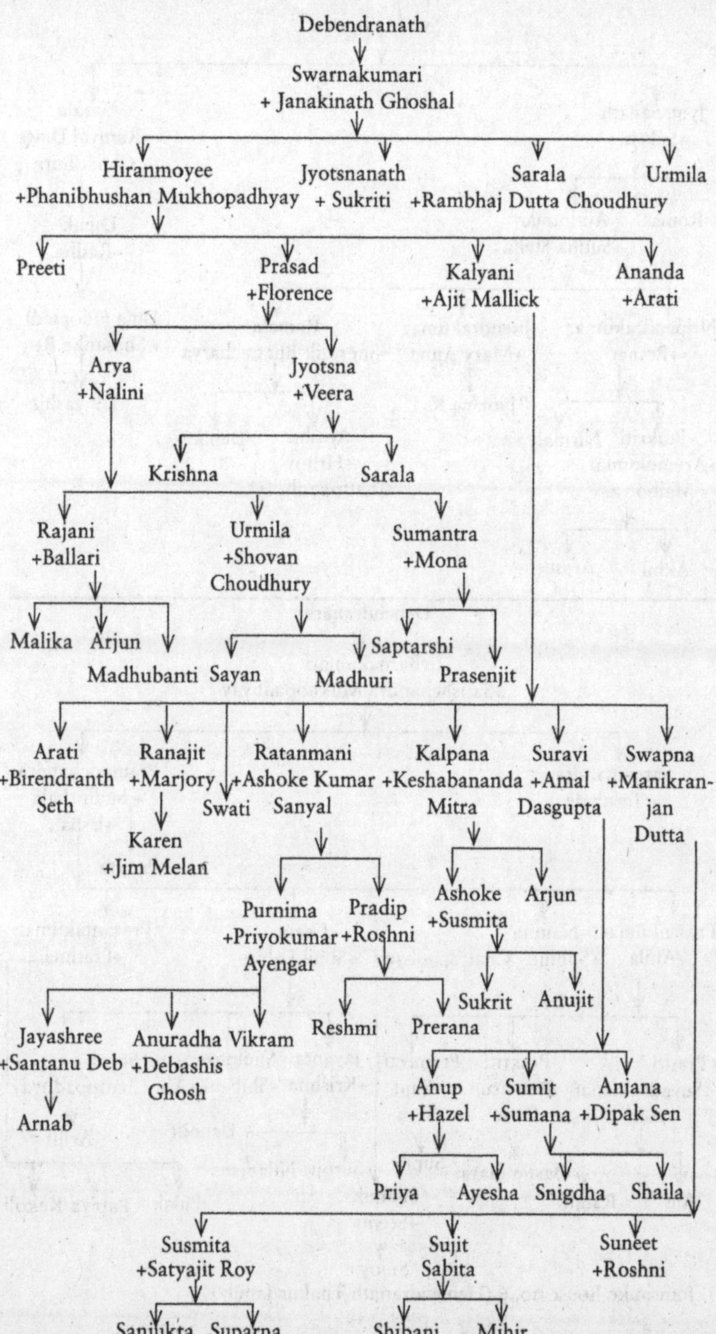
Debendranath
Swarnakumari
+ Janakinath Ghoshal
Hiranmoyee
+Phanibhushan Mukhopadhyay
Jyotsnanath
+ Sukriti
Sarala
+Rambhaj Dutta Choudhury
Urmila
Preeti
Prasad
+Florence
Kalyani
+Ajit Mallick
Ananda
+Arati
Arya
+Nalini
Jyotsna
+Veera
Krishna
Sarala
Rajani
+Ballari
Urmila
+Shovan
Choudhury
Sumantra
+Mona
Malika
Arjun
Madhubanti
Sayan
Saptarshi
Madhuri
Prasenjit
Arati
+Birendranth
Seth
Ranajit
+Marjory
Swati
Ratanmani
+Ashoke Kumar
Sanyal
Kalpana
+Keshabananda
Mitra
Suravi
+Amal
Dasgupta
Swapna
+Manikran-
jan
Dutta
Karen
+Jim Melan
Purnima
+Priyokumar
Ayengar
Pradip
+Roshni
Ashoke
+Susmita
Arjun
Sukrit
Anujit
Jayashree
+Santanu Deb
Anuradha
+Debashis
Ghosh
Vikram
Reshmi
Prerana
Arnab
Anup
+Hazel
Sumit
+Sumana
Anjana
+Dipak Sen
Priya
Ayesha
Snigdha
Shaila
Susmita
+Satyajit Roy
Sujit
Sabita
Suneet
+Roshni
Sanjukta
Suparna
Shibani
Mihir

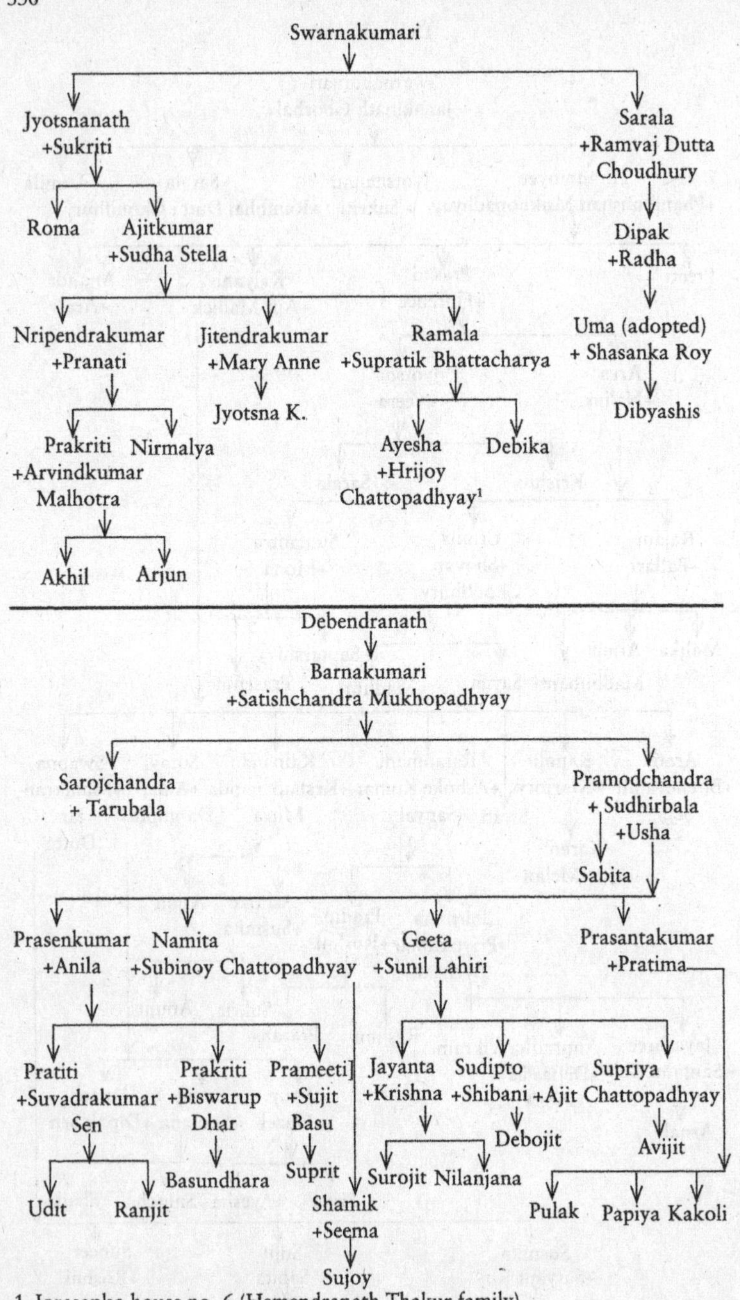

1 Jorasanko house no. 6 (Hemendranath Thakur family)

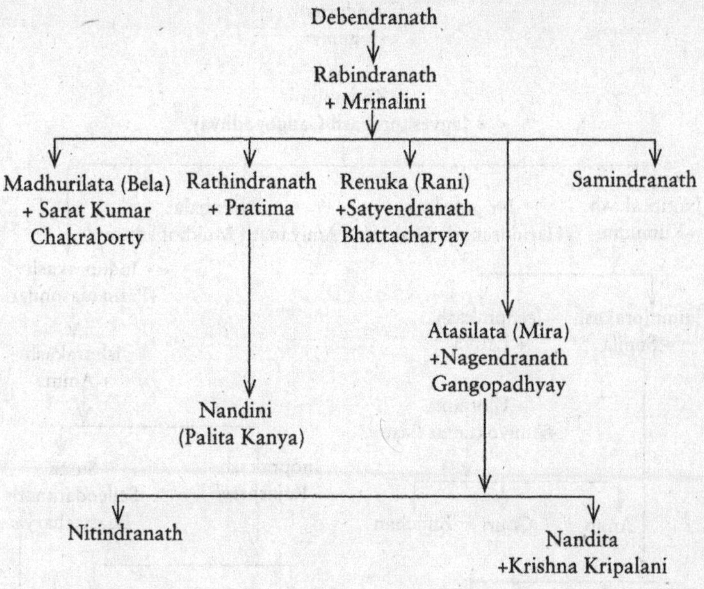
Debendranath
Rabindranath
+ Mrinalini
Madhurilata (Bela)
+ Sarat Kumar
Chakraborty
Rathindranath
+ Pratima
Renuka (Rani)
+Satyendranath
Bhattacharyay
Samindranath
Atasilata (Mira)
+Nagendranath
Gangopadhyay
Nandini
(Palita Kanya)
Nitindranath
Nandita
+Krishna Kripalani

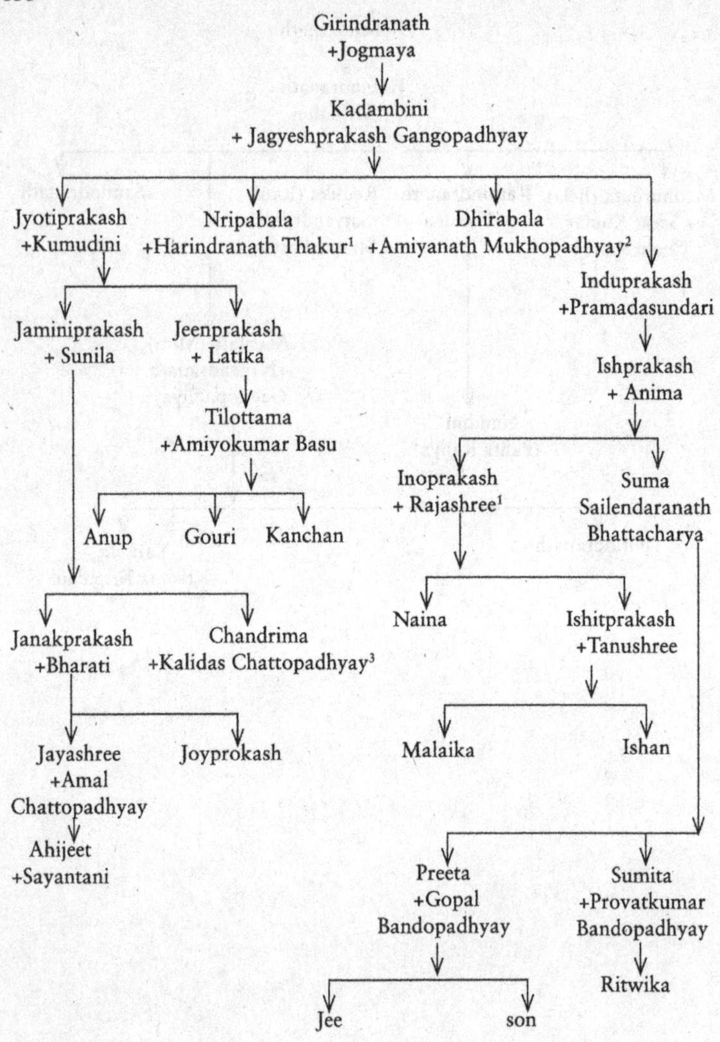

1 Ramanath Thakur family
2 Brajasundari Mukhopadhyay family
3 Prasannakumar Thakur family

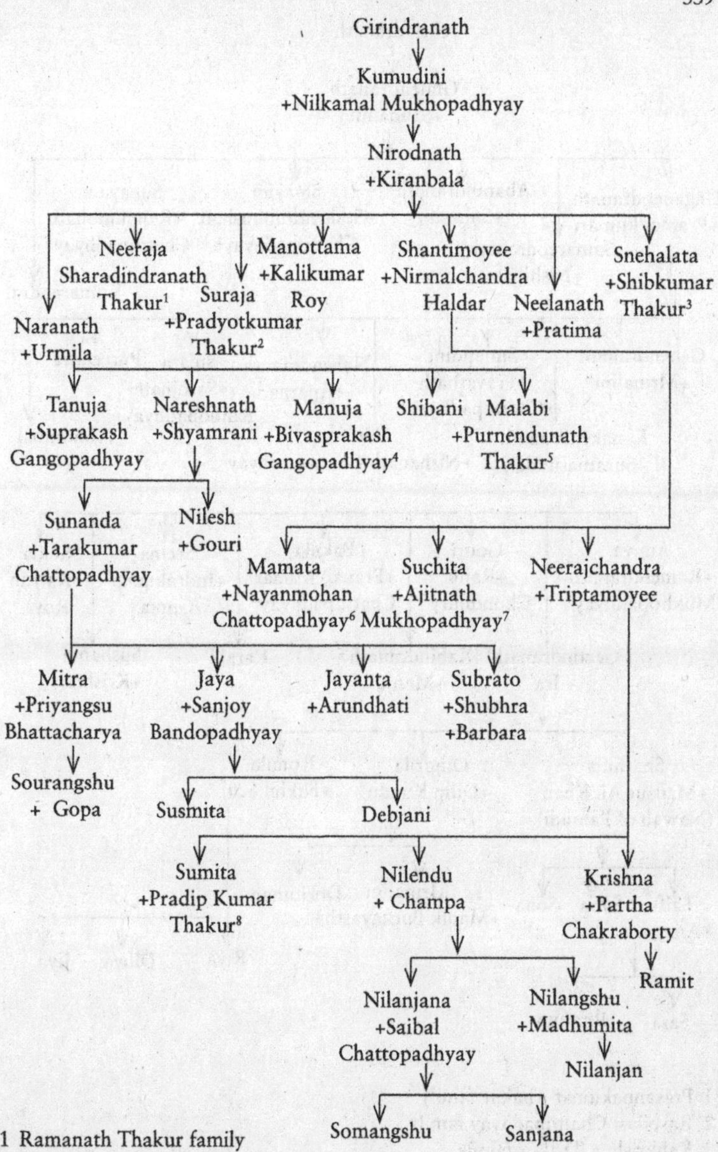

1 Ramanath Thakur family
2 Jatindranath Thakur family
3 Sourindramohan Thakur family
4 Jatindranath Thakur family
5 Kalikrishna Thakur family
6 Jorasanko house no. 6 (Dwijendranath Thakur family)
7 Brajasundari Mukhopadhyay family
8 Kalikrishna Thakur family

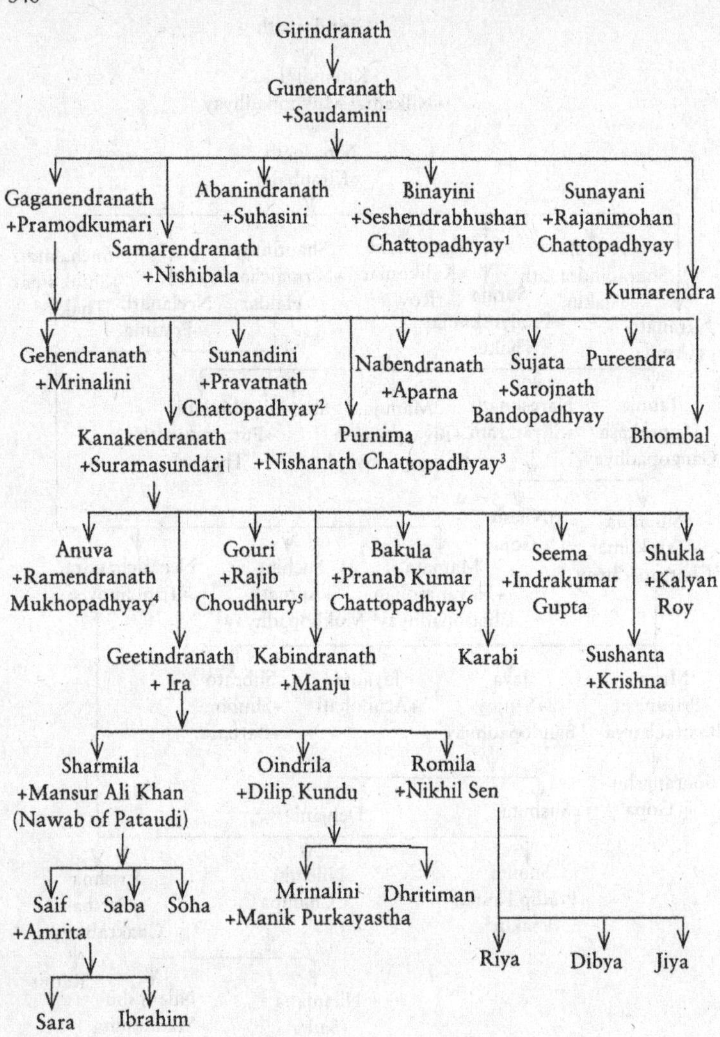

1 Prasannakumar Thakur family
2 Rasbilasi Chattopadhyay family
3 Kalikrishna Thakur family
4 Prasannakumar Thakur family
5 Jorasanko house no. 6 (Dwijendranath Thakur family)
6 Drabamoyee Chattopadhyay family

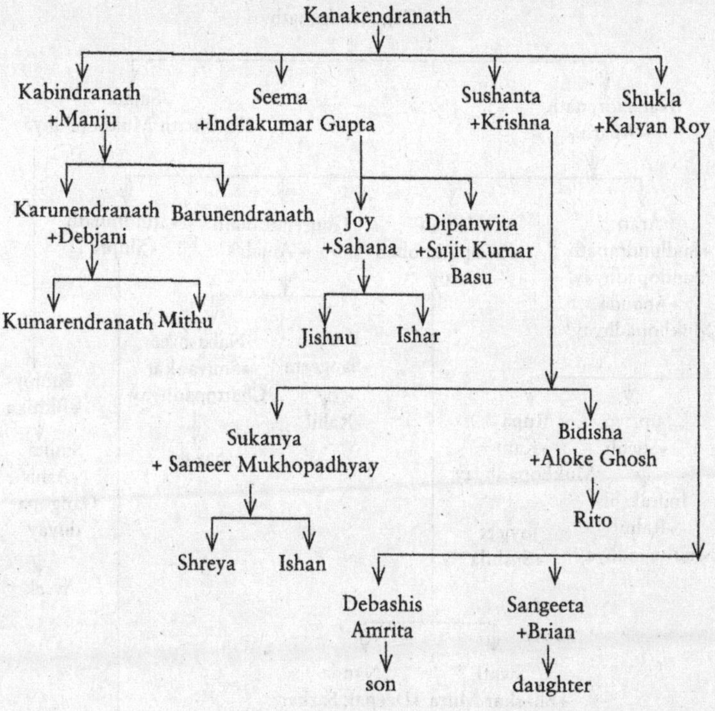
Kanakendranath
Kabindranath
+Manju
Seema
+Indrakumar Gupta
Sushanta
+Krishna
Shukla
+Kalyan Roy
Karunendranath
+Debjani
Barunendranath
Joy
+Sahana
Dipanwita
+Sujit Kumar
Basu
Kumarendranath
Mithu
Jishnu
Ishar
Sukanya
+ Sameer Mukhopadhyay
Bidisha
+Aloke Ghosh
Rito
Shreya
Ishan
Debashis
Amrita
son
Sangeeta
+Brian
daughter

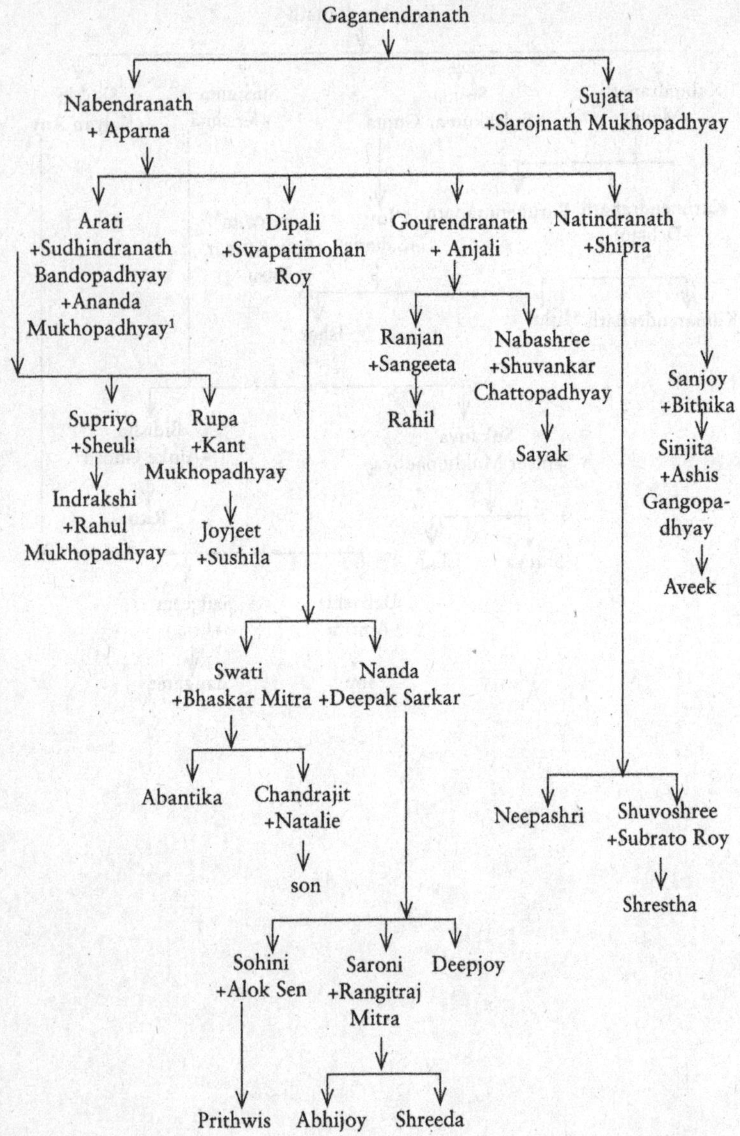

1 Jorasanko house no. 6 (Swarnakumari Ghosal family)

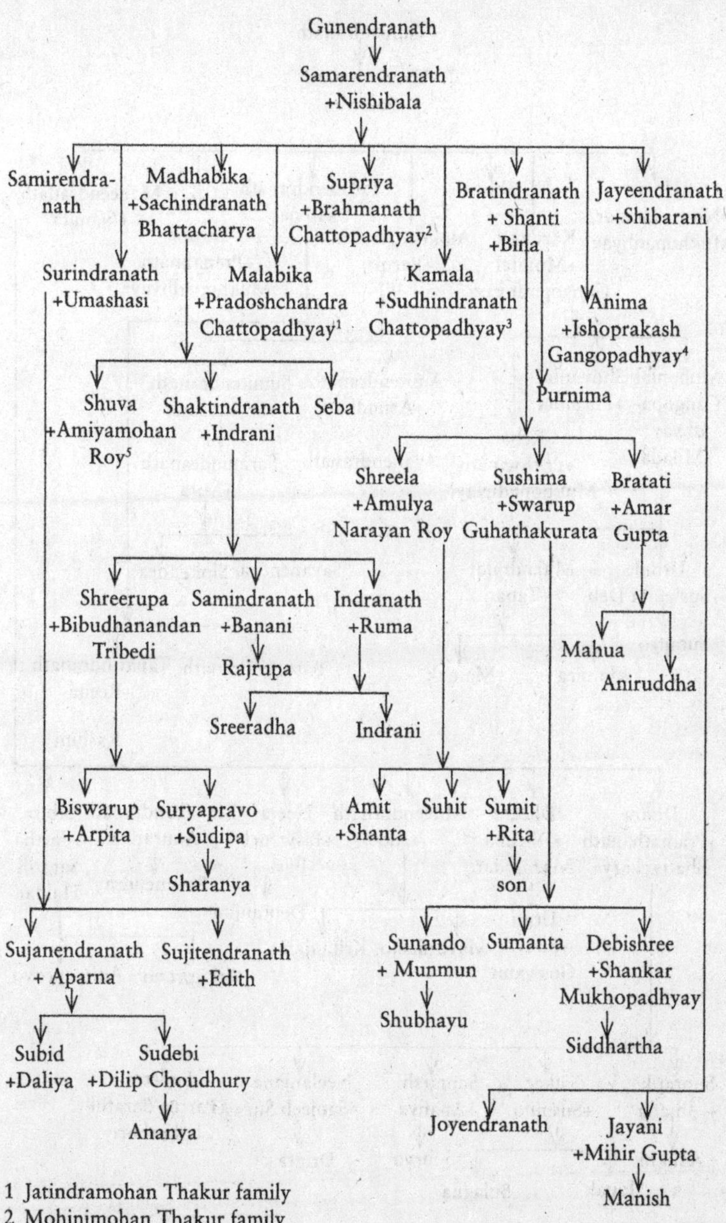

1 Jatindramohan Thakur family
2 Mohinimohan Thakur family
3 Gopal Lal Thakur family
4 Jorasanko house no. 5 (Kadambini Gangopadhyay family)
5 Anandiram Thakur family

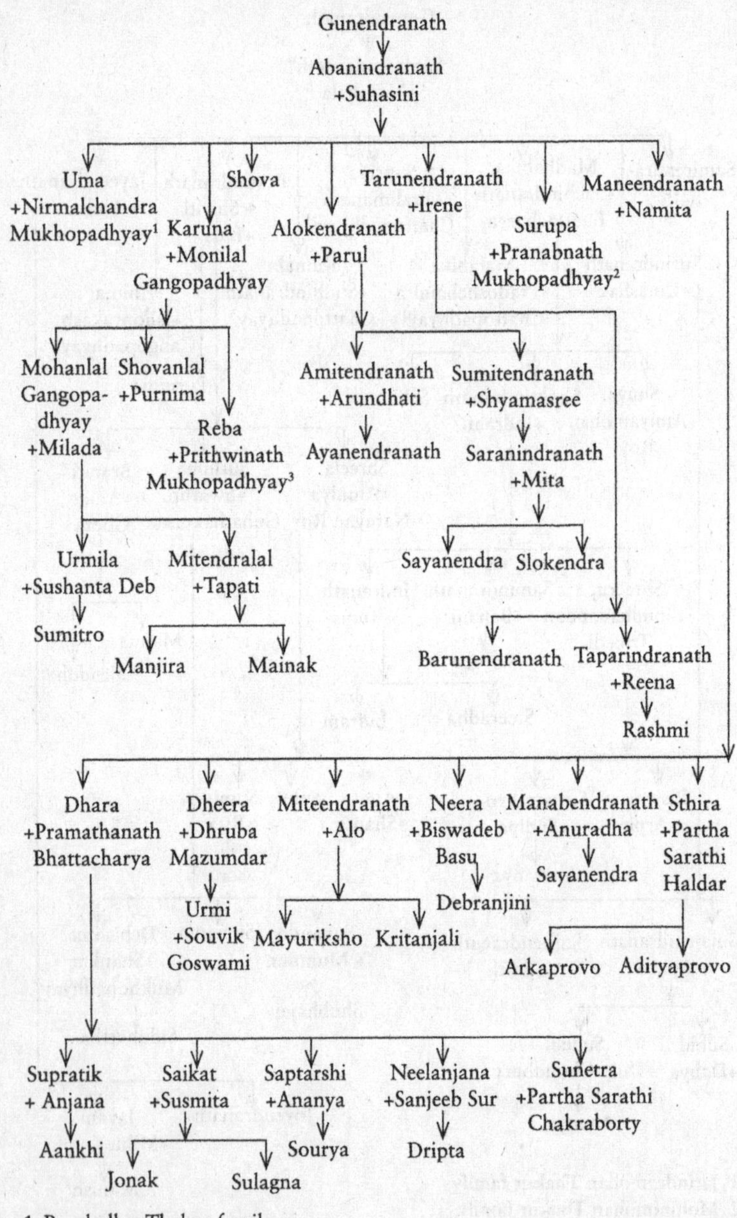

1 Ramballav Thakur family
2 Brojasundari Mukhopadhyay family
3 Brojasundari Mukhopadhyay family

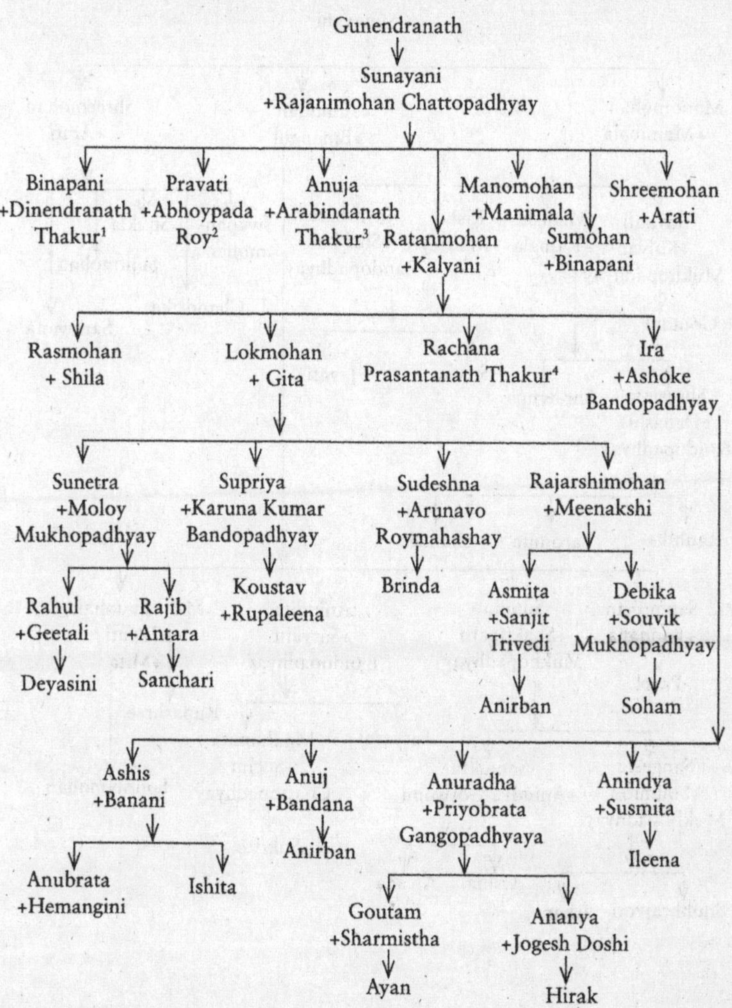

1 Jorasanko house no 6 (Dwijendranath Thakur family)
2 Anandiram Thakur family
3 Ramanath Thakur family
4 Kalikrishna Thakur family

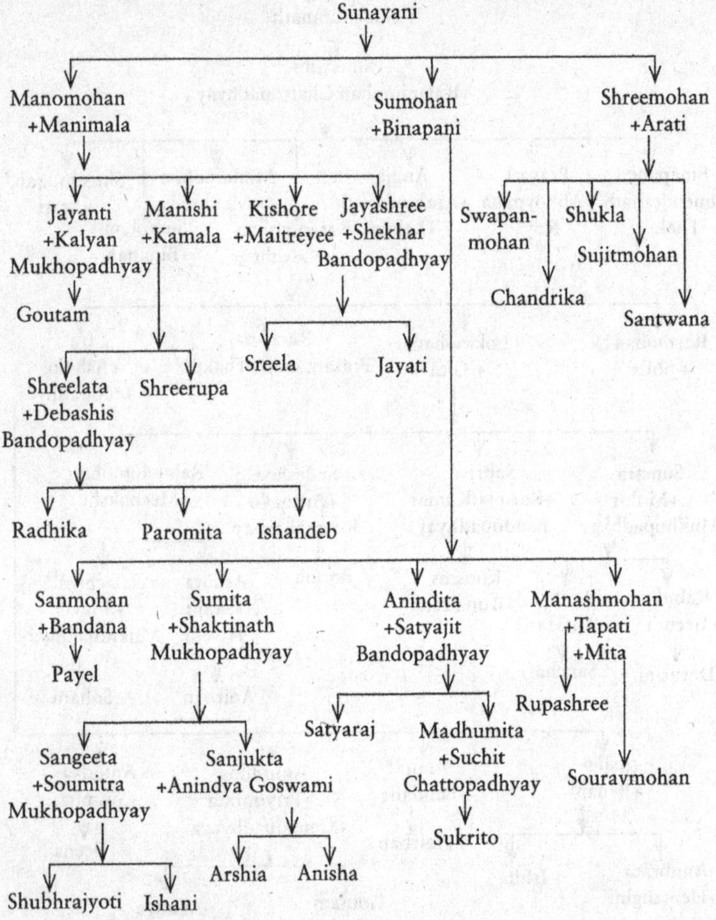

Sunayani
Manomohan
+Manimala
Sumohan
+Binapani
Shreemohan
+Arati
Jayanti
+Kalyan
Mukhopadhyay
Manishi
+Kamala
Kishore
+Maitreyee
Jayashree
+Shekhar
Bandopadhyay
Swapan-
mohan
Shukla
Sujitmohan
Chandrika
Santwana
Goutam
Shreelata
+Debashis
Bandopadhyay
Shreerupa
Sreela
Jayati
Radhika
Paromita
Ishandeb
Sanmohan
+Bandana
Sumita
+Shaktinath
Mukhopadhyay
Anindita
+Satyajit
Bandopadhyay
Manashmohan
+Tapati
+Mita
Payel
Rupashree
Satyaraj
Madhumita
+Suchit
Chattopadhyay
Sangeeta
+Soumitra
Mukhopadhyay
Sanjukta
+Anindya Goswami
Souravmohan
Sukrito
Arshia
Anisha
Shubhrajyoti
Ishani

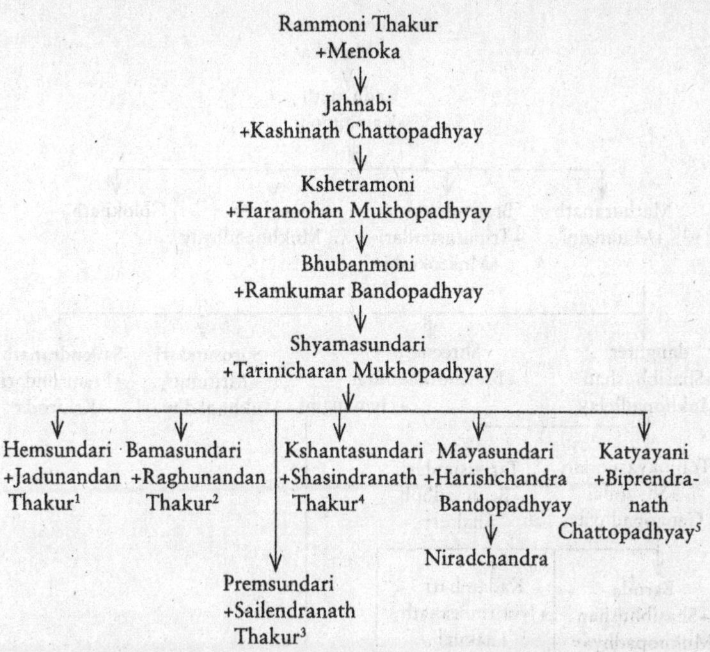

1 Harimohan Thakur family
2 Harimohan Thakur family
3 Radhanath Thakur family
4 Ramanath Thakur family
5 Rasbilas Chattopadhyay family

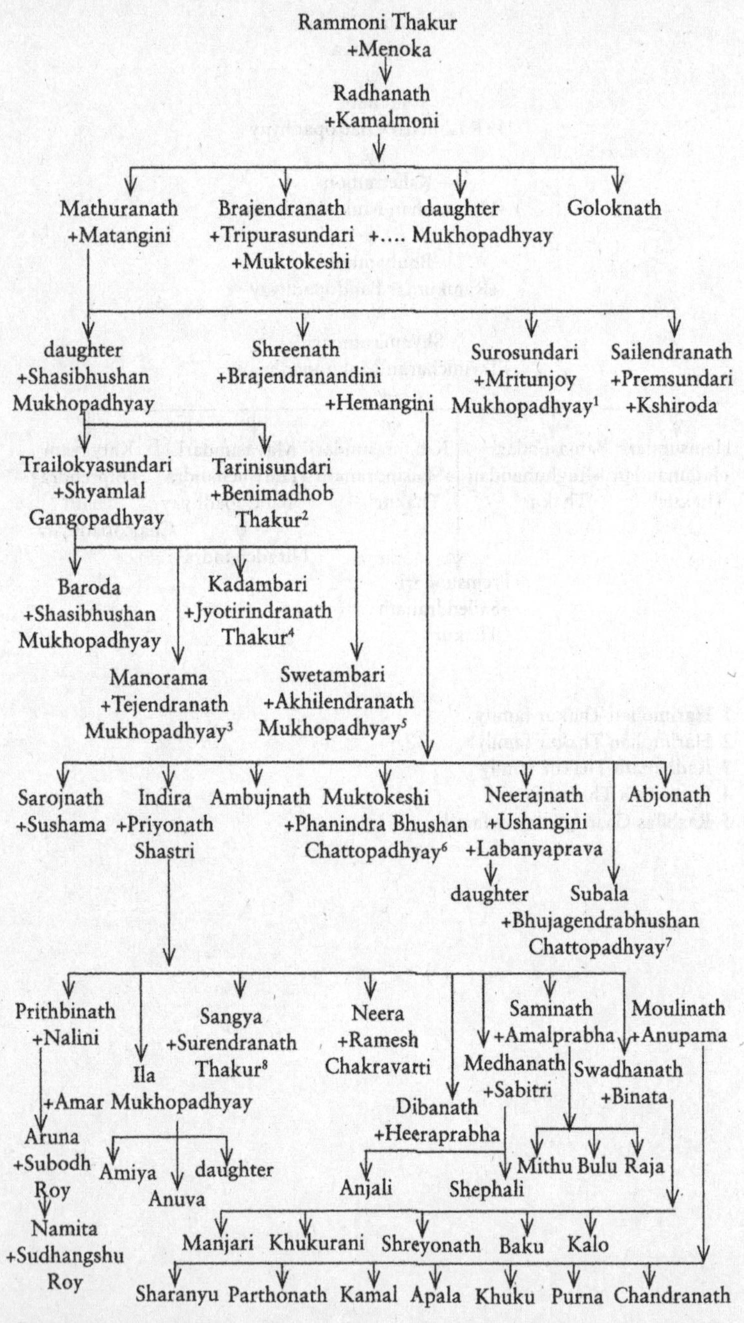

Footnotes on next page

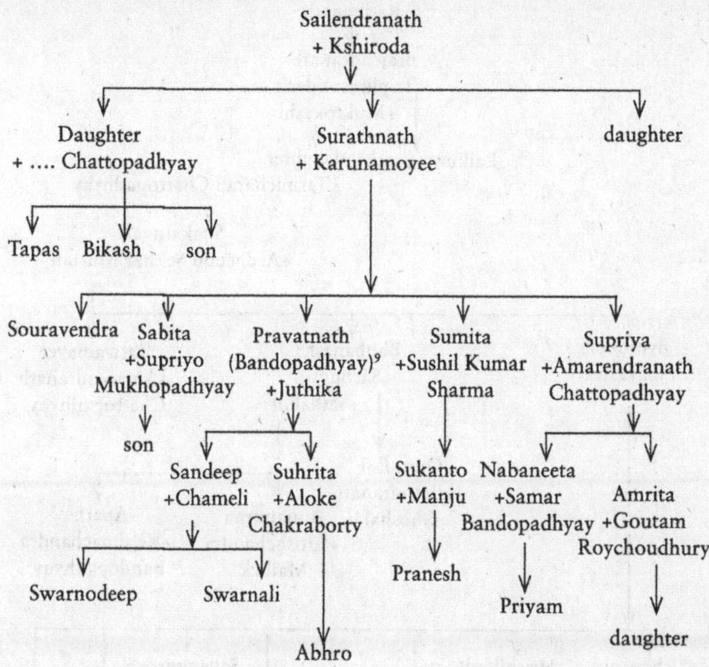

1 Pyarimohan Thakur family
2 Chorbagan Thakur family
3 Mohinimohan Thakur family
4 Jorasanko house no. 6 (Debendranath Thakur family)
5 Mohinimohan Thakur family
6 Prasannakumar Thakur family
7 Prasannakumar Thakur family
8 Jorasanko house no. 6 (Satyendranath Thakur family)
9 Radhanath Thakur's son Mathuranath was the founder of Thon-Thoney Thakurbari. Pravatnath of this family and his descendents use the surname 'Bandopadhyay' in preference to the 'Thakur' title.

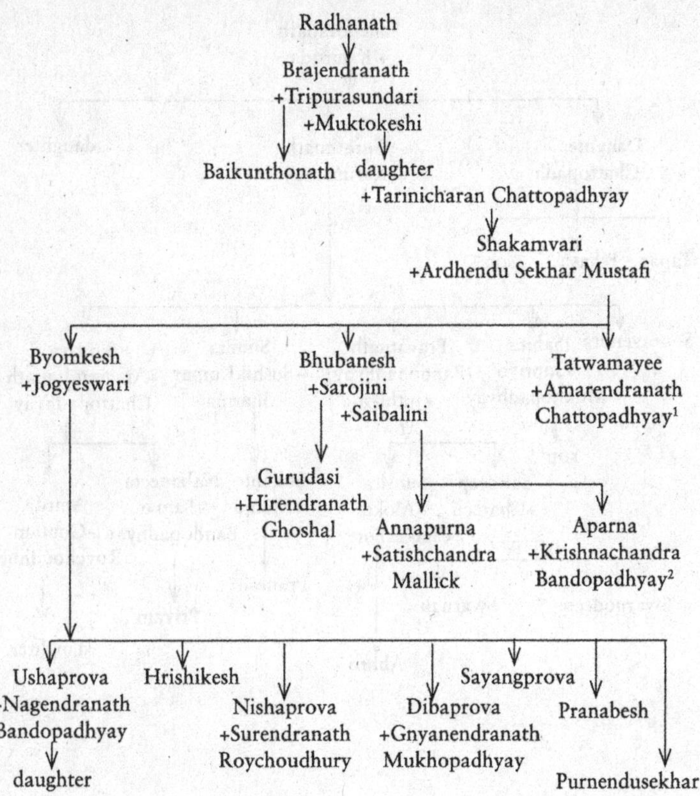

1 Rasbilasi Chattopadhyay family
2 Ramballav Thakur family

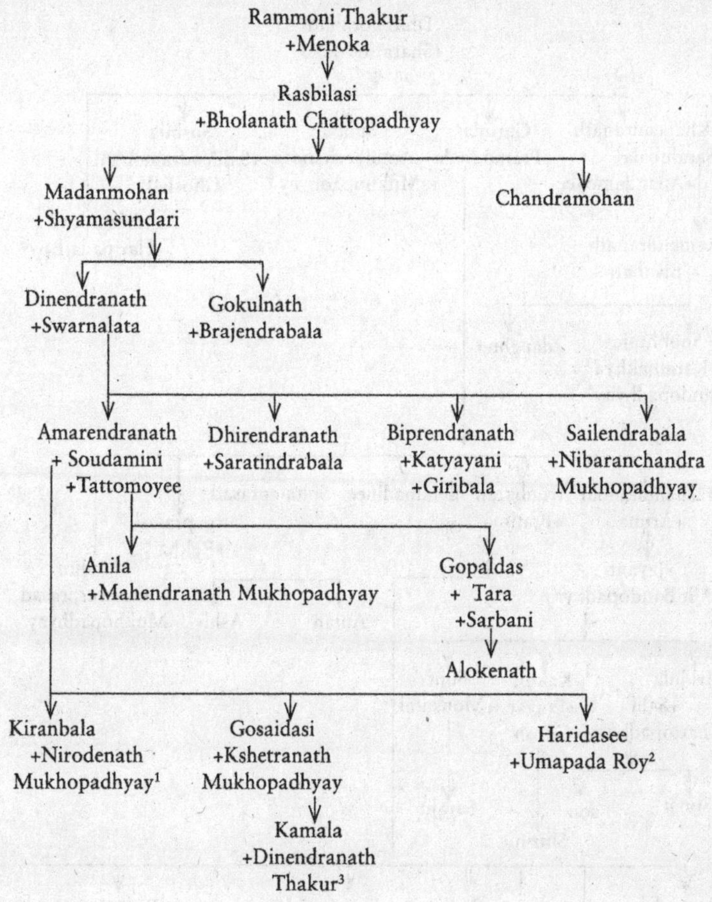

1 Jorasanko house no. 5 (Kumudini Mukhopadhyay family)
2 Anandiram Thakur family
3 Jorasanko house no. 6 (Dwijendranath Thakur family)

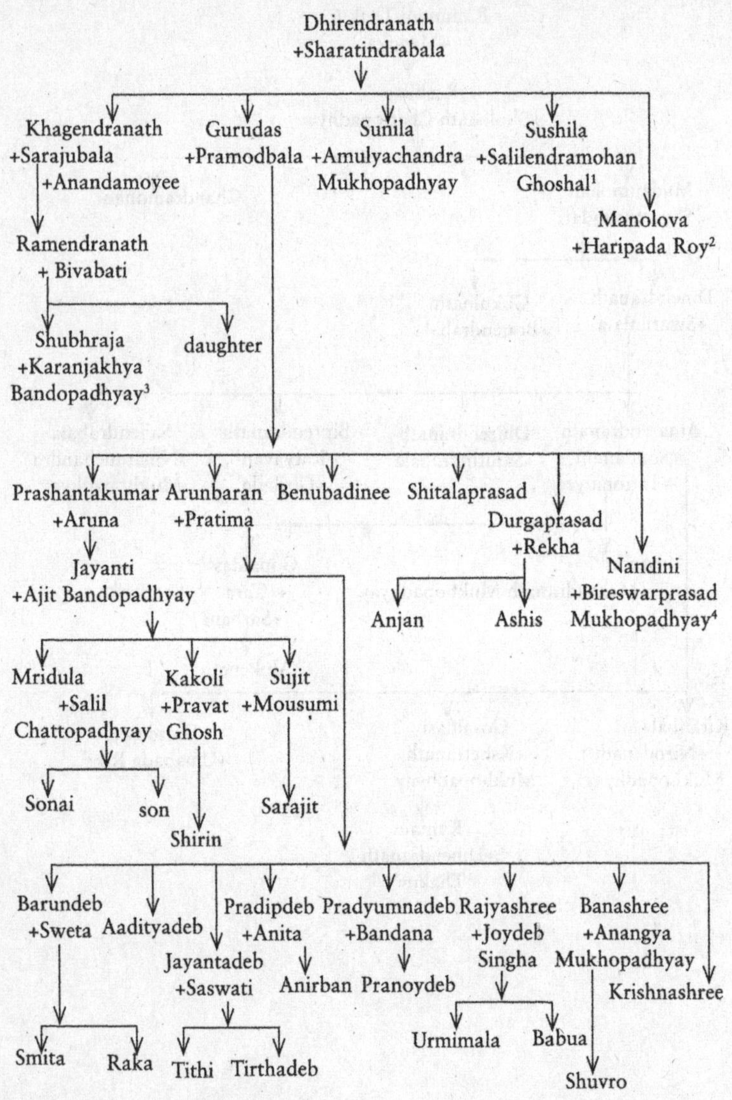

1 Kalikrishan Thakur family
2 Anandiram Thakur family
3 Jatindramohan Thakur family
4 Mohinimohan Thakur family

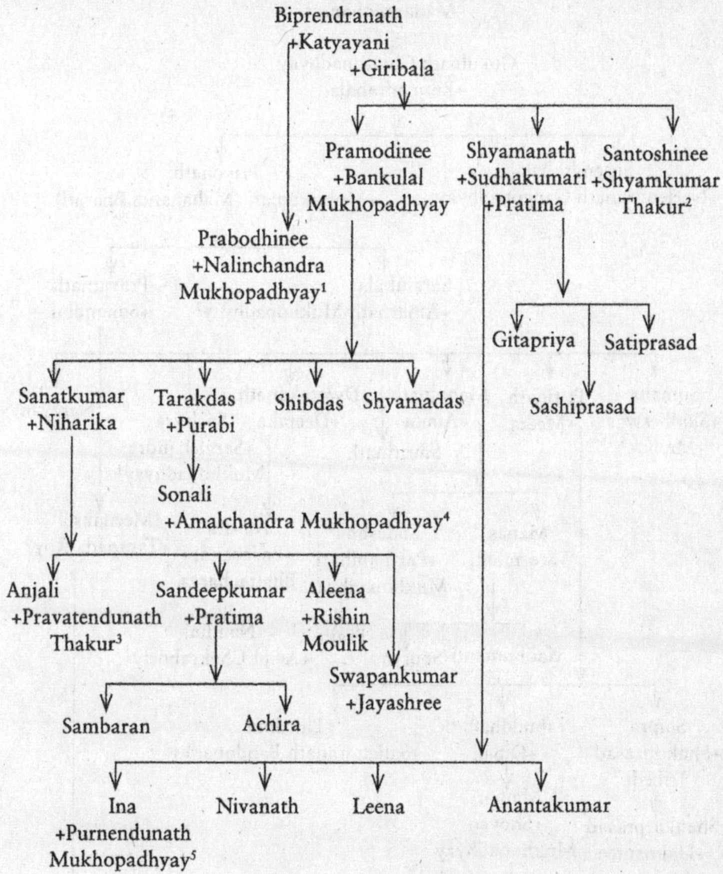

1 Ramballav Thakur family
2 Sourindramohan Thakur family
3 Kalikrishna Thakur family
4 Kalikumar Thakur family
5 Brajosundari Mukhopadhyay family

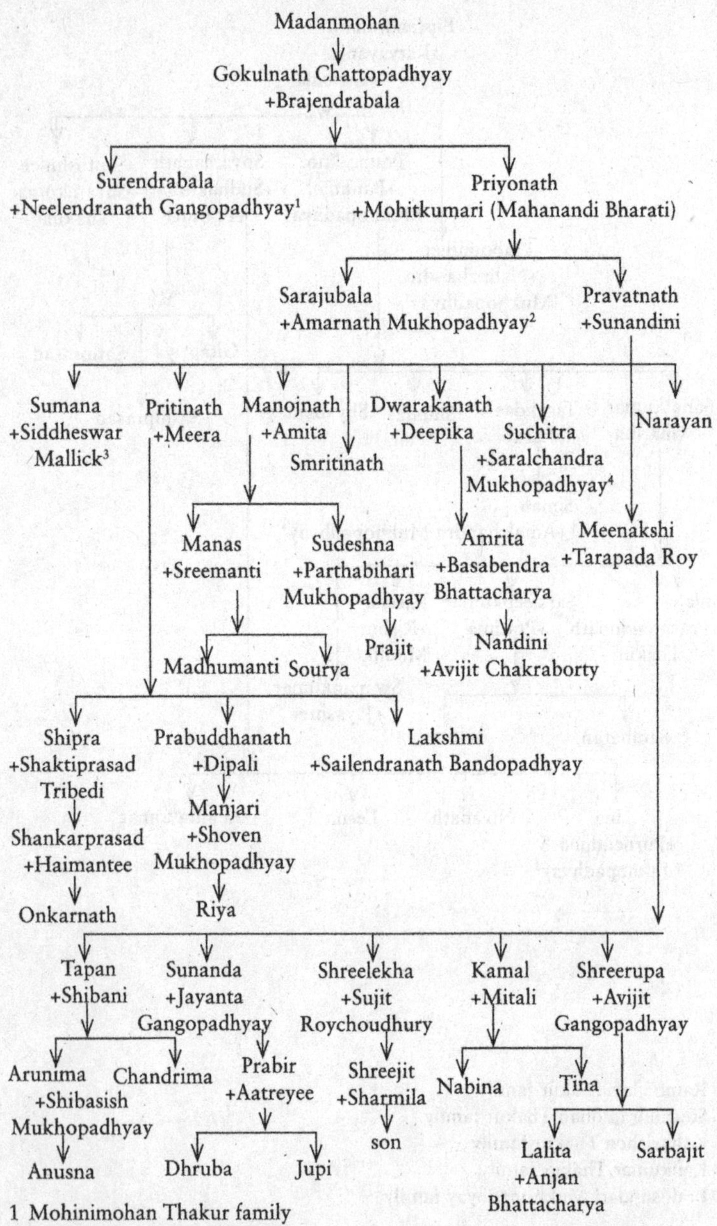

1 Mohinimohan Thakur family
2 Brajosundari Mukhopadhyay
3 Anandiram Thakur family
4 Kalikumar Thakur family. Saralchandra Mukhopadhyay married Suchitra after death of Kalpana, daughter of Sachchidananda Chattopadhyay.

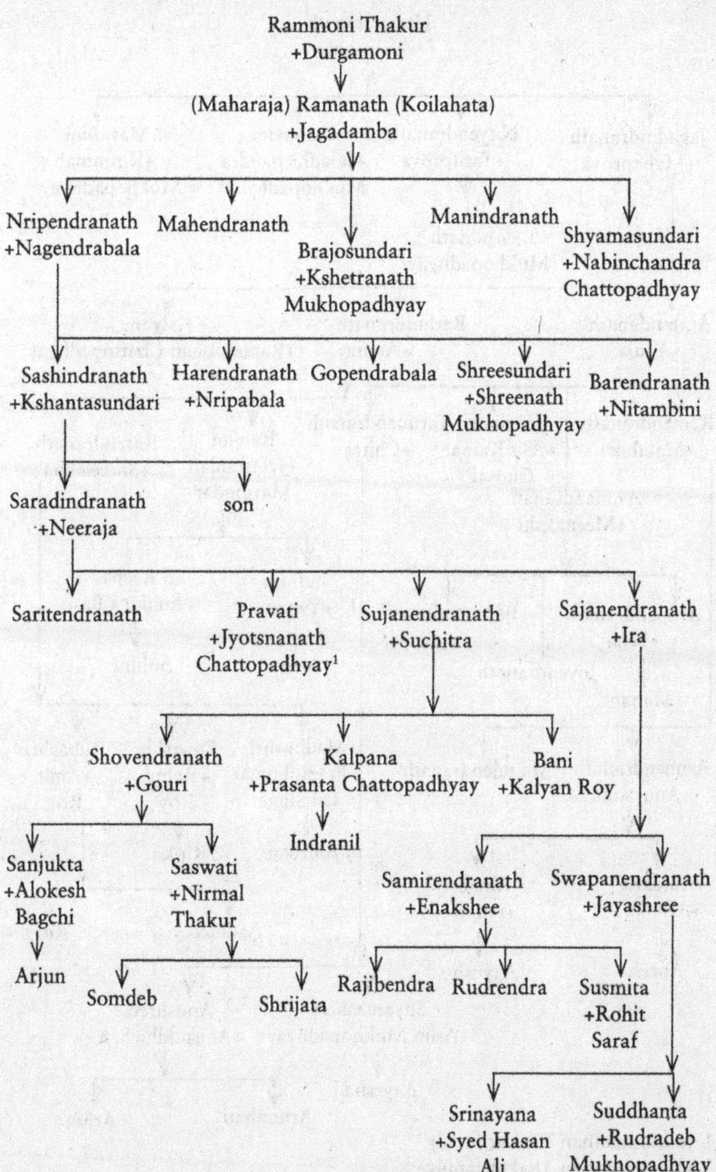

1 Kalikrishna Thakur family

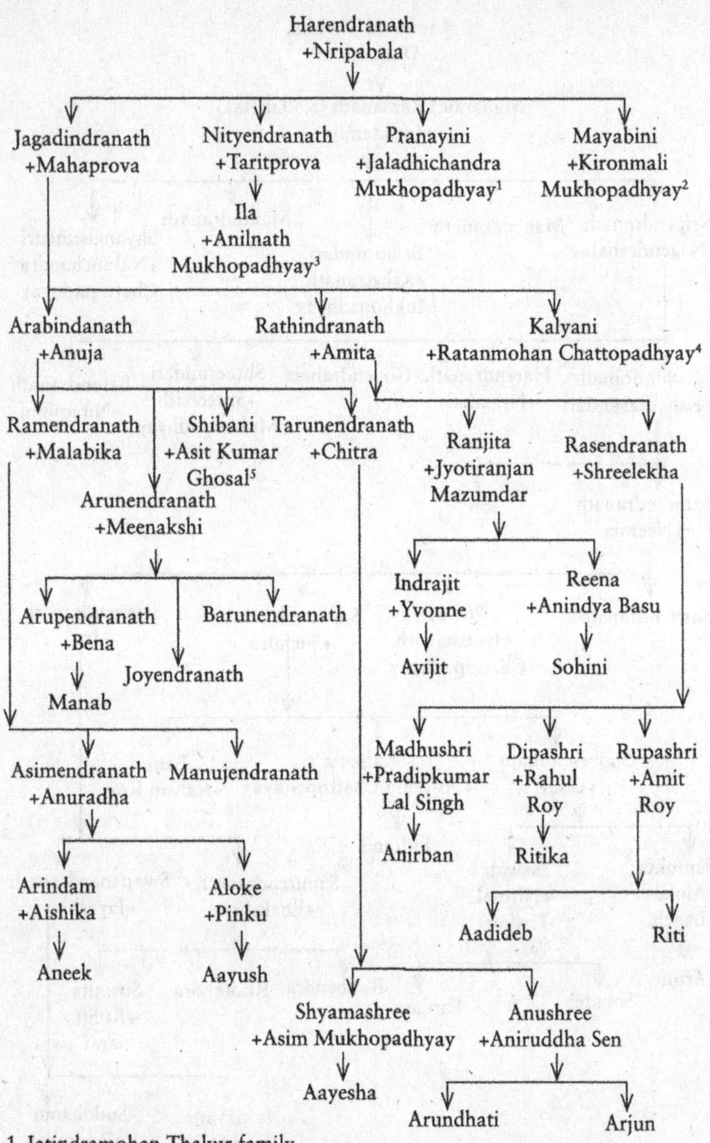

1 Jatindramohan Thakur family
2 Jatindramohan Thakur family
3 Brajasundari Mukhopadhyay family
4 Jorasanko house no. 5 (Sunayani Chattopadhyay family)
5 Kalikrishna Thakur family

Barendranath
+Nitambini

Nirajini
+Seshprakash Gangopadhyay[1]

Ushabala
+Asutosh Mukhopadhyay

Renuka
+Sanat Kumar Ghosal[2]

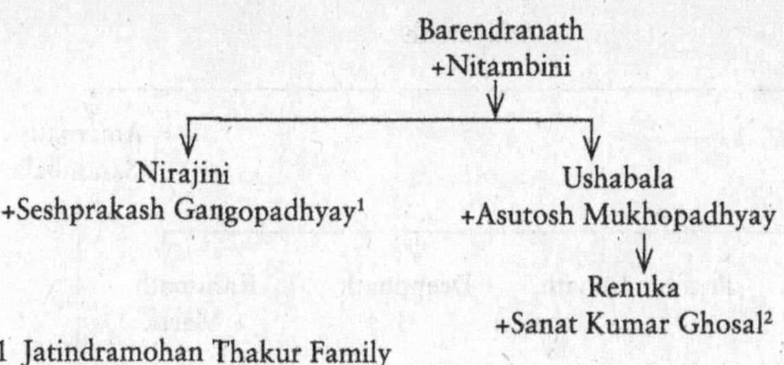

1 Jatindramohan Thakur Family
2 Kalikrishna Thakur Family

Ramanath

Brajosundari
+Kshetranath Mukhopadhyay

Amiyanath
+Dhirabala

daughter
+Jogendranath Bandopadhyay

Giribala
+Biprendranath Chattopadhyay[2]

Sharatindrabala
+Dhirendranath Chattopadhyay[1]

Amritanath
+Suhasini

Pramathanath
+Subhasini

Sarojini
+Hitendranath Thakur[3]

Amarnath
+Sarajubala

Kshitinath
+Kamalmoni

Ramaninath
+Sharatibala

Salila
+Bipin Chattopadhyay

Anilnath
+Ila

Alaka
+Ritendranath Thakur[4]

Ajitnath
+Shuchita

Purnendunath
+Ina

Purna
+Prasanta Chatopadhyay

Shibrani
+Jayeendranath Thakur[5]

Satirani
+Sunritendranath Thakur[6]

Nandini
+Biswanath Bandopadhyay

Piyali
+Debashis Sarkar

Kasturi

Kaberi

1 & 2 Rasbilasi Chattopadhyay family
3 & 4 Jorasanko house no. 6 (Hemendranath Thakur family)
5 Jorasanko house no. 5 (Samarendranath Thakur family)
6 Jorasanko house no. 6 (Satyendranath Thakur family)

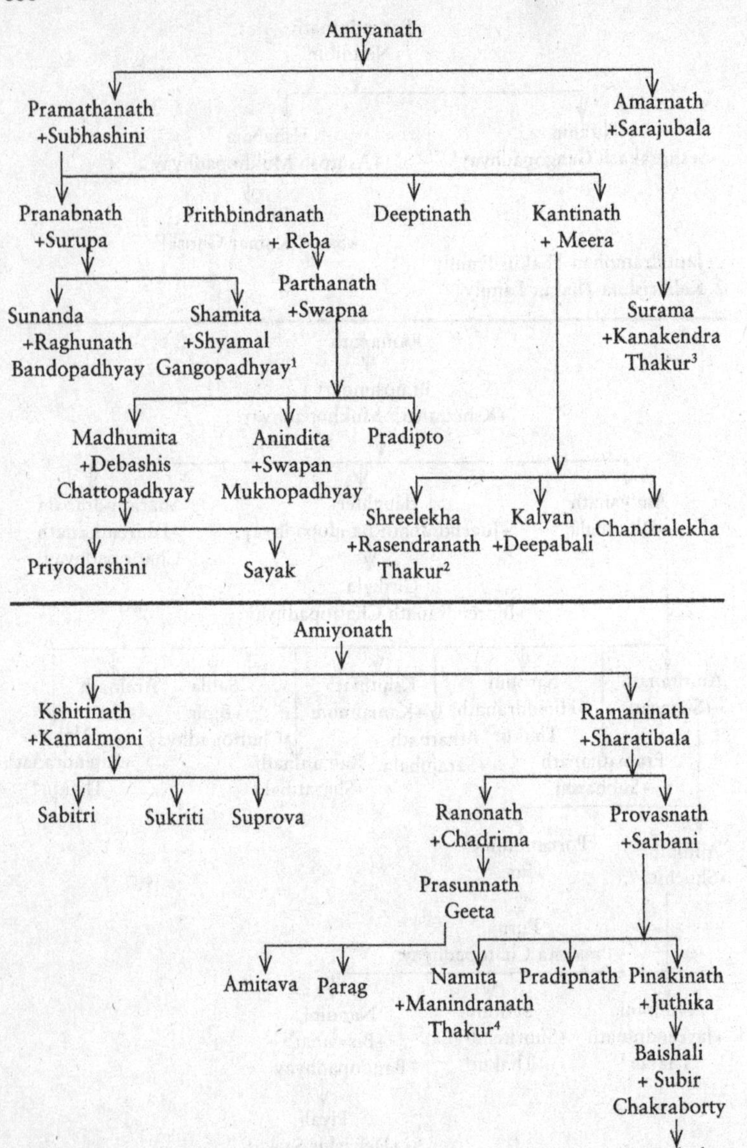

1 Kalikrishna Thakur family
2 Harendranath Thakur family
3 Jorasanko house no. 5 (Gaganendranath Thakur family)
4 Jorasanko house no. 5 (Abanindranath Thakur family)

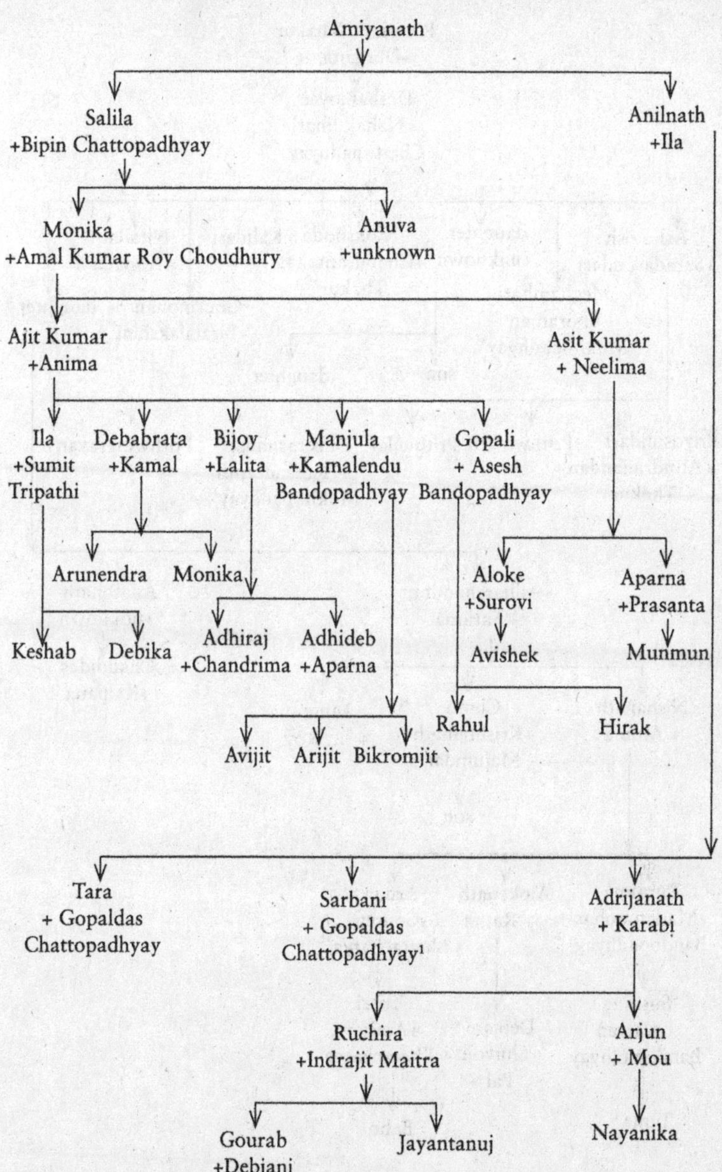

1 Rasbilasi Chattopadhyay family
Gopaldas Chattopadhyay married Sarbani after Tara's death.

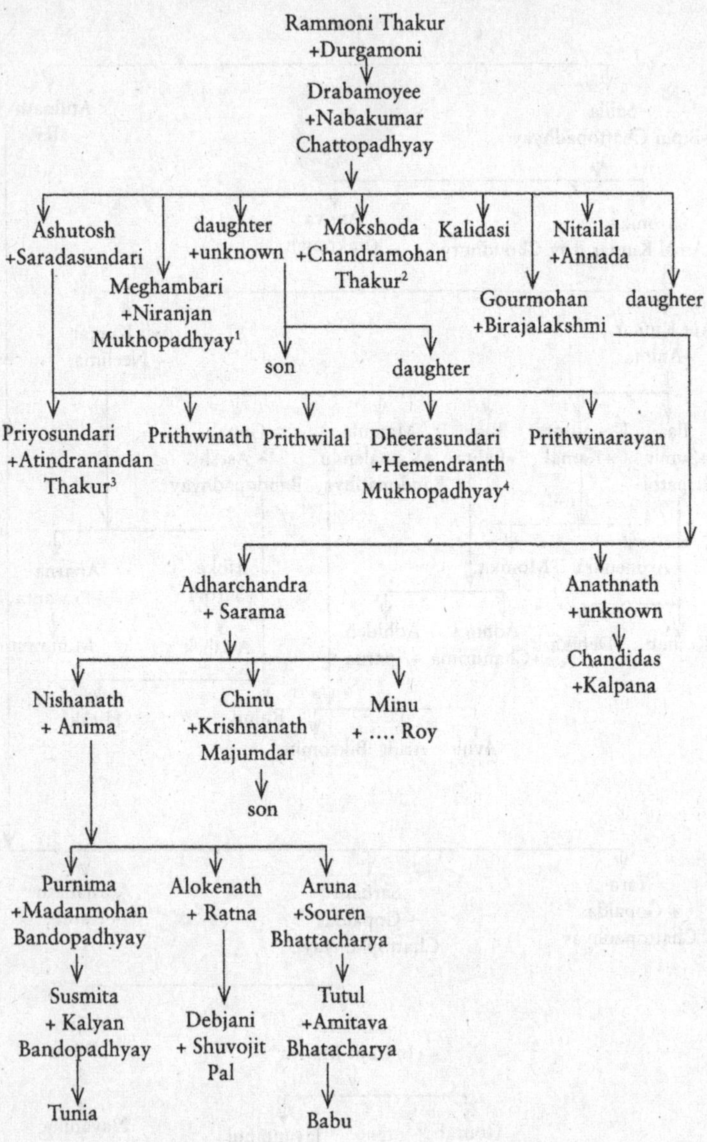

1 Suryakumar Thakur family
2 Chorbagan Thakur family
3 Umanandan Thakur family
4 Ladlimohan Thakur family

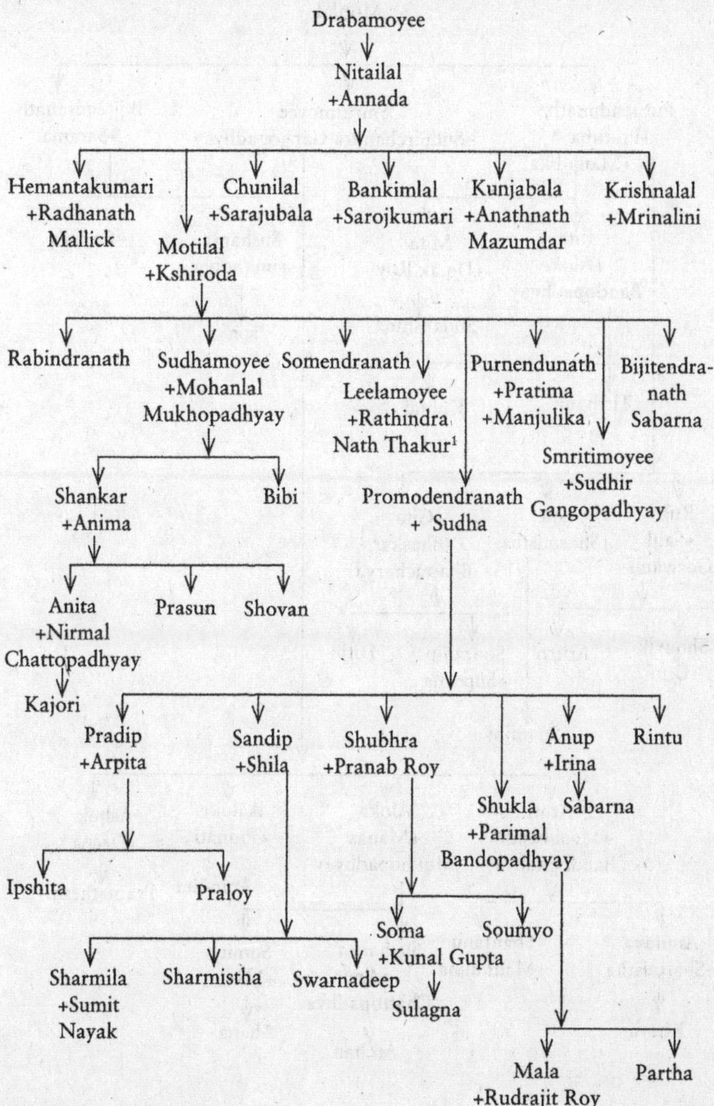

1 Ladlimohan Thakur family

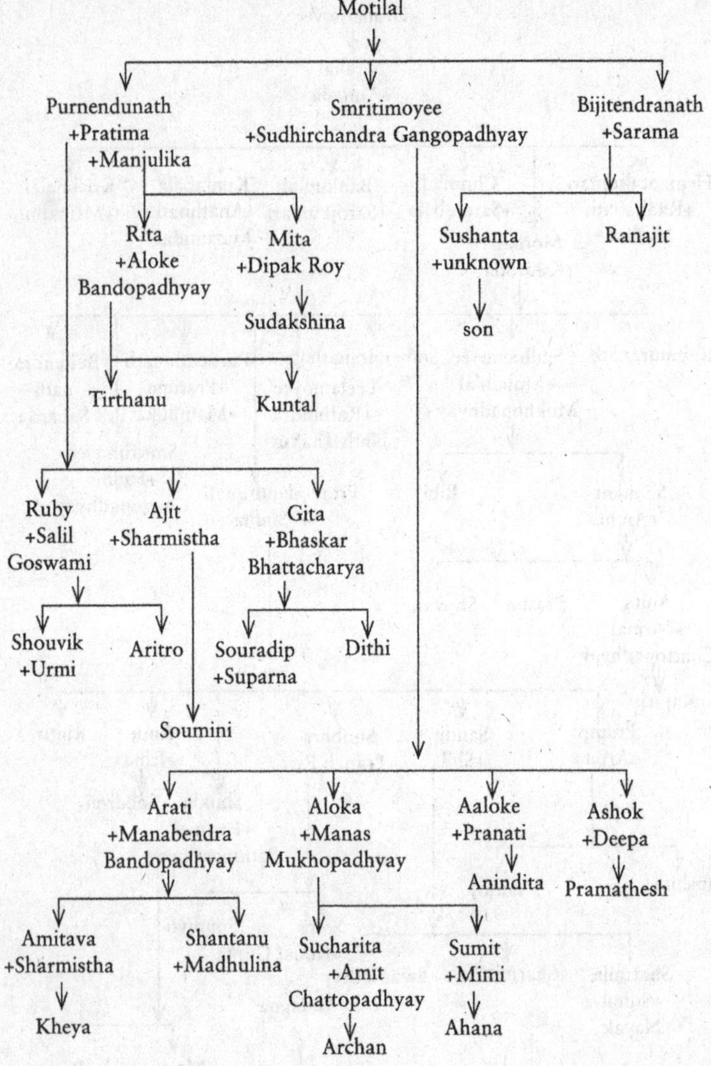
Motilal
Purnendunath
+Pratima
+Manjulika
Smritimoyee
+Sudhirchandra Gangopadhyay
Bijitendranath
+Sarama
Rita
+Aloke
Bandopadhyay
Mita
+Dipak Roy
Sudakshina
Sushanta
+unknown
son
Ranajit
Tirthanu
Kuntal
Ruby
+Salil
Goswami
Ajit
+Sharmistha
Gita
+Bhaskar
Bhattacharya
Shouvik
+Urmi
Aritro
Souradip
+Suparna
Dithi
Soumini
Arati
+Manabendra
Bandopadhyay
Aloka
+Manas
Mukhopadhyay
Aaloke
+Pranati
Anindita
Ashok
+Deepa
Pramathesh
Amitava
+Sharmistha
Kheya
Shantanu
+Madhulina
Sucharita
+Amit
Chattopadhyay
Archan
Sumit
+Mimi
Ahana

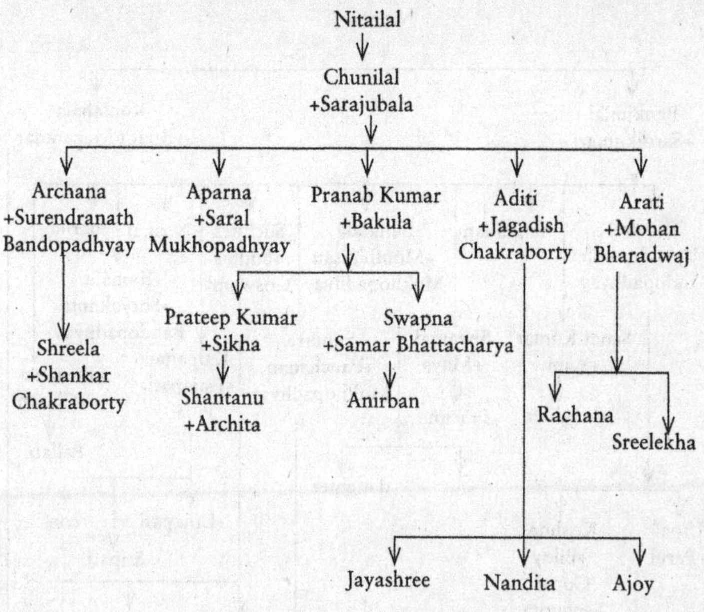
Nitailal
Chunilal
+Sarajubala
Archana
+Surendranath
Bandopadhyay
Aparna
+Saral
Mukhopadhyay
Pranab Kumar
+Bakula
Aditi
+Jagadish
Chakraborty
Arati
+Mohan
Bharadwaj
Prateep Kumar
+Sikha
Swapna
+Samar Bhattacharya
Shreela
+Shankar
Chakraborty
Shantanu
+Archita
Anirban
Rachana
Sreelekha
Jayashree
Nandita
Ajoy

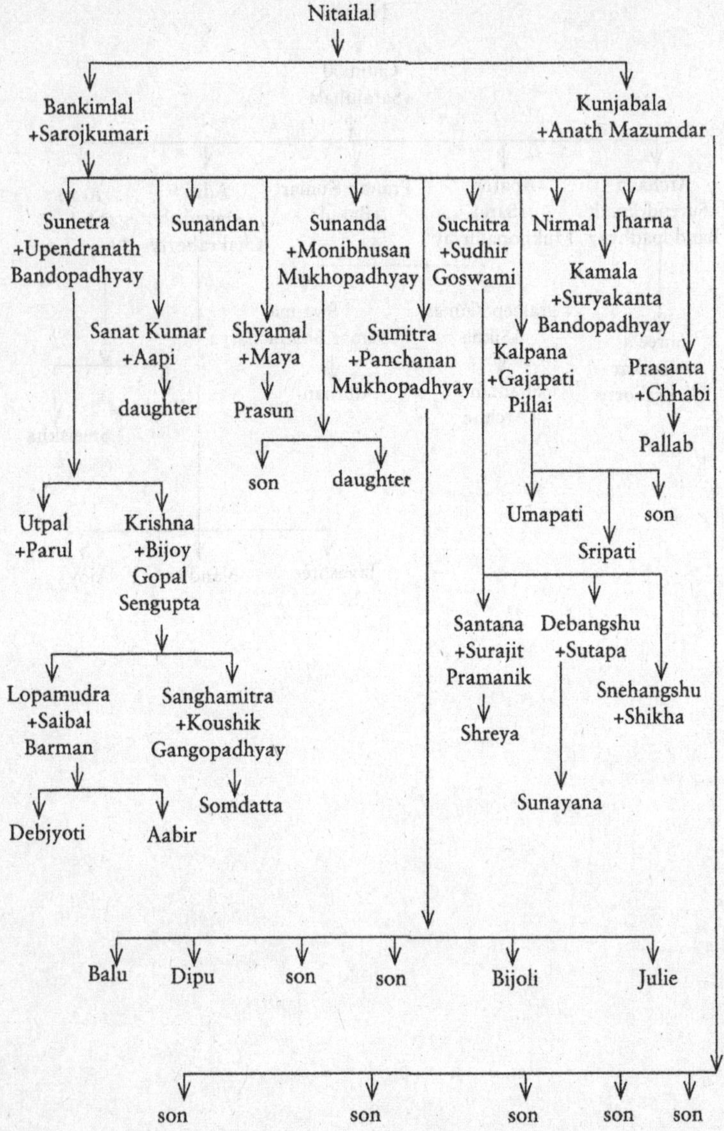
Nitailal
Bankimlal
+Sarojkumari
Kunjabala
+Anath Mazumdar
Sunetra
+Upendranath
Bandopadhyay
Sunandan
Sunanda
+Monibhusan
Mukhopadhyay
Suchitra
+Sudhir
Goswami
Nirmal
Jharna
Kamala
+Suryakanta
Bandopadhyay
Sanat Kumar
+Aapi
daughter
Shyamal
+Maya
Prasun
Sumitra
+Panchanan
Mukhopadhyay
Kalpana
+Gajapati
Pillai
Prasanta
+Chhabi
Pallab
son
daughter
Umapati
son
Sripati
Utpal
+Parul
Krishna
+Bijoy
Gopal
Sengupta
Santana
+Surajit
Pramanik
Shreya
Debangshu
+Sutapa
Sunayana
Snehangshu
+Shikha
Lopamudra
+Saibal
Barman
Debjyoti
Aabir
Sanghamitra
+Koushik
Gangopadhyay
Somdatta
Balu
Dipu
son
son
Bijoli
Julie
son
son
son
son
son

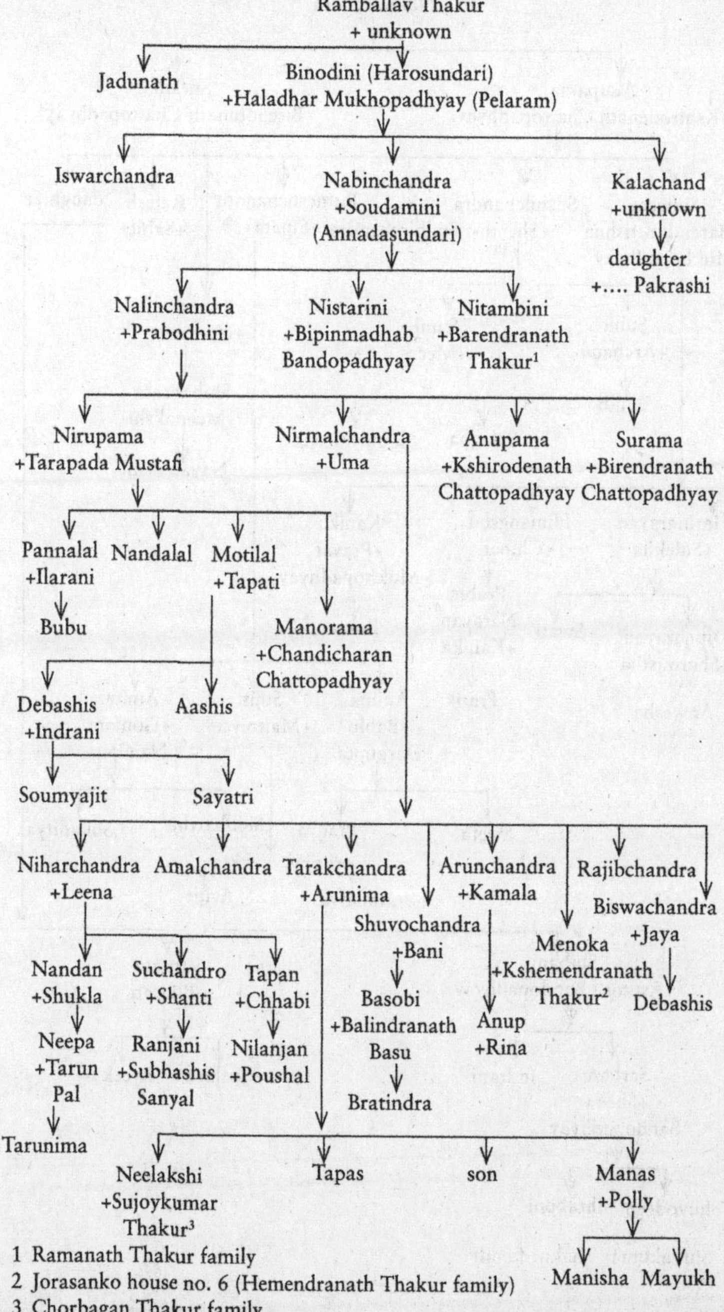

1 Ramanath Thakur family
2 Jorasanko house no. 6 (Hemendranath Thakur family)
3 Chorbagan Thakur family

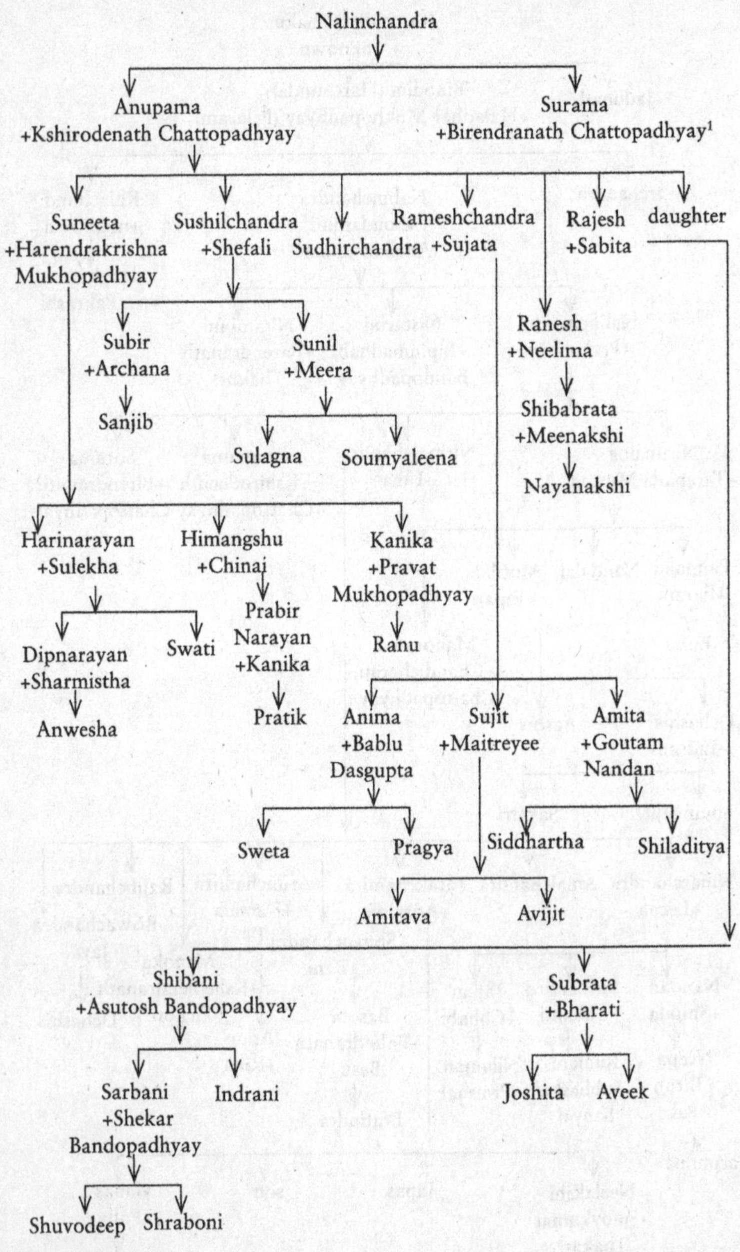

1 Suryakumar Thakur family

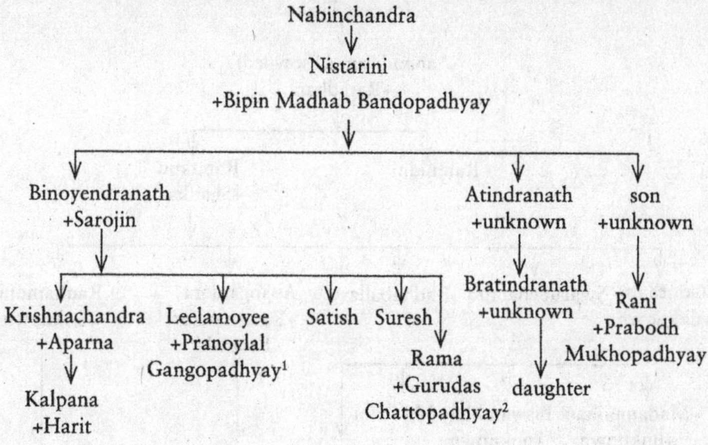

1 Siddheswari Mazumdar family
2 Sourindramohan Thakur family

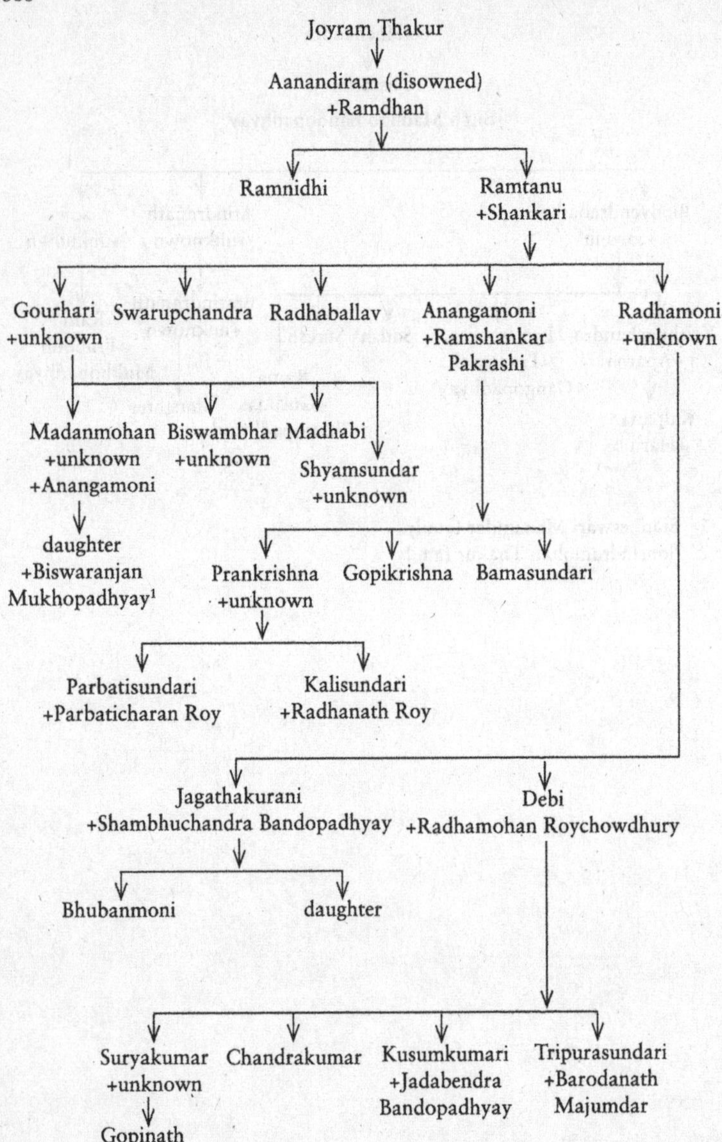

1 Suryakumar Thakur family

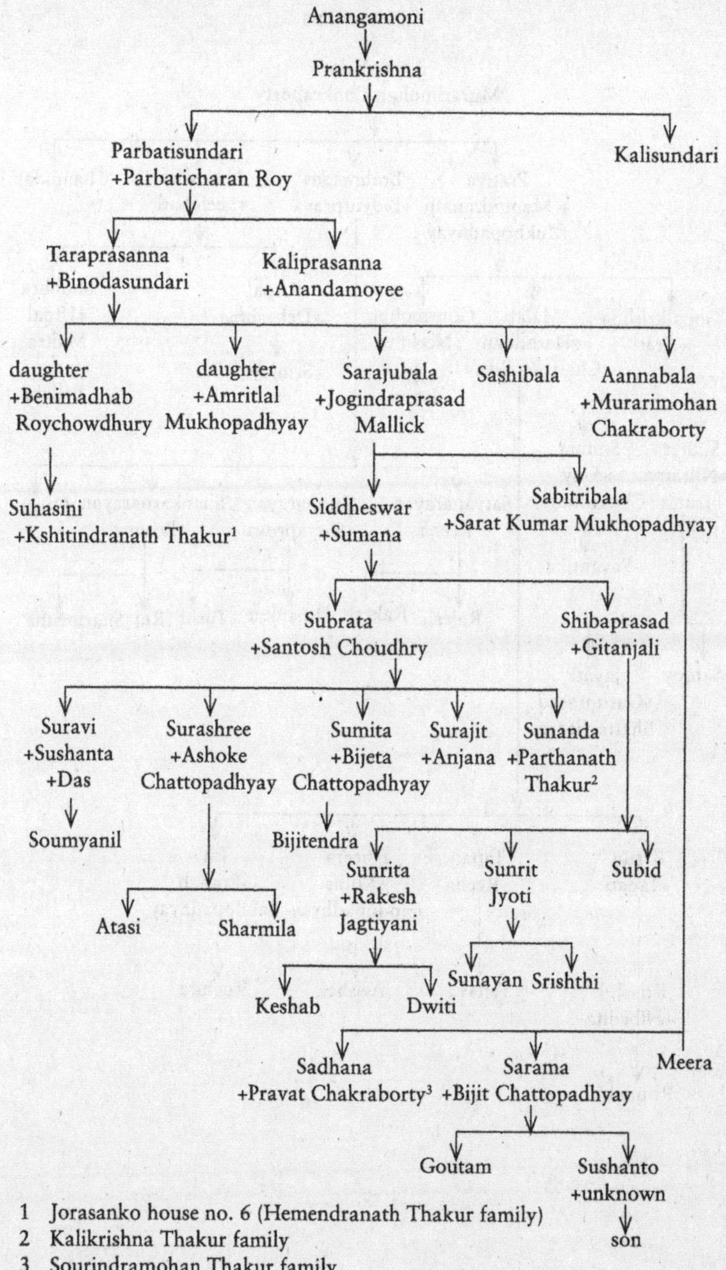

1 Jorasanko house no. 6 (Hemendranath Thakur family)
2 Kalikrishna Thakur family
3 Sourindramohan Thakur family

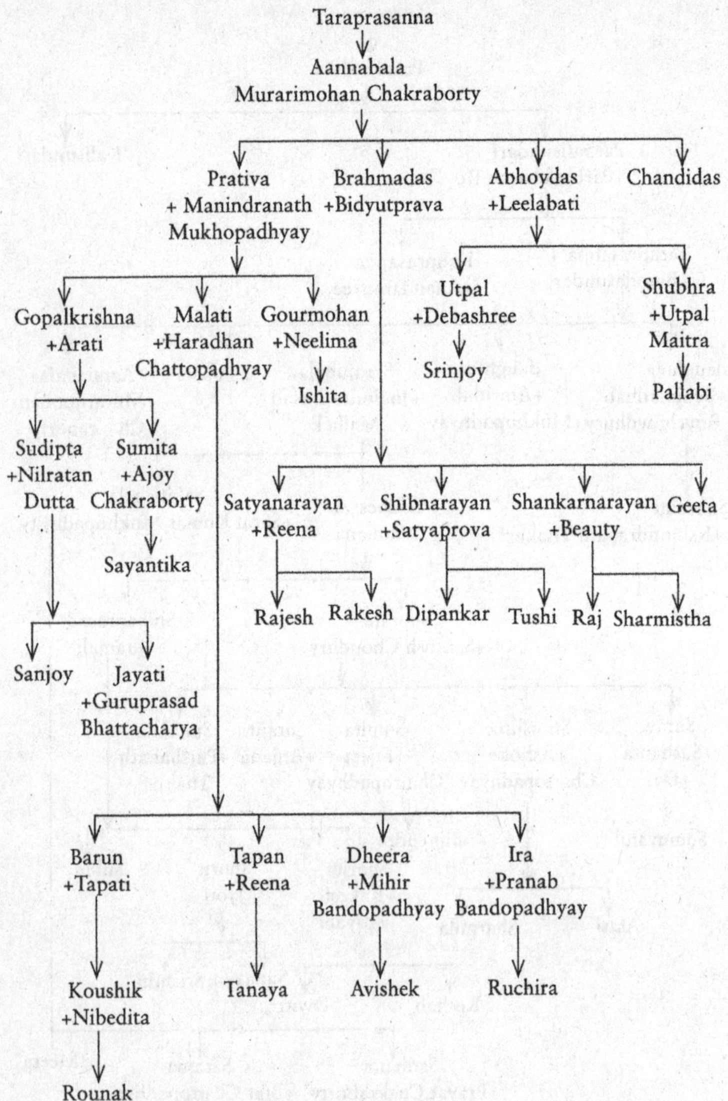
Taraprasanna
Aannabala
Murarimohan Chakraborty
Prativa
+ Manindranath
Mukhopadhyay
Brahmadas
+Bidyutprava
Abhoydas
+Leelabati
Chandidas
Utpal
+Debashree
Shubhra
+Utpal
Maitra
Srinjoy
Pallabi
Gopalkrishna
+Arati
Malati
+Haradhan
Chattopadhyay
Gourmohan
+Neelima
Ishita
Sudipta
+Nilratan
Dutta
Sumita
+Ajoy
Chakraborty
Sayantika
Satyanarayan
+Reena
Shibnarayan
+Satyaprova
Shankarnarayan
+Beauty
Geeta
Rajesh
Rakesh
Dipankar
Tushi
Raj
Sharmistha
Sanjoy
Jayati
+Guruprasad
Bhattacharya
Barun
+Tapati
Tapan
+Reena
Dheera
+Mihir
Bandopadhyay
Ira
+Pranab
Bandopadhyay
Koushik
+Nibedita
Tanaya
Avishek
Ruchira
Rounak

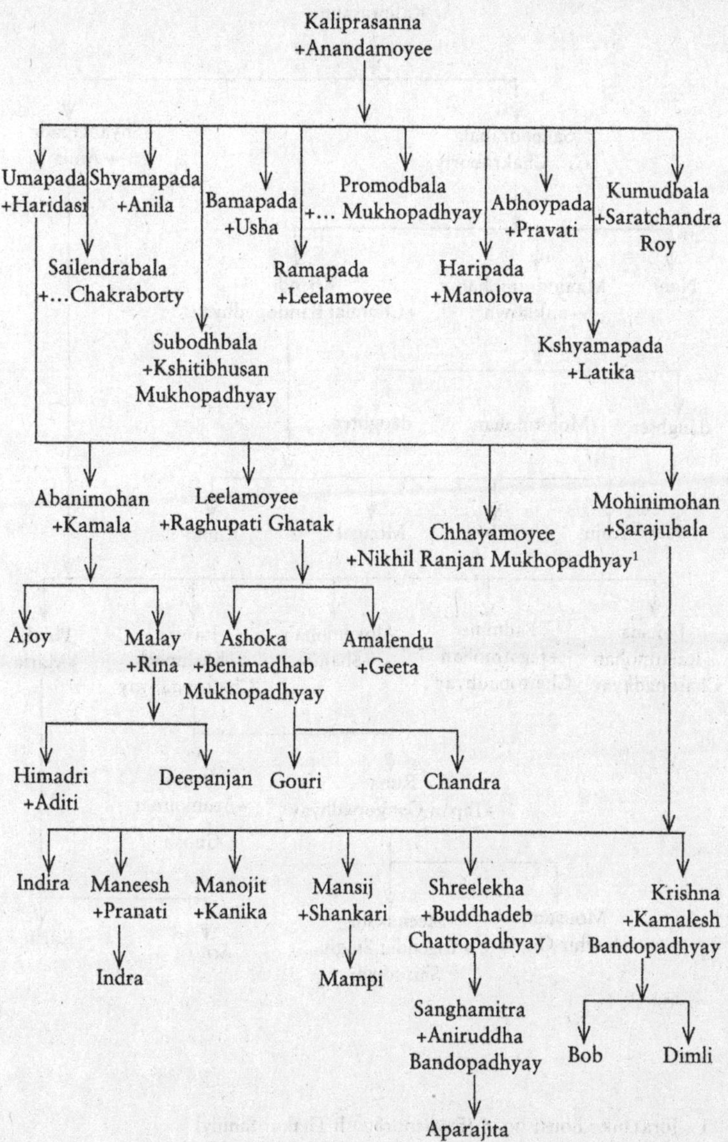

1 Suryakumar Thakur family

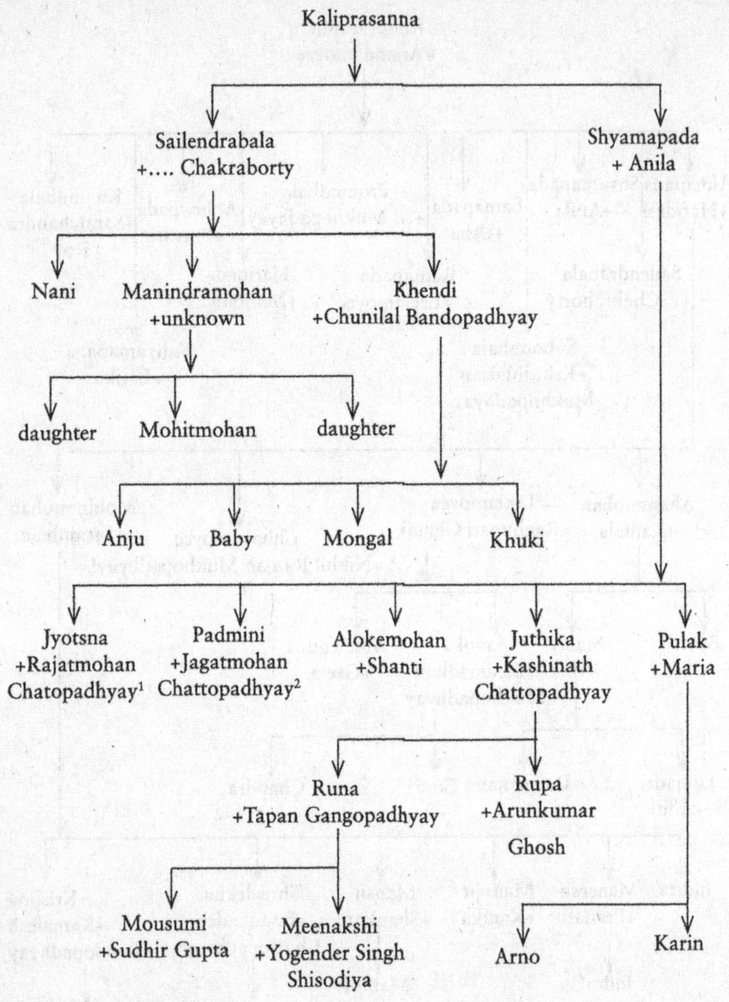

1 Jorasanko house no. 6 (Dwijendranath Thakur family)
2 Jorasanko house no. 6 (Dwijendranath Thakur family)

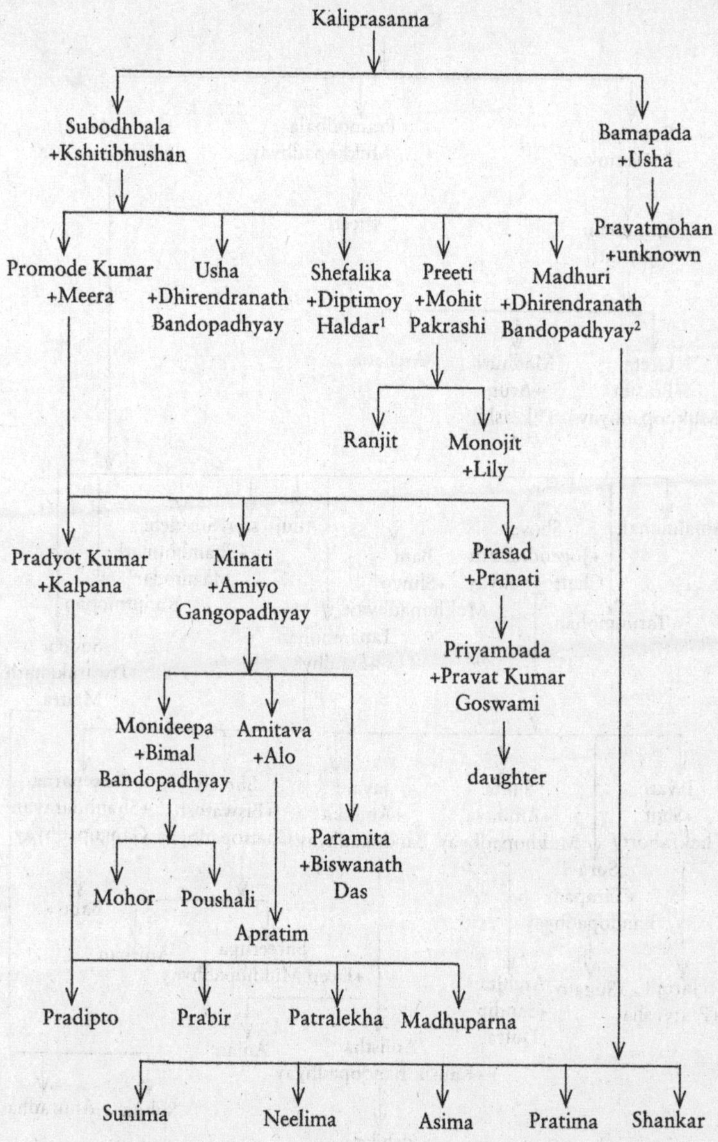

1 Jorasanko house no 6 (Sarat Kumari Mukhopadhyay family)
2 Dhirendranath Bandopadhyay married Madhuri after the death of Usha

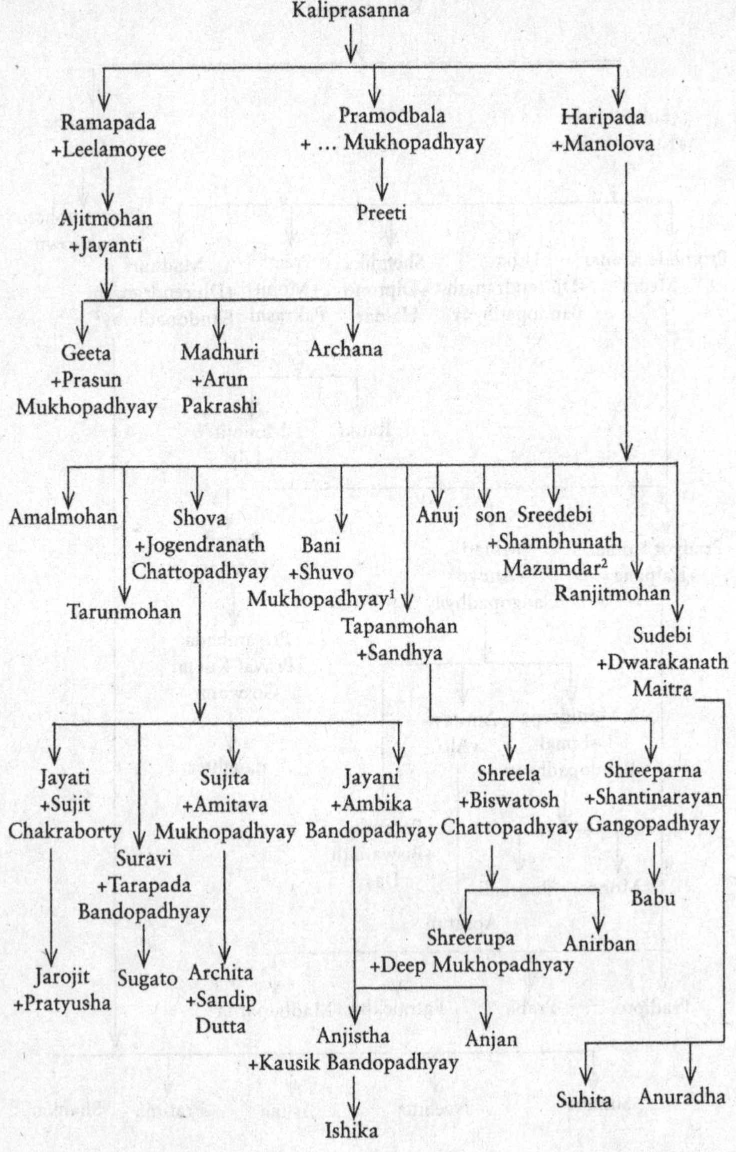

1 Ramballav Thakur family
2 Kalikrishna Thakur family

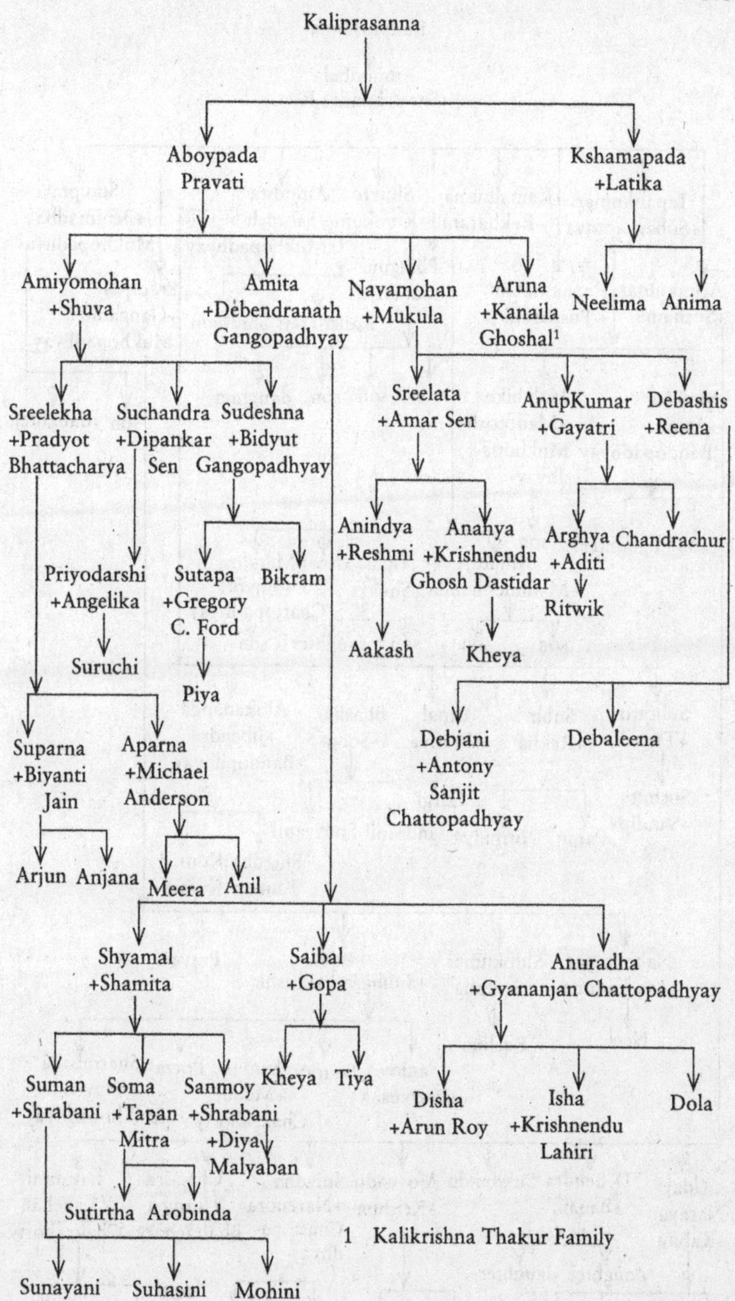

1 Kalikrishna Thakur Family

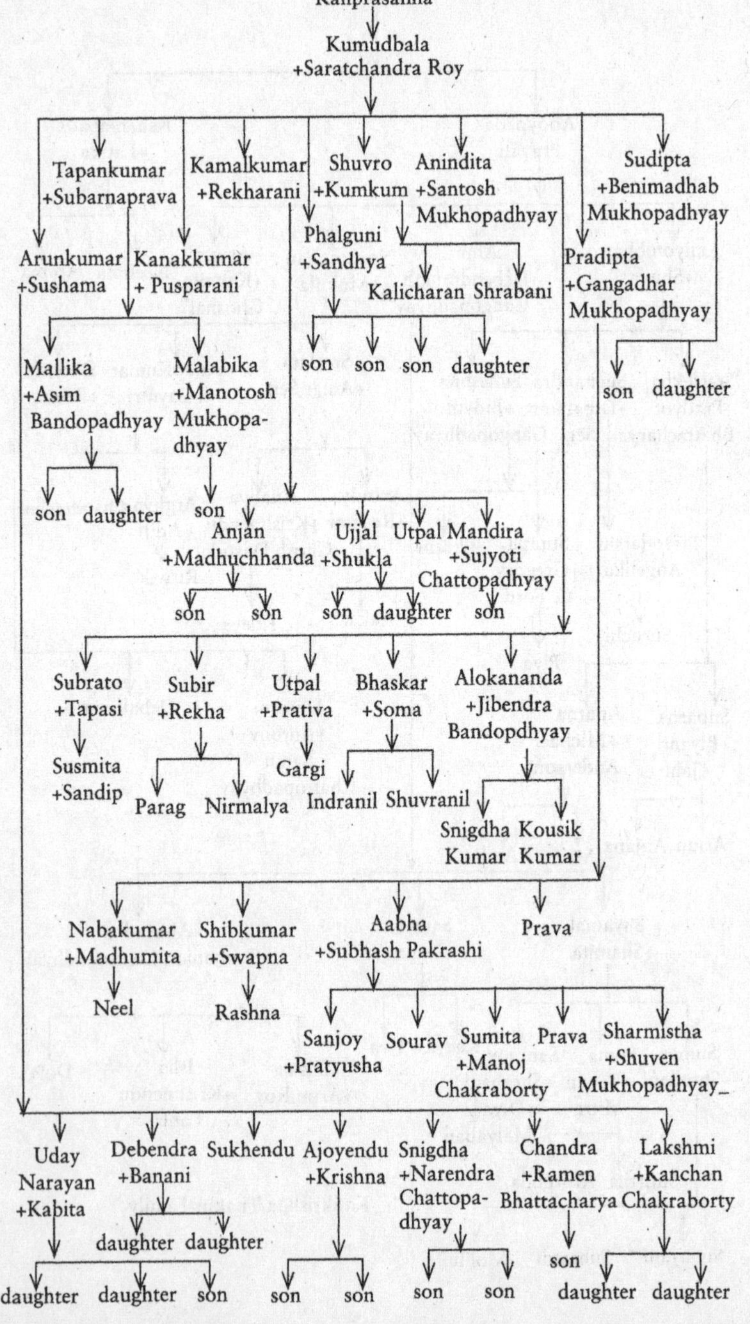
Kaliprasanna
Kumudbala
+Saratchandra Roy
Tapankumar
+Subarnaprava
Kamalkumar
+Rekharani
Shuvro
+Kumkum
Anindita
+Santosh
Mukhopadhyay
Sudipta
+Benimadhab
Mukhopadhyay
Phalguni
+Sandhya
Arunkumar
+Sushama
Kanakkumar
+ Pusparani
Kalicharan
Shrabani
Pradipta
+Gangadhar
Mukhopadhyay
Mallika
+Asim
Bandopadhyay
Malabika
+Manotosh
Mukhopa-
dhyay
son
son
son
daughter
son
daughter
son
daughter
son
Anjan
+Madhuchhanda
Ujjal
+Shukla
Utpal
Mandira
+Sujyoti
Chattopadhyay
son
son
son
daughter
son
Subrato
+Tapasi
Subir
+Rekha
Utpal
+Prativa
Bhaskar
+Soma
Alokananda
+Jibendra
Bandopdhyay
Susmita
+Sandip
Parag
Nirmalya
Gargi
Indranil
Shuvranil
Snigdha
Kumar
Kousik
Kumar
Nabakumar
+Madhumita
Shibkumar
+Swapna
Aabha
+Subhash Pakrashi
Prava
Neel
Rashna
Sanjoy
+Pratyusha
Sourav
Sumita
+Manoj
Chakraborty
Prava
Sharmistha
+Shuven
Mukhopadhyay_
Uday
Narayan
+Kabita
Debendra
+Banani
Sukhendu
Ajoyendu
+Krishna
Snigdha
+Narendra
Chattopa-
dhyay
Chandra
+Ramen
Bhattacharya
Lakshmi
+Kanchan
Chakraborty
daughter
daughter
daughter
daughter
son
son
son
son
son
son
daughter
daughter

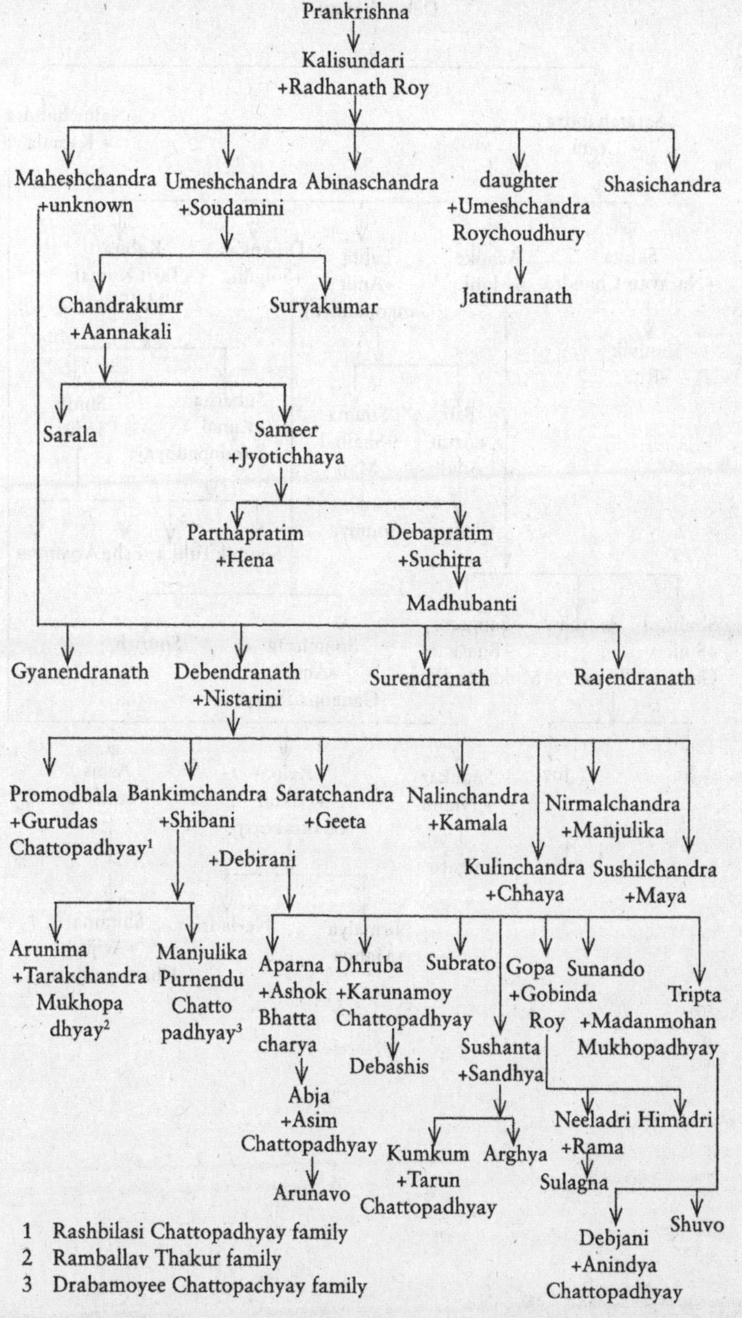

1 Rashbilasi Chattopadhyay family
2 Ramballav Thakur family
3 Drabamoyee Chattopachyay family

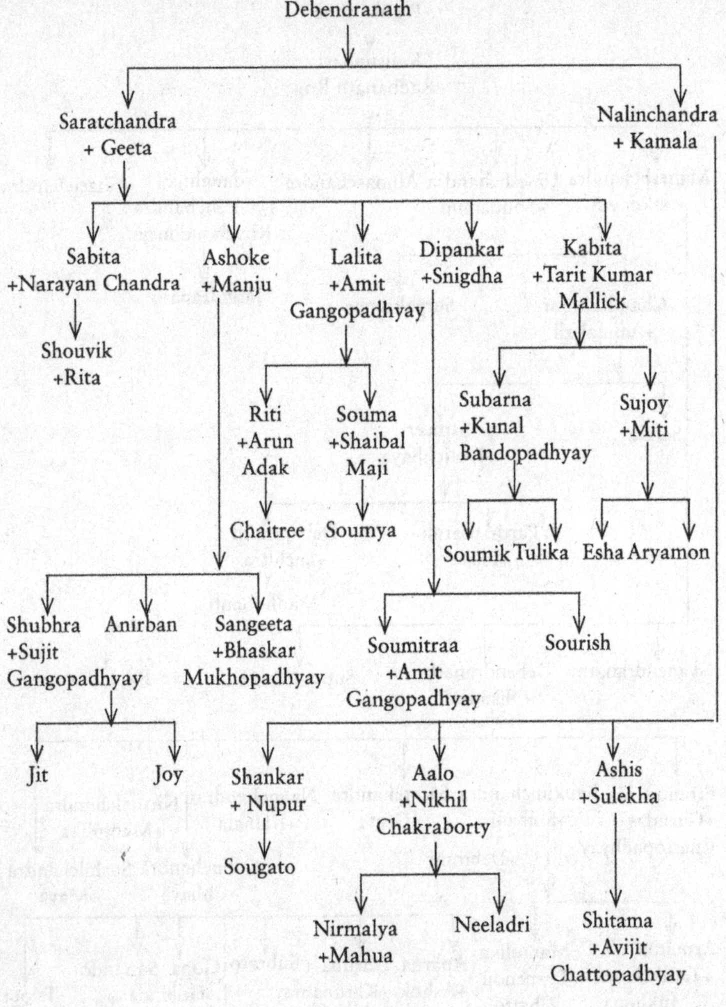
Debendranath
Saratchandra
+ Geeta
Nalinchandra
+ Kamala
Sabita
+Narayan Chandra
Ashoke
+Manju
Lalita
+Amit
Gangopadhyay
Dipankar
+Snigdha
Kabita
+Tarit Kumar
Mallick
Shouvik
+Rita
Riti
+Arun
Adak
Souma
+Shaibal
Maji
Subarna
+Kunal
Bandopadhyay
Sujoy
+Miti
Chaitree
Soumya
Soumik
Tulika
Esha
Aryamon
Shubhra
+Sujit
Gangopadhyay
Anirban
Sangeeta
+Bhaskar
Mukhopadhyay
Soumitraa
+Amit
Gangopadhyay
Sourish
Jit
Joy
Shankar
+ Nupur
Aalo
+Nikhil
Chakraborty
Ashis
+Sulekha
Sougato
Nirmalya
+Mahua
Neeladri
Shitama
+Avijit
Chattopadhyay

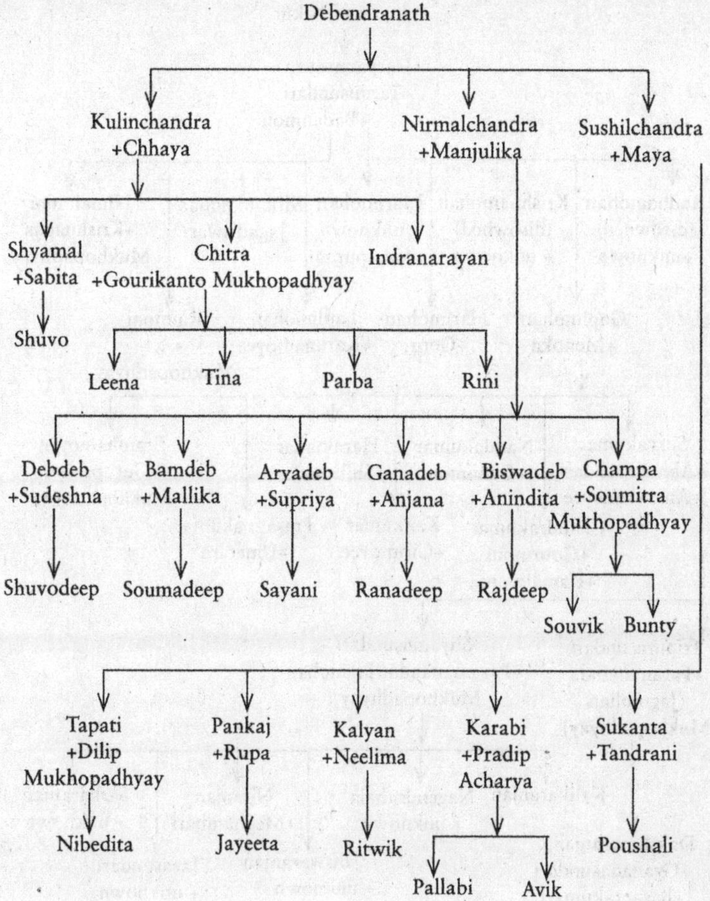
Debendranath
Kulinchandra
+Chhaya
Nirmalchandra
+Manjulika
Sushilchandra
+Maya
Shyamal
+Sabita
Chitra
+Gourikanto Mukhopadhyay
Indranarayan
Shuvo
Leena
Tina
Parba
Rini
Debdeb
+Sudeshna
Bamdeb
+Mallika
Aryadeb
+Supriya
Ganadeb
+Anjana
Biswadeb
+Anindita
Champa
+Soumitra
Mukhopadhyay
Shuvodeep
Soumadeep
Sayani
Ranadeep
Rajdeep
Souvik
Bunty
Tapati
+Dilip
Mukhopadhyay
Pankaj
+Rupa
Kalyan
+Neelima
Karabi
+Pradip
Acharya
Sukanta
+Tandrani
Nibedita
Jayeeta
Ritwik
Pallabi
Avik
Poushali

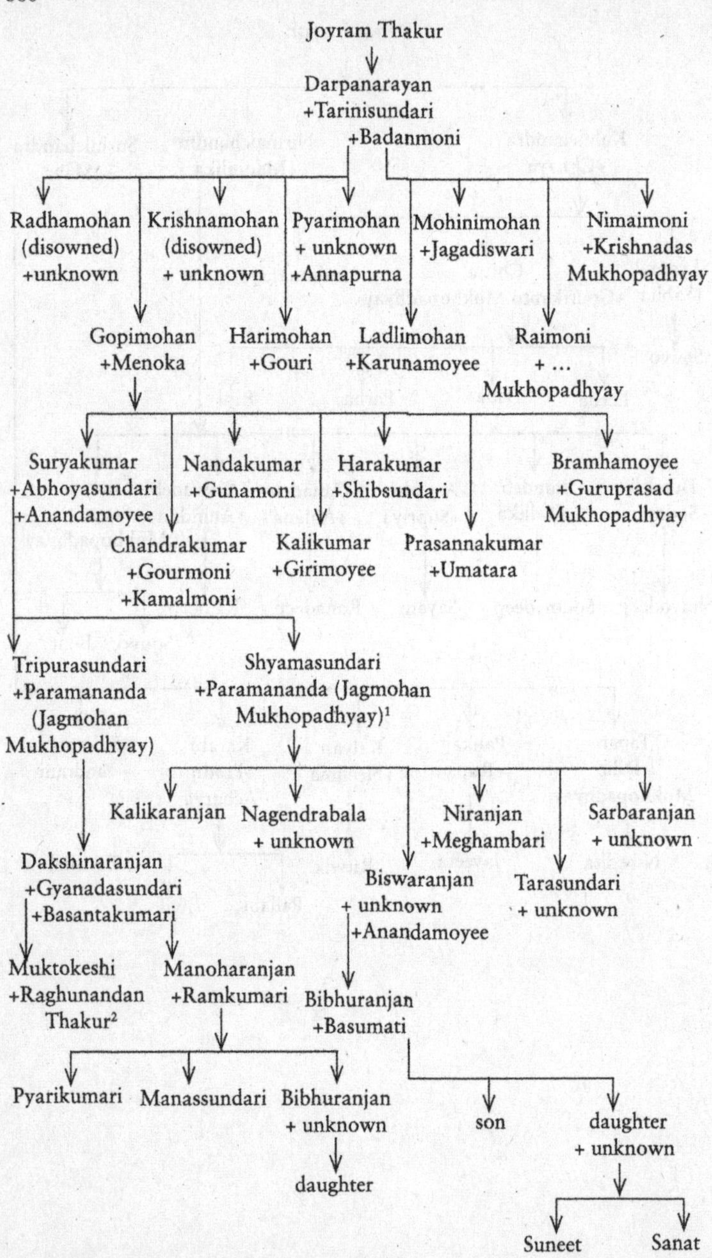

1 Paramananda Mukhopadhyay married Shyamasundari after the death of Tripurasundari.

2 Harimohan Thakur family

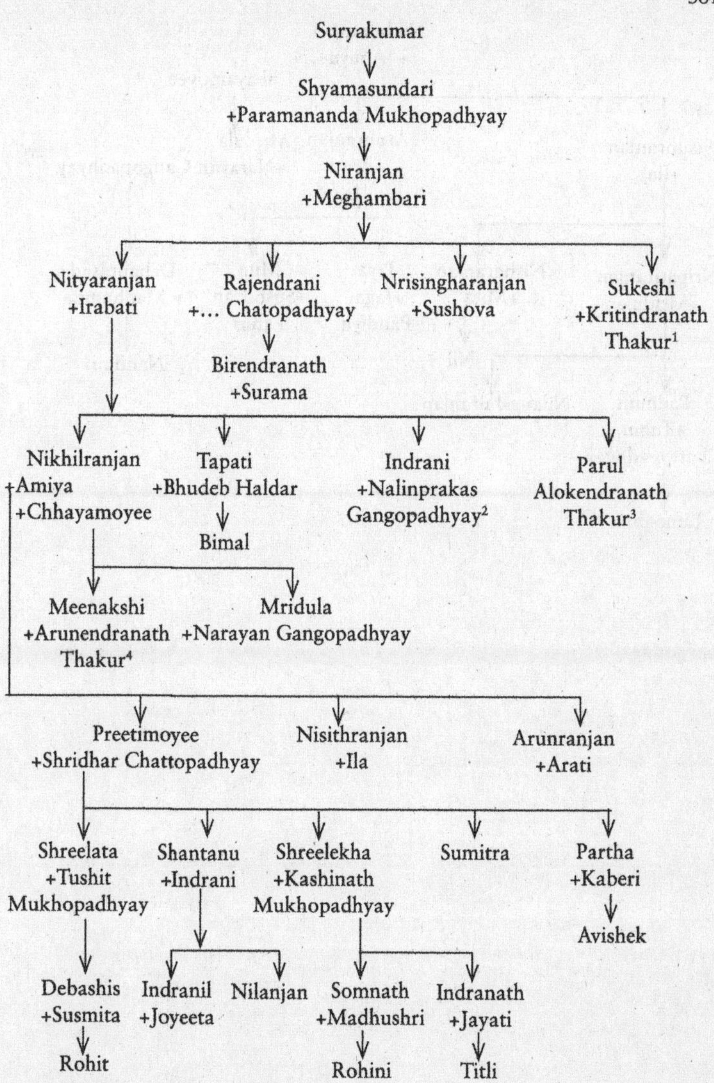

1 Jorasanko house no. 6 (Dwijendranath Thakur family)
2 Jatindramohan Thakur family
3 Jorasanko house no. 5 (Abanindranath Thakur family)
4 Ramanath Thakur family

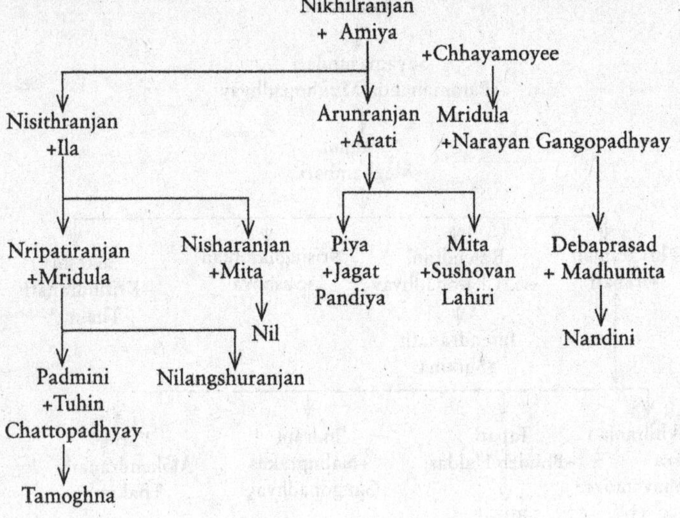

Nikhilranjan
+ Amiya
+Chhayamoyee
Nisithranjan
+Ila
Arunranjan
+Arati
Mridula
+Narayan Gangopadhyay
Nripatiranjan
+Mridula
Nisharanjan
+Mita
Piya
+Jagat
Pandiya
Mita
+Sushovan
Lahiri
Debaprasad
+ Madhumita
Nil
Nandini
Padmini
+Tuhin
Chattopadhyay
Nilangshuranjan
Tamoghna

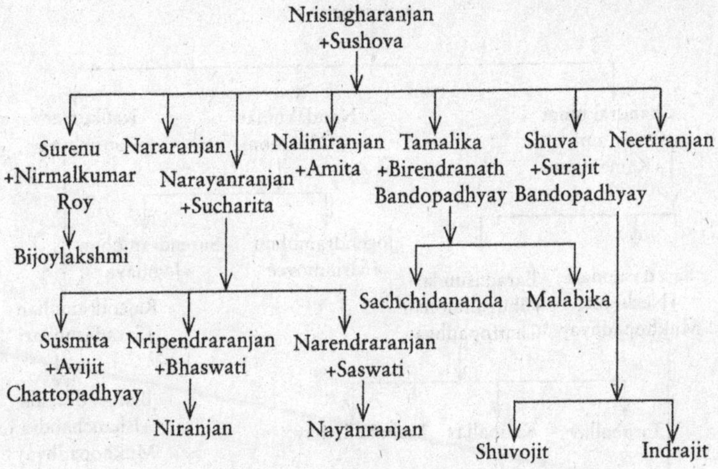

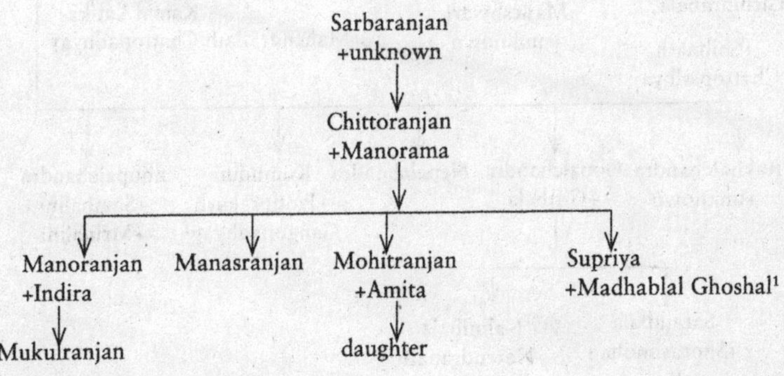

1 Kalikrishna Thakur family

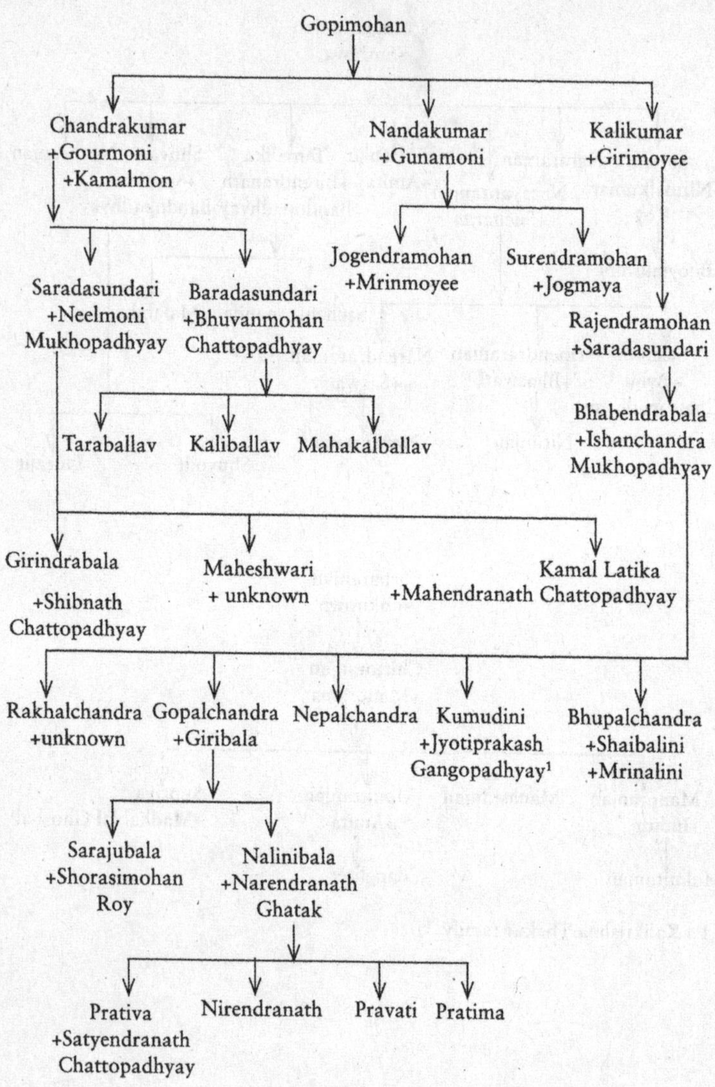

1 Jorasanko house no. 5 (Kadambini Gangopadhyay family)

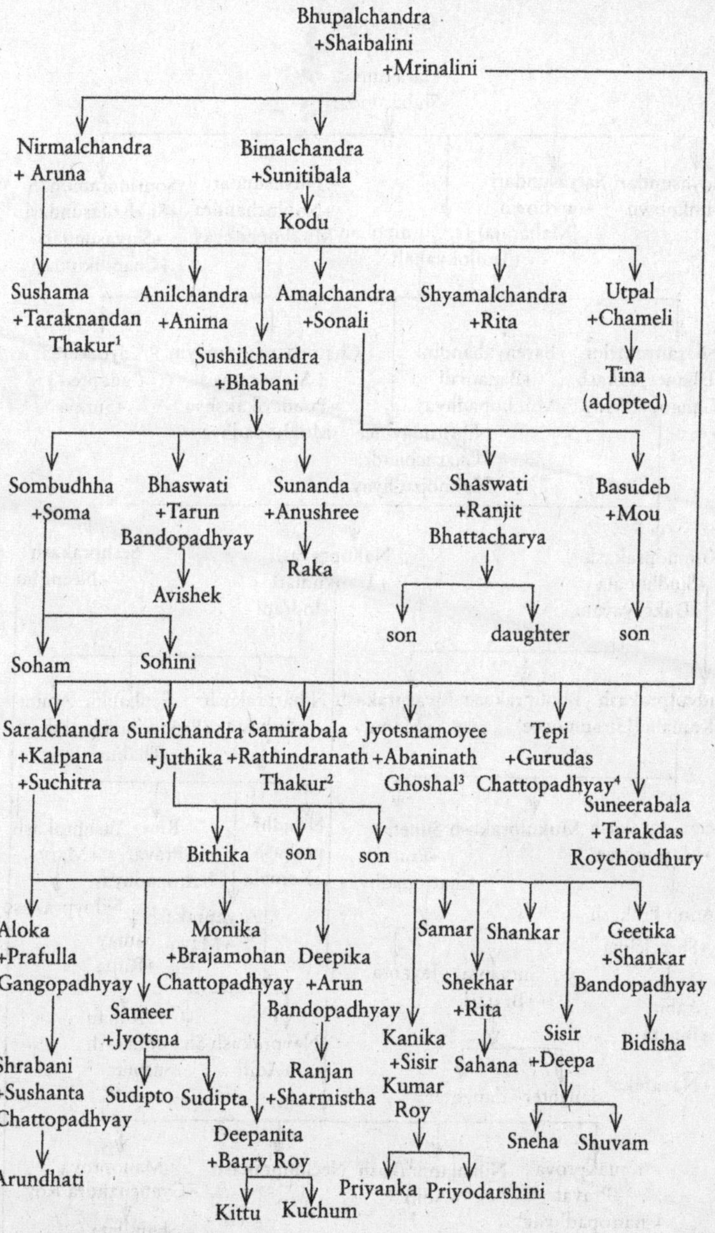

1 Harimohan Thakur family
2 Ladlimohan Thakur family
3 Kalikrishna Thakur family
4 Sourindramohan Thakur family

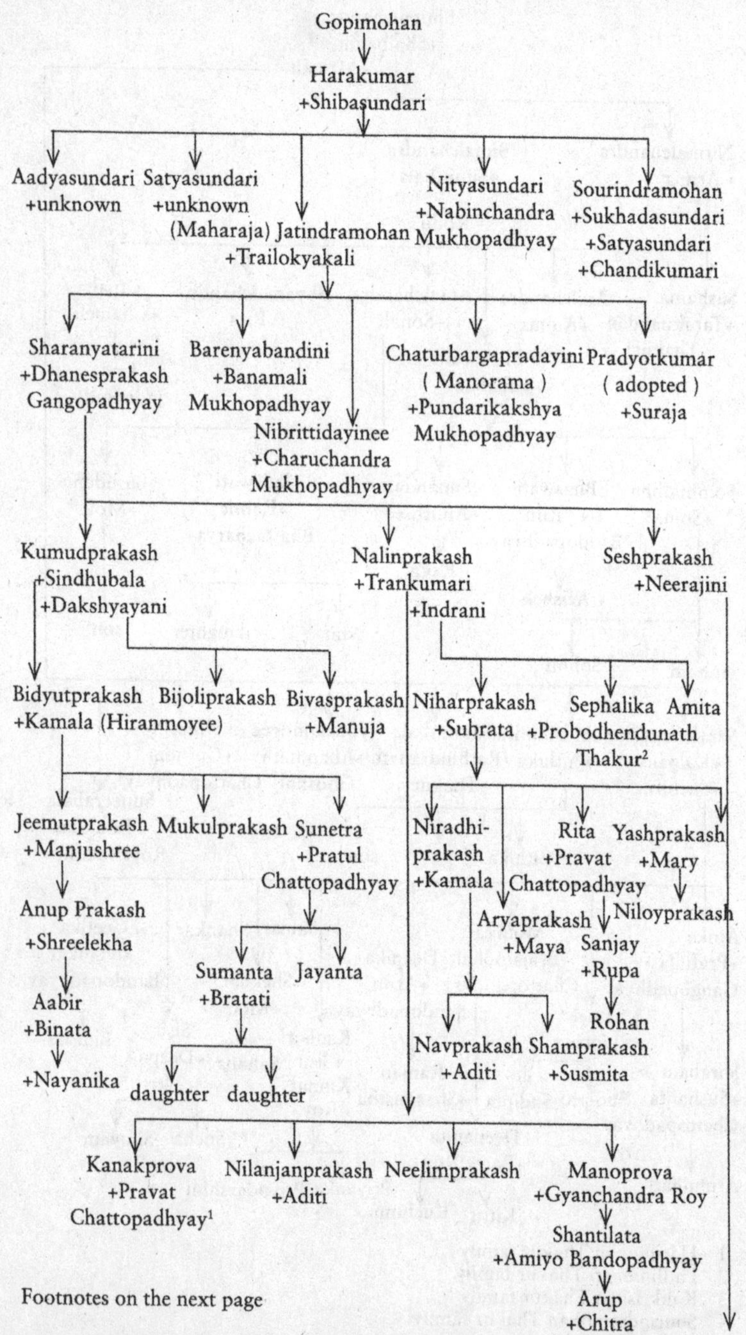

Footnotes on the next page

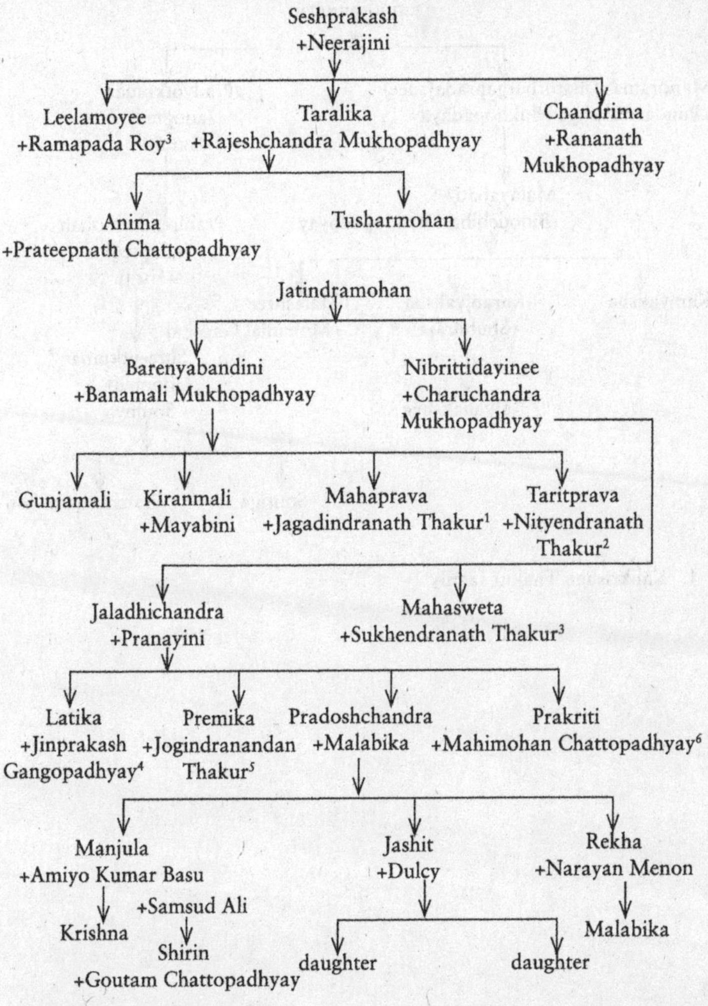

1 Ramanath Thakur family
2 Ramanath Thakur family
3 Umanandan Thakur family
4 Jorasanko house no. 5 (Kadambini Gangopadhyay family)
5 Harimohan Thakur family
6 Jorasanko house no. 6 (Dwijendranath Thakur family)

Previous page's footnotes:

1 Kalikrishna Thakur family
2 Kalikrishna Thakur family
3 Anandiram Thakur family

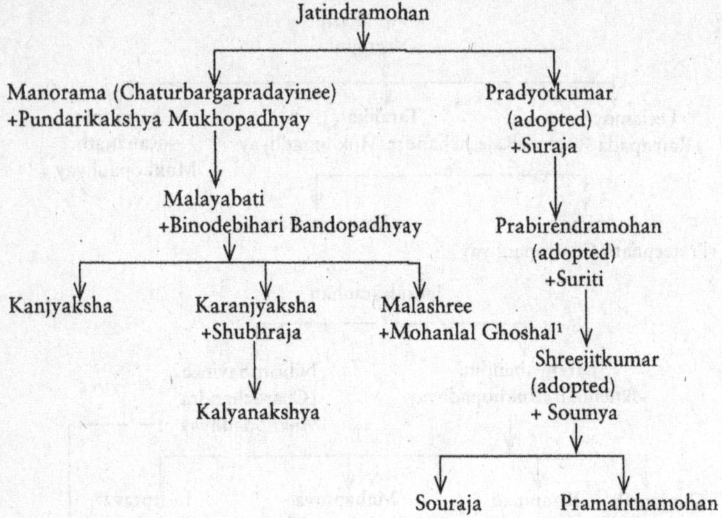

1 Kalikrishan Thakur family

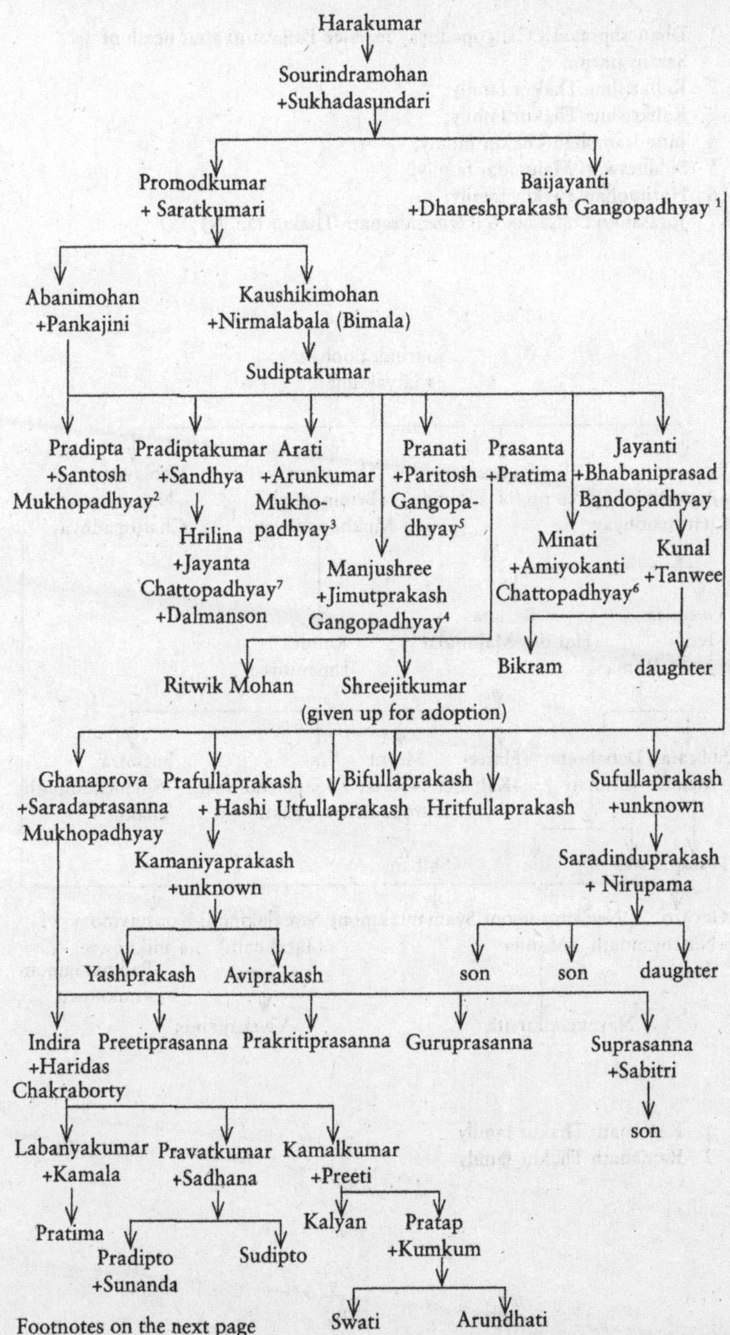

Footnotes on the next page

1 Dhaneshprakash Gangopadhyay married Baijayanti after death of Saranyatarini;
2 Kalikrishna Thakur family;
3 Kalikrishna Thakur family;
4 Jatindramohan Thakur family;
5 Siddheswari Majumdar family;
6 Harimohan Thakur family;
7 Jorasanko house no. 6 (Hemendranath Thakur family)

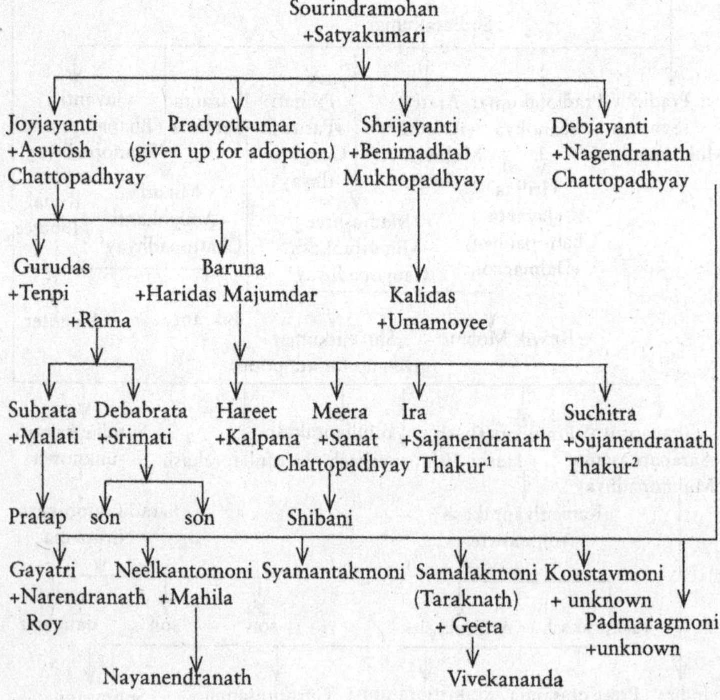

1 Ramanath Thakur family
2 Ramanath Thakur family

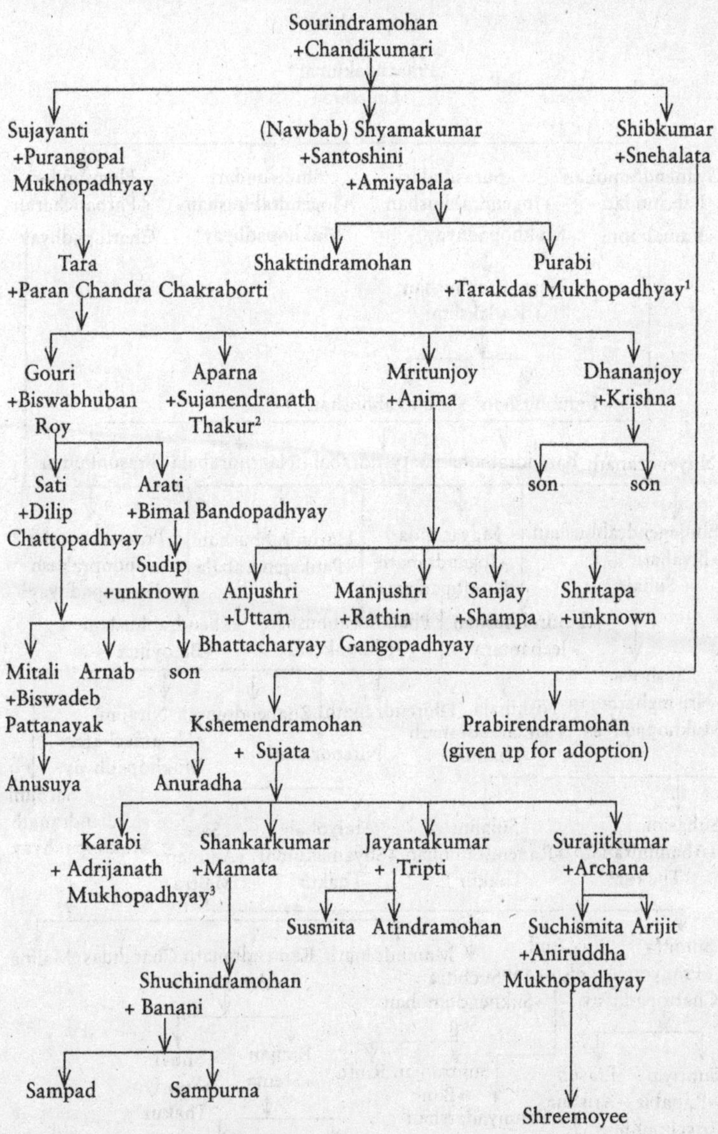

1 Rasbilasi Chattopadhyay family
2 Jorasanko house no. 5 (Samarendranath Thakur family)
3 Ramanath Thakur family

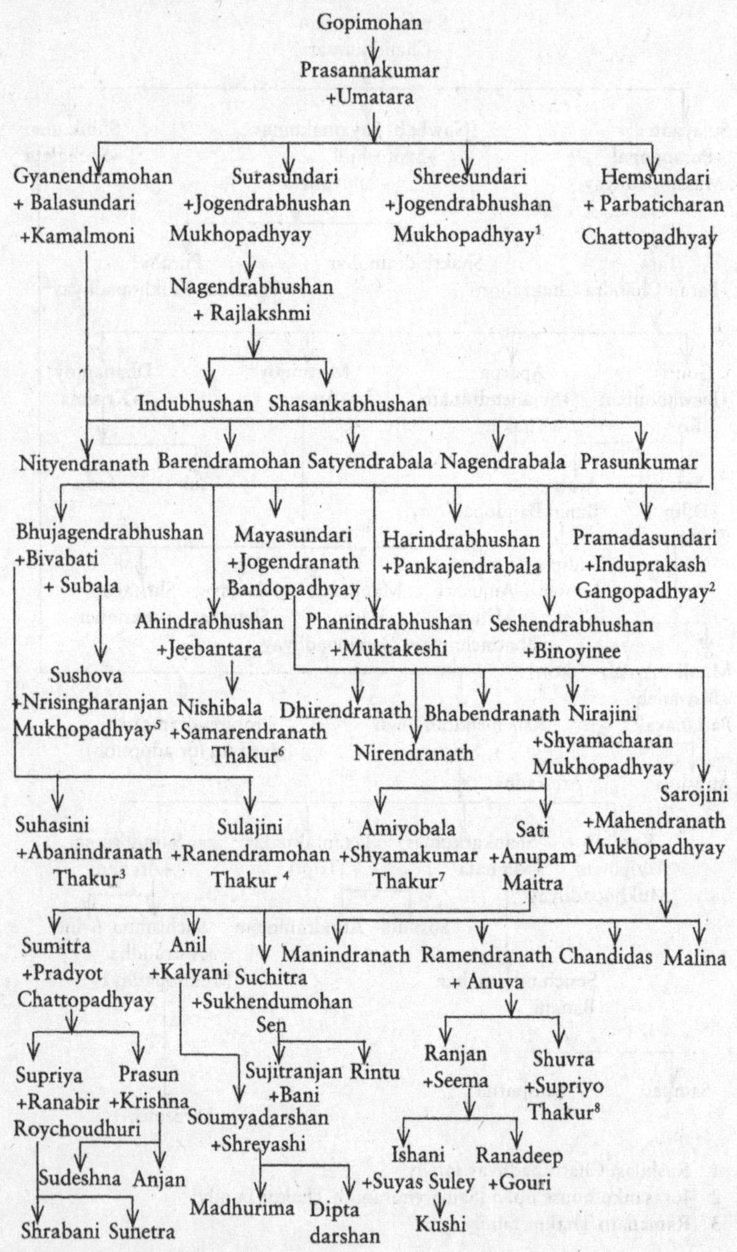

Footnotes on the next page

1 Jogendrabhushan Mukhopadhyay married Shreesundari after the death of Surasundari; 2 Jorasanko house no. 5 (Kadambini Gangopadhyay family); 3 Jorasanko house no. 5 (Abanindranath Thakur family); 4 Harimohan Thakur family; 5 Suryakumar Thakur family; 6 Jorasanko house no. 5 (Samarendranath Thakur family); 7 Sourindramohan Thakur family; 8 Jorasanko house no. 6 ((Satyendranath Thakur family).

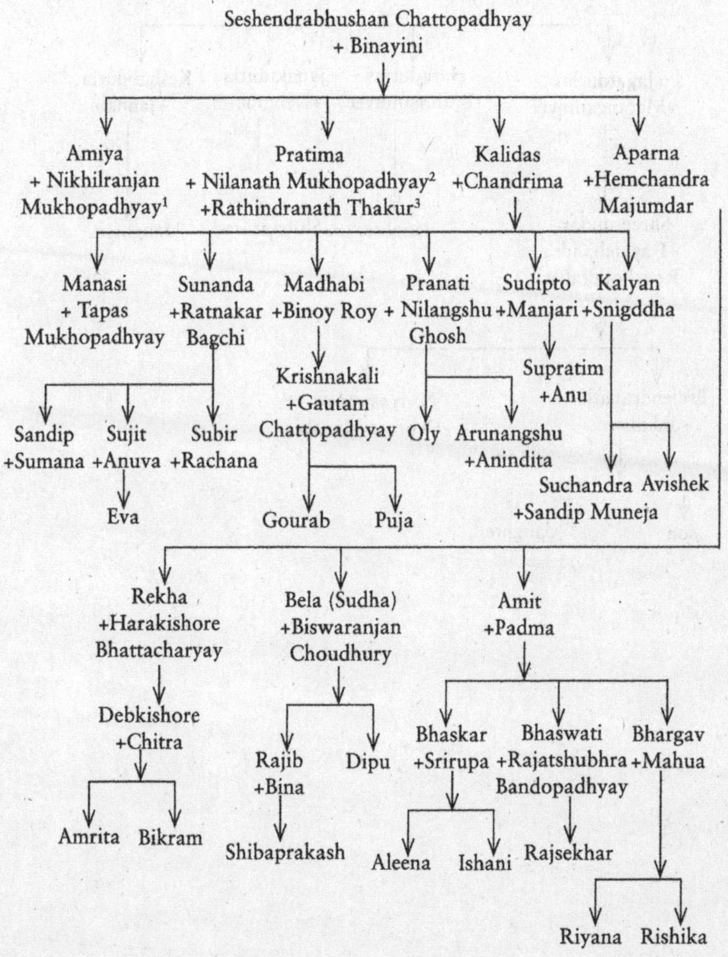

1 Suryakumar Thakur family
2 Jorasanko house no. 5 (Kumudini Mukhopadhyay family)
3 Jorasanko house no. 6 (Rabindranath Thakur family)

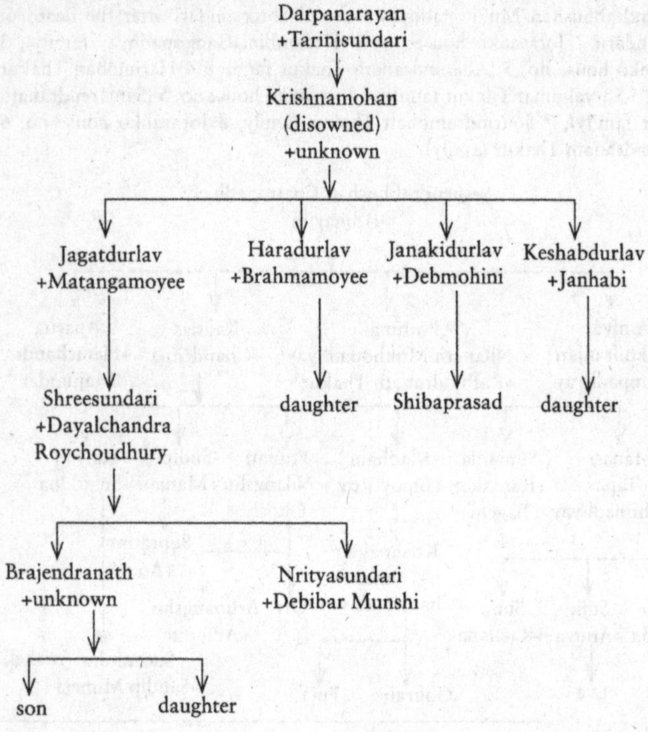
Darpanarayan
+Tarinisundari
Krishnamohan
(disowned)
+unknown
Jagatdurlav
+Matangamoyee
Haradurlav
+Brahmamoyee
Janakidurlav
+Debmohini
Keshabdurlav
+Janhabi
Shreesundari
+Dayalchandra
Roychoudhury
daughter
Shibaprasad
daughter
Brajendranath
+unknown
Nrityasundari
+Debibar Munshi
son
daughter

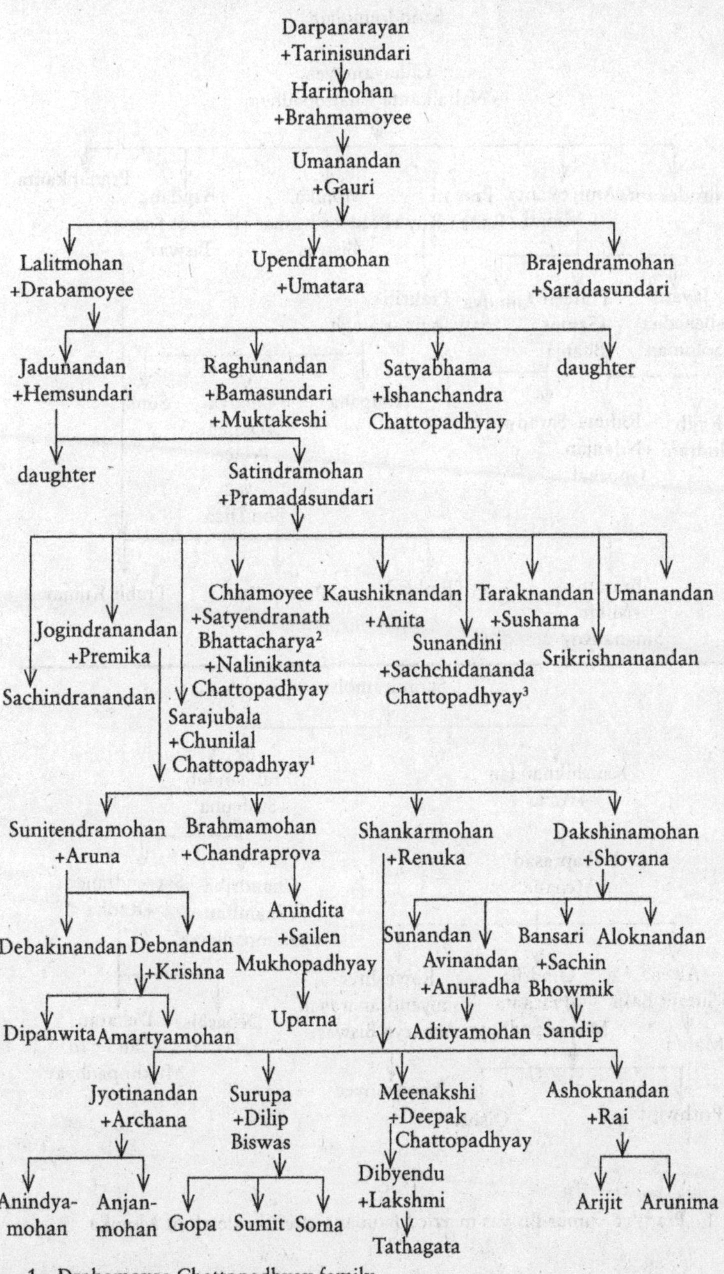

1 Drabamoyee Chattopadhyay family

2 Satyendranath Bhattacharya married Chhayamoyee after death of Rabindranath's daughter Renuka.

3 Lalitmohan Thakur family

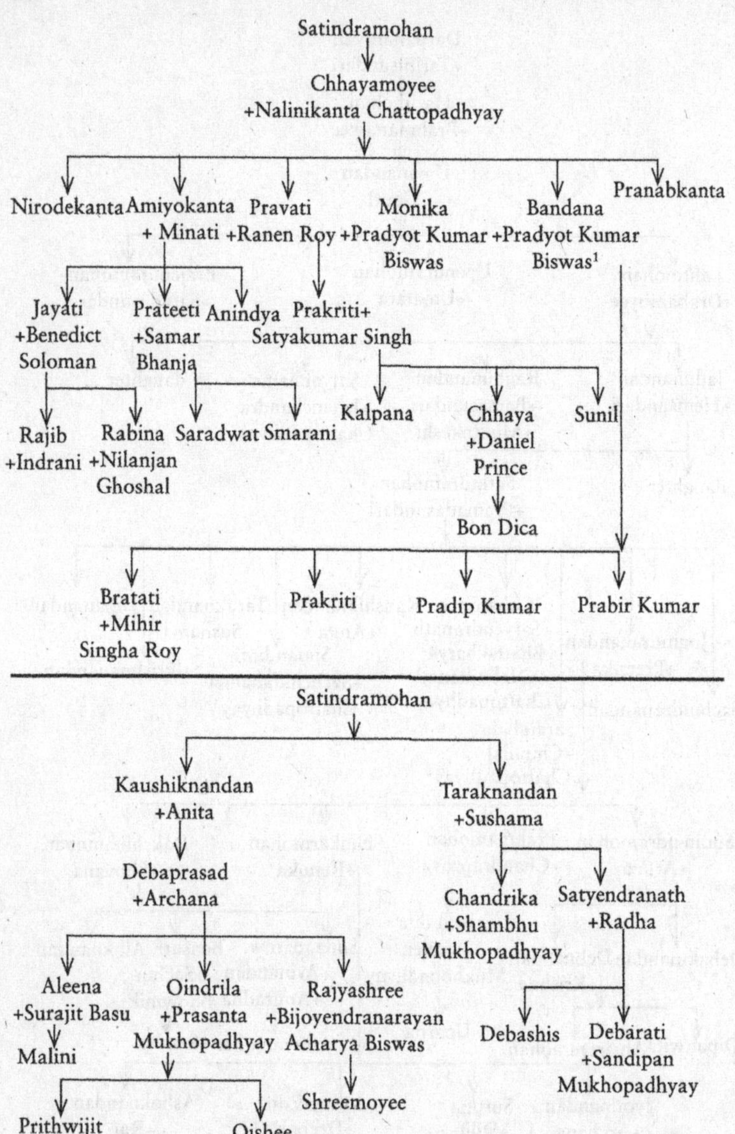

1 Pradyot Kumar Biswas married Bandana after the death of Monika.

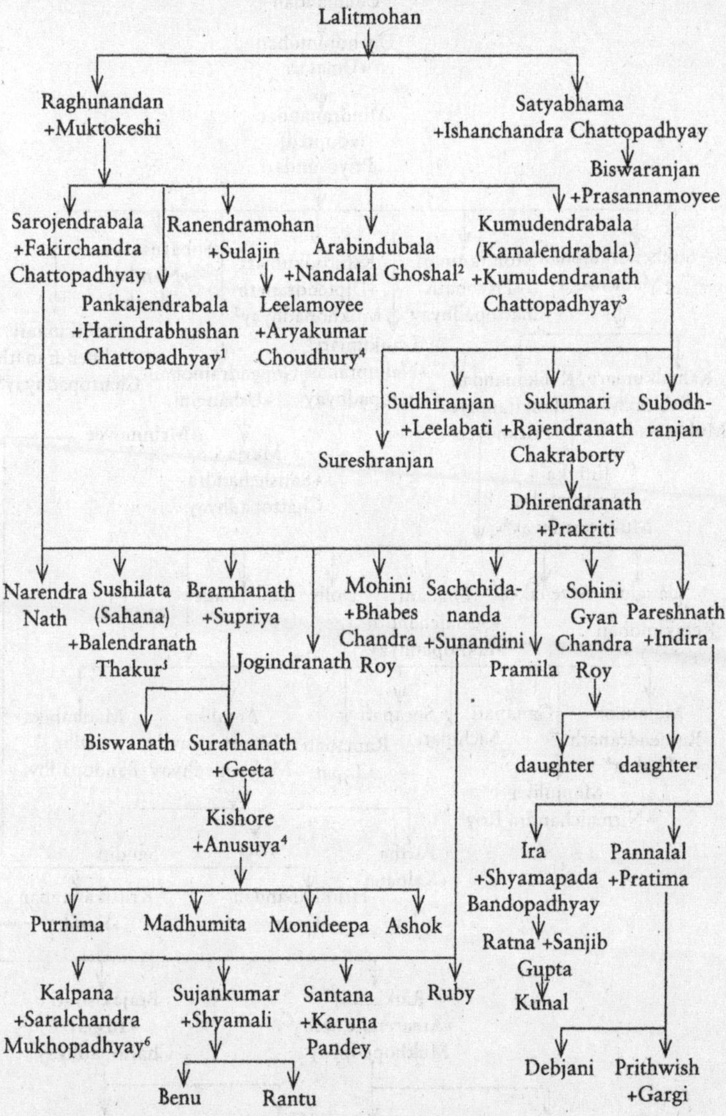

1 Prasanna Kumar Thakur family
2 Nandalal Ghoshal married Arabindubala after the death of Hemendranath Thakur's daughter Sunrita. He married Subarnakumari, daughter of Atin dranandan Thakur, after the death of Arabindubala.
3 Mohinimohan Thakur family
4 Jorasanko house no. 6 (Hemendranath Thakur family). Both Aryakumar and Anusuya are of Hemen Thakur family.
5 Jorasanko house no. 6 (Birendranath Thakur family)
6 Kalikumar Thakur family

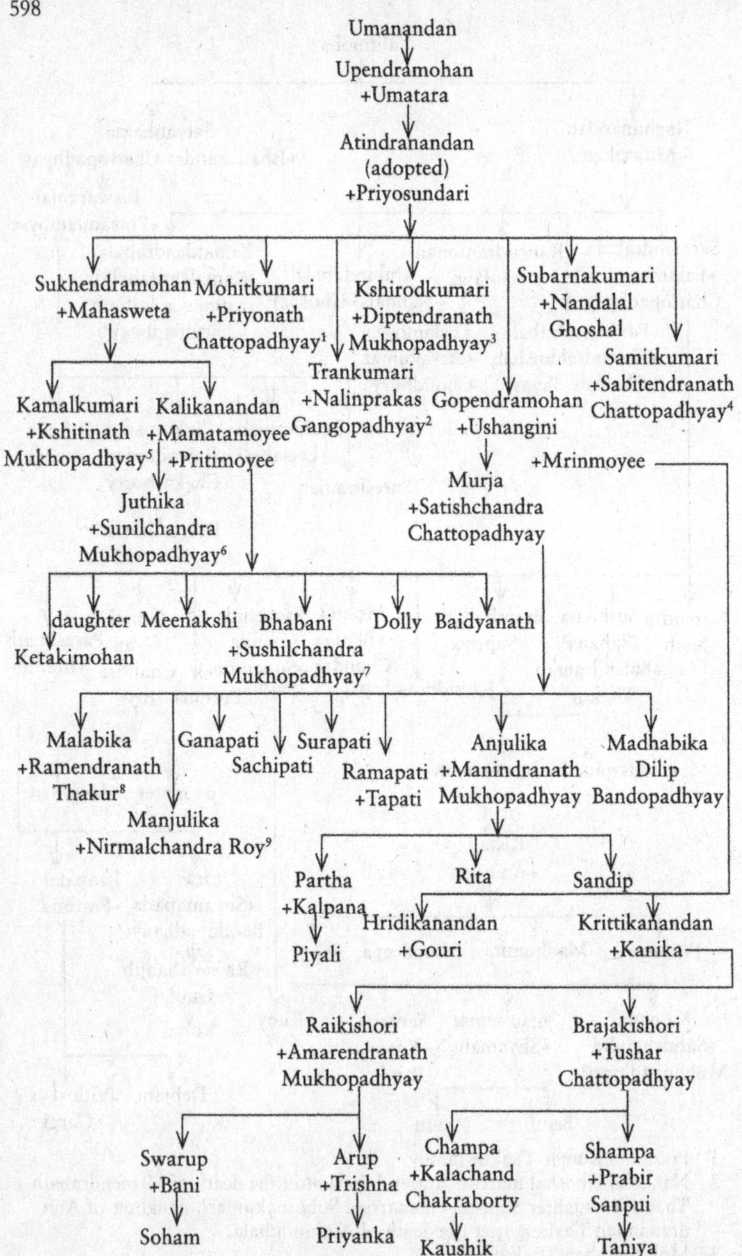

1 Rasbilasi Chattopadhyay family; 2 Jatindramohan Thakur family; 3 Brajendramohan Thakur family; 4 Mohinimohan Thakur family; 5 Brajasundari Mukhopadhyay family; 6&7 Kalikumar Thakur family; 8 Ramanath Thakur family; 9 Aanandiram Thakur family.

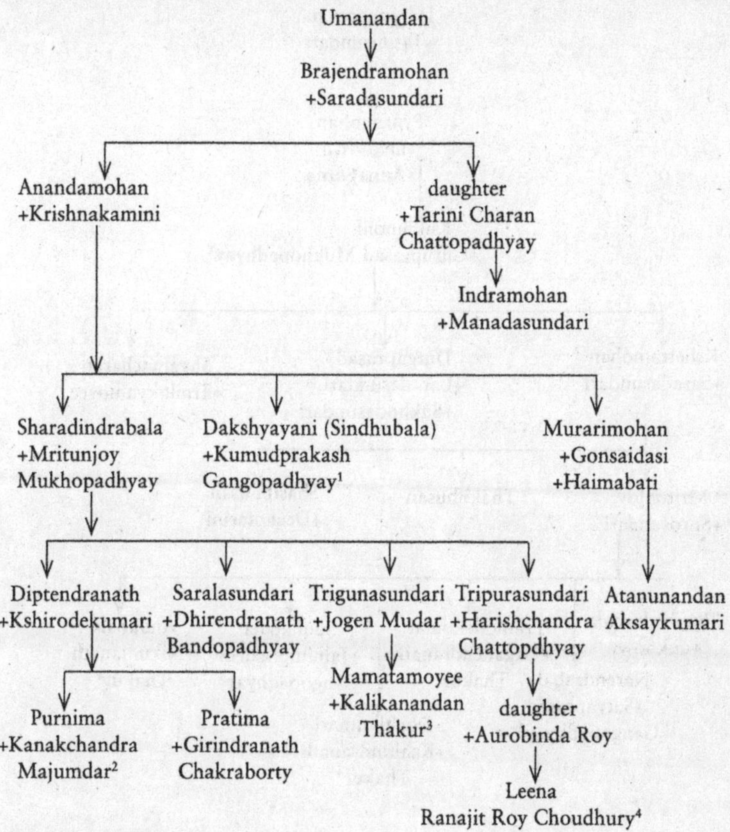

1 Jatindramohan Thakur family
2 Kalikrishna Thakur family
3 Upendramohan Thakur family
4 Ladlimohan Thakur family

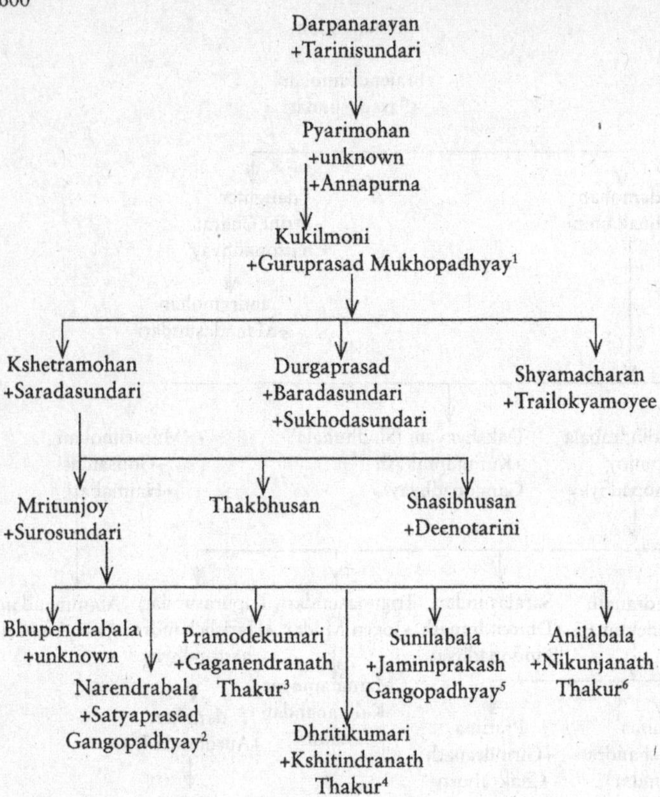

1 Guruprasad Mukhopadhyay married Kukilmoni after the death of Bramhamoyee, daughter of Gopimohan Thakur.
2 Jorasanko house no. 6 (Soudamini Gangopadhyay family)
3 Jorasanko house no. 5 (Gunendranath Thakur family)
4 Jorasanko house no. 6 (Hemendranath Thakur family)
5 Josanko house no. 5 (Kadambini Gangopadhyay family)
6 Chorbagan Thakur family

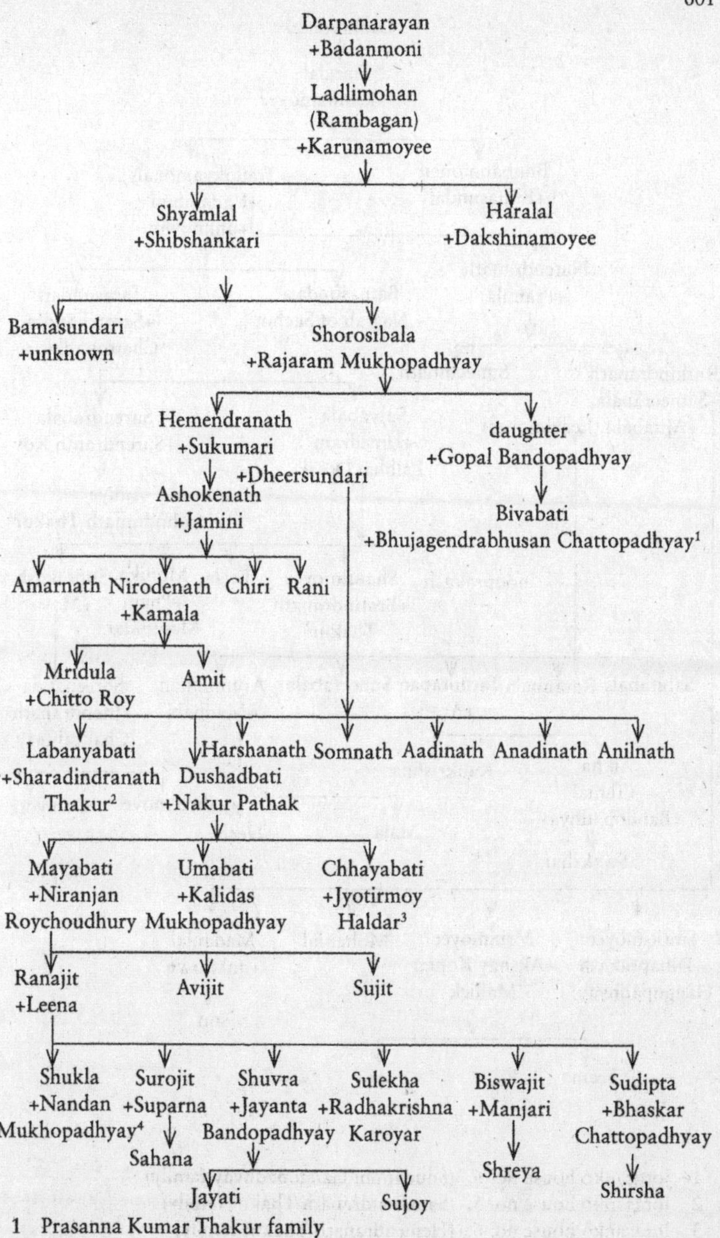

1 Prasanna Kumar Thakur family
2 Kalikrishna Thakur family
3 Jorasanko house no. 6 (Saratkumari Mukhopadhyay family)
4 Ramballav Thakur family

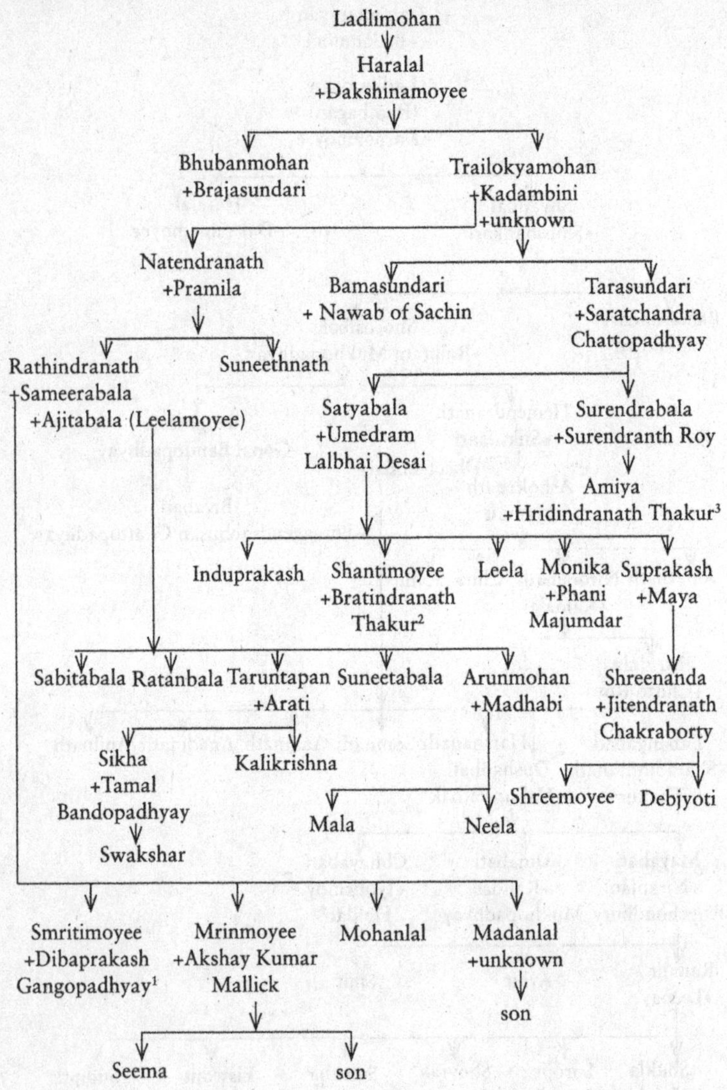

1 Jorasanko house no. 6. (Soudamini Gangopadhyay family)
2 Jorasanko house no. 5. (Samarendranath Thakur family)
3 Jorasanko house no. 6. (Hemendranath Thakur family)

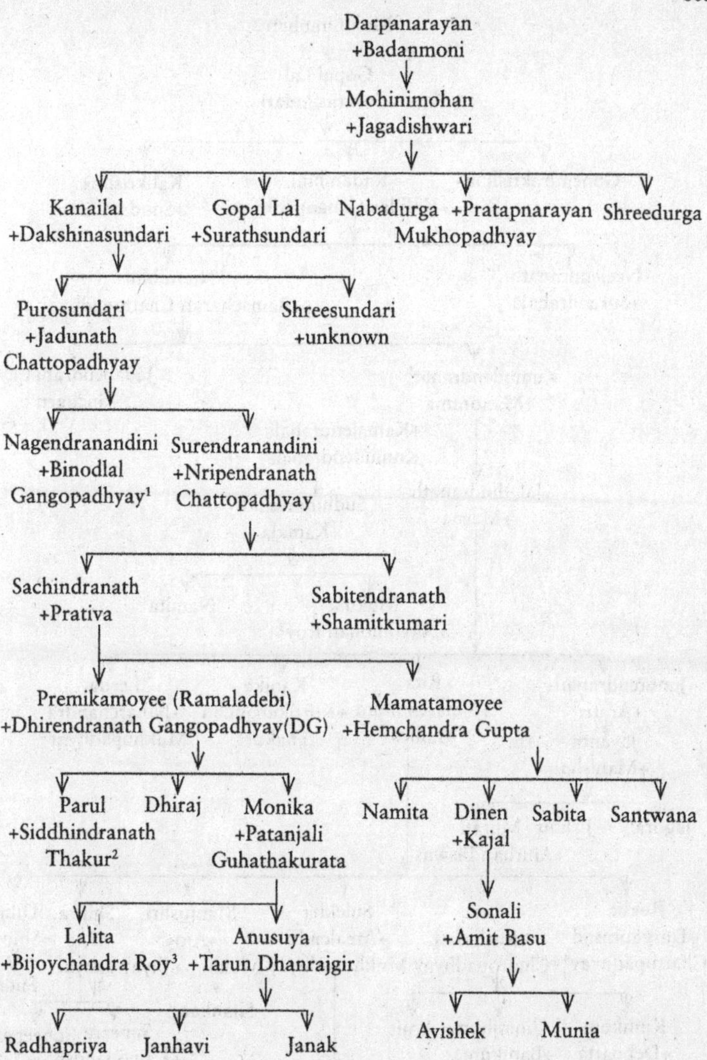

1 Siddheswari Majumdar family
2 Jorasanko house no. 6 (Hemendranath Thakur family)
3 Ramanath Thakur family

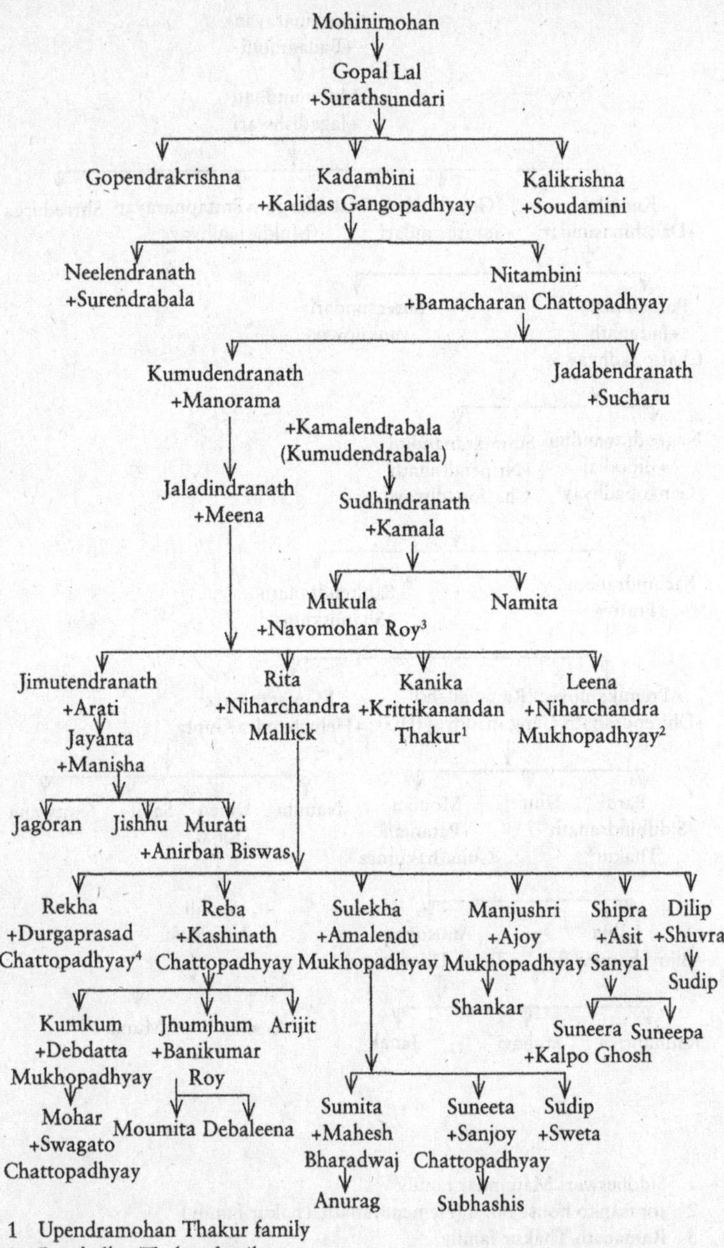

1 Upendramohan Thakur family
2 Ramballav Thakur family
3 Aanandiram Thakur family
4 Rasbilasi Chattopadhyay family

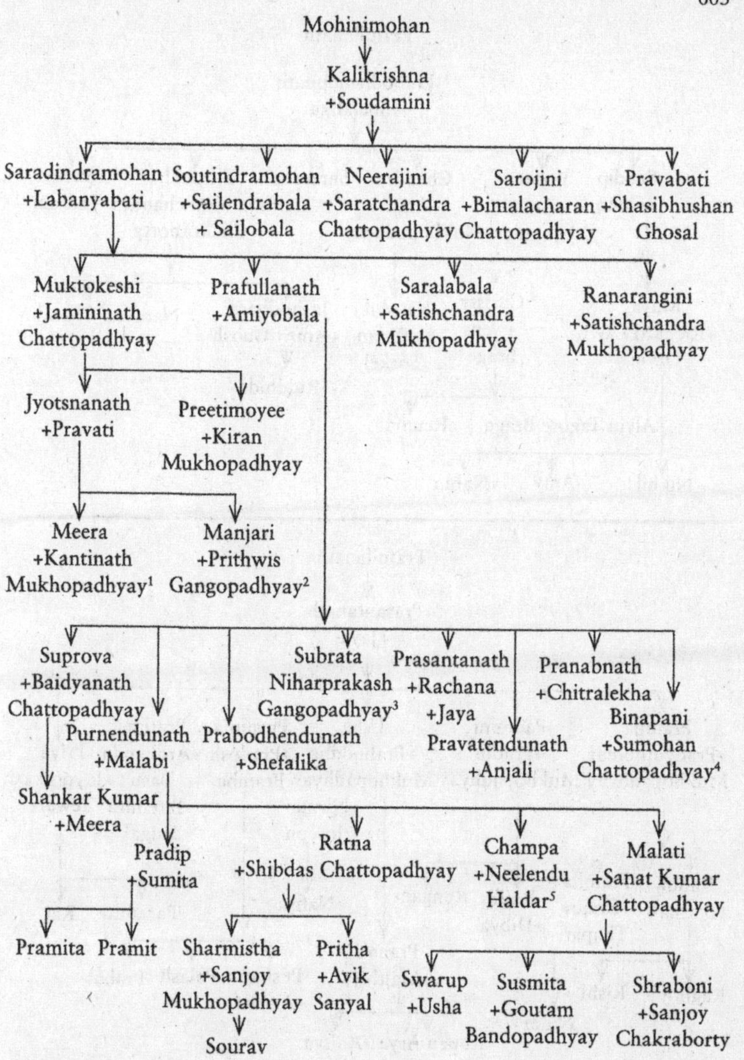

1 Ramanath Thakur family
2 Siddheswari Majumdar family
3 Jatindramohan Thakur family
4 Jorasanko house no. 5 (Sunayani Chattopadhyay family)
5 Jorasanko house no. 5 (Kumudini Mukhopadhyay family)

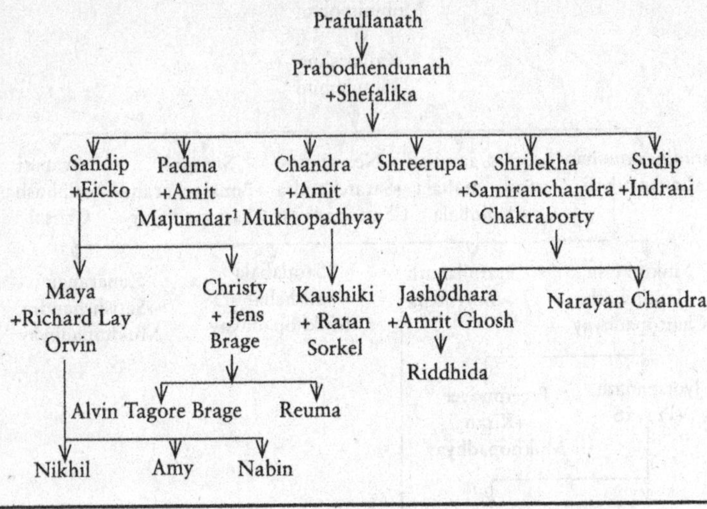

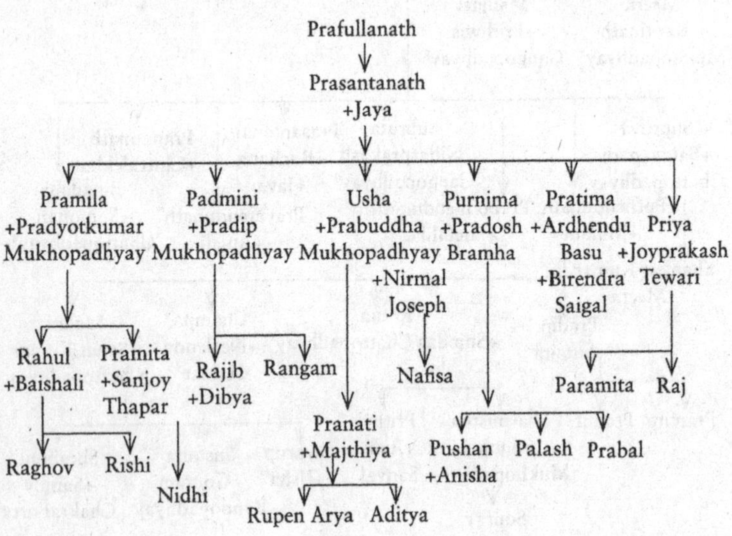

1 Prasanna Kumar Thakur family

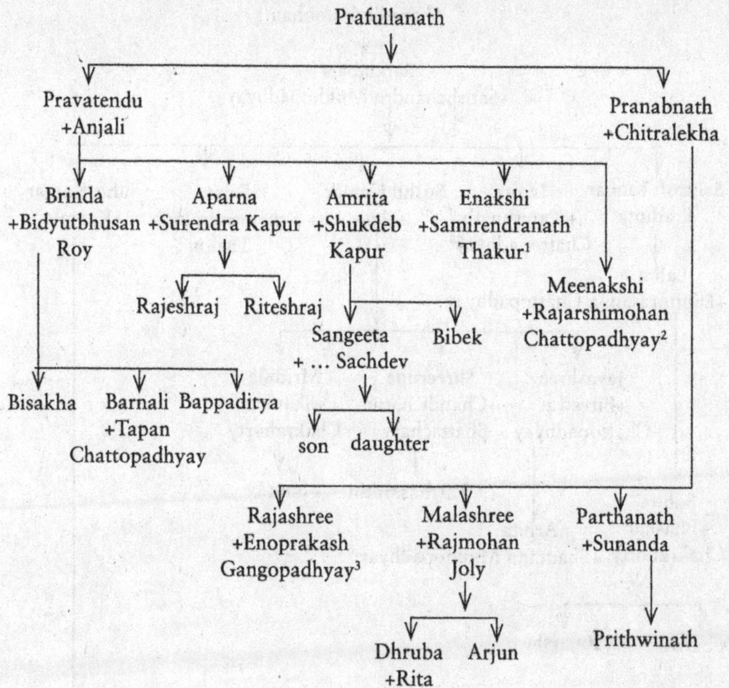

1 Jorasanko house no. 5 (Samarendranath Thakur family)
2 Jorasanko house no. 5 (Sunayani Chattopadhyay family)
3 Jorasanko house no. 5 (Kadambini Gangopadhyay family)

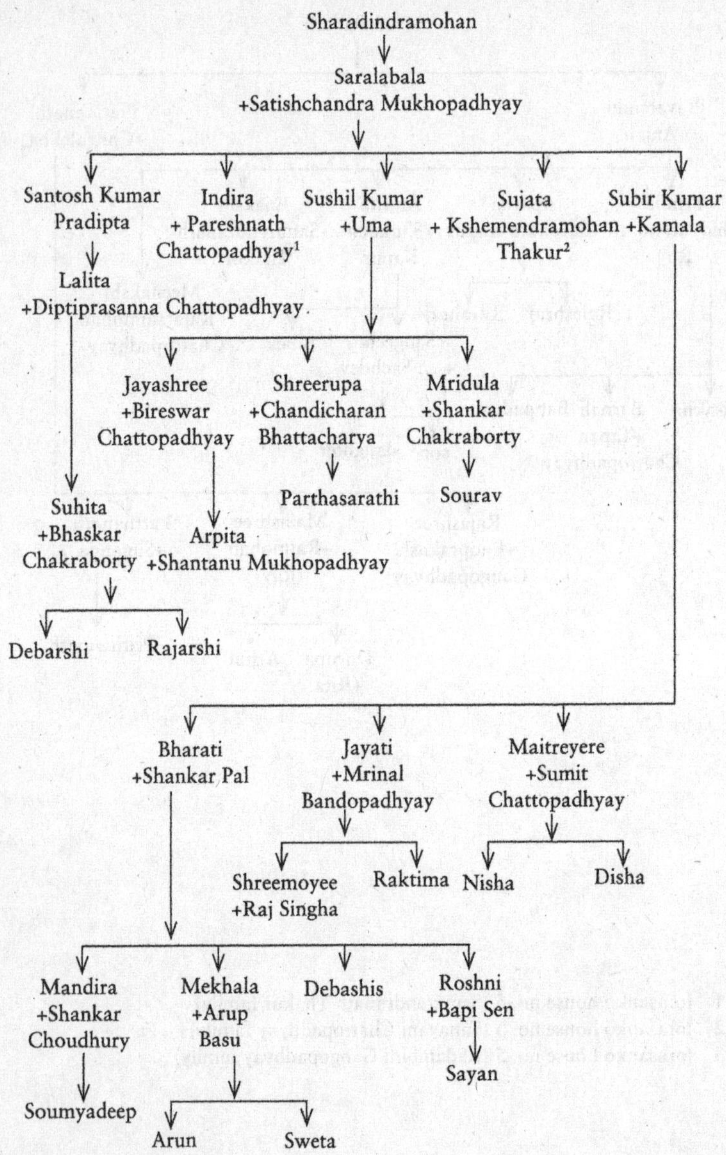

1 Harimohan Thakur family
2 Sourindramohan Thakur family

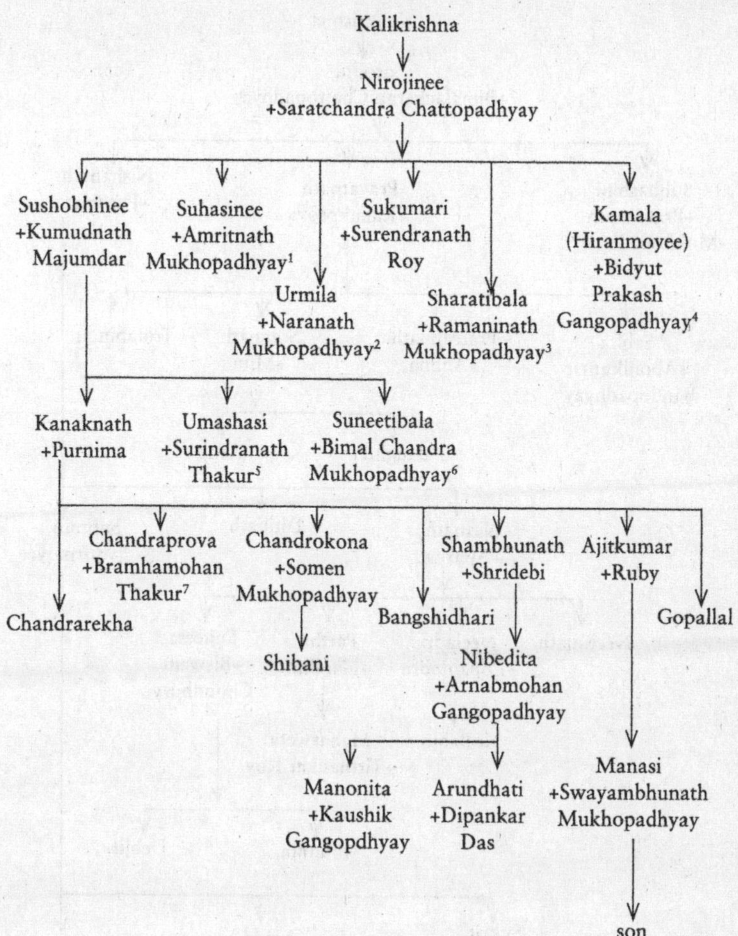

1 Brajosundari Mukhopadhyay family
2 Jorasanko house no. 5 (Kumudini Mukhopadhyay family)
3 Brajosundari Mukhopadhyay family
4 Jatindramohan Thakur family
5 Jorasanko house no. 5 (Samarendranath Thakur family)
6 Kalikumar Thakur family
7 Harimohan Thakur family

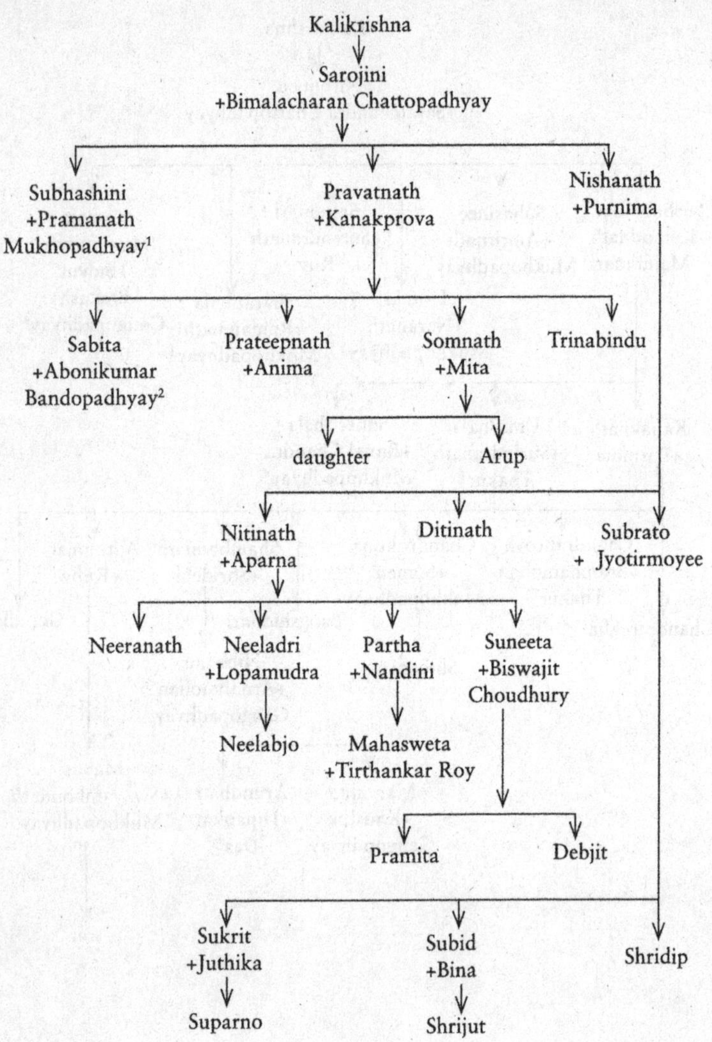

1 Brajosundari Mukhopadhyay family
2 Jorasanko house no. 6 (Sarat Kumari Mukhopadhyay family)

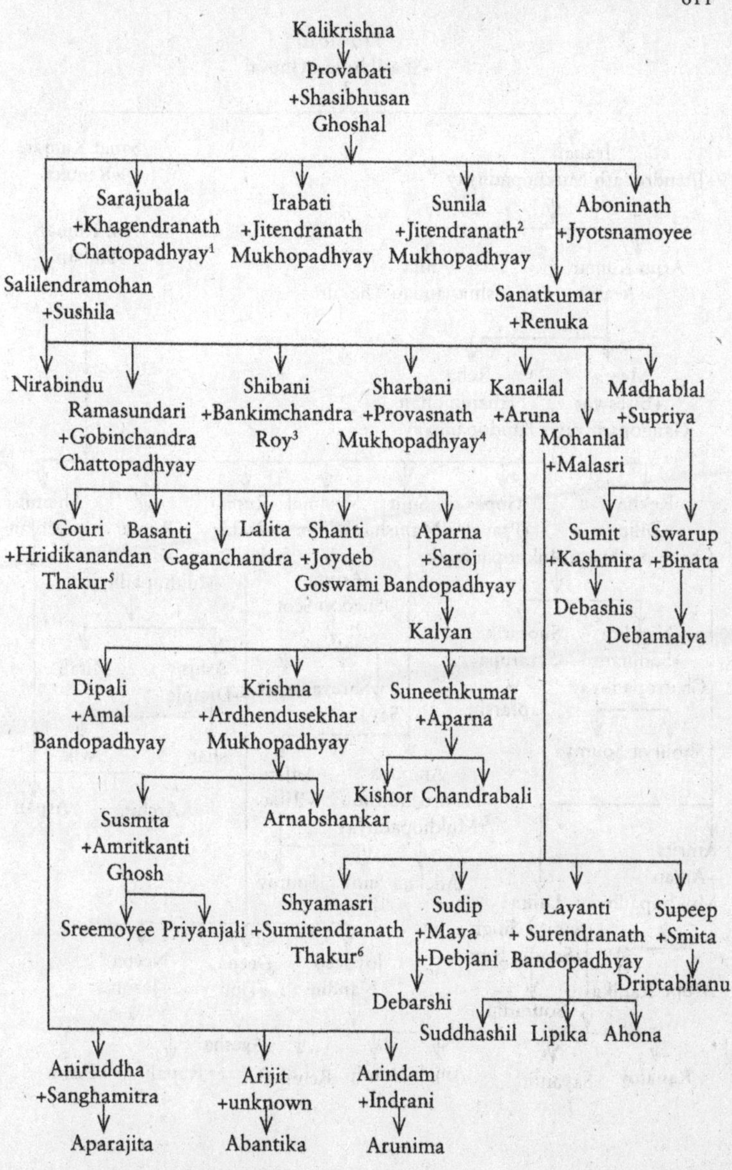

1 Rasbilasi Chattopadhyay family
2 Jitendranath Mukhopadhyay married Sunila after the death of Irabati.
3 Anandiram Thakur family
4 Brajasundari Mukhopadhayay family
5 Upendranath Thakur family
6 Jorasanko house no. 5 (Abanindranath Thakur family)

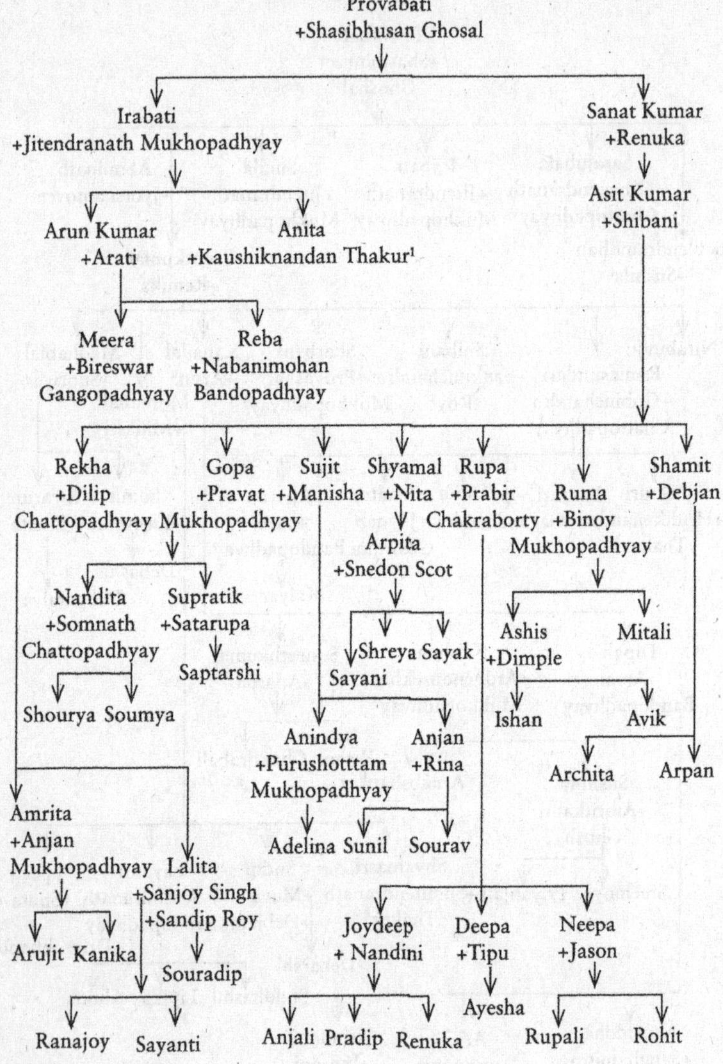

1 Harimohan Thakur family

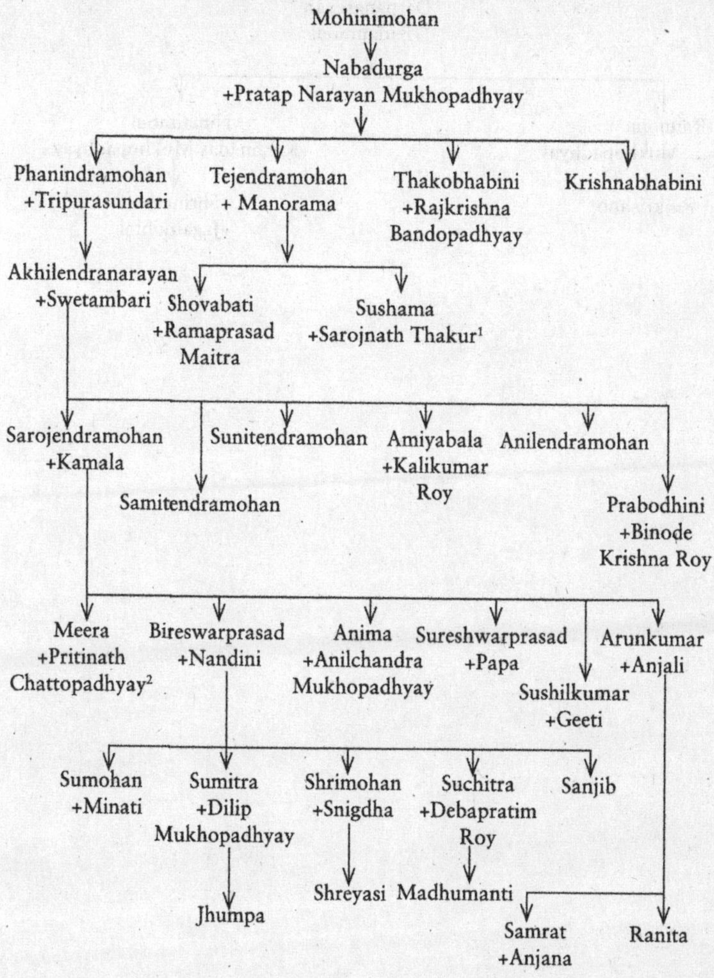

1 Radhanath Thakur family
2 Rasbilasi Chattopadhyay family

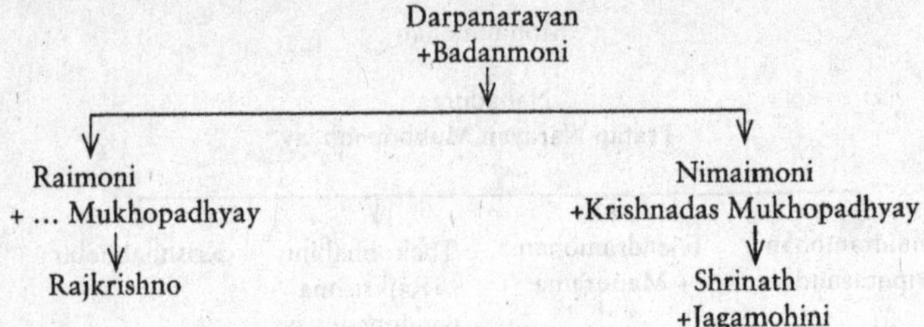
Darpanarayan
+Badanmoni
Raimoni
+ … Mukhopadhyay
Rajkrishno
Nimaimoni
+Krishnadas Mukhopadhyay
Shrinath
+Jagamohini

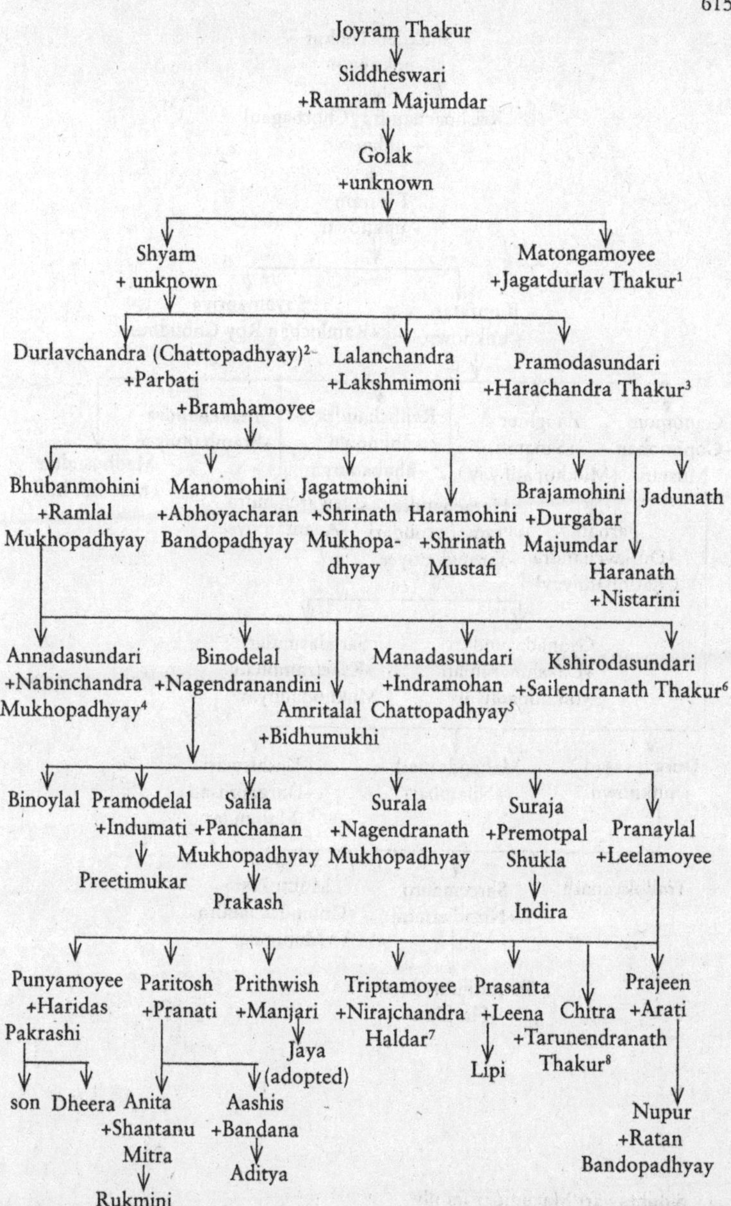

1 Krishnamohan Thakur family; 2 This family used the title 'Chattopadhyay' from the time of Durlavchandra; 3 Chorbagan Thakur family; 4 Ramballav Thakur family; 5 Brajendramohan Thakur family; 6 Radhanath Thakur family; 7 Jorasanko house no. 5 (Kumudini Mukhopadhyay family); 8 Ramanath Thakur family.

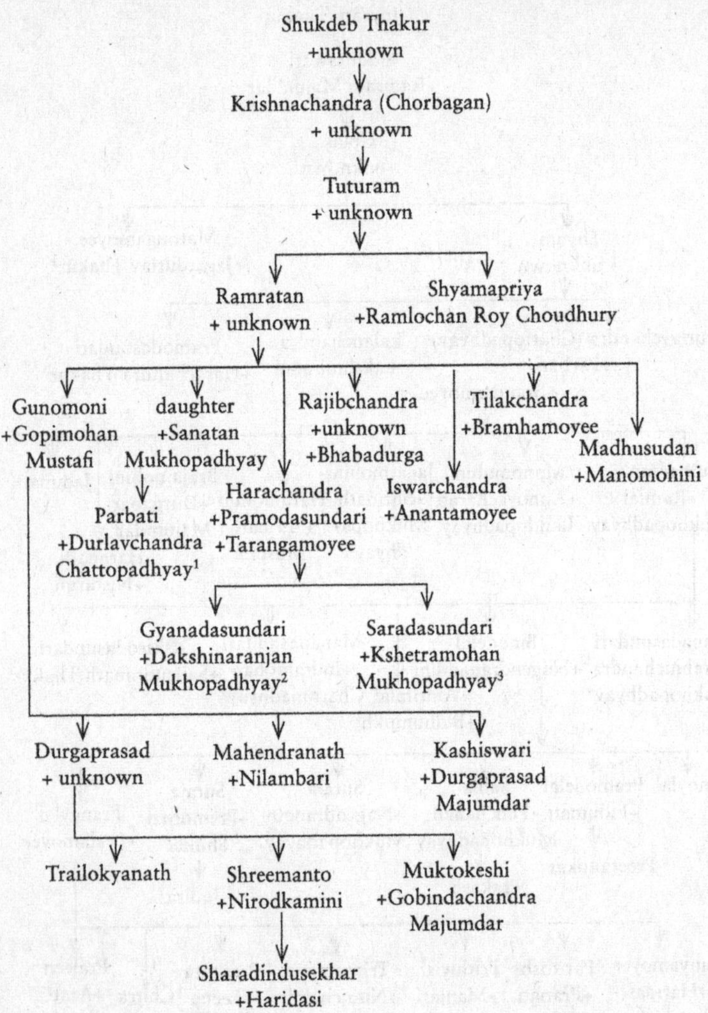

1 Siddheswari Mazumdar family
2 Suryakumar Thakur family
3 Pyarimohan Thakur family

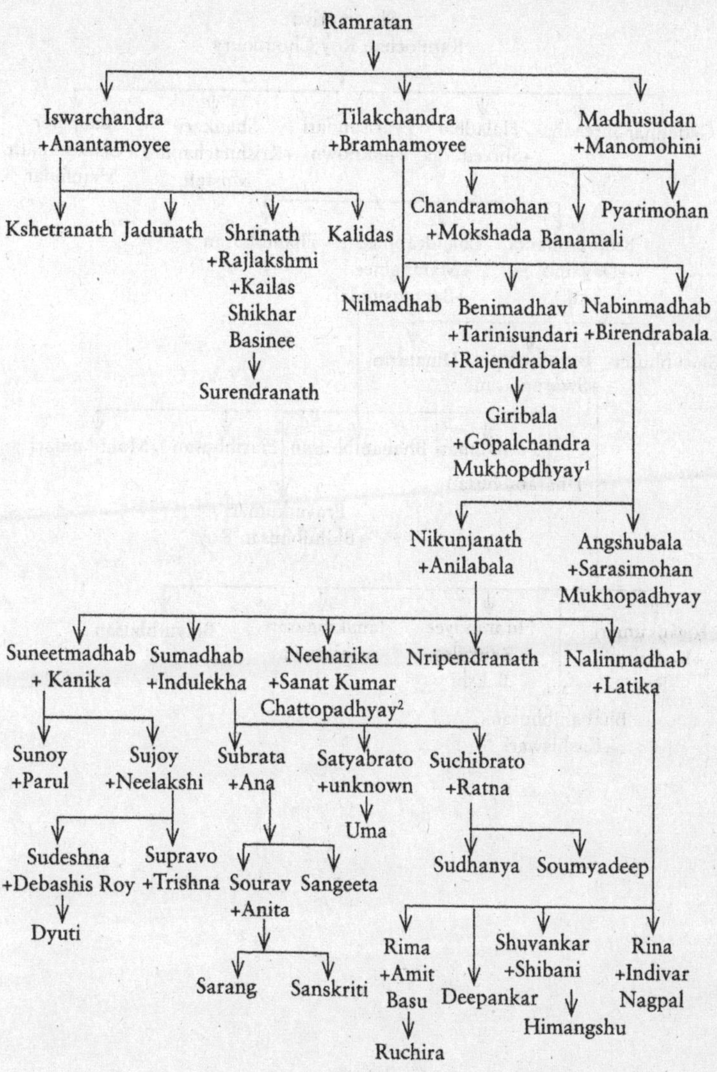

1 Kalikumar Thakur family
2 Rasbilasi Chattopadhyay family

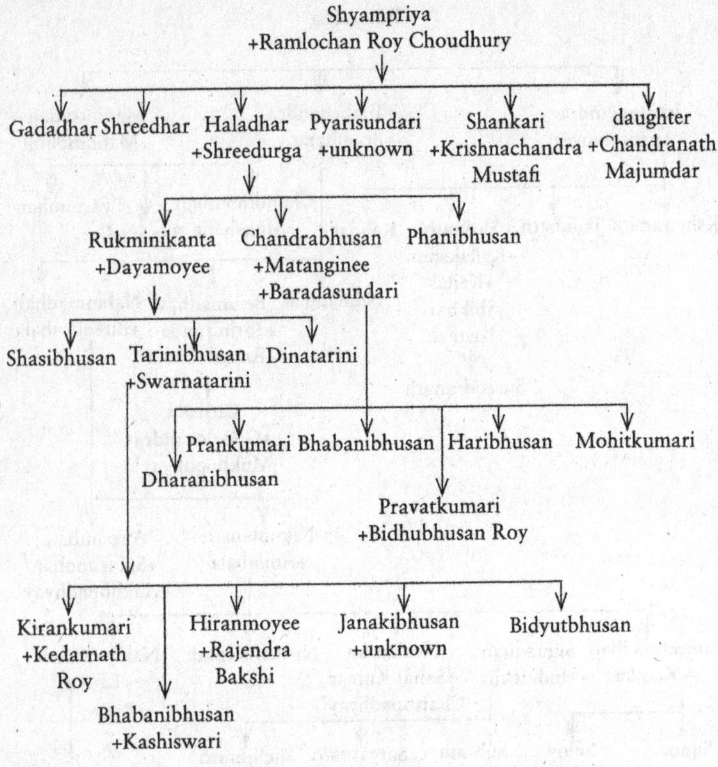
Shyampriya
+Ramlochan Roy Choudhury
Gadadhar
Shreedhar
Haladhar
+Shreedurga
Pyarisundari
+unknown
Shankari
+Krishnachandra
Mustafi
daughter
+Chandranath
Majumdar
Rukminikanta
+Dayamoyee
Chandrabhusan
+Matanginee
+Baradasundari
Phanibhusan
Shasibhusan
Tarinibhusan
+Swarnatarini
Dinatarini
Prankumari
Bhabanibhusan
Haribhusan
Mohitkumari
Dharanibhusan
Pravatkumari
+Bidhubhusan Roy
Kirankumari
+Kedarnath
Roy
Hiranmoyee
+Rajendra
Bakshi
Janakibhusan
+unknown
Bidyutbhusan
Bhabanibhusan
+Kashiswari

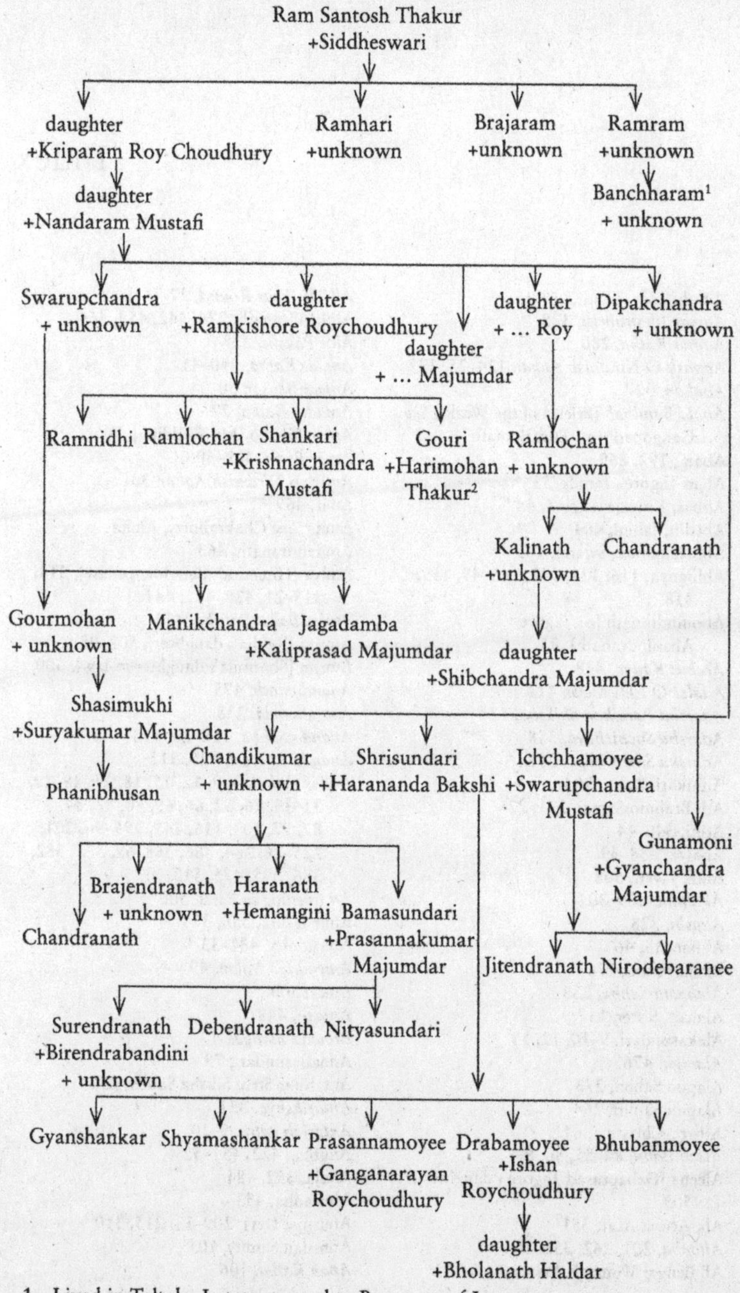

1 Lived in Taltala. Later returned to Baropara of Jessore.

2 Darpanarayan Thakur family

Index